I0885634

SOUL TIES

SOUL TIES

MISS CANDICE

Podium

To the men and women who have lost hope in true, unconditional, unwavering love. You, too, deserve love that makes you soar.

All rights reserved. No part of this publication may be reproduced, stored in a retrieval system, or transmitted in any form or by any means electronic, mechanical, photocopying, recording, or otherwise without prior written permission from Podium Publishing.

This is a work of fiction. Names, characters, places, and incidents are either products of the author's imagination or used fictitiously. Any resemblance to actual events, locales, or persons, living, dead, or undead, is entirely coincidental.

Copyright © 2023 by Candice Lewis

Cover design by Lisbeth Checo

ISBN: 979-8-3470-1667-9

Published in 2025 by Podium Publishing
www.podiumentertainment.com

Podium

TRIGGER WARNING

Because trigger warnings are also spoilers, I decided to do something different, something I saw another author do, and give you, the reader, a choice.

Scan the QR below to read the trigger warning.

SOUL TIES

CHAPTER 1

Sienna

"What you and Amiri doing for New Year's Eve?"

"The same thing we did last year," I told my best friend, Naoki, as I held my phone to my ear with my shoulder as I fished around my purse for my key fob.

As I treaded toward my car, my boots sank into the snow, and I prayed the car wouldn't be snowed in. It was as if three more inches of snow had fallen since I made it to orientation six hours ago. The only thing I hated about winter was the snow. I appreciated the quiet, and the coldness didn't bother me at all. It was the funky-ass snow that drove me crazy. A bitch could barely walk without snow covering my ankles. All I wanted was to get home and get cozy in front of the fire with my man.

"Y'all didn't do shit last year," Naoki replied.

Smirking, I said, "Exactly. He's not going to be here."

"Again? Damn, that makes two years in a row."

"Does it? Damn, I didn't notice," I sarcastically responded, as I finally found my key fob. A key fob I technically didn't need to have in my hands to start the truck. It would have started with the key at the bottom of my bag. But, hey . . . old habits die hard.

Naoki made it her business to mention how my fiancé Amiri hadn't been home for New Year's Eve the year prior, every time. I didn't need a reminder. I was disappointed as hell last year. Disappointed, lonely, and embarrassed. So, I stayed home, nursing a bottle of wine, alone, watching the ball drop on TV. Naoki invited me out but . . . hello . . . embarrassment! I pretended to be okay with it and told her I would bring in the new year in a nice bubble bath on some self-love baddie shit, to set the tone for the rest of the year.

Lies.

The lies! I didn't take that bubble bath. I wasn't on any self-love baddie shit at all. A bitch sat on the couch, drank an entire bottle of red wine, and cried, watching all of those couples on TV kiss the love of their lives. I had plans. I had big plans. I wanted to bring the year in on top of dick. I wanted to "ride" my way into the new year. But . . . Amiri had to work. This year, the news about him having to be out of town again came as no surprise. Of course, he had to be out of town. His *job* kept him pretty busy.

"You know . . . he's putting them over you, right?" Naoki retorted, pulling a heavy eye roll from me.

"Money. It's about money. It has nothing to do with them hos."

Sighing, Naoki said, "I just don't see how you're still comfortable with what he's doing after—"

"I'll call you back," I snapped, before suddenly hanging up in her face. I didn't need a constant reminder of my past . . . of *our* past . . . whenever Naoki decided she wanted to express her concerns with Amiri's career choice.

You ever been scrolling your social media feed and had to stop because a sexy-ass nigga with a thick-ass beard popped up on your timeline? Yes? That was Amiri. The one who would make you stop to double-tap. With smooth, butterscotch skin, thick eyebrows, and curly, thick tresses with the beard to match, he was an automatic panty wetter. Especially for the women who lacked in the sex department. Double-tapping and following was pretty much instantaneous. Just as instantaneous as jumping in his DMs. Which I'd had to check him about quite a few times. Being with a man who had over two hundred thousand followers on Instagram comes with challenges. Challenges I was still trying to sort through. Challenges I didn't need my best friend mentioning just because she felt like I'd swept the shit he'd done in the past under the rug. People could be very fucking insensitive sometimes.

Naoki didn't mean any harm, though. We'd been best friends since elementary school, so she was more like a sister than she was a best friend. She wanted the best for me and felt like I could do a lot better than Amiri. I didn't blame her. I couldn't. I decided to let her in on what me and Amiri were going through when he cheated. I forgave him, she didn't. Which I get. Still, I didn't need her to remind me of the shit every chance she got. It was annoying.

Once I made it to my car, I was caught off guard by a small gold envelope tucked underneath my windshield wipers. After leaning over the hood to grab it, I looked around the dark, deserted parking lot with dipped brows. *Where in the hell did this come from?* As I observed the rest of the cars, I realized I was the only one with the envelope on theirs. Off rip, I thought it was some sort of sex trafficking thing, so I went to toss it on the ground until I noticed my name was etched into the back side of it, on the envelope's flap. In a soft, italic font, it said *Sienna*, clear as day. With a frown, I ran my thumb over it, surprised at how high quality the design was. *Nah, this couldn't be a ploy to kidnap me. Niggas don't pay this type of money for targets.*

Swallowing, I looked around the parking lot again before getting into my car, ignoring the ringing of my phone. I let that shit ring. Naoki knew why I'd hung up on her and was likely only calling to further piss me off. I sure as hell wasn't looking for an apology. Every time she pissed me off, bringing up Amiri's cheating, she never apologized, claiming she had nothing to apologize about because all she was doing was trying to get me to see my worth. I didn't need her to help me with that. I was doing just fine by myself.

Once I got into the car, I started the engine and immediately turned the heat on full blast, knowing damn well that until the car warmed up, cold air was going to come out of the vents. But I did it, anyway. Like I did every single fucking time. *Old habits . . .*

Sitting there, waiting for the car to heat up, I grabbed the envelope again, running my fingers over my name. On one hand, I thought, maybe my man was surprising me with something. But Amiri didn't do things like this. He lacked spontaneity. I was the spontaneous one in the relationship. So, I tossed that theory out of the window. Then a chill ran down my spine as I thought, *Maybe it's a "Barbara, this is Shirley" type of situation where one of his bitches decided to send me something about them in a fancy envelope to fuck with me.* But the envelope was way too luxurious for that. Gold, with speckles of glitter that could only be seen if the light hit it the right way. And the way my damn name was engraved into it. *This* was something different.

Just as I was getting ready to open it, my phone rang. At first, I thought it was Naoki again, so I was going to ignore it. But when I looked at my dash and saw it was Amiri, I answered. I hadn't spoken to him all day and couldn't wait to hear his voice. We texted, checking in every now and then, but I was an over-the-phone type of gal. There was something about hearing his deep, raspy voice that did it for me every time.

"Hey, babe," I answered as I tossed the envelope on the passenger seat. Looking over at it, I thought maybe he had dropped it off and was calling to see if I had read it. Maybe he'd taken my complaining about his lack of effort into consideration. *Maybe.*

"Wassup, gorgeous? Where you at?"

Shifting my truck into drive, I pulled out of the parking space. "Just leaving. Where you at?"

"Leavin' the mall. You want me to grab something to eat on the way?"

It was close to eight in the evening, and I was starving, but I hoped he'd mention the envelope. I hoped maybe *somehow* Amiri had thought of me.

We'd been together for so long, the romance had pretty much been sucked out of our relationship. I figured that was normal. However, after talking to so many women who'd been in relationships for ten, fifteen years, I'd learned Amiri was just lazy and comfortable.

I couldn't remember the last time a bitch was surprised with a bouquet of roses or a surprise trip. I was pretty much holding on to our relationship because of comfort and because the dating pool had pee in it.

Amiri and I had been together for almost four years, but I'd known him since junior year of high school so I'd known him for about ten. Which meant I knew what to expect from him. I knew his favorite color, his favorite food, his family, his friends—I knew Amiri. So, I guess, in a way, you could say I was comfortable and lazy, too, because I stayed because I knew him.

I wanted more, I knew I deserved more, but . . . I was too afraid to put myself out there because niggas were crazy and the dating. Pool. Has. Piss. In. It. I figured, fuck it. Might as well stay where I was at. At least then, I knew I wouldn't end up on the news or some weird shit. Besides, the only issue I had with him these days was how boring we were. I needed some spontaneity. Some fun. To be romanced. I figured that should be easy to fix and wasn't worth breaking up over.

"Yeah. We haven't had Mexican in a while. I—"

"Oh my God! You be on Instagram, don't you? I follow yo' fine ass! Damn, you look even better in person. You single?" yelled some bitch in the background, cutting me off.

I took a deep breath and rolled my eyes as I gripped the steering wheel. "Tell that bitch to get out of your face, Amiri!"

Instead, he did the opposite. I heard the smile in his voice when he said, "Yeah, I'm on IG. Nah, I'm not single. I appreciate the support, love."

"I appreciate the support, love," I mocked with a grimace. "Shut yo' ass up!"

"Damn! That's too damn bad," the girl said. *"Can I get a picture with you at least?"*

Sucking my teeth, I hung up on him with flared nostrils.

I had the thick skin to deal with his large following, but at times like this, when I wanted attention and thought he had been romantic just to be let down once again, my skin was as thick as wet tissue.

When he didn't call me back immediately, I wasn't surprised. I knew what he was doing: smiling with a bitch, taking a picture, like she'd asked. That was one thing I couldn't stand about Amiri. When it came to his followers, he was very, very friendly. I didn't have a problem with it, to an extent. Today, when my skin was wet-toilet-paper thin, I had *the* biggest problem with it. Especially since he could easily hear the annoyance in my voice but chose to ignore it.

It was shit like that that always put me in the mind frame of the toughest year of my life. Every single time I felt like he was putting those bitches before me, I was reminded of a time in life that he actually had. When he was cheating. I'd call, he'd say he was busy, and I'd believe him because that was Amiri—always busy. Either he was hosting an event, at a photoshoot, or had been invited to some sort of influencer event. But back then, he was doing more than events and photoshoots. He was fucking, lying, and cheating. I should've left. I know this. Leaving, when you're in love, was a lot harder than it sounded.

Back then, in my early twenties when we first got together, I lacked a lot of self-love. But these days, I literally dared Amiri's ass to cheat. Sometimes, I wanted him to just so I could show him I wasn't that young, naïve bitch who needed him.

But for the past few years, he'd been where he said he was. I had passwords, the location, all of that. He'd been a very, very good boy. But then shit like that happened and I was in my head.

It took him ten minutes to call me back. *Who takes ten minutes to take a picture?* Instead of yelling at him about it, I let the damn phone ring.

I didn't speak to Amiri until I pulled up to the house to him waiting for me in the driveway. He stood there, running his hands over his "good" hair with those bushy-ass eyebrows furrowed, looking like a sad-ass puppy dog.

After grabbing my belongings and the shiny gold envelope I'd forgotten about, I got out of the car, hitting Amiri with the door in the process. He shouldn't have been so close to it.

"Aight, Si," Amiri said with a low chuckle. "Chill out."

I rolled my eyes and continued toward the house as I pulled my orange puffer coat closed. It was freezing out and he didn't have a coat on. I wondered how long he'd been outside, waiting for me to pull up, in the freezing cold.

Once I got into the house, I took my snowy boots off, set my things down and put my keys on the keyholder, all while ignoring Amiri, who stood right next to me, calling my name.

I rubbed my hands together and walked over the threshold, into the toasty house, with a light groan. He'd set the fire. Shifting my eyes over at it, I rolled them. He did that on purpose. He was trying to butter me up, knowing I was a sucker for a nice, warm fire.

Sitting in front of the fireplace, on a cold night like tonight, cuddled up in my big UGG cover, was my favorite thing to do. We'd lay by the fire, in each other's arms, either catching up on our Netflix shows or talking about our day. The night would always end with us laughing about me telling his messy-ass Auntie Gabby she couldn't come to our wedding. Every single night since I revoked her invitation six months ago, she'd called him, his mother, or one of his sisters, complaining about it. I didn't give a fuck. She wasn't invited. Hell, at this rate, I wasn't even sure if there was going to be a wedding *to be* invited to. I felt like calling everything off. But then again, I always felt that way when we fought. He got on my got damn nerves with that "*love*" shit. So much that whenever I heard him say or saw him comment it, I wanted to punch him in the mouth.

Walking into the kitchen, I opened the refrigerator door and pulled my bottle of red wine from it. As I stood at the island, Amiri stood in front of me, on the other side of it. Removing the cork, I finally gave him what I knew he wanted: eye contact.

"It's my job," Amiri said with a sigh as he ran his hand over the top of his head. "What was I supposed to do, Sienna?"

I glowered over at him with tight lips before turning to get a wineglass from the cabinet behind me.

"It's your job to blatantly disrespect me? All you had to do was smile and keep it moving. All that extra shit—"

"All that extra shit pays the bills, Si," he interrupted. "I don't see why we keep going through this."

With a squint, I cocked my head to the side. "You don't see why we keep going through this? Really? Don't tell me you got amnesia now."

I didn't usually trip like this but I was pissed. I was more let down than anything, to be honest. It was that damn gold envelope. *I should throw it away.* If it wasn't from him, I didn't want it. However, I was curious to see what was inside of it, so I wasn't going to toss it. The fact that it wasn't from him just upset me so bad.

The bitch walking up on groupie shit did nothing but add fuel to the fire. That, and him with that "love" shit. My God, that was such a triggering word for me. So much, he knew not to ever call me that shit.

Amiri let out an exasperated sigh before making his way around the massive island to stand beside me. With his back resting against the island, he stared into my face. "Look at me, Sienna."

Instead of looking at him, I filled my big wineglass up to the rim. Excessive? Not too elegant? I didn't give a fuck. I needed a drink. A hefty one. And sipping on a half-filled glass wasn't going to do it for me.

"You know them hos don't mean shit to me, right?" Amiri asked, with raised brows, trying to connect with me, but I refused to lock eyes with him. "All I did was take a picture, bae."

I huffed and put my glass up to my lips, taking a long sip. I knew the hos didn't mean anything to him. I'd just told Naoki that earlier. But . . . *that fucking envelope.* It was sent by the Devil. Had to be. Because before I saw it, and before he called, I was good. On top of him not surprising me with something thoughtful, the bitch in the background had really set me off. I was ready to twist this three-carat engagement ring off my finger and toss it in the damn trash.

I needed to chill.

But I couldn't.

I had a little toxicity about me. It hadn't always been there. Before, I was a sweetheart. I was understanding and so supportive of Amiri's career. I used to go to events with him. I used to sit in the crowd, sipping on drinks, having a good time while he hosted and took pictures with bitches who were dying to be me. And I used to do it with a smile on my face and confidence radiating from my infectious smile. He was mine, and for them, he was nothing more than a fantasy.

Until he wasn't.

When I found out about Amiri's cheating, I blacked out on his ass. I fucked him up. I literally fought with him, keyed his car, flattened his tires, put a candy bar in his tank, and made a fake social media page calling his dick little and weak. I was trying to do any and everything to tarnish his name but the only thing that held some truth about what I'd said was his dick being weak. It was big, long and thick, but he couldn't give me an orgasm to save his fucking life. I . . . I was getting off subject.

Yeah, toxicity.

I had some toxicity to me. When I was on one, I was on it. There was little to no stopping me when I was upset. I had word vomit. Serious word vomit. So, although I knew I needed to chill, I kept going.

"Just like the other hos didn't mean shit to you, huh?" I said, my eyes finally locked on his.

Amiri chuckled, just like I knew he would.

"Here we go with that shit again," he said before pacing the kitchen floor. "You ever gon' move on from that shit, Sienna? I mean, you told me you did, and because I thought we had moved on, I asked you to be my wife. But here we are, years later and you still punishing me for something I did when I was a completely different nigga."

I squinted and took a deep breath before taking another big sip of my drink. "I have moved on from it," I said, partially telling the truth.

I liked to think I had moved on from it. But then, shit like him addressing women would happen and those raw feelings behind what he did would come back up and I'd be right back where I was years ago: upset, insecure, and ready to bash his fucking head in. I couldn't have moved on from it like I thought, huh?

Some wounds were easy to forget about when you covered them with thick bandages. But the moment that bandage weakened, that pain resurfaced as toxic anger. That was how I looked at my situation with Amiri.

I'd covered the wounds with bandages. Some as expensive designer clothing he'd gifted me. Some covered with bandages made of words of affirmations, *I love yous*, and this phat-ass engagement ring on my finger. But any little bit of lifting and those old wounds showed their ugly faces and put me right where I was now. Standing in this beautiful, big kitchen, paid for by the very thirsty women I was threatened by. Thing was, the only thing I was insecure about when it came to those thirsty women was my relationship. However, I was secure in who I was. It took me a minute to get here, but I knew my worth. I knew I was the shit and carried myself as such. But I was afraid of losing this with Amiri. The years. The memories. The good ones. We weren't always like this. We meshed well. I'd like to say that next to Naoki and my sisters, Amiri was my best friend. Sometimes, I'd say he knew me better than I knew myself. Right now, as I stared into his sad eyes, I'd say he didn't know me at all.

"Did you? It sure don't seem like it. Let it go. Move on, so *we* can move on, baby."

And that, my friend, was what set me the fuck off.

"Don't invalidate my feelings, nigga. Don't tell me to move on, as if you didn't fuck—"

"I fucked them! That's all I did! And you chose to stay. I didn't have a gun to yo' head, Si. I didn't make you stay! You made that decision on yo' own. I say move on because if you really knew you couldn't, you shouldn't have accepted my proposal, baby."

He was right.

I hated when he was right when I was pissed off. I shouldn't have accepted his proposal if I couldn't move past it, but I thought I could. I had been moving past it. It was those fucking bandages lifting, making this shit so hard. Those bandages, and that fucking gold envelope.

Amiri stepped closer to me and grabbed my hand before I could lift the glass to my lips again. He grabbed my chin and forced me to face him. "I apologize for disrespecting you earlier, aight, cupcake?"

I swallowed and swam in those brown eyes of his. Those sensual brown eyes. I couldn't lie. Amiri was trying. In the past, that apology would have been a lot different. He would have phrased it like: "I apologize *if* you feel like I disrespected you." His apologies lacked accountability and were always formulated to make me out to be the one overreacting. Today, his apology told me he didn't invalidate my feelings, like I said he had.

As much as I'd grown, I still had a lot of growing and maturing to do. Growing, maturing, and healing.

Amiri was right. I had decided to give him a second chance and I couldn't punish him for my own decision to stay. The truth in it all was, when I weighed the pros and cons, the pros outweighed the cons, so I stayed.

I nodded. "Okay. And I apologize for tripping. You know how I can get."

Contrary to what it may look like, I'd been trying to. It just looked a little messier on my end, because I was the one who had been hurt.

"I know," Amiri said, before gripping my chin and tilting my head back. He placed his soft lips on mine and delicately kissed them. I cooed against his lips and set my glass completely down before wrapping my arms around his neck to deepen the kiss.

This was the shit Naoki and the rest of my family and friends didn't see. Us in our element. Us sorting through our shit. We were not perfect and never claimed to be. People painted a perfect picture of us on their own. For a while, before Amiri cheated, we were considered the "it" couple. The people we graduated with sent us tons of likes on social media, claiming they "knew" we would end up together. We'd even gotten a few "goals" comments, but no one knew what was going on behind closed doors and people didn't know now. Naoki, Mahogany, Hazel, my mom . . . they all speculated. They had their own opinions.

Naoki thought I was just letting Amiri get away with it, sweeping shit under the rug, but I wasn't. Mahogany supported me in my decision to forgive Amiri, but that was partially because she was married and had dealt with her own fair share of cheating. Hazel didn't have much to say besides "it couldn't be me," but that was the thing. A lot of people could say that until they were cheated on by someone they had spent many years loving and growing with. Then they would see.

My mother liked Amiri but hated what he'd done to me. She supported me, though, in the most overbearing way possible.

Regardless of what people thought, I did what was best for *Sienna*. I didn't give a fuck about what anybody had to say about my decisions. You know why? Because my decisions were my decisions to live with. I was the one going through the healing. I was the one battling the toxic insecurities. And if Amiri decided to cheat on me again, I'd be the one handling that shit. No one else. My life wasn't for anybody to understand but my damn self.

Once I calmed down, I finished my glass of wine off and poured another to take to the bathroom with me for my bubble bath. Amiri didn't stop to get us anything to eat on the way home, so he left to get Mexican like I was requesting before the bitch interrupted me earlier.

On my way up to the bedroom, I stopped at the front door to grab that gold envelope off the side table. I thought about ripping into it right then and there, but I had too much in my hands to do that, so I decided to just open it while I bathed.

I took self-care and self-love seriously. So, any time I sat in the tub, I had to have candles lit, a glass of wine, and music playing. Oh, and a lot of bubbles. Let Amiri tell it, I used too many bubbles. I didn't give a damn because I wanted to feel like royalty while I soaked, face mask and all.

After setting the mood, I undressed and sank into the tub. Before resting on the back of it, I grabbed the envelope from the bathtub tray and finally turned it over to open it.

The first line read, "You've been cordially invited." I knew it was an invitation, but to what?

"You've been cordially invited to Pandora's fifth annual New Year's Eve masquerade ball," I read aloud. "Pandora's? Who the hell is Pandora, and how in the fuck does she know me?" I thought out loud.

As I continued down the invitation, I realized Pandora's wasn't a person—but a place. Once I moved further down the invite, I noticed it wasn't *just* a place. It was a club. A secret club that could only be accessed by invite or membership. There wasn't an address listed, just a phone number with very explicit instructions on how to use it. If I was interested in attending, I would have to call with the four-digit code at the bottom of the invite, which was 6969. *How fucking ironic.* It didn't take me long to realize Pandora's was some sort of underground, off-the-grid sex club. Who would invite me to a sex gala?

As stated on the invite, whoever invited me had used their only invite for the year. Why would they waste *that* on *me*? I wasn't going. I had no reason to. I was engaged and anybody close enough to me to know what kind of car I drove, and where I would be today, knew that too.

A sex gala? That wasn't me. I loved sex and wished to have better sex, but with Amiri. No one else.

Looking at the invite, I wondered if there was a plus-one, but as I read it, I noticed it didn't state that. Shit, even if there was a plus-one, he wouldn't have been able to go. I wasn't even sure if he'd be into anything like this. I'd only thought about it because hell, maybe if we went, he'd get a little inspiration or something.

Amiri wasn't completely bad in bed, but I'd never had an orgasm. Never. Not unless I was using a vibrator, and I rarely ever used that because his ass felt some type of way any time I reached over to my nightstand. He didn't want me to like it more than I liked him. The man was in competition with a damn sex toy, when we could've figured out a way to make it work for both of us. But when it came to sex, Amiri was basic. We barely had oral sex. He wanted to fuck, bust his nut, roll over and go to sleep. It bothered me, but not to where I'd sneak off to some sort of freaky-ass sex masquerade behind his back, though. I'd be lying if I said my interest wasn't piqued. Maybe if I was single, but I wasn't, so I decided I'd just give it to Naoki.

CHAPTER 2

Jahad

"How is my daughter-in-law?" asked my mother with a sweet smile.

I nodded and stuffed my hands into the pockets of my slacks as I rested on the back of the recliner. "She's good."

"I need to get over there and see her. I just know she's so miserable."

Miserable would be an understatement. Instead of feeding more into what would end up becoming an uncomfortable conversation about my wife, I changed the subject.

"What time Pops coming home?" I asked after flicking my wrist to look at my Rolex. "It's almost ten."

Moms rubbed her bright red lips together and forced a smile. "Any moment now. I'm not sure."

There was a shift. I noticed it the moment it happened. Her mood changed, and although it was a subtle change, I noticed it immediately because I was good at noticing subtle changes. In everyone. In everything. Especially my mother.

My mother's name was Graciela, meaning Grace, and she carried it and wore it well. It was almost as if my grandmother knew exactly who her daughter would become when she looked down at her and gave her such a beautiful, classy name.

I'd never seen the woman sweat. Never seen her act out. Never even heard her raise her voice. She was classy and graceful in every sense of the word, which was why my father, Samuel, had been walking all over her for as long as I could remember. I wanted more for my mother. She deserved more. But what she wanted, and what I felt she deserved, didn't mean shit if she couldn't see it for herself. So, I stayed out of their business. Whatever kept her married to my pops had to be worth it because they'd been married for over thirty years.

Instead of addressing the shift, I chose to ignore it. I ignored and avoided uncomfortable conversations as much as I could. I already had enough shit on my plate to worry about. When I stopped by my parents' house, I wanted the atmosphere to give me a certain type of "hug." This place used to be an escape for me, but lately, it hadn't been. Coming here had been harder and harder the past couple of months. I needed another outlet before I lost it.

That "daughter-in-law" she talked about needing to see had been driving me insane. For good reason, though, and I felt like shit for running away from her as much as I could. Leighton wasn't happy. Hadn't been for some time now. There was nothing I could do to change that. Nothing she could do, either. So, being in the house—that big-ass, seven-thousand-square-foot house—was suffocating as fuck. I thought, coming here, I would be able to breathe. Shit, a nigga was suffocating here too.

"Oh, I guess I'm going to have to catch him next time," I said, before pushing up from the chair to leave.

"You're leaving already? Son, you just got here."

I smiled at her as I walked over. "I've been here for hours, little lady."

She smiled and looked up at me. "Tell my daughter to call me. Answer the phone . . . something."

I nodded. "Will do. *Renmen ou* (Love you)."

Since I didn't stay too far from my parents, the ride was only about fifteen minutes. They were older, so I stayed close by in case of emergencies.

As I drove through the community, I ran my hand over the top of my head and took a deep breath. I hadn't even made it to the house, and I already felt the heaviness of it beginning to weigh me down. Once upon a time, coming home was the highlight of my day. It didn't have the same aura it had six years ago.

I opened the garage and took yet another deep breath at the sight of Leigh's best friend's car parked in my spot. Scratching at my head, I parked in the other empty spot that was reserved for guests. She did shit like that to get a reaction out of me, but I never addressed it. That's what she wanted me to do. Spazz on her, so she could cry and call me disrespectful. The objective in my marriage was to keep the bullshit at a minimum. Adding stress on top of stress wouldn't benefit me at all, so I let shit slide. However, a nigga was reaching his breaking point.

I parked, closed the garage back up, and headed inside. After coming out of my shoes and taking my coat off, I hung it on the rack. As I made my way through the kitchen, my eyes darted over to the stove, where there were pots, pans, sauce, and dishes all over the place. I could tell Farrah had sent our cook, Evaline, home and decided to cook herself. Ms. Evaline would have never left the kitchen dirty. I took another deep breath and continued out of the kitchen.

I had half a mind to go down to my man cave without speaking. That was just how much I wanted to avoid seeing Leigh. What was fucked up was that things hadn't always been this way between us. At one point, we were inseparable. I met her when I was a twenty-year-old wild nigga with too much money and too many bitches at my disposal. She was the good girl, working at the Coney Island I used to post up at. From the first time I laid eyes on her, I wanted her, but she wasn't hearing shit I was spitting at her. Leighton knew I wasn't shit and had every right to turn me down whenever I stepped to her. However, after trying to get with her for about a year straight, she finally went out on a date with me.

That good-girl shit went out of the window the minute my lips touched hers. Leighton went from curving me to throwing her ass back on my dick in the span of a couple of days. That didn't change anything about the way I looked at her. In my eyes, she was still that "it" girl every nigga in the hood wanted but couldn't touch. I'd gotten her, though. And since getting her, I refused to let up on her.

Since we met when we were young, we went through what most young couples go through: cheating, lying, drama, petty shit like that. We broke up more times than I could count, but we always came back together. Eventually, I got my shit together and showed her just how serious I was when I proposed to her. I never stopped showing her how serious I was about her. 'Til this day, I went above and beyond to prove my love for her. But since our story began ten years ago she wasn't the same person. Shit, I wasn't either. The difference with that was, I needed the change. She didn't.

I took my time to reach the second floor. Literally dragged my feet the whole way there. Could've hopped on the elevator but I was in no rush. As soon as I made it to the top of the stairs, the sound of laughter filled my ears. That should have put a smile on my face, but it didn't. Only because I knew the minute I walked into the room, the laughter would stop. It was as if Leighton's smiles and laughter were reserved for everybody but me.

As expected, as soon as I opened the French doors to our bedroom, the laughing stopped, and their eyes landed on me. Farrah turned the corners of her mouth up and eyed me up and down.

"Jahad."

"Farrah," I greeted her back before my eyes traveled from hers to the rest of her body sprawled out on my bed like she owned it.

I didn't have to say shit for her to get up.

Forcing a smile, I walked over to the bed and ran my hand over the top of Leighton's head. "*Sak pase, lanmou* (Wassup, love)?"

Leighton leaned into my touch and tilted her head back so I could kiss her. That was new. She often played roles in front of company, but never like this. Bending down, I kissed her on the lips, letting them linger there for a moment because, shit, I didn't know when I'd be able to feel them again.

"Hi, babe," Leighton said, with a light smile, as our eyes met.

"How you feeling?" I asked her, as I caressed her cheek.

"Good, since I made sure she ate and—"

"I was talking to my wife, Farrah. You should probably dip, though. The snow's picking up," I said, interrupting Farrah as my eyes stayed on Leighton's.

The small glimmer of happiness I'd seen in them when they first met mine was quickly snatched away after I cut into Farrah. Any other time, I wouldn't have given a fuck, but because I was a nigga, hard at work putting some sort of happiness in his wife's life, that fucked with me. For the most part, I was pretty good at keeping a cool head. For the sake of my wife's happiness, I was, at least. But Farrah got up under my skin more than anyone else did because she had no idea what sacrifices I'd made my damn self to take care of my wife. Thing was, I didn't need her or anybody else to know what I did. The things I did for Leighton were done because I'd stood before our families in a church and committed myself to her and our family. It was for Leighton to notice, recognize, and appreciate. However, any time Farrah stepped out of line and tried to insinuate she took care of Leighton more than I did, I couldn't just let it go. I had to speak up and put her in her fucking place.

Farrah took a deep breath and walked to the other side of the bed to give Leighton a hug goodbye. "Call me if you need anything, boo. You know I'll be right back if you do!"

I lightly chuckled and walked away from the bed, scratching the back of my neck. Standing at the dresser, I loosened my tie and removed it with my eyes locked in on the reflection of them in the mirror in front of me.

Farrah had been in Leighton's life longer than I had. They grew up together, so they were more like sisters than best friends, but I couldn't stand her. Shit had always been off between us. The bitch loved sticking her nose in business that wasn't hers. Back in the day, I wasn't good enough for Leigh. I was too hood and didn't have enough ambition. Was a drug-dealing corner boy who wouldn't do anything but bring Leighton problems. That was the shit Farrah thought about me. Only part of it was true. I was a hood, drug-dealing nigga, but the ambition? Ambition had been embedded in me since birth.

A few seconds later, Farrah walked out of the bedroom and Leighton wasted no time whining about the way I'd handled her best friend.

"You know she didn't mean anything by what she said, right?" Leighton asked as I continued to stand at the dresser, removing my jewelry.

I reached behind me and unclamped my gold Cuban link. "Yeah, I know," I lied.

I lied a lot these days. I didn't like to, but the lies came from a good place. Little white lies that hid the way I really felt just to keep shit copacetic. Our marriage was already strained enough. Tonight, she'd greeted me with a kiss after months of nothing. So, shit, I wanted to hold on to whatever good mood she was in. Telling her I didn't give a fuck about Farrah and what she meant would do nothing but change that.

"How was your day?" she asked as she repositioned herself up on the pillows behind her.

I set the rest of my jewelry on the dresser and turned around to join her on the bed. Sitting at the foot of it, near her feet, I reached underneath the covers and touched them. She giggled and tossed her head back against the tufted headboard. Damn, it felt good to see her smile and to hear her laugh . . . with me. I started to think shit, maybe we could get back to where we used to be. I missed this side of Leighton like a muthafucka.

"Stopppp," she said, falling into a fit of laughter. "You know my feet are ticklish, Jah."

I gripped her foot and massaged its arch with my bottom lip pinched between my teeth. "I know."

Her laughs subsided, and her eyes connected with mine. With her head lightly tossed over to the side, she gave me a lazy smile. "Your day. How was it?"

I took a deep breath and moved my hand up her ankle to her calf to massage there instead. "My day was a day. You never told me how yours was."

I felt her body beginning to tense the longer I massaged her calf. I decided not to move to the other one and to slip my hands from up under the cover completely instead. I'd be lying if I said my ego wasn't bruised a little bit. It was like I couldn't touch my wife without the constant reminder of certain shit being off-limits.

Leighton rubbed her lips together and crossed her legs, likely sensing the shift in my mood. Like me, she avoided uncomfortable conversations, too, so she didn't mention it. She would, though. Eventually. That was where we differed. If I chose to ignore something, I left it where it was. However, Leighton never missed an opportunity to revisit uncomfortable moments, especially when she felt guilty about treating me like a random-ass nigga.

"It was cool, I guess. Farrah came over and sent everyone home like she owned the place."

"She has a bad habit of doing that shit," I mentioned. "I bet she didn't clean the dishes she dirtied before she backed out of my spot in my garage. She has no problem leaving her mess for muthafuckas to clean up, though. You know how I am about respect, Leigh. If she pulls that shit again, she won't be coming over here for a minute."

I was calm but stern. I tiptoed around Leighton's feelings, but when it came to Farrah disrespecting the people who worked in this house, I wasn't going for it. I treated them with the utmost respect, and I expected the people who came in and out of this house to do the same. If she couldn't, she could talk to Leighton over FaceTime until she was able to leave the bed.

"Jah," Leighton breathed out. "You know she means well. Farrah is just . . . you know."

Leighton loved to make excuses for her fucked-up best friend. I loved my wife, and I wanted her happy, but if I came home to a dirty home and no staff, she wouldn't be bringing her ass back over here. I didn't have to reiterate that to Leighton, though. She knew when I said something, it was law, regardless of how she felt about it.

"Also, Sarah isn't going to work. I didn't even put up a fight when Farrah told her she could leave. It's something about her bubbly attitude that annoys the hell out of me."

"I'll call the agency first thing in the morning. If she isn't for you, we'll find a new doula," I reassured her.

As I moved up further on the bed, my hands went back underneath the cover. Except, this time, instead of showing her affection, I rubbed her round, growing belly. Leighton was twenty weeks pregnant and on bed rest to term since her body had rejected the last few pregnancies. She was extremely high risk. The fact that we'd made it to the twenty-week mark was a blessing. Usually, she'd miscarry before week ten. Because she couldn't get around much and needed constant support that I couldn't provide around the clock, we hired a prenatal doula. If Leighton wanted a midwife, a maid, and an in-house nurse's aide, she could have them. If it would make shit easier for her, she could have whatever she wanted. This pregnancy was just as important to me as it was to her.

Leighton gave me a light smile before playfully poking her bottom lip out. "I'm being a brat, aren't I? She's the third one this month."

I lightly laughed. "Nah, you're not. You like what you like. You deserve the best, and if Ashley, Diane, and Sarah weren't the best, then shit, baby, we gon' keep hiring and firing until we find her."

Leighton sighed and looked up at me with those pretty, big, doe eyes. "You're so good to me, Jah. I wish I could show you how much I appreciate you."

"You telling me is good enough, love," I told her with a deep breath as I continued to rub her stomach.

Leighton shook her head. "No, it's not. I wish you would—"

"What did Farrah cook?"

I knew where the conversation was heading, and I wanted to stop it before it got there. I walked into the bedroom to a smile. A nigga just wanted to savor the moment, not ruin it with a conversation I was tired of having.

She shook her head. "Why won't you do it? I know you need to—"

"Because I don't want anything with anybody if she isn't you," I interrupted again.

Leighton grabbed my hand and interlocked her fingers with mine. "I know. That's why I trust you. I know you, Jah, and I know you need to—"

"What I need is for you to stop talkin' crazy," I interrupted before bringing her hand up to my lips and kissing it. "You didn't tell me what kind of food Farrah cooked that left my kitchen lookin' like that."

Leighton forced a tight-lipped smile and took a deep breath. "Chicken and shrimp alfredo, Jahad."

Her tone was heavily laced with irritation. She'd dropped the conversation, but I knew it wouldn't be long before she brought it up again.

Getting out of bed, I continued to disrobe, ignoring the desolate gaze in her eyes. I wasn't sure if I'd ever get used to who Leighton was as a whole. She was complicated as hell, and I thought after being with her for so long, I would understand her more, but I hadn't been able to. Not this new version of her, at least. The version of her who thought it was cool to offer me a pass to cheat.

When she first came to me with the crazy-ass idea of giving me a hall pass, I knew for sure I'd never be able to fully understand her. I also realized she'd never understand me either, because if she knew who I was, I mean, really knew who the fuck her husband was, she would have never come to me with that bullshit. I didn't take marriage lightly. I honored her. I honored her on every single level there was to honor a woman on. There were times her mother would playfully call me a manly man, but I was that and I wore that title with pride. Leighton was very well taken care of. I was a husband first, and then everything else right after. I wasn't sure why Leighton thought that just because she'd given me the green light to fuck someone else, I would do it. That was not who I was.

Initially, I thought maybe she thought I'd accept it because I was wild when we first got together, but I was thirty and none of that shit excited me. What excited me now was stability. Coming home to a woman I loved every day. A *happy* woman. I hadn't come home to a happy woman for a while. But today was different, and a nigga wanted to bask in it.

"You're upset," Leighton stated. "I'm not trying to upset you."

"I'm not upset," I told her before clenching down on my jaw.

Sucking her teeth, she said, "Yes, you are. Your body language changed completely as soon as I mentioned the pass."

Locking eyes with her in the reflection of the mirror, I corrected her. "I'm not upset. I'm disappointed."

"Disappointed?"

"Disappointed," I repeated. "I can't remember the last time you smiled and blushed with me. I get that tonight and you . . ."

"And I what? Try to do something nice for you? Do you know how many men would kill for a damn hall pass?"

Because we couldn't have sex, she thought the best way to show her gratitude would be by allowing me to go out and get it from someone else. Someone who didn't have restrictions. Someone who wasn't tired and depressed most of the time. Someone happier who would love to please me. Leighton said there wasn't a woman on earth who would deny me. I knew that. Didn't give a fuck about it, though. I didn't want to open Pandora's box, despite how tempting it was to.

"You know how many of them niggas *ain't me*?" I asked her before coming out of my shirt and heading to the closet to put it inside of my laundry basket. "I don't know what type of nigga you think you've married, Leigh."

"I didn't marry a nigga. I married a man. A good man. Which is why this . . . this pass won't bother me!" she yelled lightly, her eyes following me around the room.

She wanted to get out of bed and follow me around bad as hell. I knew it because that was what Leighton did before she was put on bedrest. She'd follow me, arguing, pointing and shit, trying to get her point across. Trying to be heard. Which she never really needed to do. I heard her. I could hear her clearly without the theatrics, but . . . Leighton was Leighton, and she was the epitome of theatrical. I'd say I was to blame for that. She was spoiled and hated to hear the word *no* because she never had to. My rejecting her offer was the first rejection she'd gotten from me in months. The last time, she wanted to go against doctor's orders by going out of the country for her birthday. What Leighton didn't realize was that any time I told her no, I was looking out for her. Especially when it came to that hall pass.

Why would I accept it? That wasn't what she wanted. Leighton was tweaking. She was out of her mind. If I accepted it, it would backfire. However, that wasn't the whole reason I told her no. I just wasn't interested. There wasn't a woman in the world I wanted if it wasn't her. Leighton was it for me. The hall pass wasn't attractive to me. I didn't get excited when she first mentioned it. It pissed me off, low key. Because she thought so little of me. So little of my loyalty. She thought that just because we couldn't fuck, I'd go out and fuck someone else? She thought I was that selfish?

"Jahad," Leighton said with a deep breath. "I can't . . . there isn't much I can do for you. Just let me do this one thing." I looked over my shoulder at her eyes growing misty with desperation. "Please," she begged.

Shaking my head, I rejected her offer again. "Leigh, I seriously don't want to talk about this shit anymore, aight? I'm not doing it. I won't do it."

"What are you afraid of? Why won't you accept it, huh, Jah? You're afraid you're going to fall in love with the bitch?" she snapped, despite the calmness of my voice when I spoke to her.

That was one of our biggest issues. Leighton moved entirely off raw emotion. She couldn't see I was literally trying to save her from herself because she was allowing her own insecurities to get the best of her. What she didn't understand was that she didn't have anything to be insecure about. We couldn't have sex. That was out of her control. What Leighton so badly wanted to give me now, she should have given to me before she was put on bedrest. She was so eager for me to get something from someone else now, but before, she didn't care too much about what I didn't get from her.

Sex, for Leigh, had turned into a chore. For the past three years, she'd been clocking her ovulation like crazy. She had multiple alarms set on both of our phones, specific positions she wanted to be fucked in, rules, regulations, and zero passion. It was a job. It was to a point where I had to schedule meetings around her ovulation. We were constantly at appointments. We went through numerous miscarriages. Our marriage was . . . practically over. We were pretty much just together to have a baby.

Leighton was . . . she was selfish. I hated to admit it, but it was the truth. This whole hall pass thing wasn't specifically for me, and me alone. Leighton was worried about me cheating on her, so she figured, hell, I'll give him permission before I'm blindsided. She didn't have to tell me that for me to know it because again, I knew my wife. The real version of my wife. Not this emotionally unstable, crazy-ass person. And I knew she really, truly didn't want me to stick my dick inside pussy that wasn't hers.

Turning around, I walked over to the bed and placed both my hands on the side of her, locking her in the middle. With my eyes locked on hers, I asked, "You want me to fuck someone else, Leigh? You want me to tap my dick against her clit before I stuff this fat muthafucka inside of her pussy? You want her to beg me to pull back, and then beg me to give it all to her? Hm? You want another woman to cum all over my dick? Is that what you want? You want me to bend her over and—"

"Okay, Jahad! Enough!" Leighton yelled, putting her hand up against my chest, pushing me away. "I don't need the details."

"You can't even handle me talking about fuckin' someone else, but you think you can handle me actually doing it? You know exactly what I'm going to do to her. All the shit you used to love. The shit that had you changing the sheets every night. Before you turned sex into a—"

"Jahad," Leighton pleaded, cutting me off. "I said enough."

Inching away from the bed, I rubbed the back of my neck. Gazing down at my hard dick, I sucked in air and gritted my teeth. Leighton's eyes landed on it, and I watched as her throat moved up and down with a swallow. Placing her fists into the bed, she pushed back against the headboard and licked her lips before putting her eyes back on mine.

"Come here," she offered.

With my eyes planted on hers, I walked back over to the bed. Leighton scooted over to the side of the bed and grabbed the waistband of my pants before undoing the buckle to my belt. When she got my pants and underwear down, she grabbed my dick, lightly tugging on it. She then turned on her side and pulled me closer to the bed so she could wrap her lips around it.

Leighton hadn't sucked my dick in months. She hadn't just gotten the urge to. She wasn't horny and wanting to do it because she wanted to please me. She was doing it because she'd pissed me off and I'd reacted instead of ignoring it like I usually did. Leighton was giving me apology head, and as crazy as it might've sounded, I didn't want it. What I wanted from my wife was passion, and the head she was giving me lacked that significantly. There was nothing behind it. No sloppy spit. No sensual eye contact. She hadn't tried to take it down her throat. None of the things she knew I loved. She licked and sucked me like it was a fucking chore. The same way she fucked me before she got pregnant.

Instead of standing there, accepting the bullshit, I pulled back and bent down to pull my pants up. It wasn't like I was going to nut off that shit, anyway. High key, I felt like she wanted me to walk away, just so she could get out of it.

This time, when she called after me, I ignored her.

CHAPTER 3

Sienna

I grabbed the bottle of Pinot Noir and two champagne flutes and carried them into the living room, where SZA's new album played at a low level. Before plopping down on the couch, I set the bottle and glasses on the coffee table before filling both of our glasses to the rim. We didn't do that fancy shit over here. We loved wine but refused to constantly refill our glasses after taking five damn sips.

Naoki walked from the kitchen with the charcuterie board and set it in the middle of the table before sitting next to me.

Every Saturday night, we had a little ladies' night at Naoki's house in the prestigious Beverly Hills, Michigan. She had the perfect place for it. Our ladies' nights were always classy, and the aesthetic of her home was top tier. As a traveling nurse, Naoki had bank. She was constantly on the road, so we savored these special moments.

As always, it was just me and Naoki for the first hour before the rest of the ladies began to trickle in. Mahogany, my big sister, was pretty much a married single mother who always had to drop my nieces and nephew off at our parents' house, so that always slowed her down. Hazel, my baby sister, was just lazy and constantly waited until the last minute to leave. Naoki's sister Sage had to make sure the grown-ass man child she married was good before she left. Meaning, she had to make sure dinner was done, the house was cleaned, and his balls were drained dry before she left. Me, I always showed up an hour early because I didn't have shit else going on. Amiri was out with his boys, and I wasn't working yet. We never cared about everyone else being late, though. Them being late gave us an opportunity to spend a little time alone where we could spill tea only reserved for best friends. I loved my sisters with my whole heart, but I didn't like them bitches in my business too much. Some conversations were just for best friends and best friends only. Especially the conversation I wanted to have about that freaky-ass gold invitation.

Once we got situated, I dug into my Prada bag and grabbed it, tossing it on Naoki's lap. With wine in her mouth, she looked up at me with furrowed brows. After swallowing her drink, she asked, "What the hell is this? You decided on wedding invites without me?"

I scrunched my lips up at her as if to say, *Yeah right, bitch.* "No, Kiki. Open it."

Naoki rested against the backing of the soft, curved couch and kicked her legs up under her bottom. She turned it over and gave me a look similar to the one I made when I saw my name engraved on it. She ran her fingers over it and turned her mouth down, impressed.

"This is fire. I'm doing this for your invitations," she said before opening the envelope.

"I'm not getting those people's names engraved on their invites, Ki. I don't care that much," I said with a laugh before picking my glass up. "At all."

Naoki sucked her teeth. "I said *I'm* doing it, thank you very fucking much."

Naoki and I had been best friends for as long as I could remember. We grew up together on the east side of Detroit. We used to hang with two other girls but they moved out of the neighborhood, but we stayed until we were old enough to move out ourselves.

She'd been right by my side for everything in my life, so it was only right to make her my maid of honor, despite having two eager sisters who wanted that title. They were my babies, but Naoki? Naoki was too. She was my soulmate. I was told in life, we have multiple soulmates. When I learned that, I knew for certain she was at least one of them. We butted heads every now and then, but that was only because she wanted the absolute best for me and, in turn, I wanted the same for her. Our little spats never carried on to the next day, though, and I loved that about us.

After damn near drooling over the envelope, Naoki finally opened it. I watched with a smirk as her eyes widened and she made it further down the invite. I continued to sip my wine.

"Biiiitch," she said with wide eyes. "Who invited you to Pandora's? Bitch, I been trying to get in there for years!"

I damn near spat my wine out in surprise. "Naoki!"

"What? Bitch, you know I'm a freak. Hell, you're a freak too. Your freak is just reserved for your man. Mine? My freak is unchained, baby," she joked. "Seriously. Who invited you to Pandora's?"

I shrugged. "I have no idea. The other day when you pissed me off, as I was on my way to my car, I saw it on my windshield. Somebody put it there. At first, I thought it might've been from Amiri but I knew it wasn't when he called me and didn't mention it at all."

Naoki picked her glass up and sipped from it, probably trying to choose her words carefully before saying something crazy about my man.

"Shit, it probably is from him. You said you were trying to spice it up in the bedroom, but he don't be biting, right? Maybe this is his little way to get the ball rolling."

I scrunched my face up. "Now, you know that nigga don't even roll like that. This seems like some straight-up orgy, swingers-type shit. Amiri don't even like me to use my rose. I highly doubt if he'd like to fuck me in a room full of strangers."

Since I received the invite three days ago, that thought had crossed my mind, for sure, but I knew better. Amiri wasn't the type. He was a sex symbol on social media, but he didn't live that in real life. When I said he was basic, I meant it. The most excitement I got in the bedroom was when he was away and it was just me, my rose, and Twitter. I stayed with him because love and relationships, to me, was more than just sex. Amiri and I worked well in other departments.

Naoki cocked her head to the side and pulled her mouth down as if to say *You're right.* "Well . . . Who then? They spelled your name right and everything, so you know it's someone you know."

I hadn't even thought about that. Whoever it was had to know me enough to know how to spell my name right.

"Bitch, was it you?" I asked with a squint.

Naoki gave me another knowing look. "Girl, please. You know if I was a part of a freaky club, I would've been told you and I wouldn't have put the invite on your damn windshield. I would be dragging your ass to that masquerade the day of, without you knowing a damn thing because I know your ol' faithful ass wouldn't go for it if I didn't drag you."

Naoki wanted me to get my "lick back" with Amiri so bad! I thought it was funny, but I wasn't the type. I didn't do tit for tat. Not when it came to my body, at least. If I was going to go out and fuck someone, it wouldn't be done out of spite. It would be done because I really just wanted to. I was the type of woman who lets karma do its thing. Amiri would get his, either in this life or the next. Who knows? But I wasn't for getting my lick back. At all.

"Exactly. But you can have it," I said with a shrug. "Call the number. Go have a time, sis."

With wide eyes, Naoki looked over at me. "You lying! You for real?"

I giggled and sipped from my drink. "What am I going to do with it, Kiki? Go get slutted out just how I know you want to."

Naoki danced around in her seat and bit down on her long nail. "Oh, bitch, I'm getting slutted out for sure. I hope it be some big-dick, thick niggas up in there. I want a dick in all of my holes and—"

"Naoki!" I interrupted before falling into a fit of laughter. "What is wrong with you?"

Shrugging her left shoulder, she reached for her phone to call the number on the invite. "We're here for a good time, not a long time. I got some thangs on my bucket list and being a glazed, cream-filled donut is one of them. I want all types of cream and—"

"Okay, Naoki. Just call the number. Save that shit for the party."

She laughed and put the phone on speaker after finally calling. I picked up the remote to the surround sound speakers and lowered the volume to the music. Naoki was so damn excited. I knew she would be. My girl lived life without restrictions for sure. That was one thing I loved about my bestie. She did what she wanted, regardless of what someone might think or say about her. She was the embodiment of a free spirit. I did what I wanted, for the most part, but I was nowhere near as free-spirited as Naoki. My freak was tucked and hidden, kept behind closed doors. Naoki was vocal as hell about who she was and what she wanted. Her social media pages were full of freaky shit. Hell, the Twitter page I frequented the most was hers. Her likes were full of the best shit.

"What's the code?" Naoki asked.

"Six-nine-six-nine," I told her with a laugh.

"Of fucking course," she said with a light laugh before pressing it into the keypad.

About a minute later, an operator answered the line. She asked Naoki for her full name, date of birth, what she identified as, and her sexual orientation. The minute she told them her name was Naoki Childs, the lady cut her off.

"I'm sorry. The information you entered does not match my records. Do you have another code, perhaps?"

Naoki's eyebrows snapped together. "Huh? No. My friend said I could use her invite."

"Invitations aren't transferable" was the last thing the lady said before the phone hung up.

Naoki cursed and went to call the number back but she didn't get through. Her number was seemingly blocked instantaneously.

"What the fuck?" Naoki yelled. "What type of—Si, you have to go! If I can't go, I have to live vicariously through you. As a matter of fact, bitch, I'm getting you one of those undetectable cameras to go inside of your hair or your mask. But shit, what if the nigga you fucking nut on it? I won't be able to see—"

"Girl, shut the hell up!" I laughed. "You won't be living vicariously through me because I'm not going."

"I can't believe you're going to let an invitation to Pandora's go to waste." Naoki pouted before sitting back against the couch cushions, twiddling the invite. She actually looked pretty sad about not being able to go. I almost felt sorry for her freaky ass.

"What's the big deal, Ki?"

Shifting her eyes up at me, she frowned. "What's the big deal? Pandora's is like . . . underground fetish, BDSM, kink, swingers royalty. It's not just some hole-in-the-wall sex spot. It's upscale, classy, and very professional. That's the big deal. And only big-dick, balling niggas frequent the spot. If you ain't got money, you're not walking in the building. Not without a hefty bank account or one of these high-quality invitations. I should've known a place like Pandora's wouldn't allow invite transfers. I should've said I was you."

I laughed. "The way you put it, they would have known you were lying about your identity, anyway. I'm sure places like that require medical records and identification and shit."

She cut her eyes at me and sighed. "You're right, and we don't look shit alike."

"Cheer up, ho. You'll get cream filled and glazed, eventually."

About thirty minutes later, everyone else had arrived. While they sat around, sipping wine, sharing a couple of edibles, my mind was on Pandora's and where the invite could have come from. I was tempted to ask my sisters about it, but I didn't want to, for obvious reasons. If I told them, my mother would know about it tomorrow and I didn't have time to have an uncomfortable conversation about why someone would think of me enough to take the liberty of inviting me to a damn sex club. I couldn't trust them.

Mahogany, my big sister, plopped down on the couch right beside me and rested her elbow on the back cushion. "Why you so quiet, bitch?"

I leaned forward for my glass and finished it. "No reason."

"Mm-hmm," Mahogany doubted with twisted lips. "Did Momma tell you she wants us all to come over for New Year's Eve? Is Amiri working?"

I frowned. "Come over for what? Since when? *Lawd.*"

For the most part, my family was pretty close knit. My sisters and I grew up close, being that we were only a year apart. My mother used to dress us up like triplets and everything. Most people thought we were since our names were different shades of brown. Sienna, Mahogany, and Hazel. We fed into that shit, too, for a while. You couldn't tell us we weren't triplets.

We walked around school like we were, and were often called the Mills Triplets. People in school knew we weren't really triplets, but like I said, we fed into it. We were all the same size back then and wore matching outfits and all.

It was cute, but by the time we graduated, we were over that shit. The only thing we had in common for real were our names and our looks. We were so different personality-wise.

"She says she's trying to start the year off with fresh new traditions."

"It's a little too late for that, isn't it?" I mumbled, before pouring myself another glass of wine.

My mother was okay. She was sweet as pie, but was meddling as hell. She probably figured it was okay to start new traditions with us because she felt like we wouldn't have anything else to do. Mahogany had a family, but she stayed at our parents' house faithfully since her husband, Duke, worked a lot and she often needed them to watch her kids. Hazel was wild. She didn't have anything stable going on. Shit, one week she could be fucking with a nigga, the next, she could be with a bitch, and the next, she could be in a whole-ass polyamorous relationship. Baby sis was living her best life and I didn't blame her for it! She was young, so why the hell not?

Then there was me . . . engaged to a damn Instagram model who stayed on the go. Momma just knew I wasn't doing anything. And so what if she was right?

"You know how she is," Mahogany said before she accepted the piece of gummy from Sage and popped it into her mouth.

Sage handed me a piece and I took it before grabbing my wine. I was going home drunk and horny for my man. I hoped tonight, he was on the same type of time because all this talk about Pandora's, big-dick niggas, and freaky shit had me horny as hell.

Hours later, I staggered into the house, feeling around the wall for the light switch. When I finally found it, I turned the lights on to find Amiri on the couch, laid out. Sucking my teeth, I slipped out of my Doc Martens and turned to close and lock the door. Biting my bottom lip, I tiptoed over the threshold, toward the couch. It was late, around two in the morning, and he'd just texted me a couple of hours ago to let me know he was heading home. I told him to be showered and ready for me to choke on his dick when I walked into the house. He thought I was joking and sent a laughing emoji. I was not playing.

After we got high and finished three bottles of wine, I was good and buzzed. I was the freakiest when I was drunk, so Amiri should have already known what time it was.

Apparently, he didn't, because he was sprawled out on the couch in his shoes and coat, like he sat down and passed out as soon as he hit the house. Clearly, he was drunk, too, because if he wasn't, he would have never walked into the house with his wet-ass boots on. He knew I didn't play that shit.

Me and Amiri were two different people when we were drunk. He was the pass-out type, and me, I was the freaky type. How different we were didn't mesh well because I'd be ready to fuck—like now—and he'd be dead asleep. However, tonight, I didn't care about how passed-out drunk he was. I was getting fucked.

I crouched down in front of him and rubbed his thighs through his jeans. Amiri didn't move a muscle at my touch.

"Miri," I cooed. "Wake up, daddy."

I bit my bottom lip and ran my hand up the middle of his jeans, trying to at least wake his sleeping dick up. Sucking my teeth, I climbed on his lap and straddled him. Cupping the back of his neck, I nibbled on the side of it, gyrating my hips against his warm body, hoping that all the movement and kissing would wake him, but Amiri was out.

"Amiri!" I yelled before sitting up and pushing him in the chest.

He stirred a little and lazily opened his eyes. "Yeah?"

"I told you to—seriously?" He was out again, just as fast as he woke up.

I sat there with my head cocked to the side, tight lips, and a wet pussy, mad as hell. If it wasn't for that damn invitation, I would be straight. This wasn't the first time Amiri had left me hanging when he knew I was coming home to ride his dick. It likely wouldn't be the last, but tonight . . . tonight I really, really, really needed it.

Taking a deep breath, I continued to stare down at him, snoring his big-ass head off.

Leaning down, I kissed him on his motionless lips. As I gave him soft kisses, he snored really loud, making me flinch so hard, I nearly jumped out of my damn skin.

"Fuck this," I mumbled as I got down off his lap.

If he wouldn't fuck me, I'd just have to go into my nightstand. What else was I supposed to do? I was horny as hell and he was knocked out, asleep. At least tonight, I would get the nut I wouldn't get if I was with him. It was sad to say, but the truth.

As I crept out of the living room, the sound of his phone chiming stopped me dead in my tracks. I hadn't had the desire to check his phone in months. The thought never crossed my mind because when we were together, it never made a peep.

At first, I thought it was strange and checked to see if it was on silent or do not disturb but it wasn't. The last time I went through it, there was nothing to find. It was pretty boring, aside from the thirsty bitches who stayed in his DMs. However, tonight, something told me to go back and check it.

I was the type of woman who looked at everything as a sign, and something in my gut told me the reason he was knocked out like that was because I needed to check his phone. Call me crazy, but that was just the way I saw it, and who was I to pass up on the perfect opportunity to see if my man was really as faithful as he claimed to be?

Turning around, I placed a piece of hair behind my ear and crept back over to the couch where his phone was sitting on the couch next to him. My heartbeat was heavy against my chest as I went to pick it up. I wasn't sure if I was more afraid of finding something, or him waking up and catching me, but a bitch was shook.

When I picked the phone up, my eyebrows immediately furrowed.

"What the fuck?" I mumbled. He had seven text messages.

Looking over at him, I squinted and shook my head. Something was up. Something had to be up. *Who texts someone seven times?* Because it was locked, I couldn't see who the messages were from. But lucky for me, I had the code.

Before unlocking it, I did a slow trot through the living room to the guest bathroom. Closing the door behind me, I put the toilet seat down, sat, tapped the code in, and went straight for the messages.

I'd be lying if I said I was surprised to see that the messages had come from a female. I wasn't surprised at all. But I was surprised to see the messages were from the same bitch he cheated on me with. The bitch he claimed didn't mean shit to him. The same girl he said it was only sex with. It couldn't be just sex. Not if she was still reaching out to him after two years. She was in love, begging him to come see her. Amiri was short with her, brushing her off, telling her to chill and that he'd come through when he could. I was numb to it. I had to be. Why would I be surprised? He was a nigga. Niggas lied. I was just a dumbass to believe he'd actually stopped lying and cheating.

However, when it came to the *I'm pregnant* texts and ultrasound photos, my heart broke. That . . . that was the straw that broke the camel's back. That did it for me. I didn't have one tear in my eye until I saw that. I cried. Silent, painful tears. Not for us. Not because we were over. Not because he'd cheated on me. I cried for myself. I cried for years and years of pent-up sadness because what she got, I'd never have the pleasure of getting—a baby.

For a while, since I found out I couldn't have children, I was okay with it. I accepted it. But seeing the messages, finding out he had a baby on the way, it crushed me. Since I found out *we* wouldn't be having children, Amiri was good with it. He didn't worry. He didn't care. He told me I was all he needed. He told me, yeah, a baby would be nice, but it didn't mean we were broken in any way. He told me I wasn't broken. He told me I was as perfect as I'd always been. He told me that finding out the chances of me having a child were very slim didn't change a thing. I was flawless and I'd always be flawless.

As I swiped through the messages, I wondered how long this would have stayed a secret had I not found out about it? What were his plans? What did she mean to him? Did he plan to leave me because she'd given him something I wouldn't be able to give him?

I was tripping. My crown had fallen completely off my head. It wasn't her. It wasn't the cheating. It was the pregnancy. It was the baby. We said we were okay without having children. But . . .

Shaking my head, I stood up and hit the lock button on the phone. I looked in the mirror at the steady stream of tears falling down my cheeks and swallowed, wrapping my arms around my body. Taking a deep breath, I wiped them away with the backs of my hands. I held my head high and pushed my shoulders back, refusing to be defeated. Refusing to allow this to break me. Refusing to undo so many years of growth. I was proud of myself because the tears I'd just shed had nothing to do with Amiri cheating on me. I told myself that after I forgave him that first time, I'd never shed another tear for him if those tears were because of cheating. I hadn't broken that promise to myself, and I wouldn't tonight.

I was gracefully bowing out of this bullshit.

CHAPTER 4

Jahad

I shook hands with Saint before sitting down across from him at his desk. Running my hand over the top of my waves, I tossed my head back a little and sighed.

"Damn, big bro, you need one of these?" he asked, lifting his glass of 1942.

I nodded. "Hell yeah."

He pushed away from his desk and headed over to his bar. "I got a feeling this drink you need doesn't have shit to do with business."

"Has it ever? Business is flawless. You already know," I told him, as I scrolled through my phone, scanning over emails, text messages, and missed phone calls.

Business hadn't always been flawless, but for the past five years, things pretty much ran themselves. All we had to do was sit back, delegate here and there, and make hundreds of thousands of dollars in our sleep without having to lift a finger on most occasions.

I was in the drug and gun business with my family. Along with my uncles, my father left Haiti for the United States to start a better life for us. I was five when he left, and ten when he came back to collect us. It was a transition, for sure. The States was big. Very big in the eyes of a ten-year-old. Life moved fast here. Sometimes too fast. We could barely keep up with everything, but eventually, we all transitioned very well.

When Samuel left us, I thought he'd traveled to the States for a real job. I thought that when my father came to collect us, we would touch U.S. soil with a solid, legitimate source of income. I thought struggling, stealing, and danger was over for us. But shit, all we had done was exchange one hell for the next. I went from taking care of family back home by doing odd jobs and stealing, to pretty much doing the same shit here.

I spent my first two years here shadowing him and my uncles. Initially, I didn't know what was going on. I was twelve and just happy to bond with my father after not seeing him consistently for years. But soon, I realized he'd been grooming me for the drug game. Every day after school, he'd pick us up. He'd drop my brothers and sister off at home and I'd ride with him to my uncle's place. I went on every drop and pickup with him. Back then, he was a low-level courier. All of them were. Samuel, much like me, was sophisticated in the art of hustle. He stayed low until it was time for him to come up. It took him a minute, but eventually, he moved up the ranks.

Pops went from couriering to copping his own bricks to cook up. He gave me my first rock to sell at thirteen and I was good at it. Damn good at it because I'd been a hustler my whole life, pretty much. I knew the streets well because, again, I drove around with him, witnessed transactions, and saw what that rock did to people. Literally witnessed beautiful women transform into the ugliest sack of saggy skin and bones in just a couple of months.

He didn't just show me how easy it was to move it neither. He made sure to show me what that drug money could get me. As a kid, I'd watch the big-time dealers pushing crazy-ass whips, flaunting money and shit with bright eyes. The nigga he worked for, D-Low, stayed peeling me off a couple of twenties every time I saw him. The stack he'd have on him would be stupid phat. When Samuel offered me that rock to sell, he made sure to mention D-Low and the gold chain he'd let me wear around my neck any time he was in a meeting with my pops. Told me that if I moved the sack he gave me, he would shoot me to the mall to grab my very own. That was all it took.

"Sis?" he questioned, wearing a knowing smirk.

He knew. Of course, he knew. Saint was the only person I told about Leigh's hall pass. Saint was my youngest brother, but we were the closest. He didn't find what Leigh wanted from me to be too alarming. For me, it was outrageous.

Growing up, I was taught family and loyalty were top priority. Before my father left, I was told I was the man of the house, and I was to take care of home. Whatever my mother needed, I was to do with no question asked. I was taught that she was the queen, and I was the prince. I was taught to take care of the women in my life with love, loyalty, and complete devotion. So, you could just imagine how uncomfortable Leighton's request made me feel. I didn't want to give myself to anyone else. Granted, things hadn't always been that way, but when I committed to her, I vowed to never break that commitment. I was hers, and she was mine. That was the way shit went when I asked her to be my wife. There was no room for anyone else in that equation.

Snorting was enough of a response to know it was sis. It was always sis.

Saint smirked, as he filled my glass halfway and brought it over to me. "She still beggin' you to cheat?"

Mimicking her, I said, *"It's not cheating if I'm telling you to do it, Jahad Baptiste."* We shared a laugh, and I shook my head. "I think she's lost her mind."

Saint shrugged with his mouth turned down. "Ain't that what happens when women get pregnant? They start thinkin' crazy and shit? You already know how I feel about it. You know the offer still stands."

I shifted my eyes up from my glass to him. "Nothing's changed."

"How long has it been?" he questioned with a cocked brow.

Instead of responding to him, I tilted my glass up to my mouth and drank it all. It was going on six months. Saint knew I hadn't fucked my wife since I'd gotten her pregnant, so I didn't need to tell him how long it'd been since I'd felt the inside of pussy. I didn't like to talk about it.

For a while, I ignored it by putting my focus on work and taking care of Leighton. But since Leighton had given me that bullshit-ass head the other night, all I'd thought about was sex.

"All I have to do is make a call, Jah. One call and you're in there, with no problem. No strings attached. Handle business and go on with your life like nothing ever happened," Saint continued before taking a sip of his drink. "I commend you, big brother. I really do. Because if my wife gave me a pass to go out and have sex with a random woman, I would take it. Shit, you know me . . . I wouldn't even *need* a pass. The whole faithful shit, that's you. I would've been gotten my dick wet. Especially if I was dealing with what you've been dealing with." He paused and held his hands up. "No offense. But that's me and you're you and you don't play 'bout that shit. Which is why that hall pass is perfect for you, bro. Just do it. Fuck it."

I sat back against the leather chair, stroking my beard, staring across the desk at him. Saint didn't fully understand it because he was young and unattached. He was me years ago. Free, fucking any and everything pretty with a pulse and a phat ass. Fucking random women no longer excited me. He couldn't wrap his mind around that because, right now, at twenty-three, it sounded absurd to him.

"How about this," Saint said with a sigh as he picked his phone up. "I'll make the call—"

"Saint—"

"Listen, *listen*," he stressed, locking eyes with me. "I'll make the call . . . just in case you decide to change your mind, bro. The door will always be open for you. If you don't take it, you just don't take it. If you decide you want to . . ." He paused. "You won't have to go to a bar, looking for anybody to fuck. You can just stroll up in Pandora's, get your dick sucked, fuck something, leave and go on with your life." He shrugged. "It's that simple."

It's that simple. It wasn't *that* simple. Not for me, it wasn't. Leighton was my heart. She meant the world to me and I knew if I fucked with someone else, it would ultimately crush her, despite how much she'd claimed she wanted me to fuck something. I was completely selfless when it came to shorty. As any man with a wife should be.

But I couldn't help but ponder the idea of it. I was a man, at the end of the day, who hadn't felt the velvety, creamy walls of a pussy in months. The offer was tempting as hell.

Leigh was five months, with about four months left to go. Then there was the healing process and handling the load of taking care of a newborn baby. Shit, at this rate, I probably wouldn't slide into shit for at least another eight months or so. I didn't think I could last that long. It was a miracle I had lasted this long, honestly. I had an aggressive-ass appetite for sex. I loved everything about it. To me, pussy was a work of art and I treated it as such. When I could, at least.

I felt like a nigga who had been away from his passion for too long. Shit was really eating at me, to keep it a buck. I was trapped between a rock and a hard place, for sure.

"I see you over there thinking, big bro," Saint said with a smirk. "Jump in some pussy, nigga. It's inhumane what you've been through."

I laughed just as there were four familiar knocks at the door. Blaise. I locked eyes with Saint, and he already knew what time it was. What we talked about when it came to my private shit like the hall pass stayed between us. I loved my brothers equally, but Blaise was a different type of nigga, and I kept my personal affairs to myself when it came to him.

A couple of seconds later, he walked in and sucked in air. With his hand roughly rubbing against his head, he shook it and went straight to the bar without a greeting. Neither me nor Saint was surprised. Every time this nigga showed up, it was the same shit. I wondered what the issue was tonight. He kept a boatload of them bitches.

My eyes followed him, waiting for what I knew would come at any second. Five, four, three—

"This bitch," Blaise said with a deep breath. "Every fuckin' day, this bitch finds a new way to ruin my life."

"I believe you ruined your own life, my nigga," Saint said with a laugh.

Blaise scoffed. "Pussy was too wet for a condom. I had to take it off."

"Now look at you," I said, laughing. "Fuckin' animal, G."

Blaise tossed his head back, stressed. "I love my kid, dawg. Love her to pieces. But . . . I'm mad her momma's pussy was too good for a condom. Mad I made her with that . . . that evil bitch."

"Arianna straight in my book," Saint began, egging Blaise on as he always did when he was on a rant about Ari. "Every time I pick Bebe up, Ari ain't shit but smiles. She meet a nigga at the door with a hot plate and a smile every single time."

Blaise glared over at him and pointed with his glass. "Keep playin' with me, nigga."

I tossed my head back, cracking up. Blaise liked to talk about how his baby moms got on his nerves and how he hated the bitch, but any time Saint played on his top about her, he was ready for war. It was funny as hell to me. Saint wasn't stupid enough to fuck with Ari, though. Family and loyalty went hand in hand with us. Our bond was unbreakable, and shit, unshakable too. It was solid.

These niggas drove me crazy every now and then, but when it came to them, I would murder any and everything moving if necessary. Pop instilled the importance of loyalty within us at a very young age, especially when it came to me. I was the head of it all. I led, and my brothers, they followed. Always had. Always would.

Despite how old we got, nothing about that would change. They looked up to me the most because when Pops left us in Haiti, I was father. I was the one making sure everything ran smoothly and the one who made sure they ate, got to school, and respected Mother. In them, I instilled the importance of brotherhood, blood ties, and loyalty because Pops instilled it in me. I taught them young, so regardless of how appealing Ari might've been to Saint, he'd never cross the line with her. He joked with Blaise, but that was where the flirtatious jokes stopped.

Blaise walked from behind the bar and over to us. Before he sat down beside me, he extended his hand and I stood to do our handshake. After, he did the same with Saint, just as I had done when I walked into the office. Sitting down, Blaise took another deep breath.

"She wants me to keep Bebe for a full month next month. How will I do that with everything coming up? I have to go home with Pops in a couple of weeks."

Home was and always would be Haiti, regardless of where we rested our heads. Pops left long ago, but he still had a few business affairs there that he had to check in on every couple of months. He took turns taking us every time he had to go. This time, Blaise was up. The last time, I was to go, but because of Leighton's condition, he didn't bother mentioning it and I didn't bring it up. What was understood didn't need to be addressed.

"Leave her with Moms while you go out there," Saint suggested before taking a sip of his drink. "You know she loves Bebe. Her and Natasha would love to have her there. I don't even know why you trippin' off that shit."

Blaise shook his head and sipped from his cup. "So that bitch can complain about me pawning Bebe off on Moms?"

I sat there, stoic, without an offer of resolution for him. My opinion about the situation was, Blaise should've been smarter when it came to the situation.

When I was out being wild, doing me, I was careful when it came to fucking random bitches I couldn't imagine spending the rest of my life with. I was smarter and calculated when it came to sleeping with them because I didn't want to go through what he was going through. As a young nigga, I knew off top what I wanted for my future. The woman who mothered my children would also bear my last name. Leighton didn't get pregnant with our first child until we were married. I was serious about that type of shit. I refused to have baby momma drama.

It was crazy how I did all of that planning to end up with a rocky marriage and the chances of having a child being slim to none. As crazy as it might sound, I'd rather go through miscarriages with the woman I loved than to have a child with an ignorant broad like Ari. I was smooth on that.

The buzzing of my phone in my pocket pulled my attention from my brothers. Setting my glass down, I reached into the pocket of my jeans to see who it was. Leighton.

"What up, baby?" I answered, leaned back against the chair.

"Hello?"

It wasn't Leighton. It was Farrah.

"Yeah, Farrah?"

Saint threw his hands up and yelled, "What up, Farrah? When yo' fine ass gon' stop playing with me—"

I pushed up from the chair and walked out of the office, cutting his ignorant ass off.

Farrah sucked her teeth and took a deep breath. "Are you coming home to your wife anytime soon? She's having a really rough day. I know being here is the last thing you'd like to do, but you do have obligations here, Jahad."

I was there. I left because Leighton wanted me to. She claimed I was crowding her and that she needed some space to get her mind together. We hadn't had a good day since I came home to her smiling. That day couldn't even count as a good one, to be honest. It ended the same way every day ended: with her giving me the cold shoulder and softly crying throughout the night.

Leighton had no idea what her sadness did to me. Listening to her cry, watching her struggle with being bedridden and worrying about the future of our child fucked me up just as much. I just handled my stress differently than she did.

Farrah calling me, like I wasn't taking care of my wife, pissed me the fuck off. I did a damn good job taking care of her, but there was only so much I could do, especially when she rejected me every chance she got.

"When I get to the crib, I don't want to see you there. As a matter of fact, get the fuck up out my house right now. I trust that Evaline and Maurice are still there. They better be, considering their shifts don't end until eight." Flicking my wrist, I looked at my Rolex. "And it's only five."

"Excuse me?"

"You heard what I said, Farrah. I don't know what type of power you think you have, but when it comes to my wife, you hold none."

"I've been here! Me! Not you! You—"

"Farrah? What are you . . . Who are you on the phone with?" I heard Leighton ask in the background. *"Is that Jah? Oh God! Give me my phone!"*

As I paced the carpeted hallway floors outside of Saint's office, my heart raced. For the most part, I respected women. I treated women with the utmost respect, especially, but Farrah didn't fall under the category of *women.* She was a bitch. I could have really taken it there with her, and years ago, I would have. She would have been all types of bitches and hos, but I'd matured. Besides, despite how I felt about her, she was right. She had been by Leighton's side more than I had. More than anyone had. Which was because Leighton had been having a really rough time getting professional support elsewhere.

"Jah," Leighton said with a deep breath. "I'm . . . I'm sorry about Farrah. She—"

"What did I tell you would happen if she overstepped again, Leigh? When I get to the house, I don't want to see her car in my driveway, outside of it, in front of the house, riding down the block, none of that. I want her gone."

Leighton was silent for a second. "She's . . . She's just . . . She's trying to take care of me and—"

"And I haven't been? It's crazy how you send me away but campaign for her to be there after she's blatantly disrespected me," I interrupted with a light laugh as I ran my hand over the top of my head.

"It's . . . It's different, Jah. I-I'm trying, and Farrah has been such a great support system through all of this. You know I've had a hard time finding a replacement."

"She's been a great support system through all of this? Leighton . . ." Pausing, I shook my head. "I want her out of my house."

With that, I hung up on her.

About thirty minutes later, I was back at the house, happy to see that Farrah's car was nowhere in sight when I pulled into the subdivision.

"Good evening, Mr. Baptiste," greeted Evaline, standing at the stove, cooking something up.

Evaline had been working for me for a good five years and she still greeted me the same every time we saw each other. I told her long ago the formalities were unnecessary since she was old enough to be my mother, but she refused to call me Jahad.

"How's it going, Ms. Evaline? What's for dinner tonight?" I asked, looking down into the pot.

"Mrs. Baptiste requested seafood gumbo and hot water cornbread, sir. If you'd like something else, I'll be happy to prepare a separate meal for you."

"Seafood gumbo sounds good to me," I reassured her, as I stood at the sink to wash my hands. "Has it been quiet today? You didn't have any issues with Ms. Farrah, did you?"

She nervously giggled and shook her head. "No, I didn't, sir. She did come down here, checking my pot, trying to taste things, but I shooed her away just like you told me I could."

Nodding, I told her she had done the right thing and apologized for Farrah's behavior.

After speaking with Maurice, Evaline's helpmate, I finished two glasses of tequila and reluctantly got ready to head to the bedroom. As I made my way up, I heard the sultry voice of Lauryn Hill playing at a low, subtle level. Leigh was in her feelings. Heavy. Every time Lauryn Hill played in this house, she was. I was prepared to walk into the room to see her on her side, cuddled up with one of her body pillows, facing the window with tears pouring from her eyes.

As I continued down the lengthy hallway, I rubbed the back of my neck, trying to mentally prepare myself for what I knew was to come when we faced each other. Leighton screaming, crying, blaming me for everything wrong in our lives. It had been happening for years. I should've been used to it by now, but I wasn't. I didn't think there was a nigga walking this earth who would ever get used to his wife blaming him for shit that was out of his control. Especially if that man was trying, like I had been. I was used to being Leighton's verbal punching bag.

To be real, I felt she enjoyed the shit. Going off on me, putting the blame on me, had to give her some kind of sense of relief. Every time she did it, she'd calm down and apologize a couple of hours later. And what would I do? Let shit slide because she was my wife and we were going through some shit. I didn't know how much more of it I could take, though.

As soon as I walked into the room, she turned over from the position I said she would be in. The redness swimming in her light brown eyes sent daggers to my heart. A heart that beat and pumped blood for her and her only.

"Why'd you do that?" Leighton asked, staring over at me with her eyes narrowed to slits. "You . . . You made Farrah cry! All she . . . All she wanted was to help me! All she wanted was for you to come home and be a fuckin' husband! That's it! But you put her out . . . out of *your* house. It's funny how every time there's a problem, it's *your* house! Both of our names are on the deed, Jahad Baptiste. What? Is it more yours than mine because you paid for it? With money I helped you make. Dirty money I helped you clean. If it wasn't for me, you wouldn't have this house! We wouldn't have this house! You do not have the right to put my best friend out because you don't like to be called out about your bullshit. You weren't here! Farrah was! Farrah always is."

I ran my tongue over my bottom lip, standing just inches away from the bed, quiet. She didn't stop. She wouldn't until she got the relief she wanted. She wouldn't stop until she said some shit that would shut her the fuck up. It was coming. It always did when she was like this.

Leighton was the only person walking this earth who could get away with coming at me disrespectfully. With her, I was gentle and patient because she was so fragile, and I didn't want her to break.

"You're never here! What am I supposed to do alone? You didn't find me a new doula. Evaline's old ass takes forever to come up here when I need her. And Maurice . . . Maurice is . . . you know what Maurice is. He's useless. I-I need help. You're supposed to care for me. You're supposed to honor me. What kind of husband yells at his wife's best friend just because she cares more than he does?"

I laughed and continued to run my tongue over my bottom lip.

"What's funny, Jahad? You think this is funny? You think what I'm going through is a joke? Fuck you! Fuck you, Jahad Baptiste! You get to come and go as you please, leaving me here for hours, alone. To go through all of this alone! It's always just me! You don't understand!" She bawled. "I went through three miscarriages! I loss three babies and this one . . . this one probably won't live and you know who's going to have to deal with that? Me—"

"Us!" I yelled, causing her to flinch with surprise. "Us! We have to deal with it . . . together! You act like you're the only one in this marriage that that shit affects, Leigh! That shit affects me too, but because I don't physically go through the loss, you claim it as your own and act like the only one that's loss three babies is you. That shit ain't right.

"And hell yeah, I wanted that bitch out my crib. The fuck you even talkin' about, shorty? Stop playin' with me!" I yelled, pointing my finger at her. "You keep talkin' crazy to me about how I'm not here but you told me to leave, Leigh! I . . ." Pausing, I shook my head and walked away, rubbing the back of my neck.

I didn't do this. I didn't argue with and disrespect my wife. Shit was boiling over.

"One minute, you beggin' me to put my dick in another bitch because I'm so good to you and I deserve it. The next minute, you talkin' down on a nigga, telling me I'm not shit. Make up yo' fuckin' mind, Leighton. Either I'm a good nigga, or I'm a bad nigga who don't give a fuck about you taking losses because I'm not experiencing them. Those babies were mine, too, shorty! I loss them. *We* loss them and I know we could lose this one too. That's why I've been tryin' . . . tryin' to keep you happy and straight, but shit, apparently, my best ain't been good enough."

It was over. Jahad, the loving, gentle, patient punching bag was gone. It had been years since I'd spoken to her like this. Years. I didn't curse at Leigh. I didn't raise my voice. That street shit had been left on the streets years ago. But . . . I was reverting and it was because of her. It took a lot to get me to this point. A lot of self-reflection, growing up, and realizing what the fuck I wanted. I refused to go back to the disrespectful, wild-ass nigga who had nearly lost the only woman who really gave a fuck about something other than what he could provide.

I made sacrifices and devoted my life to Leighton because she was special to me. She meant the world to me. Despite how much shit had changed over the years, I never lost sight of what she was to me. However, as I stared down at her, staring up at me with a frown, I could barely see her as who she was. The woman I fell in love with years ago no longer existed.

I was very well aware of what the losses and depression had done to her. I had accepted it, empathized, and supported her through it all, but shit . . . what about what I'd gone through because of it? I wore my pain well because, as a man, I was supposed to. I didn't cry. I didn't wallow. I didn't lay in bed, sulking and depressed because I wasn't wired that way. I took shit on the chin and carried on with life, upholding and uplifting her, despite how much she kept trying to tear me down. I was the only one in this marriage fighting. Had been the only one fighting for years now. A nigga was dead-ass tired.

"Fuck this shit," I mumbled before walking off, heading to the bathroom.

"You're probably *really* going to go out and fuck someone else now, huh?" Leighton whispered.

"Crazy how the only thing you *really* give a fuck about is me stickin' my dick in someone else," I flatly replied, refusing to look over my shoulder at her as I walked into the bathroom and slammed the door.

Every day, Leighton showed me how self-centered she was.

And every day, I let her get away with it.

Tonight, I felt indifferent.

CHAPTER 5

Sienna

I glanced over at the invitation before taking a deep breath and leaning forward for my glass of wine. I was on glass three and tipsy as hell. I knew that by the time the ball dropped, I would either be in the bathroom, throwing up, or knocked out on Naoki's couch. That was where I was. At Naoki's house. She wasn't home. She caught a flight out of Michigan early yesterday morning on an emergency nurse assignment. My girl was looking forward to partying for New Year's Eve, but she was about her business more than she was about play. She was tempted to decline the offer, on my account, but I told her ass she'd better go on and make that sixty dollars an hour. I didn't need a babysitter. What I needed was wine and she had a fully stocked wine cellar for me to choose from.

It had been a couple of days since I left Amiri and he'd been calling and texting, trying to find me ever since. I hadn't said a thing to him. Every call went unanswered, and every text sat on read. I thought about blocking him, but I enjoyed watching him beg. It gave me a certain type of satisfaction I couldn't understand. It was something like an *aha* moment. Amiri was laying all of his best shit out, too, but I'd been standing firm on my choice to leave him.

I wondered if he thought I was bluffing when I told him if he cheated again, I'd leave him. I wondered if Amiri thought I needed him. I wondered if he thought I was still that same weak-ass girl I was a few years ago. He had to think that. Otherwise, he wouldn't be begging. Otherwise, he wouldn't have cheated. He couldn't have done it with the confidence of not getting caught.

Men were stupid. They always got caught. There wasn't too much you could keep from a woman. Our intuition was our superpower, trust and believe that shit.

I was proud of the way I was handling it. I wanted to curse him out. I wanted to react the way I did before—slash his tires and all of that—but fuck him. He wasn't worth my energy. The only reason I thought about doing any of those things was because of the baby. Those ultrasound pictures. I thought about them every day. They haunted me.

As I set my glass back down on the table, my eyes found that invitation again.

"Fuck it," I mumbled as I picked it up . . .

What was stopping me now? I wasn't in a relationship. It was five o'clock in the evening on New Year's Eve and what I had going on now was what I'd have going on all night. Nothing. I wasn't going over to my parents'. For what? To be questioned about Amiri? To be asked why I wasn't wearing my engagement ring? I couldn't sit through that. I was still sorting through shit. I wasn't ready to face them with the news that he'd cheated on me again. My mother would give me a look, but she wouldn't say anything. My father . . . he'd give me one of those forehead kisses and tell me I was too good for him, or something of that sort. I didn't want any of it. I didn't need to be coddled. I didn't want to be judged. I didn't need anything but . . . dick and a distraction. And what better than some unattached, random, good dick?

Shrugging, I grabbed my phone to call the number on the invite. I bit my bottom lip, hoping I hadn't waited too long to accept it. There wasn't a cutoff time on the invite, so I should be good. But by the way Kiki was talking, I knew they'd have some requirements, like paperwork and stuff, for me to fill out.

"Damn," I said, as I bit my thumbnail, just as I was requested to put the code in. Right after I did that, the operator's sultry voice came through over the line.

"Pandora's," she said.

"He-hey, I'm . . ." I stammered over my words, a nervous wreck. What the hell was I doing? I'd always considered myself to be pretty freaky. I enjoyed porn and raunchy, unhinged sex like most freaky people did, but did I think I was underground, sex dungeon, swingers, fuck-on-a-stranger freaky? I didn't know.

"I'm . . . My name is Sienna and I have an invitation and—"

The lady giggled lightly. "Hey, Sienna. How are you? What is your date of birth?"

"April 14, 1996," I told her as I treaded across the room, heading for the kitchen, my pedicured toes sinking into the plush carpet. "I'm too late, aren't I? I'm sorry, I—"

"Relax, beautiful," she interrupted. "And you sure are beautiful."

With pinched brows, I paused. She knew how I looked? What the hell? By the tone of her voice, it was as if she was looking at a photo of me. I shouldn't have been shocked. According to Kiki, Pandora's was the upper echelon of underground sex dungeons. I kept calling it a sex dungeon because, shit, what else should I call it? Shit, to me, that was exactly what it was.

"Like I was saying before you nervously interrupted me," she continued with a giggle just as sultry as her voice. Her tone was so low, so . . . seductive. But not in a slutty way, if that made any sense. She had the type of voice that reminded me of the Quiet Storm that used to come on the radio at night back in the day. Soothing *and* sultry. Hell, the lady sounded damn good. Simple as that.

"Sorry about that," I coyly replied.

"It's all right, gorgeous. No, you're not too late. You're only too late if you don't have access to your medical records, and if your most recent ten-panel is more than thirty days old."

I nodded and picked up the bottle of Pinot before pouring a fresh glass, as if I didn't have one sitting on the coffee table. I was nervous, *chile*. I didn't know what the hell I was doing. This wasn't me. But, shit, maybe it was time to do something different.

For years, I'd done things by the book. I was faithful to a man who didn't deserve me, settling for mediocre sex, thinking it was okay, but deep down inside, knowing it wasn't. I wasn't fulfilled. I hadn't been emotionally or sexually fulfilled in . . . hell, pretty much ever. Tonight, I was letting my hair down. Why not? I needed to live a little.

"Yes, and yes. Everything is current. I have access to my chart online," I told her, as my heart raced a little.

After I found out about Amiri's cheating, I got tested immediately. I wasted no time. I should have been getting tested regularly beforehand, but whatever, it is what it is.

"All right, honey. I just have a few more questions," she told me.

I was doing this shit. As nervous as I was about everything, I found comfort in knowing that Pandora's was up on their shit when it came to tests and things of that nature. I should have known, once again. The way Naoki ranted and raved about it, I shouldn't have expected anything less than.

As I stood at the massive marble kitchen counter, listening to the lady with the Quiet Storm voice give me the rundown, I was filled with excitement. I couldn't wait to step outside of my element. I couldn't wait to see all of what Pandora's offered. *You only live once, why not be free and have fun while you live it?*

* * *

Three hours later, I was in Midtown Detroit, staring up at the dark gray building and the people heading inside, contemplating my damn life. I was so up and down with this decision, it didn't make any sense. I'd gone from sipping on wine to taking a couple of shots of Casamigos before I left the house. I'd even called Naoki for a pep talk. It was insane. I wasn't shy by far, but this . . . this was a completely different ball game.

"Do you have your mask?" Naoki asked, taking my attention off the couple walking hand in hand toward the building. The woman was blond, wearing a red dress, high heels, a fur, and a red rhinestone-adorned mask, and on the arm of a shorter, chubby man. I wondered if he was her pimp or something because the duo didn't make sense.

Looking over at my gold, gem-encrusted mask, I took a deep breath. "Yeah, I got it."

Before I headed this way, I stopped at a boutique and got a really cute mask to go with my short, champagne-colored, sequin fringe dress. I was shimmery as hell tonight with a pair of five-inch Giuseppes I'd raided Naoki's closet for. I was dressed provocatively, yet New Year's Eve appropriate too.

Instead of wearing my usual bone-straight bust-down middle part, I threw in a few barrel curls, giving my long, twenty-six-inch frontal wig voluptuous waves. Since I was shimmery and glamorous enough, I didn't do too much with my makeup. I kept it soft and neutral. Although it would be hidden behind the mask, I still wanted a nice, subtle beat.

"Girl, when you gettin' the best back shots of your life, you won't be nervous. Bitch, you probably gon' ask for a membership when that nigga is done with you. Wait . . . how many dicks you taking tonight? Two at a time? Three? One in every—"

"Kiki!" I said with a laugh. "Now you know!"

"Yeah, three at a time is more my speed," she said with a light giggle. "Anyway, take a dick for me, too, SiSi! Don't get in there and just fuck one. Fuck a couple—"

"Shut up, bitch," I said with a laugh before taking a deep breath. "I'm so fucking nervous."

"Hit the bar, peep the scenery, and get a feel of the place. On a serious note, I want you to have fun, but if you're not feeling it, just leave, girl. This is new territory for you, so I get it. Just . . . whatever you do, make sure you're completely comfortable with it so you don't leave with any regrets," Naoki said in a serious tone. "I have to get back on the floor before I end up catching a case for beating one of these jealous, ugly bitches up."

"All right, bestie boo. I'll let you know what happens."

"K. Love you!"

"Love you, too, Ki," I said before hanging up.

Sighing, I sat back against the seat and went to my text thread to click on the link the lady I spoke to earlier had sent me. It was my golden ticket inside, equipped with a barcode that likely had all of my information attached to it. I was on the phone with her for a good thirty minutes, asking questions and giving her information. It was a lot to process, but I appreciated how thorough they were. Now that I was here, I just needed to muster up the courage to get out of the damn car.

Mumbling under my breath, I said, "Fuck it." *Fuck it* had been my pep talk a lot these days.

I snatched my champagne-colored, chained-crossbody clutch and draped it over my chest before getting out. Stepping out into the blistering cold, I held my waist-length faux fur closed and put a little pep in my step. The temperature had dropped from midforties to twenties in a matter of hours. I knew it was going to be cold, but I decided to dress half-naked anyway because, shit, who showed up to a sex party covered up?

Tonight, the goal was to be desirable, although I was desirable twenty-four-seven, three hundred sixty-five. However, tonight, I wanted niggas to be drooling, damn near foaming at the mouth, wanting me so bad. I was sure I was going to have no problem pulling a few, but I planned on being very selective about who I allowed to get a piece of this cookie. I always had been.

Just as I was walking up to the door, my phone rang. Looking down at it, I sucked my teeth at the sight of *B.A.N.* Amiri had gone from *Bae* to *Bitch Ass Nigga* as soon as I found out about his cheating. I ignored his call and took a deep breath as I got closer and closer to the entrance.

The heavy beat from the music playing inside spilled out into the streets and I bobbed my head a little. As I looked around, my eyes fell on a couple standing a few feet ahead of me who were eyeing me like a piece of meat. I had to stop myself from turning my nose up at them because tonight wasn't the night for that. I wasn't at some club downtown tonight. Tonight, I was at a fucking fuck fest and I couldn't walk up in there acting like I was above freaky shit. The couple was nice looking, though. Very, very nice looking, but threesomes weren't my thing. I didn't like women enough to eat pussy and I was a selfish lover, so that would never work for me. I could appreciate a beautiful woman and watched a little lesbian porn here and there, but that was it.

Instead of giving them a stank look, I softly smiled and turned away. Hopefully, they got the clue and didn't try me later.

Once I was finally inside, my jaw dropped. The outside of the building did the inside absolutely no justice. It was every bit of luxurious. I knew it would be just from the invitation I'd gotten alone. Pandora's was astonishing. I wanted to take photos, but phones were prohibited, so I didn't have it on me.

Upon walking inside, I checked my coat in the coat check room, which was just as lavish as the rest of the place. Their colors had to be black and gold, as the place was adorned in it. Most of the décor was black, with gold accents. Huge portraits of Playboy models, well-renowned porn stars, and a few pinup girls adorned the matte black walls in immaculate gold frames.

As I scanned the place, my eyes landed on the bar, and I immediately raised my eyebrows. It was exquisite. The shelves were of the same shiny gold shade as everything else. The bar was huge, black, with a marble countertop. The barstools were matte black too. There was a huge mirror on the back wall that gave me a clear view of the other side of the club that made me want to hurry up and make my way through just to get over there.

In the middle of the room was a gigantic bed. The biggest bed I'd ever seen. It had to be custom made, but it wasn't the size of the bed that had me enthralled. It was what was going on in it that made me want to hurry up and watch up close.

There was a thick Black woman and two white men in it. The woman had her mask on, while the men who were fucking her brains out, didn't. Most of the men weren't masked. They didn't mind exposing their identities. Probably did it gladly, hoping someone they knew saw them, getting fucked all over the room. I didn't blame them. Women were more discreet when it came to their freak, so I get it. If I was on a bed full of people, getting fucked by two men like we were the only people in the room, I would wear a mask, too.

She was being fucked by one of them anally, in reverse cowgirl, laid back a little, while the other guy fucked her pussy. It was the wildest shit I'd ever witnessed in person.

Everything about Pandora's was wild. Everywhere I turned, there was something going on. It was all . . . sex. But there were a few people who weren't participating, carrying on like nothing was going on. There were three people in the middle of sex right next to a table that occupied a group of women who were simply mingling and drinking, having a good time. It was crazy.

I wondered if my newness stuck out like a sore thumb. My raised brows and parted lips had to be a dead giveaway. I just . . . I couldn't believe it. I needed a damn drink. I would need the whole bottle if I was going to have sex in front of these people. There was an option to pay for a private room, but I was in no position to fork over thousands of dollars on a VIP suite. If I was a member, it would've been included with the yearly membership fee, but I wasn't, and I wasn't rich, so I said fuck that VIP suite.

"Damn."

Looking over my shoulder, I was greeted by a smirking face. He was bold. Bold and . . . fine as hell. He didn't have on a mask. He was tall, dark, and handsome, with *a lot* of dick to offer. He was walking around, ass naked, big horse dick on full display. He was confident and had every right to be. But . . . there was something about his boldness I didn't like. He was almost *too* bold. *Too* free. I wasn't interested.

I gave him the same cute, coy smile and turned away. But because he was bold and confident, he grabbed my hand.

"I'm not interested," I told him as I pulled away.

He pulled his lips into his mouth and nodded with a furrow in his thick brows. "That's too bad. I was going to devour that li'l pussy. I bet it's fat. I can tell by the way you walk, you got some good pussy."

I nervously giggled and looked away from him. I expected him to press me a little longer, but he didn't. Of course, he didn't. There was so many beautiful women at his disposal that it made no sense. Before I made it to the bar, I was approached two more times. Once by a woman, and then by another couple. A gay couple. That . . . blew me away.

"Hey, can I have a shot of Casamigos?" I asked the naked bartender once I made it to the bar.

She was beautiful, with big, perky titties, full lips, and an ass that would put Cardi B's to shame. She clearly went under the knife a lot. It was written all over her. I wasn't hating. She looked damn good and had every right to flaunt that shit. I would've.

After I took the shot, I ordered a tequila sour and headed in the direction of that big-ass bed. That big-ass bed wasn't the only bed in the place. There were several on both sides of the club. In the middle of the room were tables where people were eating, drinking, or getting fucked. The layout of the place was very nice. There was even a small dance floor.

I sipped from my cup with a raised brow enjoying the show. The lady moaned as she aggressively sucked dick, holding onto it, gagging, her eyes rolling to the back of her head. By the way she handled them, I wondered if she'd even noticed everyone watching. Probably not.

Getting fucked good, on an orgasmic high, probably made having public sex easier. I could imagine it being exhilarating as well. As good as it looked, I could never take two at a time. I didn't think there was anything wrong with it, it just wasn't my speed.

When it came to other people's sex lives, and their lives in general, I didn't judge. If it didn't affect me directly, I couldn't give a damn about what a person did with their life. And as I watched the woman clearly having the time of her life, I mentally cheered her on, admiring her confidence and how free she was.

"You should join me up there," said someone so close to my ear, I flinched away.

Looking over at him, I sized him up. He was white. The typical white boy too. Blond hair, blue eyes, nice teeth. If I saw him on the streets, I'd automatically assume he was a stuck-up racist. And shit, I didn't put it past him now just because he'd approached me. He probably had some sick fetish for Black women.

Snorting, I gave him a smirk. "No, thank you."

Before he could press me any further, I turned to walk away, bumping into someone. He grabbed my elbows as my drink went splashing onto his black button-up shirt. I would have pulled away and embarrassingly apologized, but I couldn't. I was frozen—held captive in an unexplainable trance, staring into his low, bedroom eyes. He was masked but how beautiful he was couldn't be hidden behind some silly half mask. I could tell by the sharpness of his jawline, his thick Hebrew beard, and those piercing, soul-searching, dark bedroom eyes that he was fine. Extremely fine. His skin was so dark, nearly the same shade of night itself, but smooth as a baby's bottom. He was really gorgeous. I could tell he had nice teeth, too, despite them being covered by full, moist lips.

Finally, after standing there quietly for what felt like an eternity but had to be only a few seconds, I placed a piece of hair behind my ear and apologized, stammering over my words like a blabbering fool.

"I-I'm sorry! Ex-excuse me! I didn't know . . . I ruined your shirt. What is that? Versace? Is it ruined?" Pausing, I looked around the club until I spotted a waitress walking by not too far from where we awkwardly stood. "Do you . . . Hey! I need a napkin."

He lightly chuckled and looked down at the wet spot on his shirt. "It's not ruined. You spilled a drink on it. Unless you were sippin' on bleach, I'd say it's perfectly fine."

Oh God! Could this man get any sexier? He had an accent. One of those . . . those Caribbean accents. I wasn't good when it came to countries other than the one I stayed in, so I couldn't pinpoint where he was from by the accent, but by the color of his skin, I automatically assumed he was Jamaican. I was probably wrong, but he was from somewhere I wasn't.

I lowered my eyes until they landed on the tailored black slacks he wore and wondered how big his dick was. I bet he had one of those big, African dicks that made bitches squirt and damn near have seizures on that muthafucka.

I lightly giggled and was right back to staring at him. He stared at me too. I was waiting for him to ask me to join him in that bed. I wasn't going to hesitate.

He had the qualities of the type of man that deserved the pussy. Tall, at least six-six. It was a lucky guess since I was five-six and he looked to be a full foot taller than I was. I had to look up at him. I wanted to climb him. I wanted to get up on those shoulders, wrap my legs around his head, and let him have his damn way with me. For him, I was ready to let go every bit of reservation I had about this place. Now, after bumping into him, I was ready. It was no longer about looking around, and maybe participating. Hell no. The way my pussy responded to something as simple as his rough, big hands on my elbows, and my eyes connected with his, I knew it. I felt it. I was fucking ready.

The waitress finally came over, showing off every bit of work Dr. Miami, Dr. Curves, or whoever she had gone to for that big, ridiculous ass with the thighs to match. She was ass naked. The whole wait staff was.

This tall, chocolate god of a man never tore his eyes away from mine. Not even when she purposely put herself between us with her ass turned toward him to give me the napkins. *His. Eyes. Never. Left. Mine.*

I took the napkins from her and went to dabbing at his shirt with them. He grabbed my wrist and took them from me. "It's cool, love."

I hated that word. Hated it so much because of Amiri. But . . . the word *love* coming from him? This fine-ass muthafucka? I loved it. I could listen to him speak all day, every day. I was tripping, getting caught up in this fantasy, knowing good and got damn well, after tonight I wouldn't see him again. I mean, I wouldn't mind seeing him again if he wanted to see me. I needed to chill and heal since I was fresh out of a relationship with a fuckboy who'd broken my heart more times than I cared to admit. Now was for me, but God damn . . . A piece of man on the side while I got myself together wouldn't hurt, right?

Swallowing, I softly smiled and pulled my lips into my mouth, unsure of what to say next. I didn't think I needed to say anything. I was waiting for *him* to ask *me* to *fuck him* in front of these freaky-ass people. My pussy throbbed with heavy anticipation. He needed to ask me. I was literally fiending for him to.

But he didn't. He nodded at me and told me to enjoy my night before walking off. What the fuck was that?

CHAPTER 6

Jahad

"Another one," I said to the bartender after throwing my first shot of 1942 back.

Looking around the dimly illuminated club, I had half a mind to get the fuck out before I made the mistake of sticking my dick in something. Specifically, the curvy, brown-skinned chick with full lips and captivating brown eyes I couldn't look away from.

About five minutes ago, I had to pull myself away from her before I made good on my thoughts. My adulterous, explicit thoughts. My dick bricked right before I walked away from her. She was willing and ready to take it too. I didn't have to ask her to know it. I saw it in her eyes. And at that moment, I was ready too. Ready to rip that short-ass dress from her body, bend her over, and fuck her right there in the middle of the room, recklessly . . . on some straight savage shit. But what I wasn't ready for was what would come right after I busted my nut.

Regret.

Shame.

And most of all, guilt.

I'd come all this way from the 'burbs to Midtown Detroit for nothing. Nothing but an eyeful and a hard dick that wouldn't be taken care of. I was tweaking. I shouldn't have come out here, especially since it was New Year's Eve, but I didn't have shit waiting for me at the house.

You'd expect me to be laid up in bed with my wife, ready to bring the new year in with her, but shit had been crazy between us since I snapped on her a few nights ago. The only thing back at the house was her mean ass, Farrah, her parents, and two of her sisters. A house full of women—her bitch-ass pops included.

I'd let Farrah back in. She called me the day after everything went down and apologized to me. I was mentally drained by both of them, and life in general, so I said fuck it, I didn't give a fuck. You want to fall through after parking in my spot, barking out orders to my staff, and disrespecting me? Yeah, shorty, come through. Anything to get that pitiful, sad-ass look off Leighton's face. Anything to fill the house with something other than soft sobs all day, pointed fingers, and hatred. Fuck it. Go crazy. Do you. I was pretty much just cruising through this shit called life on autopilot, to be honest.

Somehow, I ended up at Party City, where I'd gotten this cheap-ass black mask to wear to this freaky-ass club Saint had been practically begging me to hit up. Pandora's. Pandora's was the perfect name for it.

When I walked in and looked up at the big LED sign, it was like a warning or some shit. I was getting ready to open *Pandora's Box*. The minute I decided to walk in, I had opened it, low key. Just a little bit. Cracked it open. I saw inside. . . and I liked it. Loved it. If I decided to stick my dick down the back of her throat, I'd be opening it completely. There would be no going back after this.

A couple of years ago, before I decided to settle down and leave the reckless, street nigga shit alone, I didn't have a conscience. The love I had for my wife had given me one, and it was eating at me like a muthafucka. Damn near as much as I wanted to eat at the pussy that belonged to the chick in the short-ass, sparkly-ass dress. Shorty with the captivating eyes I'd likely see every time I closed my own.

I. Was. Tweaking.

No bullshit.

It had been a long-ass time since I looked at another woman the way I looked at her. That eye contact . . . that desire . . . that hunger . . . this hard-ass dick . . . had been reserved for one woman and one woman only for years. Five minutes ago, the thought of lifting that reservation had crossed my mind. It still lingered there, for real.

"Another—"

"Give me one too!"

Before I could finish asking the bartender for another drink, she sat next to where I stood. The scent of her soft perfume immediately filled my nose as a reminder of how much I missed the sweet smell of a woman. Leighton hadn't worn perfume in months. She showered regularly, but she didn't put any effort into what she wore when she got out. I didn't mind. I understood to a degree. It wasn't until she sat next to me that I remembered how much I used to love it. Burying my face in the crook of Leigh's neck, inhaling my favorite perfume, feeling her soft hands on the back of my neck, giggling at my beard tickling her skin. I missed that shit.

She looked up at me with a smile. "So . . . What are you here looking for? Please don't tell me you're gay. I mean, if you are, no big deal, I just . . ." She bit down on her bottom lip and smiled at me again. "It would break my heart if you were."

I drew back with a frown. "Gay? Why you think that? Because I didn't ask if I could stick my dick in you?"

It was her turn to draw back. "What? N-no. I was just . . . just saying."

The bartender returned with our drinks, and she immediately tossed hers back, frowning once she swallowed. She'd asked the bartender to bring her what I was drinking, not knowing what I had ordered, to begin with. By the look on her face, it was obvious she hadn't had it before. Tequila, more specifically, dark tequila, was an acquired taste, despite how smooth 1942 was. But when she turned her mouth down and cocked her head to the side, I could tell she liked it. Especially when she called the bartender over for another one.

"To answer your question, nah, I'm not gay," I told her before finishing my shot off just as the bartender handed her her fresh one.

She looked at me, lightly nodding before taking her shot. I then went into my pocket to pay for my shots and hers as well, deciding it was time for me to go. I didn't know how long I would be able to hold up the vows I'd made to Leigh if I stayed here any longer.

"No . . . allow me. I did spill a drink on your shirt, after all," she bashfully offered.

I locked eyes with her and there they were again. Those fireworks that held me in an inexplicable trance. What the fuck was this? I couldn't see much behind her mask, but I didn't need to see anything beyond it to know I wanted her. To fuck her. To taste her. *I wanted her.*

Since I woke up this morning, I had been in a constant battle between my mind and my dick. So far, my dick had been winning. Every move I'd made today had been catered to him. Because, shit, why not? I'd catered to my mind . . . *and* my heart for years. Meanwhile, my dick had just been there, hanging, sad, and neglected as fuck.

I shook my head and stopped her from sliding her card across the bar. When my hand landed on top of hers, there was this surge of energy that rushed through my entire body. She must've felt it, too, because when she looked up at me, after I snatched away, her jaw dropped, and I watched as her throat moved up and then down again with a swallow.

With my eyes locked on hers, I handed the bartender three bills and told her I was paying for the lady's drinks too.

She took a deep breath, grabbed her purse, and sat there quietly for a moment before she turned to get off the barstool. She glanced up at me, smiled, and told me to enjoy my night. As soon as she walked off, I grabbed her wrist, stopping her. I didn't need to ask her if I could stick my dick inside of her for her to know exactly what I wanted.

Five minutes later, we rode the glass elevator up to the tenth floor, where my VIP suite was located. I wasn't the type of nigga who cared to fuck in a room full of people. When I found out about the VIP rooms at Pandora, I jumped on it. I'd let them weird-ass niggas have that shit. I wasn't opposed to public sex, I just couldn't see myself fucking in the same bed as other muthafuckas. That shit was too weird to me. There was too much over-the-top, wild-ass shit going on at Pandora's for me to ever even consider that shit. I liked my privacy. I was no exhibitionist. That was more Saint's and Blaise's style.

I looked down at the key in my hand, then looked up at the doors as I passed by each one, looking for room 1010. Each room I passed, I heard screaming, moaning, and skin slapping against skin. A few doors were wide open, giving a clear view of what was going on inside. One we walked by was occupied by five men and one woman. Another, there was a couple in the bed, and a man sitting on the side of it, watching with his dick in his hand. Another one we passed by, there was a man hooked up to some dominatrix-type shit with a gag in his mouth while a woman in leather stood behind him, clearly fucking him in the ass. I snatched my eyes away from that shit so quick. Weirdo shit. If it wasn't for me looking for my room, I would have never looked inside any of the rooms. However, shorty seemed to be fascinated by all of it. I could tell she was just as new to the spot as I was. That made me a little more comfortable about my decision.

When I stepped in here, I was on a quest for the reserved type. I was selective about where I stuck my dick, for obvious reasons. Despite Pandora's strict medical records check, the idea of fucking a woman who'd just been filled with nut from ten different niggas didn't appeal to me.

When I finally got to the room, I put the key in the door and pushed it open, letting her walk in first. My eyes landed on her round ass as she walked in, the scent of her perfume permeating the air, making my dick twitch. Before stepping in and closing the door behind me, I paused for a moment, right back in that mental battle.

"I was thinking and . . . I know this entire process has been challenging for you. I . . . I love you enough to be selfless and give you a hall pass. One night. One woman. No strings attached, Jahad. You deserve to have good sex, babe, and since I can't give it to you, I'm allowing you to go out and get it from someone else. Because I love you." Leighton's voice echoed through my mind as I gripped the door and slowly closed it.

In the back of my mind, I knew I was making a mistake. I knew it'd backfire. Eventually. But I'd come too far now to back down. I couldn't walk out of this room, not with this hard-ass dick. It was so brick, the muthafucka was starting to hurt, pressing up against the fabric of my tailored pants. I needed to bust a nut, and because my wife couldn't please me, I'd use her.

After I turned around to walk further into the room, my eyebrows lifted at the sight of her slipping out of her dress. When it dropped to the floor, my eyes stayed centered on her pretty, puffy pussy. She had a peach for sure, with the sexiest landing strip running down the middle of it. I'd never been the type to put my mouth on random pussy, but as I treaded toward her, my mouth salivated.

I couldn't eat her pussy.

That would be pushing shit, wouldn't it?

But damn, that muthafucka was pretty.

So pretty. So phat. So . . . smooth.

I couldn't believe I was actually entertaining the thought of eating her pussy and I didn't even know her name.

"What's your name?" I asked once I finally made it over to her.

Staring up at me through the holes in her mask, our eyes locked there again. Fireworks. Silence. Slow motion. That was what it felt like whenever our eyes met. Whenever we connected like that, it was like my heart beat at the speed of molasses on the pavement on the coldest day of winter. Everything seemed to slow down. She didn't blink. I didn't blink. I didn't know what the fuck that was about. It was too much, so I looked away to unbutton the top button of my shirt, waiting for her to give me her name.

"Naoki," she told me in a tone just above a whisper.

I had her name.

So, I wouldn't be eating the pussy of a nameless stranger.

"How old are you?" I continued my line of questioning as I began to further undress, sliding out of my shirt.

"Twenty-six," she replied through labored breathing.

Had an age. Perfect. She didn't look a day over twenty-one. She had beautiful, smooth, blemish-free skin. Through the makeup she wore, I could tell. It laid perfectly, almost as if it was a second layer of skin. Perfection.

"You nervous?" I asked, as I undid my belt.

"Should I be?"

I nodded as I dropped my pants to my ankles. "The good kind, though."

When her eyes fell on my dick, she gasped and stepped back. "Wait."

I looked down at it, standing at its hardest, pulsating, the skin stretching so much that even the thinnest veins were visible. Back in the day, when it was the thing to do, I measured my dick. Every young nigga did it. If a nigga told you he hadn't, he was lying. Measured it up against that Comcast remote, Glade air freshener cans, and all that. I was nine inches at seventeen. Now, as a grown-ass man, I didn't know what size I was. I just knew any time I dropped my pants, I got the same reaction. Leighton wouldn't fuck me for months when she first saw it. It took some coaching and slow strokes to get her onboard. For the first few months, I could only put half in. Now, she took all of it. Skillfully. Once upon a time, she couldn't get enough—

What the fuck was I doing thinking about Leighton? Leighton had to . . . I had to put her to the back of my mind.

I grabbed Naoki's hand and placed it on my dick, slowly wrapping it around it as much as it could. The tips of her fingers barely met, since the girth of it was pretty intimidating, too.

She looked up at me with nervous eyes. I hoped she wouldn't back out. I needed to slide in too fucking bad. But if she did, I'd respect it. But not before putting my lips on her pussy. I wouldn't leave the room without it. Eating pussy was one of my favorite things to do. Leighton had even stripped me of those benefits, claiming she couldn't handle it because she'd want to have sex, and since we couldn't, she didn't want to tease herself like that.

There I was again, thinking about that woman.

Swallowing, I kept my eyes locked on Naoki's. She began to slowly move her hand up and down the shaft of my dick, taking slow, low breaths. The nervousness in her eyes subsided a little. After a few seconds of her slowly jacking my dick, the nervousness faded completely and was replaced with desire. I backed her up against the bed until the back of her legs bumped against it, forcing her to sit down. Once she sat down, I kneeled and parted her thick thighs. A nigga was damn near drooling with hunger, I wanted to taste her so bad. A stranger, who wasn't that much of a stranger anymore. She was Naoki. Twenty-six-year-old Naoki.

"What's your favorite color?" I asked her as I parted her puffy lips and licked my lips at the sight of her budding clit.

"Yellow."

"Mm," I replied as my eyes traveled down the slit in her pussy until they landed on her tiny hole. She was a creamer. Lowering my head, I stuck my tongue out and licked her from her hole up to her clit, where I lightly sucked.

She was sweet. Sweet and creamy. The perfect combination.

"When is your birthday?" I asked her before placing a kiss on her clit.

"Mm-hmm," she moaned.

I gripped her thighs and kissed it again. "Naoki. Your birthday."

"Ap-April fourteenth." She moaned, gyrating her hips.

I grabbed her waist and placed my lips against her pussy again, this time, licking, sucking, and flicking my tongue over her clit. She wasn't a stranger anymore, was she? Naoki, twenty-six, favorite color yellow. An April fourteenth Aries. Fire sign like me. I knew her. I knew her well enough, right?

Her pussy was sweet, thick, and she didn't like to go bald. She preferred a landing strip, and right above it was a tattoo of a rose. Such a dainty, sexy rose. I knew enough about her to eat her pussy, right? Yeah . . .

"What's . . . What's your . . . your name?" Naoki asked, as I continued to feast on her.

Gripping her thighs, I pushed her legs back and she scooted up the bed until she reached the headboard. I climbed into bed with her with my lips clamped down on her clit. Instead of responding to her, I softly sucked on her clit, repeatedly, forcing her to grip the back of my neck. Her legs trembled, and that cream oozed from her pussy, coating my beard. I made a mental note to hit the connected bathroom and wash my beard vigorously before I left. I wanted every trace of tonight to be scrubbed away before I went back home to my wife.

My wife.

Pausing, I pulled back and swallowed with dipped brows.

I was cheating on my wife.

Something I said I would never do.

Sensing my hesitation, Naoki opened her eyes and looked down at me. "You . . . Is everything okay?"

I didn't know how long I'd laid there, frozen, with that revelation on my mind before she said something. When she did, and I was pulled out of my thoughts, I looked up at her. And like every other time when our eyes met, they were stuck. Fireworks. Slow motion. Silence. I could no longer hear the music playing from the speakers in the corners of the room. I could no longer hear wild fucking from the people next to us. All I heard was my own heart thumping in slow fucking motion.

"Hey," she said, with a sense of urgency in her voice before sitting up on her elbows. "Are you o—oh my *God*."

Before she could pretend to give a fuck about if I was okay or not, I dove back in, shutting her the fuck up by clamping my lips down on her clit and sucking on it. Slowly. Faster. Slow and then fast again. Dragging my tongue up and down her slit, I made sure to give her hard clit a soft suck every time I made it there. Her legs went back to quivering and she shut the fuck up.

The only thing I wanted to hear were her moans. The only thing I wanted to hear was the sound of her wet pussy brushing up against my wet tongue. Nothing else mattered. After tonight, she wouldn't even matter. She wouldn't exist. But for now, she did and I was going to enjoy it.

Tonight, I wasn't Jahad Baptiste, the loving husband. Tonight, I was Jahad Baptiste, a single man with his face inside of a sweet, phat pussy he'd just been introduced to.

After Naoki's orgasm subsided, she sat up and grabbed my face. I didn't stop her when she put her lips against mine, sucking her juices off my tongue. That was another thing I didn't do. Kiss random people. But I was outside of my element. Shit, I was outside of my element when I walked into Pandora's. Fuck it. This version of myself had no reservations.

She skillfully moved her tongue around my mouth, sucking her sweet, thick, creamy pussy juices off my tongue, moaning.

I gripped the back of her head, and the strap of her mask broke. Neither of us gave a fuck enough to put it back in place. It was in the way, anyway. When it fell off her face, we pulled away from the kiss long enough for it to get out of our way so we could go back to what we were doing. But a nigga was stuck again. She was beautiful. I would have never guessed she was this fucking beautiful behind it. I knew she was fine but got damn.

The corners of her alluring, captivating brown eyes turned up more than the mask had exposed. When she reached up and placed her hands behind my head, going for the strap of my mask, I grabbed her wrist, stopping her. But then I let her take it off. It was something about the look in her eyes when I stopped her that made me give in to it. Shit, I didn't know her, anyway, and the mask was hot, sweaty, and covered in her pussy juices, so I was happy to take it off.

Her eyes scanned my face with satisfaction before her lips were back on mine again. There was something about the masks being removed that woke something up in both of us. Maybe it was the fact that both of us were highly attracted to the other now that we could see it all.

Naoki wrapped her legs around my waist and my dick poked at her wet pussy as we continued to kiss. She ground her hips onto it and I let a light groan escape my mouth.

"Damn," I mumbled, as I looked down at my dick, streaks of her cream coating it, tempting me to just slide in without a rubber. Before I could entertain the thought anymore, Naoki climbed off me and got on her knees in front of me. I pushed up on my knees and she grabbed my dick before placing soft kisses on the head of it, swiping a thick glob of my pre-cum up from the head. She moaned at the taste and looked up at me before rolling her eyes to the back of her head. Naoki was a freak and I loved that shit.

Clenching my jaw tighter, I grabbed the back of her head and pushed my dick inside of her mouth. I had been teased enough. I needed my dick sucked and I needed it sucked good. By the way she'd sucked the pre-cum from my dick, I knew she was going to go crazy on my shit.

Which she did.

Naoki jerked my dick with both of her hands as she sucked it with slobber dripping from her lips. She took one of her hands off and slowly slid my dick down her throat as far as it would go. When she gagged, she didn't pull away; she kept going. With my lips pressed tightly together and a frown of straight-up ecstasy on my face, I gripped the back of her head and pushed it down her throat. She gagged again and looked up at me with tears from gagging rolling down her face. She pulled back a little and went back to bobbing and weaving on it.

"Fuck," I muttered, as she gripped my balls and put them both in her mouth and hummed on them. "Shit, shorty."

She moaned and threw her ass back as if she was being fucked by an imaginary dick. Reaching back, I roughly smacked her on it, and she moaned, throwing it back again. Curiosity got the best of me, and I pulled my dick out of her mouth and roughly turned her over so her ass was facing me. She looked over her shoulder and gripped the sheets with her teeth pinched over her bottom lip. I gripped my dick and moved up a little to position it with her wet-ass pussy. Looking down at it, my mouth salivated again, at the sight of a long, white, thick line of her cum oozing from it. I wanted it. So, before I put my dick in it, I leaned down and licked it. I swiped my tongue up her pussy and dipped it into her pussy hole.

"Oh my *God*!" she yelled.

I gripped her hips and moved her back and forth on my tongue. It didn't take her long to catch on before she was throwing her ass back against my face. My tongue darted in and out of her pussy, scooping up every drop of her good-ass cum. I couldn't believe how good she tasted. I wondered if she felt just as good.

Stopping, I grabbed her hips and went back to position my dick at her pussy. She tensed up as soon as I put the head in. I was all right with that because I needed a minute to get my shit together, anyway. I'd only had the tip in and knew off back that it was as good as it tasted. She was wet enough to take every inch but because she was nervous and tensing up, it wouldn't be as pleasurable as I knew I could make it for her.

Leaning forward, I whispered in her ear, "Relax."

She took a deep breath and leaned into me, resting her head on mine a little. "Okay," she mumbled, in such a small, sweet, seductive voice that I damn near nutted right then and there.

"Open up for me, baby," I grunted, as I gripped her hips and looked down at my dick, inching in deeper inside of her. "Damn."

I inched out a little, just to get a look at how much she'd wet my dick up and couldn't believe the amount of cream on my shit. She was wet as fuck. Closing my eyes, I cursed myself. It had been months since I felt the insides of a woman. The pull and tug of a woman's pussy muscles gripping my dick. The sound of a sexy-ass moan. The view of a phat ass moving back and forth on me as I dug deeper and deeper inside of her. I was going to be nutting fast as fuck and I was mad about it. Naoki had the type of pussy I wanted to stay in forever. Well, shit, for as long as I could before I had to step outside of this alter ego I had to create to get what's-her-name off my mind.

I inched back inside of Naoki, going deeper than I had been before and she gasped, tensing up again. She reached back between her legs and gripped my dick, stopping me from going any deeper.

Leaning forward again, I whispered, "Give me this good-ass pussy. Stop tensin' . . . let me in, baby."

She sighed and moaned again. "Mmmm. O-okay."

Instead of just gripping my dick to stop me like before, she pulled it closer, helping me slide further inside.

Licking my lips, I tossed my head back to the ceiling, remnants of her sweet pussy juice on my lips and tongue reminding me of just how good she tasted.

"It tastes good . . . *and* it feels good," I said with a grunt before going deeper inside of her. "Got damn."

"Yesssss!" Naoki moaned before slamming her hand against the bed. "So . . . So fuckin' gooooood!" she whimpered.

"Told you to relax. Let me give you this shit, baby," I said as I gripped her hips, giving her slow, deep strokes, enjoying every crevice inside of her wet-ass pussy. I didn't want to move fast. Didn't want to get too excited. Shit, I didn't want to move at all, for real. I just . . . wanted to sit in it because I didn't know the next time I'd be able to feel the inside of pussy again after tonight.

Naoki loosened up a bit more, slowly gyrating her hips, matching my tempo. I slapped her ass and gripped her cheeks, spreading her ass open. Looking down, I shook my head and grunted at the sight of her pretty asshole coated in her thick pussy juices. She was so got damn wet.

She clenched her pussy walls and looked over her shoulder at me with her bottom lip pinched between her teeth. When her eyes met mine, the surge of energy that rushed through me was like the surge from earlier when my hand sat on top of hers. But this shit was different. I knew she felt it because as we stared at one another, a tear trickled down her face. The sight was damn near too much for me to handle. As hard as it was for me to look away from her, I did, closing my eyes. I clenched them shut but that didn't stop me from seeing her behind my closed lids. It didn't stop me from feeling that magnetic pull. The shit I felt was crazy. Like I loved her, but I didn't even know her. She was a stranger. Not *really* a stranger. She was Naoki, twenty-six-year-old Aries, with the favorite color yellow. But I didn't know her enough to love her. I hadn't even known her for a full hour, but damn. Was the pussy *that* good?

With my bottom lip clenched between my teeth, I opened my eyes again and she was still looking back at me with a face that was the embodiment of what pleasure was. Her mouth was laid lazily agape as she moved her pussy up and down over my hard-ass dick.

I gripped her hips and pushed deeper inside of her.

"Ohhh." She moaned as her bottom lip quivered, and those captivating brown eyes rolled to the back of her head.

I flipped her over and mounted her, immediately wrapping my hand around her throat. She opened her legs wider and wrapped her hand around my wrist. I thought she was going to try to pry my hand away, but she gripped my wrist, holding on to it while I stroked in and out of her.

"Fuck—Oh . . . Oh my *God.* You fuckin' me so got damn gooood!" she cried.

I let go of her throat and held her legs up, placing them over my shoulders. Her eyes shot open and she tensed up again.

With my top teeth over my bottom lip, I mumbled, "Uh-uh. Relax on this dick, baby."

She nodded and placed her hands on my thighs, pushing me back a little. I swatted her hands away and pulled out of her. As I kissed her on her swollen clit, I told her to let me fuck her.

"Stop runnin' from it," I said against her pussy, my lips brushing against her clit with every word. "Wet-ass fuckin' pussy."

I spread her lips apart and dipped my tongue inside of it, making her pussy gush with cream, coating my beard once again. Before sliding right back into her, I tapped my dick on her clit and her legs quivered. The more I slapped it, the more they quivered. It didn't take long for her to cum again. This time, when she did, she squirted.

"Ahhh! Ohh! Oh my fucking!" she cried as I continued to slap her on the clit with my dick as her pussy juices splashed. "Oh my Goddd. Yessss."

When I slid into her again, she relaxed, and her eyes met mine again. This time, when I put both her legs on my shoulders and pushed deeper inside of her, she didn't tense and my shit slid in with ease.

"Fuck," I grunted.

"This pussy feel good, don't it?" Naoki muttered before reaching up and stroking my beard.

My eyes shot open as I took her fingers in my mouth before putting the pointer and thumb over her clit. "Rub it."

"Wait . . . It's . . . It's still sensitive—"

"Rub it," I repeated.

"Okaaay," she moaned.

She rubbed her clit as I continued to push deeper inside of her. She moved her fingers over her clit, circling it, bucking her hips against me, giving me access to all of her pussy like a pro. When I was finally balls deep inside, I sat there for a minute, savoring the moment, enjoying the way she tugged on it.

"Your dick . . . oh my God . . . it's . . . I'm so full. It's so fucking gooood," she cried, tears running down the sides of her face again.

I leaned down and her legs fell off my shoulders, and she wrapped them around my waist. I lifted her ass from the bed, and she moved her hips on me while I stroked deeper inside of her pussy. She wrapped her arms around my neck, and I slowly slammed her up and down on my dick. Although our lips were inches away from one another, we didn't kiss. We just stared into each other's eyes, while she bounced on my dick and I continued to plunge deeper and deeper inside of her.

"I'm about to nut," I grunted, as I lifted her off my dick.

She hungrily got down on her knees and grabbed my dick before wrapping her full lips around it. My dick hit the back of her throat and she gagged, while I grabbed the back of her head and fucked her face with more aggression than I'd fucked her with. She moaned as she sucked, giving me the best head I'd ever received in my entire life.

"Give me that nut," she moaned, looking up at me.

I looked at her and gave her exactly what she wanted: a mouth full of nut.

She swallowed every drop.

CHAPTER 7

Leighton

"He's not bringing the new year in with you, now? Sis, I love you with all of my heart, but you really need to do something about the way he treats you. You let him get away with every damn thing. Now this? It's New Year's Eve and he hasn't been here all day," Farrah said, sitting at the foot of my bed with her champagne flute in her hand, looking over at me with contempt in her eyes. Judgment *and* contempt.

Sighing, I reached over to the nightstand and grabbed my glass of sparkling grape juice. Sparkling damn grape juice. I wanted tequila. A nice glass of Clase Azul would be great right about now. But since I was five months pregnant, I had to settle for this. Hell, I didn't even want it. I wanted to throw the glass across the room, but I didn't want my mother to talk mess about me being disrespectful. She was here too. Downstairs, in the kitchen, fixing me a plate of wings and macaroni and cheese I wasn't in the mood for. Everyone was here. Well, *almost* everyone. My parents, my sisters, and my best friend, Farrah. My husband, however, wasn't. That was who Farrah was complaining about. She *always* complained about him. But what she needed to do was mind her own got damn business.

When it came to my life, Farrah kept her nose in it because she didn't have anything else going on. She'd been putting her nose in business that didn't concern her more than usual these days. I felt like she did it on purpose because I'd been letting her get away with so much. Much more than I would have in the past. I wasn't the same Leighton I was a couple of years ago. A lot had happened. A lot that had changed who I was.

My mental health was fried. I was an emotional wreck, and my confidence was shit. All I did was lay or sit in bed all day, every day, and it had done such a number on my personality. That fire and spunk I used to have was gone. Sometimes, I had a hard time even recognizing myself. Everybody who knew me knew I was different. My parents tried to coddle me because of it. My sisters avoided me. My husband tried . . . he tried *a lot*. And Farrah? Well, Farrah took advantage of it. She didn't think I noticed, but I had. Ever since I let her get away with saying something slick a couple of months ago, she'd been on a roll, adding little extra shit every other day. I just . . . I was mentally and physically drained and very obviously depressed.

"He'll be here," I said before taking a sip of my drink.

Farrah turned the corners of her mouth up and looked down at her watch. "When? The ball is about to drop."

I looked up at the TV, then back at her. The ball wasn't dropping for another fifty . . . no, forty-nine minutes now. I didn't have to say anything to her for her to know I knew she was full of shit.

She shrugged her right shoulder and sipped from her glass. She was drinking the Clase Azul I wanted from one of my favorite glasses. I watched as she swallowed, wishing I could have just a little bit of it. I needed something. Something to ease my mind.

The last doctor's appointment I had, I was tempted to ask if just a little bit of weed would harm the baby, but I knew better. I knew all there was to know about pregnancy. After the first miscarriage, I did extensive research about childbearing, and everything associated with it. I became obsessed. Obsessed with getting pregnant, obsessed with making it past the miscarriage stage, obsessed with carrying to term, obsessed with reading about stillbirths, obsessed with reading about SIDS. I was obsessed with all of it. And that obsession stemmed from that very first loss. I just wanted a healthy baby. So, despite how worried and mentally all over the place I was, I'd never do anything to jeopardize losing my baby.

"Well, he should be here. Period. What's keeping him tonight? Business as usual?"

Before I could answer her question, I shifted my eyes to the doorway at the sound of his voice. I glanced at Farrah and she had that look on her face. The one where the corners of her mouth turned up in dismay. I loved my best friend. I really, truly did, but she was so got damn miserable, it made no sense. I would have called her just that, but I didn't because, although she'd been wearing thin on my patience, I needed her. I couldn't do this without her. I was pushing so many people out of my life, I really couldn't risk pushing another one away. Especially not with the way things were going with my husband and me.

He walked in and immediately walked over to me. Jahad always dropped a kiss on my forehead whenever he walked into the room. We could've been arguing like a crazy toxic couple before he left, but he always came home with different energy. He always gave me a kiss. I looked forward to it, too. The look on my face might not always reflect that, but . . . if he didn't greet me or depart with a kiss, nothing in my day would go right.

"Hello to you, too, Jahad," Farrah jokingly said as he walked by her over to the dresser to take his gold chains off. "I forgive you, brother."

Jahad glanced over his shoulder at her and chucked his chin back, nodding at her. I watched with a light squint as he turned his attention back to removing his jewelry. There was something going on. I could tell by the way he stood with his shoulders lightly slumped over and the clenching and unclenching of his jaw. I shifted my eyes away from him and to Farrah.

"Hey, Farrah, give me a minute alone with Jah."

She looked at the TV, then back at me. "The ball is about to—"

"In forty minutes. Get out of my room and close the door on your way out."

She took a deep breath and pushed up from the bed, doing what I'd asked. My friend needed a new man. Ever since she'd gotten divorced, she'd been very, very clingy. I understood, though. If Jah and I ended up divorcing, I wouldn't know what to do with myself. I'd be a mess, looking for any form of a distraction from reality I could get. She and Michael were together for years before they divorced after he had an affair. I couldn't imagine.

"Everything okay?" I asked Jah, who hadn't said a thing since he'd walked into the room. I was sure he'd look at me and ask me what was up after hearing me ask Farrah to leave. I wasn't sure if he'd heard me at all, he was so spaced out. I was immediately worried about business. Jahad was the type of man who kept what he was going through to himself.

He turned to me and raised his eyebrows. "Say what?"

I studied him, eyeing him up and down. "I asked if everything was okay? You seem . . . distracted. Like something is on your mind."

Jahad ran his tongue over his bottom lip and undid the top button of his shirt. "Everything is fine."

Our eyes locked for a moment. It wasn't until he looked away from me that I knew. My stomach dropped and I placed my hand on it, rubbing it. Wondering if I was imagining things, or if that little flutter was from the baby moving or not. I knew the difference. I could tell without an issue. I just wanted that flutter to be the baby and not my gut feeling. Not my nerves. Not that . . . knowing.

Jahad had been with someone else.

Women . . . we know. It took some longer than others to figure it out, but I recognized it immediately. Not because my man was a serial cheater. Not because I was insecure. I knew because I knew him. I'd spent years with him. Learning him, picking up on subtle cues of something being wrong. I knew Jahad Baptiste as well as I knew the back of my hand. And I knew he'd been with someone else.

He *never* broke eye contact with me. When we talked, we never talked with so much distance between us. I couldn't get out of bed, so these days when we talked, he came to me. Stood next to me, held my hand, or ran his hand over the top of my head while we talked if it was a good conversation. If it was a bad one, he'd still come over. He wouldn't touch me, but he'd show me respect by standing before me with his eyes locked on mine, giving me undivided attention.

Tonight, I didn't get that.

Tonight, he was distracted.

It was because he'd been with someone else. He'd . . . he'd taken the pass.

I offered him a hall pass months ago, and when I first mentioned it, he thought I was joking. He laughed and told me I was crazy. It wasn't until he realized he was the only one laughing that he knew I was serious. Once he realized I was serious and really wanted him to be with someone else since I couldn't be with him, he flipped. He didn't yell. He didn't curse. He told me I was tripping and expressed just how disrespected he felt by the offer. I pleaded my case, telling him I trusted and loved him enough to give him the pass because I knew he needed to have sex.

Jahad's appetite for sex was aggressive. His appetite for pleasing was . . . intense. Before things changed between us, we had sex very regularly. Sometimes two or three times a day if he wasn't busy. He was skilled. Very skilled. Very passionate. The last few years had been off between the two of us. We'd gone through a lot. The chemistry was lost. My sex drive had diminished well before the pregnancy. Jahad and I went from having sex multiple times a day to only having sex when I was ovulating. It was . . . weird. It was odd. I was different. He knew it, but instead of addressing it, he went with the flow and tried to fix things.

There were many nights I just didn't feel like it. Depression . . . it was depression. A lot of times, I rejected him because I felt like it was pointless. After finding out I'd have a hard time carrying a child, I didn't feel like a woman anymore. Crazy, but that was how I felt. I felt like my womb was cursed. Every time I thought about sex, I thought, what was the point? I couldn't have a baby. Sex was all about me and . . . the baby. Now that I had the baby, I still couldn't give him what he deserved. I wanted to. I thought about it now more than I used to. But, since I couldn't have sex, we didn't have sex. At all. I was back at square one, feeling inadequate. Feelings of inadequacy and a roaming mind did nothing for my marriage.

So, I offered him a hall pass. I kept reminding him about it. Every time I did, he got upset. The last time was a little over a week ago, and by the look of things, he'd finally taken it. I didn't feel like I thought I would when he did. In fact, I felt worse. I felt alone. I felt even more inadequate now than I did before. I was afraid, afraid I was most certainly losing my husband now.

"You . . . You did it?" I asked in a tone just above a whisper.

"Did what?"

"Took it?"

"Took what?" he asked, with his eyes back on mine. "Have you eaten?"

"Jahad—"

"Have you eaten?" he asked again, finally walking over to the bed.

I swallowed and nodded. "Mom brought up a few . . . a few pigs in a blanket earlier. She's making me a plate now."

He nodded and ran his hand over the top of my head. He was doing what I told him to do if he did it. Ignoring it. Pretending it didn't happen. Putting it back inside of Pandora's box and locking it. Like I told him to do.

We weren't supposed to talk about it. If I brought it up, he was to ignore me and carry on like I hadn't asked him anything. I'd told him I didn't want to know. I'd told him I didn't want any details.

But . . . I did. At first, I thought I would be strong enough to ignore it, but it nagged at me. Those questions I wasn't supposed to ask. Questions about who she was, how she looked, how she felt, what he'd done to her. I wasn't supposed to ask but I wanted to. I wanted to so bad, my bottom lip quivered, and my eyes misted with tears that weren't supposed to surface because of that stupid pass.

Jahad kissed me on the forehead and locked eyes with me again. "I love you, Leigh."

I nodded and told him I loved him too. I didn't blink until he turned to walk away.

I shouldn't have given him that hall pass.

CHAPTER 8

Sienna

I looked up at him and gripped the base of his dick before lowering my mouth over it. He grunted and gripped a handful of my hair as I eased his dick down my throat, inch by inch. The width of him stretched my mouth to capacity. He was so thick. So long. *So damn good.* But I didn't ease up. I kept inching more and more of him down my throat. It was a challenge I accepted willingly with a wet pussy and a wet mouth. There was something about taking all of him down my throat that drove both of us insane.

Once his dick hit the back of my throat, I gagged again and looked up at him once more. He looked back down at me with the sexiest frown of pleasure on his face I had ever seen. God. This man . . . This man . . . This man. He was beautiful. The minute our eyes met, there was a flutter in the pit of my stomach that I got any time our eyes met. It was almost as if I loved him.

But I didn't know him. I'd just met him. Yet I felt so connected to him. The question of how I'd lived twenty-six years of my life without him constantly came to mind whenever our eyes met. And when his dick touched the back of my throat, and the bottom of my pussy, I couldn't believe I'd lived life this long without him in it.

He wrapped my hair around his fist and moved my head back and forth over his dick, as saliva trickled down my chin, hitting the carpeted floor.

"Damn." He grunted. "You look so good suckin' that dick, baby. Mm-hmm."

His accent and the deepness of his voice made my pussy gush. I gripped the base of his dick, stroking him as I made humming noises while I continued to suck him. Just as he fucked my face, one of our phones rang. I paused, looking over at mine sitting on the nightstand, tempted to grab it. Why? I didn't know.

He softly slapped my cheek, bringing my attention back to him. Moaning, I went right back to sucking him, trying my hardest to ignore the ringing, but it wouldn't stop. Right after it would, it would start back up. Every time it restarted, there was a sense of urgency in the pit of my stomach. After the third time, I had to answer it. I pulled back from his dick and stood up. As soon as I did, I opened my eyes. The ringing was the sound of my damn alarm, waking me up out of my dream!

I groaned with a frown as I turned over to grab my phone from the nightstand to snooze it. After I did, I turned back over and plopped down on my pillow with an attitude. I couldn't escape him. It had been two weeks since I'd had the best sex of my life, and every night, I dreamed of the chocolate sex god who made me squirt myself into dehydration. I looked at the ceiling, thinking about the way he'd made me feel.

Averting my eyes over to my nightstand, I rolled them and huffed, refusing to reach into the top drawer for my rose. I was pathetic. Pathetic and apparently in love with a man I didn't know. Okay, maybe I was pushing it. I wasn't in love with him. I was in love with his dick. His big, veiny, thick, beautiful dick.

I missed him. The guy from Pandora's. My God, he fucked me so good. I literally could not stop thinking about him. Naoki was right. By the end of the night, I wanted to get a permanent membership to Pandora's but the price range was far outside of my tax bracket. Twenty thousand for the year. It was outrageous, but worth every penny. If he was a member, it would be worth it, at least. I didn't know if he was, or if he wasn't. Hell, I didn't know anything about him. I knew he was a pussy connoisseur. He knew how to eat it. He knew how to fuck it. He was damn good at all things pussy. I knew what his dick felt like and what his nut tasted like, but I didn't know anything else about him. I didn't have his name, age, or any of that.

When I woke up the morning after, I felt like such a slut. I had no regrets, though. As soon as my pussy throbbed as a reminder of what happened the night before, I smiled. I'd finally had an orgasm without that damn vibrator. And . . . I wanted to have another one.

With him.

But I didn't know him and was sure I'd never see him again unless whoever surprised me with the first invitation surprised me with another one, which I highly doubted they would.

I had been on a hunt to find out who it was for the past two weeks, and I'd come up with absolutely nothing. I needed to stop. Felt like I was putting too much time and energy into the shit when it was really only supposed to be a one-night thing. I couldn't believe I'd gotten attached to one-night-only dick. Naoki believed it, though.

When I told her how my night went, she wanted all the details and had even cursed me out a little for giving him her name instead of mine. Hell, low key, I was mad I'd given him her name too. Just the thought of him looking her up, finding her, and thinking he was going to meet me made my stomach turn. She said that if she was approached by a fine, dark, African/Jamaican nigga, she would send him right my way. I believed her because no matter how spicy the story was, Naoki would never go behind me. I hoped like hell he was looking for me, like I was trying to look for him.

My phone chimed again, and it was the second alarm letting me know that if I didn't get up and get ready now, I'd be late for my first day of work. I did not want to go but I couldn't afford to miss a day of work. I'd just signed the lease to a very nice luxury two-bedroom apartment in downtown Detroit last week. I *had* to make my coin!

It had been a while since I'd clocked into a job, so it would be an adjustment for sure. I was excited, though, nonetheless.

Sitting on the side of the bed, I dragged my hands down my face, trying to get myself together. I had to snap out of it. I wasn't supposed to get so attached, anyway. I didn't need to get attached. I had to have tunnel vision when it came to my life now and I had no room for a new man in it. I needed to focus on healing, not a piece of dick. There was no telling what he had going on, anyway. I had to put all of my energy on me. Dick was a distraction I did not need.

"I had another one, bitch," I said to Naoki, as I stood at the bathroom mirror, giving myself a light beat.

"Damn," Naoki said with a sigh. "Was it *that* good?"

I sucked my teeth and looked into the phone camera. "I told you it was. I can't stop thinking about his ass. It's annoying."

Naoki stretched and shook her head before pulling her bonnet back off her eyes. "Anything is better than thinking about Amiri's sorry ass. Did you see his new post?"

I took a deep breath and scrunched my lips up. "True. Naw. You know I blocked his ass."

I had to. Amiri wouldn't stop calling, texting, and DMing me. After the second week, it had become very excessive. He was calling me repeatedly, texting me, trying to plead his case, begging me to come back. I was over it. It was bad enough I couldn't get my parents or my sisters off my phone.

When I got the keys to the apartment, I posted a photo on Instagram and my phone started ringing off the hook. My mother went off on me for not telling her about what was going on. My father was confused. Mahogany and Hazel were in their feelings, talking about *I bet Naoki knew*. They were right, but shit, so what? I didn't owe anybody an explanation. The only reason Naoki knew was because I needed to stay with her. Otherwise, her ass would have found out on Instagram, like everyone else.

The conversation about my failed engagement was one I did not want to have, but I would have to this weekend since my parents had basically called for a family dinner. I knew what it really was and had half a mind to skip out on it. I was trying to move forward, not stay in the past. Talking about it would do nothing to help my healing.

"I'm about to share my screen with you, hold up."

I took another deep breath and waited for her to pull Amiri's page up. When she went to the picture, I couldn't help but laugh. His corny ass was sitting in his car, gripping the steering wheel of his Range Rover. The caption really got me. *You don't just pick up and leave and leave me sick like that . . . You don't throw away what we had, just like that.* ❤🩹.

And as expected, there were a lot of bitches in his comments. Some speculating, but most throwing pussy at him.

"He so fuckin' goofy," I said with a frown of pure disgust. "Don't tell me shit else. As a matter of fact, block him, Ki."

Naoki scrunched her face up. "Hell no. I'm scanning these comments, going off on every bitch with anything foul to say about you."

I shook my head. "Block him. It's nothing. Don't even waste your time on that. I don't need you to have my back when it comes to that bullshit."

"All right, sis," she said. "Are you excited about your first day?"

I smiled and nodded, grateful she'd changed the subject.

Two hours later, Amiri was the furthest thing from my mind as I waited to start my first day of work. I crossed my arms over my chest as a blistering cold gust of wind swept through the neighborhood, making my teeth chatter. Shit, it was cold. Michigan's weather had been so up and down this season. Had I woken up early enough, I would have known the waist-length puffer jacket wasn't enough for the thirty-degree day.

I looked around the neighborhood, tempted to ring the doorbell again. It was beautiful. The homes were immaculate and everyone had those big, circular driveways. The homes reminded me so much of the ones in Naoki's neighborhood. These muthafuckas had money. I couldn't wait to reach a higher tax bracket to get a big-ass house with too many bedrooms, too many bathrooms, and pointless shit like a butler's kitchen, knowing good and damn well I wouldn't have a butler. I lightly chuckled, looking down at my boots. The minute I did, I wondered if I was dressed too casually. I had on UGGs, my puffer jacket, and a two-piece lounger set I'd gotten from Fashion Nova the other day. Shit. Looking around the neighborhood again, I swallowed. These uppity white folks were about to chew my Black ass out. What was I thinking, coming out here dressed in something other than—

The big navy blue door opening interrupted my train of thought. With dipped brows, I cocked my head to the side a little with a smile. I was pleased that the owner of the house wasn't white at all but Black, almost the same shade of brown as me. I prayed the sista gave me some grace, ignoring my casual attire for the first day of work.

"Hey, I'm Sienna—"

"Good morning, Ms. Mills," she interrupted, eyeing me up and down. "Come on in."

The bright smile I had on my face slowly diminished when I realized this sista wasn't the type of sista I fucked with. She sized me up with so much contempt, I was tempted to walk off and never come back. She had some fucking nerve. She was one of those snooty, prissy, judgmental bitches.

Once I walked over the threshold, she gestured for me to hang my coat up and told me I had to remove my shoes. Before we walked into the foyer, she told me I could put on a pair of the fluffy house slides on the shoe rack. Fancy.

As soon as I stepped into the foyer, my jaw dropped. The outside of the home did its beauty absolutely no justice. It was breathtaking.

There were two grand curved staircases leading up to the second floor where she was leading me. She talked to me, giving me a rundown about the house, telling me about the staff, but I was too enthralled by the home. There were art pieces lining the stairwell with notable Black artists like Basquiat and Kehinde Wiley, as well as a few underground artists I'd seen on TikTok a few times. I wasn't big on art, but I appreciated the artistry of it all. More specifically, Black artists. Apparently, Ms. Prissy did too. However, she didn't strike me as the type to appreciate good Black artists. Granted, I'd just met her, but I could tell a lot about a person by the energy they carried with them, and her energy was stank as hell.

Once we made it to the top of the stairs, I playfully held my chest and took a deep breath before hiking my bag over my shoulder.

She looked over at me with her big-ass nose turned up with judgment. "There's an elevator. I'll show it to you in a few."

I lightly giggled. "I was just joking. Those stairs are easy for me to get up and down, girl."

I was joking, but the look on her face didn't change at all. I took a deep breath and looked down at my watch, groaning at the fact I had eight hours to go before I could get the fuck out of here and away from her.

As I sized her up, I wondered if she was even my client at all. In fact, she gave off *The Help* type of vibes. She couldn't possibly own this beautiful house and have such a nasty-ass spirit. The client was probably white. I should have checked the report one last time before leaving the house. I felt like if I did it now, she'd have something to say about me being on my phone.

So, fuck it.

She continued to talk as we continued down a long hallway. Once we got to two towering oak French doors, she grabbed both handles and pulled it open. The bedroom was damn near the entire size of my whole apartment. I wondered how many square feet the bedroom was. Hell, how many square feet the home was. I couldn't wait to type the address into Google to be nosy.

As we walked into the room, I scanned the place and was pleased. The soft, contemporary décor didn't match her energy at all. It was too bright and airy. The long, flowy, sheer drapes hanging over the windows told a different story than the one I'd picked up from her. The story of a sad-ass, mean-ass, miserable bitch with a stick up her ass. This room gave off happiness. It was welcoming, unlike her.

"She's here," she said, snatching my attention away from the windows to the pretty, smiling woman running her hand over her round belly.

Ahh . . . *She's* my client. Not this mean, ignorant bitch. I should've known. I smiled and made my way over to the bed to give a proper introduction, but when he walked up to the bed, leaned down, and kissed her on the top of her head, my strides halted.

What the hell?

When he stood up and our eyes met, I felt it. The same thing I felt at the masquerade.

Energy. Lots of magnetic energy.

Except this time was different. He wasn't a fine-ass masked man I couldn't help but approach when he walked away from me. He was unmasked, the way he was in the room he fucked me in. And he was wearing a wedding band. One I would have surely noticed with his hand around my throat.

"Sienna Mills? I'm Leighton Baptiste, and this is my husband, Jahad."

CHAPTER 9

Jahad

With my eyes locked on hers, I gave her a subtle smile and said, "Good morning, *Sienna*. Nice to meet you."

She told me her name was Naoki.

Naoki.

Not Sienna.

Had she told me her name was Sienna, I would have noticed it on the email I got from the doula company last week. The doula company was set up sort of like a staffing agency. I didn't see the client until they came in for their first day. So, I had no way of actually finding out that this was the woman who would take care of my wife for a year or so. However, had I known her name was Sienna, and not Naoki, I would have done my research off the strength of seeing the name *Sienna* alone. I would have found out it was her and immediately requested someone new. But . . . she told me her name was Naoki. Not Sienna. So, I had no idea.

Imagine my surprise when I looked up and saw her walking through my bedroom door. My breathing got caught up in my chest a little, but because I moved very well under pressure, I greeted her with the type of eye contact that had always been a very well delivered, nonverbal warning.

She gave me a light squint and then forced a smile as well. "Nice to meet you, too, *Mr*. Baptiste. Nice . . . Nice to meet you as well, Mrs. Baptiste."

I didn't know what else to do besides jump ahead of the situation before shit got weird. She was standing there for a good twenty seconds, wearing an awkward-ass frozen grin, before I stepped up and shook her hand. I could just about imagine what was going through her mind because when I looked up and saw her, it fucked me up too. I wasn't a man who startled easily, but that shit . . . that shit shook me. Because what the fuck was she doing here?

For a second, I thought I was tripping. Imagining shit. As I had been since I left Pandora's that night. If I wasn't busy with work, I was thinking about her and the way she swallowed every drop of my nut with a smile on her face. I'd dealt with a lot of women in the past, but none of them had made an impression on me quite like she had. Not even Leighton.

"Do you need me to give her the tour, Jahad?" Farrah asked, wearing a light smile.

I was on my way out of the door to meet with my family. We had a few things to discuss about business. But because I had planned according to our new doula's arrival, I had about thirty minutes to spare before I really had to get on the road. I always scheduled things according to what we had going on regarding our child. I never missed an appointment, and I was always present whenever we got a new doula because, shit, Leigh had gone through three already and we'd just started this process about a month and a half ago.

Farrah knew what it was. She knew how asinine I was when it came to new staff stepping into my home, too, so I was thrown off a little by her offer to give the tour. She had been wearing thin on my patience for weeks, so maybe I was looking into shit the wrong way, but I was usually never wrong about shit like muthafuckas trying to be funny. Besides, the situation with Sienna was delicate. There was no way in hell I was leaving without having a conversation with her.

"I've got it. As a matter of fact, Farrah, we've kept you long enough. I'm sure you have better things to do. With Sienna here, I don't see much of a need for you to be at Leighton's bedside all day, every day."

Farrah scrutinized Sienna before putting her eyes on Leighton. "I don't mind. However, I do have a few errands to run." She walked over to the bed and leaned down to give Leighton a hug. "Call me if you need me, okay?" she stated before giving Sienna another once-over. "For anything."

Sienna lightly huffed with a smile as she looked around the bedroom, possibly trying to avoid looking at me. Which I appreciated. It was hard for me to look at her without getting stuck there, in those alluring-ass brown eyes again. So hard, my eyes went from her, to Leighton, to Farrah often just to avoid what I knew would happen if they ended up locked on her for too long. Slow motion. Fireworks. Silence. I couldn't get stuck there. I couldn't let her magnetic-ass aura pull me in. Not with my wife laying in the bed right beside me.

My wife. She'd been giving me hell these past few weeks. Literal hell on earth. She knew. She knew the moment I stepped foot into our bedroom on

New Year's Eve night. I felt her studying me as soon as I got back from Pandora's. She wanted to talk about it. I didn't. It was one of the rules. She gave me the pass, and if and when I took it, we wouldn't talk about it. I didn't want to talk about it. I didn't even want to think about it. I felt like shit, low key. More now than that night because every night since, I'd laid next to my wife with thoughts of Nao—Sienna's wet-ass pussy on my brain. And I knew Leighton noticed. I knew because I knew her. We'd be lying beside each other, eyes to the ceiling, in silence. My thoughts on Sienna, and most likely, her thoughts on me, trying to figure out what I was thinking about.

Five minutes later, I walked out of the bedroom with Sienna in tow. I felt her eyes on my back. Fiery eyes, too. She was pissed and had every right to be. I'd just made her squirt, speak in tongues, and ate her pussy like I was on death row and it was my last meal. Nice and slow. Savoring that shit. Just for her to find out I was married. I would be pissed too.

"So . . ." she said with a deep breath as we walked next to each other.

I kept my hands buried in the pockets of my dark hoodie, fists balled, trying to stop myself from touching her. Because shit . . . that was what I wanted to do. Wanted to wrap my hand around her throat, push her up against the wall, and take one of her thick-ass nipples into my mouth.

But I had to behave.

For several reasons.

Most importantly, because my wife was behind the door we'd just walked out of, and second, because that was a onetime thing. I was Jahad, the devoted husband, not that wild-ass nigga who'd stumbled into Pandora's and ended up licking and sucking on a pussy that didn't belong to his wife. I'd tucked that nigga away and had every intention of keeping him tucked away. That wouldn't be hard because I'd tucked him away before.

I wondered how she felt about finding out about my wife. I wondered because I was sure that after our night, she'd thought of me just as much as I had thought of her.

"So . . ."

"You're married," she said before pulling her lips into her mouth.

"And your name is Sienna."

"You didn't have on a ring."

"Why would I have had on my ring if I was there to fuck someone that wasn't my wife?" I boldly asked her as I stood at another set of French doors.

"Why were you out fucking someone who isn't your wife, anyway?"

I stared at her. We stared at each other. Frozen. Silence. Slow motion. That slow fucking motion. I couldn't get away from it. Not when our eyes were locked. The shit did something to me. *She* did something to me. Since she bumped into me at the club, she'd had this effect on me, so it had nothing to do with sex. It was something else. Something I couldn't put a finger on. Something I needed to stop. This was unhealthy. Unhealthy for my marriage. Unhealthy for her. For us. Because if I couldn't escape this shit, keeping that wild, young nigga who'd rubbed his face all in her pussy tucked was going to be hard as hell.

Swallowing, I tore my eyes away from hers and twirled my ring around with my thumb to ground myself.

"That's none of your business," I told her.

"How is it not? We—"

"Had sex. Consensual, no-strings-attached sex. If you wouldn't have fucked me, you would have fucked someone else. Marital status isn't on the application. The only reason you know I'm married is because you just happen to be my wife's doula."

She started to say something, but bit down on her bottom lip instead. I watched as she grabbed the strap of her Telfar bag hanging on her shoulder. Watched as she tightened her grip too. She was pissed. Probably wanted to curse me out, but she had no grounds to do so. What I said was the truth. She couldn't argue with that.

"Will working here be an issue for you?" I asked her, my eyes again locked on hers. This time was different. I wasn't stuck. There was no slow motion. None of that weird shit because this time, when I spoke to her, I was speaking from a real, genuine-ass place. I didn't do problems. Me and problems had never gotten along. I got rid of them as quick as they came before they could even actually become a problem. And I would do the same with her if necessary. I might have stuck my dick inside of her . . . might've eaten her pussy and had a hard-ass time getting her off my mind, but when it came to peace—more specifically, Leighton Baptiste's peace—I would dead anything that tried to get in the way of that. That might not mean much coming from me, but what I did didn't define who I was. And what I did would have never been done without that pass. A pass that shorty didn't need to know anything about. All she needed to know was that what happened in that room had to *stay* in that room.

She shrugged her right shoulder. "It was sex. What happened in that room, happened in that room. We leave it there. I've left it there. I was just . . . surprised to see you."

"I need you to look at me when you say that," I told her before positioning myself directly in front of her. Her eyes wandered again, so I lightly gripped her chin, forcing her eyes to meet mine.

Her brows crinkled and she nodded. "Working here . . . it won't be an issue."

I searched her eyes for any sign of a lie. I trusted that Sienna wouldn't be an issue because the only thing I saw in her eyes was desire. There was so much of it swimming in her eyes that, for a second there, I got lost in it. Only because I had already found what I was looking for beneath them.

Softening my approach, I allowed myself to get lost in them. It felt good. The things she did to me . . . without doing shit to me . . . it felt good. Possibly because it'd been a long-ass while since I'd seen so much hunger for me behind the eyes of an alluring-ass woman. For a moment, I untucked that wild-ass nigga . . . I set my reservations and the feelings I had for my wife aside. Because this shit between her and me . . . it felt good as hell. My eyes then landed on her lips. Full-ass, wet-ass, dick-sucking lips.

"Will it be an issue for you?" she asked in a tone just above a whisper, snapping me back to reality.

That was a heavy question. One I wasn't quick to respond to. I let it simmer a little because, truth be told, it *could* be an issue. If I kept giving in to the magnetic pull Sienna and I had between us . . . it could be. But at the same time, I loved and respected my wife far too much to step outside of our marriage. She gave me *one* pass. Not several. Anything I did with my dick going forward would be adultery and I had absolutely no interest in cheating on my wife. I didn't like the idea of her being here, though. Not after recognizing just how easy it was for me to fall victim to that pull. The pull that still had a light hold on me. Her working here would be a problem if I allowed it to, and I had every intention of preventing that.

"It won't be," I told her.

She cocked her right brow with a light smile. "Good, then."

"But because we did what we did . . . I don't feel comfortable with you being here," I continued.

Then there was that. In the past, when I was young and wild in the streets, I did my dirt but kept it away from Leighton. What type of nigga would I be, allowing Sienna to work here after the shit we'd done? What I'd done would eat at me more than it already was if I allowed her to prance around Leighton as if I hadn't stuffed her with dick.

She looked up at me with a frown. "What?"

As I continued to spin my ring around my finger, my eyes stayed planted on hers. "I need you to quit."

She laughed and drew back. "I'm sorry, excuse me?"

"I'll compensate you. I have your information. I'll write you a nice-ass check that'll cover just about—"

"No thank you," she snapped. "If you want me out of here, you could just fire me. You seem like a smart guy. I'm sure you'll come up with a fantastic explanation to give your wife for firing me on my first day." She boldly took a step closer to me. "I'm sorry, Mr. Baptiste. I'm not quitting because you feel guilty."

"My proposition has nothing to do with guilt," I told her. "But everything to do with respect."

"Respect? You care about respect *now*? Isn't it a little too late for that?" she challenged.

I stroked my beard and looked away from her before running my hand over the back of my neck. It was a little too late for respect. I should have respected my wife by keeping my ass the fuck away from Pandora's. But shit, I was left with little to no choice.

"I just want to work," Sienna said, as she watched me pace, stressed about what we'd done.

What *I'd* done. The guilt of fucking another woman was finally wearing off. The minute I saw her, all of it came rushing right back to me. I didn't like this. This conscience. I longed for the days I didn't give a fuck. The days I could fuck with a bird and crawl into bed with Leighton like nothing had happened. With age came maturity and a level of loyalty to the woman I loved that I never thought was possible back then, though. If I could just get a bit of *don't give a fuck* from then, I'd be straight. I couldn't *not* give a fuck. It wasn't in me. Not anymore.

"I won't pretend like working here . . . with her . . . with you two will be easy. But this is all I've got right now. I'm in no position to quit, and I for damn sure don't want a payout. I'm not like that. And I'm not a home-wrecker. I'm not the type of woman that gets a thrill from fucking with some-one's husband. I don't want a payout. I'm not a prostitute or some messy bitch you can pay off to keep quiet. And, to be honest, I'm very offended by the offer. Which is another reason you can keep that shit," she continued since I hadn't said anything.

I looked over at her with raised brows. She was pissed. I could tell by the deep furrow in her arched brows and the crinkle in her button nose.

"My intentions weren't to offend you," I reassured her.

"Well . . ." She paused and rolled her eyes. "You did."

"My fault," I said with a deep breath. "Listen . . . This . . . all of this shit is new to me. I can understand why you were offended by me asking you to quit and the offer of money. Contrary to what it may look like, this is uncharted territory for me. I don't cheat on my wife. The situation . . . our situation is complicated. And while I understand why you feel you may be entitled to an explanation, you aren't. Just like you have no obligation to me to walk away. And I won't fire you. I'd never get in the way of a person making money. Not for personal gain. That's not me."

Sienna stood with her back against the wall across from me, hanging on to every word I said. She was silent, actually listening, and I appreciated that. Why? I wasn't sure. Getting people to listen to me came easy. However, the woman I was married to didn't. Lately, she hadn't. Maybe I was taken aback by Sienna's silence because I was used to being interrupted with an explanation or an argument.

"I'm trying to process this, and I can imagine you are too. Instead of complicating shit, let's just"—I paused and shrugged, as I ran my tongue over my bottom lip—"let the shit flow. It happened. It won't happen again. We have a mutual understanding, correct?"

"Correct," Sienna said.

Nodding at her, I gestured toward the closed doors behind me before opening them. She pushed away from the wall and walked by me, into the bedroom. The aroma of her perfume filled my nostrils and, like before, I basked in the womanly scent of her. Closing my eyes, I clenched down on my jaw and made a mental note to give Leighton a reason to want to dress up and put on perfume the way she used to.

"What's this?" she asked as she looked around the modestly decorated bedroom.

"Your room. You will be with us for postpartum as well, right?" I asked with my eyes on the side of her face as she scanned the bedroom.

"Yes, I'll be here postpartum." She paused and lightly frowned. "But a bedroom? I won't need a bedroom."

"We like for our houseguests to be comfortable. You aren't the only employee here with a bedroom that possibly won't be used. The cook, Evaline, and her assistant, Maurice, have rooms here too. Except they sleep off site, in the staff quarters about a mile away from the house, through the backyard."

Sienna turned her mouth down in approval and raised her brows, impressed. "That's *very* nice."

I studied her as she continued around the bedroom, wondering what was going through her mind. But as she breezed around the room, running her hands over the smooth, off-white linen covering the king-sized bed, I could barely read her. I followed her with my hands stuffed into my pockets, my eyes scanning every inch of her. Every inch of her . . . I'd touched. I'd kissed. I'd licked. I'd thought about. I told her it wouldn't be hard for me to have her here, but shit, I couldn't stop thinking about the night we shared.

I stroked my beard and chewed on my bottom lip. She stopped at the closet doors, opened them, and giggled.

"A walk-in closet? What will I do with a walk-in closet?" she asked before looking over at me, whipping her long hair from her face.

"This is a guest room, love," I told her. "Not *specifically* for you."

"Oh. *Duh*," she said with a laugh.

"But while you're here . . . it is. You have your own bathroom as well. Which is very convenient, since the guest bathrooms are on the main floor." I nodded toward another closed door. "Right behind that door."

The ringing of my phone tore my attention away from her ass. I took a deep breath, ran my hand over the top of my head, and fished my phone from the pocket of my joggers.

It was Shelby, the head of Michigan's DEA division, and the person who helped the Baptiste family flawlessly make millions of dollars. My father built a relationship with him when he was nothing more than a rookie cop in the late nineties. They kept ties well throughout Shelby's career. The higher he climbed, the higher we did. My father didn't introduce us until I was around twenty-one.

Initially, I was skeptical of him for obvious reasons. He was a federal agent. A *dirty* fed. I hated a pig. I didn't trust them at all, especially not a dirty one. A dirty fed had to be watched under intense scrutiny. Which I did for a very long time. After a couple of years, I dialed back a little on it, but those eyes . . . They stayed on him still. I didn't trust him. Never would. He helped us make millions of dollars and I was grateful for it, but nothing would gain my trust. He couldn't even honor his badge, so why in the fuck would he honor us, a Black family from the treacherous streets of Haiti?

His transition to head of DEA helped us move work across the United States pretty much effortlessly. Our connection with Shelby made our business lucrative as hell. We had one of the most lucrative illegal businesses in all the United States. It was because of our connections that the competition was pretty much nonexistent. There wasn't a nigga in the dope game who could reach the levels we'd reached without getting knocked before they could even scratch the surface.

"Yeah?" I answered as I watched Sienna open the door to the bathroom.

"Baptiste. You got a minute?" Shelby asked, the rasp in his voice thicker than usual. He pulled from what sounded like a cigarette. Shit, what I'd bet was a cigarette. He smoked like an old chimney.

"I got a few. What's up? Where are you?"

The crackling sound of fire let me know he'd hit the cigarette again. "The yellow house."

Taking a deep breath, I pinched the bridge of my nose, realizing what Shelby wanted was serious. If he was at that small, yellow house in Armada, Michigan, that meant shit was serious and he didn't trust any of the locations closer to where he actually resided.

Armada was far in the countryside of Michigan. There wasn't anything but cornfields, farms, and shit out that way. Most of the roads weren't even lined with streetlights. There were dirt roads, and a lot of racist white muthafuckas. So, while he was safe out there, my Black ass sure wasn't.

I flicked my wrist to get a look at my watch. It was pretty early. I didn't like to be out that way past seven in the evening. I didn't want to be out there when the sun went down at all, to be honest. Not that I was afraid of what would happen to me if I was out there that late, but I was afraid of what *I'd* have to do if someone thought it was smart to even attempt to get at me on that racist shit. Again . . . me and problems . . . they didn't mix well. I liked to avoid them at all costs. If I could avoid something, then I avoided it. And me avoiding Armada after sundown was me avoiding problems I didn't need on an already full plate.

"Hello?"

"Yeah," I breathed out, as my eyes met Sienna's.

Funny how I talked about avoiding problems, but there she was . . . my biggest one . . . just a couple of feet away from me, coyly smiling like she didn't just have a mouth full of my nut a couple of weeks ago.

"Give me two hours," I told him before disconnecting the call.

Sienna approached me, her hands stuffed into the pockets of her cardigan.

"If you're busy, we can finish this later. I don't think I need to see anything else, since most of my time will be spent up here with your . . . *wife*. I mean, Mrs. Baptiste."

"Leighton is fine. No need for the formalities. Same with me. Call me Jahad."

She nodded.

"And there is more for you to see. Your boss sent over the job details, correct?"

"She did."

As we continued down the hallway, toward the elevator, I rambled off what her duties would entail. Both to create small talk and to refresh her memory in case she needed it. We didn't need much. Simple stuff, but because we had such a spacious compound and because Leighton was on bed rest, some of the things we needed went a little outside of normal doula duties. Such as picking up prescriptions and bringing food up when necessary. Nothing too crazy, though. The job was more of a personal assistant type of setup, but because Leighton did need the support during her pregnancy and after, hiring a doula was more fitting.

We stepped onto the elevator, and it was like the air immediately got thicker. Her scent . . . her *intoxicating* scent . . . filled the small space and I closed my eyes, inhaling. I felt her eyes on me, but I didn't dare to open them. I was afraid that if I did, I'd for sure end up doing something crazy to her ass. I needed to chill. I needed to get the fuck away from her. Right then and there, with her eyes on me, basking in the womanly scent of her, I decided I wouldn't be spending much time here while she was. I couldn't do it. Shit was still too fresh to effectively share a space with her without wanting to push my dick to the back of her wet-ass throat.

Ding.

The elevator dinged and both of us exhaled before stepping off. We were immediately greeted by Evaline, who was passing by, noticeably heading for the kitchen, where she spent most of her time.

"Good morning, Mr. Baptiste!" she excitedly greeted me with a bright smile as she eyed Sienna up and down. "And who do we have here?"

Sienna smiled and stepped forward with her hand extended. "Good morning, miss. I'm Sienna. I'll be working with the family as their new doula."

"Yeah, Ms. Evaline. I'm hoping this one is a good fit," I joked. "You know how Leigh likes to go through doulas."

Sienna looked over her shoulder at me with a look of concern on her face.

I lightly shook my head. "No worries. Leighton's just very selective. I'm sure you'll be a good fit."

Sienna nervously giggled and Ms. Evaline joined in.

"I think you'll be a good fit too. Quiet as it's kept, I knew them li'l timid white girls coming in and out of here wasn't going to work for a strong, cultured Black woman like Leighton."

Cultured was a great way to describe Leighton. She wore her hair in locs, loved Erykah Badu, Lauryn Hill, and of course . . . Beyoncé. She was a strong, cultured, and opinionated Black woman for sure. Had I known they existed, I would have contacted a Black-owned doula company a long time ago. Now that I knew, I was keeping that company in my back pocket, just in case.

Sienna continued to giggle as we followed Ms. Evaline to the kitchen. They made small talk, while I kept my hands stuffed in the Nike joggers and looked everywhere but at her. I couldn't understand why I was having such a hard-ass time with this. I wondered if the fact that it'd been a long-ass minute since I'd been in pussy played a part in it or not. The desire to slide back inside of her had been overwhelming. Extremely overwhelming now that she was in reach.

Looking up at the ceiling, I mumbled, "*Kaka* (shit)."

She briefly looked over her shoulder at me with dipped brows before looking away.

After introducing her to Ms. Evaline and Maurice, I showed her the rest of the house and took her off site to the staff quarters. Instead of walking, we hopped on one of the golf carts and took the short ride back there. She was quiet, but her thoughts were loud. We were so close, our arms and legs touched. Luckily, the fabric of our clothes kept our skin from touching. Yet the barrier did nothing but make me want to feel *more* of her. I wanted her bare skin on me. The way she kept squirming and trying to keep her body from touching mine was a clear sign that the subtle touching made her want more, too.

"Relax," I said with a light chuckle. "There is nowhere for you to go in this little-ass golf cart, Sienna."

She took a deep breath and placed her hands between her legs as she looked off. "I just . . . I'm trying to create a bit of distance."

Nodding, I said, "I get it. Still . . . Nowhere to go. We'll be at the house in a couple seconds."

"Is there a way Maurice or someone can drive the other one up here? It's just that—"

"I want you to relax," I interrupted, as I pulled in front of the small, quaint house. Because it was a part of the property, we'd converted it into a guesthouse. But because our families were very close knit, no one used it. They preferred to stay inside the house with us when they visited, occupying the guest bedrooms instead. So, instead of letting such a nice place go to waste, Leigh and I decided to use it as a staff house, once we realized we'd be hiring help.

I locked eyes with Sienna and said, "We've been closer. A lot closer. *Flesh to flesh.* Taking a short ride in a tight space shouldn't be an issue. Especially since I've been in tighter spaces, for longer times . . . with you."

I watched as her eyes slightly widened before she looked away and got out of the cart. Dragging my hand over the top of my head, I took a deep breath and followed suit. Maybe that was too much. It hadn't helped our—my—situation at all. My dick was brick, but because I had no time to will it down, I stepped out of the golf cart, anyway.

The minute I closed the door and headed in her direction, her eyes fell on it before she quickly looked away. Noticing how uncomfortable she was, I concealed it as best as I could by placing my hand in front of it.

Walking by her, I headed up the short stairs and punched the unlock code into the keypad. I wasn't sure if this was a good idea. Coming here with her, knowing . . . knowing what I wanted to do with her.

I swallowed and opened the door, stepping back so she could enter the house before me.

"Initially, when we bought the property, this was going to be a guesthouse for our families, but they're clingy as hell and want nothing to do with it," I started, breaking the awkward silence. "Instead of having it torn down, we converted it to a place for the staff to stay, if necessary. It has a small kitchen, a smaller bathroom, and two bedrooms. As you can see, we've made the most out of the space by converting the living room into both a living room and a dining room. So, while it may be smaller than—"

"You keep calling it small." She giggled. "It's not small. It's quaint. Very roomy and homey. It's not *small*, but I can see why you think that, considering the massive home you stay in. You're probably used to staying in castles, but most people aren't."

"I'm not used to staying in castles," I sternly corrected, narrowing my eyes at her. "I mentioned the size in reference to the main house, not to discredit its size, Ms. Mills."

"Ms. Mills?" she tossed over her shoulder. "Is that what you'll be calling me when I piss you off?"

"I'm not pissed off," I told her.

She shrugged her right shoulder. "Offended. Something happened. I apologize if me assuming upset you."

I didn't say anything. I stood at the door, watching her maneuver around the house. I didn't need to give her a tour, so I stood my ass right there, planted at the door. Her sly comment about what I was used to helped ground me. I wasn't upset, but I was offended. I shouldn't have been, considering she was only going off what she'd been introduced to.

We met at Pandora's, an upscale sex club, and had sex in a VIP room that cost more than what most people made in a month. Then she comes here, sees this massive home where we have staff and a staff quarters. It was easy to assume that I came from money, looking at where I was now. But to assume that, based on what I had now, would be asinine.

We were poor. Back home, the house we stayed in was merely that and half the size of these staff quarters. I didn't come from money by a long shot.

My father hustled and made a way for us. When we moved to the States, we didn't come here to a gigantic house and millions of dollars. We came here and moved to a three-bedroom home that was a mansion compared to where we had come from, but it was a regular, ranch-style home on the east side of Detroit, in the middle of the ghetto.

We spent many years in the trenches, and while the trenches here didn't hold a candle to the trenches back home, we were still in them, nonetheless. We didn't get more until years later, when I was nineteen. It took a lot to get to where I was.

The ride back to the house was quiet. She was more relaxed than before, and I think my quietness caused that. The tone had been disrupted, and for that, I was grateful. I had a wife and a family to think about.

CHAPTER 10

Sienna

As I sat next to the bed—*their* bed—I watched her lips move as she talked about herself. About *them*. She was giving me an introduction. Telling me about how they met. About how many times she was pregnant. About how she just knew the baby she was carrying was their rainbow baby. She smiled the biggest when she talked about the baby. Not so much when she spoke about her husband. Jahad. The man who'd given me body-quivering, pussy-squirting orgasm after orgasm. She didn't talk about him with the love that someone who had been with a man for over ten years should talk about a man. I wondered if the bleakness in her eyes as she spoke about him was because of me. I wondered if she knew. She had to know. Women . . . we always know. I'd just done some of the freakiest shit I'd ever done with that lady's husband not even a month ago. How was I supposed to offer moral support when I was probably the primary source of that . . . emptiness? That flat, lifeless smile she wore when she spoke about him?

"Tell me a little about yourself, Sienna," Leighton said with a smile. "That's a beautiful name, too, girl."

I nervously smiled and scratched my forehead with a deep breath. I'd told him I could handle working here. He offered me a buyout. Literally offered me a year's salary to quit. But because I consider myself pretty headstrong and stubborn, I told him no. Told him I was offended too. Because, hell, I was. I didn't want a buyout. Couldn't imagine quitting. I wouldn't. I needed this job. Not just for the money—he was offering to give me that—but for the experience. For the knowledge, and because, shit, I needed to get out of the house. I had to get out of the house. If I stayed in that apartment all day, every day, staring at walls, I would break. I knew I would.

This shit with Amiri was still fresh, and although I'd been handling it pretty well, I knew it was only because I'd kept busy. I'd been distracted. My mental health was on the line. But now . . . sitting beside his smiling wife as she excitedly anticipated hearing about me, I didn't think I could handle it. The guilt . . . The guilt was eating me the fuck alive.

"Well, I'm twenty-six. You're my first client, but I've been under Shonda's wing for a while now, so I'm very well trained, so you're in great hands," I said with a light giggle, trying to push away the intrusive thoughts of being in her husband's hands . . . mouth . . . and dick a few weeks ago. "I'm the middle child. I have two sisters, Mahogany and Hazel—"

"Ahhh . . . Creative!" she said regarding me and my sisters' names.

I giggled and nodded. "Yeah, my momma is like that. Creative. Always trying to be different. Anyway, yeah . . . That's about it."

"Lies," Leighton said as she turned over on her side, her hand steady resting on that beautiful round belly. "I refuse to believe that's all you've got. You told me you're twenty-six and a middle child. There's more to you than just that. Are you single? Do you have children? Want children? What made you get into doulaship? What do you like to do? Don't be coy, girl. I've sat up here and told you my whole damn life story."

We shared a laugh.

An awkward laugh on my end.

"Well, I mean . . . There is more to me than that," I told her before crossing my leg over the other one. "I am single. *Newly single.* I don't have children. At one point, I did want them, but apparently, the universe has other plans for me and this . . . womb of mine." I lightly chuckled, something I usually did in the middle of uncomfortable conversations. And just the slightest mention of this cursed womb made me uncomfortable. "I got into doulaship because motherhood is beautiful. Babies are beautiful. And, well . . ."

I paused and shrugged, letting out a few of those uncomfortable giggles because . . . I was uncomfortable.

"You're making the most out of the hand you were dealt," Leighton continued for me with a knowing nod. "Beautiful. I think that's beautiful and courageous, Sienna."

We shared a familiar look. One that said we understood each other without having to verbalize it. With my situation, I thought doulaship was perfect. Training for the certificate was pretty fast, since not much medical background was required. But Shonda, my boss, offered extensive training that lasted an additional six weeks and ended with a guaranteed position at her Black-owned and -operated company, Serene Mommy Doula Services.

It was perfect for me. I was present for numerous births, had some one-on-one time with several clients, and had even worked alongside doulas who had completed the training. I was ready. I thought I was ready. I wanted to be ready. But how ready was I, really, if I couldn't even have a full conversation about my *why* without getting emotional?

I nodded and said with a deep breath, "Yeah . . ."

She reached out and grabbed my hand. I wanted to pull away. Started to pull away, but she tightened her grip. "I'm happy to *share* this experience with you."

I just stared at her. Silent. Tears wetting my wide eyes. Drowning in guilt. I was such a fucked-up bitch. I didn't want to get too cozy with her. I didn't want her to like me. I didn't deserve it. I deserved to be hated. Her husband had an affair with me. I caused that bleakness from before. I didn't deserve her smiles. I didn't deserve her respect. I wanted her to hate me. But by the smile on her face and the twinkle in her eyes, I could tell it was pretty much too late for that. She liked me.

People always liked me. I was what my father called magnetic. I had a magnetic aura. I was a gentle soul. Someone who added light to any room I stepped foot in. And it took little to no effort. He used to always tell me that when I was a kid. I never understood it. I didn't know what the hell he was talking about then. But as an adult, I noticed it. I noticed it every time I walked into a room. The energy always shifted, and not in a bad way.

People just . . . they liked me. I'd stood in line at Starbucks and had women tell me all of their business and shit freely. Unprovoked. They felt safe to release with me. Safe and comfortable. I'd made plenty of acquaintances at the gym—male and female. I'd gone to the bar alone and left with a couple of phone numbers from women who wanted to be friends.

I didn't consider myself friendly at all. I was just . . . a beacon of light, I suppose. I didn't like it. I hated it, actually. Especially now. I didn't want Leighton to look at me as some . . . sweet, soft, magnetic soul. I wanted her to hate my fucking guts, but I'd have to give her a reason to. The problem with that was that I didn't have a nasty bone in my body. I didn't want to be rude. I didn't like to be mean, especially not unprovoked. She hadn't done anything to me. She didn't deserve attitude. She didn't deserve the raging fire I had beneath all of this light. So, I couldn't just get her to hate me. There was one way: Tell her I'd slept with her husband. But I *couldn't* do that.

I pulled my hand away and abruptly stood up. "I'm sorry, I need to use the restroom."

I was on the verge of a complete meltdown. Thankfully, I could blame my emotions on the conversation we were having. So, me suddenly needing to leave the room wouldn't come as a surprise.

She nodded and pulled her lips into her mouth. "It's okay. Take your time, boo."

Boo.

She liked me.

She *really* fucking liked me.

I quickly walked out of the bedroom. I kept the tears threatening to pool over the rim of my lids at bay until I closed the door to the guest room. My bedroom. A room right next door to hers. *Theirs.*

Once I was behind that closed door, the tears spilled over the rim with a vengeance, clouding my vision. Because I couldn't scream and sob like I wanted to, I panted heavily, the pain in my chest intensifying with every breath I took. I cried hard. Harder than I cared to. Bits and pieces of my broken heart stemming from that conversation were mixed inside of those guilty emotions too. This was why I didn't talk about it. *My reason.* My sisters . . . My family . . . they thought I'd go to nursing school like Naoki since we were usually glued at the hip, but no. I didn't have a passion for nursing. I had a passion for motherhood. Babies. Cute, chubby, bright-eyed, innocent, beautiful babies. Big, round bellies. Pregnancy hormones. *That waddle.* Pregnancy cravings. Sonograms. And what came after it. Mommy-daughter (or son) dates. Trips to the dentist and doctor appointments. First days of school. Late-night feedings. I wanted to bury my face in the crook of a chubby neck and inhale that soft, soothing new-baby smell. But because I wouldn't be able to experience those things personally, I figured doulaship was the next best thing. I just . . . I wanted a small glimpse into it. The life . . . the experience.

Never in a million years did I expect to be having my first shared experience with the wife of a man who had imprinted on my soul in unimaginable, unthinkable ways. That was what Jahad had done. Imprinted on my soul. Somehow, when he penetrated my pussy, he penetrated deeper, finding his way to my soul. It was . . . those eyes. That voice. The feelings. The chills. The . . . *everything.*

We'd only shared a couple of hours together, but my God, he'd left such a stain on me, I couldn't scrub off.

Once I made my way to the bathroom, I stared in the mirror at the mascara running down my cheeks and wondered if it was worth it. This shared experience. This glimpse into motherhood. Visions of my night—*our* night—at

Pandora's floored me and immediately gave me the answer I needed. No. It wasn't worth it.

I couldn't do it.

My first client couldn't be her.

Couldn't be . . . *them.*

I couldn't get out of there fast enough.

As soon as my eight hours were up, I grabbed my Telfar and headed for the door. As soon as I hit the front porch, I called my boss, Shonda, to get me a new client. I couldn't do it. It was too much for me.

When I had gone back to the room, there was a shift in her mood. A shift I definitely appreciated. She didn't ask me how I was doing. We didn't revisit the conversation. Nothing. She didn't ask me to talk more about myself. We kept everything strictly business and I appreciated that.

She showed me her schedule, told me about her meals and when her prescriptions needed to be filled. She talked about the duties I'd have outside of typical doula responsibilities, such as errands every now and then. We talked about the nursery, baby clothes, baby names, the baby shower . . . things of that nature. I was grateful because I couldn't have another conversation about *myself.* Felt like if I talked about *myself* anymore, I'd end up telling her just how horrible of a person I was. Felt like I would have word vomit and tell on myself.

The rest of my shift was not as heavy as the first half, but the weight of it changing didn't change my decision to quit. Today would be my first and last day in the Baptiste household.

"Hey, Si. How was your first—"

"It was . . . odd. I don't think this family is going to be a good fit for me, Shon. Is there any way I can be transferred to another one?"

Shonda was a very cool, down-to-earth Black woman like me, so we got along very well. So well, I had the privilege of calling her Shon instead of Mrs. Blake. We, along with two other women, did brunch and mimosas every other Sunday.

Shonda took a deep breath. "What's wrong with them? I told you, they were the highest-paying clients we had on the roster. They requested a sweet, caring, Black girl, which you are. I could have given the assignment to Noel, but I gave it to you because of what we talked about, Si."

I ran my hand over my creased forehead as I looked up at the massive house with a sigh, before heading to the car.

"Nothing really. I don't like the . . . the best friend. She's meddling as hell, and I can tell she'd constantly be in the way. I think it'll be a pretty stressful environment and I-I just don't want to deal with that." I lied straight through my damn teeth like it was nothing. I had to lie. I couldn't tell her I'd slept with my client's husband before meeting her. I couldn't tell her he'd eaten my pussy and fucked me in indescribable ways that made me wet at the subtlest thought of it. Shonda and I were cool. We'd swapped stories plenty of times before, but I couldn't share this one. Hell no. It was embarrassing. We were cool, but not that cool.

Shonda took another deep breath. I saw her now, sitting at that desk, rolling her eyes with her lips twisted up.

"Listen . . . I don't know about this, but I do have one other family. They're in St. Clair Shores. The wife, she has three other small children and a husband that works sixty hours a week. They're Caucasian and the pay for that family is eight hundred per week."

My eyes widened. "Eight hundred?"

"Exactly," Shonda said with a huff. "Laughable compared to that Baptiste family with the irrelevant meddling best friend, right?"

I rolled my eyes and, got into the car, tossing my head against the headrest with a sigh. It was laughable. The Baptiste family was paying fifteen hundred per week. That fifteen hundred was the reason I had signed the lease on that high-rise luxury apartment with the hefty price tag. My rent was twenty-five hundred a month. I might've gone overboard, but hell . . . I deserved luxury, right?

I couldn't go from where I had stayed with Amiri to a shabby one-bedroom apartment in the hood. I needed the stainless steel. I needed the big master bathroom. I needed the walk-in closet. I needed the on-site gym, spa, and pool.

I'd admit, Amiri had me spoiled. He paid the rent on the condo we shared. He paid for everything. My car note, cell phone bill, the utilities. I didn't have to pay for anything. The salary for doulas wasn't very high. Initially, since I thought I would marry a nigga with a hefty bank account, the money didn't really matter. I was simply passionate about it.

Since it turned out I wouldn't be marrying that ain't-shit-ass nigga after all, the money mattered. The money mattered a lot and made my situation ten times harder.

"Shit," I mumbled.

"Is she *that* bad?" Shonda asked. "Give it a week, Sienna. If you still feel the same, I'll see what I can do. I just . . . I don't know right now, okay?"

I looked back up at the house and took a deep breath. Could I last another week? In that house . . . the house he lived in? Could I stand to be in such close proximity to him without touching, kissing, feeling, and tasting him? I just didn't know. What were the fucking odds, anyway? Like, huh? How? I felt like God was punishing me for being such a nasty little slut. This was fucked up.

Something told me to look in my rearview mirror, and when I did, he was driving up. I quickly pushed the start button on my car and reversed, but he pulled in right behind me, blocking my path.

"Shon, let me call you right back." I interrupted her as she was in the middle of trying to get me to understand the importance of establishing healthy work relationships.

"Si, did you hear what I said? Right now's really not the time to walk away from a job over something so trivial. I know I just said I'll see what I can do, but I'm sorry. I can't just take you off this assignment because you don't like the friend. It's ridiculous. I love you, but you know Serene is my baby and my reputation is—"

"I hear you, Shon. I promise. I understand. I know. And I apologize for coming at you with this. It won't happen again. Could I please call you back in a couple of minutes?" I interrupted again, as my eyes met his. He was standing at my truck with his hands stuffed in the pockets of his gray pullover hoodie. I swallowed, taken aback by his beauty. A beautiful man. Was that even possible?

He wasn't a pretty boy, but to call him handsome would have been an understatement, for sure. This man was . . . everything. The best way to describe him would be by calling him beautiful. He had that panty-wetting, pussy-throbbing, drooling, *play with my pussy with my rose to the thought of him* type of good looks. Got damn.

After I ended the call with Shonda, he signaled for me to roll the window down and I listened.

"Yes?"

"You'll be back tomorrow, right?"

I looked away from him and ran my fingers through my hair, gazing out of the windshield, shaking my head. "I—"

"My wife likes you. Come back tomorrow."

"I know. I-I'll be back. I told you it's cool, I can handle it," I boasted, as if I had a choice in quitting or not. My ass was stuck. But before I showed him an ounce of weakness, I would front. I didn't need him to know that this situation . . . his situation . . . had indeed knocked me off my square. I wanted him to think I could handle anything. I wasn't just that way in this situation.

I put up this front with everything in my life. For my family, for my friends . . . Shit, for me. I was a master at faking it until I made it. And hell, it seemed to work out perfectly fine for me.

We stared at each other for a few seconds in silence before he nodded and said, "Aight, cool. See you tomorrow, Ms. Sienna Mills."

The way my name rolled off his tongue with that Caribbean accent made my coochie flood. He didn't immediately leave after telling me goodbye. He stood there for a second, in silence, just staring at me.

I nodded and turned my attention on his car parked behind mine. "Your car."

He lightly chuckled, nodded, and walked away from my car. I watched him through the rearview mirror as he ran his hand over the back of his neck. Gripping the steering wheel, I sucked in a gust of air and then exhaled.

"Get your shit together, Sienna," I said aloud. "You can do this. You can fucking do this."

I coached myself, trying to psych myself into believing that this man had no effect on me. Tried to psych myself into believing I could work with him . . . with them. At this point, it really didn't matter if I could or if I couldn't. I *had* to work with them.

Once he got inside his car and swerved over to the side of me, I avoided eye contact by quickly putting my car in reverse and speeding out of the driveway. *Don't look back, Si. Don't look back. Don't even check the fucking mirror.* Despite telling myself not to look back or check the mirror, I did both. And he was standing outside of his car, watching me drive away. That bulge in his joggers reminded me of the way he'd hit the bottom of my pussy two weeks ago. I clenched my thighs together and sighed.

"How in the fuck is that shit going to work? Hell naw!" Naoki exclaimed on the other end of the phone. I pulled it away from my ear and frowned at it before putting it on speakerphone and setting it on the counter.

I was home. The minute I hit the door, I called Naoki. I would have hit her on the way home, but Shonda called me. She was so worried about me quitting on her, she didn't even give me a chance to return her call. I reassured her I wouldn't be quitting.

Serene was her baby, for real. I respected her hustle. I respected her. I would never put a business she'd started from the ground up in jeopardy. Serene was one of the first Black-owned doula companies in the country. I had issues, but I'd never been selfish. I looked up to and admired Shonda and her business far too much.

We talked the entire thirty-minute ride back to my house.

"I don't know. I really don't," I stressed as I stood at the stove, stirring alfredo sauce I'd just whipped together. "I could go looking at other doula companies in the meantime, but you know how I feel about Shonda. I can't do that to her. Besides, ain't nobody out here paying like them."

"I bet," Naoki stated with a light *hmph*. "Black, rich, fine, with a big dick—"

"And a wife."

"And a wife," Naoki repeated. "A wife he apparently don't give too much of a fuck about."

"He does. He cares about her. I saw him with her. He's . . . He's delicate and patient with her. So sweet and . . . just . . . perfect. If he hadn't sucked on my pussy two weeks ago, I'd think he was a great husband. The way he talked about her on the tour. The way he . . . he looked at her. He cares." I shook my head and turned the stove off. "I just don't get it. It was like he was two different people."

"Most cheating-ass men are."

I nodded. "You got that right. How is your night going?"

"Like shit. I can't wait to get out of here. Are we still on for this Saturday?"

Naoki was out of town again. She was always out of town. But that was okay because she lived the type of life that was suitable for traveling.

"My parents want to have that dinner this Saturday, girl," I said with an eye roll as I strained my pasta.

"Oh. The ambush."

I giggled. "Yeah, the ambush."

"Well, maybe we can do brunch. Just me and you," Naoki offered.

"Brunch sounds good to me."

"Nurse Childs. Nurse Childs, to the nursing station," I heard in Naoki's background before she sucked her teeth.

"Ugh. A bitch can't even hide in peace. I'll talk to you later, boo."

I laughed. "Okay. Love you."

She told me she loved me too and I hung up. And then . . . it was back to that deafening silence. Sometimes I found comfort in it. Sometimes it made me put music on. I was still trying to get used to living alone. I'd never really lived alone. I moved from my parents' house right in with Amiri, so this was different. It was peaceful, but sometimes, too damn peaceful to where a bitch was lonely. Especially on nights like tonight, after I'd found out the man whose dick I'd fallen in love with belonged to someone else. That shit was a knife to the gut. Sitting with his wife, listening to her talk, seeing her sweet, soft smile . . . that shit fucked me up. I felt like shit. How was it I had turned into the type of bitch I couldn't stand? The other woman. I mean, technically, I wasn't that, but it still bothered me the same.

After fixing myself a bowl of chicken and shrimp alfredo, I went to the living room where I only had a futon, a flat-screen TV on the wall, and an old coffee table Naoki let me have. I hadn't had time to go out and shop just yet, so the crib was pretty bare. I wasn't tripping, though. At least I had peace of mind and didn't have to share a space with a lying-ass, cheating-ass piece of shit. For that, I was grateful.

Kicking my feet up, I grabbed the Roku remote from the table and turned the TV on to catch up on *Kindred.*

CHAPTER 11

Leighton

I responded to a text from my mother and set my phone down. Taking a deep breath, I shifted my eyes to the window. I didn't even like the snow, but as I lay there, looking out of the window, I wanted to be out in it. Resting my hand on my belly, I sighed and looked away at the sound of the doors opening. Jahad was home right after my new doula, Sienna, left a few hours ago. Perfect timing. We hadn't been speaking much, but I was sure he'd made his schedule centered around hers to make sure I wasn't home alone, unassisted. He was the same way with the other doulas. Always making sure to come home when they left, regardless of where we stood in our marriage.

Jahad never let frivolous things like an argument come between us when it came to his duties as a husband. He was here, yeah, but he'd peeked his head in hours ago to let me know he would be in his office if I needed him. Most of his time at the house was spent away from me and I couldn't say I wasn't the cause of that.

"You hungry?" he asked, that head in between the doors again. "Evaline should be finished by now."

I nodded. "Yeah, I'm hungry."

"Aight. I'll grab it really quick," he told me, before inching out of the doorway to leave.

Stopping him with the suck of my teeth, I said, "Why won't you just let her bring it up? What are we paying them for—"

"Don't be that way, Leigh," Jahad interrupted.

I swallowed and shifted around, trying to get comfortable. "You're right. Thank you, Jahad."

He nodded and closed the door, leaving me there feeling like a damn fool. Sometimes, I questioned why Jahad hadn't divorced me yet. Especially when I got beside myself and got a little self-centered.

Evaline and Maurice were great people. They had been working for us for years. Evaline had gotten older and slower, so she couldn't move as fast as she used to. I knew this, yet I complained about them not pulling their weight. Her assistant, Maurice, was autistic and pretty much only helped with cleaning around the kitchen when she was finished. At one point in time, I was more considerate of those things. Lately, I hadn't been. It was Farrah. She'd sit up, complaining about them all day, and somehow, I'd let her rudeness rub off on me when I'd never been that way.

I massaged my temples and leaned back against the headboard with closed eyes before peeling them open a bit to get a glimpse of my supplies sitting in the corner collecting dust. Supplies. Paint supplies, to be more specific. I hadn't picked up a paintbrush in months. I missed it. There was so much about my life that had changed since I'd gotten pregnant. So much so that when I looked in the mirror, I didn't even recognize myself anymore. I wasn't that vibrant, creative, eccentric young woman I used to be. I still had my youth. At twenty-eight, I most certainly did, but I didn't *feel* like I was twenty-eight. I felt like an old woman, trapped in the house with no control over her body. It was odd. Sometimes, when I thought about my old life, it would literally be like thinking of two totally different people.

A couple of minutes later, Jahad walked into the room carrying a food tray. My mouth salivated at the smell of parmesan-crusted salmon, potatoes, and asparagus. I was starving. I couldn't wait to eat.

Jahad set the tray over my lap and headed for the door. I wanted to ask him if he would stay and eat with me, but I didn't have it in me to ask.

As if he could read my mind, he looked over his shoulder and asked me if I wanted to eat together. Because I was stubborn as hell, I didn't say what was on my heart.

Shrugging, I dug into my food. "If you want to. Whatever."

I watched as he dropped his head and shook it before continuing his stride out of the door. My heart sank down to my stomach. I wanted him to stay. I wanted him to stay so bad. We had so much distance between us, it was really as if we were roommates instead of husband and wife. I wanted to reignite that flame, but too much had happened. *So* much had happened. He'd given his body to someone else. He'd given a part of himself that had always been reserved for me to another woman. And yeah, I told him to, but so? He wasn't supposed to take it. I wanted him to. I encouraged him to. But I've been out of my mind these past few months. He should have known better. He should have known I was too sensitive and emotionally unstable to handle something like that. I loved Jahad. I loved him with every fiber of my being. And because he had always been so good to me when I had been nothing but ugly toward him, I wanted to give him something I couldn't. Sex.

I thought it was a good idea. I thought I was showing a side of myself he needed to see. Selflessness. Vulnerability. But I had made a mistake. I didn't want him to sleep with someone else. Every time I closed my eyes, I saw him with another woman. A faceless woman. Sometimes I'd put a face to her. I'd make her beautiful. Very beautiful. Soft caramel skin, long eyelashes, a smile, and deep dimples to die for. By the end of it, I'd realize the face I'd put on this woman was my own, but she wasn't *me*. She was who I *used* to be. The version of myself Jahad fell in love with. She was perfect. She was free. She was freaky. She was his personal slut. And although I'd visualized him with who I used to be, my heart broke a little more every time I thought about it. Because he hadn't been with me, he had been with someone else.

"Jah," I called out, just as he was closing the bedroom door. "You . . . you want to watch something?"

My husband had been with another woman, and we hadn't spoken about it. That was where I was mentally. I was *always* there mentally. We hadn't spoken about it because I told him we wouldn't, but still. It was weird. I wanted to ask questions. Sadly, I'd become insecure, wondering if he was with her when he left. Wondering if they were in contact. It was constantly on my mind, around the clock. I could be talking about something totally unrelated and that hall pass and the look in his eyes that night would come to mind, and I would just stare off into space, knowing I'd made a huge mistake.

I wasn't sure if the time was right for it. My emotions. My anger. My sadness. It was all too much to sit down with him and have a meal. I was too in my head to sit up and laugh at TV, pretending he hadn't stuck his dick—dick that belonged to me—in someone else. I didn't want to ruin a moment I really needed.

Togetherness. I was lonely. I longed for him all day, every day, despite what might've come out of my mouth. It was just . . . hard for me to express the way I truly felt without everything erupting out of me like a volcano. Despite my emotions getting the best of me, I didn't want to be alone. I'd been alone enough, and I missed us. I missed this. You know . . . eating together. That had always been our thing. In the past, I wouldn't touch my food until my husband came home. I wanted to get back to that.

He looked inside the room and nodded. "Yeah. Let me go grab my plate."

I lightly smiled with a nod as he walked out of the room to go back downstairs. Taking a deep breath, I shook my head from side to side, trying to adjust my attitude. All I wanted was a good night. One good night with my husband. I told myself I could handle this. I was strong enough to set my insecurities aside to enjoy a meal with my damn husband. I had to.

A couple of minutes later, he walked into the room. As I looked up at him, my heart rate picked up a bit. He was so damn fine to me. Still. After all the years we'd spent together, it was as if Jahad had only gotten finer. How fine he was used to excite me. These days, it made me nervous, like I was when we first met. I often wondered if I felt so on edge and nervous around him again because we were reverting, drifting apart. That terrified me.

He sat down and grabbed the remote to the TV off the nightstand.

"What you want to watch?"

I shrugged again. "Anything. It don't matter."

Jahad lightly sighed but didn't say anything about my standoffish attitude.

He turned the TV on and hit the Netflix app. Because he knew me, he scrolled to *Bridgerton*. We'd been stuck on season one, episode three for months. We hadn't watched it, and regardless of how I felt about him sometimes, I wouldn't watch without him. He didn't care too much for the show. He didn't like it at all, actually. Jahad wasn't a Netflix-and-chill type of guy. He did those types of things with me because *I* wanted it. Because *I* enjoyed it. He did it for me. He didn't complain, though. He actually watched and would crack a smile or snicker every now and then. I used to snuggle in his arms, or lay in his lap, watching TV, eating fast food neither of us really needed because we had a cook who could put those restaurants to fucking shame. We did it because we enjoyed it. It took us back to our roots. To a time when we didn't have cooks and fancy food. It was the nostalgia, honestly. I missed that shit so much. These days, even sitting beside him made me nervous.

"How was your day?" Jahad asked me before digging into his plate.

I took in a spoonful of parmesan mashed potatoes and lightly moaned with my eyes closed. When I opened them, he was staring at me. The way Jahad stared when something rattled his soul. In a good way. Shying away, I dabbed at the corners of my mouth with a napkin. "It was good."

He nodded and slowly took his eyes away from my lips to put them back on his plate. "How were things with Sienna? Is she a good fit?"

My face lit up a little at the mention of my new doula. "She's a *great* fit. I think I've found my girl."

Jahad put his fist up to his mouth and cleared his throat a bit before digging back into his food. "That's good. I'm glad you like her."

"We should have looked at Black-owned companies a while ago. She's so relatable and down to earth. She's nothing like those other women."

"Yeah, we should've. They're not easy to come by."

"Sure aren't," I told him. "I've been thinking about posting about it on my Instagram to get them a little traffic."

Jahad looked over at me with raised brows. "Free promo?"

I lightly grinned. "Yeah. Free promo."

Free promo hadn't been my thing in years. I didn't mention companies unless they had paid to be mentioned. However, I wanted to spread the word about Serene Mommy Doula Services. Sienna had left such a lasting impression on me, I felt like I had to. Free promo from me, with over three hundred thousand followers, would certainly get them the attention they deserved.

Sienna was a gift, honestly. Our conversation earlier got a little emotional and I was happy to be there for her. Like me, she'd experienced losing a baby . . . or babies . . . I wasn't sure. I didn't pry. The conversation was heavy for her, and because I knew how tough the conversation of miscarriage was, I let it go.

I just wanted to wrap my arms around her. God. I couldn't believe how much we'd clicked and today was only her first day. I couldn't wait for her to come back tomorrow. Sitting with and talking with someone other than Farrah was a breath of fresh air. Sienna was a light. She was positive and uplifting, whereas Farrah did a lot of complaining. About my man, her old man, my family, her lack thereof. It was draining but I kept her around because I really didn't have anyone else.

I, of course, had Jahad, but sitting with and talking to Jahad was too much pressure. It wasn't the same. The tension was always thick. There had been too many arguments, too much finger pointing, and then there was that pass. We had a lot of unresolved issues lingering, and sitting with him all day, talking, avoiding those big elephants in the room was too much. So, I pushed him away. However, tonight, it was light. Not nearly as heavy as I thought it would be, considering.

"You must *really* like her," he added with a grin.

"I do." I softly smiled and nodded before looking up at him. "What do you think about her? Shonda said she was new, but she seems like a natural."

Jahad licked his lips and shrugged. "She's straight. As long as you're happy, I'm happy."

"She's young, beautiful, and sweet as ever," I said with a smile before giving him the side-eye. "Saint would love her," I added.

Jahad drew back with a frown. "Man, hell naw. I'm not about to put the Devil on that woman."

I laughed and playfully hit him. "She just might be able to tame baby brother. You never know. She's got her head screwed on right and she comes from a big family like you, so I think they'll have a lot in common. They're the same age, too."

"Saint is twenty-three," Jahad stated. "She's twenty-six, not too much younger than you."

With a crinkled brow, I looked at him. "How do you know how old she is?"

He looked over at me with furrowed brows that mirrored mine. "Her file."

"You *remember* her age. That's the point I'm making," I said with a side-eye. "Look at you," I added with suspicion. Unnecessary suspicion.

Suspicion brought on by my insecurities. Insecurities, I planted my damn self. I was tripping.

There was a point in time I never second-guessed what I was to Jahad. The way he was about me, I had no reason to second-guess anything. In the past, before we got it right. Before he showed me how much he'd changed . . . I would have had a reason to second-guess. But for the past six, seven years, I didn't have to. And I wouldn't have had to now if he hadn't taken that hall pass. But . . . There was a gray area in our marriage now. It was tainted, and yes, I was to blame, but I couldn't have the same confidence in him . . . in our marriage . . . as I used to have. There was a stain on it. I hated it. I hated to feel insecure about him checking on things regarding our doula. In the past, I never had. In the past, he'd done just that. Jahad wasn't letting anybody into this house without doing extensive research on them. He was careful in that sense, so of course he knew how old she was.

"What's out of the ordinary about that, Leighton?" Jahad asked with a lightly cocked brow.

Leighton. He was pissed. I giggled, trying to neutralize the mood in the room again. Tension was building. It had always been there, but since we'd started to casually chat, it had lessened. Now it was rising again and, well, I didn't want to send him running out of the room.

"I was just joking. I know how you are about stuff."

He didn't say anything, but the deep furrow in his dark, thick eyebrows told me enough. He was annoyed. Neutralizing the mood was a fail.

From the corner of my eye, I saw the side of his head slightly pulsating. That only happened on two occasions: when he chewed or when he was pissed and he'd clench down on his jaw. He hadn't put any food in his mouth, so clearly, he was pissed.

My eyes filled with tears. We were so far off, it was heartbreaking. Years ago, a joke like that, whether it was tainted with a bit of truth or not, would have never upset him. We would have laughed about it and moved on from it. Everything was so strained now. We didn't joke. We barely laughed. We just existed. And a lot of times, not even together.

Jahad and I were drifting so far apart, it was as if we were already miles away, although he was right next to me. My heart was broken. I hated to admit it, but this distance was mainly my fault. I was the reason for the strain on our marriage. I could blame it on him taking the hall pass I offered, but I'd be lying to myself. I put the strain on our marriage long before the hall pass even came up. There was no joy in our marriage because I'd sucked the joy out of it. Before the pregnancy. Before the one before this one . . . and the one before that one. At this point, I was really just clawing for something. Drowning, drifting further and further away from shore, clawing for it. It was right there, yet so far away from my grip.

But what about him? It wasn't all my fault. I played a major role in where we were, but what about the lack of effort on his end? He saw me clawing. He saw me drowning. He saw me practically dying. Why hadn't he come to save me? Save us?

Jahad shouldn't have taken that hall pass. He should've kept pushing back. He should've grabbed my face a couple more times and told me why he didn't want it. He should have told me no a million times. He shouldn't have taken it. He knew I couldn't take it, but he took it anyway. He had the nerve to sit next to me with an attitude, as if my sly remarks weren't justifiable. As if there wasn't an elephant in the room we had yet to address.

"Are we going to ever talk about it?"

"Talk about what?" Jahad asked me with his eyes steady locked on the television.

"You know what I'm talking about."

"Let it go," he dismissed.

"I think if we talk about it, we will finally move past this weirdness."

Finally, he turned to face me. "Do you? Is that what you really think, Leighton? Or will it make things worse?"

Our eyes briefly met before I looked away and pushed food around my plate. He then leaned over and kissed me on the forehead, forcing me to close my eyes to bask in the short moment of intimacy. "*Kite l ale, renmen* (Let it go, love)."

When his lips left my skin, I opened my eyes and looked at him. I *couldn't* let it go. I knew for sure I'd never be able to let it go because the minute his lips left my forehead, I wondered if he'd given her forehead kisses, too. And I wondered if, when he did kiss her there, she, too, closed her eyes and basked in it the way I did. Jahad gave the best forehead kisses. I wondered if she missed them the same way I missed them when I was without them. I wondered if she *had* to miss them at all.

CHAPTER 12

Jahad

I dragged my hands down my face and took a deep breath before stepping out of the car. After pulling the straps to my beige trench coat tighter, I blew into my hands and rubbed them together. The sun was deceiving as a muthafucka. It was closing in on twenty degrees and the sun was shining like it was a good forty out. I then hit the alarm on my Mercedes G-Wagon and treaded up the walkway to my parents' house. As soon as I made it to the stairs, I smelled the eggs and plantains. My stomach immediately rumbled. I left the crib without eating because I knew Moms was going to have a nice-ass breakfast on the stove. She stayed in the kitchen. It didn't matter that they had more than enough money to afford a cook—Natasha refused to hire a cook. I appreciated it because there wasn't a soul on earth who could cook like Moms.

Despite being in America for over fifteen years, she stayed true to our Haitian roots, and I appreciated that.

I used my key to let myself inside and immediately removed my wheat Timbs before taking my coat off and hanging it on the coat rack. I lightly smiled at the sound of laughter and talking coming from my family from the kitchen. Nothing made a nigga happier than family. There was something about it that always relaxed me. Being able to hear them at the front door from the kitchen meant their spirits were high. Just what I needed.

This place . . . it hadn't been an escape away from the shit back home for a minute. But this morning, hearing my mother's laughter, my father's flirting, my sisters bickering, and Blaise and Saint going back and forth about a football game, home away from home gave me just what I needed.

As soon as I walked into the kitchen, my mother approached me with a bright smile on her face, something I always appreciated. I was her favorite, despite how much she denied it in front of everyone else. I knew what it was. Whenever someone said it, she would deny having a favorite, then secretly look over and wink at me.

She cupped my face and kissed both my cheeks. "*Bonjou, pitit gason* (Good morning, son)."

"*Bonjou, Manman* (Good morning, Mama)," I replied before addressing everyone else. "*Bonjou, fanmi* (Good morning, family)."

"Pitit gason," Pops spoke, before giving me a handshake.

After my brothers and sister greeted me, I sat at the island and Moms immediately set a plate of food in front of me. "*Mesi* (Thanks)."

"Soon as I walked in, I'm getting cursed out. This fool comes in and gets king treatment," Blaise complained as he dug into his food with his bare hands. Stuffing his mouth, he shook his head. Nigga was a straight-up savage.

I liked to eat with my hands, too, but the way this nigga ate . . . it was like he hadn't had a meal in days. Blaise was a big nigga. Standing at almost seven feet, over three hundred pounds of straight muscle, he had the build of a linebacker. And he had the appetite of one too.

As messy as he was, Moms never complained. She watched all of us eat with a smile on her face, happy to have all three of her boys under her roof.

"Because you make poor decisions. What would you have me do, Blaise? Pat you on the back? Congratulate you for finding the worst woman in the world to bear your child?" she fussed before uncrossing her arms to wave him off.

"I made a mistake—"

"*Oh!* Here we go with that again. No man makes a mistake like that. That"—she paused and shook her head—"is a poor excuse and your father raised you better than that."

His brother raised him better than that. I raised him better than that. Not his father. I was the one who took care of him. I took care of them. *All* of them. While Pops was here, in the States, doing what he had to do to get us all here together. Maybe I shouldn't have taken credit for the way Blaise was raised, considering the stupid decisions he'd made, but I had raised and taught him better. I expected more. I expected more from all of them. Saint had his head screwed on right, to an extent. I had to check Natasha every now and then about the niggas she entertained, but that was nothing. Blaise? Blaise was like an untamed animal with no common sense. I couldn't stand it. You'd think the nigga was raised in the jungle, with savage animals, the way he conducted himself.

Out of the four of us, he was the only one without a business. Without a legitimate business of his own, at least. Everything Blaise had was linked to one of us. He had nothing for himself. Saint had his clubs, bars, and things of that nature, I was heavy in real estate, and Natasha loved fashion. Blaise . . . Blaise hung on to Pops's coattail. He was a partner in just about everything Samuel had attached to his name. Despite the many conversations we had about the importance of establishing his own direct stream of income, he never took heed.

The idea of Moms coddling him and applauding him for making yet another reckless decision was laughable. None of that shit deserved a pat on the back. Regardless of the way I felt about the direction his life was going in, I didn't judge him. Only wanted more for my brother. That was it.

As Mom continued on, Blaise didn't utter another word. He knew better than to say anything else. Instead, he continued to dig into his food, stuffing his frowning face, refusing to clean his mouth as he went. I awkwardly ran my hand down the back of my neck, listening to the way Moms handled him. Me, Saint, and Tasha sat the same way—quiet, waiting for the shit to fold over.

Pops was silent for the most part, but his disappointment in Blaise was evident. So evident, he never had to utter a word about the way he felt. The dismay he felt toward Blaise's incompetence was blatantly known throughout the family. I didn't particularly care for the way either of my parents handled Blaise. They chastised him and scolded him for doing wrong, but enabled him at the same time. It didn't make any sense to me. They wanted Blaise to be a man, yet they took care of all of his mishaps as if he were a child. Moms fussed and scolded him, but when I walked in, I noticed Bebe's things by the door. I was waiting for her little bubbly self to bend the corner at any given second.

"How was yo' mornin', *gro fré* (big brother)?" Saint asked me with a grin. A knowing grin that only he and I would be able to decipher.

My morning had been awkward. Okay, but awkward as hell. I made sure I was out of that house before eight. I told myself that the easiest way for me to deal with Sienna being there would be by leaving when she got there and arriving when she was leaving. But this morning, we'd crossed paths. And it was there. That magnetic energy. That shit I was trying to escape. I couldn't escape her, though. Not even in my dreams.

I gave him a light smirk and shook my head. "Straight."

"And Leighton? How is she? How is she adjusting to the new girl?" Moms asked, finally laying off Blaise with a smile she always wore when she talked about Leighton.

They were close. Very close, at one point. Before Leighton was put on bed rest, they did brunch every Sunday morning at the Brunch House in Rochester. It was a little too bourgeois for my subtle mother, but because Leighton enjoyed it, she went. Mother loved Leighton. So much that, sometimes, I would catch Natasha rolling her eyes when Moms mentioned her. Natasha liked Leighton, but not enough to be comfortable with her mother oozing and bonding with someone who wasn't her.

Natasha had it hard. She and Moms bumped heads often. Moms wanted more for Natasha. She wanted her to get married and start a family of her own, but Natasha moved how she wanted to move. Moms often complained, saying that if Natasha hadn't been raised in the States, she would have more going for herself. She called sis uncultured often. How hard she was on her made Natasha resent me and our brothers. I got it, though. Because regardless of how much of a fuckup Blaise and Saint could be, when it came to love and life, she didn't give them nearly as much slack as she gave Tasha.

"She's adjusting," I said.

"How you adjusting, though?" Saint continued.

I shot him a look and ran my tongue over the corner of my mouth. When I lightly squinted, he nodded and looked back down into his plate. He thought shit was funny.

On Sienna's first day, I told him. Talked about it on my way home from the meeting with Shelby. It was just the lighthearted conversation I needed to take my mind off the shit that went down at Shelby's. Saint joked about me *finally* having in-house pussy, but I didn't find it funny. He told me to lighten up about it, but how could I when all I wanted was to put my face in Sienna's pussy whenever I saw her?

I was worried about her handling working for us, but I was the one having a hard time. My dick bricked every time I laid my eyes on her, which was why I really needed to keep distance between us. I loved my wife. Loved shorty with every fiber of my being, but I'd be lying if I said fucking with Sienna hadn't made my flesh weak. A nigga with weak flesh was powerless around a beautiful woman. Especially one with a pussy as pretty and creamy as Sienna's.

I propped my feet up on the barstool and lightly shook my head at the way my dick was starting to respond at the simple thought of her. Cutting my eyes at Saint, I damn near wanted to strangle his ass.

"That's beautiful. How is my grandchild? How are things progressing?" Pops asked.

I nodded and looked up at him. "Flawlessly. Strong heartbeat."

He nodded, balled his fist, and tapped it on his chest. "Just like a Baptiste. *He* comes from a long line of men with heart."

After we ate, it was straight to business. That was how meetings at my parents' house always went. Moms would make sure we were nice and full, then we would depart to the other side of the house, where business was handled. The side we frequented the most.

Pops didn't have a man cave—he had an entire wing dedicated for him and him only. Oftentimes, Moms would complain about it, regretting her decision to allow him a whole wing to himself because he spent most of his time on this side, rather than with her.

Saint closed the massive oak doors to Pops's office behind him before he and Blaise took their usual seats at his desk. Saint on the left, Blaise on the right, with me standing in the middle. My seat was in the middle, but today, I stood. Because I stood, the tone of the meeting was set. What I had to discuss was important. Very important.

Shifting my eyes down at my father as I waited for him to be seated at his desk before I began.

"Walker's under investigation," I told them, my eyes locked only on my father's briefly before putting my attention on my brothers. Their looks mirrored mine after I got the news. A look that was only easily recognized between the four of us. A look that often went unnoticed by anybody outside of us. Murderous gazes that came off as a soft look of content. We'd given each other that look several times before, in rooms full of oblivious niggas who didn't know what was coming to them until Blaise had split their *man's* head wide open with a blick they never noticed him pull. By the time they'd realized what was what, they would be too slow to react and would soon meet the same demise as the nigga slumped with his brains splattered on the wall he once stood in front of.

Yesterday, as I sat in a meeting with Shelby and one of his crooked agents, Walker, listening to them tell me how Walker was under investigation, they thought I really was okay when I said I was. Walker thought he was safe. I actually saw his chest rise and fall after he let go of the breath he held after Shelby explained what was going on. When I nodded at him and told him everything would be okay and we'd figure things out together, he believed me. My brothers and I might've had similar poker faces, but my ability to keep a nigga calm enough to keep him at bay had always been an advantage I held over the other men in my family. I was the one who made people comfortable. The one who kept situations at a steady level right until *I* was ready for it to be elevated. *I was in control.*

I was foolishly mistaken as the poised and rational one of the Baptiste clan, when I was, in fact, the most vicious in the family. I was a bigger problem than Blaise with his temper, Saint with his weird obsession with knives, and Samuel with his torturous ways. People knew what to expect from them. When it came to me? They knew nothing.

"Under investigation for what?" Saint asked with raised brows.

"What do you think?" Pops asked him with his eyes narrowed to slits.

Dragging my hand over the back of my neck, I sighed.

"What does that mean for us?" Saint asked, mirroring a scowl just as deep as our father's.

"Nothing," I intervened. "Absolutely nothing."

Blaise shot me a knowing look and gave me a subtle head nod.

Walker's investigation could change a lot for us. We paid him handsomely—somewhere around a million a year. A salary that made the money he made with the DEA look like crumbs. There was a chance he could fold on us, despite how much we'd kept his pockets laced. When niggas like Walker fell under scrutiny, the chances of them folding heightened tremendously. And before we risked our own livelihoods, the risk of murdering an DEA agent trumped everything else. There was far too much on the line not to.

The minute I heard the words *under investigation*, my thoughts went straight to Leighton and our unborn child. I was needed out here. I couldn't imagine leaving Leighton to care for a newborn baby without me. Couldn't imagine leaving my child to live in this fucked-up world without me. I couldn't imagine losing everything, leaving them with nothing. Before I allowed that to happen, bodies would drop. DEA agents and anybody else who threatened that.

"Walker's investigation puts him under a microscope," Father mentioned as if I hadn't thought of just about every way taking care of him could go wrong.

I nodded once more. "I'm aware. Shelby too. I'm not going into this alone. Why do you think he told me? You think he would have told me Walker was under investigation if he didn't want me to do anything about it? As soon as that nigga left, we got to scheming."

Shelby knew what it was. He wouldn't have told me if he didn't. I was sure he told me because he knew how I would handle it. He couldn't handle it himself and knew he could for sure count on me to do it. His life was on the line just as much as my and my family's lives were.

Pops stood up and ran his hand over his short salt-and-pepper beard before he paced. "Can you trust him?"

"It's not about trust. It's about survival," I pointed out. "Shelby's desperate. Walker testifying will sink all of us. He wants him dead. We have a common problem. I trust that he'll come through with this because he has no other choice."

He stopped pacing and placed his hands flat on the top of his oak desk. With his eyes locked on mine, he nodded as a gesture to show me his trust. Pops was old. If it wasn't for his old age, he'd have his brothers in this room with him, cooking up a scheme. But Samuel was pretty much out of the game. He spent his free time at sporting events and lounges, on vacation with my mother, and a host of other bullshit he had no business doing. The business was mine and my brother's, for the most part. However, he still reaped the benefits because despite who was the head of it—me—Samuel would always be the one in charge. We'd always answer to him. For as long as he lived on this earth, things would go that way.

Most of the time, he looked to me for answers, but that didn't mean I would go over his head or make a move without his approval.

"What did he say?" Blaise asked with the same frown of disapproval on his face. "How will this affect us?"

I adjusted my slacks before finally sitting down. "He's concerned. Nervous. Antsy. He spoke about his notoriety and what an investigation of that magnitude would do to his family. What it would do to his legacy. He assured me he would do everything in his power to make sure things stayed as clean as possible, as long as we handled business as proficiently as he know we can. He cares too much about his legacy to fuck this up. Too much about himself. I told him it would be handled. Y'all know how I am when it comes to us. Anything that threatens the Baptiste bloodline gets handled. Regardless of power, rank, whatever."

I adjusted the sleeve on my black Givenchy crewneck sweater and pushed up from the chair. Stepping toward the desk, I extended my hand to my father. We slapped hands and I locked eyes with him. "It will be handled efficiently," I assured him.

"I need a blueprint and a timeline, Jahad," he told me. "Even with Shelby backing us . . . this . . . this is big."

I understood his apprehension about it, but there was nothing more for us to do in this situation. The fact that this was important should have told him I wasn't going to go in with any half-assed scheme. It would be handled efficiently. Professionally. The way I handled everything else in my life.

I didn't play about anything, but the one thing I never, ever played about was my family. I had been protecting them for more than half my life—why would I half step now?

We faced treacherous shit back in Haiti. I literally had to put my life on the line several times as a child. Now, with a family of my own, putting my life on the line wasn't an option. I had to go into every little thing with them on my mind. I loved my pops. Loved my brothers, my mother, and my sister too, but when it came to *my* family, the one I created, I would slaughter a million niggas if it meant saving myself just to get back home to them.

"I understand," I told him before turning to Blaise and Saint. I nodded at them, and they stood up and followed me out of the office.

CHAPTER 13

Sienna

"Good morning," Evaline, the house cook, greeted me when I walked into the kitchen.

"Good morning, Ms. Evaline," I said with a smile as I opened the Sub-Zero refrigerator.

"No, no. Call me Evaline, child."

"I would never. My mother would curse me out if she found out I had called an elder by her first name and her first name only," I told her, after retrieving the orange juice carafe. Freshly squeezed orange juice at that.

Yesterday, Ms. Evaline told me the juices were always freshly squeezed every day at five in the morning. I thought that was crazy, but she said Mrs. Baptiste liked her juice. So, I understood, I guess.

Ms. Evaline laughed and playfully waved me off. "Oh Lord. What you doin' here so early?"

I giggled and closed the refrigerator with my hip.

Lifting the carafe toward her, I said, "Figured I'd carry Mrs. Leighton's OJ up to her this morning."

I'd just gotten to the house, but because I knew how Leighton was about her juice, I decided to take her up a glass and the carafe with me, as a good morning.

Today, I showed up thirty minutes earlier, just to bring her something up. I figured I'd apologize to her for fucking her husband by being a great doula since I was in no position to just quit. My conscience was eating at me like a muthafucka. I had to do something to make up for that. But, honestly, me being a good doula attested not only to my guilt. I just wanted to be good at my job in general. I just told myself that the good work I did here would make up for being her husband's mistress for a night. I was coming up on a full workweek and I'd say I had been doing pretty damn good!

That first night, I tossed and turned with worry, guilt eating at the lining of my fucking stomach. As if she could sense something was wrong, Naoki called me at one in the morning to soothe my worrying mind. She said a lot of shit that made a lot of sense. There was no sense in stressing and beating myself up over something that was already done. The only thing I could do moving forward was the right thing. And as comforting as that might've been, all it did was worry me more.

I wanted to do the right thing. I wanted to stop thinking about her husband. I wanted to stop dreaming about him and thinking about his big dick, but I couldn't.

That man was still heavy on my mind, but I hadn't seen him much. I felt like he had been staying out of the house on purpose. I was happy about that.

When I started my shift, he was usually already gone. If not, I'd stay in the room until I heard him leave. The only time we really saw each other was at the end of my shift, in the driveway, when I was leaving. We'd pass each other as he was pulling into the driveway and I was pulling out of it. We'd lock eyes and that was just about it. No waves. No head nods. Just . . . eye contact. So much was in that brief moment of eye contact, though. Tension. Familiarity. Desire. Memories. It was crazy. But it never lasted more than ten seconds. I was fine with that. I'd been avoiding him, just as much as he had obviously been avoiding me.

Ms. Evaline smiled. "Thank you, sweetie. You just saved an old lady a trip."

I lightly laughed. "No problem."

Setting the carafe on the island, I busied around the kitchen for a glass.

"You're a good fit here. Them poor girls before you didn't last but a couple of days," she said with a laugh as she playfully swatted at me with an oven mitt. "Here, this one is her favorite."

I coyly smiled, tucking my guilt as much as possible. "That's good to hear! Thank you, Ms. Evaline."

I grabbed the glass and carafe and headed for the elevator. I never used the stairs. I told her stuck-up-ass best friend I wasn't tripping about the stairs, but bitch, I was. Fuck that. There was an elevator for use and she thought I wasn't going to use it?

On my way to the elevator, I was greeted by Maurice, Ms. Evaline's helper. He was nice and always greeted me with a shy wave. I thought it was the cutest thing.

"Hey, Maurice, you doing okay?" I asked, as I hit the up button on the elevator.

He nodded. "I'm okay. You okay?"

"Yep. It's a beautiful day, the sun is shining and stuff."

He shook his head and put his eyes to the floor. "Uh-uh. It's a snowstorm comin' later."

I sighed and lightly rolled my eyes. "Aw, man, I had no idea. Okay, thanks for letting me know."

He nodded and walked away just as the elevator doors opened. When I stepped inside, I caught him looking over his shoulder at me. Since I couldn't wave, I lifted the carafe as a goodbye. He smiled and the doors closed. Maurice was all right with me. Everyone in the house was. They had other staff who only came around every now and then. There were housekeepers and a groundskeeper who kept the snow shoveled and stuff. It was pretty amazing to be a part of, honestly. Black luxury always made me feel some type of way.

I was grateful that my very first clients were Black. I worried about where I'd go once this assignment was over, since the Baptistes had me so damn spoiled with all of this luxury. I couldn't imagine going to a family like the other one Shonda said she had available after this one. Hell no.

I stepped off the elevator and headed down the hallway. I admired the paintings adorning the walls. Before going to her room, I stopped at mine to put my things away. Looking around, I was still in awe at how these people had me set up in my own damn room. I wasn't friends with many other doulas at Serene, but the one I was cool with, Jennifer, hated her clients. She complained about feeling like a babysitter and a maid, rather than a doula. I couldn't imagine.

After putting my things away, I went next door to their room. I knocked a couple of times before Leighton called out for me to come in. She was sitting in bed, up against the headboard, eyes closed, with a pair of headphones on and her Doppler to her stomach. She looked so at peace. There was a light smile on her face as she likely listened to the sound of her baby's heartbeat. For a split second, a wave of jealousy washed over me. Jealousy that was likely only brought on by life's recent events. You know . . . the baby. Amiri's baby. A baby he said he didn't care about having when we found out I couldn't.

I took a deep breath and regained composure before I ended up falling down a rabbit hole I'd have a damn hard time climbing out of. A rabbit hole I had no business falling into at work as a doula with a high-risk, paranoid mother. I'd taken this career choice because I was mentally strong enough to. This weak shit, it wasn't me. I'd already had a meltdown once before; it wasn't happening again.

I softly set the carafe and glass on the nightstand and tiptoed toward the door, trying not to disturb her. I didn't want to take her moment away from her. I glanced over my shoulder to make sure she hadn't been disturbed and was taken aback by a wide grin on her face as she rubbed her belly. In that moment, the question of why came to mind. Why had he cheated on her? What in the fuck was he at Pandora's for? He had this beautiful, radiant woman as a wife. What did he need with a place like Pandora's? Why had he eaten my pussy like he was on death row, and it was his last—

"Sienna," Leighton softly called out just as I grabbed the handle to the door to creep out.

I bit my bottom lip and winced a little. Slowly turning around, I greeted her with a pained expression. A pained expression brought on by guilt about what I'd done—by disturbing her and fucking her husband. How was I going to let this shit go? What the fuck . . .

"Good morning, Mrs.—"

"Leigh is good, girl. How many times am I going to have to tell you that?" she interrupted with a smile and a wave of her hand.

I was being polite. Calling her Mrs. Baptiste ate me the fuck up damn near as viciously as her husband had that—there I was again, reminiscing about a man I shouldn't have been reminiscing about.

But yeah, calling her Mrs. Baptiste, since I knew who Mr. Baptiste was, made my skin crawl.

"Okay, okay," I said with a light laugh. "You caught me sneaking out. You looked so . . . peaceful. I didn't want to interrupt you."

She pulled the earbuds from her ears. "It's perfectly fine. I do this every hour. The morning time is just when she's at her busiest." She wrapped the cord around the Doppler and set it on the nightstand before grabbing her glass of orange juice.

"This morning, I didn't even need the orange juice to get her going. She woke me up, active as ever."

"Oh, is that why you like your orange juice in the morning?" I asked, as I walked away from the door to sit next to her bed.

She took a sip from it and nodded. "Mm-hmm. I . . . Sometimes, I need it. Sometimes, she's not as active as she was this morning and I . . . Well . . . I worry and this . . . it just gives me a bit of comfort. That's all."

I nodded. "I understand. So, your best friend caved and gave you the sex of the baby, huh?"

She laughed and shook her head. "Naw, girl. Farrah's not giving that up. Not until the big reveal. I always call her a girl." She rubbed her stomach.

"That's what she feels like. Boy or girl, it doesn't matter. I just want her to be healthy."

"Yeah, and that she is," I reassuringly said with a light smile.

At first, I thought Leighton would be just as snobby and stuck up as her friend, but I was pleasantly surprised. She was pretty sweet. Sitting with her didn't feel like a job most times. We talked. A lot. Which didn't help my situation much. She talked about *him* a lot, too. About eighty percent of our conversations were about them. I learned a lot about him. About them. He was Haitian. He was big on family. Big on those he loved. Serious about business. To sum it up, Jahad was the fucking shit. Aside from the cheating, of course.

I wouldn't even call when he was brought up in conversation, though. She did all the talking. I just listened. Both uncomfortable and intrigued. Most of the time, when she talked about him, there was this look in her eyes. This look of gloom. Sometimes she'd talk about him with so much sorrow in her eyes, it would be like she was mourning him, or what they had at least. I wondered if that look of sadness was my fault. I wondered if she knew. If they were going through something because she'd found out he was cheating . . . or had cheated. I wondered because she had to know. Women . . . we always know.

She spoke about him like he was perfect. Put him up on a pedestal. But those eyes. Those beautiful hazel brown eyes of hers twinkled with sadness. With the look of a woman who'd been scorned. Freshly scorned. I recognized it because I had the same look in mine when I was alone. When I didn't have to pretend to be all right. *She* was familiar. I was her. That heartbroken, scorned woman. We were one and the same. How she was able to keep him up on that pedestal with that look in her eyes was like a fucking magic trick or stupidity. Stupidity. Had to be stupidity. How could she call him a great husband with that look? Is that what marriage was? Denial? Delusion? I couldn't imagine.

So, I knew she knew. That had to be the reason for the look in her eyes when she talked about him. Knowing she knew, witnessing what knowing was doing to her, fucked with me. Every time I laid down to go to sleep, I thought about that look of sadness in her eyes but ended up playing with my pussy at the thought of him right after.

It was sick.

I was sick.

Fucked up and cruel, even.

"What's on the agenda for the day?" I asked, to shift gears.

She nodded at the cluttered desk in the corner. "Painting. I need to pick my brush back up. It's been so long."

With raised brows, I asked, "You paint?"

She smiled and looked up at me with a sparkle in her eye I had never seen before. "Mm-hmm. Most of the art on the walls are mine. You know, except for the ones by Basquiat and Kehinde."

I wasn't too surprised. She gave off a creative vibe. She wore her long locs up in a bun on top of her head and usually wore a headwrap with it. She wore crystals and eccentric rings on her fingers, along with the big-ass rock sitting on her ring finger. She had the whole artistic vibe going on.

She didn't really fit in with the house, to be honest. I really thought she would be like her best friend, but I was so wrong. Leighton had a beautiful vibe about herself, which always made me circle back to her husband being at Pandora's. Why?

I couldn't get the shit out of my head. I didn't think anyone would be able to, to be honest.

"That's amazing. Wow," I complimented her. "How long have you been painting?"

"Since elementary, if we're being literal. I've always loved to paint. I didn't get serious about it until middle school, though. After high school, I took a few classes, started my socials and stuff. I gained a big following on Tumblr. From there, I only grew more. I wouldn't consider myself big-time, but I make a little noise in a couple of underground spots."

I smiled. "That's cool, Leighton. I think that's very cool, actually. I'm not too big on art, but I can definitely appreciate a nice piece. Especially from Black artists. Our shit just—" I cupped my hand over my mouth. "My bad. I mean, our stuff just—"

"Girl, if you don't be yourself. I curse. You can curse. You know, you're my fourth doula. The other three were very stuffy and just . . . I don't know. Stuck up. I like you because you're down to earth and true to who you are. Don't change that for me. Don't change that for anybody."

I nodded and pulled my lips into my mouth. See? How was I not to feel horrible? She was a sweetheart. It would've been easier to hate her if she was a bitch. Like that Farrah. Not even a bitch. If she didn't have this calming, sweet, centered vibe about her, it would have been easier to be comfortable with what I did, in a way. I wanted Leighton to punish me, honestly. Was this *God's* way of punishing *me* for being a li'l loose kitty slut? I shouldn't have gone to Pandora's. This just had to be my karma. Our karma. Because, what? It wasn't even eight in the morning, and I wanted a glass of wine.

"I—"

Before I could say anything else, the door to the bathroom opened and he walked out with a towel wrapped around his waist, all of that fine-ass chocolate on display. He was like a fucking god, stepping out of that steamy bathroom with beads of water on his chest, running a white towel over his head.

Before I could be caught gawking over him . . . before my eyes lowered to the bulge I knew would be there against that white towel, I jumped up and covered my eyes. I had no idea he was here. The staff had a separate garage to park in. It was attached to the house, but still, separate from the main one. So, it wasn't like I had a car to look for or anything. But of course, he was here. I arrived thirty minutes before my scheduled time. Duh. I should've just come in, set the carafe down and left like I intended to do. But no, I got caught up in conversation with his wife and now look.

"Oh my—"

"Leigh," Jahad stressed. "You didn't—"

"She just got here, sorry," Leighton quickly said.

"I'll come back. I'm sorry," I said before quickly heading for the doors.

As soon as I got into the hallway, I took a deep breath and rested against the doors. I tossed my head back against it and put my eyes on the cathedral ceilings. God. My fucking God. I didn't like to use the Lord's name in vain, but my fucking God! I didn't think he could get any finer. Didn't think I could be more attracted to him than I already was. But . . . fuck! He was literally like an African god—no, *Haitian* god.

I closed my eyes as my pussy throbbed with desire. I wondered if Leighton was in there doing what I would have done: putting that thick, fat dick down her throat. I wondered if she'd snatched his towel off his waist and pushed his dick to the back of her throat like I would have done. Was she gagging? Was he fucking her face like he'd fucked mine? I held my breath and tried to listen. Tried to hear for those grunts. Those low moans. That low "Fuck, baby" he gave me as I drenched his dick with my saliva.

But I didn't hear anything but the low sound of bickering. They were having a disagreement but tried to keep it on the hush. Was it me? It sounded like Leighton was chewing him out because he'd come out in a towel.

"I know you heard us talking," she angrily whispered. *"You did that on purpose."*

"Aight, Leigh," Jahad said.

He didn't whisper. Leighton did. She was stirring the pot but didn't want anybody in their business. He didn't give a fuck, though.

"Aight, Leigh, what? You did that on purpose, right?"

"I came out of my own bathroom, into my bedroom, wrapped in a towel like I do every fuckin' morning. I didn't know the woman was here. What type of childish-ass games you think I play? All of a sudden, I play games, huh?"

"Why are you so loud?"

"I'm not loud. You're whispering like a child. I won't."

"Because I don't want people in our business."

"Oh, you don't? Damn, that's new."

I walked away from the door. I felt like I was being intrusive. I didn't want to be up in their business, especially since I was private about my shit. Besides, they were my clients, and I had no business eavesdropping.

When I got to the bedroom, I plopped down on the bed and laid back, looking at the ceiling again. I had to get that image of him out of my head. I had a whole shift to work with his wife. That couldn't be etched in my mind all day. It was already bad enough I worked with guilt all day as is.

I dug into the pocket of my duster and texted Naoki. I was dressed down again. On my first day, I asked Leighton if there was a dress code she wanted me to adhere to and she told me she wanted me comfortable and decent. She'd only said a word! I had a closet full of three-piece loungewear outfits to wear, coupled with a variety of UGGs to choose from. Since we had to remove our shoes at the door, I'd taken the liberty of bringing my UGG slippers too.

Me: He walked out of the bathroom in a towel.

Naoki: Oh my fuckin' God. Did you stare? I hope you didn't stare, Si.

Me: No, I got the fuck out of there. They're arguing. Well, she's arguing with him. She's mad. They goin' through some shit.

Naoki: Maybe that's why he was at Pandora's then.

Me: Going through shit doesn't give him the right to cheat, Ki. The fuck?

Naoki: True, true.

Before I could respond to her, there was a knock on the door. I quickly sat up and smoothed my hair over. It was him. It had to be him. Who else would it be? She couldn't just roam the halls. I got up and walked over to open the closed door. Once I did, my eyes met his. They were angry, initially, but the longer we stared, the softer they became. Tearing my eyes away from his, I took in the rest of him. He was dressed in a crisp white T-shirt—the brightness of it against his dark skin reminded me of the marshmallows I used to roast over the fire as a child. He had on a pair of black jeans that were held up by a Hermès belt. His shirt was slightly tucked, but not in a way that was done purposely to show off the brand. Jahad didn't *need* to do that. His wealth oozed from his pores with the way he carried himself. The sharpness of his attire, the way he walked, the subtle jewelry he wore, and the way he smelled screamed money. He was just a boss-ass nigga in every sense of the fucking word.

"Your shift starts at eight. Please come at eight. Not a minute sooner," he sternly told me, all businesslike. *This nigga.*

I nodded with a slight smirk. "You've got it, *boss.*"

He squinted and rubbed the back of his neck. "Leighton wants to go downstairs to paint in the sunroom. The wheelchair is sitting beside the bed. If she refuses to use it, she won't be painting anywhere but that bed."

I saluted him, and he squinted again. I was playful. I had to be because he was being an asshole, but I couldn't take it personally. I got it. The easiest way for me to handle what was happening was for me to approach it in a not-so-serious way. Besides, why make my stay here miserable and stuffy? I had to make the most out of my situation.

About thirty minutes later, I was in the sunroom with Leighton while she painted in silence. She hadn't said a word to me since Jahad came out of the bathroom in that towel that left little to the imagination. I could tell by the furrow in her brow she was pissed. That, and the way she kept slamming material around with deep sighs. She was frustrated.

"You need me to do anything? How about some tea? That always—"

"No thank you," she interrupted before moving her hands around her locs, making them messier than they already were. I was supposed to be here to alleviate any stress, yet she wouldn't allow me to help her. I felt useless, sitting on the chaise lounge, watching the snow fall.

At the sound of the door to the sunroom opening, she took a deep breath and pulled her lips into her mouth. I didn't have to look up to see he'd come into the room. Not only did I smell him—I felt him too. There was something about him. I couldn't put a finger on it, but he made me feel in ways I never felt before. Any time he was in my presence, it was as if every nerve in my body ignited as tingles shot through my entire being. He was electrifying.

"You need anything before I go?" he asked Leighton, standing beside her, giving her his undivided attention.

She shook her head with a heavy frown on her face. She barely acknowledged him as he leaned down and placed a kiss on her forehead. I wondered if it was as delicate as it looked. As he turned to leave, he looked over his shoulder at her and told her he loved her. I held my breath at the tension in the room and wondered if she would be so cold to him, she wouldn't even return an *I love you too*. She couldn't be that mad.

I let go of the breath when she replied to him with a dry "Love you too."

For the first time since he walked into the room, I *actually* looked over at him. The emptiness in his eyes as he stared at his wife as if she was the only woman in the room made my heart sink. What in the hell was going on between these two?

After about ten seconds, he took his eyes off her and put them on me. It took him a second or two, but eventually, he sent me a light head nod and told me to have a great day.

"Thank you, Mr. Baptiste. You have a great day, too," I sincerely told him, hoping he recognized it. Hoping he actually would.

CHAPTER 14

Jahad

As soon as I walked into Blaise's house, I immediately blew into my cold hands. The weather had gone from sunny and cold to straight-up freezing and heavy snowfall in a matter of hours. After closing and locking the door, I stomped snow from my wheat Timberland boots and hung my coat up on the coat rack. The heavy scent of good-ass green filled my nostrils as I bobbed my head to one of my favorite Jay-Z tracks, "Family Feud," blasting from the surround system speakers.

It was early in the afternoon. The last time I checked the time, it was inching in on 1:30. I'd been busy as hell all fucking day and hoped that when I sat down with this nigga, I wouldn't have to put more work on my schedule. I had a couple of hours before Sienna's shift ended, so I had to head back home to make sure Leighton's evil ass wasn't alone. As painful as sharing a roof with her had been these past few months, I wasn't going to abandon my responsibilities.

Stepping over the threshold, I scanned the massive room, shaking my head. The place was a mess, and sprawled out on the big sectional couch were three women, ass naked, passed out at damn near four in the afternoon.

Steady scanning the room, my eyes fell on several pieces of clothes scattered on the floor, liquor bottles, drug paraphernalia, and condom wrappers. Evidence of a good-ass night.

Running my hand over my thick beard, I clenched my jaw and stepped over another woman laid out on the floor, blocking my path to the back area of the house where I was sure I'd find Blaise in the kitchen.

I was right. I walked in to him bobbing his head with a blunt dangling from his lips. He moved around to the loud-ass music, standing at the stove, whipping some eggs up. He was in his element, sprinkling salt and pepper into the pan. Because I wanted to test him, I subtly untucked my burner from my waistband, ensuring the safety was still on, and wrapped my hand around the handle. Creeping up on him, I upped it.

"Aight, nigga. You know the law. You up it, you better let it loose too. And if you let it loose, you better make sure my soul leaves my body before you get comfortable too, fool," Blaise said, his back still on me. Not even a second later, he turned around, aimed his gun at my forehead, and smiled at me.

"*Sak pase, fro* (What's up, bro)?"

I gave him a lazy smirk and tucked my burner back into my waistband. "I see you on yo' shit."

"Always," he said with a smirk, before putting his gun back into the holster strapped to his shirtless chest. "I learned from the best."

Me. He learned from me. Ensuring my brothers' awareness was always on point was instilled in them before we left Haiti. When I said we were bred in the trenches, I meant that shit. We didn't come from a place of beauty and safety. We came from the slums, where it was either eat or be eaten.

Back home, muthafuckas were always looking for an opportunity to better their situation. People weren't eating out there. Meals were scarce. Money was scarce. It was the survival of the fittest, and although my brothers were young, I made sure they had the survival instincts of a cheetah. Fast, smart, and hard to catch slipping.

I leaned with my back against the counter, next to the stove, and nodded in the direction of the living room. "You had a night."

"Invited a few people over." We locked eyes as he took the pan of eggs off the stove and dumped them into a big steel bowl. "I had to make sure the women were occupied while I took a brief intermission."

With my mouth turned down and my arms crossed over my chest, I nodded, understanding. The women . . . The party . . . He was giving himself a solid alibi. Blaise might've been the fuckup of the bunch, but when it came to getting down to business and handling shit efficiently, he never half stepped. I was happy I wouldn't have to pick up any of his slack. But then again, Blaise was never a slacker when it came to putting in work for the business. The *drug* business. Anything outside of it, the nigga was a mess.

"Cooking them breakfast now?" I asked, switching gears.

The kitchen was no place for the conversation we had to have. Even with the music blasting, I didn't trust it. *We* didn't trust it. The women passed out in the living room were Blaise's women. Women he collected over time. He had four—the first three had been with him for years, but we didn't trust them enough to speak freely around them. Shit, I barely spoke freely around Leighton, and she was my wife. She knew about the trivial shit. Big shit, like conspiring to murder a DEA agent, she had no clue about. There was no way in hell I was about to talk about what we had going on in front of them bitches.

Blaise looked over at me with a half smirk. "A nigga felt generous today. I'm in a good-ass mood."

Chucking my chin up, I gave him a nod. "Had a good-ass night, huh?"

"A *great*-ass night," he emphasized. "You hungry?"

Rubbing the back of my neck, I shook my head. "I stopped by Moms this morning."

"You ever eat breakfast at home, nigga?" Blaise asked, as he pulled a sheet of beef bacon from the oven. "You have a cook that will make you anything you want, but you drive to Momma's for breakfast. Momma's-boy ass."

"Don't worry about what I do, bitch," I joked. "You should worry about those burnt-ass eggs."

Blaise frowned and looked down at the bowl of eggs. Sucking his teeth, he looked back up at me with a deep furrow in his thick brows. "Fuck you. I like my eggs well done."

I laughed and shook my head as I looked down at my phone. It was Leigh. She'd sent me a simple *I apologize* text. Running my hand over the top of my head, I replied, telling her it was cool, and that I loved her.

This morning, I walked into the bedroom wearing a towel while Sienna was there. Had I known she had come to work early, I would never have done that. Despite the way I felt about Sienna, I would never disrespect my wife in that way. Shit might sound crazy coming from me, but regardless of whatever, my morals stayed in place. I hadn't blatantly conspired to cheat on my wife. I wasn't that nigga anymore. However, since Leighton knew I'd accepted the hall pass, every little thing ticked her off. She was showing signs of the same insecurities from before, and the shit was killing me.

We hadn't been in the best place lately, but before New Year's Eve, we didn't argue. Not as often as we were now. Before, there was distance and light arguments about that pass. Since taking it, things had shifted. Things had shifted a lot.

Regardless of what we'd been going through, though, I still loved her ass. I didn't measure her beauty or our love by the battles we were currently facing. I knew who Leighton was. I knew her heart. Because I knew what she was and who she was, I pitied my brothers.

"Good morning," yelled one of the women, boldly walking into the kitchen, ass naked.

I looked away and ran my hand over the top of my head. Wild.

Blaise looked over his shoulder at her with a scowl. "It's not morning. Go put some clothes on. Have some fuckin' respect!" he barked. "*Tét zozo* (Dickhead)."

I dragged my hand over my mouth before placing my hands flat on the countertop with my back to her.

"What did you call me? You think you slick, sayin' shit I don't understand! Hey Siri!" the girl yelled as she stormed out of the kitchen. "What does *Ted Zoo Zoo* mean?"

Blaise and I looked at one another before we both laughed. Shaking my head, I said, "I don't know how you do it, bro."

He smirked and set plates on the table. "Like a king, nigga."

"Yeah, aight. Kingdom unstable as hell," I joked.

Blaise took a deep breath, his big shoulders rising and falling. "I thrive in chaos, my nigga. You already know."

We laughed and I watched him maneuver around the kitchen, fixing plates for his women. I thought the shit was hilarious, to be honest. I had nothing against a man cooking for a woman. When it came to who I loved, I was a simp. Couldn't front on it. Everybody who had witnessed me with mine was already hip. If Leighton asked me to travel ten miles for her favorite ice cream in the middle of the night, I would with no questions asked. I had at the beginning of her pregnancy. And because she loved it so fucking much, I basically had a weekly subscription to them muthafuckas that didn't even exist. For me, they made an exception because I paid triple what they were asking for just to make sure Shorty had what she loved.

So, yeah, I wasn't the type of man who turned his nose up to affection. But this nigga Blaise? Blaise was a bachelor who wanted to be worshipped by women. He wanted them waiting on him, hand and foot.

Monogamy was a joke to him. He had never been a one-woman man, which was why the number of his women had gone from five to four. Ari, his baby moms, was a part of his cult. I called it a cult because to me, that was what the shit seemed like. Before she was pregnant, she wanted him to herself, but Blaise wasn't having it. So, she left and created problems in his life.

Like Saint, Blaise lived a wild-ass life. One filled with meaningless wild sex, drama, and instability. They were the complete opposite of me. Well, who I was *now*. In the past, we were similar. I had matured quicker because I was the one who'd fallen in love. Found someone I deemed worthy enough to step away from the wild shit for. As crazy as things were between Leigh and me now, I had no regrets. Not one. I didn't look at my brothers' lives with envy.

In fact, I pitied them. Felt bad they hadn't experienced what I experienced yet: contentment and satisfaction with one woman.

Once I realized just how badly the bullshit I was on was affecting us, I pulled back and got serious about my shorty. The risk of losing her made a nigga's chest hurt. The more bullshit I did in the streets, the further and further she seemed to drift away from me. That last time I fucked up, Leighton didn't shed a tear and that was when I knew if I didn't fix my shit, I'd lose her forever. The fact I cared about losing her at all spoke volumes to me. She was worth deading all the immature bullshit. She was the one for me. Even with the bullshit we were going through, I still saw her as the one.

I said I pitied my brothers because there was no greater feeling than finding someone worth that. Loving wholeheartedly, freely, beyond the ugliness, beyond the rough times, knowing the shit was reciprocated without ulterior motives. The love was genuine. Leighton didn't give a fuck about what I had because she was with me before I had it all. That shit stood for something with me. Meanwhile, the bitches I was doing her dirty over fucked with me off pure vanity. Nothing more. And the women my brothers fucked with were the same. Not one woman on their team was solid. I knew this because, if she was, if they had that feeling of fulfillment that made me chill, Blaise wouldn't need four bitches and Saint wouldn't frequent Pandora's.

Fifteen minutes later, Blaise and I were in his office. The women were in the kitchen, eating, talking shit, and far out of earshot. However, they could be standing right outside of Blaise's office door and wouldn't be able to hear a thing. His office was soundproof, just like mine, Saint's, and Pops's were.

For us, caution was on the same level as loyalty. Without caution, how balanced would the loyalty be, anyway? An unstable foundation, messiness, and carelessness left room for imbalance on every level, and an imbalance in the business we were in was detrimental to the Baptiste family.

We sat down at the desk. Blaise pushed his plate of food aside and interlocked his fingers. "He won't be in the land of the living much longer, *gro fré*."

I nodded, lightly stroking my beard. "It's done?"

"Of course. Just the way we talked about," he reassured me. "I personally made sure the job was done to maximum capacity."

Closing my eyes and reopening them, I clenched down on my jaw. "You went?"

"I went," he told me, as if he had done the right thing.

"B—"

"Relax. I was careful. I couldn't trust Benny to do the job alone. A job this big . . . I needed to be there personally to make sure everything would go as flawlessly as we need it to."

"That wasn't a part of the plan. You could have been seen. How many big, Black, six-seven niggas do you think is roaming around the suburbs, Blaise? The fuckin' country at that? None. You stand out, nigga. You—"

"It was four in the morning. Quiet. Not a soul out to that bitch," he interrupted before placing his food back in front of him. "No one saw us. We were in and out. You know he keeps it in the garage. We entered through the cornfield, handled business, and was out of there in under fifteen minutes. I know what I'm doing, nigga." He dug into his food and talked with a mouth full of food. "I'm not new to this, bitch, I'm true to this."

I sat back against the chair and ran my hands down over my pants. I felt like he'd fucked up. The plan . . . It was flawless. Shelby convinced Walker to stay at his house in Armada to keep him "safe." He gave Walker access to everything. His old car included. Because Shelby is the head of DEA, he's in charge of who watched Walker when, so in that situation we were good too. No one wanted to travel out to fucking Armada. Out there, he didn't have eyes on him often. All Benny had to do was go out there at a certain time, loosen the lug nuts on the tires of the car and that was it. Simple. This nigga Blaise, bro. I just couldn't understand it. Blaise liked to think he knew what he was doing. Out of the three of us, he was the one who had a hard time lying low and keeping his hands clean.

Transitioning into this corporate, blue-collared façade was hard for him. As the main one of us who stayed breaking niggas' necks with his bare hands, how hard it was for him was no surprise. That was why we kept the nigga out of the field. Blaise had a team of niggas we used to get rid of problems.

We didn't use anybody on his team. We went to Benny, our cousin, specifically. We didn't trust anybody outside of the Baptiste bloodline with moves like that. Benny, just like Blaise, was heavy in the sanitation department. They were similar in many ways, except Benny wasn't a big-ass, burly, seven-foot nigga. Nothing stood out about Benny, except for the long scar across his face. A scar that stayed concealed by face masks whenever he was on murder shit. Blaise . . . Blaise couldn't hide who he was.

"Trust me. It was dark as hell, and quiet," Blaise said, attempting to quiet my mind. "I handled it. You just make sure that nigga stand on his word."

I huffed with a sly smirk. "Make *sure what*? I don't need reinforcements, bitch. Never have."

Blaise held his messy hands up before digging back into his plate. "I'm just sayin'. I'm just sayin'."

I leaned forward, resting my forearms on the desk with my eyes locked on his. "Don't just say. When it comes to me, I don't need you to just say. You should have made sure you did what you were supposed to do. I'm strict about staying on course for a reason, Blaise. You itching to do something? Itching to get your hands dirty? You could have waited until you left. Here, on U.S. soil, where we rub shoulders with the very organization you just made a move on is a no-go."

The top corner of Blaise's lip twitched as he stared back at me with fire behind his dark, slanted eyes. "*Konprann* (Understood)."

Blaise hated to be told what to do. That was why he rebelled against our parents so much. Rebelled against me too, which was why him joining Benny on a job specifically for Benny came of no surprise. Blaise, although thorough, was like that. But he had the nerve to be in his feelings about the way I handled him because of his rebellious attitude.

I pushed up from the chair and nodded at him. He picked his napkin up and wiped his hands and face before standing and extending his hand to me. With our eyes locked, I shook his hand and told him I loved him. Nodding, he told me he loved me too. Regardless of the way he felt about how I'd cut into him, respect and love were two things we would always have for one another.

About twenty minutes later, as I was turning into the subdivision, I noticed *her*. Sienna. She was standing outside of her car, making a sad attempt at digging herself out of the mountain of snow she'd turned into.

Squinting, I took a deep breath and pulled over on the side of the road. The snow had gotten crazy as hell. It was so thick, being able to see out of the windshield was damn near impossible. I passed at least five car accidents on my way to the house. As much as I needed her as far away from the house as possible, I wasn't the type of nigga who would send her on her way, knowing how dangerous the roads were.

After pulling over and shifting my car into park, I hit the hazards and hopped out. Not only was it snowy as fuck, but it had gotten colder too. The last time I peeped the weather on my dash, it said it was twelve degrees out.

My Timbs sunk into the snow as I made my way over to her. There was a predicted ten inches in the forecast, and by the looks of things, we were going to get every bit of that shit.

"Aye!" I called out.

She looked over at me in a crouched position and tossed her head back in annoyance. I could tell I was probably the last nigga she wanted to see. I couldn't blame her. I was an asshole to her this morning. Pissed because I'd walked into the room in a towel, putting both of us in an awkward position. Pissed because it was the only position I *could* put her in, although I could easily think of five off the top of my head I *wanted to* put her in.

"Come on, ain't shit you can do about that right now," I told her, my hand extended.

She was covered in snow. Her hair was white, her eyebrows were white, and the cute-ass coat she had on did nothing to cover the bottom portion of her body, so her pants were just as covered. She didn't have on any gloves either but was out there shoveling snow from underneath her tire with a floor mat. Shorty was wilding, for sure. Wilding and wasting her time because the minute she removed snow, it was replaced with more. It was a damn blizzard.

She looked up at my hand and then went back to trying to shovel the snow. "I'm good! I got—"

Before she could say anything else, I grabbed her by her arm and pulled her to her feet. "Come on. That shit will have to be taken care of tomorrow. You out here with this li'l-ass coat on, no gloves, covered in snow in below-zero weather in a fuckin' blizzard."

The dash might've said twelve, but with the windchill, it was easily below zero. Although I'd been in the States for years, the cold weather was something I still hadn't gotten used to. I was useless in it and did everything in my power to stay out of it. I might've been overstepping by putting my hands on her, but I didn't give a fuck. I wasn't about to be standing out in the cold, debating shit with her. She was getting in the car with me, one way or another.

"I said—"

"And I said fuck that shit. I'll handle it tomorrow. Right now, you're going to get in the car and drive back up to the house with me. Cold as shit out here and you want to be difficult."

With that, I led her to the car, and she reluctantly followed.

About two minutes later, I pulled into the garage. I shifted my eyes over at her. She was nervous. Her knee bounced profusely. I wondered if she was nervous because she was in such closed corners with me again, or if she was just that nervous about sleeping under the same roof as me. I'd bet it was a combination of both. I was sure it was because I had the same reservations. Although, I didn't show it.

It was hard for me, sitting beside her, the scent of her perfume filling my nostrils. The sound of her shallow breathing and that magnetism pulling my orbs in her direction. I could barely focus on the snow-covered road as we headed back up. The urge to place my hand on top of her bouncing knee became too much for me to ignore, and I found myself doing just that.

"I can't stay here," she mumbled.

I understood what she meant. She could . . . but she *shouldn't.* There was a lot of shit we shouldn't have done, but that shit was done and over with and I refused to spend another day, beating myself up over the shit. Especially since Leighton had been a fucking headache.

I had been beating myself up every day about making a decision she forced on me, and for what? The situation we were in was one she put us in.

She looked over at me the minute my hand landed on top of her thigh. "Relax."

Her eyes softened a bit and, like before, mine got lost in hers and time seemed to slow. My eyes then traveled from hers down to her lips just before she pulled them into her mouth. When I was in her presence, I felt weak, and *weak* was a word that could never describe Jahad Baptiste. However, there was something about this woman that made me that way. Made me want to say fuck the vows I made to Leighton. Shit, hadn't she, in a way? But then I'd be hit with the realization of what those vows entailed. For better or for worse . . . in sickness and in health.

Taking a deep breath, I looked away from her and finally got out of the car before those vows quickly became another afterthought and I ended up doing something wild, like kissing her. I'd asked her if working here would be an issue for her, but shit, she'd been doing perfectly fine. It was me. I was the problem.

Standing up out of the car, I adjusted my hard dick and placed my hand in front of it. Soon after, she got out of the car, and I told her she could go ahead inside after giving her the unlock code. I needed to get my shit together. I couldn't walk into the house with my dick on stiff. She nodded and walked inside and my eyes landed on her. They always landed on her. Even when I didn't want them to. She was the first person I looked at when I stepped out of the bathroom this morning in only a towel, body still damp with water. In that moment, I wanted her to take the towel from around my waist and wrap her soft lips around my dick.

When the door shut, I placed both of my arms along the roof of the truck and leaned my head down. *Mèd* (Fuck).

Taking a deep breath, I ran my hand over the top of my head and looked down at my twitching dick.

"Calm the fuck down, nigga," I mumbled, shaking my head.

Once I was comfortable and my dick was soft, I hit the alarm on my car and headed inside. After removing my shoes and hanging my things on the coatrack, I went searching for Ms. Evaline. I needed to realign myself with my marriage. My mind had been so clouded with thoughts of Sienna, I hadn't recentered myself after that hall pass the way I needed to.

Walking into the kitchen, I found her where I always found her: in the kitchen.

I chucked my chin up at Maurice, who was sweeping, before giving Ms. Evaline a mischievous grin. "So, Ms. Evaline, I need a favor."

CHAPTER 15

Leighton

I picked up my phone and checked the time before looking back over to the window, watching the snow fall. Sienna had left about ten minutes ago, so I was expecting Jahad to walk in at any moment. My anxiety was through the roof. Things had been so rough between us that simply seeing him had me on edge.

This morning, before Sienna came in early, it was awkward. I was awkward. Any time his phone made a sound, I looked over, hoping to get a glimpse of his screen. I was driving myself crazy with insecurities that I'd literally lost sleep over it. Most nights, I laid wide awake, thinking, creating scenarios. One night, it got so bad, I cried. I questioned every little move he made. If he said he was out handling business, I second-guessed it. Jahad could tell me the sky was blue and water was wet, and I'd question it.

All of this shit was my fault. We needed to have that conversation. The conversation we were not supposed to have. The one about that hall pass. Because I couldn't do anything all day, my mind wandered like crazy. All I did was sit here and think. Think about him with her. Think about him fucking her. Think about him stepping out on me, outside of our agreement.

Women don't fuck Jahad once. He was like good dope. You always wanted a hit, even if you were in rehab. There was no way in hell this woman fucked him, had him how I had him, and just let him go. And who was to say she didn't have him hooked? Jahad hadn't had pussy in months before fucking her. There was much possibility hanging in the air. So many unanswered questions. So much uncertainty, insecurities, and bad days because of that uncertainty and those insecurities.

I flinched when my phone rang. Sucking my teeth, I slid the phone over to answer Farrah's call.

"Hey, boo," she said, sounding more chipper than usual. "How was it today?"

"Are you going to ask me that every day? You act like Sienna is incapable of doing her job," I snapped, before closing my eyes with a sigh.

"Ugh. What the hell is wrong with you?"

"Nothing," I flatly responded. "My bad. Today was just . . . rough. I tried to paint today and couldn't."

Painting was my passion. I was only passionate about two things: painting and motherhood. It was almost as if I was cursed. I couldn't have them both at the same time. When I was creatively flowing, I couldn't hold a pregnancy to save my life. I was sure that creativity came from stress. I had to pour into something. Had to cling to something I had control over because I sure as hell didn't have control over my damn body. I was like that. Obsessive over the things I really couldn't control. Grasping at possibility. Clinging onto hope when everything around me gave me every reason in the world to let go of it.

I'd spend hours on top of hours in my studio, just painting. Painting with Erykah Badu on full blast. I'd stay in that room, locked away from sunup until sundown, obsessing over time. Obsessing over the day of the week. Day after day, it was a continuous countdown to when I'd be ovulating again.

I waited for that day like a kid waiting for Christmas Day. And then, after making sure Jahad's schedule aligned with my ovulation days and making sure he was here, on time, to nut in me, I'd wait. Wait a few days before my late period to take a test, and in between that time, I'd be painting.

Now that I had my rainbow baby, I couldn't paint. The way my mind was scrambled now, I could barely think without having a fucking panic attack. I was a mess. A complete mess and I just . . . I missed me so much.

Farrah sighed. "It'll come back. You haven't been out. You haven't been around anything to give you creative inspiration."

"I've never needed creative inspiration, though, Farrah," I stressed, rubbing my forehead. "You know that."

"Yeah, but things are different now, babe. You're under a lot of stress. Do you need me to come over?"

I rolled my eyes to the back of my head before tossing it back into the pillow. "You see the weather, right? You don't need to come over here. I'm fine."

"You know I don't give a damn about the snow. If you need me—"

"I don't *need* you," I interrupted.

The last thing I wanted was to get into it with my girl. I had enough conflict in my life.

I was losing my husband. Literally felt him slipping through my fingers. One of my biggest fears was being alone. Completely. No husband, no friends. I'd have my family, but they had their own things going on. My sisters and I had never been close. Ashleigh was thirteen years older than me, so we had nothing in common. Shiloh was ten years older, so yeah, same with her. I was the youngest. My parents had me when they were close to forty. I had a pretty lonely childhood. A lonely childhood with siblings who pretty much resented me for getting all the attention since I was the baby.

Farrah was the closest thing I had to a sister, and I couldn't lose her. The thought of it with everything going wrong already really scared me. I was doing a very shitty job at keeping my husband; I couldn't do a shitty job at keeping my friend.

The silence that followed was deafening. Rubbing my temples, I let out an exasperated sigh. "I didn't mean it like that, Farrah."

I really didn't. Because *hello*! I did need her. I just didn't like people to think I needed them, although I did. I didn't like how weak I'd become, dependent on people, afraid of losing them, making rash decisions to keep them. Putting up with sly remarks and shit like that to make sure they stayed in my life. This wasn't me. I didn't like how she'd insinuated I needed her. That ground my fucking gears. I could've taken it the wrong way, but still. That was triggering for me. For me, an independent woman, to become so dependent on people was a change I still hadn't been able to adjust to.

"Girl! It's cool! I know you didn't," she responded with forced excitement in her tone.

Before I could address it a little more, Jahad walked into the bedroom. I swallowed as my eyes fell on him, walking over to me. He chucked his head back and continued toward me. He was on his way to deliver his kiss. A kiss that used to make me blush and butterflies fill my stomach like crazy. Now, his kisses felt poisonous. Instead of loving them, I questioned them. Wondered if he greeted and said goodbye to her the same way he did to me.

"Sienna is back," he told me after kissing me on my forehead. "Saw her stuck in the snow at the exit. I told her she could stay until the roads clear up."

"Hubby's home?" Farrah asked.

"Mm-hmm. I'll call you right back," I said before we hung up.

Setting my phone on the bed, I pressed my fists into the mattress and scooted back a little, wincing a bit.

"You good?" Jahad immediately asked. He was like that. Attentive and always there to fix anything that was wrong.

"Yeah. I told her she could stay earlier, but she was determined to leave. You should have left her hardheaded ass out there," I joked.

Jahad lightly chuckled and turned his attention back to the dresser he stood at, removing his jewelry. I ran my hand over my round belly, watching him as he prepared for his shower. A shower he took every time he came home. There was nothing out of the ordinary about it, but because I felt like he'd been cheating on me, I was suspicious. Had he been showering when he made it home now because her scent was on him?

"Where were you?" I questioned.

He looked over his shoulder with a crinkled brow. "I told you I was going to see Blaise today."

"Yeah, but . . . where did you go after? You were over there the whole time? You left the house before noon."

He eyed me with skepticism before turning away and lightly shaking his head. "Stopped at my mother's for breakfast, Leigh."

"Oh," I said, still studying him. "How is she? I haven't seen her. I should call and see how she's doing."

"Yeah, you should," he told me. "Especially since she's been calling to check on you and you haven't answered."

At one point in time, Mrs. Baptiste and I were close. Very close. Sometimes, she and I would be closer than me and my own mother. It wasn't until being bedridden and losing more of myself that I pulled away. I hadn't pulled away from just her and Jahad—I pulled away from everyone. Farrah too. She just didn't *let* me pull away. I felt like if she was still married, she would have let me pull away too. She needed me. I was all she had left. It was ironic, how now I clung onto her for that very reason. That unsettling fear of being alone.

I sighed. "You know how I am. I've just been under a lot of pressure."

He didn't say anything, just nodded. For some reason, that annoyed me. Like he didn't believe me, or like he didn't care. Something about his disinterest in carrying on a conversation with me ticked me off.

"Why are you so quiet? Something on your mind?"

Jahad ran his tongue over his bottom lip before pulling his shirt over his head, giving me a pensive stare. That body . . . those muscles. This man . . . He wasn't the one-night-stand type. I'd watched him effortlessly captivate bitches. All Jahad had to do was smile. He had superpowers. The kind that made women fall to their knees and want to please him.

Before we changed, I enjoyed watching them practically drool over him. I enjoyed the flirtatious looks he was given. The smiles he received. The attention. I liked to see women swooning over him because I knew that, despite how much swooning they did, he would never swoon over them the way they did over him. He was too busy swooning over me.

That confidence took a lot to build, though. I wasn't always that confident in our relationship. It was crazy how it'd taken me a while to build it up, just to be the reason it was torn down.

I shouldn't have given him that pass.

He shouldn't have taken it.

"Nah, I'm good. Something's clearly on your mind, though," he said, before tossing his shirt over into the dirty laundry basket sitting right outside of the walk-in closet. "What is it?"

I eyed him up and down as he made his way over to the bed. When we talked, there was rarely ever any distance put between us. That was the red flag that told me he'd taken the hall pass *that night*. Just imagine how that felt, starting a new year, knowing your husband had been with someone else. But here was the catch—there was nothing you could do about it because you gave him permission to be with someone else. And because you told him you never wanted to talk about it, you had to sit with your thoughts all day, every day because you were confined to a bed. Meanwhile, he was roaming the streets, most likely seeing her, fucking her, kissing her, and giving her things that were rightfully yours.

That was where I was at with it.

Where I'd been at with it since I found out three weeks ago.

I was fucked up.

"Have you been with her?" I asked, inching in on having that forbidden conversation. Hoping he'd take the bait. We needed to talk about it.

"Have I been with who?" he asked, feigning ignorance.

I squinted and ran my hand over my belly, just as she moved. "You know who."

Jahad shifted his eyes away from mine and placed them over my rolling belly. She was so active, and since he was rarely around when she was, he lifted my shirt and ran his big hand across my belly, ignoring me. Goosebumps immediately covered my skin. I wondered if my cheeks were as red as they always were when he touched me. Regardless of what I was going through mentally, my body had a mind of its own. The way it responded to him was its instinct. We could be in a full-fledged argument, but let Jahad kiss or touch me and my body always responded in a way that said I loved him, still. Which was true.

"Jah."

"Shhh," he told me as he leaned over and pressed his ear against my stomach.

I sucked in air at the feel of his prickly facial hair digging into my skin.

"*Bonjou, bebe. Se papa ou. Komon ou ye? M pa ka tann pou m rankontre w. Nou gen anpil trape jiska fè.* (Hello, baby. It's your father. How are you? I can't wait to meet you. We have a lot of catching up to do.)"

He never spoke to the baby in English. Any time Jahad spoke to my belly, it was in Haitian Creole. He had it in his mind that if he spoke to her in his native language now, when she was born, she'd recognize it. Jahad said he was going to speak to her in Creole and Creole only and how I could speak to her in English so she would know both.

Initially, he didn't like to make plans for the baby, as he handled our losses in his own way. But once we made it past the twenty-week mark, he opened up more. He talked about her a lot now, though. Talked about how he was going to raise a child who was heavy into his heritage. He planned on buying land in Haiti to build a home on so we could visit often. He not only wanted her to know the language, but he also wanted her to know their roots. He was proud to become a father. I knew he was going to be an amazing one solely based on how he was an amazing husband to me.

When he kissed my belly, I gripped the bedding and pulled my lips into my mouth with a slow blink. God. He hadn't kissed me anywhere but my forehead for weeks. His lips felt good against my skin. So good, I almost forgot about what I was asking him.

"Jah—"

"Evaline cooked white chicken chili, cornbread, and a side salad. It's been a minute since we've eaten in the dining room," he interrupted with his eyes bearing into mine. "I know you can use a change of scenery. So, after I get out of the shower, we're going down. Together. Put on that perfume I like. The Baccarat."

"Why do you keep ignoring my question? You've been fucking her, haven't you?" I asked with a fiery squint. "Don't lie. Don't try to change the subject because I'm not going to let you. You already know how I am. I'll keep asking—"

"No, Leighton. I haven't been fuckin' her," he boldly stated in such an even tone, it was like a sharp razor blade gliding against my skin. "Dead that shit. Have a better attitude when I get out of the shower."

With that, he walked away. I watched him in complete silence, an argument sitting on the tip of my tongue. However, I couldn't speak. Jahad rarely ever spoke to me like that, and when he did, it hurt my feelings to the damn core, as if he'd cursed me out and called me bitches and hos.

* * *

About thirty minutes later, Jahad and I left the room. He was pushing me in the wheelchair I hated. Neither of us had said a word to each other since he'd hurt my feelings. The elevator ride was just as quiet and intimidating.

I busied myself by scrolling my Instagram to get back at him for the way he spoke to me. Jahad hated when I brought my phone to the dining room. We had a strong no-phone rule for dinner time. Because he was big on family and communicating, he liked to spend that time catching up and shit like that. Well, tonight, I wasn't in the mood for laughing, talking, and intimacy. I knew what he was trying to do. Fix us. Get back to doing things we used to do before we had this bridge between us. I wanted things to get better between us, too, but so much had happened, I just didn't know where I was mentally.

As he stood behind me, against the wall of the elevator, I felt his eyes on me. So much so, the hairs on the back of my neck stood up and my heart rate picked up. His stare, even with my back turned, was just as intense and intimidating as it was when we stood face to face with those piercing eyes on mine.

I could tell he had so much to say, but he said nothing. His silence, that stare, it worried me. Jahad was a ticking time bomb. Never with me, always with other people. However, with his eyes on my back and the coldness of his energy, I was afraid of who and what he would become when he did finally blow.

Ding.

The elevator sounded and he gripped the handles of the wheelchair to push me out. I could have wheeled myself, and I would have if I didn't have my phone in my hand. But because I was sitting on this high horse of "pisstivity," I let him push me. I wanted him to feel what I felt. Disrespect. Anger. And all the things in between.

The fact that he'd pretty much told me to shut the fuck up and fix my attitude when I inquired about the bitch he'd given "my" dick to pissed me off beyond reason.

When we made it to the dining room, he froze, and me, I smirked.

"Hey, Sienna. I'm happy you decided to join us," I said with a smile as I grabbed the wheels and escorted myself further into the dining room, since he'd stopped walking. I felt him seething with anger and didn't have to look over my shoulder to see his face to feel it, either.

Inviting Sienna down for dinner was another dig at him. I did feel a little bad once I realized how the table had been set. We had two dining rooms—a formal and a regular one that could be classified as formal as well. We were in the regular one, which was our favorite place to have dinner at one point in time. It was massive, decorated in black and silver. The eight-seater, black marble tabletop dining room table sat on X-shaped thick gold legs. The walls were matte black and geometrically textured. Hanging from the high ceiling was an enormous, luxurious crystal chandelier, adorned by black and silver accents. It was a statement piece, for sure, and my favorite part about the room.

The décor was nothing new to me; however, the table setting was. Which was why I felt a little bad about my cattiness. Jahad had obviously planned for us to have dinner here, as the table was romantically set for two. Our plates sat across from each other at the end of the table. Instead of placemats being at each end of the table, they were directly across from one another. There were candles, too, and the lighting on the chandelier had been dimmed.

"Hey," Sienna said as she pushed back from the table to stand. "Ms. Evaline said the table was only set for the two of you. I don't want to—"

"Don't worry about it," Jahad interrupted, finally speaking. "Have a seat. I'll set it for three."

I glanced over my shoulder at him before placing a loose loc behind my ear. I didn't feel a little bad anymore; I felt horrible. Through the ears of someone who didn't know Jahad, you'd think he was really okay. But since I'd known him for the better part of ten years, I heard the truth. He was disappointed. Heartbroken.

"I didn't realize this was . . . a dinner for two. Jah, I'm sorry. Sienna, please—"

"Nah, it's cool. You're here now, Sienna. Please." Jahad motioned for her to sit where I usually sat, as if she wasn't already standing at the chair she'd just stood from. "Have a seat."

Her eyebrows crinkled with just as much confusion as mine did. I cocked my head to the side a little but said nothing, as I wheeled myself to where the chair was, stood up out of my wheelchair and sat in it. Jahad was testing me, and I couldn't lie and say I didn't deserve that disrespect.

"Oh, hey, Mr. Baptiste. I was just getting ready to call and ask if I should make accommodations for Ms. Sienna," Evaline said, emerging from the kitchen with her hands wrapped around the cordless phone assigned to the staff. She looked over at me, gave me a sweet smile, and spoke. "Hello, Mrs. Baptiste. It's so good to see you out of the room, sweetheart."

I gave her a forced smile as I swiped around my phone, trying to busy myself with something to stop myself from erupting at Jahad. I didn't have the right to. I knew he wanted to eat together. I had called Sienna down. How he reacted to seeing her was my fault and mine only. However, I wanted to explode!

To keep my damn mouth shut, I grabbed the wineglass of water and took hefty sips from it, wishing I could have a glass of Opus One. I needed it. I needed it, badly. I'd heard long ago that red wine during pregnancy was okay. As long as it was one glass. I thought that was outrageous and completely reckless, but now I wanted it. I needed something. I couldn't sit here, forcing smiles all night, pretending I was happy when I was fucking miserable. And whose fault was that? Mine. I loathed myself. I was a miserable fucking woman and there was nothing I could do to escape myself. I was just . . . stuck. Stuck with living with a version of myself I'd truly grown to hate.

That was the hard, cold truth. The realization I sat with every day was that, and because I'd beat myself up enough, I took it out on the man who loved me more than life itself sometimes. And you know what? I hated myself even more because of that. What a sad-ass life.

CHAPTER 16

Sienna

I couldn't sleep.

Every time I looked at the clock, only a minute had passed, but my God, it felt a lot longer. I'd been lying in the same spot, with my eyes to the ceiling, thinking about him for hours. Dinner was weird. I tried to excuse myself from the table, but Leighton was adamant about me staying and relaxing. What she didn't know was that I badly wanted to relax on her husband's lap. As I sat there, eating pasta, I thought about how it felt to have his dick slide down my throat. Every time I slurped a noodle or sucked sauce from the fork, I thought of him and the way his creamy nut tasted. I wanted him so got damn bad.

I felt like such a fucking slut.

Who in the hell was I?

And to make matters worse, there was this energy between us that couldn't be ignored. The whole time I sat there, my heart raced and my eyes wanted so badly to be on him. So much, I had to steal a glance every now and then. I swear it felt like if I didn't, I would have died. It was just that intense.

Apparently, he felt it, too, because every time I glanced at him, he'd be stealing glances at me too. I didn't know how much more of this I could take.

As I laid there with my eyes to the ceiling, my hands found that sensitive bud between my legs. The bud he had sucked and licked on until I quivered and squirted all over his face. I closed my eyes and pinched my top teeth over my lip as a light moan escaped my lips. Looking over at the wall that separated our rooms, I began to yet again imagine I was in bed with him. Except I wouldn't be snoring. I would be choking on dick.

I began to vigorously run my fingers over my clit as I heard his deep baritone voice in my ear, saying, "Rub it." I moaned, recalling our moment in *that* room. His aggression. His precision. His . . . allure. My God, I wanted him so fucking bad.

With my eyes lazily locked on that wall, I continued to fantasize about him. I thought about us. I imagined him fucking me from behind, tugging on my hair, pulling my head back so that he could attack the thin layer of skin on my neck with his teeth. Those perfect, white teeth against that smooth, deep, rich chocolate skin. I thought about him gripping my ass cheeks and—

The ringing of my phone interrupted my little fantasy.

Good.

My sick ass had no business fantasizing about that man while he slept with his fucking wife. Taking a deep breath, I rolled over and grabbed my phone from the nightstand. It was Naoki. Sliding the phone over, I answered.

"Yeah, girl," I said, the sound of desperation heavy in my tone.

"It's three in the morning," she said, stating the obvious. "You're wide awake . . . with that dick on your mind, ain't you? You about to fuck that woman's husband in her house, ain't you? You freaky little—"

"No, bitch," I interrupted with pained laughter.

She giggled. "But you want to."

I exhaled and ran the back of my hand over my forehead. "So got damn bad, Ki. I need to leave."

"The roads are horrible. I'm trapped at the hospital. At least you've got a comfortable, big bed to sleep in. I'll be sleeping in one of these damn patient rooms," Naoki complained.

"At this point, I'm ready to risk it," I said, biting my bottom lip and swinging my legs over to the side of the bed to stand.

Treading over to the window, my feet sunk into the plush carpet, and I wiggled my toes a little. I stood at the window and swiped the curtain aside to get a look out of it. My eyes widened at how much snow had fallen and was still falling. By the looks of things, the snow wouldn't be stopping any time soon.

"How? When your car is buried in snow half a mile up the road and AAA won't be there for hours, Si? Don't be stupid now," Naoki said, reminding me about my car.

"Fuck," I muttered before sitting on the window ledge with one of my arms crossed over my chest. "I forgot my car was buried."

The snow . . . It was beautiful. I always found it fascinating. It was something about the quiet that came with heavy snowfall that gave me a bit of solace.

As a child, I was the same way. I'd lay in the snow, my eyes to the sky, snowflakes falling on my face. I'd lay out there for hours, fully covered in a snowsuit, snow boots, and mitts. Sometimes, as a grown-ass woman, I still appreciated it. However, now, I hated heavy snowfall. It made life for me a pain in the ass. Now, especially. I was stuck here until the service call I'd put in to roadside assistance was answered, which most likely wouldn't be until the morning. I was trapped. Trapped inside of a house with a man and his wife. A man I wanted to fuck so bad, the seat of my panties was drenched with pussy juice. If he so much as breathed on me, I'd probably have a damn orgasm.

It was sick.

"Yeah, exactly. Just . . ." Naoki sighed. "Just try to get some sleep, boo. And don't fuck that woman's husband in her house, Si."

I pushed up from the window ledge and repositioned the blackout curtains. "Oh, trust me, I'm not." I paused and rolled my eyes. "I'll talk to you later."

I wanted Jahad, but not bad enough to lose my dignity. I knew he had a wife. Sleeping with him now would be foul as fuck. I couldn't help the fantasies—trust me, I've tried. As long as I stayed away from him, I would be good, and since working here, I'd done a great job keeping distance between us, and for good reason.

I avoided that man like the damn plague. If I heard him in the hallway, I'd stay in my room until he was gone. Any interaction with him was dangerous. Honestly, I'd never in my life been as powerless in the presence of anyone as I was in the presence of him. Not even Amiri could make time slow and my heart race at once. There was something about that man that was like kryptonite.

"Love you."

After I told her I loved her, too, we hung up. I took a deep breath and tossed my phone onto the bed. In order for me to sleep, I'd need a stiff-ass drink. I'd had a glass of wine over dinner, per Leighton's request. She told me there was a whole walk-in cellar in the kitchen that I could help myself to—off hours, of course.

We shared a dry, awkward laugh. Little did she know, I didn't just want to help myself to the wine—I wanted to help myself to her damn husband, too. Since I couldn't have the latter, I'd help myself to that wine. I didn't know the name of the wine I had earlier, but it was exquisite.

I walked out of the bedroom and stood in the dark, quiet hallway for a moment. The house was so quiet and still, I felt like if I took one step, I would wake them up. The only light illuminating the hall was from the snow falling over the skylight, and the luminosity coming from the small pendant lights lining the staircase. Aside from the soft sound of snoring, the house was completely quiet. So quiet, I could nearly hear my own heart racing.

I took slow, careful strides toward the staircase. Biting my bottom lip, I hoped and prayed they didn't creak once I walked down them. Thankfully, they didn't.

Once I got to the bottom of the stairs, I let go of the breath I'd been holding. Since I was on the main floor, and not literally next door to them anymore, I was a lot more comfortable. I hurriedly treaded across the glistening white marble floors, toward the kitchen that wasn't too far away. Just like upstairs, the main floor was just as dimly illuminated. However, it was a lot brighter since there was more space.

Turning into the kitchen, I opted out of turning the light on since the light above the stove was bright enough to help me on my quest to finding the wine cellar. Walking barefoot across heated floors was a luxury I could really get used to. I had never been the type to walk around anywhere barefoot, but it felt like wearing socks and shoes on these floors would do me a disservice.

It took me a little while to finally find the wine cellar. When I did, I looked around for a good five minutes before deciding on a bottle of red wine. Shutting the light off, I walked out and closed the door with my hip. I set the wine bottle on the huge, white marble island top and turned around to eye the many closed cabinets. Now which one of these could hold wineglasses?

The kitchen was massive with about fifteen ceiling-high cabinets. I turned around to look underneath the island to see if they had some shit specially made that held wineglasses. I was annoyed to see they didn't.

Pushing up off the island, I started my search. After a couple of minutes, I finally found a wineglass and a corkscrew too. By the time I found both, I didn't even want to pour a damn glass. I sat down and sipped an elegant, seven-hundred-dollar bottle of wine straight from the neck of its bottle.

As I sat there, looking around the big-ass, state-of-the-art kitchen, I lightly snorted and shook my head. This was what I wanted with Amiri. Luxury. We were heading in that direction. With his influencer career and with me getting my foot in the doula business, we were setting up for a promising future. We had the nice luxury condo, cars, and hefty bank accounts, but I needed devotion and happiness too. Without that, I didn't want any of this shit.

I wondered if I'd ever get that. *This.* With the happiness, the devotion, and the baby too. The baby . . . well, the baby would probably never come. I'd come to terms with that. I accepted it. Only because I was okay with no baby as long as I had him. Amiri. My eyes misted with tears when I was hit with the realization that this, without the baby, probably would never even happen for me. Hell, even if I did get a glimpse into a lifestyle similar to this one, I was far too damaged to fully accept it without giving it the side-eye.

Amiri had ruined my trust in men. Amiri, and shit . . . Jahad too. He seemed like such a great man. He took care of his wife. The way she spoke about him, he seemed like a great man, and if I hadn't fucked him, I would think he was too.

Hooking my warm toes over the barstool's footrest, I sat against its small backing and picked that bottle up again. Taking another swig, I frowned at the bitter taste. I liked my wine to have a bit of sweetness to it, but if I wanted to feel the wine, I had to go for something with a high alcohol content and Opus One was hitting just at under fifteen percent. I was going to be good and drunk after I finished this. Yes, a bitch was finishing the whole bottle.

Leighton might not have meant I could finish a bottle of wine when she said I could help myself to the cellar, but I had a strong feeling she wasn't going to miss it. Especially since she couldn't drink, and there were over a hundred bottles back there.

I sat in that big-ass kitchen, drinking, crying, and thinking for a good thirty minutes. I was good and drunk too. So tipsy, I didn't realize the bottle was damn near empty until I went for another sip. Because I wanted every drop, I finally poured what was left into the stemless wineglass I'd found. I wasn't finished drinking either, just because the bottle was empty. I needed more. I didn't know what exactly I was trying to accomplish by drinking, but I couldn't stop now. I was too far in it.

I got up and headed right back for that cellar, glass of wine in hand. This time, I staggered around, looking for something lighter. After settling for a random bottle of Moscato I lucked up and found among an ocean of reds, I headed out, careful not to bump into anything on the way out.

"Oh fuck!" I shrieked when I walked out of the cellar and bumped right into him.

It was like déjà fucking vu. When I bumped into him, the little bit of wine I had left splashed onto his white wifebeater. Jahad didn't even look down at his shirt—his eyes stayed on me. I couldn't tell if he was upset or not. One look at the deep furrow in his thick, silky black eyebrows, you'd think he was extremely pissed. But his eyes, those dark orbs of his, held a certain softness.

He was so close, I could smell the heavy scent of liquor and the faint scent of his cologne. A scent that had been burned into my nostrils since Pandora's. He was so tall, towering over me. I'd be lying if I said I didn't like it, though. I appreciated how close he was, how close we were.

With my eyes on his, I was a bit speechless. They were so captivating, and sultry, and dreamy, and intense, and magnetic. I could stare into them for hours. But I couldn't. I didn't need to. I needed to put some distance between us.

So, I tore my eyes away from his and maneuvered around him, careful not to lose my footing. I didn't even want to stagger. My steps were careful and calculated. I was sure he could smell the wine on me, but I didn't *want* to *look* like I was as drunk as I was.

I walked back over to the island, setting the empty glass and fresh bottle of wine down. I felt his eyes all over me. Those magnetic orbs bored into me so deep, it was as if he was staring into my soul, searching for something.

"I'm so sorry about that. You scared the shit out of me," I finally said, once I was comfortable with the distance I'd put between us.

He finally looked down at the wet, red stain on his shirt. "Oh, you good."

And then his eyes were right back on me. He watched me the entire short walk to the sink. He didn't stop watching me until his back was to me, finally giving me time to discreetly ogle him. He was wearing a white wifebeater, a pair of red and black checkered pajama pants, and he was barefoot. Of course he was. Walking on these heated floors with shoes would really be a fucking disservice. However, seeing a man confidently walk around barefoot was new. Amiri kept his feet in a pair of slides or designer house shoes. I was surprised to see that Jahad had pretty nice feet, too.

"Couldn't sleep?" he asked before turning around, forcing my eyes to the empty glass.

I shook my head. "You?"

He shook his too. "Hell naw."

I swallowed and looked down into the empty glass, wishing I could take a hefty sip.

"Too much on my mind to sleep," he continued.

I was sure his mind was cluttered with whatever was going on between him and Leighton at dinner. She called me down moments before they arrived. When I walked into that dining room and saw the way the table was set, I just knew I wasn't supposed to be there. Just as I was getting ready to get up and leave, they walked into the dining room. The look on Jahad's face was stone cold, flat, and emotionless. But his eyes? His eyes told another story. He was upset. Pissed. I didn't know him well enough to pick up on cues like that, but I'd seen anger like that many times in my own reflection, so I knew. The eyes told no lies.

The tone of voice usually didn't either. When he told me I could stay, after Leighton tried to clean up whatever mess she'd caused, I knew for certain. These muthafuckas were going through some *thangs*.

However, unhappy, happy, miserable, or not, those weren't grounds to cheat on his wife. In my eyes, nothing gave him the right to do that. So, I still looked at Jahad like an ain't-shit nigga. Except he was an ain't-shit nigga with a good, big dick I couldn't seem to get off my mind.

Within all of that "ain't shit" was a good man too. I couldn't quite put a finger on it, but there was something strikingly different about Jahad that somehow separated him from the ain't-shit niggas I was used to. Amiri more specifically. Jahad had an air about him. As I looked over at him, I figured it out. It wasn't an air. It was that BDE. Big Dick Energy. Amiri didn't have that because he didn't have *that*. Jahad was indeed a different caliber of man.

Still a dog-ass nigga, nonetheless. A dog-ass nigga I wanted to fuck me.

Fuck. Who was I?

"You want to talk about it?"

He clamped his top teeth over his bottom lip and slowly shook his head. "I can't imagine that helping me." He paused and his eyes traveled from my eyes to the rest of me. "At all."

What the fuck was I thinking? Asking him if he wanted to talk about it? I was tripping. I needed to be taking my ass up to the bedroom. But the room was beginning to spin just a little, and I was afraid that if I stood to leave now, I would expose myself, as if the two bottles of wine on the island hadn't exposed me enough.

"I hope me being down here is okay," I said, lifting the bottle of wine. "Leighton said I could help myself to the cellar."

"Help yourself to whatever you like. It's cool," he casually told me, not knowing he was pretty much telling me I could help myself to his dick. Because that was what I wanted. More than this wine. More than this job. More than anything else in the fucking world. But the wine would have to do, since his dick was someone else's.

He smiled and nodded toward the bottle of red. "Looks like you've helped yourself already, though."

I coyly smiled and wrapped my hand around the Moscato, like a damn alcoholic. I bet I looked like a fool, coddling a bottle of wine, like I was afraid he'd take it from me or something. I quickly unwrapped my hand from around it and placed a piece of hair behind my ear. He was making me nervous. He always made me nervous. The way he looked at me made me feel like there was something on my damn face.

"Yeah," I awkwardly breathed out.

"What's keeping you up, love?" he asked. "Bad dreams?"

I snickered. "In a way. Depends on what you consider bad."

Hmph was the only sound he made as he turned to finish dabbing at his shirt. I watched him as he turned the water off. He was quiet as he opened one of the cabinets and grabbed a glass. When he turned back around, his eyes were on me. It was like they were programmed to fall on me any time we were in a room together. The shit was intimidating. Tonight especially, since I was drunk and probably had dried-up tears on my face. I wondered if I looked as bad as I felt. Hopefully not.

Jahad stood at the island, reached into a cabinet under it, and came back up with a bottle of Clase Azul. A bottle I had never seen before, but because it had Clase Azul's signature look and style, I figured that was what it was. However, the bottle wasn't white and blue; it was black and silver. Fancy and undoubtedly expensive. Just like everything else in the damn house.

We awkwardly sat there in silence for a couple of minutes. I wanted to reach over and grab the corkscrew, but because it was right next to him, I stayed put. I was afraid that if I got too close again, I would make good on the intrusive thoughts of putting my lips on him.

Instead of moving an inch, I circled my finger around the rim of my glass and gazed around the room, trying to look everywhere but at him. His energy was so fucking compelling, and not because he smelled good. Not because I knew that when I looked at him, I'd be looking into the face of a fucking god. But because . . . *it just was.*

The longer I avoided eye contact, the more I wanted to look at him. It was insane. I needed another got damn drink, but I needed the damn corkscrew.

I swallowed as I was forced to look in his direction. He had that half-filled glass to his lips. Those fucking lips. Lips I wanted on me. Lips I wanted *all* over me. I was jealous. *Instantly* jealous of that tequila. I wanted him to drink *me* the way he had before. The way I'd dreamed about for weeks. The way I'd fantasized about. His lips. His tongue. Those hands. All of him. God, I wanted him on me, so bad.

"You all right?" he asked after setting his glass down.

No. I wasn't okay. Because I *really* wanted to ride his dick on the kitchen island while his pregnant wife—my client—slept upstairs. I felt horrible. I couldn't shake the unwavering, gnawing feeling. The feeling of wanting him. Inside of me. On my face. In my mouth. *Everywhere.*

I felt like such a fucked-up person. I didn't want to be the source of another woman's agony after I'd been that woman on more than one occasion.

I just . . . God, *I wanted him.* Didn't give a fuck about what they had going on. Why should I care about what he was doing, right? I didn't owe Leighton any loyalty. But I did, in my opinion, owe her respect.

Never in a million years did I think I, the brokenhearted, would be okay with being an accessory to breaking a heart. Regardless of how okay I was with it, at the moment, I couldn't do it.

"Yeah," I told him as I eyed the corkscrew. "I need that."

He looked down at the corkscrew and raised a brow before running his eyes all over me. Studying me. Yeah, he could tell I was drunk. Oh the fuck well. "You do?"

I drew back with a light frown. "Yeah, that's kind of why I'm asking for it."

I licked my lips and wondered if I'd licked them as slow as it felt like I had. Seemed like everything was moving in slow motion, and not only because that was what time seemed to do when he was near me.

I was drunk. Every passing second I stood there, I felt the liquor consume me more and more, and I needed to take my ass upstairs before I really did something I'd regret in the morning.

"It looks like you've already had enough to drink," he said before putting that glass back up to his lips.

I swallowed. Swallowed because I had never wanted to be a glass so bad in my fucking life. "I'm a grown woman, Mr. Baptiste. I can drink as much as I . . . as much as I want."

He nodded and corrected me. "Jahad."

"I know your name," I told him, nodding toward the corkscrew. "The corkscrew, please."

"Use it. Mr. Baptiste is my father," he told me as he finally slid the got damn corkscrew across the island.

"Ms. Evaline calls you Mr. Baptiste," I reminded him.

He eyed me from head to toe again. This time, in such a seductive way, the seat of my panties was immediately drenched. "You're not Ms. Evaline."

A chill ran down my spine as our eyes met again. I was stuck there. My limbs were useless. I wanted a drink. Needed one, even. Had gotten the corkscrew to take that drink, yet I hadn't done anything with it.

I didn't have time to pick it up before he made his way to my side of the island, where I'd surely lose the use of my limbs. I would have to. Felt like if I did move, it would be to touch him, and because I couldn't do that, I stood there as stiff as a board, with labored breathing as he got closer and closer to me.

He grabbed the neck of the wine bottle and opened it for me with those fucking eyes on me. I swallowed and finally found the strength to move away from him.

That magnetic force pulled me in his direction with so much aggression, I damn near gave in to it. But I didn't. I was able to move an inch. However, I needed a lot more than an inch. I needed to carry my ass upstairs.

Darting my eyes away from his, I looked toward the wide walkway leading me out of the kitchen, wondering if I could make it that far. Wondering if I did move, if I would stagger and fall. Wondering if I did move, would I just end up in his arms, my lips pressed against his. I was afraid it would be the latter.

Gripping the countertop, I turned my gaze to it and took slow, deliberate breaths as my heart rate continued to quicken. Again, I was powerless against him. I'd known this since Pandora's. The way he commanded me in that room . . . the way he made me do some of the freakiest shit I'd ever done in my life . . . he had to have some sort of hold on me. I happily choked on his dick. Happily swallowed every drop of his fucking cum.

I never did that with Amiri. Never wanted to. Never even thought about it. But with Jahad, a man I didn't know, I let go of all of my inhibitions. Gave myself to him freely and I wanted to give myself to him again, knowing he had a wife. Knowing she was upstairs. This was why I needed to stay the fuck away from him. Why I needed to move more than a fucking inch away from him!

Once he opened the bottle for me, he went as far as pouring my glass, too. When he stopped midway through, I motioned for him to continue, and he chuckled.

"Right up to the rim, *Mr. Baptiste*," I said, finally finding my voice. It came out just as cracked up as I knew it would. A telltale of just how drunk and horny I was.

"Jahad," he stressed, again, after filling my glass. "What will I have to do to get you to listen?"

He slid the glass over to me and stepped closer as well. That inch I stepped away from him? Useless. He was right back in my personal space, ogling me.

My heart raced as I kept my eyes on my glass of wine, refusing to look up at him. He was watching me *again*. Because I didn't have clothes of my own here, Leighton had given me a brand-new set of pale pink silk pajamas. The shirt was buttoned and short-sleeve. They came with shorts but I chose the oversized pants, for obvious reasons. However, despite how modestly dressed I was, I knew he could see how hard my nipples were through the thin silk fabric.

As I shifted my gaze up to him, my eyes locked with his. I expected him to shy away, but he didn't. In fact, his stare grew more intense. And in that moment, it was as if the rate of my heart slowed. How? It dropped significantly from its racing. Not only did time slow more than before, but everything did. Him lifting the glass of Clase I didn't notice him bring over with him to his lips. My breathing. The ticking of the clock on the wall. Everything . . . seemed to slow. The slower things moved, the more I wanted him.

My pussy throbbed with desire. So much desire, I wondered if it was possible to have an orgasm with no physical contact because that was what I was on the verge of.

My cheeks grew hot, and I sucked in a hefty gust of air, grounding myself. I needed to go. Suddenly, that fear of whether I'd fall or not didn't seem too scary anymore. I'd take my chances.

I hoped that when I did pass him, I wouldn't let that undying hunger for him win. If I took the long way out of the kitchen by walking on the other side of the island, I'd be fine.

"Good night, *Mr. Baptiste*." I turned to walk away and lightly staggered. Holding up the hand with the glass in it, I giggled. "Whoa."

I looked up and Jahad's eyes were on me, as fucking always. With raised brows, he said, "Maybe you should have a seat."

I shook my head. "Uh-uh. I'm fine. I got it."

I swiped a piece of hair from my face and took a deep breath before taking another wobbly step. Fuck. I lowered my head and shook it. Got damn it. I'd sat up here, cried over a bottle of wine, and drank the whole thing like I was at home. I couldn't even walk a few steps, how in the hell was I going to make it to the elevator? The stairs, I wouldn't dare tackle. But apparently I couldn't tackle the elevator.

Jahad twisted the cap on his bottle and shook his head. "Sit down."

"No, thank you. I said, I got it," I said with an attitude. "I have to go upstairs."

I really did.

I couldn't be around him. I wanted him so bad, my mouth literally salivated with desire. The desire to taste him. All of him. The pre-cum that oozed from the tip of his fat, mushroom-shaped head, the thick, veiny skin over his long dick, his balls, and his bitter cum. I wanted to taste him so damn bad. So, I needed to carry my horny, pathetic, desperate, drunk ass upstairs.

With my hand firmly wrapped around the bottle of wine, I took another step to leave and, like before, I stumbled. Except this time, when I stumbled, he was there to grab me before I could hit the floor.

I closed my eyes at the feel of electricity shooting down my spine. At such a simple, meaningless grab of my elbow, my entire body heated. Not in a bad way. In the same way that electricity shot through my body. First, it started at the contact point, my elbow. Then it rapidly made its way throughout my entire body, shocking and igniting me in a way that made me completely fucking powerless.

He carefully took the bottle of wine and the wineglass from my hands, our fingers brushing up against one another, creating more jolts of electricity. More . . . heat. More desire. My God.

I shifted my eyes up and away from the floor and at him. He felt it too. He had to. The look in his eyes was familiar. That passion. That desire. The way his full lips laid lazily agape was like an invitation to them. Or was I just imagining things? They were delectable. I wanted them on me just as badly as I wanted the rest of him on me. He felt the same way because, before I knew it, his hand went from my elbow to the back of my neck, where he delicately pulled me forward. I exhaled and melted into his arms.

Finally.

Finally, being in his arms again after wanting to be for so long was like an addict getting that first hit after being without it for far too long. I needed to be careful. I had to be careful. But in this moment, with his lips against mine and his tart, tequila-tainted tongue roaming around my mouth, I didn't care to be careful. I wanted to overdose. I wanted to consume him just at the brink of overconsumption, because who knew how long it would be before I felt this again? These sparks? This . . . heat? This passion? Probably never.

In that moment, as we stood in the middle of his state-of-the-art kitchen with his wife upstairs, it was just the two of us. Nothing else existed. Not his wife. Not Amiri. Nothing. The world didn't even exist. We were floating. At least, that was what it felt like. I felt like I was levitating. It could have been the liquor, but in my heart, I knew it was him.

Slow, passionate kisses turned into aggressive, animalistic kisses. Our tongues didn't do that two-step. There was no rhythm, just hunger.

Jahad backed me up against the island and immediately picked me up. With my arms wrapped around his neck, we went back to hungrily kissing one another. And then came the fucking emotions. It was the liquor. Had to be the liquor. The levitation? No. But these tears? The tears that rolled down my cheeks and seeped into our hungry mouths? The liquor was surely to blame for that.

It was just that I wanted this man so fucking bad. I'd been avoiding him. I'd been professional. I'd tried to avoid this, but it was as if fate wanted us together. What were the odds of him and his wife being my clients after that night we shared? And this . . . ? How was this happening? I hated cheaters and women who willingly gave their bodies to men they knew were spoken for. However, here I was, with another woman's husband's tongue down my throat and . . . I fucking loved it.

I felt horrible.

But I felt so got damn good.

Too good to stop it. Too good to give a *muthafuck*.

Jahad pulled away from the kiss and aggressively ripped the pajama shirt open, sending buttons scattering about the marble floors. I moaned and tossed my head back when he greedily attacked my sensitive, hard nipples. His mouth was so wet. So warm.

He lightly tugged on my nipple with his teeth after every suckle, giving me the right amount of pleasure and pain. He then cupped my other breast and went back and forth between both titties, making my pussy gush.

I grabbed his face and pulled him away before I slid back on that massive island, inviting him to more than just my titties. As if he could read my mind, he grabbed the waistband of my pants and tugged them down. Grabbing my waist, he pulled me closer to the edge of the counter. For a couple of seconds, Jahad just stared at me. I watched as his brown eyes slowly washed over my body, studying it in a way that was like he wanted to remember every little detail about it. He brushed his thumb over my rose tattoo before leaning down and placing a kiss on it. I moaned and ran my hand over the back of his neck.

"Pretty fuckin' pussy," he mumbled, before he rubbed his face against it.

I moaned and slapped my hand against the marble countertop. His face against my pussy felt so fucking good. He wasn't a man who was afraid of getting his face wet. At all. He welcomed the pussy juice. The way he moaned into my pussy as I felt my juices run down the crack of my ass, spilling onto the countertop, told me everything I needed to know. Jahad *loved* pussy. The way he pampered it. The way he made love to it with everything, and not just his dick, told me exactly who he was.

A pussy connoisseur.

The first brush of his tongue against my clit made my entire body quiver. I whimpered. It felt so got damn good, and when he grabbed my hips and pulled me further to the edge of the island, closer to his face, I yelped.

"Ooh!"

He held a vise grip on my waist as he wildly moved his head from side to side, softly licking and sucking simultaneously. My eyes rolled to the back of my head and, for a brief moment, I couldn't move. I was literally paralyzed with pleasure. However, those tears continued to run down the sides of my face.

With my lips parted, my eyes rolling to the back of my head and the way I couldn't move, I was sure I looked possessed. And I felt every bit of it. My eyes finally found their rightful position and landed on the ceiling. The ceiling that separated us from her, where she laid, asleep while her husband's head moved skillfully between my legs.

In that moment, I was grateful.

Grateful for whatever issues they had that made him eat my pussy like he hadn't been fed in years. As fucked up as it was, I felt it. And I felt it without a remorseful bone in my body. In this moment, while she slept, with his head between my legs, Jahad was mine. Regardless of how much he wasn't, he was now, and I was going to enjoy it.

Sucking in air, I tore my eyes away from the ceiling and looked down at him.

To my surprise, he looked up at me, planting soft kisses on my pearl tongue, causing me to shudder. I was in the middle of my third orgasm, my eyes locked on his, easily making this the most intense of the three. I loved him. I loved him so fucking much. At least, I did now. For the moment. I was sure that when it was over, I'd hate him and I'd probably hate myself more. But, right now, I loved his ass.

What he did to me, the way he pampered my pussy and made love to my soul, how was that even possible? My soul was intangible, inaccessible, but Jahad had made his way to it, bypassing my heart with such ease, it scared me a little.

Who was this man?

And why did he make me float?

He stood up and the rate of my heart quickened at the sight of my juices painted all over his face. It was beautiful. The best piece of art in this muthafucka, for sure. He grabbed one of the strings dangling from his pajama pants and pulled it. Moments later, they fell, and I laid eyes on what truly was the best piece of art, not only in this house but in the fucking world.

His dick was beautiful. A real work of art. Bigger than I remembered. Maybe because he was harder now than he was in that room. Maybe because he'd wanted this, just as badly as I'd wanted it. Dreamed of it. Fantasized about it.

I arched my back and bit down on my bottom lip when he slowly slid inside of me. "Fuck," I moaned with deeply furrowed eyebrows.

I placed my hands on his thighs to push him back a little and he smacked them away. "Relax. Take it. Let me fill you up," Jahad said into my ear with his hands back around my waist, pulling me closer to him. The closer he pulled me, the deeper he went, the more he stretched me.

"Waaait," I moaned.

"Wait for what? Hmm?" He grunted before pulling back a little. He looked down at his dick and bit down on his bottom lip. "Fuck."

His dick was drenched in my cream. I didn't think his dick could get any more beautiful but I was wrong. Covered with my creamy pussy juices, it was breathtaking. So much so, that when he went back to slide inside of me, I relaxed, grabbed his waist, and pulled him toward me while he pulled me closer.

"Ahhhh," I moaned, once his dick hit the back of my pussy, venturing off into places no one else had ever been.

He sat there for a moment, hands wrapped around my waist, face buried into my neck, savoring the moment. I immediately imagined him savoring it because he knew, like I knew, this would be the last time. It had to be. We shouldn't have been doing it. That was an unspoken truth neither of us needed to *address*. We just didn't give a fuck. Desire won.

Jahad slowly pulled back and I contracted my pussy muscles around his dick, wanting him to stay right where he was. I watched as he slowly closed his eyes and clenched his jaw muscle. When he opened his eyes and looked down at me, I saw it again. That hunger. That desire. The desire we couldn't let go of. The magnetism neither of us could avoid. For me, it was too much, so I closed my eyes to avoid it. However, I felt his eyes burning into mine, forcing me to open them again. When I did, he clamped his top teeth over his bottom lip and quickly flipped me over.

I bent over on my knees while he plummeted his dick in my gushy pussy from behind. He fucked me mercilessly with his fist gripping a handful of my messy hair. I groaned in pleasure, forgetting to muffle my moans, and he quickly clamped his hand over my mouth, steady giving me death strokes, making my eyes roll to the back of my head and my pussy violently squirt where Ms. Evaline and Maurice would prepare breakfast in a few hours.

Through a muffled moan, I said, "You fuckin' me so good, Mr. Baptiste."

In response, he grunted and took his hand from my mouth before then gripping my neck. He buried his dick deep inside of me when he pressed his face against mine and whispered in my ear, "Jahad."

I threw my ass back and bit my bottom lip before murmuring, "Mr. Bap—"

Before I could finish my statement, he slid out of me. I looked over my shoulder at him lightly stroking his dick, chest glistening with sweat, remnants of me still dripping from his beard, and wanted to slap him. I was right at the brink of another fucking orgasm.

"What are you doing?" I whimpered.

"What's my name?"

"What?" I exasperatedly asked him, panting.

He roughly slapped me on my ass. "My name."

"Seriously? Come . . . come on." I moved my ass back and placed a piece of hair behind my ear.

Because I was still drunk as hell, the room spun a little, and my words slurred. All I wanted was his dick inside of me. Everything else—frivolous shit like his name—was the last thing on my mind. Games too. I wanted him inside of me.

Since he hadn't come back to me, I turned around and got off the counter with my bottom lip pinched between my teeth, but he stopped me. He gripped my neck again and tilted my head back by moving his big hand up my chin.

"Where you goin'?" he asked.

"Come on . . . *Please*," I begged, reaching out to touch his dick.

I was fiending, literally. So much so, I could barely stay still. I was a quivering, horny mess and he couldn't have cared less.

"Please, who?" he taunted before stepping back and rubbing his pre-cum-dripping dick over my lips.

I looked up at him and ran my tongue over its head and moaned. "Jahad."

He groaned and pushed his dick in my mouth, straight to the back of my throat, without giving warning. I gagged so hard, I damn near threw up on him. But that didn't stop him. He grabbed the back of my head, and this time slowly pushed his dick to the back of my throat, giving me time to relax enough to take it.

"Open it," he directed.

I did. I opened my mouth as wide as I could and he gyrated his hips in circular motions, slowly and sensually fucking my throat. It was the sexiest shit I'd ever done. And his face? The sexiest shit I'd ever seen. A second or so later, he pulled his dick from my mouth, grabbed me by the waist, and sat me in a puddle of my squirt. Opening my legs, he slid into me this time and there we were again. Eyes locked, fireworks erupting, time moving slow, just connected. This time, he didn't run from it. Neither did I. We stared into each other's eyes so deep, it was almost as if I could see his soul. It was screaming out for me, the same way I knew he saw mine screaming out for him.

Jahad hooked his arm under the bend in my leg and held it up. He scooted me to the very edge of the island and gave me slow, rhythmic strokes without breaking eye contact. The furrow in his eyes was questionable. I couldn't tell if it was there because he was confused, or if it was there because the pussy was drenching his dick. Either way, it was sexy as hell. An image that would surely be etched in my mind until the day I died.

He ran his thumb over my cheek, swiping away a tear I didn't realize had fallen. He then brushed that same thumb over my parted lips. He was so gentle. So . . . passionate. So much so, the thought of never having him again petrified me. I should have stayed in bed. Shouldn't have come to this kitchen. Had I not, I wouldn't have gotten too drunk to run away from him. Wouldn't have gotten too drunk to escape this. This was torture. The good kind. The kind I wanted to last forever. The kind of torture that was only torture because it wouldn't last forever.

Jahad looked down at his dick and shook his head before clenching his lips together and throwing his head back. He was about to cum, and I wanted to catch it. Couldn't wait to catch it. But light suddenly filling the dimly lit kitchen caught both of us off guard and he came inside of me.

CHAPTER 17

Jahad

I stood at the sink in the bathroom connected to my office and took a deep breath. With my head down, I shook it from side to side. Looking over at the glass of tequila, I picked it up and finished it. I couldn't look at myself. Avoided that mirror like I should have avoided Sienna. I wanted to. I wanted to because I knew I *needed* to. I'd done a pretty good job at that, but avoiding her wasn't enough. Sometimes the shit felt impossible.

She was supposed to be a one-night stand. She wasn't supposed to be here. If she wasn't here, I wouldn't have fucked her. I had no way of contacting her. Didn't know shit about her at Pandora's. Now I knew her. Knew her name wasn't Naoki. Knew she was really twenty-six. Knew her favorite color was really yellow. Now I knew her address, and her phone number too. I knew her Instagram name. Knew her Facebook name too. I knew too much. Too much to stay away from her. Wanted her too much to stay the fuck away from her too.

I knew she was in that kitchen before I entered it. I sat at my desk and finished a half-empty bottle of Clase Azul while I watched her finish and cry over an entire bottle of wine. It wasn't purposely done. I'd only sat there and watched her for so long because I was trying not to join her. But temptation forced me out of my chair. That, and my hard-ass dick.

I didn't leave the office until she went into the cellar. I wanted her to bump into me. Wanted to feel her as much as I could.

A nigga was bugging.

I could blame my actions tonight on the liquor—a weak-ass nigga would—but I knew better. I would have done what I did sober, and I knew Sienna would have done the same. Alcohol wasn't to blame for either of our actions.

Desire was. Chemistry, too. We had it. In a quiet room, it was there. I felt it, she felt it, but we ignored it. Ignored it until we couldn't ignore it anymore.

I was in my office because I couldn't sleep. After dinner, I never went up to the room. Left Leighton up there to sit in the shit she'd pulled. Regardless of the red flags that were constantly thrown in my face, I never stopped trying. I stepped out, accepted her hall pass, and had sex with a woman. A mesmerizing woman I couldn't get off my mind. But . . . she wasn't enough. Regardless of what I felt with her, she was no Leighton, so I set my feelings for her aside and decided to put effort into my marriage. Tried to look beyond the tension, the awkwardness, and Leighton's constant unhappiness.

After the ride from Sienna's car, I stopped in the kitchen and asked Ms. Evaline to prepare a special dinner for Leighton and me. I was stepping into my romantic bag. Since she was confined to a bed and didn't like the idea of having to be wheeled into a restaurant for dinner, I said fuck it, we'll have dinner at home. Did that a few times before she turned into this woman I didn't know. Hadn't done it in a few months so I thought tonight would be good. I was wrong. She knew if I wanted to have dinner in the dining room, there was obviously a reason. But she invited Sienna, and I told her she could stay.

I relished having her there. Didn't give a fuck about prancing the woman I'd fucked in her face. Boldly locked eyes with shorty every now and then too. I just . . . didn't give a fuck. Leighton didn't notice. Not with her face in her phone most of the night.

My plans were pointless. It was like Leighton wanted me on animal shit. Like she wanted me to snap on her, give her a reaction and turn into the nigga she didn't like years ago. So, I fucked shorty. Fucked her on the marble countertop Leighton had specially made. Leighton loved that fucking island. And now I did too.

Taking a deep breath, I finally looked up in the mirror and ran my hand over the top of my waves. Tilting my head back, I ran my tongue over my bottom lip. Traces of Sienna's cum was still there. I was tempted to leave it. Leave it and greet Leighton with a good-morning forehead kiss she didn't deserve. I was fucked up and pissed, a combination that had never mixed well with me. Not only was her taste on my lips, but there was dried-up cum in my beard too.

As pissed as I was at Leighton, I couldn't leave traces of Sienna anywhere on me. Disrespecting my wife, regardless of how I felt about her, was something I'd never do, despite my past actions.

Turning the hot water on, I let it heat up, cupped my hand under it, and splashed my face with it until it was drenched. I was immediately reminded of what it was like to have her juices in my face just a couple of minutes ago and my dick immediately bricked. Looking down at it, I sighed and shook my head.

I reached over to the floating glass shelf and grabbed facial cleanser and beard wash before erasing evidence of my betrayal from my face. However, regardless of how much I scrubbed, it would always be a constant reminder on both my heart and mind.

Five minutes later, I walked out of the bathroom.

"Sorry to keep you waiting," I said to Ms. Evaline before sitting in the big recliner across from the couch she was sitting on, a nervous wreck.

Her nerves were warranted. She walked in on us, just as I came inside of Sienna's pussy. Caught us red-handed and walked right out of the kitchen as if she hadn't seen a thing. But because I was a man and she was an employee here who'd just witnessed her boss cheat on his wife, I refused to brush it under the rug and pretend what happened didn't happen.

"It's okay. Listen, Mr. Baptiste. You don't have to worry about me telling Mrs. Baptiste anything. I'm here to work and work only. Your business is your business and yours alone. I can assure you that—"

"Hang on," I interrupted with my hand up. "You don't need to assure me anything, Ms. Evaline. I didn't call you down here to my office to make sure you kept what you witnessed between the three of us. I'd never ask you to keep a secret. I would never purposely put you in an uncomfortable position. I called you down here to apologize."

Her face washed over with a mixture of relief and confusion. "Apologize? Mr. Baptiste, this is your home."

"And you're a guest here," I told her before clearing my throat and pinching the bridge of my nose.

This was an uncomfortable conversation. I didn't like to have uncomfortable conversations. Not ones like this. I'd just been caught with my dick inside of the doula, while my wife slept upstairs. As a man who prided himself on integrity, I hated how this made me look. I'd never been the type of man who really cared too much about opinions, but I never wanted to be pegged as an unfaithful husband. But that was who I was now, an unfaithful husband who not only had a hard time speaking about his infidelities but had a hard time looking at himself in the mirror as well.

The fucked-up part about it all was that if Sienna walked into this office, ass naked, and put her pussy on a platter, I would fucking feast. Not because I wanted to, but because she made me weak.

I could admit it. Inwardly. I would never say that out loud. There was only one woman who'd held power on me before her and she bore my last name. This thing . . . this hold Sienna had on me was unholy and detrimental to my life.

"I was wrong. My actions do not reflect who I am as a man, a boss, and they most certainly do not reflect who I am as a husband," I told her, my eyes centered on hers, watching, waiting.

There it was.

It was subtle, but I noticed.

The doubt. The judgment. I noticed it. I couldn't say I didn't blame her. My words didn't hold much weight. Not even against myself. I'd just pondered giving my wife a forehead kiss with another woman's cum on my lips. The fuck type of husband was I, really? I'd just fucked that woman on a piece of furniture she'd spent days sketching for constructors. I wasn't as noble as I claimed to be, now was I? Couldn't fucking be. So, as much as it stung for Ms. Evaline's eyes to shimmer with doubt, I couldn't feel anything toward it because I'd given her reason to doubt me.

"I understand, Mr. Baptiste," Ms. Evaline said, fiddling with her fingers.

"Have I made working here uncomfortable for you?"

"No, you haven't." She paused and pursed her lips together. "But . . . if it's not out of my place, can I say something?"

I motioned for her to go ahead as I leaned back against the chair, resting my arms on the armrest, my hands dangling over the edges.

"I've been working for you for years, Mr. Baptiste, and within those years, I've only seen you as a noble man who loves his wife. You cherish the ground she walks on. And Mrs. Baptiste, she loves you the same.

"I'd be lying if I said I haven't noticed some changes around here over the past couple of years, though. The house, it's gotten a little colder and you know I'm not talkin' about the temperature. The air is thick. Somethin' in my spirit is tellin' me that somethin' isn't right.

"But I see you every day, with a smile, coming down here, treating me and my nephew with so much kindness and love. You've always been a good man to us. I say all of that to say this . . . don't let anything change who you are as a man. Don't let the Devil tempt you, Mr. Baptiste. Don't lose your integrity. Keep lovin' your wife through the hard times. Hold on until you can't hold on no mo'. New, shiny things always look better than the old stuff." She winked. "But what you don't know is that the old stuff holds a lot of value. You only let go of when that 'old thing' no longer serves you mentally, spiritually, and emotionally. The physical?" She waved me off. "The physical, son, is weak! Eventually, the physical breaks down. At the end of the day, the only thing all of us gon' be left with is this." She paused and pointed to her heart. "If your heart ain't in it and it's not serving you on a mental, spiritual, or emotional level, then it's not for you. Until then, hold on until your hands bleed, son. You don't want to make the mistake of letting go too early just because something newer and shiny comes along. Now . . . I'm in no position to tell you what to do. I'm just an old lady with some experience with love, giving you some advice."

Standing up, I stood up in front of Ms. Evaline and opened my arms for a hug. She stood up and accepted my hug by wrapping her little arms around me. "I hear you, Ms. Evaline. Thank you. I hope you'll still view me as the noble man you've always viewed me as."

"One mistake won't change that. However, how I view you don't matter. How *you* view *you* is what matters, Mr. Baptiste."

Hours later, I woke up on the couch in my office. Bright sun rays gleaming through the sheer curtains forced me to squint. Turning over on my side, I scowled when my head pounded, thanks to all the drinking I had done just hours prior. I had a hangover. I hadn't had a fucking hangover in years. But then again, I hadn't drunk as much as I had last night in a long-ass time.

Reaching over to the coffee table, I bypassed a Stanback and two bottles of water to grab my phone. The first thing I checked was the time. It was 12:13 p.m. I never slept in late. The second thing I checked was my messages. At the top of a plethora of unread text messages was one from Sienna. A group text she'd sent to both me and Leighton. Her resignation. I'd be lying if I said I didn't see that coming. The reason she gave for resigning was personal conflict. She and I knew it ran deeper than just that. I didn't read anything beyond that. Didn't read Leighton's response either. Didn't need to know she was heartbroken about it. I was sure that when I went upstairs, she'd let me hear all about her devastation.

I set my phone down and grabbed the Stanback and the bottles of water to mentally prepare myself for what was to come when I finally did decide to go upstairs to the room. Dry apologies, empty promises to fix her attitude, excuses, and then . . . begging. Leighton was going to want me to fix it. She was going to beg me to go over to Sienna's and beg her to come back. She was going to nag me, profusely, until Sienna was back at her bedside, making life easier for her and life harder for me.

I cracked the bottle open and sat back against the soft couch cushion before taking the Stanback and chugging the water. Rubbing my temples, I sat up, grabbed the other bottle, and chugged that one, too. Reaching over, I grabbed my phone to finally look at the other text messages. Natasha wanted to get in contact with the real estate company I used to list my properties. My mother wanted to throw something at the house for Leighton to lift her spirits. Saint checked in about where we were meeting to discuss business later. Pops hit me to confirm our meeting at his hall later on tonight at eight. In the meantime, I had a meeting at three to finalize design plans for the high-rise luxury apartment building that was set to begin construction this spring.

I took a couple of deep breaths and then finally pushed up off the couch to begin my day. I didn't have time to sit and wait for my hangover to pass. I had to push through it like I pushed through everything else in life. I was always on the go. Always had been. Life never slowed down for me. Shit kept moving, regardless of what I had going on.

As I made my way through the house, on my way toward the elevator, I made sure to stop in the kitchen where Ms. Evaline and Maurice were finishing up lunch. I greeted them and thanked her. I didn't have to say for what. She knew I was referencing the talk, and the little hangover kit she had left for me.

Once I got on the elevator, I crossed my arms at the wrists and leaned back against the wall, waiting, with my eyes closed. Leighton's text message was the only message I left unopened. I didn't want to start my morning off with lengthy, emotional text messages from her. Didn't want to feel the weight of her tears spilling through her words off the screen as I read them.

Ding.

The elevator opened, and I again released a labored breath, continuing down the hall. Lauryn Hill's "Nothing Even Matters" filled the halls. I wondered *who* would be looking back at me when I walked into the room. Would she be sitting up against the headboard, in a bra and panties, legs crossed, smiling, her hand on her belly with locs pulled up? Or would she be laying underneath the covers, crying because of me? Because I let her sleep alone, knowing she hated that shit. She probably tossed and turned all night while I was down in the kitchen, while she cried . . .

Damn.

I felt like shit.

I dragged my hand down the back of my neck as I stood at the bedroom doors, heart pounding. I needed her up against the headboard with that big, beautiful belly on display, smiling at the feel of our blessing moving around inside of her. That was what I *needed.*

I walked into the room and didn't find her in the bed at all. She was sitting on the chaise lounge, staring out of the window, wearing a sheer robe. Her locs were pulled back and she wore her usual headwrap over them. She seemed so at peace, but I knew the minute she put her eyes on me, that look of serenity would be replaced with something else. Hatred. That was what it felt like sometimes. Stepping into this room, staring into my wife's eyes, it felt like she hated me. She was ice cold, and since I'd taken that hall pass, she'd only gotten colder.

Leighton didn't realize I'd come in until I closed the door behind me. She turned away from the window to face me. I was surprised to see it wasn't hatred looking back at me this time. She was sad.

She ran her hand over her belly and reached over to the side table next to her for the remote to the surround sound system.

"You slept in the office," she stated, after turning the music down.

I nodded.

"Sienna quit. Did you see her messages? She quit because we're . . . our household is a mess. Yesterday was horrible. From the time she got here, 'til the time she left this morning. Dinner was fucking insane. We're toxic. We pushed her away." She paused and scratched at the back of her head with a huff that told me tears would soon follow. "No . . . *I* pushed her away. You didn't want to sleep with me. She don't want to work for me. Am I *that* hard to deal with? Am I *that* horrible?"

Regardless of where we stood in our marriage, Leighton's tears still fucked with me. Before all of this, multiple pregnancies that came with multiple miscarriages, and then this one that came with all the risks, Leighton was a strong woman. She was resilient. Sometimes I'd joke with her and say she had a heart of steel. She was a powerful, confident woman who, although a little timid when we first met, fit in perfectly in my world because of that power and confidence.

Shorty held me down in unimaginable ways. In situations where most women would have folded, Leighton stayed right by my side. Not just as a companion but as a solid partner. A rock. My rock. I didn't choose her to be my wife because she was beautiful, had good pussy, and took me back after I cheated on her a couple of times. I asked her to be my wife because she was my rib, someone I looked to for guidance and strength when I couldn't find what I needed from within.

She wasn't weak.

She wasn't horrible.

She wasn't hard to deal with.

She'd been dealt a fucked-up hand in life. The one thing she wanted more than anything I had power to actually give her seemed intangible, and it broke her. It broke us, because shit, I wanted that intangible thing just as badly as she did. She couldn't see it breaking me, though. That was where our wires got crossed.

I didn't allow her to see it. I had to be strong. I had to hold her up, even though I really didn't want to. Even though I detested the fuck out of her for the moment. I loved my wife, loved her more than anything, but sometimes I hated her. I was human.

An hour ago, I hated her ass. Last night, I hated her so much, I fucked another woman in her kitchen. But as I stood before her, watching her, the broken woman I married who hadn't always been broken, I loved her. Loved her more than life itself.

That was marriage, though. The real shit about marriage. The shit people don't talk about. Shit's not always sunshine and roses.

I walked over to her, sat at her feet, and ran my thumb over her cheek, brushing away her tears.

"Sienna quitting has nothing to do with you, love," I honestly told her. "You're not horrible. You're not hard to deal with. Baby, you're tired. *We're* tired. *We're* not toxic. It's all right, though, because we're going to come out on the other end of this shit the way we came into it: happy."

Leighton leaned into my touch and looked up at me with sad eyes. "I hope so."

"I know so," I told her before dropping a kiss on her forehead.

CHAPTER 18

Leighton

"She quit? On her off day? She's only been working here . . . what? Four days? And she didn't even have the decency to tell you goodbye this morning? Why would she quit? I knew it was a bad idea, going with that Black-owned company. Jahad should have known better. Black women—especially Black women like *her*—can't be depended on. She came here dressed in a two-piece lounger set, for crying out loud. Ghetto and classless as hell. That right there should have been a dead giveaway. She's probably some hood rat who couldn't handle the pressure of working for a beautiful, successful boss-ass bitch such as yourself. Did you see the way she looked at Jahad when she walked into the room? As if she wanted to suck his dick right then and there? I say you dodged a bullet, Leigh. Don't worry—"

"Farrah!" I yelled, as I massaged my temples. "Please . . . shut the hell up."

Farrah drew back with offense and raised her brows. "What? Why? Did I lie? I'm just saying. Everything happens for a reason. You've called her three times since I've been here, and she hasn't answered not one of your calls. Fuck her. I don't understand the infatuation, anyway. Isn't she new? At this point, I can just stay here and look after you. We do good together. That way, you know you can trust the person under your roof." She smiled. "You know we've always taken great care of each other."

I stared at her blankly as her lips seemed to move a hundred miles per hour, rambling on and on as if I hadn't told her to shut the hell up. This was why she couldn't work with me. This was why I'd rather go through ten doulas before I settled with her ass. She talked too much, and most of what came out of her mouth was complete bullshit.

Her energy stunk of negativity and had been ever since Mike left her for his secretary. She was miserable, and as I listened to her go on and on, the meaning of misery loving company couldn't be clearer.

The minute I told her Sienna quit, she was on her way here. She claimed she was coming to take care of me because, in her words, "No one else could like her, anyway." I didn't even have help on the weekends, so her reason for coming was complete bullshit. Farrah only came to run her mouth and be negative.

I was drained. Mentally and emotionally drained. This hall pass and my insecurities had been weighing heavy on my heart. We hadn't done anything but argue over the past few weeks. Well, I did the arguing. Most of the time, he'd just stare at me with this blank expression on his face that did nothing but worry me further. I thought about the way Farrah used to describe Mike's behavior before he asked for a divorce, and it sent a crazy chill down my spine. I didn't want to lose my husband, but it felt like I'd already lost him.

Dinner last night was a disaster. We ate in silence. Dead silence. Silence that was loud as hell. The longer we sat there, eating but consumed with more than just food, I felt it. Jahad . . . slipping away from me.

I had gone overboard. Jahad had pretty much disconnected from me completely, and I couldn't say I blamed him. I felt it happening with every passing second we sat there, quiet. That hatred I had for myself? It had doubled. I was so disappointed in myself. I was losing my mind. I never intended to push him away, but I had done just that. Jahad just . . . he didn't care anymore.

Last night, he slept in his office. After dinner, he asked Sienna to escort me up to the room. I thought about arguing that I wanted him to take me up, but I was already embarrassed enough. I wasn't going to fight for him to take me up, just for him to snap at me or give me a shoulder so cold, even she would feel a breeze from it. To save face, I told him I loved him with a smile. He responded with a dry *"I love you, too,"* but didn't even bother looking up from his phone. He just . . . He was gone. Mentally and emotionally, at least.

The ride up to the second floor with Sienna was just as painful. She was quiet . . . I was too. When I woke up to her text, I was sure she'd quit because, although the house seemed to be pretty put together, we were toxic as hell. I'd pushed her away, too. And I was just so fucking fucked up about it. I'd finally found a doula I could tolerate. One I could relate to and have a conversation with, and I pushed her away. Another reason to hate myself.

I was intolerable. So intolerable, the doula didn't even last a full week. How pathetic. She tossed us aside just like I tossed those other doulas aside. *Is this how they felt? Betrayed? Bewildered? Abandoned? Disliked?*

Before Jah left, he tried to reassure me that there was nothing wrong with me. Despite me being a total bitch last night, he apologized for sleeping in the office and gave me reassurance. He spoke life into me, into us, even though I didn't deserve it. We spent about an hour just talking. But even then, it didn't feel the same. I could tell he felt the same way. He said in time, we'd be back to where we used to be. Happy. But I had doubt in my heart. I honestly didn't know if I would ever be able to move past him and that hall pass. Fucked up, right? I made the bed, I should lie in it. Welp, I couldn't.

"So, I can just stay here."

That was the only thing I heard Farrah say. That was enough to snap me out of my trance.

"No, no, you can't. Farrah, I love you but—"

"But what?" she asked with a cocked brow.

"Your ass is a lot to deal with every day," I finally mustered up the courage to say.

I'd only held so much down because I was afraid to lose our friendship, but I felt like our friendship was strong enough to withstand some brutal honesty. True, Farrah was the only friend I had, and most of the time, the only person who came to see me. But she was draining as hell.

"How, Leigh? I'm just keeping it real."

"Maybe you should dial back a little on 'the real.' Most of the things you say are disrespectful and negative as hell."

She crossed her arms underneath her chest and rubbed her lips together. "Well, Leigh, I honestly don't mean to be. I just want the best for you. I've always wanted the best for you. You know that."

"I know that, babe. And I have that. The doula quit, okay? So what? Big deal. She'll be back. I'll get her to come back. You don't know her to judge, Farrah. She's been through a lot, just like I have. I can only imagine how rough working here, watching me live a life she's dreamed of . . ." I paused and shook my head, trying not to disclose too much of Sienna's business. "She didn't quit because she couldn't handle working for a"—I paused and made air quotations—"'beautiful, successful, boss-ass bitch such as myself.' *Trust.* Sienna's not some hood rat, okay? And yes, I can say this after only knowing her for a couple of days. You don't have to attack anyone's character to make yourself look like a better contender. You're my best friend." I made eye contact with her, widening my eyes. *"My best friend,"* I reiterated. "Okay? Nothing will change that. You don't have to feel threatened by everyone I take a fucking liking to, Farrah."

Farrah was territorial. Very territorial. Always had been. For a long time, *we* were territorial over each other. Our friendship, growing up, was called unhealthy by both of our parents. Shit, not only our parents—everyone in our lives thought it was weird and sickening how we stayed glued to one another's side. We spent every day with each other.

We met in the first grade and had been best friends ever since. We went to the same schools after that. Same high school, same college, and we had the same jobs. We got our first tattoos together and even made a virginity pact, agreeing that we would both lose it to twin brothers, Michael and Matthew, seniors at Eastern Michigan University. We did.

Farrah ended up engaged, and I ended up in a toxic-ass relationship that ended with me dropping out of college and taking my ass back to the hood, where our lives seemed to steer off road. That was where our bond got a little shaky and Farrah felt threatened by every little thing. The job at the Coney Island—it wasn't in our plan. And me falling for bad boy Jahad Baptiste, who ran around the hood, shirtless, slanging drugs with his mannish little brothers? Oh, he definitely wasn't in the plan. He was so out of the plan that any time she saw us together, she would damn near foam at the mouth with anger. And don't let me call him my best friend! Oh God! Farrah would lose it! I didn't realize how right our family and friends were about our friendship until we took time apart and Farrah was the only one still so dependent on me. How careful I was with her dated way back then. She was fragile, despite how tough and bitchy she led people to believe she was. Farrah couldn't take much. She for damn sure couldn't take losing me.

Farrah pulled her lips into her mouth and nodded. "Mm-hmm. I know." She forced a smile and plopped down on the bed. "So, what did Mama Baptiste want earlier?"

I sucked in a deep breath and released it, glad for the shift in conversation. She'd changed the subject because she was on the brink of tears. I saw them building in her eyes while I talked. Before Farrah shed a damn tear, she would force a smile and pretend everything was perfectly fine. She and I were similar in that way. She didn't like to appear weak, and I appreciated that because I was in no mood to deal with someone else's emotions when I was drowning in my own.

"She wants to have some sort of dinner, girl. I don't know," I said with a light laugh. "She just wants to get me around some people. You know her."

"Well, she does know the gender reveal is happening next month, right? Why won't she just chill and wait for that? I've got it under control."

"Speaking of, have you reached out to them about the plans? You know the family wants to be involved, Farrah," I stated, giving her the side-eye.

She twisted her lips up and playfully rolled her eyes. "They can handle the baby shower. The reveal is all me."

Before I could respond, my phone rang.

"This is Rome. Hold on," I told Farrah with an eye roll, before answering. The last person I wanted to speak to was Rome, but I'd ignored enough of his calls.

"Hello?" I answered.

The smile in his voice was loud when he said, "What's up, Leigh? How you holdin' up, mama?"

I ran my hand over my belly as she moved a bit more. "Pretty good. Hey, listen. It's been a little hectic for me. If possible, could you give—"

"What did I tell you a couple of months ago, Leigh?" he interrupted. He was on the move. I heard people in the background. I wondered if he was in Manhattan. Roman was a big name in the art business. We met in college, where we both majored in fine arts. His career took off in ways mine didn't because I dropped out. I took the long road to success, and he'd been there every step of the way, helping me on it. He owned several art galleries here in Michigan, but in New York, he was larger. The market there was insane, and I had been given an opportunity to have a few of my pieces placed in one of his biggest art galleries there. It was an opportunity of a lifetime. One of my biggest dreams, to be exact. But here I was, six months later, and I hadn't produced a single piece for him.

He might've been patient with me, but I wasn't patient with me. I needed to get out of this funk.

Shifting my eyes down to my rising and falling belly, I sighed. The funk was this pregnancy. I hated to say it, and I'd never say it out loud, but the pregnancy was an inconvenience. Despite how much of an inconvenience it had been to my usual busy life, I wanted her. I wanted this. More than I cared about having my pieces in the biggest Black art gallery in the world. Yes, the world. Not just Manhattan. Not just the U.S. The fucking world. If I could just migrate between this pregnancy, the hormones, the emotions, my failing marriage, and that hall pass, I would be fine. Pretty soon, hopefully, things would recenter themselves. I'd have a cute, chubby baby and those pieces on display. Beautiful pieces, painted effortlessly, too.

I'd been worried about my creativity, but I knew I just had mommy brain. Everything was twisted and foggy up there.

"I know. I just . . . You know how I am," I said with a sigh.

"Tell her she'll be painting before she knows it, Roman!" Farrah yelled. "She's been so hard on herself."

Roman softly chuckled. "Yeah, Leigh, listen to your friend. I wasn't calling to rush you, woman. I was just calling to check up on you. How's the little one? You been aight? Taking care of yourself, I hope."

"I appreciate that," I said with a light smile. "Yeah, I've been taking care of myself. Not much I can do these days, you know? She's doing great. She's a busybody for sure."

"A girl? A little Leighton? Oh, she's going to be beautiful. A beautiful firecracker," he said. "Just like her mother."

I laughed and shook my head as if he could see me. "No, I don't know what the gender of the baby is just yet." I cut my eyes at Farrah to see if she'd give me a clue what it was, but she remained stone-faced as she looked down at her phone, scrolling. I rolled my eyes and scrunched my face up. "I just call her a girl."

He laughed and said, "Ah, all right. I get it. Hey, I'll be in Michigan next month. The husband all right with me stopping through?"

"Of course," I reassured him. "You know you're always welcomed here, Rome. Our gender reveal is next month, too. Hopefully, you're in town then."

I heard the smile in his voice when he said, "Cool. I'll hit you in a couple of days and let you know when I'll be down."

As soon as we hung up, Farrah was in my face.

"Rome's coming to the gender reveal?" Farrah eagerly asked. "Shit, I'm single now. He's not leaving without me sucking his dick first."

I laughed. "Bitch!"

She laughed. "I'm just saying! You know how I feel about Roman fucking Johnson. I've wanted his ass since the first frat party."

"A lot of bitches did," I reminded her. "And a lot of bitches had him that night too."

"A lot of bitches that wasn't me," she joked. "Is he coming?"

I giggled and shook my head as I scrolled my contacts for Shonda's number. "I'm not sure, whore. He said he's coming to town next month. He'll let me know exactly when in a few days."

She nodded. "Aight. Well, he's coming. That's all I need to know. I need to get this fucking jungle between my legs chopped down so I can be ready for his ass."

I looked up from my phone and cracked up laughing. "Farrah! It is not a fucking jungle down there, bitch!"

"But it is!" She laughed. "Shit, I wasn't going to be getting waxed, damn near getting my pussy lips snatched off, and I wasn't getting any dick!"

I shrugged. "Tiffany is here religiously, every month. I keep 'Priscilla' pretty at all times. It makes me feel like a *laaady.*"

There wasn't much I could do these days, but I did make sure I stayed up on my maintenance. I kept my kitty waxed, a pedicure, and a full set. I could use a fresh retwist, but I kind of liked it when my new growth got a little unruly. I didn't dress up much, but I didn't stop pampering myself. That was the one thing I made sure I held on to. I didn't want to lose too much of myself. Whenever I got pampered, it made me feel like me again.

CHAPTER 19

Sienna

I lay in bed with my eyes to the ceiling, dreading the call I had to make. I wasn't going into work. Not today, not tomorrow, not the next day, neither. I quit. After we were caught by Ms. Evaline, I did the walk of shame right up to that bedroom I didn't deserve. I showered and tried to scrub every bit of what I'd done off me. But no amount of scrubbing would change what happened. It was imprinted in my brain. In both a good and a bad way. Luckily, after the shower, I got a notification from roadside assistance, letting me know they were five minutes away. I got dressed and ran out of that house so fast. Trekking down the street in the snow didn't bother me at all. The farther I got away from that house, the better.

The minute I got situated at home, I sent them a text, letting them know I wouldn't be returning Monday, due to personal reasons. I figured I was doing them a favor by telling them ahead of time, giving them enough time to make arrangements for Monday. Leighton had called me three times since then and had sent a long-ass text message. He hadn't called once. However, I wasn't expecting anything from him. I was sure he felt just as shitty as I did. Leighton's messages were kind and uplifting, about persevering through pain. She thought I'd quit because I couldn't handle being around her pregnancy. She had no idea I quit because her husband was my biggest weakness. I'd done the unthinkable. Doing the things I'd done to him at Pandora's before I knew he was married was one thing, but doing those things after finding out, meeting his wife, and working with her . . . That was completely different.

I felt low.

Low as hell.

So, as I laid in bed with my eyes to the ceiling, I felt nothing but disgust. What the fuck was wrong with me? How was it I was turning into the type of bitch I hated? The side bitch. The messy bitch who fucked with a nigga, knowing he had a girl. What I'd done last night was unjustifiable. I was turning into something I wasn't comfortable with.

At the sound of knocking on my door, I sat up with furrowed brows. Who in the hell? Naoki didn't get home until eight this morning, so our brunch date was canceled, so it wouldn't be her. She was the only person in my life who had my address. Literally. I hadn't given any of my family members my address, but I knew by the end of dinner tonight, they would have it. So, I had no idea who could've been knocking on my door.

Sucking my teeth, I laid back down. The knocking continued, so I threw my comforter off my body and got out of bed. I stormed down the hall to the door with a frown.

Standing at the door, I looked through the peephole and my eyes widened at the sight of Shonda pacing back and forth. Backing from the door, I covered my mouth and mumbled, "Shit."

The call I'd been dreading to make was to her. I'd fucked up. She was a sweet woman, just trying to make a name for herself in an industry that was white dominated, and I'd probably fucked her business up by quitting the way I had without letting her know what was up. I said I wouldn't and what had I done, anyway? Allowed the shit I had going on to spill over into her business.

If Serene was owned by anybody else, I wouldn't have given a fuck, but Shonda was cool. She didn't deserve what I'd done.

"I heard you walk up, Si. Open the damn door," she said before knocking again.

I tossed my head back and my bonnet fell on the floor. It was after twelve in the afternoon, and I was still in bed, in pajamas, looking a damn mess. This little self-love journey was going terribly wrong, wasn't it? Felt like I had taken ten steps back.

Unlocking the door, I opened it and stepped aside so she could come in. Shonda scrunched her face up and eyed me up and down as she walked into my apartment. She was, as always, dressed cute as hell, in a pair of high-heeled, thigh-high boots. Shonda was the epitome of a bad bitch. Next to Naoki, she was the most confident woman I knew. I considered myself confident, too, but the way this bitch carried herself? It was like she owned every room she stepped into. The confidence and bad bitch just *oozed* from her pores. So, her little size-up made me feel some type of way, since I was dressed down in a holey, bleach-stained tank, and old leggings I'd cut into shorts. Listen . . . I was having a morning, okay?

Taking her fur off, she draped it over her forearm and placed her hands on her hips. "Si . . . what's going on?"

Closing the door, I turned and faced her. I scratched the back of my head and shrugged. "I was going to call you. I told you the best friend was a lot to deal with, but you wouldn't listen."

She squinted as I walked by her to sit on the futon. My life was a complete fucking mess. I thought getting this high-rise apartment, drinking wine from classy glasses, taking bubble baths, and repeating affirmations every day was going to fix things. I thought taking my ass down to Pandora's and hopping on new dick was going to fix things, too, but sadly, all that had done was make my situation ten times worse.

All I had to do was make the most out of an odd situation. You know, getting hired to be their doula. All I had to do was be professional. Unfortunately, I was prone to self-sabotage, wasn't I? I kept myself in a hopeless relationship, constantly forgave a man who didn't deserve my forgiveness until he hurt me in a way that forced me to finally choose Sienna. Then, I went to Pandora's and got attached to one-night-stand dick. Who was I kidding, going to something like that in the first place? I wasn't the one-night-stand type. But . . . I put on that mask and did my "big one," huh? Things would have been okay if I hadn't ended up working for them. Seeing him, being around him, I couldn't control myself. I thought I could. I just knew I would. But it was like I wasn't *me* when I was around him.

"Sienna, who do you think you're talking to? Some stranger that don't know you?" Shonda asked, shaking her head. "*I know you.* You don't give a fuck about a meddling best friend. If anything, you'd use a meddling, petty best friend to your advantage. You kill bitches like that with condescending kindness. I know because I've witnessed it. Cherice can't stand you to this day because she couldn't get underneath your skin. And you're going to sit up here and tell me you quit working at a job that pays close to five thousand dollars a month because her friend was difficult? With this new apartment and all the responsibility that comes along with it?" She took a deep breath and treaded over to me, her heels click-clacking against my dirty hardwood floors. "Yeah, fucking right. Am I pissed about you quitting, knowing how important my company is to me? Hell yeah. We'll get to that, eventually. Right now, I need the truth. I'm coming to you as a friend, not a boss. What's going on? Is it Amiri?"

I swallowed and quickly turned to look at her, slightly embarrassed. Shonda and I were cool, but not cool to where we talked about the shit I went through with my relationship. We weren't *that* close. The only person I spoke freely with was Naoki. I didn't even talk to my sisters about my and Amiri's problems. I was closed off, and for good reason. I didn't like to give people room to judge me.

Any time something got out about Amiri and me, it got out because of the blogs. Like I said, Amiri had a big following. We were "relationship goals" for many people. Surprisingly, nothing had gone up on the blogs this time. People were speculating and that was it. Of course, if you knew me, those speculations were pretty much confirmed with me moving out, regardless of how private I had been about everything.

"I don't mean any disrespect, Si. I promise. I'm just saying," she continued. "Are you depressed? Is it interfering with work? Like . . . talk to me."

She had that look in her eyes.

That look of pity that was often disguised as concern. I hated it. Hated it so much.

"Don't look at me like that," I said with an angry squint. "I'm going through some shit, but I'm not broken."

I wasn't . . . was I?

Shonda put her hands up in surrender. "Hey, like I said, I'm not trying to be disrespectful. I'm just trying to figure out why a woman I considered a friend would do what she did to me with no explanation."

Did I dare tell her? Did she deserve an explanation? The truth, at least? She did, but was I privy to telling her? Hell no. I didn't want her to know anything about what Jahad and I had done. It was already bad enough we'd been caught by the fucking cook. The look in her eyes was unsettling enough and I didn't even know her for real. I didn't think I could take it if Shonda looked at me that way. With that disgust. The same disgust I felt for myself every time I thought of him. I couldn't handle it.

"It's just heavy . . . working there. It's heavy, Shon," I said, diluting the truth a little.

It was heavy. Very heavy. That was the truth. I didn't need to go into detail about *what* was heavy because Shonda was going to make her own assumptions about what I meant based on my history. Based on what I'd told her about the miscarriages. As fucked up as that may be, I was okay with her assuming I couldn't handle it because of my inability to bear children.

Shonda's face softened as she advanced toward me. *Good. It worked.* She wrapped her arms around me and rubbed my back.

"What did we talk about before you started?" she asked, looking into my eyes with sympathy. I was okay with sympathy; with pity, I wasn't.

"You told me that if it gets too hard, to just call you," I said, remembering our talk over brunch and mimosas a few days before I started.

She nodded. "Exactly. You could have called me. We could have gotten through it together."

Shonda was no stranger to miscarriages. Except she had three children already. She didn't struggle with conceiving. Her issues came after the first three, so, in my opinion, she couldn't understand how I truly felt. Yeah, a loss is a loss, but the loss hits differently when you don't have a child to raise at all. I appreciated her, though, just didn't think she understood my pain completely. It might not have been the reason I quit, but it still applied. She couldn't truly understand, for real.

"I know," I said, as I twiddled with my fingers. "I'm sorry, Shon. I was going to call. I've just been . . ." I scratched my head. "It's been kind of crazy."

She nodded. "I understand, Si. So, where are you going from here? Because I love you and want the best for you, my door is always open, but I understand if you've chosen another career path."

My eyes widened a bit. "Oh, no, I don't want to give up on it, Shon. If you'll have me, I'd love to stay with the company. Just . . . I can't work for that family. It's too much. She's got a background similar to mine, and now that she's gotten her baby, she won't stop talking about it. Her rainbow baby. I don't think she's purposely doing it, though. I mean, I get her excitement . . . I just can't handle that right now," I continued to lie. God, I hated to lie.

Leighton rarely ever showed me her excitement about finally getting her baby. She was careful with me, in that sense. Since we had that talk when we first met, she'd been careful not to talk too much about it. Little did she know, I didn't struggle with conversations about the baby nearly as much as I struggled with conversations about her husband.

"All right, I have a new list of clients. Since Leighton mentioned us on her Instagram, things have picked up," Shonda said before standing up. She approached me and wrapped her arms around me. "I'll call you in a few days with new details."

"Thank you so much, Shonda. I really appreciate you."

She gave me a friendly kiss on the cheek before pulling back from the hug. "Mm-hmm. Keep this between us. If Jennifer finds out I got you a new client after she'd been complaining about the family she's with for weeks, and you quit, I'll never hear the end of it."

I laughed and playfully zipped my lips.

* * *

"Good luck, boo," Naoki said with a laugh.

Looking up at my parents' house, I sucked my teeth. "I don't need luck, I need a shot of Patrón."

After Shonda left, I looked around my messy, empty apartment and decided to get my shit together. I had been drowning in guilt all week, but it was time for me to come up for some damn air.

I threw on SZA, cleaned, and hopped in the shower. The bright, natural sunlight bouncing off the white walls in the expensive-ass high-rise apartment, coffee, music, and a good, long cry in the shower helped boost my mood tremendously, so I actually put some effort into my look today. I decided on a pair of light wash, skintight, high-waisted jeans, a brown pair of thigh-high, heeled boots, and a tan cropped sweater that hung off my shoulder. I wore gold jewelry and my favorite Louis Vuitton mini bag. I even straightened my twenty-eight-inch frontal wig and threw on a little bit of makeup. I looked damn good. I felt good, too, but I looked a lot better than I actually felt. Looked like my shit was all the way together. Just the mask I needed for tonight.

"Period!" She laughed. "Call me when you're done. Maybe we can hit a bar or something. After last night, and the night you're about to have, I know you need a *few* shots!"

Yep. I told Naoki about my shameful night last night. I tell the bitch everything. I could do that with her. She was my safe space. Someone I could vent to freely, without the fear of judgment. All Naoki ever was was a listening ear and sound advice when I needed it most.

She told me not to sulk in it. Told me jokingly if I was going to be a ho, don't be ashamed of it—own the ho-ness. On a serious note, she told me to enjoy life and not to take it so seriously. Everyone made mistakes, and beating myself up about it wasn't going to change anything. She'd been telling me the same thing since I started working for them, and so far, it was like her advice had fallen on deaf ears.

"All right, girl," I told her with a laugh before we said our *I love yous* and hung up. I took a deep breath and tossed my head back against the headrest. I was in no mood for the question game my mother was about to play with me. I knew the minute I walked into the Mills household, I was going to be under scrutiny.

I ran my thumb over my bare ring finger and sighed again. I wasn't ready to face the music. I wasn't ready to hear the tone of straight-up disappointment in her voice. My mother's. She cared more about me getting married and having children than anybody else, me included.

Marriage would be nice, but I didn't center my life around it. I was trying to center my life around happiness, and after getting fucked and licked on by a married man while his pregnant wife slept upstairs, marriage didn't seem appealing at all. I just wanted to be left alone, but my mother, she'd think something was wrong with me if I told her that.

Snatching my seatbelt off, I mumbled, "Let me get this shit over with so I can go get drunk."

I got out of the car and closed my coat tighter. My teeth chattered as I thought about the comment Jahad made about my "little-ass coat" and couldn't agree with him more. I needed to get a longer, thicker coat. Winter had been brutal this season.

As I climbed the stairs, I shook my head at the Christmas decorations my daddy had yet to take down. I just knew Eve had been giving him the fucking blues about that shit. Knowing him, he kept them up longer each time she complained about it, just to get under her skin. If there was one person Eve was powerless against, it was Big Reggie.

Because I hadn't added my new house keys on my old keys yet, I didn't have my key to the house, so I rang the doorbell. I blew into my hands and rubbed them together, hoping they'd hear the bell over all the noise spilling from the inside onto the porch.

A few seconds later, my dad answered the door.

"Hey, SiSi, baby girl," my daddy greeted me with a hug as soon as I stepped into the house.

I closed my eyes with a smile and hugged him just as tight as he hugged me. My daddy gave the best hugs and it always seemed like he gave the best ones when I needed them most.

"You all right?" he asked after we pulled away from the hug.

I looked over my shoulder at him as I hung my coat on the coat rack. With a forced smile, I nodded. "Yep! I'm good." Changing the subject, I deeply inhaled. "It smells good up in here."

The smell of fried catfish, chicken, collard greens, and macaroni and cheese hit my nostrils as soon as I walked into the house. My favorite. My momma was doing what she always did—adding a little cherry on the top of shit to smooth things over. She'd made catfish for me. That meant I was either going to leave here crying, or we were going to get into a screaming match that ended with her crying. Both of which I was in no mood to deal with.

"Yeah, she just threw some sweet cornbread in the oven, too," Daddy said with a smile and a wink.

My stomach growled with anticipation. Yeah, this was about to be a shit show. I'd almost backed out of it, but there was no avoiding the inevitable. I figured, shit, why keep prolonging it? I couldn't keep distance between us forever, so might as well face the music.

On my way to the kitchen, I hugged and spoke to my nieces and nephew. They were, as always, in front of the TV, playing the game, and off on their phones. My brother-in-law sat on the couch, nursing a beer. I was surprised to see him. *Great. My mother is going to have a field day throwing Mahogany's marriage up in my face.* That was what she did. I could hear her now. *"Mahogany . . . Duke, y'all's union is so strong. I wish more young couples took relationships and marriage as serious as you two. Nee, I'm so, so proud of you."* Even though Mahogany's marriage was a fucking joke, and her husband spent more time on the clock than at home.

After giving Duke a one-armed hug, I continued into the kitchen, where Aretha Franklin was playing. There was laughter too. They were having a good-ass time but I knew when I entered the kitchen, I would make it awkward. The elephant would be in the room and muthafuckas would tiptoe around the question of what happened between me and Amiri. They loved to tiptoe around shit until there was no room left for tiptoeing. Then they'd just bombard me with questions, all at once.

"Hey," I sang with a smile as I walked into the kitchen.

My momma was at the stove, stirring a big pot of greens; Mahogany was buttering corn on the cob, getting ready to put it in the second oven; and Hazel was sitting at the island, most likely scrolling TikTok. They looked up at me and spoke with smiles on their faces. My mother stepped away from the stove, wiped her hands on her old apron, and walked over to me. She wrapped her arms around me and kissed me on the cheek before pulling away to cup my face.

"Hey, baby," she said, with one of those comforting smiles. Except I didn't want a comforting smile. I didn't want to be treated like something was wrong.

"Hey, Momma." I smiled and walked away from her. "It smells good in here! I'm starving. The only thing I ate today was a banana!"

"You're not eating?" Momma said with concern heavy in her tone. "You all right?"

I frowned. "Yeah, I'm eating. I just knew it was going to be a big dinner, so I saved room for it. I'm all right, Momma."

My momma didn't miss a moment to scrutinize me. The fact that I'd suddenly upped and moved without telling them, to her, meant I was depressed, suicidal, and starving myself. She meant well, but that shit could be draining.

I couldn't make a drastic move without her meddling in my business. You'd think I was the youngest, the way she stayed on me. She wasn't even on Hazel as heavy as she was on me.

Sometimes, I felt like as the middle child, I was the one expected to be the failure or something. When I was younger, damn near everything I did was done in pursuit of approval from my parents. As time went on, and I got a personality of my own that wasn't tailored for their approval, I stopped giving a damn as much.

"Okay, baby," she said with a smile. "I'm just making sure you're okay. Considering everything."

Considering everything.

Whew.

She didn't even ease the meddling in this time. I just knew she'd save her line of questioning and sly remarks for dinner. Not after, but during. That was when Eve dropped most of the bombshells. In front of everyone, right in the middle of laughter, catching up, and face stuffing. Momma eased the bullshit in at that moment every time. I guess she'd been waiting too long to wait for dinner.

"Everything?" I asked with a cocked brow. "Or me moving?"

She shrugged her shoulder and shuffled around the kitchen, pretending to be distracted. Pretending that what she wanted to talk about was no big deal to her. Pretending to be casual, knowing good and got damn well what she really wanted to do was point her big fork at me and run her mouth about shit she had no business concerning herself with.

My love life and my uterus were two things Eve had always somehow made her business. I needed to have a baby. I needed to get married. I needed to stop being so mean to Amiri and give him some babies.

When he proposed, it was *"Oh Lord, now my SiSi can give me some grandbabies! Lord knows they overdue!"* Totally clueless about the horrors I'd experienced regarding childbirth. Completely clueless about this broken uterus I was cursed with. I basically had it and titties for no reason, right? Since, technically, breasts were there to feed babies.

"I mean, you know. Everything associated with that, Sienna."

"What's associated with me moving, Ma?" I asked, challenging her with my head cocked to the side before reaching into the strainer for a wing drumette. They were my favorite. I didn't know why they got so much slack. I preferred them to the flats, unlike a vast majority of the world. The only reason there were any drums in the strainer at all was because *I* ate them. No one else in my family cared for them. Otherwise, my mother would have slapped my hand and told me to get my hands out of the food. But because they were mine, I could eat them freely.

She gave me that forced, coy smile as she wiped her hands on a towel. "We don't have to do this right now, Sienna."

"We honestly don't have to do it at all," Hazel mumbled with her eyes fixed on her phone.

"Exactly," I said, tossing my bone into the trash. "Aubry!" I yelled, calling my thirteen-year-old niece as I walked out of the kitchen. "Come on! Let's do a TikTok! You know my hips go crazy, right?" I smirked.

I wasn't even the TikToking type, but because I needed to change the tone, I said, *Fuck it, let me find one of my nieces and have some fun.* I couldn't be in that kitchen with them. I should have been helping with the food, but fuck that food and fuck helping. The energy in there was suffocating. More suffocating than I imagined it to be on my ride over. My mother was . . . a muthafucka, man.

Ladies' night with my bitches sure didn't sound bad, but I'd never hear the end of it if I left right now. My mother would end up forwarding me the pastor's phone number to call for prayer or just to talk if I felt like it.

"Okay, Tee-tee," Aubry giggled. "Come on."

I rubbed my chicken-greased lips together as if I'd just put on a new coat of gloss and smoothed my hair over, making sure I was camera ready. I wasn't big on TikTok, but since I had a little following on Instagram, anytime Aubry posted a video with me, she got a lot of traction on her page. And any time she put a video up with me in it, I made sure she cut the comments off. I didn't need anybody posting any bullshit under my niece's shit. Somehow, those videos always ended up on some low-level blog site with all the comments they couldn't leave under Aubry's post under it.

After we did three videos, Hazel and my mother set the table. She shot me a look that said *Get your ass in the kitchen and bring some food to the table.* Regardless of how crazy she drove me, I stopped playing around and took my ass to the kitchen to help. When I walked in, Mahogany was scrolling her phone with one hand and trying to carry the tray of macaroni with the other.

"You drop that macaroni, I'm smacking you, Mahogany," I threatened.

Next to drumettes and catfish, macaroni and cheese was my favorite. And my mother made the absolute best. Hell, there wasn't a dish Eve didn't excel at. She could cook her ass off. Meanwhile, I was just all right. Hazel had been blessed with Momma's good cooking gene, though. Me and Mahogany were the carryout queens! You hear me?

Once the table was set, everyone sat down for grace.

"You don't get off that phone right now, I'm going to take it, little girl," Momma said to Aubry.

She raised her eyebrows, pulled her lips into her mouth, and tucked the phone under her thigh. I giggled and shook my head before joining hands with Hazel and Mahogany, since I was in the middle of them, like always. Middle child in the middle, oldest to the right, youngest to the left. It was the natural order of things in the Mills household.

"Dear God, thank You for blessing us with this glorious meal, prepared by these glorious hands," said Momma, joking a little like she did at the start of every grace. "We give thanks for bringing us all together, my Lord. Every day above ground is a blessing, and every day we get to spend with family is an even bigger blessing. Family, good food, love, and grace like Yours is all we ask for. In our times of need, despair, and loneliness, we all ask that You guide us and shield us from unholiness."

I sucked in air and rolled my eyes before shutting them again. Here we go.

"We thank You, Father God, for everything You have blessed us with! Bless the unions of my children! The grandchildren—those here at this table and those that are to come. I—"

"Amen," my daddy interrupted.

"Amen," everyone else added in scattered, low tones.

"I wasn't done. Don't be rude! Hold hands and bow y'all heads," Momma pressed.

Daddy cleared his throat. "Enough of that. You thanked the Lord. That's good enough, Eve. Son, pass me the cornbread."

With that, Eve let it go and we piled food on our plates. I looked across the table at him and he gave me a smile and a wink. In response, I gave him a smile.

"Look at her ass," Hazel mumbled before lifting her On the Rocks margarita to her lips. "Trying to pretend she's busy."

Mahogany giggled, bouncing my youngest niece, Sparkle, on her hip. "I give it twenty minutes. Momma is about to burst, she wants to say something so bad."

Dinner ended about thirty minutes ago. Since then, my momma had been acting weird as hell. She was trying her damnedest to tiptoe around what she'd really called this dinner for. I thought it was funny, but that was Eve. She played that good, motherly role until she couldn't play it any more, especially when something of this magnitude fucked with her. Me moving without telling them, to her, was just as much a red flag as someone getting caught in a locked bathroom with a loaded pistol. She was a lot to deal with sometimes, but her worrisome ways came from a good place, I suppose.

My sisters and I were sitting in the living room, on the couch, sipping mixed drinks, talking and watching Eve damn near lose her shit. My dad and Duke were in the kitchen, washing the dishes, since the ladies had done the cooking. My nieces were back on their phones, and my nephew was busy upstairs, playing Fortnite or whatever popular game the kids were going crazy about these days. It was just an overall good-ass vibe, but I knew pretty soon, Eve would kill it.

I pulled the cork from the On the Rocks mixed drink I got from the freezer and took a sip from it. "Just twenty? Naw, I give her five. She don't know what to do with herself."

"Why did you just up and move without telling us?" Mahogany boldly asked before leaning over and laying a sleeping Sparkle in her bassinet. "That was foul as fuck. We were just together a couple of weeks before you moved, Si."

"Mm-hmm," Hazel added, with a twist of her lips.

I took a deep breath and lowered my head before taking another sip of the strong little drink. "I needed time to clear my mind. Y'all know how I am. I have to sort through my shit first."

"You called Kiki," Mahogany argued.

I locked eyes with her. "We already talked about this, Nee. Let it go."

"I'm just saying. You could've called me. You could've come over to my house."

"I could've? Girl, you have four kids. Your hands are already full. I wasn't about to just put my shit on you," I stated before putting my eyes on Hazel, who wore a frown that mirrored Mahogany's. "And you? Don't even say shit because you've been couch hopping for months. I went to Naoki because I have my own room there, y'all know that."

My sisters knew how I was about my personal business. Mahogany, especially. She was the goody two shoes out of us. She was the one who'd gotten married, had the kids, and had the stable family. She was the apple of Momma's eye. She was the one who could do no wrong. Momma's best friend. I definitely couldn't trust her with any of my business.

Growing up, Mahogany used to snitch on me and Hazel so damn much. As I got older, I stopped telling her ass shit. I didn't trust her. Hazel, I didn't tell her anything because hell, why would I? The girl didn't give a damn about anything except having a good time. My sisters and I were similar in some ways, but different in so many more. I'd rather not tell them my business.

"I guess. I just know, next time you make a move like that, I better not find out on no damn Instagram. I'm not some random follower, Sienna. I'm your big sister and I want you to know you can come to me for anything. Both of you. A lot has changed since we were teenagers and I miss the way we used to be. Now, all we do is meet up every Saturday for ladies' night. We need to do more than that. With just us. Naoki and them cool, but I miss us. The triplets."

Hazel and I laughed.

"We're far from triplets now, shit," Hazel said, stroking her short, curly, red hair.

"Yeah. Bitch, you going through some type of identity crisis?" Mahogany joked. "The hell? You just had a bone-straight bust down the middle part the other day!"

Hazel laughed. "I just like to switch it up a little. Ain't nothing wrong with that."

"Say you switch your hair like you switch your bitches, huh, sis?" I joked.

"Exactly!" Hazel said before we slapped hands.

It felt good to kick it with my sisters. That was the best thing about these dinners. Spending time with my sisters, just talking about a bunch of bullshit. It put things into perspective every time.

Sitting back, watching my nieces and nephew play, listening to my sisters talk, and watching my parents made me think about life and how fast things were moving. Apparently, Mahogany felt the same way. Unlike me, she voiced her feelings about it. Me, I just watched and let life, life.

The speed life was moving at scared me. I'd be lying if I said it didn't. It didn't scare me before . . . before Amiri and what he did. But now, sitting back, watching them, it worried me. I was twenty-six, single, and barren. I wondered if I'd die alone. Wondered if—

"Hey, hey, family! We leavin' doors unlocked around here now?"

At the sound of *his* voice, I turned around. I nearly lost my mind when I saw Amiri at the entryway, hanging his coat up. *Amiri was here. Why in the fuck was Amiri here?* My eyes immediately went to Mahogany and Hazel, who did nothing but return the same bewildered looks.

"I know you fuckin' lyin' to me," Hazel mumbled.

Me? I was too stunned to speak. Literally. Speechless. Really, more heartbroken than anything. Felt like my heart was beating out of my chest, it was racing so fast. I was pissed. So pissed, I felt the anger pulsating through my entire body. I wanted to scream.

"Hey, son!" my momma said, rushing from the kitchen with a smile, drying her hands on a towel. She shifted her eyes back and forth between me and Amiri. "You just missed dinner. I put you up a plate."

My momma and Amiri had always been close. My whole family loved his bitch ass. But what about me? What about me moving out of the condo said it was okay to invite him to dinner? Shit, what about me showing up without him, said that things between him and me were good? I didn't have to tell any of them we'd broken up for them to know. The shit was clear as day. That and me not having on my engagement ring. They knew. She knew. She knew before this dinner, and she still invited him! The reason for her nervousness was clear now. She'd been sitting on pins and needles, waiting for this bitch nigga to show up.

"Why is he here?" I asked, with my eyes centered on her, seething. I was so mad, I could curse her the fuck out, and I'd never, in all of my twenty-six years of life, disrespected my mother. But this? This was some straight-up bullshit.

She pulled away from their embrace and nervously smiled at me. "You know I extended the invitation to Amiri. We talked the other day, and—"

"And did he tell you he has a baby on the way?" I interrupted with my top lip turned up into a snarl.

I knew it was going to be some bullshit tonight. I knew it. But never in a million years did I expect this. This was low. Eve was meddling, but she'd never gone this low before. I couldn't believe her.

"Si—"

My momma put her hand up, interrupting Amiri. "He said the baby isn't his, Sienna," she said in a tone just above a whisper. Looking around the quiet living room, she looked back to me. "This isn't how I wanted to do this. Not in front of everybody. Let me . . . let me talk to y'all in private. Come on. Come up to my room."

She had clearly lost her fucking mind. I couldn't even look at him. I refused to. Amiri didn't exist to me. I hated him. I hated him to my core, and I didn't use that word loosely. I hated him so much, I wouldn't bat an eyelash if he dropped dead right beside me.

That was the thing about me. If I cut you off, I cut you off. There was no getting back on my good side. Amiri, especially. He'd played with my heart too many times before for me to give him even a little bit of grace. I'd never cut him off completely in the past when I should have, for sure. But this time, I'd walked away from him. I closed that chapter in my life and there was absolutely no looking back for me. I hated him. I didn't want to be friends. I didn't care about the history we shared. I literally hated his fucking guts.

"That's foul, Ma. You knew this nigga had a baby on the way and still invited him? That's dirty," Hazel said, shaking her head, sizing Amiri up like she wanted to smack the fuck out of him. I wouldn't put it past her, at all.

"Oh, Hazel! Hush, this is grown folk business. You wouldn't know a good man if he—"

"All right, Eve," Daddy said as he approached us from the kitchen. "Amiri, you gotta go."

He sent me a sentimental gaze, but I was somewhere else mentally. Mentally, I was on the bathroom floor, sobbing with yet another negative pregnancy test, and Amiri was right there with me, his arms wrapped around my trembling body, making promises he did not keep. He told me we were okay. We didn't need to have a baby. We had each other. He told me he loved me so much and that he would always be there. Amiri promised it would always be us. With tears falling down his own cheeks, he made those promises to me and this was after I'd found out about him cheating on me . . . for a second time.

The pain I dealt with was unimaginable. I was stuck living with him after he'd cheated because I was too dependent and embarrassed to go back home. I hadn't called him into the bathroom, he just heard me. While I cried in his arms about him cheating and losing another fucking baby, he promised to make things better. He promised to never cheat on me again and I believed him and took him back. I believed him because he was so fucking convincing.

Just for it to all be a lie. Eve . . . inviting him here, after all I'd gone through with this man, was unforgivable. Without warning, I jumped up from the couch and headed for the door and Amiri was on my heels.

"Si! Wait! Let's talk! We never got to talk," Amiri pleaded. "Please! Please, Sienna!"

"The fuck I just tell you, boy? She don't want to talk, she don't have to talk!" my father yelled.

Reginald Mills might've been in his late sixties, but he didn't look a day over fifty and he didn't play about his daughters. At all. He cared for Amiri the same way he cared for Duke, but tonight, after seeing me so distraught, that was dead.

My daddy had good sense and respect for me to know that something wasn't right, and if something wasn't right, then Amiri was no good in his book. Eve just didn't give a fuck. She wanted me married with babies and she was going to get me there one way or another. Fuck my feelings.

I hurriedly slid my boots on and snatched my coat off the rack. Amiri was right next to me, snatching his coat off the rack too. He was still fucking with me, following me, ignoring my daddy.

When we left out of the house, my dad's yelling faded. I didn't have to look over my shoulder to know he'd gone upstairs to his room to get his gun. If Amiri was smart, he'd leave me the fuck alone. Just like Mahogany was the apple of my momma's eye, I was the apple of my daddy's. He loved us all the same, but I was his sweet baby.

My feet sunk in the snow as I hurriedly rushed to my car with trembling hands, trying to hurry and get the hell away from Amiri and my mother too. I heard her apologizing, and my sisters telling Amiri to leave, over his pleading, but really, everyone's voices were muffled. It was too much. Seeing him. What my mother did. What happened last night. It was just too fucking much.

"I know my word ain't worth shit right now, Si, but I swear to God on my momma's grave that that girl's baby isn't mine! How you gon' just up and leave me like that, baby? We couldn't talk? You don't think I deserve a conversation? A nigga just wake up and you gone? You know how worried I was, Si? I thought something happened to you! I thought you never made it home that night! You had me callin' around, looking for you and shit and—Wait! Wait! What the fuck?"

Right in the middle of Amiri's pointless-ass talking, I yanked my car door open, hitting him with it, and got inside. I didn't waste any time letting it warm up. I pushed the start button and immediately shifted the car in reverse, although his car was right behind mine. I'd bet every dollar in my bank account he'd parked there on purpose. He wanted to block me in, but if he really knew me, he would have known he wasn't stopping shit!

Once the back of my car bumped into his, I pressed down on my brakes harder and backed out of the driveway, pushing his truck out of my fucking way.

"What the fuck you doin'? Hold up! Si! What the fuck?" Amiri yelled with his hands up.

"Move it, then! Move it now, bitch!" I screamed as I slammed down on my brakes.

"Aight, aight! I just want to talk to you! Why you on crazy shit? Damn!" Amiri yelled, standing at my window like I wasn't prepared to really back his shit out of the driveway completely.

Because he hadn't moved, I put my foot back on the gas and continued to back out. His pleas fell on deaf ears as I kept backing up until his car was nearly in the driveway across the street and I was able to turn off and speed away. I didn't cry until I reached the stop sign.

CHAPTER 20

Jahad

"Thanks, Terry, we really appreciate all you have done," I said before I placed my hand on my chest. "Seriously."

Terry, the newest doula on Leighton's chopping block, gave a forced smile and climbed into her car. "Yep. Thank you, Mr. Baptiste. I hope your wife finds what she's looking for."

She did find what she was looking for, she just didn't work for me. And I didn't work for her.

I stepped away from the car and nodded at her as she backed out of the driveway. Stuffing my hands in the pockets of my Moncler, I looked up to the house, then to the snow-covered ground. Leighton was bugging and driving me fucking insane. We'd gone through three doulas in the three weeks we'd been without Sienna. Every fucking girl Shonda sent us, Leighton found something wrong with her. There was nothing wrong with any of them. Well, except for one. Shorty couldn't stay off her phone. I caught her doing TikToks and shit, fronting like the crib was hers. That was about it. The other two, Terry especially, had been straight. I was surprised Shonda still did business with us. I was sure she'd only kept us on as clients because she felt obligated since Leighton helped build her clientele by posting the company on Instagram. She didn't owe us shit, though.

Taking a deep breath, I ran my hand down the back of my neck and headed inside. Once I made it in, I caught the tail end of a newscast I'd been waiting for.

"What a tragic accident."

"Yeah . . . Such an unfortunate situation. Agent Hershel Walker will be greatly missed by family and friends. Our hearts go out to all the lives that were lost today."

After closing and locking the door behind me, I came out of my black Givenchy boots and walked over the threshold.

"Agent Walker, Agent Walker, that name sounds so familiar, son," Moms said after lowering the volume on the television.

It was because of her the TV in the sitting room was even being put to use. She'd been at the house for the past three hours.

I came home to a house full of women about fifteen minutes ago. Leighton was in the kitchen with Natasha, Farrah, her sisters, and her mother too. Initially, Leighton was upstairs, while they discussed plans for the gender reveal Farrah wanted to take control over. But the minute she came at my mother with that shit, it went from Farrah's little project to a group project everyone had a part in. Farrah was pissed, but if there was one person Farrah was defenseless against, it was Graciela Baptiste. Everyone was. Moms killed people with kindness. Every fucking time. She was the sweetest person I knew, but her tongue was as sharp as a machete. So, instead of Moms throwing a party together, the gender reveal would be *that* party.

"Walker? We went to his commemoration ceremony when he was promoted a few years back. Why?" I asked, feigning ignorance.

Our connections with the DEA ran deep, which was why I was so pissed at Blaise for making the dumbass decision to ride out with Cuz to do a job he could have done flawlessly on his own. We didn't just rub shoulders with law enforcement—we funded political campaigns, donated to charity, were invited to balls, brunches, and dinners. We put ourselves in big rooms with the purpose of hiding in plain sight. We stood in rooms with politicians and law enforcement that wanted the malicious people responsible for the rise in gun violence, drug trafficking, and military weaponry flooding the streets of America buried under the prison, and they hadn't a single clue they were standing, drinking, and partying and had shaken hands with the very people they were searching high and low for. I wouldn't go as far as saying we were responsible for it *all*, but if it was illegal and profitable, the Baptiste name was linked to it in *some* way.

Moms snapped her fingers. "You know what! That's right." Shaking her head, she sucked her teeth. "I knew the name was familiar. That big accident on the news this morning? He was in it. He was the driver that lost control of his car. They say he was going eighty miles per hour when his tire came off. Eight cars were involved. Three people died, including him."

We'd all been sitting on pins and needles, waiting for Walker to finally take a ride in Shelby's old-school Chevelle. When I got the call he'd finally pulled it out of the garage this morning, weight lifted from my shoulders. But right after that weight was lifted, it was replaced with more. The fee. How much would the move I made against Walker cost me?

Tanbou bat nan raje, men se lakay li vin danse (The drum is beaten in the grass, but it is at home that it comes to dance/Acts that are done outside the home end up having repercussions in the family).

The shit we were off into? It linked *me* directly to karma. I tried to make up for the bad with good, but the scales were imbalanced. I'd done some unethical shit. I had blood on my hands, and lots of it. For every action I took, there was always a reaction for it. For every drop of blood I spilled, I lost plenty. Always. Every time. I never got away with shit without repercussion. It might appear that way on the surface because I'd never been placed behind bars. To me, there was no greater repercussion than the wrath of bad karma. Karma hits me where it hurts the worst. And I knew . . . when it came to what happened this morning, those two innocent lives . . . I would have to answer for it, eventually. Just like I'd had to answer for every not-so-pretty decision I had to make because it was either them or us.

A nigga longed for the days when all I did was hit the block, serve a couple rocks, get a few hours of sleep, and do it all again the next day. I missed the days when Samuel was the head of the business. The *true* head of it. Back then, shit was simpler. Everything fell on that nigga's shoulders. But the minute he decided he was too old to handle what he and his brothers started, he pretty much forced the torch in my hand. The same way he forced the torch in my hand back home. I wasn't given a choice. I'd *never* been given a choice. Why couldn't Jacque run shit? What about Emu? They weren't capable? Apparently, since Samuel started it, it had to continue with his direct bloodline. It had to be handed down to Samuel's firstborn. However, I felt like shit; if Blaise was older, this job would still be mine because I was built different. I was built for this. Built to hold the heaviest of loads on my shoulders because I could carry it. I could hold it all up because I wouldn't fall. I'd just keep piling shit on. *They'd* keep piling shit on. I could take it. That was who I was. The strong one. The warrior. The fighter . . . since the fucking womb.

I wore my stripes, though.

Wore the crown with pride.

I didn't complain. Complaining didn't solve problems.

"Mmmph. Damn," I grunted under my breath as I stroked my beard. "I'm going to have to give Mrs. Walker a call, see if she needs anything."

I was going to do just that. Planned on attending his funeral and the wake too. And if they started a charity or shit? I'd drop a crazy, stupid donation on that muthafucka too. With a clear conscience and a smile on my face because that was what I did. I wore masks. Several of them. For several occasions, for several people, in several situations. Shit, I wore one every fucking time I stepped foot in this got damn house.

After giving my mother a kiss on the cheek, I walked off and headed into the lion's den. The ladies were having a great time. There was music playing. Beyoncé. The *Lemonade* album, Leighton's favorite. It didn't matter who or what was going on in the kitchen, every single fucking time I walked into it, I saw *her*. Tasted *her*. Felt *her*. Heard *her*. Shit was sickening. So sickening, I avoided the kitchen as much as I could. It didn't help that the women were gathered around the island where I'd devoured *her* pussy. Where I'd stuffed *her* with dick *she* took like a good girl.

Running my hand down the back of my neck, I swallowed and twirled my ring around my finger to ground myself.

The island was covered with finger foods, champagne and wine bottles, neutral color palettes, phones, plates, and wineglasses. The housekeepers were going to come in tomorrow morning to a surprise for sure.

Reaching over to the island, I grabbed a chocolate-covered strawberry and took a bite out of it. "Leigh, I gotta shoot a move."

"Already? You just got here." She pouted.

I leaned over and kissed her on the lips. She licked the chocolate I left there from the strawberry and then motioned for me to grab her one.

"Yeah, I know. Something came up. I won't be gone that long, though, love," I said before feeding her the strawberry I grabbed for her.

From the corner of my eye, I saw Farrah roll her eyes and pick her wine-glass up. Bitch stayed in business that didn't pertain to her. I made it my business to be here as often as possible but my business was unpredictable, and Leigh had a house full of muthafuckas who could help her if she needed it.

Leighton and I had been *straight* over the past few weeks. She still had her ways and I still had mine. The good days had been outweighing the bad, although we still had a lot of fucking bad days. The affection we showed? Shit was a front. Most of the time, what we did in public was a front. On her end, it was, at least. Leighton would never show her people just how bad things were between us.

She pouted and let me feed her a strawberry on some cute shit, but I saw the insecurities swimming in her hazels. I saw what no one else could because we were connected, eye to eye, while everyone else was busy looking at their phones or buzzed off whatever they had been drinking. Leighton thought I was going to fuck with the woman I'd used the hall pass on, and I would have to do everything in my power to prove to her I wasn't.

We were sharing locations. That was what I'd been subjected to. We never did that shit in the past. The fuck was she sharing her location with me for when all she did was sit here all day? It was cool, though. I did what I did to soothe her wandering, insecure mind, although it didn't help much. It didn't help at all, actually.

Despite knowing my location twenty-four hours a day, she still questioned me. There was no pleasing her but I kept trying. What Ms. Evaline say? Hold on? Don't let go? Yeah . . . I'd been holding on. So tight, my fucking hands were bleeding. How much longer was I supposed to hold on? Until they were raw? Until I was left with nothing but bones?

"Where are you going?" she asked.

"Vault. I need to see my brothers," I told her.

Natasha jumped down off the counter. "Can I come? I've been here all day."

I looked over at my baby sister and saw the misery written all over her face. Nodding, I said, "Fa sho."

With her hands together, she dramatically bowed. *"Mesi."*

I laughed and shook my head before turning my attention back to Leighton. With my eyes locked on hers, I lightly squinted, as if to ask, *Would I let Natasha come with me if I was going to stick my dick in another woman?*

"You're leaving already? Have you heard? She fired *the girl*," Farrah said with a huff. "That's what . . . number three? You need to find a different company. Leigh is clearly miserable with Serene Mommy and—"

"I'm not miserable, Farrah," Leighton interrupted. "I just . . . I don't like any of them."

Farrah rolled her eyes. "Because you have this sick infatuation with *that girl*. What's her name? The girl that wore the tacky outfits and complained about the stairs? Sierra? Her. Yes . . . Let it go. She's shown you who she was. Either you find another company, or I'll step in and just look after her full time because this is ridiculous."

"What happened with the last girl?" Shiloh, Leighton's sister, asked, as she poured herself a glass of wine.

"She quit," Farrah stated. "And Jahad has yet to find a suitable doula—"

"You're suitable. You sit here. You do the job. You got it, right?" I interrupted before shifting my attention to Leighton. "That's cool, right, love? She's here every day, all day, anyway. Why not? Might as well make it official."

Leighton looked up at me with wide eyes. "We discussed what I wanted, Jahad. Farrah—"

Farrah shrugged. "I don't see the issue. I can do the job perfectly fine. I'm always here. Always have been. I can take care of Leigh with no issue. It won't be any different from what I've been doing, anyway."

I locked eyes with her and gave her a cold smile. Our eyes stayed locked for a good five seconds before she was forced to look away. Leighton didn't want this bitch here with her for eight hours a day, five days a week. She would be miserable. Leighton wanted Sienna. That was the *only* doula she wanted. She wouldn't stop firing them until she had her.

"Farrah, that's ridiculous," Leighton said with a sigh.

"How come, dear?" Beverly, Leighton's mother, asked, nursing a glass of what I could easily guess was Chardonnay. "You and Farrah are close."

"I don't want her to have to take care of me, that's all."

"She might as well. She's always here," Ashleigh, Leigh's oldest sister, added.

"Exactly!" Farrah beamed with excitement. "It's going to be amazing! You won't have to worry about a thing! And when your husband has to leave, right after *finally* making it home, I won't mind staying over. You know it's nothing for me. I can stay as long as you need. Your health is *my* top priority."

I clenched down on my jaw and stared across the island at her. She was really tempting me. Farrah wanted me to disrespect her. She wanted me to call her bitches and lose my cool. The way I used to when she would come out of her mouth on some slick shit back in the day when Leighton and I first got together. But I was a different nigga, and I wouldn't give her the satisfaction of proving herself and Leighton's family right. They had opinions about me. None of them respected who I was growing up. They knew I was in the streets. Shit, they still knew who I was, but because I'd made it look sophisticated by dressing it up in a suit and tie and secured myself a few legitimate businesses, they didn't mind standing in my state-of-the-art kitchen, sipping on my thousand-dollar wine. They didn't judge me anymore. Not to my face, they didn't.

But if I nodded at Natasha, giving her the green light to beat the shit out of Farrah, they would. They would call us thugs, animals, and tell Leighton she should have never married me, despite me being the best thing that had ever happened to her and them.

It had been years since I had to give Natasha that head nod, but time wouldn't matter. If I told her to go, she would go, especially at Farrah. She couldn't stand her ass but we were grown as hell, and I was a different nigga.

So, instead of giving Farrah what she wanted, I smiled and put my eyes on Leighton. Winking at her, I subtly let her know everything would be okay. She gave me a smile of relief. Kissing her on the forehead, I told her I loved her, told them to have a good night, and left the house with baby sis in tow.

* * *

"You should've," Natasha said, with her arms crossed over her chest. "I would have gladly beat her ass, Jah. I sat there all day, listening to her talk like she was really in charge of everyone. Momma cut into her a few times, too. It was a shit show. You really saved me."

Thirty-five minutes later, I was pulling up to the curb at Vault nightclub with Tasha, talking about Farrah. It was a busy night at Vault. *Every night* was busy, but Fridays and Saturdays were the busiest and the easiest way to find Saint if you needed him. Vault was his. He owned it and did a damn good job running it too.

Vault was one of the hottest nightclubs in Royal Oak, MI, for young Black people. It stayed to capacity, but nothing ever popped off at Vault. Niggas knew to keep that bullshit as far away from Vault as possible. The only muthafuckas getting through the doors with heat on them had Baptiste blood running through their veins and security. The place was heavily guarded and professionally run. People fucked with Vault off the strength of who ran it, the strong drinks, and the bad bitches who frequented the spot.

"I'm already hip," I said, shaking my head, as I swiped around my phone to shoot a text to the group chat.

I'd texted both Blaise and Saint about the linkup before I left the house. Pops was busy doing whatever he did on Friday nights when he wasn't with Moms or handling business, so I would get with him tomorrow. I was sure he'd gotten a whiff of what happened already, anyway. It was Blaise and Saint who needed to be informed because they never watched the news or stayed up to date on current events. They should've, but that was another thing that was my responsibility. I was the one who was to make sure everything was everything.

"What's going on?" Natasha asked, looking over my shoulder, trying to get a look at my phone. "Why are we here?"

I looked at her from the side of my eye and stuffed my phone into my coat pocket. "You're here to sit at the bar and have a couple of drinks," I told her.

We kept Natasha out of the business for obvious reasons. This wasn't a business for women. The less she knew, the better. She knew a lot, though. She'd never gotten her hands dirty and that was all that mattered. We protected Natasha from the lifestyle. Many people didn't even know there was a Baptiste sister, she was so protected from it. A lot of times, how shielded she was from it made her feel like an outsider. Inside of our home, and outside of it. I tried my best to include her, which was one of the reasons I told her she could come along with me when she asked me. Natasha was rarely around. Sometimes I even forgot I had a little sister. So, the relationship had always been a little shaky. With me being six years older than she was, we didn't have much in common, but I always made sure to assure her I was always a phone call or car ride away. I was more of a father figure to Tasha than I was a big brother because of the way our family dynamic was growing up. Anything she needed, she got it.

She cut her eyes at me. "Okay, Jah."

CHAPTER 21

Sienna

"Just think about it, okay? You're miserable, they're miserable . . . Shit, all of y'all are making *me* miserable. Might as well just make everybody happy by just going back, Si," Shonda said.

I sighed and tied the rope to my fluffy robe around my waist. "Bye, Shon."

"Promise me you'll think about it, at least," she pressed.

I rolled my eyes and walked into the bedroom. "I promise."

I heard the smile in her voice when she said, "Thank you, friend. You're the best! Enjoy your weekend. Call me with *good* news Sunday morning, okay? Bye!"

She hung up and I tossed my phone on my bed. I stood at my vanity and placed my hands flat on the glass tabletop before lowering my head with a deep sigh.

Looking over my shoulder, I eyed my phone, contemplating. Shonda wanted me to go back to work for the Baptistes. The thought had crossed my mind several times since working for this new family. Every single time I really gave it some serious thought, I was reminded of what it meant to work for them.

He was there. I couldn't go back there. I needed to. My bank account was screaming for me to. What I made working for the Baptiste family in one week took me three weeks to make with the McIntyre family. It was ridiculous. The salary difference was insane. I'd even worked for DoorDash on the weekends just to make a couple of extra dollars. A bitch was practically struggling. I'd been digging in my savings so much, I'd been dreading checking it for days now. Pride and the fact that I knew I needed to stay away from him was sending me straight to the poorhouse.

Every morning I woke up to go to work, I wanted to cry out of misery. My life had really been subjected to working for pennies. I was working, again, as an antepartum doula, which would have been fine if I hadn't been treated like a nanny. I was stuck with Jennifer's old client and every day had been hell. I rarely ever spent time with my client, Eileen. She had toddlers who ran around all day, fucking shit up, eating shit up, and drinking shit up. I complained to Shon about it, but she just said I was supposed to be there to alleviate stress from the mother, so *in a way*, I was doing my job.

That was bullshit.

But I rolled with the punches because shit, what leverage did I really have? I had to take what I was offered, considering Shonda didn't have to give me a job at all. She really could have fired my ass for the shit I pulled. So, I just sucked it up and went in every day with a smile on my face and dealt with two bad-ass kids who constantly called me Hershey's milk chocolate. Bad-ass white kids who were rarely ever around Black people, so they didn't know how to fucking act.

Snatching my chair out, I sat down and took another deep breath. Work was the last thing I wanted to think about. I was off for the next two days and wanted to enjoy it and planned on doing just that.

Tonight was ladies' night. We usually did our thing on Saturdays, but Naoki's unpredictable-ass schedule had us partying on a Friday night. It threw everything off for all of us. I'd just gotten in a couple of hours ago, Mahogany had to rush home from the office, Hazel couldn't get tonight off so we were just going to party at her job and leave her fat-ass tips all night, and Sage was on vacation, so our ladies' night would be a little different tonight. Maybe not a little different, very different since I had cut back on drinking.

A bitch had to start somewhere, right? I hadn't given it up completely. I was just spiraling and trying to drown all my problems with liquor. Wine, tequila, vodka, whatever I could get my hands on. I was overindulging, and for no reason because, by the end of the night, I'd have a face full of tears, or a mouth full of cum that belonged to a man who didn't belong to me. Well, not often. Just . . . that one time. The last time, I ended up with a coochie full of his cum, but that was neither here nor there. The problem was the liquor. I was in pain and thought liquor was the cure. It got worse after seeing Amiri.

Seeing him that day put so many fucking raw emotions inside of me. I couldn't hold back. I was, however, proud of myself for saving my tears for the car. I didn't drop one fucking tear in front of him. I refused to allow him to see me weak, but what power did that really hold if I was still weak, regardless?

Why hadn't anyone told me how tough this was? This . . . grieving process. That was what this breakup was. Death. And I was smack-dab in the middle of grief. It was tough. Tough as hell.

Bubble baths, spa days, affirmations, wine—none of it took the pain away for real. These days and weeks, I'd been sprinkling glitter over shit, calling it mental growth. Calling it self-love. Calling it healing. I said I was good. I thought I was good. But until I could be face to face with Amiri and not feel a single fucking thing for him, I'd simply be a broken woman, sprinkling glitter over shit, trying to find the beauty in such an ugly situation.

There was no timeline on healing. No true cure to a broken heart. I had to give myself time and I hadn't done that. Not at all.

Rushing my ass to Pandora's, just to end up falling in love with a dick that was attached to a married man, did nothing for my healing process. Rushing out and leasing this lavish high-rise apartment with rent I could barely afford had done nothing for me. I was lonely. Lonely, sad, and damn near broke, since I was basically working for pennies. I was a fucking mess. The *Fragile* sticker planted on me had gone completely ignored because I was broken. Sometimes I felt like I was broken beyond repair.

But it was over for that sad shit. Tonight would be a good night because I said it would be. I was affirming every single day and night, choosing to be happy. Choosing not to think about *him*. Or *him*. Choosing to let go of the past. Choosing to be okay with just being Sienna. No babies. No husband. Nothing.

Every day, although I hated my job, I chose happiness. I had to remember that everything I wanted took time. I'd been rushing growth. Rushing happiness. Rushing every fucking thing, but I was taking a new approach to things by slowing my ass down and living through the pain and not trying to move around it.

Taking a deep breath, I opened the drawer to my vanity and started on my makeup.

About an hour later, I was dressed and walking into Mahogany's house. I was her designated driver for the night. She didn't want to drive because she wanted to get drunk and let loose tonight. She'd even had me stop by our cousin's house for edibles. I didn't know exactly what Mahogany was going through, but I'd bet it was a midlife crisis. Out of the three of us, she was the one who'd jumped into marriage and the family lifestyle the quickest.

Growing up, she was much like Hazel. Free-spirited, fun, wild, and free. The minute she got with Duke, all of that shit seemed to go right out of the window. It was crazy.

"Hey, Tee-tee!" Aubry yelled, and threw her arms around my waist. "You look cute! I want my hair like that, but my momma said goddess locs are too grown."

I laughed and ran my hand through my locs. "They are. Maybe she'll let you get them on your fourteenth birthday."

Aubry was thirteen, going on twenty-one! She was a sassy little something, but my favorite out of my nieces and nephew.

I gave Aubry a wink and she smirked at me and walked away. I laughed and shook my head before speaking to my other niece, Honesty, and my nephew, Gabe. The baby, as usual, was asleep, bundled up in her car seat, ready to go. I leaned down and gave her a kiss on her juicy cheek.

Standing up, I looked around the house and really took it in. It was clean, for the most part, but there were toys all over the place. Mahogany wasn't going through a midlife crisis, sis just needed a damn break. These ladies' nights were probably the only thing keeping her sane.

Duke's ass stayed at work. He made good-ass money, both of them did, but his job kept him away most of the time, leaving the bulk of the housework and caring for the kids to Mahogany. It was no wonder she wanted more togetherness with me and Hazel and wanted to get drunk as fuck tonight. All of her drinks were going to be on me. Fuck that. I made a mental note to get the kids for her every now and then, too, just to give her a break.

Sitting on the couch, I looked down at Sparkle and smiled. I really couldn't wait to get some quality time in with her little butt. I loved babies. I leaned down and rubbed her tiny hand, wishing I could pick her up and kiss her chubby little cheeks. She gripped my finger and a chill ran down my spine. I could never get tired of this.

A couple of seconds later, Honesty ran up to me wearing a crooked mask. She was four, and just as busy as anybody would imagine a four-year-old being.

"Tee-tee! Tee-tee! Look at me! I look pretty!"

I giggled. "Shhh. You're going to wake Sparkle up," I whispered as I rocked the car seat a bit. Looking up at Honesty, I asked, "You do look pretty! Where you get that mask from?"

My voice trailed off and my eyebrows furrowed as I cocked my head to the side. Taking it off her face, I held it in my hands and examined it.

"Mommy's office." She giggled before she grabbed it and tried to put it back on. "It's pretty!"

I sat there, watching as she tried to put the mask on in a daze. I was speechless, and I probably looked just as crazy as I felt because, eventually, Honesty ran off, wearing the mask I watched her mother get slutted out in with two men at Pandora's.

Thirty minutes later, Mahogany and I walked into the club. I had no idea how we'd even gotten there. I drove there, yes, but I couldn't remember the drive. A bitch had been moving on autopilot since Honesty ran up to me in that mask. I was in complete disbelief. What in the hell was Mahogany doing at Pandora's? A married woman? With four kids? I couldn't get it out of my head. Her in that big-ass bed, getting fucked like that. I thought she was at Momma's house. She was supposed to be at the little family function with them for New Year's Eve. What was she doing at Pandora's?

Mahogany usually brought the new year in with her family. Why was she at Pandora's? Did she stay there the whole night? I had so many questions. How often did she go? Was she a regular? Did Duke know? Oh God. Were they freaks? Did he put her up to that shit? Was he slutting her out? Nah. He couldn't have known. Why did she invite me? What the fuck? She knew I was with Amiri. *I had so many questions* but I couldn't ask her shit.

I didn't know what Mahogany talked about on the ride over. Shit, I didn't know if I'd responded. I did remember my daddy coming to the car to speak when we dropped the kids off at my parents' house. Remembered him saying something about my mother being sorry, but that was about it. My mind was really stuck on the fact that my sister was a freak. A stone-cold, adulterous freak who liked to be fucked by two men at once in a room full of people. And she'd invited me to that freaky-ass party to participate in the freaky-ass shit. Why?

I said I wouldn't have but two drinks tonight, but I needed four. I needed a whole bottle because . . . *what?*

"You heard me?"

"Huh?" I asked, snapping out of my trance.

Mahogany's eyebrows dipped. "Bitch, you've been out of it since we left my house. Did you already have a piece of candy?" she asked, referring to the edibles.

I shook my head. "Naw. I'm good."

She laughed. "You sure?"

"Yeah, Nene. I'm sure." I laughed and lightly frowned. "What did you say?"

"I asked if you wanted to find Hazel or go to the bar first?"

"Bar," I blurted out.

The club was packed. There were people everywhere, wall to wall. Every table was occupied. Luckily, we had a section. I needed to sit down. Couldn't imagine standing after the shit I'd just found out. I had forgotten all about the invite. I hadn't forgotten about Pandora's at all but I stopped thinking about where the invitation could've come from a long time ago. It was crazy how the minute I stopped looking and trying to figure it out, it was literally put right in my face. That tripped me the fuck out and it came from the person I would have least expected. Hazel? Yeah. Never in a million years would I have guessed it came from Mahogany's sneaky ass!

When we made it to the bar, I untucked the locs that had gotten caught underneath my cropped white faux fur and winced in pain. Standing at the bar, I shifted my weight back and forth between my feet, wishing I'd opted out of the orange, over-the-knee, four-and-a-half-inch high-heeled boots I'd coupled with a simple black one-piece jumpsuit. But they were cute and matched my orange Chanel bag to a T.

She was talking again. Her lips were moving but I didn't hear a thing coming from her mouth, and not because the Lil Baby track was too loud for me to hear her. I was dazed *again*.

Looking at her, all I saw was the way she took those dicks. I laughed. Literally laughed. I couldn't control it. Looking back, literally putting Mahogany in that room . . . on that bed . . . the shit was insane! I gave Mahogany a once-over and shook my head. Thick ass. Just like the bitch back at Pandora's. *Because she was the bitch at Pandora's.* The woman I complimented and mentally cheered on and applauded for the confidence. Wow. Mahogany was her.

Tonight, she exuded that same confidence, too. She had on a tight red bodycon dress and a black, floor-length mink. Hers was real—unlike mine. On her feet were a pair of black thigh-high leather boots. Her long weave was bone straight with a part down the middle. She looked damn good, like the type of bitch who could afford that twenty-thousand-dollar membership at Pandora's. Because . . . she was the type of bitch who could afford it. Wow. Nothing in life surprised me anymore. Shit was really insane.

"Right? That shit is crazy," Mahogany said in response to me laughing.

Her crazy and the crazy I laughed at were two completely different things. I was sure of it.

"Mm-hmm." I hummed with a shake of my head. "Crazy as hell."

Finally, after we had been standing for a couple of minutes, the gentlemen sitting on the barstools in front of us offered us their seats. I politely thanked them and sat down. A bitch's dogs were barking! If I would've been thinking about something other than going back to the Baptiste household, I would have sprayed my feet with numbing spray before I put my boots on. I said I would stop thinking about it but I hadn't. Especially not after I'd checked my savings.

"Damn, you smell good," said the man who'd given up his seat for me. "Look good, smell good . . ."

I looked up at him with a cocked brow, daring him to finish his statement. Instead, his eyes met mine with a sly smirk and we shared a light laugh. He was attractive, very attractive, but not attractive enough to steer me off my little self-love, no-new-dick journey. So, I thanked him, looked away, and signaled for the bartender.

"Whatever she wants, I got it," he said before picking his cup up and sipping from it.

I didn't argue with that.

"And whatever she's drinking, I got," said his friend, motioning toward Mahogany, who quickly flashed her phat-ass wedding rings.

"No, thank you," she said with a smile. "I'm married."

I turned the corners of my mouth up into a light smile. *Oh, now you care about being married? Yo' ass didn't care about being married when you were taking two dicks at the same time in a room full of muthafuckas.* There was no telling what she did once I walked away. I wondered if she'd stayed there all night. Couldn't have. She had a family to go home to. Man, I had so many damn questions but I was too fucking shook to ask her anything.

"Damn, that's too bad. He's a lucky-ass man," the guy said.

Was he? I felt bad for Duke. Honestly, I did. He wasn't perfect, but I hadn't heard anything about him cheating in years and even then, that was before they were married.

"That he is," Mahogany said with a grin as she adjusted her diamond rings.

I ordered a shot of Casamigos and she cut her eyes at me. I ignored the look. I was going to take it easy. I just had to start off heavy because I'd really been hit with a fucking curveball.

Fifteen minutes later, we were sitting at our booth with Naoki, talking, laughing, and drinking. Well, Naoki and Mahogany were laughing and talking. Me? I was still in that trance of disbelief. I didn't know why I couldn't get Mahogany and Pandora's off my mind. I wondered if it was because I couldn't see her in that light. I wondered if it was because my mother had always held Mahogany up on a pedestal while she secretly judged me and Hazel, disguising it with condescending remarks every time we were together. I didn't know what it was exactly, but the one shot of Casamigos hadn't loosened me up nearly as much as I thought it would.

A couple of minutes later, Hazel walked over with her little tray in hand, dressed skimpily in a white high-waisted skirt, blue lace tights, and a red lace bodysuit. She looked cute, despite the odd color coordination. The colors did, however, match the club's aesthetic with its red and blue lights, the flags adorning a few of the walls, the plastic wear, and a few accent pieces I'd seen scattered about. Hazel could rock a bag and she would look good in it. Baby sis looked good in everything.

"Heeeey!" she yelled over the music, dancing with her tray up.

She leaned over and gave me a hug.

"Hey, boo. You look the fuck good," I complimented her before playfully smacking her on her butt.

"Don't I? I already know. I made enough for my car note already and the night just started," she said with a grin as she gave Naoki and Mahogany hugs. "What y'all drinking?"

As she took their orders, my eyes landed on a guy mingling near our section. He was *very* good looking. He wore a navy blue tailored suit that I could tell was Tom Ford because of the plethora of Tom Ford that lined Amiri's closet, Tom Ford shoes, and a thick Cuban link chain.

Every crowd he walked into seemed to part for him. He was very well respected and greeted everyone with the same respect they greeted him with—soft smiles, handshakes, and pats on the back. He was a boss and I automatically wondered if he *was* the boss.

I swallowed when I realized he was coming our way. I hadn't come out to meet anybody new. Shit, after I took my shot, I practically ran away from the bar to get away from the man who'd bought it for me because a bitch didn't have time. But there was something about this man that said he wouldn't be easy to turn away.

"What you want, Si? Casamigos?"

"Shit, she don't need anything for real. She's my designated driver," Mahogany mumbled.

Before I could tell Hazel to get me a double shot of Casamigos, regardless of what the fuck Mahogany's cheating ass had said. Mr. Fine Ass approached our table.

"Wassup, ladies? How is everything going? Having a good night, I hope," he said, his eyes lingering on mine before he looked at everyone else.

I wondered if I looked like a deer caught in headlights because that was exactly what I felt like, staring at him. Hearing *his* voice come out of this man's mouth caught me completely off guard. His accent. That cadence. The ruggedness. It sent a chill down my spine. One so aggressive, I had to run a hand down the back of my neck.

"It's gotten better, that's for sure," Naoki flirted.

He nodded and sent Naoki a flirtatious wink before looking at Hazel. "You taking good care of them, Haz?"

Hazel nodded. "Yep. I'm just waiting for my sister to tell me what she wants."

"Your sister?" he asked as he looked around at the three of us.

Hazel nodded at me, and I quickly told her I wanted a double shot of Casamigos. Right after, I fished around my Chanel for my phone, avoiding the daggers Mahogany shot my way and the pensive stare the guy had on me. I didn't want to talk, and I didn't want him to talk. At all. What his voice did to me was just a cruel reminder of what *Jahad* had done to me. Imprinted on me. Staked claim to me. Literally owned me . . . and I could and would *never* be his. But he would always be a part of me, regardless of how much I tried to forget him, and that shit drove me insane.

But then . . .

Something changed.

The air in the room grew thicker and heat ran from the top of my head to the tip of my toes. Not the type of heat that comes from liquor hitting your system. The type of heat I'd only experienced when I was around *him*.

I squirmed in my seat and took a deep breath, attempting to ignore the feeling, deciding it was probably brought on by the guy's accent. His accent probably wasn't even Haitian. Shit, I didn't know how to differentiate between Caribbean accents. He could be Jamaican. My ass was tripping.

"*Li isit la* (He's here)."

My eyebrows snapped together, and I slowly lifted my eyes from my Instagram feed to look up. They traveled up from his dark jeans and lingered at that Hermès belt buckle before they landed on his hands, where that diamond-encrusted wedding band sat. The one he didn't have on that night at Pandora's.

I swallowed and slowly closed my eyes before opening them to his eyes on mine.

I couldn't escape this fucking man. *Why couldn't I escape him?*

CHAPTER 22

Jahad

I didn't believe in coincidences. Never had.

Either Sienna was stalking me, or we were being pulled together. She didn't pique me as the stalking type. I didn't know her, but I knew enough about her to know she wasn't a deranged stalker. It had to be something else. I wasn't religious. Never had been. I was raised by a spiritual mother. Most of the people back home were. Growing up, I was taught that everything happened for a reason. Nothing . . . absolutely nothing in the world was coincidental. The shit with her ending up our doula? Not even that. However, I chose to brush it off. Just the way I'd brushed everything else off. The way time seemed to move when our eyes met and the jolts of electricity that ran through me any time her skin touched mine. I ignored the shit because I didn't want it to mean anything else.

Tonight couldn't be ignored. I was still at Vault. Walked in with Natasha about two hours ago and had been here ever since, waiting for Blaise to show up. He was out with Bebe, so he couldn't get with us when I texted. I understood, so I kicked back and sat at the bar with Natasha for a minute, chopped it up with bro in the office for a few, too, until he had to walk around and do the owner thing. I was in no rush to go back home to Leighton and the vultures. A house full of emotional women and a nigga who was nearly at his wit's end wouldn't mix well.

While I waited for Saint to come back, Blaise hit me and let me know he had pulled up. I left the office to find Saint. I didn't know that when I found him, I'd find him standing in a section with Sienna in it. When I walked up and told him Blaise had made it, I immediately felt her. It didn't take me but a second to sense she was there. I didn't have to scan the faces of the other women to spot her because I *felt* her. And she felt it too. I *saw* the feeling wash over her.

There was something about this woman.

It wasn't the taste of her pussy. It wasn't the feel of her velvety walls clenching my dick. To me, that shit was shallow. I'd never been the type to get hooked on a woman because she had good pussy. It was something else. It was *her*. And I barely even knew her. Knew things *about* her but I really didn't know Sienna. I knew the subtle things too. The subtle things she didn't think anyone knew. The shit she hid from the rest of the world. The things she only did when she didn't think anyone was watching. But . . . I didn't know her. However, I felt something for her. Wanted to get to know her. Wanted her to tell me she felt the shit I felt when we were near one another.

"Sienna." I spoke with a head nod.

She gave me a nervous smile and nodded back. "Hey."

Saint looked over at me with raised brows. "You two know each other?"

I locked eyes with him and nodded. He knew who Sienna was. He knew *exactly* who Sienna was. Knew her name too. So him asking if we knew each other after I'd said her name was just Saint being a dumbass.

He concealed his smirk by dragging his hand over his mouth. "Damn. Small world. She's my waitress's sister."

"Small world indeed," I said after putting my eyes back on Sienna, who had gone back to looking at her phone.

However, I could tell she didn't give a fuck about what was on the screen. My eyes traveled from her face down to her bouncing knee. She was nervous. Always so nervous. I thought it was a thing that only happened when we were in tight spaces, but tonight proved otherwise.

Looking away from her, I chucked my head toward the back of the club where Saint's office sat. "Come on, bro. Business."

Before we walked off, I gave Sienna another look and said, "It was good seeing you, Sienna. You ladies have a great night."

"You too," she replied.

"Damn, she fine," Saint said, shaking his head as we walked away from the group of women.

I nodded and stuffed my hands into the pockets of my coat. I didn't have anything to say to that, except for the nod I'd given him. Sienna was fine as hell. Tonight was the best I'd ever seen her. The new hair and makeup looked good on her. Her titties were sitting nice as fuck in the one-piece, too. Yeah, she looked good as hell, but her eyes told another story. A regular nigga could easily look at Sienna and see what we saw—how fine she was. How thick she was. The titties . . . shit like that. But me? I looked past that shit. I didn't look often. Hell, I didn't look at all. But at Sienna, I did. And what I saw in her was more than what was on the exterior. I saw the tears she hid from everyone sitting behind those pretty-ass brown eyes. Brown eyes that would be seen as plain and sultry to anyone else, but brown eyes that were beautiful and told so much of her truth to me.

We stopped by the bar to check on Natasha before we headed in the back for the meeting. She was having a better time here than she was having at the crib for sure. Sis had herself a few drinks and had been sitting, talking with the bartender all night. What she didn't know was that I'd put a bug in dawg's ear and told him to keep an eye on her and the niggas off her. He kept her company with friendly conversation and watered-down drinks, and she hadn't a clue. All Natasha cared about was the good time she was having. I didn't have to get chewed out or told I was overbearing and overprotective in the process because she had no idea I was controlling shit.

We caught Blaise right before he turned the corner into the back area where Saint's office sat. Slapping hands with him, I pulled him into a brotherly embrace and then he did the same with Saint. I felt the stress coming off bro when he leaned against the back wall while Saint unlocked his door.

The minute we got inside of the office, Blaise hit the bar. Instead of sitting at Saint's desk, I sat in the lounge area where the surveillance monitors were. I *could* say I sat there to keep an eye on Natasha. But I didn't need to do that. We had eyes all over the club. She was protected; it was Saint's. I sat there to watch Sienna. I always wanted to watch her. This obsession I had with her was unhealthy and that was exactly why I needed Leighton to let the infatuation she had with her go. She wouldn't. And in a dark, twisted part of my mind, I really didn't want her to. I wanted Sienna in the house. I wanted her close. However, what I wanted and what I needed were two completely different things.

"I was supposed to drop Bebe off hours ago," Blaise said, approaching with a glass of liquor I hadn't seen him pour because my eyes were too fixated on the monitor with the camera pointed straight to the section where Sienna and her girls were seated.

"Bitch wouldn't answer the phone, and when I pulled up at the house, she wasn't there. I drove around for hours, trying to find her, calling her and shit. The bitch did that on purpose. When she finally did pick up, she was drunk and out with some nigga. I ended up having to leave Bebe at the house with the hos."

I tore my eyes away from the monitors when he said that. "You did what?"

Hearing that my niece was practically at a ho house alone snatched my attention away from Sienna with the quickness. I didn't like it. I didn't like it at all. Blaise needed to get his shit together. The decisions he made were asinine. Every time this nigga vented to us about his baby momma problems, I thanked God I wasn't as reckless as him with my dick when I was coming up. I was wild as hell, but reckless with my nut? Never.

Blaise held his hand up. "Relax. I trust them with her."

Saint shook his head. "This nigga, man."

"They know if even one of them touch a hair on my daughter's head, I will bleed every one of them bitches dry, one by one," Blaise said through gritted teeth before grabbing his pants and sitting down. "What's this shit about, anyway? I hope we don't have any more surprises. You know I'm still adjusting after the trip back home."

Blaise and Pops had just gotten back from the business trip back home a week ago. Lazy-ass nigga. He barely did anything except for the bare minimum but complained about a spur-of-the-moment meeting. The problem with the way shit was set up for us now was that niggas had gotten too comfortable. Comfortable with the structure. Comfortable with me handling everything on the back end. Comfortable with just collecting money. If it wasn't about bodying a nigga, Blaise didn't want to talk about it. He wanted to get his hands dirty. The suit-and-tie, meeting-type shit wasn't for him. He hated it and I hated to have him around for it. Loved my brother, would body any-fucking-body behind him, but the nigga was annoying as hell.

"Walker's dead," I said, shifting my eyes away from him and back to the monitor.

My nostrils slightly flared when someone new came into the frame. He was talking to Sienna. She'd looked up at him, smiled, said a few words, and picked her shot up. Whatever she said to him didn't send his ass the other way because he sat next to her with his arm draped over the back of the couch, grinning and shit. While she sat there and allowed him in her space.

Fuck did I care for, right?

I was married. Had a whole wife at home. A *pregnant* wife.

So why did I care? I couldn't care.

I ran my tongue over my bottom lip and squinted at the monitor, watching, waiting for him to leave. But he didn't. She continued to smile. Continued to entertain him. When he ran the back of his hand over her cheek, I snorted and ran my hand down the back of my neck. A nigga was bugging. Taking a deep breath, I dragged my hand down my face and shifted my attention to my brothers.

"When?" Blaise asked.

"This morning. Heard it on the news a couple hours ago," I told him before shifting my eyes back to the monitor. Once I took them off the monitor, I looked over at Saint and he was watching me, wearing that stupid-ass smirk.

I sat up, resting my arms on my knees, while I ran my hand over my waves. How uncomfortable I was was crazy. The nigga was still there. And Sienna? Smiling the same. She had a fresh drink. Her sister was at the table, dropping it off, and the nigga sitting next to her paid for it. Why did she allow that nigga in her space? He didn't deserve to breathe the same air as her.

Blaise took a deep breath and sipped from his cup. "Shit. That's some good-ass news."

I nodded. "It is, but now we wait."

"Wait for what?" Saint asked with dipped brows.

I nodded in Blaise's direction. "To see if this big, stupid-ass nigga fucked up."

"I never fuck up," Blaise cockily retorted before finishing his glass off. "I'm out."

He pushed up off the couch and Saint and I stood to shake hands with him before he left. As soon as he was out of the room, Saint was on my ass about Sienna.

"You about to run after your girl?" he asked, nodding toward the monitor. "Look like you 'bout ready to break dawg's face."

I drew back with a frown. "What? Nigga, you wild."

Saint shook his head and maneuvered around the couch to walk over to his bar. "Nah, nigga, you wild. I get it, though. Shorty is bad as hell. She got a vibe to her too. She's dangerous. Would be fun for a nigga like me, but for you?" He made a noise and whistled. "Dangerous as hell."

I rested on the back of the couch with my arms stretched out and my eyes fixed on the monitors. Saint kept talking; however, my attention wasn't on him. I was sure he noticed and had probably said something about it, too, but I wasn't hearing that nigga. I was too gone. It was no longer about the nigga in the section. It was about her. My eyes were on her and her only. I didn't give a fuck about him. My eyes were drawn to her smile. It was wide. Bright . . . but lifeless. She was in so much pain. I wondered if the people around her noticed. I wondered if the nigga with her, sitting beside her, practically feeding her liquor, noticed. He didn't give a fuck. He had one thing in mind: pussy. He wanted to fuck. I felt like Sienna was smart enough to know that, but in too much pain to give a fuck about it. I didn't know her well enough to really say but I *saw her*. Saw her without her mask. I saw past it because I'd seen her without it once. While she cried at my kitchen island and drank a whole bottle of wine. The one from Pandora's wasn't the only mask she wore. She wore them often, just like me.

I jumped up from the couch, startling Saint, who yelled, *"Kaka!"*

I walked over to him with my hand extended. "I'm up. Take Natasha home."

With a smirk, he shook hands with me. "Why can't you? About to grab the mistress and get up out of here?"

I locked eyes with him. "I don't have a mistress, Saint."

He shrugged. "You sure about that?"

We stood in silence for a few seconds before releasing hands, and I walked away. I didn't have a fucking mistress. I had a problem. Except this time, I had no idea how I was going to get rid of it.

Two minutes later, I was at the bar with Natasha. I let her know Saint would take her home. She asked a bunch of questions I didn't answer, and when she tried to follow me, I told her to sit down and wait for him to come get her. She listened, but that didn't stop her from trying to watch me as I made my way over to Sienna's section. I was sure I'd wake up to a couple of missed calls and text messages from her tomorrow morning. Natasha wasn't Leighton's biggest fan, but if she felt like I was cheating on her, she'd have some shit to say. I wasn't cheating on Leigh, though, and had absolutely no intentions of doing that tonight.

When I walked up to the section, everybody but Sienna looked up at me. She knew I was there, though. She sighed heavily, took a long sip from her drink, and turned her attention on the guy next to her, attempting to ignore my presence.

I cocked my head to the side and lifted my eyes up at her as an attempt to get her attention. Where I stood was in perfect alignment with her peripheral vision, although she didn't need to see me in it to know I was there.

"Si," one of her girls said, tapping her on the arm.

The guy she was with sized me up, but when his eyes met mine, his brows raised and he drew back a little, recognizing me off top. He didn't get up and walk away. I didn't want him to. Like I said, I didn't give a fuck about him. All I cared about was her. I wanted her to get up and walk away with me. I'd never been the type of nigga to make a scene for the sake of bitching a nigga off the strength of a female. It had never been that. The only time I'd ever been on murder shit with a nigga was about my respect. That was one thing I'd been known to never play about. As long as he sat there quietly, didn't touch her, and didn't address me . . . we'd be straight. Which I knew he would because the nigga knew of me. Yeah, he could sit there, sipping from his drink, stone-faced and shit all he wanted to. I got it. He didn't want to seem like the bitch he was in front of women. He was saving face. For his sake, I hoped he cared just as much about saving his life.

"Hm?"

"Jah—"

"I know," Sienna said, interrupting her.

"You cool?" the guy asked with his eyes fixed on her. He hadn't looked my way since I approached the section.

I shifted my eyes from her to him. He didn't look at me, but the tapping of his finger on the table told me he felt my eyes on him. She looked at him, gave him a tight smile, and nodded. I ran my thumb over my bottom lip, then reached over him, grabbed her coat, and shook it to straighten it out.

I draped it over my forearm and reached out for her to grab my hand. She looked up at me with crinkled brows and glossy eyes, swimming in sadness. Her lips slightly parted and her shoulders fell a bit as if she'd exhaled. Still, she sat there, unmoving. And the nigga next to her? He ran his hand over his head, stressed. He was quiet. At least to me, he was. The sound around us seemed to fade out, the same way it did back at Pandora's. It was just her and I. In a club full of muthafuckas, at a table full of people, we could only see each other.

I didn't know how much time passed before her small hand fell into mine. This time, I wasn't surprised by that surge of electricity that transferred between us. I expected it. I would have only been surprised if it hadn't happened. I pulled her to her feet, and she stood up. Once she did, she walked over to me, and I slid her coat over her shoulders. I closed my eyes when the soft scent of vanilla and cashmere filled my nostrils. I was tempted to bury my face in the crook of her neck, inhale deeper, and kiss her there, but I knew better. My hunger when it came to this woman was aggressive. However, tonight was more about freeing her than it was about my fulfilling my appetite.

Fifteen minutes later, we headed to her spot. She was bundled up in her little-ass coat, leaned over on the door with her leg crossed over the other one like she'd move further over if she could. I understood. She wanted space between us. She didn't want to be here with me, but she couldn't help herself. When she was around me, there was pretty much nothing she could do to stop that magnetic pull that forced her closer to me, despite the warning signs. I could assume with confidence because I felt that way, too. I knew I shouldn't have had Sienna with me. I should've spoken to her, finished business with my brothers, took Natasha home and went back home to my wife. But . . .

"I'm my sister's designated driver," Sienna mumbled, her soft, slurring voice cutting through the silence.

I gave her a quick glance before putting my eyes back on the road. "Designated driver? You need a designated driver. We went over this already." I tugged on my beard. "Shorty's straight."

Before we left the section, I had a short talk with the women she was with. Her sister, Mahogany, and her best friend, *Naoki*. Imagine my surprise when she introduced herself. By the smirk she gave me, she knew her best friend was out giving niggas her name instead of her own. Mahogany didn't like the idea of me taking Sienna. Naoki was open to it, which told me she knew more about Sienna and me than Mahogany did. Mahogany didn't know anything. She mentioned Sienna being her designated driver, but then considered all the drinking Sienna had done and said she'd find another way home. I offered to drop her off, but she wasn't ready to end her night. Sienna wasn't ready, either. But it was over for that shit. She was one drink away from barely being able to stand on her own two feet. Tavious and Kim made strong-ass drinks, and I refused to give the nigga feeding her the shit an all-access pass to a body that should only be touched by me. My first thought was my truest. That was the way I felt about it. Shamelessly.

"We shouldn't be together," she mumbled before scooting over, closer to the door, trying to escape me. There was no escaping me. Not here, it wasn't. I glanced up at the roof of my car and drew in a deep breath. Not at all, it seemed. The truth behind that statement was a little unsettling.

CHAPTER 23

Sienna

I wanted to crawl inside of a deep, dark hole and stay there for the rest of my life.

How much life would I have left to live if I crawled inside of a deep, dark hole, anyway?

Probably not much.

I still wanted to do it.

How was this loving myself? This was weak. *He* . . . made me weak. I'd gone from being weak for one man to being weak for another. Where was my strength? Every time I closed my eyes, that popular TikTok sound replayed in my head. *You weak in the knees! Stand up!* I needed to stand up. Seriously. How much did I really love myself? Did I give a fuck about Sienna *at all?*

A few hours ago, I was all *Oh, I'm just having a drink or two. I love myself. I'm not drowning my problems in liquor anymore. It doesn't work, anyway. I always end up with a face full of tears, or a mouth full of cum.* I was all self-love, self-righteous, I'm healing, right? So, how did I end up here, with him walking me up to my apartment building? His arm was hooked around my waist, while I staggered in boots I needed to pull off.

I clumsily fished around my purse for the small-ass keys to my building because I still hadn't put them on my regular, fuller key ring. My life was a mess. I was a mess. I didn't have time to put keys on a fucking key ring? What the fuck?

I stopped walking, took a deep breath, and placed my hand on my forehead. I wanted to snatch away from him. *Needed* to snatch away from him but I was afraid that if I did snatch away, I'd end up falling. It was too cold to fall. How embarrassing would that be? I'd already embarrassed myself enough. I was drunk. More drunk now than I was in that kitchen. That beautiful kitchen where I'd lost every bit of self-respect I thought I had.

Fucking slut.

Nasty, side-piece-ass bitch.

That was who I was.

That was who I wanted to be.

And that was why when the nigga from the bar came to our section, I welcomed him. I let him buy me two drinks, knowing I didn't need them, but I needed to drink. I *had* to drink. I'd just found out that my sister was an adulterous slut who'd cheated on *her husband* at an underground fuck fest she invited me to, while I gave my pussy to a man who was also an adulterous slut, cheating on *his wife*.

What in the entire fuck?

I needed the bottle.

The entire bottle of Casamigos.

I was perfectly capable of buying my own drinks, but the thing was, I allowed him to pay for them. Let him sit with me, flirt and shit because I wanted to get *him* off my mind. It didn't work, though. *Ain't that some shit?*

I stared into that man's face, smiling, laughing, and talking, with tears in my eyes. I was losing my mind. Losing my mind because I couldn't stop thinking about *that man. This* man.

"Here, let me see," Jahad said, motioning for my purse.

I looked over at him, took another deep breath, and handed him my purse. He found the keys in less than ten seconds. I stood back with my arms wrapped around my body while I waited for him to unlock the door to the main entrance to the building.

Once he got it open, he reached out for me and I looked down at his hand before grabbing hold of it. His arm was around my waist again. Except this time, he held me closer, tighter, like he didn't want to let me go.

He smelled so fucking good. As callous as I tried to be, the truth was told by the goosebumps that ran down the back of my neck, forcing me to put my free hand there. Jahad had an intense effect on me. One that no one had ever had on me, and it had absolutely nothing to do with the way he treated my pussy. It was him. It had been him since I bumped into him at Pandora's. Before he put his mouth on me. Before I put my mouth on him. Before he slid his long, thick, veiny dick inside of my pussy. It was just . . . him. His aura. It was captivating. Magnetic. Drowning. Intense. *Every-fucking-thing.* Which was why I had to stay away from him.

Jahad held me close to his side until we were at my apartment door, where I slid out of his embrace to unlock the door. I didn't have a key for that. I had an unlock code.

I looked over my shoulder at him with a squint. "Turn around, please."

Jahad laughed lightly, shook his head, nodded, and then slowly turned around.

"I don't *trust* you," I mumbled with an eye roll, lightly staggering as I struggled with the keypad. I put the wrong code in twice before I finally got it right.

I opened the door and stepped inside. Turning around to face him, I gripped the door, placing myself in between the small crack in it to hold myself up on it and to keep him out. When he took a step to come inside, I placed my hand on his chest and my breath seemed to get caught up in my throat. The electrifying tingle that shot through my fingertips through my entire being forced me to pull my hand back. With raised brows and misty eyes, I wondered if he'd felt it too.

He looked down at his chest, and then up at me, with furrowed brows, before taking a step into my apartment, basically letting himself in. I really couldn't even call what he'd done pushing himself into the apartment because when he advanced, I didn't put up too much of a fight to stop him. I was weak, remember? I wanted to be his side bitch. Wanted him to cum down my throat. Wanted to squirt on his face and watch him lick my juices from his lips. I'd never say that out loud. My thoughts . . . here . . . it was a safe space. I was free to be me. Didn't need to pretend. Couldn't pretend if I wanted to. I just gave a little resistance so it wouldn't look as easy as it would be for him to have me if he wanted me. Fucking ridiculous. *Where's your dignity, Sienna?*

I sat down on my new entryway bench and pulled my boots off. I couldn't wait to come out of them. Jahad stood quietly at the door, watching me. I hadn't looked up at him. I felt his eyes on me. Those piercing-ass eyes of his. Any time they were on me, they literally bored into me.

"Why are you still here?" I asked, tossing my boots into the corner. "You said you wanted to take me home. I'm home."

"Can we talk?" he asked.

I tossed my head back against the wall and closed my eyes. The room spun a bit. I'd overdone it. As always. I hated this. I hated this so much. I wanted to curl up in bed in a fetal position and sleep. But it was never that easy for me. I never went to bed and just went to sleep. I always cried first. Crying was like that bedtime feeding for newborn babies. I didn't sleep without it.

"About what?"

I swallowed when I felt him come near me. I pulled my legs back underneath the bench and my heart raced. Ugh. I was yet again disgusted with my damn self. I wanted him so bad. Wanted to unwrap my arms from my body to hold on to him. Wanted to feel his strong body against mine again. He felt good. Manly. In his arms, I felt safe. The safest I'd ever felt in my entire fucking life.

I hated this so much.

Hated it more than I did Amiri.

Crazy, right? Desiring a man I couldn't have was torture. Who in the fuck was I? I had to ask myself that at least twenty times a day. Why was this happening to me? What was life? *My* life?

Why couldn't I have met him first? Before her? Before Amiri? I wanted forever with Jahad, and I barely even knew him. I didn't need to know him to know I wanted forever with him. I knew because I wanted *the feeling*. The feeling of him. The exhilarating rush of energy that shot through my entire fucking body any time he was near. I wanted to feel that forever. For an eternity. I never wanted to go without that electrifying pull of gravity. The pull . . . it was always so got damn good. But when we touched? Oh God. When we'd finally collide after resisting that fucking pull? It was like floating. It was like soaring. In the sky. Free. Free of every fucking thing. Limitless. Nothing existed but us when I was with him.

The reality I faced was depressing as hell. That was what pissed me off. That was what nearly brought me to tears. Reality. He was married and, to him, I was nothing more than an easy fuck. Some bitch he met at a freak party who had good-ass pussy he couldn't get enough of. A woman who'd let him fuck regardless of the ring he had on his finger. *She* didn't care about any of it. *She* let him fuck on the kitchen island his wife once prepared meals on before she was bedridden. *She* let him fuck while that bedridden wife laid upstairs, pregnant with his child. That was who he saw when he looked at me. That was reality. The soaring, the electrifying high he gave me, that was bullshit. That was fantasy.

He sat down and his knee brushed up against mine. I flinched away and slid over, closer to the wall. He took a deep breath and his eyes landed on me. My eyes stayed closed. I felt his on me. Piercing fuckers.

"Leighton wants—"

"Please go home," I interrupted with a laugh. *"Leighton wants, Leighton wants,"* I mocked in a horrible Haitian accent with my mouth turned down like I was a little-ass kid. "Leighton wants you at home! Not here with me in the middle of the fucking night! You care about what Leighton wants . . .

now? Did you care about what Leighton wanted when you fucked me in her kitchen? When you fucked me at Pandora's? Did you care about what Leighton wanted when you pulled me out of the club, just to fuck me at my spot since I'm not at yours anymore? No! Please get the fuck out of my apartment and stop pretending this is about what Leighton wants because you don't give a fuck!" I screamed.

I snapped.

I snapped.

I fucking snapped.

Her name was a trigger. What about what I wanted? Hm? I wanted to be loved. I wanted a big house. I wanted a family. I wanted him. I wanted to be seen as more than an easy piece of sad-ass pussy. What about me? What about my happily ever after? Didn't I deserve that shit? I was losing my fucking mind.

"Si—"

"I said get out!" I screamed at the top of my lungs, finally opening my eyes to find him crouching in front of me with his arms resting on his knees.

When did he get there?

How drunk was I? Yep. I was losing my muthafucking mind.

He stood up and held his hands up. "Aight. I'm leaving."

I stood up, nodded, and followed him to the door. "Yep. Go home. Go home to your wife. Sorry to disappoint! You won't be getting any more pussy out of me, my nigga! I'm not a side bitch. I'm not an easy piece of pussy to slide in when you feel like it! Clearly, you've gotten the wrong idea about me!"

I couldn't shut up. What Cady Heron say? A bitch had word vomit. I had it. Always had it when I was on one. Once it started, getting it to stop was pretty fucking impossible. I screamed at him. Yelled at him about not being a side bitch or an easy piece of pussy to slide in, but that was my own insecurities jumping outside of my damn body. I was crumbling. *I* had the wrong idea about me. I didn't know who I was. I was ashamed of who I had become. I just . . . I wanted Jahad.

Leighton didn't deserve how much I wanted her husband. If she knew. My God . . . if she fucking knew. That would destroy her. I didn't want to hurt anybody. I couldn't help what happened. Couldn't help the way I felt. I wished I could. It would make this so much easier. Feelings were a bitch. Honestly.

Jahad stood facing the door and glanced over at me. "I didn't come here to have sex with you, Sienna."

I frowned and sized him up and down. "Yes, you did. That's all you want from me. You look at me and you see me as the girl from Pandora's. That . . ."

I grabbed the wall and held my other arm out for balance. "Had sex with you . . . did all of that nasty shit to you . . . and I didn't know you. You think I'm a ho. I'm . . . I'm not a whore. You just . . ."

And then my equilibrium was thrown completely off. The room began to violently spin, and I lost feeling in my limbs. I went from holding on to the wall to staggering all over the place with flailing arms. It wasn't like that for long, though. Before I could hit the floor, Jahad had his arms wrapped around me. And there it was. That fucking feeling. That feeling that had me on the brink of tears a moment ago because I wanted it forever, but I couldn't have it forever because forever with him was impossible because he belonged to her. He was already someone's forever.

The deep, dark hole?

Where was it?

I needed it.

I pulled away from his touch and staggered away, trying to stop the trembling of my bottom lip. Trying not to fall. He was right behind me, though. There to catch me if I stumbled too much. I was on the brink of losing it. I didn't know how much longer I could hold my tears inside before they erupted. I was a fucking mess.

"Listen, let me just carry you to your room at least," Jahad said from behind after catching me for a second time.

I turned around and faced him, searching my brain for a snappy comeback about him trying to get me to bed, but I came up with nothing. Looking up at him, that beautiful brown—almost black—skin glistening. Those dreamy brown eyes piercing so deep inside of me, it was as if Jahad could see every teardrop I had been holding back. I was rendered speechless. Or just incoherently drunk. Whatever the case, when he gripped my waist tighter and went to lift me, the dam broke. He froze, and I stood there violently crying in his arms. My body shuddered with every tear I spilled on his chest. The tighter he held me, the harder I cried. In his arms, I felt safe enough to do so. I cried in Jahad's arms as if he was my pillow and I was alone.

After about five minutes of boohooing, my crying subsided a bit, but Jahad didn't loosen his hold on me. His strong arms stayed wrapped around me. When he dropped a kiss on the top of my head, I liked to fucking lose it again. This man . . . he needed to leave. He was no good for me, and apparently, I was no good for him. This was unhealthy. This was toxic. He was a married man, and I was a woman with a battered heart. A heart that needed healing. A heart that needed to stay as far away from this married man as possible because, my heart, it couldn't take any more battering.

"You have to leave," I said, my voice slightly muffled.

"I know, but I can't," he admitted. "I can't leave you like this."

I swallowed and rested my head against his chest, listening to the heavy thump of his heart. With wide eyes, the unsettling gut feeling of pure fear filled my being as the revelation of what I'd gotten myself into hit me. Like a powerful blow to the gut, or to my heart, rather, I was unintentionally falling for this married man. Falling headfirst, at full speed, with nothing but concrete beneath me. No. Concrete would be too easy. Beneath me was the biggest, deepest body of water. The Pacific Ocean. I was falling headfirst there on a freefall to the bottom where the truth lay. The truth of what falling for him would do to me. To my life. Things were only going to get worse. I saw it. I felt it. I tasted it.

Saw it like that big, endless body of water. Felt it like the impact of hitting that cold, immeasurable ocean. Tasted it like the sea salt that would fill my mouth, drowning me once I sank.

Standing in my living room with his arms wrapped around me was like I was standing at the edge of a cliff, looking down at it. Did I dare take a step off? Did I dare take that fall to a certain death?

Looking up at him as his beard tickled the top of my forehead, I knew. I knew I was going to take that step off and knowingly, willingly fall. Because got damn it, this man felt so fucking good. He was like an escape, an escape that would end badly, of course. But for the moment, I wanted to bask in the beauty of it. I needed it. My soul craved it. It craved him. It needed the hug he gave me. The hug he gave me with his arms wrapped around my body. The hug he gave my heart whenever he was in my presence.

The ring didn't matter.

The wife . . . my issues . . . my broken heart. None of it mattered. Why should it, anyway, when all we really have in this life is the moment? I couldn't step away from it. I couldn't allow outside shit to interfere with the moment. This moment. This forbidden moment with him.

He looked down at me and eagerly, but in such an unrushed way, placed his lips on mine. With one arm wrapped around my body, he held me closer, while the other one snaked up the back of my neck and gripped me there as we deepened that forbidden kiss. I moaned into his mouth, and he groaned into mine as our tongues did a familiar dance. A two-step I'd quickly memorized. One that was fit for just the two of us. A sensual, hungry, passionate two-step. I wanted to do this dance with him forever. It felt so got damn good. His velvety, thick, wet tongue sliding, gliding, and sucking on mine.

Self-sabotage . . . I wore it like a new tattoo.

Without warning, he pulled away from the kiss, leaving me standing there, drunk, horny, and confused. His arm never left my waist, though. I wasn't sure if he left it lingering there to hold me up, or because he wasn't ready to let go of me just yet. What I did know was that he regretted his decision to kiss me. Through drunken lenses, I could see that. Felt it too. The grip he had on my waist lessened. Not too much, but enough for *me* to notice.

"I didn't come here for this," he reiterated with those eyes locked on mine.

"Uh-huh. What did you come here for, then?" I asked with my head slightly cocked to the side, struggling to keep my eyes open. "To drop me off? Yeah, okay."

He just stared into my eyes, and I stared right back into his, struggling. The comfort I felt nestled in his arms was indescribable. I could fall asleep right there in his arms, standing on legs that felt like wet noodles, and I was sure I'd get the best sleep of my life. I'd already had my nighttime cry. Cried good and hard too. I'd for sure sleep like a damn baby.

Finally, he spoke. "I don't know."

I huffed and laughed lightly. "Exactly."

"To make sure you were okay," he said with a pause before pulling his bottom lip into his mouth. "I wanted to make sure you were good."

I nodded with my mouth turned down. "Sure, you did. You came here to fuck me. So . . ." I shrugged. "Fuck me. That's what we do. We fuck . . . and we don't see each other for weeks. And then . . . when we do see each other, you play like a gentleman. You do shit like pull me out of the snow. You make sure I get home safe. Stuff like that . . . Charm me. But . . . listen . . ." I burped and covered my mouth with a giggle. "You don't have to do that." I flicked the tip of his nose with my finger. "Because you own me."

His eyebrows furrowed before he swiped a tear away from my cheek. Was I crying again? God, I was crying again. Drunk, burping, crying, confessing.

"I don't want sex from you, Sienna," he softly said, before lifting me and carrying me down the hall.

I tossed my head back against the crook of his arm and closed my eyes as he carried me. Closed eyes in a spinning room was a recipe for disaster, but I closed them to keep the tears contained. Locked behind my lids. Hidden from him. If I wasn't so damn drunk, I would have realized just how silly that was. Tears . . . they slip through cracks. They *always* slip through the cracks.

A couple of seconds later, he laid me down on my bed. To hide my pain, I opened my eyes, quickly swiping away at the tears with the back of my hands, and smiled.

"This is the part where you lean over, kiss me, and then . . . you know."

Jahad took a deep breath and leaned over me. I waited for his lips to kiss mine. Closed my eyes and anticipated the feel of those silky soft lips on my lips. But they never touched me there. He kissed me on the top of my head instead and told me to get some rest.

I woke up to a pounding headache.

Literally felt like my head would explode. It hurt so badly, I could barely open my eyes. Turning over on my side, I winced and felt around my bed for my phone. *Where was my phone? Where'd I put it? How did I even get home?* The last thing I remember was seeing *him* at Vault. After that, my memories were just a blur of shots of Casamigos and fruity, alcoholic concoctions.

Frowning, I took a deep breath and finally opened my eyes. God. It hurt so got damn bad. When my eyes landed on the bottles of Motrin and Gatorade, I snatched them both up. How they got there, I didn't know. Mahogany had to end up driving us home because I sure as hell couldn't remember driving anywhere. I wondered if everything was so foggy because my headache was so bad.

I slowly sat up on the side of the bed and cracked the Gatorade open first. After taking a long drink from it, I opened the pill bottle, popped two, and finished the Gatorade off. I wanted to lie back down and let the pills do their job, but I had to use the bathroom and I needed to find my damn phone.

I sat there for another five minutes, collecting myself before standing. My legs were wobbly, but I made it to the master bathroom. Before I could turn around and sit down, bile rose to the pit of my stomach, my mouth began to violently salivate and I threw up. Leaning over the toilet, I tossed my goddess locs back, grabbed a hold of the toilet seat and continued to throw up. *Never again.* I didn't want to see another bottle of liquor.

"Yeah, good looks. *Na wè pita.*"

I flinched, and my eyebrows snapped together at the sudden sound of *his* voice. He was here? Why was he here? My eyes widened when I heard him enter my bedroom. I quickly shot up from my bent-over position and darted to the door to shut it. Right after, I was back at the toilet, throwing up. I dry heaved and my body jerked forward, searching for more of the *nothing* I'd eaten to throw up. That was why I was here. Throwing up because I'd drank like a fish on an empty stomach. Just . . . stupid.

When it finally stopped, I reached over to flush the toilet before walking over to the sink with my hand on my stomach. As I stood at the sink, waiting for the hot water I'd turned on to heat up, I stared at myself in the mirror, disgusted by what looked back at me.

I was a mess. My eyes were bloodshot red, and there were heavy bags underneath them. Then I remembered I'd cried. Cried my eyes out against his chest. He'd held me.

As I cupped my hand under the hot water, those foggy memories of my night rushed back to me. I remembered. I remembered every damn thing. Cursing him out. Crying. Telling him to leave.

Knock. Knock. Knock.

But he was still here.

He hadn't left . . .

After I washed my face and brushed my teeth, I opened the bathroom door. He hadn't knocked again, just waited. He stepped aside so I could walk through. I could barely even look at him, I was so damn embarrassed.

"What time is it? Why are you still here?" I asked, before tossing things around the room, looking for my phone.

He walked over, handed it to me, and said, "A little after two. I told you I couldn't leave you like that and I didn't."

Just after two? Damn, I got drunk quick and early. I just knew it was around five in the morning. How long had I been asleep? What time did we get back if it was only two in the morning?

I unlocked my phone and walked back over to the bed, where I climbed in and checked my text messages and missed calls. I had eight missed calls, all from my sisters and Naoki. They had been blowing me up in the group chat too. Mahogany was worried. Hazel raved and talked about how I was lucky to be with a Baptiste brother. Naoki pacified Mahogany's worrying with jokes about how Jahad was far from a stranger. Said him and my coochie were very well acquainted. That made me chuckle.

He sat near the foot of the bed. "Plus, we need to talk."

I took a deep breath and sat my phone on the nightstand. I stayed underneath the covers, bundled up. Both because I felt like shit and because I was still very embarrassed. I remembered everything. Every single thing. What taunted me more than everything else I'd said was when I told him he owned me.

"About what?"

I listened to him inhale. Shortly after, he pulled my cover off my shoulders.

"Sit up."

"For what? I feel—"

"Please," he pressed.

I swallowed and listened, pulling myself up and against the headboard. He leaned over and hit the switch on the lamp on my nightstand to bring some light into the dark room. I wanted to reach over and turn it right back off. I looked a fucking mess and probably had droplets of vomit on my top. I needed to hop in the shower, but here, in bed, was the safest place for now.

"About the things you said to me earlier—"

"I was drunk."

"Liquor doesn't make a person lie. It makes telling the truth easier," he said with his eyes locked on mine.

Touché.

"I don't see you as a piece of easy pussy, Sienna." He paused and his eyes slowly washed over me before he put them back on my face. "I see you as much more than that. If I didn't, I wouldn't be here."

I huffed and shook my head in disbelief. "You drove me home to have sex with me."

"I drove you home because the last place you needed to be was at a nightclub, being fed liquor. If it was about sex, I could have easily taken you to the bathroom, fucked you, and left you there to be handled, however, by whoever."

"It would've been that easy, huh?"

He locked eyes with me and sternly said, "Yeah, it would've been that easy."

"And you think that because you think I'm some side bitch . . . someone with no morals or self-decency."

"That's not why I think that. If I thought that, again, I wouldn't be here. We wouldn't be having this conversation. I would have fucked you and left you in that bathroom." He ran his hand down the back of his neck and took a deep breath.

"Why do you think that, then? If that's not the case, why are you just so sure I would have let you fuck me in a club full of people? Because I'm a slut. A slut that let you fuck her in a sex dungeon. A slut that let you fuck her in your kitchen, knowing your wife was upstairs. Just tell the truth."

We sat there, in silence, staring at one another for a good minute before he slid his hand underneath the cover where he delicately touched my leg. I took a deep breath and grabbed a fistful of the bedding at the tantalizing surge of energy that traveled down my spine. His hand continued up my leg, ran over my thigh, and stopped about an inch away from my pussy. My clit pulsated with desire and my breathing quickened just before he suddenly pulled away.

He inched up the bed, closer to me. Our eyes stayed locked the entire time. He then lifted his hand and ran the back of it against my cheek. I closed my eyes and basked in that feeling. That feeling I wanted forever. I was, once again, on the brink of tears.

When he pulled his hand away, I still felt him there. My cheek tingled, an aftereffect of his touch. My thigh, it tingled the same way. When I opened my eyes, I found his lips inches away from mine. He was so close to my face. I should have backed away. I wanted to back away. But I couldn't.

"When he touched you, did you feel it?"

"Feel what?" I whispered, my eyes traveling from his eyes to his lips. Lips that were so close, I could feel his breath on mine just as much as I could feel my own. I wanted to kiss him. So fucking bad. I gripped the sheets of the bed tighter, trying to ignore the pull.

"This."

I shook my head before our eyes met again. He didn't need to elaborate on what "this" was for me to know what he was talking about. The "this" was the electricity. Every time it happened, I wondered if he'd felt it. He felt it. There was so much passion behind Jahad's gaze, I nearly jumped into his lap and straddled him.

"Let's be real, tho'. I wouldn't have had to take you to the restroom, Ms. Mills," he said, before lowering his eyes to my lips. "I could've fucked you right there, in that section, in front of everyone. And you would have let me. Not because you're a slut, but because against me . . . this pull . . . whatever the fuck it is . . . you're powerless." He paused again and licked his lips.

Jahad backed away and the air between us lessened. I took a deep breath and followed him with my eyes as he stood to pace.

"The way you think I see you isn't how I see you at all," he continued. "I see you, though. I see you clearly and, Sienna, if I thought for one second you were a slut . . . a home-wrecker . . . whatever, what we did would have truly been left at Pandora's. I wouldn't have fucked you in my kitchen while my pregnant wife slept upstairs. I would have left you at Vault. I wouldn't have come back. I wouldn't have stayed here this late, knowing the risks. I'll tell you what you are. A problem. A problem for me because I'm powerless against you, too."

He looked over at me and I just sat there with raised brows, speechless. I didn't know what to say. There was so much I could say, but I couldn't find the right words.

"You asked me why I drove you home. I told you I didn't know. Told you I wanted to make sure you were good. That's only half the truth. I'm here because I couldn't help it. I couldn't leave Vault without you." He redirected his pacing in my direction, stopping next to me. "You asked me why I stayed. I stayed because I couldn't leave you here with those thoughts about me. That's not who I am. I told you my why was none of your business but that was unfair. I owe you that. After what you said . . . after hearing what you think . . . I realize that's the picture I painted. That's not me, though, love."

And here comes the lies. *He's different. He cheated on his wife by mistake. It was supposed to be a onetime thing, but he's falling for me. It's just something about me.* Same ol' bullshit.

Jahad cheated on his wife because he's an ain't-shit-ass nigga, just like Amiri and the rest of them. We just have this thing between us, that's it. I'd respect him more if he just told the truth. *"I cheat and you're one of many."*

"Leighton gave me a pass. One night, one woman. It took me months to accept it. Every day, she pressed me about it. I didn't want it. I couldn't imagine sleeping with someone who wasn't my wife.

"Back in the day, before we got married, I would have jumped on some shit like that. I didn't need a pass back then, though. The minute I asked that woman to be my wife, I devoted myself to her, and to her only. The only woman I wanted was her. Somewhere along the line, shit got blurry. Things changed. I ended up at Pandora's during a moment of weakness. Before you came to the bar, I was about to dip. Realized the mistake I was making and decided to leave. But then . . . You happened. That pull. I couldn't escape it then."

I believed him.

I couldn't explain why. I just . . . did, and it annoyed the fuck out of me, because who believed a story like that? Who believed that a woman as beautiful as Leighton would give a man as captivating as Jahad a hall pass? No one would. So, why did I? But . . . I did, and it made me sad. For Leighton. For Jahad. For all of us.

CHAPTER 24

Leighton

Bright lights beating against the white bedroom walls told me Jahad had finally made it home. At four in the morning. I was wide awake. Waiting, while time continued to tick on. I hadn't spoken to him in hours. Not since he was at Vault, but he had left Vault hours ago. Spent an hour and a half at one location, before he ended his night at Saint's. Talking and laughing with Farrah, who laid sprawled out at the foot of my bed, snoring fast asleep, kept me from losing my mind. It wasn't until she began to snore that I allowed myself to feel. Feel the pain of what was happening to my marriage. I was losing it. Just like she'd lost hers.

We sat up for hours, talking, watching old movies, and eating popcorn. She talked about how she was happy to be spending the night with me. Said that big, five-bedroom house was lonely without Mike. Her divorce, although over a year old, was still pretty fresh. Farrah dealt with a lot. Looking at her while she reminisced . . . I mean, really *looking* at her . . . I saw it. The pain she hid behind forced smiles and negativity was clearer than ever as she talked about what home was for her now. I felt sorry for her.

Farrah and I had been friends for a very long time, but it wasn't until we had that talk that I realized just where a lot of her clinginess stemmed from. Loneliness. Sadly, I saw so much of myself inside of her. The attitude, the bitterness, the fear of being alone. I saw it. I was becoming her. I didn't want that. The thought of turning into what she had petrified me. Divorced, lonely, bitter, angry, unhappy, negative. I was already heading down a slippery slope. I wasn't too far off. Not at all. I was four out of five and heading straight for that fifth one. I didn't want that.

"Farrah," I said, as I softly kicked her, trying to wake her up.

"Mmm." She groaned before pulling the throw blanket she was covered up in over her shoulders.

"Get up, Jahad is home," I said before snatching the blanket off her.

She sucked her teeth and sat up, scratching her head. "What time is it?"

"Time for you to go to the guest room," I told her.

She'd only asked for the time so she could make a snarky remark about him coming home so late. I was sure of it. I had no time to go back and forth with her. Jahad would walk in at any moment, and the last thing I wanted was for him to see her asleep in our bed.

"Okay, okay," she said with an attitude as she got up and out of the bed.

My heart uneasily raced against my chest as I waited. I didn't know what I would say to him once he walked in. I just . . . I wanted my marriage to go back to the way it used to be. I didn't want to argue with him. I didn't want to yell. I didn't want to give him an attitude. The last few weeks had been hell enough. I'd done enough screaming, yelling, and arguing to last us both a lifetime. I was exhausted. He was exhausted. Arguing had gotten us nowhere.

I wanted to talk. I wanted to get back to where we used to be. I wanted to get back to where *I* used to be. Happy. I missed that. I missed staring into the mirror and just being happy with who looked back at me. I longed for the days that I actually enjoyed my own company. The days where I enjoyed his company, and he enjoyed mine. The days where the house, this big ol' house, was filled with so much love, the size of it didn't swallow me.

A few minutes after Farrah walked out, Jahad walked in. I lay on my side, watching him, quiet, hoping the heavy beating of my heart didn't give me away. He closed the doors and immediately came up out of his shirt. Getting rid of evidence? Did he smell like her? Were there traces of her on the collar of his shirt? *Get your shit together, Leighton Baptiste.* Once he was out of his shirt, he walked over to the bed and leaned over to deliver that kiss. His chain brushed against my shoulder, tickling me, and forced me to move.

I opened my eyes, and they met his. "Hi."

It's late. It's four in the morning, and you're just getting here. Where the fuck have you been? With her? I bit back so much. If he was with her, that was my fault. I'd opened Pandora's box. I had to accept that everything I'd been experiencing this past month and a half was my fault. I offered the man a damn hall pass. He wouldn't take it, but I pressed him to. Pretty much forced him into another woman's bed. That was my fault. That was on me. That was the cold, hard truth I'd had a hell of a hard time facing.

"Bonjou, amou," he softly said. "Forgive me for coming in so late. I—"

I leaned up and kissed him on the lips. "It's okay."

The minute my lips left his, a chill ran down my spine. It had been so long since I'd taken the initiative. I hadn't shown Jahad affection in a very long time. He was just as taken aback by my assertiveness as me. He expected something else. He expected me to yell and accuse him of cheating. He expected me to ask him about that address he'd spent an hour and a half at. I wanted to. I wanted to so got damn bad. But would his answer really matter? My brain was so cluttered with insecurities, I wouldn't believe him, anyway. I decided to play blind. I wasn't sure if that was the best approach to take, but for now . . . it worked. I didn't have the strength to do anything else.

We stared into each other's eyes for a few minutes before he placed another kiss on my lips. I closed my eyes and sucked in a deep breath when he pulled back and walked off. The silence was loud. Very loud. I didn't need to ask him if he'd been with her to know. Felt like he'd just given me confirmation by saying nothing at all about where he'd been.

"Can I join you?" I asked with tears in my eyes, as I watched him at the dresser, removing his jewelry. When I got a glimpse of his wedding band on his finger, I swallowed. Wondered if he'd put it on in the driveway, or if he had to remove it all when he was with her. I closed my eyes and looked away as a tear rolled over my cheek. I quickly swiped it away and shook my head before turning back in his direction, hoping the evidence of my sadness wasn't on my face.

I was tired as hell and my showers couldn't last but ten minutes, but so what? Ten minutes of intimacy, in the shower together, would feel like a lifetime for us since it'd been so long since we'd done that.

I couldn't get that look of sorrow in Farrah's eyes out of my mind. I didn't want to become her. Felt like I was heading in that direction, and well, I really wanted to avoid that. As nervous and awkward as I felt about taking the initiative to spend some quality time with my husband, I had to start somewhere, right? I couldn't just give him to *her*. Tonight scared me. Jahad coming home so late signified just how fucked things were between us. I had to fight for my husband. He was worth the fight.

He looked over his shoulder at me, the moonlight hitting him just right, showcasing the lazy smile he wore. "What you think?"

My behavior was erratic as hell, but he didn't seem to care. Jahad, too, had been clawing for *something*. I saw him claw every day. The forehead kisses, the random *I love yous*, the effort he put into our marriage every day, his undying determination to make sure I was happy. Egotistically, I could say I'd been clawing too. I could say I tried my hardest, considering the circumstances, but I'd be lying to myself. I'd been selfish. Selfish with my love.

Selfish with my smiles. Selfish with . . . everything. Hell, honestly, the hall pass was offered out of selfishness too. But there was no room for selfishness inside of a marriage.

I smiled and pulled my tank over my head. Jahad's eyes immediately fell on my breasts as he walked back over to the bed. Because I was a little self-conscious about the way they were changing, I covered them. The size of my areolas had doubled right along with my bra size. I always had cute, little, round areolas. Now they were big as hell, nearly the size of my palm. However, when I covered them, Jahad pried my arms away from them and brushed his thumb over my nipple. I sucked in air and swallowed. My God.

It had been so long since he'd touched me like that. So long since I had allowed him to touch me like that. He kept looking to my eyes for reassurance and it really broke my heart, to be honest. My husband, a man who had always had complete access to every part of me, kept looking at me, making sure it was okay for him to touch me.

When our eyes locked, I smiled at him, and he tossed the comforter from the bottom half of my body. When his hands inched up the side of both of my legs, I sucked in air again as chills ran through my entire body. This was what Jahad did to me. Gave me chills. Made goosebumps cover every inch of my skin. Since it'd been so long since I gave him freedom to touch me the way he wanted to, I forgot how good his touch felt.

When he grabbed the waistband of my shorts, I tensed up a little. Only because it'd been so long since I'd let him take my bottoms off. He took it as rejection and pulled away, but I grabbed his wrists, stopping him.

"You can take them off, Jah. I want you to," I reassured him.

I hated what I'd done to him. This wasn't Jahad. He was assertive. He staked claim to every inch of me before I was officially his, so for him to be so hesitant to do something as simple as pull my shorts down was crazy.

He rubbed his full lips together and pulled them off. The feel of his rough hands against my bare thighs made me shiver again. Instead of helping me to my feet so I could walk to the bathroom for my shower, Jahad lifted me from the bed and held me in his strong arms. I giggled with my arms wrapped around his neck as he cradled me. I laid my head on his chest as my smile lightly faded. Not because I was sad or wanted to back out of this but because I missed this so much.

Once we got to the bathroom, he sat me on the chair at my vanity and kissed me on the forehead. I watched him as he walked off, over to the walk-in shower to turn it on. God. He was so damn good to me. *Too* damn good to me, knowing good and damn well I didn't deserve it.

As I watched him setting the water temperature to one hundred degrees, I smiled. It was shit like that, that showed me how lucky I was. Before I got pregnant, I kept my showers hot—at around one hundred and ten degrees, but now I couldn't go above one hundred, since anything over it could harm the baby. Jahad always started my showers and he always set the temperature to one hundred. Every day, he got it ready for me, and every time I got inside, I never had to adjust it. He was considerate, loving, assertive, forgiving . . . just the total fucking package.

And I'd given another woman access to him.

My entire body heated with fear. Running my hand down the back of my neck with worry, I silently prayed to God that the only thing he'd given her access to was his body. Nothing else.

I was so afraid of losing him, my bottom lip trembled a little. I gave him that pass because I wanted to control a scenario I had never controlled before. Infidelity. That was the truth. The God's honest truth. I was afraid he would cheat on me. Afraid he'd go back to his old ways because I couldn't perform. So, I got online, did some research, and found out it wasn't uncommon for women in my situation to give their husbands hall passes. I read the horror stories and still gave it to him. Figured it would be easier this way, but I was wrong.

Taking a deep breath, I ran my hands through my locs just as he turned to face me. With his arms opened, he approached me. A second later, I was back in his arms again, giggling like a little-ass girl. I could have easily walked to the shower from this distance, but Jahad refused to let me.

Once I was inside of the shower, I sat on the bench and watched him continue to undress through the frosted, steamy glass. My mouth salivated when he dropped his pants to his ankles. My clit throbbed and I bit the corner of my lip. Taking a deep breath, I tried to push the question of how good the sex with her might've been out of my mind. Did she love it? Of course, she loved it. I loved it. I loved it so damn much that when we were younger, we had sex regularly while I was on my period. Loved it so much that when I was horny at my family reunion, I fucked him in my auntie's bed. Loved it so much that there was a point in time, I used to just suck his dick and cum all over myself with no penetration. No touching. Nothing. Just . . . passionate, unadulterated fucking desire.

So.

Of course, she loved it.

The bigger question here was, did *he* love it? Was she tight? Did her pussy walls clench on his big dick the way mine used to? Did he tap his dick on her clit? Did he make her squirt? Did he . . . did he eat her pussy? Her ass? Did he—

Jahad stepping into the shower with me killed my train of thought.

"Come here," he said with his hand extended. My fingers brushed up against his diamond-encrusted wedding band as our hands met, and a sense of calmness washed over me. Whether he removed it with her or not no longer mattered. Regardless of what he did, what she did, or how she felt . . . He was *mine*. Jahad Baptiste and *everything* attached to him was mine. His dick. His heart. His fucking soul. It was mine. And everything on me belonged to him. It was time I acted like it.

He pulled me to my feet, and I lightly exhaled. Showering together. Being completely naked together, close and intimate, was awkward. And that was crazy, considering we used to shower together every morning if our schedules aligned.

When he stood behind me and placed a soft, subtle kiss on my shoulder, I shuddered. The good way. A light moan fell from my lips. Since I could only shower for ten minutes, I was sure Jahad was going to make those ten minutes feel like thirty.

He set the tone as he lathered my loofah with my Native body wash and ran it along the shoulder he'd just kissed.

"I missed this," I admitted in a tone just above a whisper.

His response was a kiss to my nape, immediately pulling another moan from me. I backed up against his hard dick pressed against my ass and wanted him to fill me up so bad. So got damn bad, a bitch liked to cry! I hadn't felt him inside of me in months. *This* was one of the reasons I didn't like to do this anymore. One of the reasons why I had been so affectionately closed off. Because the desire for him when we were like this . . . when he touched me . . . was too much to bear. How much I wanted him was unbelievable. I wanted him as bad as a man on death row, waiting for his lethal injection, wanted freedom.

"I missed *this*," Jahad said before I felt him kneel, just moments before his lips touched my left ass cheek.

I gasped and bit down on my bottom lip. "Jah . . ."

"Shhh," he interrupted before going from one ass cheek to the other, planting soft, wet kisses there. "Let me take care of you."

My pussy throbbed with desire as I leaned forward on the shower wall. When I felt him grip my waist and bend me over further, my knees buckled a little. I was damn near embarrassed by how turned on I was. I was on the verge of tears, his lips felt so good against my skin. Jahad didn't have to do much to get my pussy wet. It wasn't what he did that got me there. It was how he did it.

I sucked in air when he finally stood up again and went back to washing me up. He took his time, running that loofah over my body, careful to linger on my most sensitive spots the longest. He was so thoughtful and attentive that when it was time to wash my pussy, he switched loofahs and used my unscented body wash. Hiking my leg up on the bench, he ran the loofah over my pussy, delicately, before leaning forward and placing a kiss on my clit. Such a fucking freak. It was covered with soap, but he kissed her anyway. I moaned and bit my bottom lip, wanting another one, but he stood up and continued to bathe me.

Gazing down at his dick, I wrapped my hand around it and watched as his eyelids slowly fluttered closed. My touch still did the same thing to him. I wondered if she had that same effect on him.

Instead of worry and insecurities filling my mental, I was fueled by something else. Competition. Rage. I wanted him to remember why I was the one for him. I wanted him to remember just how good I used to take care of him. I slowly stroked his hard dick as he continued to bathe me, our eyes locked on one another. I saw the hunger in his eyes as soap covered my hand, lathering his dick, giving just the right amount of friction. With our eyes locked, there was so much familiarity. So much desire. So many unanswered questions. So many conversations needed to be had. So much . . . pain. But above everything, there was that passion. Passion that overshadowed our issues. Passion that forced us to push past the bullshit and just simply enjoy one another.

Jahad grabbed my waist and pulled me closer to the waterfall showerhead, which in turn brought me closer to him. We stood under the showerhead with water cascading down over our heads, my hand on his dick, his lips pressed against mine, his fingers digging into my ass cheeks. Jahad gave me hungry kisses. He sucked on my tongue and groaned in my mouth with aggression that matched how rock hard his dick was. His dick was hard as steel, pulsating in my palm, begging me to put my lips on it.

So, I did.

Without interrupting our kiss, I backed up out of the water, over to where the bench was, to sit. Jahad, although engulfed in our kiss, directed me there by keeping a firm hold on my waist. Once I sat down, I was at eye level with what was once my favorite meal: his dick and the pre-cum oozing from it.

Licking my lips, I gripped his dick a little tighter and inched it into my mouth. The minute the head of his dick hit my tongue, I moaned with furrowed brows. His hands found the back of my head, where he gripped a handful of my wet locs.

He wrapped a handful of my locs around his big hand and began to slowly fuck my mouth. When his dick hit the back of my throat, I gagged and pulled away.

I looked up at him with slob dripping from my chin with wide, unsure eyes. He took a step closer to me, gripped my chin, tapped his dick on my lips, and said, "Mm, mm. Open this pretty-ass mouth. Wide too."

My pussy pulsated as I listened by opening my mouth as wide as I could. He gripped the base of his dick as he slowly inched it into my mouth. He looked so got damn good with his bottom lip pinched between his teeth and his thick eyebrows furrowed with desire. I missed that look. The look that only Jahad could deliver. One that said he was for no games, and if you entered this realm with him, then you had better deliver or he was going to fuck you and your mouth until you did.

I used to love it.

Now it frightened me . . . in somewhat of a good way, though. I was up for the challenge. Up for getting back to who I used to be. His slut. His personal dick-sucking, deep-throating slut. I relaxed my throat as he got closer to my tonsils. When he hit them, I lightly gagged. Instead of pulling back this time, I gripped his dick, forcing his hand away, and slowly stroked it, inching more of it down my throat. With my eyes locked on his, I took all of his dick down my throat. He gave me a nod of approval and clenched down on his jaw before tightening his lips.

"Uh-huh . . . Just like that. Eat this dick wit' yo' pretty ass," Jahad grunted, before gripping my hair tighter.

There was something about the ruggedness in his voice that awakened something inside of me. The way he talked to me, handled me, reminded me of the old Jah. Not the Jah I married. He was a fucking savage, too, but Jah from the block? The mannish-ass hood nigga who used to bring his ass up in my Coney Island every day fucking with me? Oh, that Jahad Baptiste was a fucking problem. And tonight, with his dick in my mouth, and the sound of his rugged voice with that Caribbean drawl in it, did something to me.

I sucked his dick like there was no tomorrow, and he matched my energy by fucking my face with just the same amount of aggression. I moaned as his balls slapped against my chin and his pre-cum coated my sore throat. It was sore, all right. But shit, it hurt so damn good. I was making up for missed time. I was showing him I was *all* he needed. Not only was I showing him, but I was showing myself too.

Adding other people into our mix was pointless. I could be all things for him. Coming to that realization took longer than necessary, but I was here, and I prayed it wasn't too late.

Without warning, Jahad pulled his dick out of my mouth and immediately kneeled in front of me. Before I could adjust to what was going on, he had my leg propped up against his shoulder and his mouth on my pussy.

"Oh my God!" I yelped as pleasure shot through my body, his tongue sending surges of electricity through every nerve.

He gave my clit soft strokes with his thick, wet tongue, and I purred, massaging my sensitive nipples. Jahad made love to me in every way possible. Mentally, spiritually, physically. But the way he made love to my pussy? With his mouth? It was indescribably passionate. So passionate, I whimpered when he separated my puffy lips, pushed the hood on my clit back and softly sucked on it. He was so good with his mouth. So good with everything.

"I missed this sweet-ass pussy," Jahad mumbled against my clit. "Don't keep it from me again." He paused and locked eyes with me. "You hear me?"

I responded with a moan, and he dug his nails into my thighs, gripping them tighter before softly slapping me on my pussy. "I can't hear you," he pressed.

My eyes shot open and I rapidly nodded. "I-I won't. I'm . . . I'm sorry," I moaned.

His fiery eyes left mine and he went back to devouring my kitty cat. He gripped my calves and moved his head from side to side, eating my pussy with so much passion, my legs began to violently shake. I hadn't had an orgasm in so long and he felt so damn good. It was like I was in no control of my body as I slid down the bench, forcing Jahad to hike my legs up and turn me around, so I could lie down comfortably. He didn't miss a beat as he continued to eat my pussy. He groaned and moaned into it as if it was the sweetest thing he'd tasted in months.

He mercilessly pushed my legs back as much as my round belly would allow and dragged his thick tongue from the crack of my ass to my sensitive clit where he softly sucked, coating my pussy in his thick saliva. I grabbed the sides of the bench and held on for dear life as I felt the earth-shattering orgasm coming on. Tingles traveled from the tip of my toes to the top of my head as I violently shook in his hands as he held on to my waist, sucking on my clit as if my pussy juice wasn't squirting all over his face.

"Ahhhhh!" I yelped. "Ohh! Mmmmm! Yesss! Fuck! Pleeeease eat this pussy, Jah! Ohhh, you eat my pussy so goooood!" I screamed, slightly possessed by the orgasm that was taking over my entire body.

Once my body calmed down, Jahad placed soft, careful kisses on my clit as he sensually massaged my thighs. I twiddled my nipples as I slowly gyrated my hips, lightly shuddering any time his tongue brushed up against my sensitive clit.

When I opened my eyes, he was on his feet, staring down at me with my juices dripping from his thick beard. He licked his lips, shook his head, and grunted, "Mmm."

I sat up and wrapped my hands around his hard dick before wrapping my lips around it. With his head tossed back, he grabbed my head and began to slowly gyrate his hips, matching the rhythm of my sucking. I lifted my eyes up and moaned at him licking his lips, devouring droplets of my juices like he was dying of dehydration and all he had left to drink was me.

Moaning, I sucked him with more passion as my pussy thumped at how turned on I was by how obsessed he was with my taste. He was zoned out, licking his lips, moving his hips, fucking my mouth with his eyes closed.

For some reason, I wanted him to look at me. As turned on as I was by sucking his dick, those insecurities crept in a little and I wanted his eyes on me. I wanted him to focus on me . . . not his thoughts. Because, hell, he could have been thinking about anything.

"Look at me, baby," I pressed as I rubbed his pre-cum-coated head over my wet lips.

Jahad lowered his head, opened his eyes, and looked at me. I moaned and moved my hips back and forth over the bench, as if I was riding his dick. I was just that turned on. He lightly smacked me on the cheek and told me to take it all down my throat. He gripped my jaw and pushed his dick further down my throat, making me gag just a little bit. The whole time I inched his dick down my throat, his eyes stayed connected to mine. When my vision got cloudy from tears brought on by gagging, I kept them on his still. I couldn't break the eye contact. Both because I was stuck there, held captive by his persuasion, and because I was afraid if I did look away, he'd close his eyes and think of her. I needed to forget about her, and I needed him to, too. So, I sucked his dick like our marriage depended on it, because shit, it did.

Within minutes, Jahad was shooting his thick, creamy nut in my mouth. Instead of swallowing it like I would have months ago, I spat it out and rubbed it all over my lips, face, titties, and pussy, giving him a little show.

Hours later, I woke up to two dozen roses and a handwritten note from Jahad that read: *Bonjou, amou. Get dressed and join me in the dining room. Today you will have a day almost as beautiful as you are. Mwen renmen ou.*

At the foot of the bed was a satin turquoise, orange, and navy wrap dress and white Hermès sandals. My wheelchair was right next to the bed, and there was a glass of orange juice on the nightstand. I took a sip of it and then grabbed the robe and house shoes.

Waking up to roses, a handwritten note, and an outfit laid out for me attested to just how good of a night we had. I couldn't remember the last time we connected like that. I never wanted to go back to that dark place in our marriage. That was the lowest we'd ever been. I doubted if I'd be able to forget about *her* and the hall pass, but I couldn't wallow in it anymore. What was done was done. It was time to move forward.

I refused to bring a baby into a world full of mess. Mommy and Daddy were going to be all right. Running my hand over my belly, I smiled as she moved around.

Just as I was about to get out of bed to head to the bathroom, there was a soft knock on the bedroom door before it opened. Farrah. I'd forgotten all about her ass.

"Great, you're finally awake," she said before sitting down. "I heard y'all last night. You really sucked his dick like he didn't come home at four in the morning? You know, that's how it started with Mike. Where do you think he was all night? With another woman, Leigh. And you—" She paused and looked around the bed. "Roses? A note?" She eyed me up and down. "What are you up to? That's new?"

I sucked in air and stood to sit in the chair. "What are you still doing here? What time is it?"

She sucked her teeth and grabbed my phone from the nightstand. "Twelve. I'm still here because I wanted to talk to you. I'd been cooped up in the guest room for hours, waiting for you to wake up. I heard him leave about an hour or so ago. I peeked my head in right after he left. Since you were sleeping so good, I didn't bother you." She paused, but only long enough to switch subjects. "What did he say? What bullshit excuse did he give you for coming home at four in the fucking morning? Must've been good. You sucked his dick. Was that before or after he ate your pussy? Probably after. That's probably what made you suck his dick. He hit you with some good head and got you, didn't he? Mike used to do that too. He'd come home with gifts." She paused again and motioned toward my dress and sandals with a cocked brow. "Wake me up with head, bend me over, fuck me good, and I'd be—"

"Jahad isn't Mike," I interrupted as I sat on the side of the bed to slip my pink and gold Versace slippers on. "And don't worry about who did who first. Freak. Me sucking his dick had nothing to do with any of the shit you're talking about, Farrah." I laughed. "Mind ya business."

She drew back with offense. I'd said it jokingly, but I meant that shit. She really did need to mind her business. I refused to allow her to sit up and poison my brain with negativity. She'd done enough of that. After seeing just how sad and miserable she was last night, I decided the last person I needed in my head was her. I was trying not to become her but she was forcing me in the opposite direction of that. Farrah needed to go. She and her unsolicited advice was poisonous to my marriage.

"Mind my business?" she asked with a nod. "Okay. Don't forget you said that when shit goes bad, and you come to me with that business you want me to mind so damn bad."

I ran my hand over my forehead and closed my eyes. I wanted to have a good day. That was all I wanted. One good-ass day with my husband. One good-ass day with my damn self, honestly. I just wanted to be happy. To smile, laugh, and to be surrounded by love. Not misery. Not negativity.

"I didn't mean it like that, Farrah," I reassured her, that fear of being alone still gnawing at me, forcing me to tiptoe around how I really felt about her toxicity.

She held her hands up. "It's cool." She picked the note up, read a few lines, and tossed it back on the bed. "Sounds like a man that for sure got his dick wet last night and not with saliva, either. But . . . I'll mind my business." She got up and walked away. Before she walked out of the room, she looked over her shoulder at me. "I would say don't call me when he breaks you, but I love you too much to turn my back on you like that. Call me. I'll be here when he hurts you. And he will hurt you."

Fuck you, Farrah.

Fuck you!

She sighed and said, "See you Monday."

Instead of saying anything to her, I picked my roses up, closed my eyes, and buried my nose in them. I didn't look up from them until she was out of my bedroom. I set them down and stared at the carpeted floor with my fists pressed into the soft mattress. Here they come. The tears. The fucking tears. I was so happy before she walked into my bedroom.

Taking a few deep breaths, I sucked those tears up and dried my eyes. There was a chance he would hurt me. A huge chance. That chance scared me every fucking day. But before I settled with those chances, I would do everything in my power to prevent it. Farrah was just mad. Mad because she didn't have a man who cared as much as mine. Mad because Mike had never given her roses. He'd never handwritten her a note. The only thing she got from him were empty promises. She hated that I had someone who cared enough to make our marriage work. She hated that we couldn't bond through misery.

Today, would be almost as beautiful as me.

CHAPTER 25

Jahad

I ran my hand over the top of my waves and glanced over my shoulder through the glass pivot door into the sunroom. With my phone pressed against my ear, I paced the back deck.

"Emu. Have you spoken to Emu?" I asked my cousin Nix.

"I called him first. I kept getting the voicemail," he replied with a deep sigh. "If I didn't think it was urgent, I wouldn't have called you, Jah. You know I don't do this."

I needed a day.

Just one fucking day that I didn't have to worry about shit but taking care of home. My wife was at the top of my priority list today. It was like the minute I put it out into the atmosphere, bullshit came flying at me from left and right. There was a delay in our shipment from Mexico. We never experienced delays. Our operation ran impeccably. When I said it ran itself, I meant it. There was no hard work and labor for us to do anymore. The hard shit stopped for us the minute Samuel secured a Mexican connect. We went from dealing with a middleman to securing a link with the direct source.

We had various logistics companies that were in partnership with UPS and FedEx that helped us get across the border. The logistics companies weren't just for transporting drugs. Shipments of fruits and vegetables were transported to warehouses across the country that distributed to various grocery stores. At every warehouse, there was a Baptiste who delegated a small team that was to separate the boxes that were being shipped to the grocery stores from the ones that were full of kilos of cocaine and guns. We kept our family in the business. There wasn't a department within our organization that didn't include a Baptiste.

So, imagine my surprise when I got a call from my cousin Nix, all the way in fucking Texas. *Texas* . . . where Emu ran things. Nix ran the warehouse, and Emu was in command. The company, our company, was run somewhat like the Mafia. We had appointed chiefs in every state we did business in. Nix shouldn't have had to call me. He wouldn't have had to call me if it weren't for Emu's incompetence.

"The trucks were supposed to pull in fifteen minutes ago," Nix said, panicked.

"Mete dlo nan diven ou," I told him. "I'll call you back in a few minutes."

After hanging up, I sat on the steps of the deck and called Emu. He didn't answer the first three times. The longer his phone went unanswered, the more patience I lost with him. Shit, with everything. A nigga was tired. Most of the niggas in this game got in for one of three reasons. Struggle forced them into it, they saw the shit on TV and wanted to see what it was like, or three . . . they were forced into it because of the bloodline they were born into, like me. I never wanted it. Never wanted any of this shit. It was an inconvenience to my life, my family, and the way I loved them, too. I resented the dope game, and everything associated with it. Yeah, it came with its perks, but if I had a choice, I would have never gotten into it.

"Sak pase," Emu answered.

"*Sak pase?* Business, nigga," I said through gritted teeth. "Nix called me. You want to tell me what the fuck is going on down there?"

He sighed. "*Manman.* I took her to the hospital this morning. Unc didn't tell you?"

"Tell me what?"

"Complications after her surgery. She's back in the hospital," Emu said with a grunt.

Much like mine, Emu's hands were constantly full. He was the eldest of his siblings. We were the same age, left with the same responsibilities. He, too, was left to be the man of the house at five years old. Of course, the bulk of the responsibility still fell on our mothers, but once we grew older and stronger, we stepped into the role of taking care of everyone.

At seven, I started to hustle and put food on the table. Emu too. The hustling and stealing I did back home was done with Emu right by my side. We were close as hell, more like brothers than cousins. When we moved here, things changed. Our bond was broken by their move to Texas. It was heavy as hell for us. We went from spending every waking moment together to telephone calls and rarely ever seeing each other at all. It was heavy. We kept in touch now as much as possible, which was barely.

"Shit," I said, as I ran my hand down over my head and glanced over my shoulder, back into the house. "Listen, give Nix a call. Let me know what's going on. If necessary, I'll come down."

"Konprann," he replied before hanging up.

I stuffed my phone into the pocket of my pants and rested against the steps with my head tossed back. A delayed shipment could mean a lot of things. Good and bad. For the sake of the business, I hoped it meant traffic was backed up.

Pulling my phone from my pocket again, I thought about calling Shelby. He assured me that getting rid of Walker wouldn't cause complications for the business. In fact, he promised me things would continue to run smoothly. If that turned out to be a lie, I wasn't sure how I'd take it. I couldn't imagine getting rid of one problem just to end up with another one. We had mouths to feed. Several. Thousands. The drug business kept the family afloat. Without it, we would survive. We had a lot to survive with. However, the business going under wouldn't just hurt pockets, it would hurt on a larger scale.

I took a deep breath and stood up. Dusting my blue jeans off, I headed back inside. There was nothing for me to do right now. All I could do was wait for Emu's call. In the meantime, I was going to enjoy as much of my day as I could with my wife. It had been a long-ass minute since I could say something like that.

I walked through the sliding doors and chucked my head back at Ms. Evaline. "She hasn't come down yet, has she?"

She smiled and looked up from the dish she was rinsing off. "Nope. Not yet." I felt her eyes follow me as I headed out of the kitchen. "Mr. Baptiste."

"Wassup, Ms. Evaline?" I asked, looking over my shoulder at her.

She winked. "Keep holding on."

I nodded. "I am."

We hadn't revisited the conversation about what she'd seen that night since we had our little talk in the office. When we left out of that room, we kept that conversation right there in it, but her words stayed with me. I'd been holding on for dear life, and for the first time in months, it felt like my wife was holding on with me.

When I made it to the crib early this morning, around four, I expected to be met with shouting and tears. I'd mentally prepared myself the whole ride home. I cooked up a bogus-ass story to feed her and felt like shit behind it too.

While Sienna laid passed out, drunk, I had Saint come grab my phone so my location would put me at his spot. That shit ate at me. I wasn't on that type of time. That was the shit young niggas with no direction did. I was secure. I had my forever. But the minute Saint pulled off from the parking lot with my hitter, I felt like I'd taken ten steps back. I told myself the lies were necessary. What I should have done was left and carried my ass to the crib, but I couldn't. I was stuck. Hated that shit too.

However, when I made it home from picking my phone up at Saint's, Leighton didn't greet me with anything but love. We had a good-ass night. We showered together. She finally sucked my dick with passion, like she wanted to, instead of sucking it like it was an inconvenience. *She let me touch her.* Intimately. Wet my whole fuckin' beard up. We were good. Damn near perfect. But, despite the love she gave me, I saw insecurities and pain swimming around her hazels.

The lies and the way I felt about Sienna haunted me the minute the room was quiet and filled with nothing but Leighton's soft snores. Shit ate at me so much, I couldn't sleep. Once the time hit ten, I got out of bed and planned our day. I decided I never wanted to see that look in my wife's eyes again. That look of desperation . . . failure . . . and fear. It fucked with me. I hated who I had become. Hated who I had turned her into. We'd worked hard as fuck to get where we were in our marriage. I couldn't undo what I did, but I would work hard as fuck to correct it.

It was no secret at this point.

Sienna had an immense effect on me. We had an immense effect on each other. But before I left her last night, we not only came to that conclusion, but we built a mutual respect for my marriage and each other too. I loved my wife. *She* could see I loved my wife. We were going through some shit, and in the midst of it, my soul had somehow intertwined with hers. But . . . I loved my wife.

Sienna might've made fireworks erupt and ignite every nerve in my body, but my heart and my complete devotion belonged to Leighton Baptiste. She understood. She respected it. Which was why I didn't bother asking her to return to the house. I couldn't, regardless of what Leighton wanted. She would never find out, but in letting the Sienna shit go, I was saving her. That pull was too much for either of us to ignore. I was a warrior, the strongest of the Baptiste tribe. But . . . against her, I was completely fucking powerless. She told me I owned her, but sometimes when I was around her, it felt like she was the one who owned me.

A couple of minutes later, Leighton turned the corner, into the dining room, and I stood to greet her. She was beautiful. Always had been. Her beauty had never wavered. She wore her thick, golden locs up in a high ponytail, accentuating the beautiful features that made me fall in love with her.

I wasn't surprised to see she'd decided to wear a headwrap. I fucked with it. Found it sexy as hell, but Leighton hated them. She only wore them when she needed a retwist. I preferred her with the wrap. But, shit, I preferred her any way . . . as long as there was a smile as beautiful as the one she wore today, gracing her gorgeous face.

I bit my bottom lip and looked down at her. "Damn, you beautiful."

She blushed and tilted her head back for a kiss before I gripped her chin and kissed her. I couldn't help but notice how with Leighton, I didn't feel what I felt with Sienna. The pull. Time slowing. Fireworks and shit. It didn't matter, though. I never needed any of that shit before, so I didn't need it now. I hated to even compare, to be honest. The two couldn't be compared. Leighton's wedding rings brushing up against my fingers when she intertwined hers with mine signified that.

"If you need to leave, you can leave, babe," Leighton said, looking back at me.

My phone had been buzzing nonstop since earlier. After we had brunch, Emu called and told me there was an issue at the border. The truck was a part of a random search. Luckily, we ran a tight business. The paperwork checked out, and the product was so well compacted and concealed, the truck was let through without an issue. Anybody else would look at that as a win, but me? I took it as a red flag. I needed to link with Shelby. Needed to like, two hours ago, but I said today was for Leighton and I wanted to keep it that way.

I kissed her on the top of her head and ran my hand over her smooth, round belly, flutters from my unborn child thumping against my fingers. "Nah. I'm chillin' tonight."

I wanted to live like a regular-ass nigga with legitimate businesses that didn't require half as much attention as the drug business did. I wanted to do the family thing. Sit up with my wife, eat ice cream with her, and watch her favorite corny-ass British TV show. For once in my life, I wanted to be able to enjoy a Saturday evening with her without interruptions from my phone. I was having a good-ass day. *We* were having a good-ass day. I wasn't ready for it to end.

Despite having two other sons who were very capable of having a civilized meeting with Shelby about the mishap in Texas, Samuel wouldn't stop calling me. He knew I was chilling. I'd spoken to him right after speaking to Emu. I told him to send one of them niggas to speak to Shelby. I told him I wanted to just kick it with my wife for the day. Told him whatever couldn't be handled today would have to wait for tomorrow. I didn't give a fuck. Them niggas had the luxury of chilling with bitches and running through freak bitches at underground sex spots on Saturday nights with no fucking issue. Me? Nah. I had to put life on hold.

Fuck that.

I'd put life on hold long enough. Nothing was more important than what I had going on tonight. For the first time in months, the future of my marriage looked promising. It felt good to have Leighton laid out on my chest, staining my white tee with chocolate ice cream that had slipped from her mouth during one of her uncontrollable laughing fits. Shit was really nostalgic. For a minute, I did feel like a regular-ass nigga. Right until my phone vibrated again, letting me know I was far from it.

Leighton sat up and looked at me. "We both know if your phone is ringing like that, you can't *just* chill."

I locked eyes with her and clenched down on my jaw. Shit was quiet everywhere but the dope game. I hadn't gotten a call from any of my property managers all week. Shit with the construction of the condominiums downtown had even been quiet. But this drug shit? Phone stayed going crazy. You'd think that since I was no longer on the block, it wouldn't. But it did. *Everyone* called Jah. Just like Nix hit my line, all the way in Texas, I had family all over, doing the same shit. If anything ran off course, it was me they got in contact with first.

Leigh was right. I could complain about it, and pretend to live this regular life, but the truth would always be there. I wasn't regular. I could complain all I wanted to; it wasn't going anywhere. My phone would never stop ringing. Ignoring it and putting shit off would only make things worse for me.

I took a deep breath and picked my buzzing phone up off the nightstand.

Fifteen minutes later, I was driving to meet with Shelby with my father in the passenger seat. The car was silent, except for a low grunt here and there from Samuel. He was disappointed. It was written all over his scowling face. I didn't give a fuck, though. He devoted his life to this shit—not me. He got in the game and neglected his obligations as a husband and father for it. I wouldn't. His devotion saved us, but scarred and damaged us too. Shit, a nigga would've been good with Pops punching the clock at a factory or something. That would've been good enough to save us.

"Is this what I have to look forward to after my grandchild is born?" Samuel asked, breaking the silence.

"If you're asking me if I'll put my family over this business, the answer is yes," I told him before glancing over at him. "Nothing is more important than family to me."

He stroked his salt-and-pepper beard, that frown deepening. "Nothing should be. But—"

"When it comes to my family, there are no buts," I interrupted. "Respectfully."

I respected my father. Would always respect him, but he and I saw things differently. Vividly. He thought it was sensible to leave his wife and children in another country for six years to chase the American Dream. I appreciated the hell out of him for that, but that didn't mean I respected it. He thought it made sense to groom his children to become mini versions of himself. He put drugs in our hands, when most parents told their children to go to school and stay out of the streets. That was the type of man he was. He forced me into this position. Didn't give me an option but I wouldn't become him. I learned a lot from my father, but the most important thing I learned was how not to raise children and how not to treat my wife. He was good to my mother, but a blind man could see his infidelities. He didn't honor his vows. I did. I made a promise to. Which was why this shit with Sienna had been eating at me the way it had been. I didn't want to become Samuel. I wouldn't. I would do everything in my power not to.

"I don't ask for much," I continued before he could speak. "Show me the same respect you expect from me. Respect the fact that nothing will ever be more important than family to me."

"I'm family. Your mother, your brothers, your sister."

"And nothing but the family I've created on my own comes before you."

We locked eyes for a few seconds before I turned away to give my attention to the road. I gave this family, the one I came from, everything. My childhood, my teenage years, most of my life. Samuel could go to hell if he thought I'd give him more than I gave my own.

"If I say I'm spending the day with my wife, respect that I'm spending the day with my wife. Blaise is—"

"Incompetent."

"Only because you made him that way," I added. "Saint . . . the same. If you can't trust them to handle things when I cannot, then you handle things yourself. You're capable. One day . . . All I asked for was one day and you couldn't give me that when I've given you years."

My father and I had a peculiar relationship. I could sit and kick it to him on some real shit. Samuel and I could talk like this because, in a sense, we were equals. If I were Blaise or Saint, there would be no back-and-forth. Because I spent so much time with him, we were alike in many ways. But the ways in which we differed was clear as hell.

Samuel put money and business over the family. Always. I would never. I had no reason to. Even with reason, I couldn't fathom putting drugs and money over them. I had enough. I'd never been a greedy nigga. I came from nothing, so what I had now was plenty. I could sleep easily without this shit. Every move I'd made while in it was strategic. Samuel could die with his hands still in the dope game, I wouldn't. I'd had my hand in it long enough.

If he told me he wanted me to step down right now, I would pull this whip over and switch sides with him with no fucking problem. He would never do that, though. Samuel's plate had been damn near cleared off because he'd piled everything up on mine. He was an OG, but he was in his late fifties. He wasn't equipped to handle the magnitude of bullshit I handled on the daily. Despite his disdain for the way I handled today, he would take it because, at the end of the day, the business needed me—I didn't need it.

"This business requires a certain amount of dedication."

I looked over at him. "I know. I've dedicated half of my life to it. Am I to turn my back on my family for it?"

He glanced over at me and shook his head. "Find a way to find a balance."

"I have found a way. Speak to Blaise. Put him in position."

"I can't do that," he said, steadily stroking his beard.

"I don't know what to tell you then, Pops," I dismissed.

He could do that. He just didn't want to do it. But that wasn't my problem. My American Dream and his were two different dreams. This was his shit, not mine. I refused to compromise anything just to pour into this shit.

About thirty minutes later, we pulled in the driveway of the yellow house behind Shelby's pickup truck. After tucking my burner, I hopped out and Samuel followed suit. As we treaded up the walkway to the house, Samuel lightly tapped me on the arm.

"Listen, I understand. I do. But—"

"Told you," I interrupted with my eyes locked on his. "When it comes to my family, there aren't any buts. If you understood the way you say you understood, the conversation would be over."

Samuel nodded and ran his hand down the back of his neck. "You were made for this." He stuffed his hands into the pockets of his peacoat. "Blaise will create problems. You handle them. I can't put my business in the hands of that . . ." He shook his head. *"Vakabon."*

I cut my eyes at him but said nothing. If Blaise was a bum, it was because he made him that way. I couldn't stress that enough. The discussion was over. I was finished bending over backward for him. I'd given him enough.

The minute we knocked on the door, Shelby let us in. We shook hands and stepped over the threshold into the small, dusty house. The home was so dusty, there was always a cast of it permeating the air. He didn't come here for shit but private linkups. Other than that, the house sat, rotting, untouched.

"How was the drive—"

"Cut the small talk," Samuel interrupted. "I need an explanation."

I stuffed my hands into the pockets of my Moncler and lightly cocked my head back.

Shelby's eyes shifted between the two of us before he pulled from his cigarette. "Things are hot right now. Getting rid of Walker was only half the battle. There is still a microscope hovering over the force. Walker's unfortunate accident did nothing but put fire under my ass. I have to act accordingly, guys."

Samuel nodded and grabbed his pants before sitting on the couch. I stood by the door. Had no intentions of getting comfortable. Besides, any time I came here, I stood, refusing to sit on the outdated floral couches that were covered in the same dust in the air.

"How long will things be hot?" I asked. "You know we run a very tight schedule. What happened today can't happen again."

Shelby shook his head and stabbed his cigarette into the glass ashtray on the wooden coffee table next to him. "I can't give you a timeline. What I can do is assure you that things will blow over soon. Right now, eyes are on Reek and his team out in Jersey. No one is looking at you guys. No one. We nail Reek, this blows over. Give me time to work on things on my end. I've got it under control. Nothing will happen. I can confidently promise you that."

I locked eyes with him and nodded. "You know how I feel about promises, Shelby."

He nodded and placed his hands on his slender hips. "I know, I know. Just make sure your paperwork and the trucks are in tiptop shape. The drivers, too, man. We can't have any fuckups."

My mind instantly went to Blaise and his foolish decision to get involved with tampering with Walker's car. I sucked in air and ran my hand down the back of my neck.

"What's going on with Walker's death? Any suspicion of foul play to worry about?" I questioned.

He turned his mouth down and shook his head. "Nothing. Clean. The car was old. Hadn't had any maintenance on it in over five years."

Samuel looked over at me with a squint that I chose to ignore. He didn't know about what Blaise did. I intended to keep it that way, especially since I'd basically just told him to put Blaise second in command and take me out of it. I was tweaking. Putting Blaise in control would be a bad move. Today was just a day. A day the weight of it on my shoulders was the heaviest.

I nodded. "That's good to hear. Listen . . ." I paused and took a couple of steps closer to him. I needed him to see my eyes when I told him, "Fix it. Whatever you have to do . . . fix it. There are a lot of variables at play. You know this. One problem causes a domino effect of problems and . . ." I rubbed the back of my neck. "I have no room in my life for any more problems. You get me?"

The trucks getting searched at the border made things shaky between the connect and us too. I didn't need any of those niggas looking at us as incompetent. We'd been in business with them for years. Good business. I needed it to stay that way. I might've wanted to pull back from the business, but for now . . . I was in it. Regardless of the disdain I had toward it, I'd always give one hundred percent effort to it. That was one thing Samuel would never have to worry about. As long as I was his second, I would put in work like number one. I looked over at him and nodded. As I'd always done.

"I get you," Shelby said with a shaky voice.

Slamming my hand down on his shoulder, I gave him a light smile. "Perfect."

Pops stood up, adjusted his coat, and gave Shelby another handshake before we walked out of the house.

When we got into the car, my phone buzzed. Pulling it from my pocket, I checked it. My dick instantly bricked at the sight of Leighton's pink, pretty, puffy pussy. I couldn't remember the last time Leigh sent me a pussy picture. She had me feeling like I was twenty-five again.

Wife: We miss you. Hurry back.

I untucked my burner, set it on the armrest, and put my phone in the cup holder. "I'm off the clock for the rest of the night, old man. No calls . . . no texts. I did what was asked of me and I'd appreciate it if I was given the privacy of spending the rest of my day with my wife."

"Konprann," he said with his hand extended and his eyes locked on mine.

I shook hands with him, then pulled out of the driveway.

CHAPTER 26

Sienna

I gripped my steering wheel and shifted my eyes to the clock on my dashboard. It was 7:45 a.m. I was five minutes away from my destination with the urge to turn around and go straight home. My heart raced against my rising and falling chest as I continued to wrench my steering wheel with so much aggression, a few of the rhinestones that covered it began to fall into my lap. I closed my eyes and ran my hand over my cramping stomach. I didn't know if I was cramping because I was nervous, or if it was because my period was finally coming, but I'd been cramping since I woke up. The closer I got to my destination, the worse they got.

Taking a deep breath, I pulled away from the green light. I was on my way to work—and not to the McIntyre house. Sunday morning, as soon as I opened my eyes, I called Shonda and said the first thing that came to mind. I was going back to the Baptiste household. Saturday night, after endless hours of thinking and beating myself up about what to do, I told myself that the first thing that came to mind on Sunday was the decision I would go with. When Sunday came, I opened my eyes, and my first thought was of Leighton. It wasn't Jahad. It wasn't me. It wasn't the way I felt about him. It was her.

Her and the oath I took when I became a doula. It was my duty to take care of her. I couldn't run from my responsibility as a doula because I had some kind of connection with her husband. This wasn't about him. It wasn't about money. It wasn't about guilt. It was about taking care of her. My first client. I went into the job with confidence and the excitement to be there for a woman with similar struggles as myself. I specifically asked Shonda for an antepartum doula assignment because I wanted to be there for the mother every step of the way. Somehow, someway, my first client just happened to be *his* wife. That shouldn't have changed anything. It wouldn't have, had I conducted myself like a professional, rather than an emotional drunk. Leighton deserved better. I hadn't been my best self. I'd been an unethical, emotional wreck. However, she still wanted me.

I couldn't understand it, but a lot of the tears I'd shed over the weekend, after talking to Jahad, were for her. I wanted to hug her. I wanted to give her so much love. I didn't judge Leighton. I didn't think she was weak for giving her husband a hall pass. I thought she was strong. I pitied her. I wanted to tell her she was far too beautiful and too strong to feel the need to give her husband a hall pass. I wanted to tell her she was special. I wanted to tell her she was more than sex. More than what she couldn't give him. I sympathized with her because I understood her. I knew what it was like to feel inadequate. To feel like I wasn't enough. I hated that for her. I hated that for *us*.

My phone rang, snatching me out of my thoughts. I looked at the screen on my dash and saw it was Naoki.

As soon as I answered the phone, she asked, "You sure you want to do this?"

I twisted my steering wheel, and more rhinestones fell. "Mm-hmm."

"You don't sound sure. You know you don't owe her shit, right?"

I sucked in air and made a right turn. "I know. It's . . . It's not just about her, Kiki."

"You sure it's not? It sounds like guilt to me. You fucked her husband. She gave him permission to fuck someone else and that someone else happened to be you. Oh well. It's not your fault she made the dumbass decision to give her husband permission to cheat."

I rolled my eyes. "A lot of women in her position give their husbands hall passes."

After Jahad left, I did a little research on pregnant women on bed rest and, surprisingly, it happened often. Some women did it because they felt obligated. Some women did it because they felt like their husbands deserved one night of passion. And some women did it because they felt like if they didn't, he would end up cheating anyway. It was sad . . . sad as hell. I didn't know Leighton's why. I didn't want to know why, per se. Regardless, it was a sad-ass situation. The more stories I read, the sadder I felt for her.

"So? What, it's supposed to make it less stupid because a lot of people do it? It's stupid. And you feel you owe her something because, why? You fell in love with her husband? I don't get it. What point are you trying to make, sis?"

Of course she didn't get it. She never had to deal with feeling insignificant because she stayed on the move. Naoki didn't have time to fall in love. She recycled dick. Went back to old niggas who really didn't deserve her or her coochie because of convenience. And attachments, too. More for convenience than anything because her job kept her too busy to find someone new.

I sucked my teeth and ran my hand over my stomach. "I'm not in love with her husband. I made an oath," I told her. "Say you walk into work one day and Denim's wife is your patient. She's sick as hell and needs to be treated. You're the only Black nurse on shift and she requested you. What you gon' do? Leave? Walk off the job because you stay fucking her husband? Or are you going to put that shit aside and do your job?"

"Really?"

Denim was a sensitive subject. And one of the dicks she used for both convenience and unhealthy attachment. They had history, and a lot of it. We were all childhood friends, but Naoki ended up losing her virginity to him. They were together for most of high school and our early twenties, but their shit was toxic as hell. They fought and argued all the time but couldn't stop fucking around with each other. Not even after he proposed to his wife. Not after he got married. Not even after he had three kids.

"Yes, really. The fuck?" I snapped. "My oath as a doula might not be taken as serious as yours as a nurse, but I still took an oath. I quit on her because of my own selfish reasons. She didn't deserve that shit. That lady didn't do shit to me. So, to answer your question, I'm not going back because I feel guilty, I'm going back because I have a job to do. Unless she does something to hurt me, or is nasty in any way toward me, I'm going to do my job. I won't let you, me, or him get in the way of that."

"What about Mrs. McIntyre?"

"What about Mrs. McIntyre? Jennifer is going back to her. We switched cases because of what I did. Leighton didn't like her. It didn't work out. So . . . she's going back to them and I'm going back to *them*."

"Oh. The oath you made don't apply to Mrs. McIntyre, huh?" Naoki challenged. "You're full of shit, Si. You're going back to that house either because you feel guilty or because you want to be around him. You know what? Fuck guilt. It is about him, period. You should've seen yourself at Vault. Bitch, you were under some type of spell."

I frowned. "What? Bitch, this has nothing to do with him."

"Yeah . . . Keep telling yourself that. Either way, I love you and would never judge you."

"You couldn't judge me if you wanted to because you would take Keisha on as a patient and fuck Denim in their bed that same night, while she's laid up in the hospital on her deathbed."

"Sure the fuck would!" Naoki yelled with a laugh. "I own my ho-ness. You know this about me. You're the one who would rather pretend you're honoring some oath instead of just admitting to wanting round two on that big-ass kitchen island. Stop—"

I hung up on her and went back to twisting my steering wheel. I was pissed. My heart raced against my chest so aggressively, I had to pull over. I sat on the side of the road, trying to calm down, but only ended up crying and gasping for fucking air. Naoki called back, but I sent the bitch to voicemail. I was pissed. Pissed, pissed. I wasn't sure who I was madder at—myself or Naoki because . . . she was right.

Not completely.

But . . . she was right.

I did want to be around him. I didn't want to let him go. I couldn't. I was addicted to the way he made me feel. I couldn't have him. Not the way I'd had him before. Not in my hands. Not in my mouth. Not on my skin. He made that very clear. We made it very clear to each other. Leighton deserved better than that. I deserved better than that. I couldn't be the other woman. He wouldn't allow me to be, anyway. He cared too much about his wife and I was far too damaged to be the other woman. However, all I wanted was a small dose of him. I couldn't imagine never experiencing that again. Him. That pull. It was torturous. It would tease me. But so? I just . . . I wanted to see him. *Feel* him. Smell him. Talk to him.

That was why it was sad. For her. For him. For us. I couldn't walk away from what I had with him. Life wouldn't let me. That pull wouldn't let me. I felt it twenty miles away from him. And the closer I got to his house—their house—the stronger it became. I didn't want round two on that nice-ass kitchen island, as Naoki had put it. I couldn't control whatever it was that drew me to him. I wanted to control it. Hated that I couldn't. Naoki tried to paint me out to be a home-wrecker . . . to be that slut I'd been calling myself since I met him. But I wasn't that. I was . . . just . . . his . . . in the most unattached, attached way imaginable.

Once I calmed down, I cleaned my face of tears and touched up my makeup before pulling off. Naoki called again and I ignored her for a second time. She didn't want shit and I didn't want to sit on the phone, trying to explain something that not even I could understand. To her, it would always look like I was just playing a role, pretending to give a fuck about Leighton to get close to her man, and that was not the fucking case. I cared about her . . . but I cared about him too.

Five minutes later, I was parked and climbing out of my car. The weather was nice. The snow had melted, and the sun was shining. It was a beautiful day. A cold-ass thirty degrees, but it was beautiful, still. Before I left the house, I told myself it would be a good day. I repeated that shit over and over again. Said I wouldn't cry either and look . . . Naoki had already fucked that up for me. I was determined to have a good day, though.

I dressed in bright colors, did my makeup, and put my goddess locs up in a cute, messy bun. I was still shoveling glitter on top of shit, but hey . . . it worked. Pretty soon, the shit would be covered completely, and I'd just be shoveling glitter on top of glitter.

After ringing the doorbell, I was hit with a serious case of déjà vu. Especially when Farrah's big-nose, caked-up-makeup-wearing ass answered the door.

She looked me up and down with a frown of disgust on her face. "What are you doing here?"

"Hey, Farrah," I said with a forced smile. "Your makeup looks so good! I'm here to work." I fished around my Telfar bag and pulled my Serene Mommy Doula badge out as if the bitch needed to see it, and showed it to her. "See."

She squinted and turned her nose up at me. "You quit."

I locked eyes with her. "And I'm back." Pausing, I looked past her. "Are you going to let me inside?"

She looked over her shoulder and gripped the door. "I'm taking care of Leighton now. We no longer need you."

I cocked my head to the side and frowned a bit. "You sure? She's been requesting me to come back for weeks. Let me just call her and see—"

"You know what? Come on inside. I'll let her tell you herself," she interrupted with a tight-lipped smile before stepping aside so I could walk in.

I gave her that same bullshit-ass smile and walked inside, purposely hitting her with my bag as I put it on my shoulder. "Oh, sorry about that."

She stared at me with fire behind her eyes before she closed the door and locked it. I took my boots off and slipped into the fresh, unworn slides they kept by the door. I had my slides with me, but I wasn't sure if I would stay, so I didn't put them on. I knew Leighton would welcome me with open arms since she'd been on Shonda's head about getting me back here. It wasn't Leighton I was worried about. It was Jahad.

When he left my apartment that night, we were good. I walked him down to the lobby and everything, but before, when we talked, I saw just how desperate he was to fix his marriage. He didn't sugarcoat a damn thing. He told me Leighton meant the world to him. He told me she was the love of his life. Thing was, he didn't have to tell me that. I knew it already. I didn't expect anything less. What happened between us was just . . . something. Something that led to an intense connection. One I knew he wanted to disconnect from. Me being here would make it hard for him. I knew that when I made my decision to come back. Regardless of what Naoki thought, my duty was to take care of Leighton and I wasn't letting anything come in between that. The only way I'd leave was if he blatantly fired me.

Once I came out of my coat, I crossed the threshold into the foyer. I didn't bother waiting for Farrah's bourgeois ass to escort me anywhere. I went right to the kitchen, where I knew Ms. Evaline would have Leighton's orange juice waiting.

"Where are you—"

"Getting her orange juice, girl. You know she just gotta have her orange juice in the morning. Did you grab it?" I interrupted with a squint as I continued toward the kitchen with a racing heart and a steady cramping stomach. God, I was nervous as fuck. Not only about being in this house again, but about seeing Ms. Evaline, too.

I wasn't ready to face her. At all. After she walked in on me and Jahad that night, I ran my ass out of the kitchen so fast, you would think I'd gotten caught by my grandmother. I felt like such a slut, and I knew she thought I was one, too. She had high hopes for me and my future in the Baptiste household, and what did I go and do? Get drunk and fuck my client's husband on the kitchen island like I didn't have a lick of sense or common decency.

"No, I didn't. I came down to get it when—"

"Good morning, Maurice!" I said, purposely interrupting Farrah. I didn't want that bitch saying a damn thing to me. She walked around this big-ass house, trying to run shit like she was important. I wanted the bitch to know she didn't mean a damn thing to me. Farrah might've intimidated the bitches before me, but I wasn't the one.

Maurice looked up from the counter he was wiping with a big, bright smile. "H-hey, Sienna!"

Before I could go into the refrigerator, Ms. Evaline emerged from the butler's pantry, carrying a few pans. We made eye contact and I swear I saw a flicker of disgust run across her face. I could've been imagining things, but the tension for sure grew thicker.

"Good morning, Ms. Evaline," I said with a timid smile.

"Good morning, Sienna. You're back? To stay?" she asked, her brown eyes on mine with a light squint.

I nodded and swallowed. "Mm-hmm."

"Mm-hmm." She groaned. "Mrs. Baptiste is going to be delighted."

What was that supposed to mean? Did she tell Leighton what she saw? She couldn't have. Was she being funny? Sincere? I couldn't read her. Not for real, anyway. I nodded and pulled the refrigerator door open and grabbed the carafe full of fresh orange juice out. Before I could go for Leighton's favorite glass, Farrah was in the cabinet, grabbing one.

When she handed it to me, I shook my head and said, "She has a favorite, and it sure ain't that one."

I lightly bumped her out of my way with my hip to look into the cabinet. Once I grabbed it down, my eyes met Ms. Evaline's again. She squinted at me and took a deep breath before setting the pans on the stove. Yeah, she hated me. Why in the fuck did I even care? I shouldn't have. But I did. I swear the way she looked at me reminded me of the time my granny caught me sneaking this corner boy, Zay, out of the back door of her house when I was seventeen. She cursed me out so bad but she never told my parents what she saw. Every time she saw me, she gave me a look. Shit, she still gave me that look to this day. That was probably why Ms. Evaline's glower was so got damn unsettling.

I ignored the patronizing stare Farrah gave me as I walked off with the carafe and glass in hand. She lingered behind a little, but I felt her eyes on me, even behind the thick, big-ass eyelashes she wore. Just as I was almost out of the kitchen, Ms. Evaline called me.

"Hm?" I asked, turning around to look at her.

"When you get a chance, could you come down and help me with something?" she asked.

I nodded. "Yeah . . . I can."

I turned away and sucked in air. She didn't want help with a damn thing. When I walked off this time, I heard the click-clacking of Farrah's heels behind me. She must've been an exception to the no-shoes rule. No wonder the bitch thought she ran everything.

I stopped right at the elevator and hit the up button. She walked by, snorted, and shook her head. I didn't give a fuck. I was taking the elevator. I didn't have shit to prove to her miserable ass.

It took me no time to get up to the second floor. The minute I stepped off the elevator, she was walking by. I, again, ignored her and continued down the hallway. My heart raced and my stomach cramped again. And . . . that pull . . . I felt it. I rubbed my lips together and tried to mentally prepare myself to see him again. I closed my eyes, just for a second, and images of him while I laid in his arms Friday night flooded my mind in an instant. When I opened them,

I could still see him. Inches away from kissing me, I could feel his hands on my skin and his breath on my eager lips. Could feel his tongue passionately gliding along mine.

Fuck.

Farrah opened the double doors to the bedroom and walked inside. I could hear her telling them I was back before I even walked in. *Bitch.*

"She's back," Farrah said in a cold tone.

"Who's back?" Leighton asked, just as I stood at the doorway and knocked on the frame.

Farrah stepped aside, out of Leighton's view, and when she saw me, her eyes lit up. She was so happy to see me. The smile that spread across her face warmed and broke my heart at once.

"Hey, Mrs. Baptiste," I said with a light smile, ignoring the feel of his eyes burning into my skin. My pulse raced. I felt it beating against the thin skin on the side of my neck. I wondered if they saw it. If he saw it. His stare was so penetrating.

"Sienna," she softly sang. "Come in, boo."

Boo. The smile on her face and the love in her eyes only made my stomach turn more. God, why did she like me so much? If she knew . . .

I swallowed and took a deep breath before entering the bedroom.

"Didn't you cut ties with them, Jahad?" Farrah asked with her arms crossed over her chest.

I still hadn't looked in his direction, but since she'd addressed him, I had to. I tore my eyes away from Leighton and painfully put them on Jahad. I hoped he saw how sincere I was behind them. God, he looked fucking good. He had a fresh fade and the lineup of his beard and goatee was immaculate. For a brief moment, time did its thing when we were in the same room. Slow motion. But . . . he looked away, breaking it. I felt slighted. Just a teensy-weensy bit. Like I had the right to. *Tuh.*

I smiled and nodded at him. "Good morning, Mr. Baptiste. I spoke with Shonda yesterday morning, and she reassigned me as Leighton's doula. She didn't mention anything about your contract with her being severed. Should I call her?"

Jahad locked eyes with me again and shook his head. "That won't be necessary."

My eyes traveled from his eyes to the Dior loafers on his feet before taking in the rest of him. He looked so got damn good. His tailored black pants did nothing to conceal that bulge between his legs. Damn. A big-ass dick. One I dreamed about last night. Big hands . . . big dick . . . big feet. Big every-fucking-thing. Leighton was so lucky. So got damn lucky.

"Right," Leighton chimed in before cutting her eyes at Farrah. "We did not cut ties with Shonda's company, Farrah. I told you, I didn't need you to be my doula, crazy." She looked at me and smiled before putting her eyes back on Farrah. "Go ahead and handle your business today, bestie. Sienna's got this."

Farrah was pissed with a capital *P*, honey! Especially when I walked over to Leighton's bed, poured her glass of orange juice, and handed it to her. "If you don't mind, I'd like to speak to the both of you alone. You and Mr. Baptiste, I mean."

Leighton nodded and looked over at Jahad. "Babe, you got a little while before your meeting, right?"

Babe.

I'd never heard her call him that. They were happy. That was good. She was happier. She didn't have that look in her eyes anymore. That familiar look. The look that told me she knew. Today, her smile reached her eyes. She was truly happy. That was good. So good. I was happy for them . . . honestly.

"Yeah." He paused and looked down at his watch, undoubtedly to keep his eyes off me. "I got a few."

Farrah laughed lightly and shook her head. "Okay, then. I really hope things work out this time. Otherwise, you really need to reevaluate what's best for your wife."

Jahad glared at Farrah with so much fire in his eyes that if it was possible, her ass would've been set ablaze. She had to feel it because her eyebrows rose a bit and she looked away from him. She walked over to the bed, gave Leighton a hug, and told her to call her if she needed anything. Before she grabbed her purse, she cut her eyes at me and told me to take good care of her friend. I just gave the bitch a forced smile and looked away.

As soon as she walked out, I took a deep breath and stepped away from the bed a little to put myself in the middle of the room. I was nervous as hell. To have both of them with their eyes on me was very intense. I was in such a weird space. How in the hell did I even end up here?

"I just wanted to personally apologize for the way I handled things before," I said, my eyes locked on Leighton. I was afraid that if I looked over at Jahad, she would see *it*. The lust. The pull. The desire for him. Naoki said it was like I was under a spell at Vault. She had to see something in me. I didn't want Leighton to see the same thing.

"I handled things very unprofessionally and that's not a reflection of who I am. I made an oath. An oath to offer comfort, where there is fear. To bring hope, where there is despair . . . Encouragement where there is reluctance . . . and a loving companion if there is loneliness. I came here to help you, Mrs.

Baptiste, on your path from womanhood to motherhood, and I didn't do that. The way I handled things was very unethical." I glanced over at Jahad, then back to Leighton. "I allowed my emotions to get in the way, and in doing that, I lost sight of what was important. You. My oath.

"Despite my shortcomings, you showed me so much grace, Mrs. Baptiste. Because of that, I'm going to do everything in my power to show you just how much I appreciate that."

Why in the hell was I getting choked up? My God! My emotions had been all over the fucking place. At this point, I was sure I needed to seek professional help. Honestly. I needed to sit on somebody's couch and get everything out. I was an emotional, heartbroken, self-loathing wreck.

"I'm sorry," I said as I tossed my head back to keep my tears at bay. "So sorry."

"Come here," Leighton said, reaching out. "Don't cry, hun."

I looked from her to him. He stood on the other side of her bed, watching me as I took slow, undeserving steps toward her. *Please don't hug me. Please don't,* I thought with a racing heart, just inches away from her bed. As soon as I was next to the bed, she opened her arms. She wanted a hug. *Fuck.*

I hesitated by wiping tears from the corner of my eyes. Not that that helped at all. She moved her fingers, gesturing for me to hug her. I briefly glanced at Jahad and finally gave her a hug. She hugged me so tight, I could literally feel how much she cared through it. She whispered in my ear, telling me she understood and that her pregnancy was mine too. A sentiment toward my reason for getting into doulaship in the first place.

Tears got caught up in my throat as I hugged her. I kept my eyes closed to avoid his. I felt them on me. He was staring directly at me. I kept my eyes closed because I was afraid of what I would see when I looked into his. Anger? Resentment? Hate? I slowly peeled them open, my heart racing faster, while Leighton ran her hand over my back. The minute I opened my eyes, they fell on him. As expected, he was looking directly at me. Surprisingly, when our eyes met, I didn't see anger. There was no resentment. Hate neither. Jahad's gaze held the same compassion and guilt I was sure he saw behind mine.

Thirty minutes later, I was finally putting my work bag away in the guest room. After my little emotional breakdown, we sat and talked for a while, catching up. Leighton told me about the gender reveal happening in a couple of days; she let me know about her upcoming appointments, prescriptions that needed to be refilled, and contractors that would be on and off the premises to prepare for renovations they were having done on the guesthouse.

Leighton was approaching her third trimester, and being that she was high risk, there would be a lot for us to do. It was a lot to take in, but I was excited. I hadn't really been able to fully step into my position because I quit, and I was nothing more than a glorified nanny at the McIntyres'. I really couldn't wait to fully get into my role.

The whole time we talked, Jahad was there, and I kept my focus on Leighton. That was huge, since that fucking magnet stayed pulling me in his direction. The fact that I was able to do my job without having to work hard to keep my focus told me I'd be able to do this with no problem. I felt victorious as fuck. Over my feelings for him, and over the shit Naoki had said.

After using the bathroom, I headed out of the bedroom to grab her breakfast. That was something else Ms. Evaline and Maurice usually did, but I was very hands on and had no issue grabbing her food and drinks. They appreciated me for it too. As soon as I walked out of the bedroom, I bumped into him. We had a habit of doing that . . . bumping into one another.

We stood, awkwardly staring at each other in silence for a couple of seconds before I decided to say something.

"I—"

"Not right now," he interrupted before taking a step closer to me. "I'll hit you later."

I felt like I owed him an explanation. I wouldn't be surprised if he thought I came to blow his spot up when he looked up and saw me in his bedroom doorway. I was sure he had a lot of questions about my why, considering everything we'd talked about and the feelings we both clearly had for one another. Feelings we both agreed were weird, intense, and a distraction that neither of us needed. Anybody would wonder why. Anybody would question my motive. Jahad made it very clear to me he didn't see me as this wild, home-wrecking slut, but I don't know. From the outside looking in, it would look like I was. And . . . I really didn't want him to think that.

I pulled my lips into my mouth and nodded before he gestured, allowing me to lead the way. Butterflies filled the pit of my stomach as I walked in front of him. I wondered if he was being a gentleman or if he only wanted me in front of him to look at my ass. I was sure it was a combination of both. I felt his eyes on my ass with every step I took toward the stairs. Yes, the stairs. Taking them down was a piece of cake. It was the trek up I refused to do!

The walk down felt longer than usual. And my feet? They were heavy, like I was walking in quicksand. The urge to turn around and throw my arms around his neck was insane. I wondered if he felt it too. That pull, urging our lips to touch and our tongues to intertwine. He did. He had to. The only thing stopping me from turning around was the smell of Leighton's perfume on my clothes.

When I finally made it to the bottom of the stairs, I looked over my shoulder at him and his eyes were on me. All over me. He didn't shy away when I caught him ogling me, either. He slowly lifted his eyes to mine and dragged his teeth over his bottom lip. I wished I could read his mind.

"Have a great day, Ms. Mills," Jahad said, all professional like, with a head nod.

I gave him a light smile. "You too, Mr. Baptiste."

He gave me a squint. "Jahad."

His reminder to call him by his first name made my pussy tingle. The last time I wouldn't call him Jahad, he forced me into submission with his dick. Damn, it would be nice to have that again.

But because it was over for that, I just smiled and said, "Jahad."

Something flashed across his face before he lightly nodded with his mouth turned down. Could it have been finality? Something about me calling him Jahad made the end of our thing real. It was like putting nails in a coffin.

When he walked away, a rush of realization consumed me, and my heart began to race. I said I was okay with settling for the pull, but was I? Really? God . . . I wanted *everything*. The pull was just too got damn heavy without collision.

I rested against the wall next to the stairs and took deep breaths. With my eyes closed, I tried to ground myself in the present moment and the bigger picture. Grabbing a fistful of my top, I brought it up to my nose and took a hefty whiff of it. Leighton deserved better, so I had to find a way to be comfortable with never having him again.

"Shit!" I yelped with my hand on my chest when I opened my eyes to find Ms. Evaline standing a few feet away from me, watching me with that look on her face.

She eyed me up and down, and in return to her judgmental-ass glare, I rolled my eyes. I was taught to respect my elders, but she only had a few more of those looks to give me before I popped off on her ass, and everything I was taught was a damn afterthought.

"Why are you sneaking up on me?" I asked with a swallow. I pushed up off the wall to walk away.

"Sneaking up on you? Child . . . I didn't sneak up on you. Your mind must've been *somewhere else*," she grumbled before giving me that look again.

Ms. Evaline was the epitome of an old-school granny. Curvy, dark skin, high cheekbones dotted with dainty textured moles, and long, thick salt and pepper hair she kept in a low ponytail. She was just as meddling and messy too. Mm-hmm. I saw through the soft smiles and side eyes like she was made of glass.

I ran my hand over my forehead. "Ms. Evaline, stop looking at me like that."

"Lookin' at you like what? Like you've lost every bit of sense the good Lord gave you?" She cut her eyes at me and we walked off, heading for the kitchen.

I lightly laughed and stuffed my hands into the pockets of my duster. "Yeah . . . Like that."

"Have you?" she questioned, eyeing me up and down.

I took a deep breath. "No, Ms. Evaline. I haven't. I just—"

She shook her head. "Uh-uh. Don't even try it." She paused and grimaced in disappointment. "Look, it's not my place to say, but keep your little kitty off that married man. You hear me?"

I planned to! If it was really up to me, my "little kitty" wouldn't even like that married man so much. I was ashamed of how much she liked him.

I looked over at her with pinched brows and another soft laugh. "I hear you, Ms. Evaline. And . . . I . . . What you saw—"

She put her hand up. "Ain't my business. I don't need no explanation. I'm just offerin' a li'l advice to a beautiful young woman that clearly needs a little guidance. Hell, self-love and respect, too, might I add." She cut her eyes at me again. "I don't know why you came back, and I really do hope it's to do your job. Mr. Baptiste is a fine young man, but he belongs to somebody else. And you're too beautiful and sweet to be anything other than the only one."

I pulled my lips into my mouth and nodded. She was right. I left Amiri because he refused to see my worth. I deserved to be the only one, not number one. Not one of many, either. It was crazy to me how I left him because he wouldn't see my worth, but here I was, not even three months later, not holding myself to that same regard.

CHAPTER 27

Jahad

"She just left. What time are you heading back?" Leighton asked.

I pinched the bridge of my nose and set my glass of Clase Azul on the coffee table. "In a couple hours. Still waiting for bro to touch down."

Leighton sucked her teeth. "Again? What's been going on with him and time these days?"

"Hell yeah," I said with a sigh before running my hand over my waves. "Ari making it hard for that nigga."

"Figures." She sighed. "Well, Mama just got here. She brought me a plate over. Legim and—"

"Did she bring me one?"

Leighton laughed. "You know she did."

I laughed and tossed my head back, resting it along the back of the couch. "Bet." Pausing, I said, "Listen . . . *Mwen renmen ou* (I love you)."

I heard the smile in her voice when she said, "*Mwen renmen w tou* (I love you, too)."

We hung up and I tossed my phone on the coffee table. I dragged my hands down my face and shook my head. Shortly after, Saint snickered. I didn't need to lift my head to know he was watching me, wearing a goofy-ass smirk.

"It's gettin' easier, ain't it, bro?" Saint asked.

"What?"

"Lying to sis. It's getting easier."

I took a deep breath and said nothing. It wasn't getting easier. In fact, it was hard as fuck for me to lie to her. Especially since we were in a good space. The last thing I wanted to do to Leighton was lie to her. But I had to. I thought that shit was dead, but I knew it wasn't when I looked up to find her standing in my bedroom.

She was back. Sienna.

Why was she back? She told Leigh she wanted to finish the job she started. Hugged her, cried in her arms, and gave a heartfelt apology, but something in my spirit said there was more to it than just that. I needed to talk to her. On some one-on-one-type shit, away from the house.

In the back of my mind, I knew linking with her was a bad idea, but a nigga had been prone to bad ideas these days. I couldn't stop myself.

Blaise left about an hour ago. I'd been kicking it with Saint since, tossing drinks back, venting, talking about shorty and the connection we had. Tomorrow, I'd regret even letting him in my head as much as I had. But right now, I needed to vent. I couldn't understand why I couldn't get this fuckin' woman off my mind. Felt like I was losing my mind. My reality didn't even seem like my reality. Felt like I was living someone else's life.

Back in the day, when I did my dirt, it wasn't because I felt a connection with any of those hos. I did it because I wanted to. But with Sienna? Nah, with Sienna, it was different. I couldn't understand how one night had thrown me off so heavy. Every time she came to mind, I was hit with the question of why? Saint kept talking about I was hooked on the pussy, but I knew it wasn't that. Not that alone, at least. I'd had my share of good-ass pussy. Shit, Leigh was sitting on gold. It wasn't that. This was something different. It was the feeling. A feeling I couldn't decipher. It ate at me on a daily.

How different it was literally drove me insane. I couldn't close my eyes without thinking of her and the way the air in the room seemed to thicken anytime she was in it with me. I couldn't sleep without dreaming of her. The past couple of nights had been spent with Leighton sleeping in my arms, but Sienna always made her way into my dreams. I couldn't remember the last time I dreamed of my wife. That was unsettling. One of the most unsettling things about this whole situation, honestly.

That fucked with me more than the lying did.

I sat up and picked my glass up, ignoring the pensive stare from Saint. I was on drink number three. I'd really been tossing them bitches back. Between Leighton, Sienna, and this drug business, I couldn't help but toss drinks back. A nigga was drowning. Drowning and constantly sinking further away from the surface. I'd come here, hoping I could get a little leeway. Sat down with Blaise, discussed what I needed from him since Samuel refused to, and the nigga laughed in my face. Told me I knew the suit-and-tie, corporate-boss-type shit wasn't for him. I knew that shit already. Still tried to put the bitch nigga in position because I didn't give a fuck. A nigga was tired. Desperate and tired. Blaise wasn't hearing me, though. I was stuck. Stuck in a business I never wanted to be a part of. Stuck on a woman I never wanted.

Leighton had done this shit to me. To us.

She was just as bad as Samuel.

"Jah," he called out.

"What, nigga?" I snapped.

"She worth losing Leigh over?"

I shifted my glare from the black marble coffee table up at him. "You stupid?"

"Nah . . . *I'm* not stupid. But are you? You sitting there looking like you about ready to risk it all over a bitch—"

"Aight, nigga. Be careful," I warned with a smirk.

Saint cocked his head to the side and gave me a confused look. "You defending her now, too? Yeah, my nigga, you gone."

I was gone. Too far gone. So far gone that twisting my ring around my finger no longer grounded me. Nothing could ground me. Not with her in my life. With her in my life, I floated. Floating would be straight if she was my wife. But since she wasn't, I needed to find a way to ground myself. Thing was, grounding myself was the furthest thing from my mind. I was past that.

Instead of responding to him, I looked over at him and sat back against the couch. Dragging my hands down my face, I let his question marinate. She wasn't worth losing Leighton over. No one in the world was. Leighton was my everything. I told myself that shit every fucking day. Saint didn't understand. He couldn't . . . because not even I could understand what it was. Did he think I wanted to lie to my wife? Did he think I wanted to fuck another woman in her house? I couldn't control it. No matter what I did, I couldn't. I didn't ask her to come back to work for us because I wanted to let it go. I wanted the flame to die. I needed it to. And what happened? She showed up at my shit. I couldn't escape the fucking woman.

I thought about taking the bitch nigga route and forcing her to leave, but that shit didn't work before and wouldn't work without Leighton raising an eyebrow, anyway. Especially after the apology Sienna had given her. There was no way out of it.

"You know why I asked you that? A couple years ago, I asked you how one woman was enough, and you told me Leigh was enough because nobody else was worth the risk of losing her. You been sittin' here for a good hour, talkin' about shorty's ass and how you can't escape her. Sis call and you lyin', talkin' about we waitin' on bro and that nigga skated over an hour ago. I'm already hip to what type of time you on. At least this time, you won't have to call me to grab yo' phone so your location will ping here, huh?" He nodded at my phone sitting on the coffee table. "You gon' leave that bitch right there, huh, bro?"

I looked down at the phone, sat up, and grabbed my glass instead. He was right. I was leaving the phone here. I had to. Hated that I had to, too. Fuck it, though. I hadn't been able to look in the mirror and be cool with the nigga looking back at me for years. I'd done worse. Tonight, my intentions were pure. At least I wasn't scheming and moving fucked up to go stick dick to her. I wasn't on that type of time. Didn't that count for something?

"Chill, nigga. I know what I'm doin," I said, slightly tipsy, before finishing my drink.

He cocked his brow. "You sure? You still ain't answered my question, tho', nigga." He paused and moved closer to the edge of the couch he sat in across from me. "I'm kicking it with you on some real shit, bro. Like, I been on goofy shit, joking with you about the situation, but today showed me that this shit ain't for play. You serious 'bout this broad."

I pushed up from the couch and grabbed my coat from the armrest.

"You might want to think about what I asked you before you head out, brodie," Saint warned before taking a shot of the Clase Azul.

"I think about that. I think about it every fuckin' day. And regardless of what it might look like, she ain't worth it. What I said still stands, Saint."

"What you tell me?" Saint asked with a cocked brow. "The way a nigga talk don't mean shit if the way he move don't match. You goin' back on your own philosophy, nigga? You taught me that. It don't apply to you, huh, *fré*?"

Sometimes, I hated how good I'd raised the nigga. He took heed to everything I told him. Even the shit I didn't think he listened to, he heard. In this case, I wished he'd shut the fuck up and let me do me. The philosophy applied to me, for sure. But this was different. Despite what it looked like to him, I was moving the way I talked.

I looked over at him. "I need to talk to her. I'm not on bullshit."

"About what, nigga? She showed up to work. She told y'all what it was. What more do you want from her? Let that shit go. Let 'er work. You don't need to talk to her. You *want* to talk to her. Keep it a stack."

I clenched down on my jaw and walked over to him with my hand extended. He stood up and we shook hands. He pulled me into his chest and said, "You had your fun, bro. Play time is over."

We locked eyes and I said nothing. Did he think this shit was fun? Did he think fucking with her at Pandora's was fun? Fucking her on the island? None of that shit was fun. It gutted me. Broke my heart to stick my dick in someone other than my wife. I didn't get a thrill out of it. This wasn't fun. It was torture.

About twenty minutes later, I was in her parking lot, calling her for the third time. Just like the last two times, it went to voicemail. Instead of leaving, like I should've, I got out of my car and treaded up to the building with my hands stuffed in the pocket of my coat. I told myself I couldn't leave without having a conversation with her. Told myself the conversation was necessary. She hit me from left field, coming to work today. We had to talk about that.

Standing at the apartment's entrance, I buzzed her apartment number and waited. With my hands stuffed into the pockets of my coat, I waited, and waited. I rang it and her line three times before someone walked out and held the door open for me. Didn't ask me if I stayed there or anything. Just let me inside, not knowing what type of time I was on. Shit was crazy.

Her not responding to my calls, or answering her doorbell, should have told me she didn't want to be bothered. But it didn't. In fact, the silence did nothing but worry me. Something in my gut told me she wasn't ignoring me because she didn't want to be bothered. She knew I was linking with her today, so why would she just up and ignore me all of a sudden? The unsettling feeling in the pit of my stomach wouldn't allow me to just leave. I should've. But from the parking lot, I felt it. That fucking pull. It wouldn't let me just dip. There was a voice in the back of my mind that said, *Just go to the crib, nigga. Kick it with the wife . . . do the good husband thing. Turn around and go home.* But . . . I couldn't. All common sense and rational thinking went out of the fucking window when it came to shorty.

Hated that shit.

When I finally got to her floor, I knocked on the door. She didn't answer. It was dead quiet on the other side of it. That eerie feeling in my gut magnified, and I began to pound on the door. My mind was flooded with memories of her sitting at the kitchen island, drowning herself with wine, crying. I thought back to the emptiness behind her beautiful eyes when I stared at her on the monitors at Vault. Something was wrong. Tonight, something was very wrong. I felt the shit. My heart began to race, and panic rushed through my veins.

"Sienna!" I yelled. "Aye!"

"Everything cool, man?"

I looked over my shoulder at the short, scrawny-ass white nigga and scoffed.

"Aye, man . . . She's in there. I saw her about an hour ago. If she's not answering, she must not want to be bothered. Maybe—"

"Maybe you should mind yo' fuckin' business," I flatly interrupted.

"Hey, am I going to have to call the police?" he asked before pulling his phone from the pocket of his leather coat. "I have them on speed dial, you know? You might want to leave before they get here."

I ran my tongue over my bottom lip and turned to face him. "Call 'em. Make sure you tell 'em to send an ambulance with 'em, too, pussy."

He drew back with a frown. "Excuse me? Is that a threat?"

Before I could tell him it was for sure a threat, the door cracked open, revealing only one side of her face. She eyed me up and down, then put her red, puffy eyes on her neighbor. "Hey, Adam. I'm fine. This is my friend."

"You sure?" he asked, sizing me up before looking over at her.

The type of time I was on, I was liable to really smack the piss out of him. It had been a while since I'd had to put my hands on a muthafucka. That type of shit was behind me, but my patience was running thin. Especially after seeing the redness of her eyes and the dried-up tears on her face.

She lightly smiled and nodded. "Yeah. I promise."

Adam took a step closer to the door with dipped brows. "You okay? Looks like you've been crying. Did he—"

I grabbed him by the back of his jacket and yanked him away from the door before lightly pushing my way inside, softly closing the door behind me. Sienna walked away. With furrowed brows, I watched and followed her. She didn't have on any pants, but still had on the shirt from earlier. Something was wrong. I could feel it. Her aura was gloomy. Her eyes held no life, and there was so much defeat in her stride. I expected her to yell or complain about me showing up after she didn't answer my call or her intercom, but she gave me nothing. She didn't seem to give a fuck about anything. I was sure she'd only answered the door to stop me from banging.

I followed her to her bedroom, where she got into bed and pulled the covers over her shoulder. She turned over on her side and curled up into a fetal position before she began to slowly rock and softly cry.

I sat next to her and ran my hand over her shoulder. "Sienna."

She didn't say anything, she just continued to rock and cry. I didn't know what the fuck was going on. With dipped brows, I scanned the slightly dark room for her phone. Had something happened? Did she get some bad news or something? I didn't know why, but my heart ached for her. For some reason, this didn't feel like it was my fault. If it was my fault, she would've let buddy's ass call the police on me. Shit, she probably wouldn't have even answered the door for me. This felt more serious than what we had going on. It was alarming as fuck. My thoughts immediately went to her ex-boyfriend. Had the nigga showed up and done some bullshit? I'd never spoken to her personally about him, but I knew shit. While I scanned her social media accounts, I found out about him. About them. They were Instagram famous. Posted the type of content that made young, inexperienced women yell "couples goals," although they were the furthest thing from that shit. Dawg was a piece of shit. But who was I to talk, right? I had a whole-ass wife, yet I was sitting in the bed of another woman, heart racing and aching because she was in pain, and I had no clue why.

Type of sense did that make?

I pushed up off the bed and walked around the room, searching for her phone. I pushed the slightly cracked bathroom door open and flicked the light on. Her phone was there, sitting on the floor next to her pants. I swallowed as I walked inside, bypassing the phone. The pants were the focal point. Not just the pants, but what sat in the middle of them. Blood. Dark, thick blood. Blood that made me lightheaded. The blood wasn't from her menstrual. Nah, this was something else. Felt like déjà vu. I'd walked in on Leighton several times in the past with the same clotted blood in her panties.

Sienna had had a miscarriage.

CHAPTER 28

Sienna

How many times could a heart break before it gave out completely? Mine had been broken plenty of times and I just kept working to repair it. Kept pushing. Kept fighting. But, honestly, I was tired of fighting. Tired of the pieces of this battered heart coming back together just to break again. Today, my heart shattered again. Months of trying to fix it had gone to waste. This time, it didn't break because of a man. Jahad hadn't done anything. Amiri couldn't do anything. It was this cursed-ass womb. Why did I even have a uterus? It hated me.

I loss another baby. This time, I didn't even know there was a baby to lose. Had no idea I was pregnant. Had no idea because I figured my period was late because I was stressed the fuck out. It had happened before. So, I thought . . . welp, here we go again. I was stressed out so my period was late. Nope. I was wrong. I was pregnant. And then . . . I wasn't.

Turned out, those cramps I was having earlier weren't because my period was starting or because I was nervous. I was losing my baby. When I made it home, things progressed. The cramping got worse and worse and worse. They got so bad, they forced me on the floor. I couldn't walk, my stomach hurt so got damn bad. On my hands and knees, I crawled to the bathroom where the miscarriage finished, and my baby sat in the seat of my panties. I laid there for hours, crying and mourning a baby I didn't know I had inside of me. A baby I'd conceived with a man who belonged to someone else. Laid there crying and mourning Sienna Mills, too, because she was dead. I didn't know who the fuck *I* was anymore. A woman pretending to be Sienna. A woman pretending everything was okay. Still a woman shoveling fucking sprinkles on mountains of shit. Shit that kept piling up on top of shit; it seemed like it was never-ending.

This was payback. Payback for fucking that woman's husband. Payback for falling in love with the feel of him. He was here. In my bathroom, probably looking at what I couldn't. *It* still sat in my panties. I was afraid to look at it. Clumps of what remained. A reminder of what would never grow. The end . . . before a beginning. A realization that only made me cry harder. Cried so hard, for so long, eventually, I fell asleep with those pants that housed a baby that would never become a baby right next to me.

It was the banging on my door that woke me up. Before I fell asleep, the sun was up. And then it wasn't. I had no strength—absolutely no desire—to answer the door. I laid there, ignoring them, hoping they'd just walk away. I didn't know it was him until I heard his voice. *That fucking voice.* That Caribbean drawl that made my heart flutter and ache at once. I hated him. Loved the way he made me feel. Hated him for making me feel it. And he made me feel. Deep. Deep, deep. So deep, that when he crawled into bed with me a second ago and wrapped his arms around me, I melted into him and felt peace I'd never felt before.

We laid there in silence, but it was so loud. I felt the question of if the baby was his oozing from his fucking pores. It was. I got pregnant right on that forbidden kitchen island. I couldn't tell him that, though. I wouldn't. Before I opened my mouth to tell him the baby I'd just loss was his, I'd die. I didn't even want to face that reality myself. The reality of what I'd done was unsettling as fuck. Had been unsettling since I did it.

I wondered if he'd ask me. Wondered if he felt like he needed to ask me. As he began to softly run his hand over my stomach, I got my answer. He knew. Didn't need to ask me to know. Jahad just . . . he knew shit. And I knew shit too. And I hated it. Couldn't, for the life of me, understand this connection. I felt at home in his arms. Like, I deserved to be there. Like the places I'd been before had never been home. Like . . . home wasn't found until we found each other. It was weird. So weird. But I loved it. Loved and hated it. Hated it because, despite how at home I felt, I wasn't there. He was home for someone else.

"You need to go home," I said through muffled crying.

He held me tighter. "I know."

I closed my eyes and took a deep breath. I was floating. We were floating. While we floated, I thought I could do it. You know, be okay with being the other woman. The minute that thought came to me, I opened my eyes and moved away from him. He didn't let me. He moved with me, tightening his grip and burying his face in my nape. And . . . I moved again.

He sighed, the smell of tequila heavy in his breath. "Stop."

"Go home."

He didn't say anything, just continued to hold me. His heart raced against my back. He was afraid. Just like me. Afraid of what we were doing. Afraid of this unhealthy addiction. Afraid of what it would do to him. To me. To her. To us.

"Jahad . . . Please," I cried.

"Shhh. Just . . . let me," he whispered.

So, I let him.

Let him hold me.

Let him caress me.

Let him comfort me.

Because it felt good. And I needed to feel good because I felt so bad. I loss my baby. Our baby. The racing of his heart began to subside a bit. My tears dried up, and before I knew it, I was sleeping again.

Hours later, I woke up to him staring at me. He was lying on his side, just . . . staring at me. We stared at each other. Once again, that silence was loud. Screaming. Intense. Just like that pull. A pull I ignored, but he gave in to when he pulled me closer to him.

"Did you know?" he asked, cutting into the silence.

"No."

"It was mine," he stated.

I closed my eyes and took in a deep breath. "It wasn't."

I lied with a straight face. Had to lie. Felt like the lie was necessary. He needed to get out of my bed. And if I told him the baby was his, he would stay. For some reason, I felt like he'd stay, regardless. There was absolutely nothing in the air that said he would leave anytime soon. I needed to fix that. He had to go. He felt too good. Too good to be so bad for me. I couldn't do this. The fact that I'd almost given in to that desire—that need—and settled, petrified me. There was nothing good that would come out of this. Things would only get worse, and I'd suffered enough, hadn't I?

I couldn't carry on like this. I had been too nice. Too naïve. Too receptive. Things had to change because if they didn't, life would continue to run on a slippery slope.

He grabbed my chin. "Look at me when you speak."

I yanked away from his touch. "Just go home, Jahad. God. Remember what you said? You wanted to work on your marriage. You wanted to right your wrongs. We both agreed that this"—I paused and gestured between the both of us—"isn't good. Whatever it is, it's not right. I told you the baby wasn't yours, so just go home."

He shook his head and scratched at his cheek. "The baby wasn't mine, Sienna?" He paused and looked at me in doubt. "Yeah, aight."

He didn't believe me. His nonchalance really annoyed me. He reached out to touch me again, and this time, I quickly moved and got out of the bed. I paced and shook my head. "Why would I lie? The baby wasn't yours! You're not the only nigga I've been having sex with. The fuck? You have all of this faith in a bitch you don't know, and for what? Does it even matter? The fucking baby is *dead*! Let it go. Go home to your pregnant wife, Jahad! There is nothing here for you!"

I was bawling. And he was sitting up against the headboard, watching me. Always fucking watching me. His stare was so pensive, I couldn't look at him for more than a few seconds. Felt like if I did, he'd see the lie. Felt like if we stared eye-to-eye, I'd crumble. I'd tell him he was the father. I'd tell him just how unfair life had been to me. I'd tell him that, secretly, I wanted the baby. Maybe . . . maybe we could've had some kind of future.

I was losing my mind, losing my grip on reality. A baby in this situation would have never worked. I was smart enough to know that, but then . . . there was delusion. Sometimes, I found comfort in that shit. Just like I had a minute ago when the thought of being a mistress didn't seem so bad.

It was fucking horrible. I was fucking horrible. I didn't know who I was anymore. I really didn't. The smiles I wore were forced. The laughs. The . . . everything. Every day, I woke up, stared in the mirror, and repeated some bullshit-ass affirmations about self-love and growth and strength and didn't believe any of it. How was I supposed to love myself when I was disgusted in who I had become? A woman who was attached to another woman's husband. I was a reflection of the type of women I hated. How was I supposed to grow when all I kept doing was the same shit?

My life seemed to be on a recurring cycle. How was I supposed to be strong when everything in my life gave me reason to be weak? When he made me weak?

He was the problem.

He stood up and approached me. I put my hands up and shook my head. "Stay away from me," I coldly said. "I-I don't want you near me. I don't want this." With disgust in my tone, I eyed him up and down. "The fucking baby wasn't yours. You don't have to pretend to give a fuck about me losing it. This ain't my first rodeo. Instead of staying here with a bitch you barely know, you really should go home to your wife. That baby wasn't yours. Even if it was, it doesn't matter because it's in my panties!"

He approached me. "Sien—"

"No! Go! Get out! Why did you even come here? To talk about why I decided to go back to work for Leighton? I told both of you why already! And you don't have to worry . . . I'm sticking to that oath. What happened today won't change that." I swallowed and looked away from him, toward the bathroom.

I needed a shower. Needed one badly, but I was afraid of stepping into that bathroom and seeing it. The baby I'd spoken so disrespectfully about. That hurt. Pained me deeply. But I couldn't care. Not in front of him. I couldn't show him just how badly my heart had broken. I just wanted him to go so I could feel. So I could breathe. So I could stop floating and deal with reality. I needed this to stop. The feelings. The . . . everything. So, I chose to pretend I hated him. I hadn't tried that yet.

Looking away from the bathroom, I sighed and put my eyes on him. The pain that briefly flashed in his brown, almost black eyes would surely haunt me every time I thought of him. I didn't want to hurt him. Didn't think I could, actually. Not until I saw it. That pain. Pain that was necessary because, if I didn't hurt him, I would hurt me, and I'd done that enough.

Jahad nodded and pulled his lips into his mouth. "All right. Take care, love."

With that, he walked out of the room, then shortly after, out of the apartment.

I stood there for a moment, allowing the silence and that pull to drift away. I was relieved. With my arms wrapped around my body, I looked toward the bathroom again. The door was slightly cracked, and the light was on, inviting me inside. I had another bathroom to use, but I *had* to use this one. I couldn't avoid it forever. Eventually, I'd have to face the horrors that sat on the floor inside of it.

I took slow, deliberate steps toward the bathroom as my heart raced. I didn't think I'd have this happen to me again. Since I'd come to terms with never having a baby again, Amiri and I took strong precautions not to get pregnant again. I absolutely loathed birth control, so we avoided sex during ovulation and used the pull-out method. I thought the days of me having to go through this were over. But then I met *him* and lost every bit of sense I had.

When I pushed the bathroom door open, I was surprised to see the floor clean. As I stood there, staring down at it, baffled, the rumble of the washing machine filled my ears. He did it. He cleaned it up and washed my clothes for me. That couldn't have been easy for him but he did it, anyway.

I took a deep breath and went over to start the shower. While the water heated, I went back into the bedroom for my phone. Naoki had called me five times. If she was in Michigan, she would have come over a long time ago. Thank God, she wasn't. Hazel, my momma, and Mahogany had called too. Hazel, I would hit her up in the morning. I hadn't spoken to my mother since she invited Amiri to dinner and had absolutely no plans of talking to her anytime soon. Mahogany, I'd been avoiding like the plague. I wasn't ready to talk to her just yet. Especially not after what happened today. If it wasn't for her, I wouldn't have even met him, and then . . . so forth. The things I'd been through these past couple of months stemmed directly from that fucking invitation.

Five minutes later, I was standing in the shower. I scrubbed my skin with so much force, if I were light, my skin would for sure be red. I scrubbed every bit of negativity, sadness, and desire for him from my body. Told myself over and over again I was cleansing myself of everything that had caused me pain. Scrubbed remnants of Amiri that lingered and made life hard. After every negative emotion went down the drain, I turned the shower off, took a deep breath, and stepped out.

I grabbed my towel from behind the door and wrapped it around my body. Standing in the mirror, I stared at my reflection. There was so much sadness behind my eyes. So much hurt on my face. I wondered if my daddy saw me now, if he'd think I still radiated that light that drew people to me. Doubt it.

"Saturday at twelve works," I said into the phone, holding it up on my shoulder.

"Okay, great. I'll send over confirmation shortly. Have a great day."

"Okay, sounds good. You too," I said before hanging up.

I tossed my phone on the bed as I busied around the room in my bra and panties, getting ready for work. Did I want to go? No. Did I have to go? Absolutely. It would have been easier to just lay in bed, sulk, and feel sorry for myself, but I had done that for two days straight. It was time to get up and get to the damn money. Besides, I couldn't just lay in bed, anyway. Work was happening whether I wanted it to or not. I told Shonda about the miscarriage, and she gave me time off. She was surprised when I hit her this morning around six and told her I'd be going in to work. She wanted me to take more time off, but I refused. Three days had passed since the miscarriage, and I was ready to go back to work. Mentally, I was pushing. Didn't have much of a choice but to. No one was coming to save me. I had to save myself. Giving up would've been easy, but nothing about my life had been easy. So, I pushed. Even when I didn't want to. Even when I didn't have the strength to. But I was over shoveling glitter on top of shit. Honestly. I couldn't keep faking it until I made it. So, I took the first step to really working on myself by scheduling an appointment with a therapist. The daily affirmations weren't working. I needed to sit on someone's couch, and I was going to do just that this coming Saturday.

It took me a minute to really come to terms with it, but I was broken. Seriously broken. The type of broken that wouldn't fix itself with daily affirmations, spa days, and endless bottles of wine. I needed help. Real help. Help Pinterest and TikTok couldn't give me. I needed to release. The miscarriage really almost sent me over the edge. Honestly. I was ready to check out. Sadly, despite how many miscarriages I'd had, I wasn't numb to them. Didn't think I ever would be. This one showed me just how numb I wasn't. It was easy for me to pretend not to care, but pretending only lasted so long.

As I rummaged around my closet for my pale pink three-piece set, there was a knock on my front door. I looked out of the closet's doorway and just stared into the hallway. Who in the hell? Turning away, I looked up at the white and gold clock hanging on my wall. It was seven in the morning. Taking a deep breath, I chose to ignore the knocking and went back to looking for my outfit. Today was Leighton's gender reveal, so I was dressing the part. How resilient I was astonished me. The strength came easy. I was just tired of having to be strong. Tired of having to deal with uncomfortable shit. This situation was insane. I wished I could look forward to it ending soon, but nope. I was her postpartum doula too. Fucking crazy.

So, since I couldn't escape him, I had to find a way to make an uncomfortable situation comfortable. I was taking the first step toward that Saturday. Technically, I'd already taken the first step by cutting off all communication with him. He called me every day—

My phone suddenly rang, interrupting my train of thought. I frowned and walked over to it, sitting on my nightstand. It was Mahogany. I still hadn't worked up the nerve to speak to her. Talking to her right now, after everything that had happened, would be too much for me to bear. Realistically, falling for Jahad and losing my baby was her fault. If she hadn't sent me that invitation, I would have never met him. But then again . . . I made the decision to go. Still, she played a major part in it. Right?

Bang! Bang! Bang!

"I just heard your phone ring! Let me in! You got these people looking at me like I'm some kind of maniac!"

With wide eyes, I looked out of the bedroom again. Mahogany was here. What in the hell was she doing here? She should've been at work. She was an interior designer with a high-profile clientele list. Couture Interiors, her company, was just as much her baby as my nieces and nephew. She never missed a day, although technically, she didn't have to go in to work at all, unless she was working on a project.

After sliding my feet into my house shoes, I padded out of the bedroom to reluctantly answer my door.

I unlocked the door and opened it. She eyed me up and down with a frown on her face. "So, you *are* alive!" she dramatically said, before pushing herself into my apartment.

I rolled my eyes and closed the door behind her. I wasn't surprised when she started to give herself a tour of my apartment, looking at and touching just about every little thing I had. She had never been over before. I didn't want her to come over until I finished furnishing and decorating. I had done a little something. Added a bench by the door, finally got rid of the futon and replaced it with a beige sheepskin couch. I had two matching chairs and a stone coffee table. That was about it. I still had some ways to go. It was cute, just bare as hell. Which was why I hadn't invited her over. Having her, the queen of interior design, tour an unfinished apartment was just as bad as serving a professional chef underseasoned food!

"How did you get my address?" I asked, with my arms crossed over my chest.

Mahogany looked over her shoulder at me before setting her black Birkin on the couch where a pillow should've been. They were coming. Wayfair was taking forever to deliver them. I was tempted to give an explanation, but fuck her. She didn't tell me she was an undercover, cheating-ass freak.

"You're my sister. I had your address before you told us you moved out," she boasted, steady looking around.

"Stop judging my apartment," I snapped, before adjusting the brown throw blanket draped over the armrest. "I'm not done yet."

"I'm not judging your apartment, Sienna. I'm looking at it," she replied after crossing her arms over her chest. "Why haven't I heard from you since the club? Don't give me no bullshit, either. You've been avoiding me."

I wasn't ready to have the conversation yet. But I felt like Mahogany wasn't going to leave until I gave her a real explanation. She was only a year older than me, but God, she had this thing about her that made you feel like you were in trouble. Maybe it was because she was a mother. Moms had that. Shonda had that same thing about her.

"I have to be to work at eight. Aren't *you* supposed to be at work?" I walked off, heading to my bedroom with her on my heels.

"One of the perks of being the boss is going in whenever you want to," she humbly bragged. "And I know. So, you better tell me what's going on, so you won't be late."

I squinted and went back to looking for my outfit. She was doing it again. Looking around. She'd walked into the walk-in closet with me, into the bathroom, and back into the bedroom and I couldn't read her. I said she didn't deserve an explanation, but man! I felt insecure about it.

"I'm not done decora—"

"Stop doing that shit." She interrupted with a sigh before plopping down on the chair across from the bed. "I'm not studying your damn apartment. But I mean, I'd be lying if I said I didn't feel some type of way. My little sister moved into a big-ass luxury apartment with gorgeous, large windows and an open floor plan and she didn't even ask me to go furniture shopping with her."

"I ordered off Wayfair," I told her, with an eye roll.

"Lies. Not everything. I saw that bench by the door at Home Goods. And I bet you went with Naoki."

"Here we go," I pouted, after finally finding my three-piece set.

"Here we go," she repeated. "I told you I wanted us to get close again, like we used to be, and you don't ask me, a professional interior decorator, to help you shop? Shit, we could've sipped on wine and browsed Wayfair together. You know I get a discount." She rolled her eyes. "We can circle back to why you treat me and Hazel like stepcousins after you tell me why you been acting funny."

I cut my eyes at her and took a deep breath. "I do not treat you bitches like stepcousins. Stop lying." I tossed the outfit on the bed and picked the shirt up before pulling it down over my head.

I felt Mahogany's eyes on me while I continued to get dressed. As unprepared as I was to have a conversation about her inviting me to a sex club she shouldn't be a member of, I appreciated the distraction. Thinking about something other than having to face him after the way things ended the other night had my nerves rattled. I cursed him out and lied to him, just to find out that he'd cleaned my bathroom of evidence of the loss I was afraid of facing. Despite me cursing him out and treating him like shit, he kept calling. Kept texting. Kept trying to check up on me. I ignored every last one of his efforts to talk. I had to. However, today, I wouldn't be able to ignore him. I was glad to be returning on the day of the gender reveal, though. That way, he wouldn't be able to give too much attention to me.

"How did you find out?" she suddenly asked with a deep breath.

I looked over at her with dipped brows. "What?"

"About the invitation. How did you find out?"

"What invitation?" I asked, feigning ignorance as I pulled the chair to my vanity out.

She crossed her left leg over the other and snarled at me. "Really?"

I rummaged around the top drawer for my moisturizer. I didn't have but about twenty minutes before I had to leave, so I was only doing a soft, natural beat using BB Cream instead of foundation.

"Mm-hmm. You can't be talking about the invitation I got to Pandora's, that sex dungeon. Because the invitation came from a member and there is no way in hell you, a married woman with four kids, is a member of a sex club."

Mahogany scratched at the back of her blunt-cut bob and looked away with a sigh. "You weren't supposed to find out it came from me. How did you find out?"

"I wasn't supposed to find out about how you like to fuck two men at the same time, in a room full of people either, was I?" I asked, as I roughly applied moisturizer to my face. "Duke know he married a freak ho?"

She took a deep breath and cocked her head to the side. "That's none of his business."

With wide eyes, I looked over at her. "What? How is it *not* his business?"

She looked me square in the eyes and said, "The same way it's not yours."

"Do you hear yourself? You really sitting there, acting like you being a member of a sex club as a married woman is okay."

"Yeah, I hear myself. I'm doing what works best for my marriage. I asked you how you found out I gave it to you. This ain't ask Mahogany questions about what she does with her coochie."

I condescendingly laughed. "Wow."

"So, how did you find out?"

"Honesty. She was playing with the mask I watched you get fucked by two men in," I sternly told her as we stared at each other through the mirror.

"Shit!" She ran her hand down the back of her head.

"Yeah, shit. You might want to do a better job hiding shit if you don't want your husband to start snooping around."

"Duke isn't going to be snooping around for shit because he's too busy doing his own dirt to give a damn about what I do," she told me, shocking me once again. "You might as well wipe that judgmental look off your face. I can do without it. This . . . Pandora's . . . it's for me. Let me have that without the judgment. I've always done right by him. By my children. By my job. By everyone but Mahogany. I want to have fun. I want to feel desired and sexually liberated. I don't get that from Duke anymore because he's constantly giving what he used to give me to everybody else." She nonchalantly shrugged with tears in her eyes. "So, yeah, from time to time, I like to let loose. I like to become someone else. Someone nobody knows, but everyone desires. I want to be free. Free of everything. Obligations, kids . . ." She threw her left hand up. "These fucking rings. If you want to judge me for it, then so be it. I don't give a damn, really."

I felt sorry for my big sister. Honestly. From the outside looking in, Mahogany had it all. The promising career, a beautiful family, a loving husband with the big-ass house and in-ground pool. She was living the dream. But, realistically, she wasn't living the dream at all. I wanted to hug her. So, I did what she told me to do: wiped that judgmental look off my face, got up, and wrapped my arms around her. We hugged for a few minutes, with her shedding a few tears on my shoulder and me shedding a few I wiped away before she could notice them.

Pulling away from the hug, I sighed and asked, "Why did you invite me, Mahogany? I wish you wouldn't have invited me."

She waved me off and dabbed at her eyes. "Oh, hush. Sex is sex. No biggie. We've seen each other naked countless times—"

"I mean, finding out your sister was the woman you watched get slutted out is pretty traumatizing, but that's not why I wish you hadn't invited me." I interrupted with a laugh we shared. "It's . . . that invitation really caused a lot of bullshit."

With a cocked brow, she asked, "Bullshit like what?"

I swallowed, wondering if I should tell her about Jahad. My sisters wondered why I didn't open up to them as much as I did when we were teenagers, and it was because the bitches couldn't hold water. If I told Hazel something, she'd tell Mahogany, and Mahogany would run to Momma and tell her. It took me a minute to shut them out of my personal business, and since I'd done it, I'd been good. Momma didn't know my business and there was no room for them to judge me. It was freedom. However, I knew her secret. A secret I knew she wouldn't want to get out. So, I felt like I was in a safe place.

I glowered at her. "You tell anybody what I'm about to tell you and I will tell Momma her golden child likes two dicks at one time. Mm-hmm. I will tell her all about the freaky shit I saw you do. Don't even—"

"Okay, bitch, relax. Just tell me."

I squinted and first said, "I'll tell you . . . after you tell me why you invited me."

She pulled her lips into her mouth and said, "Hmmm . . . Well, remember that ladies' night we had for Friendsgiving? When we were playing Never Have I Ever? You didn't take a shot when Sage said something about never cumming from sex. You said you only have orgasms when you use your vibrator." She shrugged. "That made me sad. I realized that even Hazel was more sexually liberated than you were. I wanted to give you the gift of multiple orgasms with multiple men if you wanted it. Because I know you, I figured the masquerade would be perfect. You wouldn't have to show your face, so you would feel comfortable to go." She tossed her head back and sighed. "Please don't tell me you fucked around and caught something. I will sue the shit out of them if they let someone get past with an STD."

I was shocked. Literally stunned. I hadn't put on a lick of BB Cream, I was so shocked. I sat at my vanity, listening to her reason with my mouth open. She was full of surprises. She'd been plotting and scheming on my coochie for months. I thought it was hilarious. My sister cared so much about me catching a nut that she invited me to an exclusive sex club to get it. That was so *Naoki* of her.

"I didn't catch an STD, Mahogany. Shit, I feel like an STD would've been easier. Easier to get rid of, at least."

"You're pregnant?" she blurted, making my stomach drop and my heart ache all over again.

I lowered my head and shook it. With my eyes to the floor, I told her, "Not anymore. I had a . . . I loss it. I didn't get pregnant at Pandora's, though."

She got up and ran over to my side, ready to hug me, but I put my hand up. I didn't want to be comforted. I didn't do it in a rude way. Just . . . I didn't need her arms around me. Didn't need her to tell me everything would be okay. There was nothing anybody could say to make it okay. I just told her I was good and didn't need a hug. She hugged me, anyway. Didn't tell me it would be okay. Didn't give me any words of encouragement. I was grateful for that. Sometimes a hug and silence were all a person needed.

"Now, see, you know something Naoki doesn't. Happy?" I joked to lighten the mood and to stop myself from crying.

I hadn't told Naoki. I would, but for the moment, I wanted to forget it even happened.

"I do? Wow! I guess I'm pretty special after all," she said with a laugh.

I then took a deep breath and untwisted the cap to my BB Cream. Then I spilled my guts. Told her about Jahad. About his wife. About the kitchen. About the club. About going back . . . the obsession. The feelings. The connection. That pull. Literally released it all and she let me. I was surprised. Mahogany loved to run her damn mouth. Not this time, though. Felt like she might've sensed just how badly I needed to talk.

"And you're going back?" she asked with a look of suspicion.

I shrugged and added the finishing touches to my eyebrows. "Yeah. I have to go back."

"You really don't *have* to do anything," she pointed out. "I understand the oath. I understand you wanting to honor it. It's commendable. But I'm going to tell you what I think it is. From a spiritual standpoint."

Mahogany was spiritual. That was the only thing our mother didn't like about her. We were raised in a Christian household. My momma had us reading the Bible at a young age. Shit, we were in church every Sunday, faithfully. However, when Mahogany got older, she let go of those beliefs and got into spirituality. Despite her telling our mother she believed in God and not the Bible, that lady still scolded her over her religious choices.

"It's a soul tie," she added.

"A soul tie? Girl, what the hell—"

"A soul tie is a spiritual connection. What you explained to me . . . that's what it sounds like to me. You feel connected to him. If you felt connected to him before y'all had sex like you said you did, then baaaaaby." She shook her head. "It's deeper than that. You two are linked. That's why you want to go back. *Truly.* The logical explanation would be the oath. You don't know it, but it's not that. Not at all. That's just the black and white part about it. But nothing about what y'all have is black and white. It's not simple. It's deeply rooted. Regardless of what path y'all take . . . the road will always lead back to each other. This isn't y'all's first rodeo, baby. Your soul has most likely been connected to his for many, many lifetimes." She paused again and laughed. "And you're talking about the invitation ruined your life. Little sis, y'all would have met regardless. Because . . ." She winked. "It's predestined."

I took a deep breath and stepped on the elevator with Leighton's orange juice. I made it to the house a minute ago and couldn't believe how many people were already here. Leighton's mother, her sister, Farrah, caterers, the whole fucking nine. And it was only eight in the morning.

On my way in, Leighton's nail tech was leaving. Today was going to be insane. I didn't mind it, though. I needed as many distractions as possible.

The entire thirty-minute ride over to the house, what Mahogany said had been on my mind. It was predestined. We were soul ties. Is that really what it was? I mean, it would explain a lot. I just didn't really believe in that kind of shit. My disbelief might've come from the fact that, for a long time, I thought Amiri was my soulmate. Thought we'd be forever. And since we weren't . . . I don't know . . . the notion of anything or anybody being connected on a soul level didn't really resonate with me. And it still really didn't. I refused to believe Jahad and I would have met regardless.

I stepped off the elevator and first stopped at the guest room to put my things away. A bitch was stalling. I knew he was here. Saw his car parked in the driveway when I got here. I had to get myself together before I stepped into that bedroom. Seeing him today would be different from seeing him when I came back after I quit. I had a miscarriage. Literally loss a child he knew belonged to him, regardless of what I'd said. I hadn't spoken to him. Had mistreated him . . . Shit would be weird for sure.

I swallowed and walked out of the bedroom. The trek down the hallway was heavy. The sound of laughter coming from the room told me things wouldn't be that tense. Again, I was so grateful for the distraction of the gender reveal being today. I knocked on the door and then, a second later, he answered it.

It was like time stood still. We couldn't have been face to face for more than a few seconds before he stepped aside for me to walk inside. But God, it felt like we stood there, eye to eye, for hours, staring into each other's souls. The laughter around me muffled. The world around me even faded. It was just him and me. Today, we didn't float. I didn't, at least. I didn't know what it felt like for him. But for me, it felt like I was dying. Like I had certainly stepped off that cliff and fell to my death in that big-ass body of water. It was crazy how many emotions rushed through me in just a few seconds. It wasn't until he broke eye contact that I felt like I could breathe again. I sucked in air, looked beyond him into the subtly crowded bedroom, and walked inside to play the role of the loving, caring doula, whose heart wasn't shattered into a million pieces.

CHAPTER 29

Leighton

"Leigh, dear, did you hear what I said?" asked my mother, snapping me out of my trance.

"Huh? No, what did you say?"

"I said Ashleigh has to work late, so she won't be able to make it to the party."

"The party"? My very first gender reveal, that could very well be my last. Yeah, she couldn't make it. Sure. I snorted and closed my eyes with a sigh. Ashleigh not being able to come to my very first gender reveal was no surprise. They didn't care about me. Not like they cared about themselves. To her, me finally having a child was minuscule. It was *only* a baby. No big deal. She didn't get the big fuss. Ash was too busy wasting her life away at the hospital to give a damn about starting a family. She couldn't understand why I cared so much about having children, said they slowed you down. I didn't need her to understand, but I would've liked for her to pretend to at least care.

"I'm going to video call—"

"Don't worry about it, Mom," I interrupted. "If she really wanted to be a part of this, she would be here."

"You know she wants to be a part of it," my mother pressed.

I opened my eyes and laughed. "Of course she does."

She swatted at me. "Oh, stop being so mean. You've been mean all week! Your sister means well."

I just stared at her until she kissed me on the forehead and walked away. She always made excuses for them. I knew the truth, though. We just didn't mesh well. We had no bond. I was pretty much an only child. The baby they resented because our parents made them keep me all the time. Shiloh was okay. She showed up. She'd been helping Farrah all morning. She was actually excited for me. Since she had children of her own, she understood. Her kids were practically grown, but still . . . she got it.

I didn't think the day could get any worse. Life was already doing a number on me. Today was supposed to be a good day. I should've been happy. I should've been smiling. My heart . . . it should've been full. But it wasn't. It was broken. I wasn't happy. I hadn't smiled. Not all week. Not since Monday. Before he lied. Before he came home after midnight. Jahad. We were doing so well. We were . . . happy. I thought we were. I thought he wanted me smiling more and nagging less. I thought he wanted me to be affectionate. I thought the night in the shower, and the brunch he planned with snacks and *Bridgerton* to follow, was a restart, another chance at fixing what I broke. I thought . . . I thought we were making progress toward forgetting about the past. I was, at least. I'd forgiven him. I'd forgiven myself. I was ready to pour into my marriage.

But he lied. Lied and told me he loved me right after. The lie . . . he made it sound so got damn good. So good, I really did believe he actually was at Saint's house, waiting for Blaise. If it wasn't for Blaise calling Momma Baptiste shortly after I got off the phone with Jah, I would have believed him. Blaise wasn't on his way to Saint's. In fact, he told Momma he'd just left and was heading to pick Bebe up from Natasha's. How was that possible when Jahad told me Blaise was late because Ari had been giving him a hard time? It wasn't possible. Jahad was lying. Again. It was the only thing I'd been able to think about for days. That and the scent on him when he finally climbed into bed with me late that night.

I didn't know what time it was when Jahad came home. I stopped checking the time after midnight. Just lay there with tears rolling down my face, waiting. Waiting for those lights to bounce off the white walls of our bedroom. Waiting to hear the garage open. Waiting for him to walk into the room, kiss me on the forehead and shower. That night was different. Very different. He didn't park in the garage. He didn't kiss me on the forehead and shower. He walked into the room, climbed into bed, and wrapped his arms around me. Held me tight . . . with the scent of another woman's perfume on his clothes.

That was three days ago. And for three days, all I'd done was wish things could go back to the way they were before that fucking hall pass. Things weren't great, but it wasn't this. We were right back at square one. That night, I let him hold me because I felt that something was very wrong. I was frozen. It was alarming and I was paralyzed with fear. I didn't know what to think. Had my husband come home and wrapped his arms around me with the scent of another woman on him because he had plans of leaving me? Because he was conflicted? Did he hold me as tight as he had because he planned on letting go of us? Something was up. And because I knew he'd been lying, I was afraid of what would come out of his mouth if I actually asked him what was wrong.

But then, that morning, we woke up and he carried on like nothing happened. Like his behavior before hadn't been erratic. So, I asked him. And he lied . . . again. Said he was tripping last night because he'd had too much to drink. I didn't know what was going on, but what I did know was that he was not at Saint's. His location said he was there, but something in my heart told me he wasn't actually there. So, I did something I saw on Instagram: placed a bogus DoorDash order to Saint's house. I asked her to look for Jahad's car. It wasn't there. So now, I didn't trust Saint's sorry ass either.

"You look so beautiful," Sienna said with a smile, as she approached with a drink for me.

Yep. Sienna was back. She came back Tuesday. When she called out Monday, I was afraid she was quitting again. I couldn't imagine running through doulas again. Not because the girls Shonda sent over were bad, but because they weren't her. She was the only doula I wanted to share this experience with. She was only with us for a week before she quit, but I felt such a strong connection to her. I liked her. I knew the minute I laid eyes on her. She had a magnetic air to her. Soft, sweet, caring, and . . . *wounded.* I saw a lot of myself in Sienna. Maybe that was why I was so drawn to her.

I took the drink from her and put it to my lips. God, I wished it had alcohol in it. But the virgin daiquiri would have to suffice. The gender reveal was happening. Had been happening for the past thirty minutes, but I felt miles away. Mentally, I was in my bed with that scent stuck in my nostrils, while my husband laid beside me, snoring, with a death grip hold on me. That was where I had been for days.

There was music playing. Friends, family, and old business partners scattered about my home, but I hadn't interacted with them much, besides the basic catching up we did when they arrived. I honestly felt like I was suffocating. Farrah had gone too far. She'd invited damn near all of Michigan's underground artist community, friends I hadn't seen in years and family I couldn't give a fuck about. And lawd . . . don't let me get on Jahad's family. It was huge. I had a house full of rowdy Haitian men and sassy Haitian women. It was insane. It felt like my wedding reception all over again. Except this time, I wasn't happy. Not at all. But . . . nobody seemed to notice.

"Thanks, boo," I said, with a light smile.

"Mm-hmm," she said with a light bump on my shoulder after she sat next to me. "Too pretty to be sitting over here spaced out. You sure you okay?"

She noticed, though. I couldn't understand why. Probably because it was her job to notice. I did look pretty. Beautiful. Breathtaking even. I had on a white, strapless tulle gown with a long split up the front side of it. I wore a neutral color because I was on neither side—boy or girl. I just wanted a healthy baby. But Jahad surprised me this morning with a pink corsage because he knew in my heart, she was a she. Literally put me in the mindset of prom. But it was cute and very *Jahad* of him. That got a smile out of me. That was the only smile he got out of me all day, sadly.

I nodded. "Yeah, I'm good. It's just . . . a lot of people here."

She nodded and looked around. "It really is a lot of people here. Farrah went crazy with the guest list, huh?"

"She really did. I haven't seen most of these people in years," I said, as I watched Farrah work the room.

Sometimes, I felt like this gender reveal was more for her than it was for me and Jahad. She'd been working the room like crazy, talking to people, smiling, taking pictures and shit. She was mingling more than I was. She was me, in a sense. Who I used to be, at least. I used to work rooms like that. I was the social butterfly. Any time I was at or hosting an event, I lit the room up. But I wasn't that person anymore. Every time someone new walked through the door, my palms grew a little sweaty with nerves. I hadn't been around a large group of people in a very long time. On top of stressing about my marriage, social anxiety about this gender reveal had been building all week.

Leighton Baptiste and social anxiety had never been synonymous. Only stepping foot outside of the house for doctor appointments for the last six months had done a number on my mental health. Listening to Farrah ramble on and on about everyone she'd invited made my heart race. I should have told her to keep it small and intimate, but I didn't have it in me. A small and intimate event for Leighton? Hell no. That didn't make any sense.

"They shouldn't be here, then," Sienna leaned in and whispered with a light smile.

My eyebrows snapped together as I got a quick whiff of the scent of her perfume. I gestured for her to come back. "What kind of perfume are you wearing? It . . . it smells familiar."

She made a face and leaned in again. "Umm, it's Chanel."

I cocked my head to the side. Could it be a coincidence? She was wearing the same perfume Jahad smelled like that night he came home. That was why the smell was so familiar to me. When she hugged me that day, I smelled it on her then. And now. No. It had to be a coincidence. I refused to believe Jahad was fucking with Sienna. That wouldn't make any sense. Why would—

"Bestie!" Farrah yelled as she approached, breaking my train of thought. "You cannot sit over here in the corner all day! This is your party. Come on, let's move around, boo!"

I rolled my eyes and shook my head. "Uh-uh. I'm staying right here." I forced a laugh. "The only place I'm going is the backyard when it's time for the reveal."

Farrah sucked her teeth and placed her hands on her hips. "Don't be like that. Everyone came out to support you. Mingle with them, boo."

She looked good. The baby blue spaghetti-strapped midi dress clung to her curvaceous hips with perfection. When I first saw that she had on a blue dress, I was certain the baby was a girl. But then, I noticed the hot pink heels and Chanel bag and wasn't as confident anymore. Her face was beat to the *gawds*, and her hair? Baby, her hair was laid. Her bone-straight, thirty-inch, middle-part frontal wig stopped just at the crack of her best asset—her BBL. The bright smile, and the way she moved around the room, said she was doing better than ever. One look at her and you'd think she had it all together. But I knew better.

Ever since we had that little talk that night, I knew the real. She was sad, lonely, and miserable. Farrah was for sure putting on. And for a bunch of people who really didn't give a damn about her. Because most of my friends were her friends, too, she thought she had something to prove since they knew about Mike's affair and their divorce. I couldn't blame her, though. I was doing the same thing.

Looking past Farrah, I noticed Jahad in the crowd. He stood in a group with his brothers and cousins. I thought he'd noticed me, too, but his eyes weren't on me. He was looking past me. When I turned to look over my shoulder to see who he was gawking at, my stomach dropped. He was staring at Sienna. But when I turned back around to look at him, his eyes were on me. What the fuck was that about? Was I tripping? Naw . . . I had to be imagining things. The lies, the hall pass, and the perfume . . . it had me going crazy. My insecurities were at an all-time high.

When our eyes met, he walked away from the crowd and in my direction. I gripped the armrests on my chair and dug my nails into them. What did he want? I didn't have anything to say to him. Shit, we didn't have anything to say to each other. He refused to give me details about this bitch, and I refused to let it go. I was, once again, obsessing over the details. I asked him, countless times, about his whereabouts the other night. Told him I knew he was lying and everything, but he gave me nothing. Just would stare at me and tell me it was complicated, but nothing for me to worry about. How? How was I not to worry when my husband was cheating on me? He swore he wasn't, but I knew better.

I was one second away from getting a divorce. The thought really petrified me, though. Didn't want to get a divorce. Wanted to fix it. Wanted us to be a family. I did not want to become a single mother. A bitter single mother. That wasn't the plan. That was not how I envisioned my family. I wanted us happy. I'd do anything to go back. I would never have given him that pass.

"I don't want to mingle. I don't know why you invited all of these people anyway," I complained.

"Because—"

"Leighton Baptiste," a familiar voice from behind said.

I smiled and looked over my shoulder, away from Jahad. Roman was here. He greeted me with a friendly hug and snuck in a kiss on my cheek. If it wasn't for Farrah blocking Jahad's view of us, he would have never done it. The kiss was friendly, but everyone knew how territorial Jahad was over me. I wondered if that was still true, though. Didn't feel like it. Felt like he was doing everything in his power to get rid of me.

"Roman! You made it!" I said with a smile.

He drew back with a frown as to say *Duh*. "Of course. Wouldn't have missed it for anything in the world, baby girl."

Roman looked good. Better than he did the last time I saw him. He'd traded his usual coily 'fro in for short locs he wore barrel twisted. His beard had thickened and connected with his mustache perfectly. His caramel-complected skin was blemish free, except for a few small moles dotting it, right underneath his left eye. He looked really good. Farrah was practically drooling from the mouth, he looked so good. She wasted no time throwing her arms around his neck to hug him. They rocked back and forth like old friends. She locked eyes with me and widened them before mouthing the words *Oh my God*. I thought it was both funny and pathetic. I couldn't blame my girl, though. She probably had cobwebs on her kitty.

"It's been a minute, hasn't it?" Farrah asked once they pulled away from the hug.

"Hell yeah. Too long of a minute," Rome said with his eyes briefly on Farrah before he put them on me. When Jahad made it over, he gave him his attention and extended his hand. "Jahad, my man. How's it going?"

Jahad chucked his head back and shook hands with him. "It's goin'. What's good?"

There was always tension between the two of them. Well, Rome was always cool. It was Jahad with the tension. He said he didn't trust Roman. Claimed he could see his true intentions when it came to us and our friendship. Roman wanted me. Always wanted me and had stayed around, waiting for his turn. That was what Jahad thought. Me? I didn't think anything. Roman was a good friend. We went back to college days. If he wanted me, he would have made a move long before I even met Jahad. And he didn't. It had always been platonic between the two of us. Jahad was just an overprotective man, staking claim to his wife, as always.

"Did you eat?" Jahad asked, immediately putting his attention on me.

I nodded. "Not since this morning."

I was dry. The tension between us was thick. I wondered if everyone else felt it. I had no desire to pretend we were good today. We were cordial, but that over-the-top shit I usually did when people were around when we were in a fight? I wasn't on that today. I didn't have it in me. My dryness seemed to tick him off. I didn't know if it was because Roman was here or what but I watched as his top lip twitched with annoyance before he took a sip of his drink. Jahad had been drinking more than usual. I noticed it. He was on cup number two and it was barely three in the afternoon.

"Oh! Roman, this is my doula, Sienna. Sienna, my old friend, Rome. We went to college together. You were impressed with my pieces, but they have nothing on his!" I boasted, finally introducing them.

Roman turned to Sienna, smiled, and extended his hand to her. "Don't listen to her. She's being modest. I have yet to come across an artist as talented as her." He looked over at me and winked before putting his attention back on her. "Nice to meet you, Ms. Sienna."

Sienna smiled. "Modesty must be one of her strongest traits, huh?" She lightly laughed and rubbed her lips together. "Nice to meet you, too."

Rome's eyes stayed locked on Sienna's for a while. I got it. She was beautiful, but she had this thing to her. Something that made you want to know her. He hadn't even pulled his hand away from hers yet. I smiled. They would be cute together. A definite better fit than Saint's lying ass. I didn't know much about Sienna's personal life, but I did know she was single. Hopefully, by the end of the event, she would have something set up with Roman.

"You mind grabbing Leigh a plate, Ms. Mills?" Jahad asked Sienna, with his eyes locked on hers.

Since when? Since when did Jahad care to send someone to get me food? Hell, he didn't even like to bother Evaline and Maurice at dinner time. But he asked Sienna to grab me food?

Sienna nodded and lightly smiled before pulling her hand away from Rome's. "Not at all." She took a deep breath and turned to me. When her eyes met mine, I noticed a glimmer. I wasn't sure if it was tears or what, but I noticed something. "I'll be right back."

She walked away and Farrah immediately grabbed Rome. "You must be starving. Come . . . let's go get you something to eat too."

Funny how just a minute ago, Farrah was campaigning for me to mingle, but as soon as Rome showed up, she couldn't care less. When they were out of earshot, I put my eyes on Jahad.

"You fuckin' her?" I asked with a smile. A smile I put on just to hide the truth. That I was far from happy with my husband.

He drew back. "What?"

"Sienna. You were watching her and she's wearing the same perfume you had on you when you came home late as hell the other night. And now . . . you send her to get me food to get her away from Rome. You think I'm stupid?"

He ran his hand down the back of his neck with a laugh. "I sent her to get food because it's her job to take care of you. You should've had lunch, and you haven't." He paused and took a step closer to me. "Also . . . because I wanted to speak to you in private."

I looked up at him with raised brows. "Sure. I notice you didn't say anything about watching her or the perfume."

"You been tweaking for days. You gon' believe what you want to believe if I say something or not," he rudely spat. "I'm trying . . . trying to keep you happy, but every time I turn around, you have this attitude."

"You're trying to keep me happy, Jahad? How? By lying to me? By going behind my back—"

"Right now isn't the time or place for this shit," he harshly whispered, causing me to shudder.

I hated when he cursed at me.

"I came over here with good intentions, love. I really did. Today is supposed to be a good day but you haven't said more than a few words to me—"

"And whose fault is that?"

"If we're being technical . . ." He paused and made eye contact with me. "Yours."

I swallowed and a chill ran down my spine. Was it my fault? What was my fault, exactly? Was Jahad admitting to being with her? Seeing her behind my back after he was only supposed to see her for that one night? Did he mean it was my fault he was cheating? This attitude . . . these problems . . . were they really my fault?

He grabbed my hands and brought them up to his lips. "*Mwen renmen ou.* Just you. Let me."

Tears wet my eyes, as I tried to pull my hands out of his. But he wouldn't let them go.

"You don't love me—"

"With everything in me," he interrupted. "So much, the shit hurts sometimes. We will talk. Eventually. Right now, let a nigga love you, aight? The conversation you want to have . . . we will have it. Not today. Today is about us." He finally let my hands go, but only to run them over my stomach. "And him."

He was draped in all white, too. The tailored white tux and white shoes looked good on him. Like me, he just wanted a healthy baby. However, the blue handkerchief told exactly what side he was on.

"Him?" I asked with a cocked brow.

He smirked and nodded. "You gon' let me do that?"

"Do what?"

"Love you?" he sincerely asked before grabbing my hands and kissing them again.

I took a deep breath and rubbed my lips together. Despite everything, Jahad still made my heart smile. I wasn't ready to walk away from us. I was just as at fault in this situation as he was. Since he was finally open to talking about it, there was hope for us. This marriage was worth fighting for.

"Yes, Jahad. I'll let you love me."

He closed his eyes and enveloped my hands in his before putting them to his chest. He leaned down and kissed me on the forehead just as Sienna returned with my food. The glimmer I'd noticed in her eyes before was most definitely tears. They might've been dry now, but the smeared eyeliner was a dead giveaway. Before I could ask if she was okay, a sharp pain ran down the side of my stomach.

CHAPTER 30

Jahad

"How is she?"

With my head tossed back against the wall behind me, I kept my eyes closed. I was tired of that question. I was asked it at least ten times a day. How was she? Did she need anything? What did the doctors say? Three days ago, Leighton went into preterm labor at our gender reveal. For three days, we'd been in the hospital, trying to stop our daughter from coming. For three days, my wife cried nonstop. For three days, she'd been silent. How was *she*? Shit, how was I? A nigga was tired. Exhausted. Both physically and mentally. Hell, spiritually too. When we got to the hospital, she was dilated to three centimeters. They needed her to stay pregnant for at least another four weeks since she was only at week twenty-seven, but it wasn't looking good. They gave her medicine to stop the contractions, but shit didn't seem to work.

"She's hanging in there," Sienna said to my mother, speaking up, since I hadn't said anything. "The biggest thing they want right now is for her to rest."

My mother nodded and sat next to me and began to recite a low prayer. Next to me, Sienna delicately ran her fingers over the palm of my hand. My arms were crossed over my chest, so my hand dangled beside her. Every now and then, she'd do that. I had no idea why, but it comforted me.

I was grateful for her. More than she'd ever know. Not only had she been extremely supportive to my wife, but she'd been supportive of me too. Our . . . whatever it was . . . was shaky. We didn't talk. Not about *our* loss. Not about what we felt for each other. Not about that pull. It was straight-up business between us, although there was and most likely always would be much more. Regardless of her personal feelings toward me, she'd shown up and supported me in a major way. Sienna didn't owe me shit, but in moments where I was weak, she was there to handle things for me and to subtly run her fingers over the palm of my hand when I was at my weakest.

That was where I was at with it. Weak. Every time something like this happened, I knew what it was. It was me and the shit I'd done. When I said karma handled me in different ways, this was what I was referring to. The only thing I wanted out this bitch was a seed. Something of my own. Something I created. That came straight from me. But . . . I couldn't have it.

The last three times Leighton miscarried, I lost hope. They never stayed too long. She'd usually miscarry around week ten. When she wanted to try this time around, I wasn't with it. Didn't have it in me to go through another loss. But . . . Leighton gets what Leighton wants, so despite my reservations about it, I did what was necessary. It took me a minute to embrace this pregnancy. I didn't want to get my hopes up. I didn't even really acknowledge the pregnancy until we crossed that twenty-week threshold. For me, the pregnancy didn't officially begin until seven weeks ago. For me, it was still fresh. The excitement. The anticipation. And for nothing.

I was angry. My little blessing, she gave me hope. I thought I was going to finally be a father. I dreamed of trips back home to show her where I'd come from. I dreamed of a future with a child. I thought about trips to the park. Daddy and daughter dances, or our first basketball game together, shit like that. I'd looked forward to fatherhood. I planned on being everything to my child. Everything Samuel wasn't.

But it was all a waste. That type of shit wasn't for me. I couldn't have children. Physically, yeah. Spiritually, I couldn't. I had done too much shit, and because of that, a future with children was unobtainable. Out of reach. That fucked with me. Me and Sienna's loss was proof of that. Why would I be blessed with something so beautiful when I'd done some of the ugliest things? *Tanbou bat nan raje, men se lakay li vin danse.* The family thing wasn't for me. The only family I'd ever have was the one I came from. Sitting with that fucked with me on a different level. Nothing out this bitch bothered me more than not being able to have children.

I suffered in silence. Wore the shit on my heart rather than my sleeve so no one would ever know. Not even Leighton. However, I needed her to understand more than anybody. She was the reason I was in the hallway instead of the room with her. This was her alone time. The time she spent enjoying *her* pregnancy and the soft flutters of *her* baby kicking. She wanted to savor it, but did she think for one second I wanted to savor it too? The future of our child was uncertain. The time we had right now, with her safely inside of Leighton's womb, was the only time that was guaranteed. I wanted to spend time too. I hated that I gave a fuck but I opened myself up to that possibility, and now my heart was torn to pieces.

The sound of heels click-clacking against the floor caused me to sit up and sigh. Farrah was here.

"Yes, she's in room 234. You can come visit. I'm sure she'll be happy to see you, Rome. I—"

"No visitors outside of family," I interrupted, with my eyes on hers.

Farrah frowned and drew back. "Rome *is* family. He's been in her life longer than you have."

I ran my tongue over my bottom lip and pushed up from the chair. My mother grabbed my arm, but I lightly shook away from her touch.

"Jahad," she whispered. "Not right now."

Farrah looked up at me with wide eyes as I walked over to where she stood, moments away from walking into Leighton's room. Once I made it over to her, I took the phone from her hands. She tried to protest, but I snatched it.

I put the phone to my ear, and locked eyes with her as I said, "Yo, no visitors. Come up here, we gon' have a major fuckin' problem."

"Aye, man, I under—"

I took the phone from my ear and immediately slammed it on the floor, shattering it into pieces.

Farrah gasped and shielded her face from flying debris. "You did not just break my fucking phone!"

I did, though. Type of time I was on, I was liable to break her jaw. I didn't hit women, but I'd gripped it with so much force, I would snap that bitch in half. Farrah had been skating on thin ice for months. I was itching to shut her the fuck up. But instead of catching a case when my family needed me most, I walked away.

I massaged the back of my neck and opened the door to Leighton's room. The minute I stepped inside, the pitter-patter of my little girl's heart filled my ears. I closed my eyes and rested on the closed door as the sound of Farrah's annoying voice began to fade to the back. She was arguing with Sienna, who wouldn't let her inside of the room. My mother had intervened too. She was pissed, speaking in our native tongue, cursing Farrah only the way Graciela could. Soon, though, I couldn't hear any of it. The only sound in my ears was the sound of my daughter.

Thump. Thump. Thump. Thump.

Her heart was racing. She wanted out but it wasn't time yet. I needed li'l mama to chill for as long as possible. Swallowing, I pushed away from the door and treaded over to the bed, where Leighton was asleep with a frown on her face. My wife was under so much pressure, she couldn't even sleep peacefully. That gutted me too. Leighton without a smile on her face would *always* gut me, regardless of where we were in life. I loved my wife. She was flawed as fuck, but I was too.

I pulled my chair closer to the bed and sat down before leaning over and laying my head on Leighton's stomach, accidentally waking her. Instead of pushing me away, she ran her hand over the back of my head as I talked to my baby girl.

"*Bonjou, ti bebe dous. Fè m 'yon favè . . . fredi pou jodi a. Mwen bezwen ou rete mete pou yon koup plis semèn. Souple. Pou nou. Pou ou menm. Mwen konnen, mwen konnen . . . ou kontan sou reyinyon nou. Nou kontan rankontre ou tou, men yon sèl bagay mwen pral anseye ou lè tan li se enpòtans ki genyen nan pasyans. Mwen konnen mwen te di mwen pa t 'kapab rete tann pou rankontre ou. Men, mwen kapab. Mwen reyèlman kapab . . .* (Good morning, sweet baby. Do me a favor . . . chill for today. I need you to stay put for a couple more weeks. Please. For us. For you. I know, I know . . . you're excited about meeting us. We're excited to meet you, too, but one thing I will teach you when it's time is the importance of patience. I know I said I couldn't wait to meet you, but I can. I really can.)"

Was it silly, me speaking to her in our language still? A language I'd probably never get to hear her speak. It felt silly. Heartbreaking, to be honest. I'd never experienced a pain with anything remotely close to this.

I lifted my head from Leighton's stomach, and our eyes met. There was so much sadness behind them as a lone tear rolled down her cheek. I hated to see her cry. Hated knowing there was nothing in the world I could do to stop it. I wish I could fix this. Wished I could give her the one thing she really wanted from me. Wished I could give it to both of us.

"Jahad," Natasha whispered as she gave my arm a light tug. "It's . . . it's time, big brother. Are you ready?"

With my head lightly cocked back and wide eyes, I clenched down on my jaw and finally blinked after staring off into space for I didn't know how long.

"No," I honestly told her as I slipped out of her grip and walked through the door to Leighton's room as one of the nurses held it open for me.

I wasn't ready but that didn't mean shit. What was happening, was happening whether I was ready for it or not. Leighton was in labor. Our angel, our sweet baby girl, she was coming, and she wasn't even fucking *ready*. Her heart rate went from racing to declining in a matter of hours. Things were getting bad. Fast. She was in distress and there was nothing they could do at this point to stop the labor.

When we found out, I lost it. Physically, I appeared fine. But mentally? Mentally, I was having a tantrum. I was the fixer. I was the one that made problems go away. But here, I couldn't. I couldn't fix this. I'd tried. Switched doctors, got her a doula, made sure we followed the rules. But nothing could fix it because nothing I did now would fix what I did in the past that'd cursed me.

A minute ago, I'd stepped out to give her and her parents a bit of privacy. That was what I told them. I stepped out to breathe. I had to go to the restroom to get myself together. I couldn't contain my rage. I had to release, and I did. I put a massive hole in the wall of one of the bathroom stalls. Blaise and Saint tried to follow me, but I told them to let me be. I wanted to be alone. Nah, on second thought, that wasn't what I wanted. What I wanted was to be at home, in bed with my wife, watching that fucking British TV show I hated, while she laughed, eating ice cream I had special delivered because she just had to have the shit. And in the middle of her gushing over a corny-ass show, I'd scoot down the bed to place my ear on her stomach to have a conversation with the best part of me. The beautiful part. The untainted, innocent part. My child. What I wanted meant nothing because . . . *Leighton was in labor.*

The walk inside of the room was a blur. The only thing I saw was Leighton. My beautiful, beautiful Leighton. She was broken. This was breaking her. There was nothing behind her eyes. I wondered if as she stared back into mine, if she saw nothing too.

I stood next to the bed and immediately grabbed hold of her hand. I brought it up to my lips and softly kissed the back of it before leaning down and kissing her on her forehead. She exhaled and then came the tears. The sound of her gut-wrenching scream would stay seared into my brain until the day I died.

I wrapped my arms around her, and she shook against my chest as she cried harder than I'd ever heard her cry before. This was different. We were too close . . . too close to finally becoming parents for it to be snatched away from us. It was unfair. Unfair to her. Leighton didn't deserve this curse. She didn't deserve to catch the back end of my karma. Shit wasn't right.

Because only me and the birthing partner, Sienna, were allowed in the room, our families, Farrah's nagging ass included, stayed out in the hallway. It was just us, the doctor, and the nurses. But the air was thick and heavy. Shit didn't just weigh on my shoulders—it penetrated me and weighed on my heart.

"Mrs. Baptiste, I need you to push." Dr. Griggs's soft, mellow voice ripped through our moment.

Leighton and I locked eyes, and I stood up straight to give her room to push. Her eyes stayed on mine, and mine stayed on hers.

"Mwen renmen ou," I told her, repeatedly in between kisses on her lips.

"I . . . I love you, too, Jahad." She cried as she shook her head. "I can't do it. I can't . . . She's . . . she's not ready. I don't want to."

I ran my hand over the top of her head. "You have to, my love. You have to push."

Leighton shook her head again. "I . . . Just a little longer. I want . . . I want her to stay a little longer. Why? Why is this happening to me?"

"Mrs. Baptiste, you—"

I put my hand up, silencing Dr. Griggs. "I don't know, beautiful, but it's happening. And, baby, you have to push. I know it's difficult but we get through the difficult things together, don't we? I'm here." I looked over to Sienna, standing on Leighton's side, rubbing her head. "And Sienna's here. We're here. We'll always be here."

"Promise?" she cried with her head tilted and her eyes upturned in a way that ripped my already broken heart into tiny shreds.

"I promise," I said, as I swallowed the knot in my throat.

Sienna wouldn't always be here. Today would be her last day because her assignment would end with the life of our baby. I hoped Leighton would understand that. I hoped I would learn to understand that.

I kissed her on the lips. "Do me a favor, love. Give me a big push."

She nodded and finally pushed. I exhaled and closed my eyes at the scream that erupted from her. It sounded like it came from the depths of her soul.

For a split second, I looked away from Leighton and put my eyes on Sienna, who repeated words of encouragement. The look of sorrow on her face as tears rolled down her cheeks resembled Leighton's. I hadn't, for one second, in the middle of all of this, thought of how she must've felt. Just six days ago, she experienced a loss of her own. *We* suffered a loss. She said it wasn't mine, but I knew better. I would say I couldn't believe I was experiencing another loss like this, back-to-back, but I believed it. This was one thing I could count on. The only thing in my life that was promised to me.

The hospital room was quiet as Leighton screamed and pushed. Every now and then, Dr. Griggs would tell her she was doing good. Every now and then, I told her I loved her. Every now and then, Sienna would encourage her. But for the most part, the room was silent. An eerie silence that was loud in its own way. Loud in knowing that, despite the hope in Dr. Griggs's voice when she told us there was a chance the baby would survive, we knew it was too soon. We knew when Leighton left the hospital, our daughter wouldn't be going home with her. That realization tore my heart to shreds. I was fucked up. I was right in the middle of a mental meltdown but my hand, it never left hers. And every time a tear rolled too far down her cheek, I kissed it away. I was her rock, even when I was crumbling.

"Why?" she screamed, as she gave another big push.

Why? I knew why. I was a poison, that was why. She thought I wanted to stop trying for babies because I wanted to give up. I wanted to stop because I was tired of losing them. Tired of the shit I'd done coming back to haunt us. That was why I wanted to stop. Because it was pointless, and the more we tried, the more damage I did. She kept losing them. Kept having D&Cs. They weakened her cervix. We knew this going in, but she wanted to keep trying. Was straight with bed rest. Even with the low chances Dr. Griggs gave her. She wanted to keep trying. Leighton never lost hope. When she wanted something, she'd go to the end of the earth to get it, but my God, I hoped this was the last time. These losses . . . they didn't just do damage to her cervix, they did damage to her. To me. To us. I couldn't handle another one. I would for sure lose my shit.

"All right, just one more big push, Leighton," Dr. Griggs coached.

Leighton's eyes found mine as she gave the final push. My baby was petrified of what would happen next. Her bottom lip trembled as we both waited. Waited for that sound that gave all parents hope. That cry.

"She's okay?" Leighton asked, eagerly looking over at the doctors working on our baby just a few feet away.

Sienna gave Leighton a light smile. "What's her name? You got a name?"

She was trying to distract her.

"Huh?" Leighton confusingly asked with pinched brows, looking back and forth between Sienna and me, and then back to Dr. Griggs and the nurse. "Is she okay? Why isn't she crying? Jahad. Is she . . . She's supposed to cry."

"You had three names, Leigh. Remember? You said . . ." Sienna paused and took a deep breath. "You had, um, Shia because it meant 'gift from God.' And Anaya because it meant 'God answers,' and Aleyah Lavelle for 'glorious soul.' You . . ." She lightly giggled through tears. "You never picked boy names because you just knew it was your girl. It's . . . it's your girl, Leigh. Pick . . . pick a name, boo."

Her face was full of tears. Shit, mine, too. I couldn't handle it. I went from standing at the bed to pacing. Pacing because the shit was just too fucking heavy. My wife kept asking Dr. Griggs questions, but she was busy. One of the nurses was between Leighton's legs again, telling her she needed to deliver the placenta. No one had answered Leighton, and our baby, she hadn't cried. I looked over every now and then at her little body, watching them giving her compressions. Watched as they tried to bring her back. Watched until they stopped. I went back over to the bed when they did, leaned over to Leigh and told her it would be okay. But I knew it wouldn't. This was going to break her. This shit was going to break us. I just prayed this was it. I needed this to be it. I couldn't handle this shit anymore. She couldn't, either.

Leighton stared off, unblinking, with a flat expression on her face. "I had four names." I watched as she put her eyes on Dr. Griggs walking over with our daughter wrapped in a blanket. "Leia. Child of . . . Heaven."

"Take care of her . . . Okay?" Sienna said with a tear-filled smile.

I nodded. "Always."

It was late. Sienna was supposed to be gone hours ago, but she stayed by Leighton's side until she fell asleep. I didn't want to leave Leighton's side at all, but I had to walk Sienna out. It was the right thing to do. We stood in the secluded garage, quiet, staring at each other. Was this the end of us? Felt like it. It needed to be. It had to be. I couldn't imagine stepping away from my wife to see her. There was nothing for me to have her in my life anymore.

Leia was gone. Just like that. One minute, we were parents, the next, we weren't. One minute, we needed a doula, the next . . . we didn't. Life didn't surprise me anymore.

"Take care of you, too," she said, as she opened her car door.

I nodded and stepped closer to her. Regardless of what it was, that pull was still there. Now more than it'd ever been before. I wondered if it was because this was the end, or if because my soul needed to feel it. *Her.* The *it* I could only get from her. Still, I kept a respectable amount of space between us.

"We appreciate you." I paused and locked eyes with her. "I appreciate you."

Sienna pulled her lips into her mouth and nodded. I watched as a tear slowly ran over her top lip and slid between the small space between her closed lips. Lifting my finger, I brushed away another one that was heading in that same direction. She closed her eyes, and I felt her exhale. I did too. That electrifying tingle transferred between us, but all I could do about that was pull my hand away from her face. Whatever it was between us, that was over. Had to be. I needed it to be.

"Are you going to be okay?" I asked. "I . . . I know being here was heavy. I hope—"

"I'm okay. I'm going to be okay," she said with a forced smile. "You just . . . you just make sure she is . . . and you are."

Unspoken words transferred between us. Unspoken words I understood perfectly. She was telling me it was the end. I knew it was without the unspoken confirmation. Neither of us wanted it. I saw it through her lenses, and I was sure she could see it behind mine. But like she told me before—this wasn't about us. It was about Leighton. Leighton was the common denominator for both of us. Now more than ever.

"If you need any—"

"I won't need anything," she interrupted before her gaze fell to the ground. "I told you, just take care of her. *She* needs you."

I chewed on my bottom lip and nodded.

"And you don't," I stated, and waited for confirmation she never gave me.

I couldn't help it. That jarring need to keep her in my life somehow, some way. I wanted to feel this—whatever it was between us—forever. That "this" I never felt with my wife before. That "this" I knew I would *never* feel with her. There was something about Sienna Mills. Always had been something about her. I couldn't help but wonder if she was only meant to be in my life for a season. A short season. To show me the importance of what I had at home. Could it be that? Was she a lesson? That was what she felt like. Hadn't I failed, though? Didn't feel like I'd passed anything. I gave in to her. Gave in to Leighton's persuasion of the hall pass. And found her. Found her and she imprinted on a nigga's soul so aggressively that not even sleeping beside my wife kept her out of my dreams. Not even the pain my wife was in was enough to pull me away from her. I felt like shit. As bad as I did with my stillborn daughter in my arms.

Leighton deserved more. She deserved nightly dreams. She deserved all of me. But in giving myself to Sienna, Leighton only owned pieces of me. So much belonged to Sienna, and I couldn't, for the life of me, wrap my mind around why . . . around how. Realistically, shorty was a stranger. But fuck, she felt familiar. Like home.

Losing my daughter in such a horrific way should have kept me grounded in my marriage. But there was this gnawing feeling in the pit of my stomach that told me to run. And not toward Leighton. Toward her. My kryptonite. Sienna.

We stood there, awkwardly silent for what felt like hours. We were unfinished. I felt it, and I knew she felt it. But regardless of what it felt like, this was the end. A necessary end. Just like Leigh deserved more, Sienna did too. What I wanted, it didn't matter. What I wanted didn't make sense. It would paint me out to be as fucked up as I knew I was. I was, as always, concerned about everybody but me. That was, and probably always would be, what life was for me.

"Good night, *Mr. Baptiste*," she said with a tear-filled wink.

Against my better judgment, I closed the space between us and hugged her. She didn't resist. She wrapped her arms around me and hugged me just as tight as I'd hugged her. I didn't want to let go. I had to. But I didn't want to. She felt too fucking good. The hug put bandages on wounds. Wounds I kept hidden from the rest of the world because if I showed them, I'd come off as weak. But I felt. I had wounds. Deep ones. But in her arms, none of it mattered. She felt good as fuck. So good that when she tried to pull away, I held on to her. It was the end. I wasn't ready for the end of us yet. There was still so much for us to unpack.

Why did she cry when no one was looking? What troubled her? What was she doing at Pandora's? Why was there this magnetic-ass pull between us? Why, when she was in my arms, did I feel like I was floating? Why did I feel like I knew her, deep, and I'd only known her for a couple of months? I knew her favorite color. Knew her birthday was coming up. Knew how to make her cum. I knew what her face looked like just moments before orgasming. But I didn't know her favorite food. I didn't know what type of movies she liked to watch. Didn't know if she wanted children someday. I wanted to learn more about her. But shit, it was the end of us and a nigga just did not want to let go.

She exhaled and her shoulders dropped defeatedly. "Jahad. You have to let me go."

I swallowed but said nothing. Kept my arms wrapped around her with my eyes closed, savoring the feel of peace. Freedom. I needed to savor it for as long as possible because I knew when I let her go, that peace and that freedom would come to an end. Fantasy . . . shit felt amazing.

"What if I don't want to?"

"What we want doesn't matter. You know that," she said as her tears seeped through my T-shirt.

"What's your favorite food?"

"Pasta. Any kind of pasta. Alfredo the most."

"What kind of movies do you like?"

"Psychological thrillers," she breathed out, sinking deeper into my chest.

I swallowed. "Why were you at Pandora's?"

"My sister sent me a secret invitation. Said she sent it because I said I'd never had an orgasm. I almost didn't go."

I lightly grunted with a short laugh we shared.

"Are you happy you did?" I asked.

"Jahad—"

"Just answer the question," I interrupted. I wasn't ready for the moment to end.

I was in no rush to go back to the room where my wife slept, and our child slept . . . eternally. She was still there. Right beside the bed. Leighton wanted to take her home. I didn't. I wanted it to be over. She didn't want to let go. I did.

"Yes and no," Sienna finally responded.

"No? Why no?"

"Because I met you," she said with a sigh.

With raised brows, I said, "Damn. Why yes, then?"

She softly cried. "Because I met you."

I understood. Understood completely.

"You have regrets?"

"I do."

"Like what?"

"Not meeting you first," she whispered, like it was a secret.

Understood that too.

Was it bad that I wished I'd met her first, too? I didn't regret Leighton. I really didn't, but it was the feel of this woman. The way every nerve in my body ignited when we touched. She brought me so much peace, right in the middle of a storm. How was that shit even possible?

"Why do you cry when you think no one is watching?" This time, I whispered. I wasn't the whispering type, but the magnitude of my question warranted one.

"I need to go—"

"Please," I begged.

Time stood still while I waited for her to answer me. Her breathing picked up and more tears wet my shirt. Her hold around my back tightened, and suddenly, it was like I felt everything she felt. Sadness. Sorrow. Heartbreak. It knocked me off my square a little. What was crazy was that I already felt those things, but for a brief second, the feelings multiplied, and I knew they were hers. I didn't know how I knew . . . I just knew. I had never been so sure about anything in my entire life.

"Because it's the only time I'm me. When no one is watching, I can . . . I can take my mask off and be . . . free," she whispered back.

This time, when she pulled away, I let her. She looked up at me and rubbed her lips together with a light smile. A smile that didn't reach her eyes. She got into the car and I stepped back so she could pull off. With my hands stuffed into the pockets of my coat, I watched her leave.

I didn't say goodbye.

Didn't have to because this wasn't the end. Regardless of what I felt before, I knew it wasn't. We would see each other again. That was how *this* worked between us. Life . . . it *put* us together.

CHAPTER 31

Leighton

"You ready?" Jahad asked when he walked into the nursery. A nursery we only used for three days.

I looked up away from Leia and shook my head with tears rolling down my face. "No. I'm not. Call and tell them—"

"We can't do that, love," he interrupted with a sigh. "We told them we would take her back today. We have to take her back today." He walked further into the nursery and sat on the other side of the room. I frowned with tightened lips. I hated him. "I understand—"

"You don't understand. How could you understand when you haven't held her since she's been here? And you treat her like . . . like nothing? You won't even sit with us. You don't understand anything. You want her out of the house. You—"

"Leighton, baby, please," Jahad pleaded before his head fell into his palms. "Don't do this right now—"

"Don't do what? Talk about how you've treated our daughter like . . . nothing? Talk about how you haven't acknowledged her at all?"

He looked up at me and said nothing, just stared at me. Stared me in my eyes so intensely, I was forced to look away. Looking down at her was painful, so I put my eyes on the window instead. She . . . it was time for her to go back but I wasn't ready to let go of her. Why couldn't anybody understand that? Why was I treated like a crazy person because I wanted to spend time with my daughter? It was the only time I could spend with her. I didn't have weeks. I didn't have months. I wouldn't see her grow up. I wouldn't see her take her first steps. I wouldn't get to see her crawl. There would be no first words, no first days of school, no first foods, no first smile.

I had nothing. I got nothing. All I had was this. So why couldn't I just enjoy it? Just a few extra days with her in my arms? A few extra days with her in the nursery I finally got the opportunity to design? I just didn't want to let go. I wasn't ready to. I had to. I knew this. I just wanted more time. I *needed* more time. I didn't think more time was good, since she was changing, but I still wanted it. The illusion was fading.

I'd wake up in the morning, come in here, pick her up and sit with her. Read her stories. I was happy. But this morning when I picked her up, she was different. She didn't feel the same. She didn't look the same. It broke my heart. She was changing. Leia, my sweet, precious baby. Her skin. Her lips . . . things were changing. It was *really* time to take her back. I could barely look at her now. So, instead of looking down at her face, I kept my eyes on the window. There was snow falling. Big flurries. Huge snowflakes. We wouldn't have snowball fights. We wouldn't lay in the snow and make snow angels. There would be no putting up Christmas decorations together. No light shows. No sleigh rides. Nothing. This was so fucking unfair.

While I was zoned out, staring out of the window, wishing I had more time, Jahad approached. He ran his hand over my shoulder, and I shuddered. He didn't pull away. He kept his hands there. Never left my side. Never returned my anger with anger. Always repaid me with love and compassion. I hated him for that. Hated myself again for it. But my anger, it was justified. This was his fault. All of it. Every bit of it.

Dr. Griggs said these things happen. Preterm labor. They happen. It was common for women with my history. An extensive history of repeated D&Cs and pregnancy loss. There was no explanation for it, besides history. But I knew better. I had an orgasm. I let him put his mouth on me. I gave him my body. I pleased him. I spent too much time in the shower. Took that risk because I was afraid of losing my husband to the woman I told him he could have sex with. Desperation cost me my baby. There was no proof of it, but in my heart, I knew it was that. I told Dr. Griggs that, too, and what did she say? *"Oh, Leighton, you can't look at it like that. We spoke about the risks when we first learned about the pregnancy. You could have gone into preterm labor regardless."* Blah, blah, fucking blah. Jahad did this to me.

I took all of those fucking risks and what did he do? Still lie. Still cheat. Still see her. I hated him. I hated him so fucking much. This anger had been building and marinating for days.

Every time I walked into the nursery to silence and a lifeless baby, it grew. I thought my baby was my chance at true happiness. I thought she was our do-over. I was hopeful, even when I had no reason to be. Realistically, I knew the odds were stacked against us, especially when she went into distress, but I kept hope. I just knew God wouldn't punish me like that. I just knew I would get my girl. She was my rainbow baby. But when I didn't hear her cry, when the nurse put her lifeless body in my arms, it was over. I was done. *We* were done. Me and Jahad.

He promised to always be by my side, and before, there was no other place I would've wanted him. But the minute I realized she was gone, I wanted him away from me because I knew she was gone because of him.

"When you sleep, I hold her," Jahad said, breaking my train of thought. "I sit in here for hours and I talk to her, too. So, please, don't say I don't understand because I do. Taking her back is hard for me, too, Leigh."

I didn't say anything, just stared out of the window, silently crying, wishing my life was different.

An hour later, we were pulling into the hospital's parking lot. Before we left the house, Farrah showed up and drove down with us. My parents were right behind us, too. I was grateful for my support system, but I really just wanted to be left alone. I was tired of being asked how I was doing. It was a stupid question. My baby was dead. How did people think I was doing? I wasn't rude to them, though. I smiled and nodded like I was okay, but I wasn't. I wouldn't be for a very long time.

Farrah ran her hand over my thigh when Jahad parked. "It's going to be okay, babe."

It wasn't.

I was in the backseat, sitting with my baby. You know, like new mothers do. They sit in the back in case the baby wakes up and needs to be fed. Leia, she wouldn't need anything, but I sat in the back, anyway, wishing she would. Hoping, feeling like she would. Waiting for her to cry. Literally. I was losing grip on reality. Maybe bringing her back was the best thing to do. Her little lips. They were so . . .

Jahad turned around and gripped my chin, bringing my eyes to his. "We can do this."

We. We. We.

I carried her for nine—no, for . . . how many—for six months. Not *we*. I would have carried her for nine if it wasn't for what he did. For what he made me do. That hall pass. He made me give it to him. Forced me to. Laid beside me all of those nights, looking like a sad-ass puppy dog who wanted his fucking dick wet. Laid next to me, thinking about cheating, wanting to go out and fuck someone else. He didn't think I knew, huh? Jahad, the master fucking manipulator. He manipulated me into giving him that pass. And then he wanted to act like he didn't want it. Toyed with me just to go out and use it on New Year's fucking Eve. The got damn holiday? What a bitch made nigga. Then he gets with the bitch, fucks her and tells me nothing even though he sees me losing my mind about it. So what I told him I didn't want details? Why not tell me? Then he made me feel insecure. Insecurities that led me straight into desperation. Insecurities he planted! That made me get in the shower with him. Made me suck his dick. Made me open my legs and cum so fucking hard. Made me think we were okay. I thought we were good, then he lied. And then that insecurity that led me in that shower made me lose the only thing I cared about.

I would have carried her full-term if it wasn't for what he did. *We* can do this? Hadn't *he* done enough? *I* can do this. *I* can take *my* baby to the morgue.

If someone were to ask me how the process went, I wouldn't be able to tell them. I must've been on autopilot or something because the only thing I remembered was getting out of the car and then I was back in the car again. Except, this time, without my baby. I remembered the car ride home. It was quiet. And I was in the front seat. I had absolutely no reason to ride in the back now. Farrah asked me to, but for the fuck what? So she could keep rubbing on me and telling me it would be okay when I knew it wouldn't be. She asked me if I wanted her to stay. I told her yes. But not because I wanted her to keep me company.

"You want to watch that show?" Jahad asked once we made it up to the bedroom.

I looked over my shoulder at him and shook my head. "Your phone was ringing the whole ride home. You're needed, aren't you?"

He leaned against the dresser and ran his hand over the top of his head. "You know I don't give a fuck about that shit right now."

"Why not? There is nothing here for you to care about," I lowly said as I swiped a tear from my face and walked into the bathroom to go to my closet.

He was coming. I wanted him to stay where he was, posted up against the dresser. I didn't want him anywhere near me. Not only because I hated him but because it would be easier to do what I needed to do if he kept his distance.

"Leigh, what are you talkin' about?" he asked exhaustively, stepping into the bathroom. "And what are you doing?"

I was in the closet, pulling my luggage from the back of it. "I'm talking about how . . . how there is nothing here for you to care about. You might as well just go. I'm leaving, going to stay at Farrah's for a while."

He laughed. He didn't chuckle. He was literally cracking up, like something was hysterically funny. It was scary. So scary, I had to look up from the luggage at him to see if he was on the phone or something. Because what was *so* funny? But he wasn't on the phone. He leaned up against the sink counter, rapidly running his hand over the top of his head, cracking up. He pushed up from the counter, paced, and continued to laugh. Then he stopped pacing and stood at the closet door.

He placed both his hands on the doorframe and looked down at me with a sadness behind his eyes that I'd never seen before. "Why you doin' this shit to me?"

"Why am I doing what shit to you?" I yelled. "What did I do to you? Do you know what *you* did to *me*? To us?"

I walked up on him and shoved him. He didn't move. He was solid, like a brick wall. And for some reason, that only made me madder. I kept pushing him and he never moved. Just stood there, gawking down at me with that sadness. Sad eyes, glossed over with tears. Sad eyes that ultimately made me cry. Why was he sad? He didn't even want to try for another baby. I had to beg him. I had to make him come home when I was ovulating. I had to beat the importance of certain positions in his head. He wasn't happy about my pregnancy for most of it. Didn't touch my belly. Didn't talk to her. Didn't acknowledge it. Not until about a month ago or so. Now he cared? Now he wanted to be sad? After he made me lose her?

I pushed him again, and this time, he caught my wrists, grabbed me and pulled me into his chest before wrapping his strong arms around me. I stopped fighting. This was why I didn't want him near me. Hating him wasn't easy when he was in my space. But I had to hate him. He took her away from me. He took our chance away from us. But my God, being in his arms felt so good. Too good. How good it felt only lasted a minute because I was immediately flooded with thoughts of them. Him and her. Wondered if he held her like this that night he came home smelling like her. After all I'd done to fix us. After all I'd done to make up for my mistakes.

I tried to pull away from him, but he wouldn't let me.

"Let me go!" I screamed and cried.

"Mm-mm" he grunted. "Don't do this to me, love."

"I'm not doing anything to you!" I cried as my legs began to grow weak. "You did this to me! You did this to us! She's not here 'cause of you!"

The silence after I said what I'd been thinking for the past three days was thick. Loud and heavy. With wide eyes, I stood frozen on shaky legs with a racing heart. I didn't . . . I didn't mean to say it. I didn't want to hurt him. But it *was* his fault, and I was in pain. I couldn't stop it. I just . . . I just said it. And there was no taking it back.

He pulled me away from his chest and looked down at me with a menacing scowl on his face. Those sad eyes? That glimmer of tears? Gone. "What the fuck you just say to me?"

I shook. My entire body shook. It felt like my legs were going to give out on me. And if they did, I wouldn't fall because the grip he had on my arms was so tight, I wouldn't be able to.

"What did you just say to me, Leighton?" he asked with flaring nostrils, backing me up into the closet.

"Let me go!" I cried. "Let me go!"

"Repeat what you just said to—"

"It's your fault!" I screamed with wide eyes before kicking, finally finding feeling in them so he'd free me. "I went into labor because of you! If . . . If I didn't . . . If we hadn't done that—" He let me go and walked away, and it infuriated me. "Don't walk away from me! Don't shut me out!"

I followed him as he gripped the back of his head with both of his hands. He was on his way out of the bedroom. Farrah was downstairs. The staff wasn't here. Thank God they weren't. Giving Farrah front row seats to our mess was already embarrassing enough.

For months, I pretended everything with Jahad and me was okay. I didn't tell her I gave him a pass. Didn't tell her I didn't trust him. None of that. Didn't tell her about the scent of perfume. Was too ashamed of all of it. The only thing she had on us was how often he stayed out of the house. *We were happy*. She *thought* we were happy. But now she knew. She saw it. The ugly. She heard it. I knew she could.

We were in the hallway. He was running away from me. I should have stopped. I should have turned back around and went back to packing but I didn't. I followed him. I bullied him. Cried and blamed him. Called him names. Told him he ruined our family.

"I hate you!" I screamed at the top of my lungs once he made it to the last stair.

He stopped walking. He stopped rubbing the back of his head. His arms dropped to his sides and he slowly turned around to face me. I looked over my shoulder at the mountain of stairs I'd have to run up to get away from him if he advanced toward me, and knew I wouldn't get too far before he caught me.

I didn't even have time enough to think before he was on me, though. Jahad stood in front of me in a matter of seconds with his hand gripped around my small jaw. He tilted my head back and forced me to look into his eyes. I tried to close mine, but I couldn't. I was stuck. Numb. Could barely feel my heart beating.

"You hate me?"

"Jahad, that's enough," Farrah said from behind. "Let her go before I call the police."

Jahad didn't move a muscle. His eyes stayed locked on mine, like he didn't even hear Farrah.

"You don't have to answer me, Leigh, because I believe you. You didn't just start hating me, tho'. You been hating a nigga. You tolerated me. Gave me weak-ass pussy for years just to get a nut up out me so you could get a baby. I gave you that baby and you still refused to give me the only fuckin' thing I wanted from you. Passion. Didn't give a fuck about pussy. Could've easily gone nine, ten months without that shit. But you . . . you don't fuckin' think." He pressed his finger into his temple and continued to talk over Farrah, who kept threatening to call the police. "You thought the best thing to do was to give me permission to put my dick in something else. But all I wanted was my wife to treat me like she gave a fuck about me. And now . . . now that the one thing, the only thing you really wanted from a nigga is gone, you ready to pack yo' bags and move in with a miserable bitch that loves to see shit unfold like this. The only reason you leavin' is because you know I'm done. You know I won't give you another baby because I refuse to go through another loss alone."

He then pushed my face out of his hand and walked away.

"Come on. Let's get out of here, Leigh," Farrah said as she looked away from me, and at Jahad, who walked up the stairs. "We can come back for your things tomorrow."

I stood there, shaking and crying for a good minute. This wasn't how things were supposed to be! We were supposed to get through this together. There wasn't supposed to be a "this" to get through. However, there was. But I was so got damn mad and bitter, I just couldn't. I couldn't look at him without thinking about the *what ifs*. I couldn't look at him without blaming him. How was I supposed to get through this with him if I blamed him? If I hated him because of it?

The sudden sound of our bedroom door slamming made me flinch.

"Come on!" she pressed.

I looked down at her and still could not fucking move. I didn't want to go with her. I didn't want to be here. I didn't want any of this. I wanted my daughter. I wanted a family. This wasn't supposed to be my life. I wasn't supposed to become Farrah. But as she grabbed hold of my arm and led me down the rest of the stairs, I felt it happening. I was slowly but surely morphing into her and there was nothing I could do to stop it at this point. I'd done and said too much. There was no coming back from this.

I was her.

CHAPTER 32

Sienna

ONE MONTH LATER

"Serene Mommy Doula Services, how can I help you?" I answered as I twirled around in the office chair with my eyes locked on the wall clock.

Every day, ten minutes before the office closed, someone always called.

"Hey! So, I saw an ad on Instagram. I'm eight weeks pregnant and I want to know what it is y'all do up there? This an abortion clinic? How much y'all—"

"I'm sorry. This isn't an abortion clinic," I quickly interrupted with a heavy eye roll.

"Serene Mommy . . . Services. It sure sounds like an abortion clinic to me! Confusing-ass name!" she yelled before hanging up in my face.

I set the phone on its receiver and tossed my head back, dangling it off the back of the chair. God. Today had been a long-ass day. That was the fifth call I'd gotten like that this week, and it was only Tuesday. It was ridiculous. The calls made me think Shonda had the company classified under the wrong category on Google until I realized all the calls we received came from the Instagram ad she had running. It was blatantly stated in the ad that we were a doula company but people just didn't pay attention.

I was working in the office. Mentally, I couldn't handle being in the field. The trauma that came with working as an antepartum doula was too heavy for me to handle right now. A month had passed since Leighton and Jahad loss their baby and a month since I loss ours too. I was traumatized and didn't want to work with mothers at all.

The past month for me had been like a literal roller coaster. I had good days. I had bad days. I had days I missed him. Days I was happy he was out of my life. Days I wanted to check on him. Days that pull was aggressive but not aggressive enough for me to actually give in to it. Days there was an angel, my therapist, Diamond, on my right shoulder, telling me to let that go and to move on with my life. But then the little demon on my left shoulder, Mahogany, would tell me to call him and that it was destiny. That we were meant to cross paths and become more than what we were. I didn't believe in destiny, so naturally, Angel Diamond would win. That chapter of my life was finally over. I hadn't seen or talked to him in over a month.

"You have to do something about that Instagram ad," I said to Shonda, who was walking out of her office.

It was time to go. I couldn't wait to get home, take a shower, order something I had no business eating, and binge watch old episodes of *Snowfall*. I was content with going home to an empty apartment these days. Before, it bothered me. The silence. The emptiness. I loved it now. My space was coming together, although sometimes, I felt like it was too big of a space for little ol' me. The Sienna I was today didn't need a big-ass, luxury, sixteen-hundred-square-foot, two-bedroom, two-bathroom apartment with floor-to-ceiling windows, stainless steel appliances, and fancy countertops. I didn't need the big-ass walk-in closet, the master bathroom with the double sink, walk-in shower, and soaker bathtub. Back then, I was putting a price tag on self-love. True self-love doesn't come from outside sources; it *literally* comes from within.

"What happened? We got another abortion call?" Shonda asked with a laugh, shaking her head.

I shut my computer down and turned the call forwarding on. "Girl, yeah. The shit is ridiculous at this point. You want me to make another flyer?"

"It's not the flyer," she said, hiking her Gucci bag over her shoulder. "Those bitches are just illiterate."

I grabbed my Brandon Blackwood bag off the desk and laughed. "Yeaaah, you've got a point."

"What you about to get into?" she asked, as we headed to the exit, turning lights off on the way there.

"Absolutely nothing."

She and I were the only ones at the office. Before, it would just be her. She answered the phones and handled all the clerical duties. The girls stayed in the field. But now that I'd been in the office with her, she was thinking about opening an office position for when I went back out into the field because having me around had been so helpful. Shonda didn't know, but I didn't plan on going back out into the field any time soon. I told her I needed six months in the office, but what I really needed were six months to start my own doula company. She knew I wanted to start my own company, but she thought that was a long-term plan. Hell, I thought it was, too, but the experience with Leighton really shook me. I couldn't go back into the field. I didn't want to be a postpartum doula, didn't want to be an antepartum doula, and I didn't want Shonda to keep doing me favors. So, once my six months were up, I would hand in a resignation letter. I planned on telling her before then, of course, but I was taking my time because that was a touchy subject and I hated uncomfortable conversations.

I wasn't giving up on doulaship altogether, my wounds were still fresh. I thought I could handle doulaship with my history, but that was just me shoveling glitter over shit. I was done doing that. I was at a point in my life where I was facing my problems head on. I didn't wear masks. I didn't hide my emotions and only cry when no one—or I thought no one—was watching. I didn't pretend I was okay, because pretending only hurt me more. I just couldn't do that shit anymore. Doing that was what damn near made me an alcoholic.

Just as we were approaching the front door, Naoki walked in with a big smile.

"Surpriiise!" she shrieked, as she charged at me with open arms.

She wasn't supposed to be home until Thursday.

We hugged and rocked back and forth. God, I was so happy to see her. She'd been out of town more and more these days. I saw her more on FaceTime than in person and I hated that for us. We both did.

"What are you doing heeere?" I yelled before we pulled away from the hug.

"I lied, I lied. Forgive me. I wanted to surprise you," she said with a smile. She looked over at Shonda. "Hey, girl."

Shonda spoke back. "Hey, boo."

We walked out of the building and Shonda locked up. I told her I would see her in the morning and Naoki and I interlocked arms as we walked to the parking lot. With my free hand, I pulled my bomber jacket closed as a gust of wind blew in. It was a little chilly. It was mid-March with spring on the horizon, but it was still a bit chilly. Earlier, the temperature was around fifty, but since it was after six, it had dropped significantly. We hadn't had snow for a couple of weeks, but in Michigan, that didn't mean a damn thing. I wouldn't be surprised to wake up to snow in the morning.

"We turning up on a Tuesday, *fren*?" Naoki joked.

I laughed. "We?"

I didn't drink anymore. At all. That cutting back shit didn't work for me. How I handled "cutting back" that night at the club was proof. So, I'd gone cold turkey. I didn't need that. I hated what it did to me. Wine was my go-to. I drank tequila every now and then, but wine? Wine was my shit. But it wasn't for me anymore. I couldn't handle it. I always overdid it. That last time was it for me.

The day Leia died, I got home and could barely breathe, I was so distraught. As soon as I made it inside of my apartment, I snatched the refrigerator open and grabbed two bottles of wine from it. Don't ask me why I had wine on stash, and I was cutting back, I just did. I drank both bottles that night. I was a crying, drunken mess. I woke up the next morning on my kitchen floor, with puffy eyes and a throbbing headache. That was when I knew something had to change.

"Oh shit, I'm sorry. I forgot. Damn. I wanted to hit the bar. But—"

"No, we can go. I was going to order food and binge watch *Snowfall* from season one on some granny shit. Might as well get some food from the bar. I mean, why not? My best friend *diiiid* surprise me and shit. That's the least I can do."

"We can binge *Snowfall* tomorrow night," she said with a smile, and leaned her head against mine. "Franklin fine as fuck. How big you think his dick is? I bet it's black and thick as hell. And veiny. You think he circumcised? They do that where he from? He Haitian? Like ol' boy? Is he circumcised—"

"Bitch, if you don't shut the fuck up," I said with a laugh.

She cracked up and shrugged. "I'm just saying."

Then there was an awkward silence. Ol' boy was a sensitive subject. We didn't talk about him. Ultimately, I told her about the miscarriage and about the emotional moment we shared at the hospital the last time I saw him. It was heavy. Very heavy. Walking away from him was one of the hardest things I'd ever had to do in my life. Harder than leaving Amiri, which was fucking insane, considering the history I shared with his ass. Jahad was just different.

"Sorry," she said.

"It's cool," I said through a sigh.

I didn't like to talk about him. Talking about him only made me remember he constantly stayed on my mind. Every now and then, she was there, too. Leighton. I texted her a couple of weeks ago and asked her how she was doing. She replied, said she was breathing and that was it. After an hour, she asked me how I was doing. I replied, *Same*. Life was *lifing* for everyone.

After we left my job, we went straight to my apartment, and I got ready while she talked about work and one of the doctors she'd been fucking. And then, as always, we got on the conversation of Mahogany and that damn invite. I told her, only because Mahogany didn't say anything about keeping it a secret. Had she asked me not to tell Naoki, I wouldn't have. Naoki had been pressing me about asking Mahogany to get her inside, but I refused to. I wasn't bringing Pandora's up to Mahogany again. Especially not to ask if she could get Naoki in. She might not have asked me not to tell Naoki, but I was sure she didn't want her ass to know.

After I got out of the shower, she put fresh crimps in my twenty-six-inch middle-part frontal wig, while I put on a little makeup. I was happy she was here. I had no problem sitting in the house, but it did feel good to catch up in person rather than over FaceTime. I really did miss my best friend. During times like this, when I was healing, I wished she was closer. Sometimes, I needed a distraction. On the hard days, days that FaceTime calls and text messages weren't enough, I wished she was a car ride away. But not having a crutch was good too. Coping alone helped me keep that mask tucked away. If she was just a car ride away, pulling that mask out and pretending I was okay would be too easy. So, in a way, Naoki being thousands of miles away at work so often was good for me.

Once I was dressed in a black leather strapless corset, baggy, stonewashed, high-waisted jeans, and a pair of pointed-toe pumps, we were out of the door.

For a Tuesday evening, SavannahBlue, a Black-owned soul food spot I'd started placing carryout orders from, was pretty crowded. But then again, this was the "it" spot for the grown and sexy.

After checking our coats, we were seated at the bar, which was okay with me. It wasn't like I was a full-blown recovering alcoholic. I had a problem, but not a big one. I could sit around liquor with no problem.

"What did Nene say?" Naoki asked.

I picked the menu up and cut my eye at her. "About what, bitch?"

She cocked her head to the side. "About pulling up, ho."

I laughed. "Oh yeah. She can't make it. You know she works tomorrow. Hazel didn't reply."

"Sage can't either," she said with her bottom lip poked out. "I leave in two days."

"Two days? I thought you were here for the weekend, Ki," I complained.

She shook her head and signaled for the bartender. "Nope. I told you I lied. I have to go to Texas for an assignment I'm starting Saturday."

I just nodded and continued to flip through the menu. I understood. I swear I understood, I just missed my damn friend. She was here and then she wasn't. A bitch was pretty lonely. I was spending more time with my sisters, but it wasn't the same. Since Mahogany had opened up to me, we were closer, but it still was not the same. I thought I had Naoki for at least five days.

We stayed at the bar until they closed at eleven. She had two drinks, but when it was time for us to go, she'd pretty much sobered up. We talked and curved niggas the whole night. I was surprised because Naoki was usually game for new niggas. Tonight, she wasn't, though. I was sure it had a lot to do with the way I reacted to her telling me she would be gone in two days. She followed me home and we agreed to link up tomorrow after I got off to watch *Snowfall* as promised.

I got off the elevator and fished my phone from my pocket to text and remind her to let me know when she made it to the house. I ran my hand down the back of my neck as a chill ran down my spine. She had a bad habit of forgetting since the ride from my house to hers was so long. After I hit send and looked up, I stopped dead in my tracks, caught off guard by who sat at my apartment door with his head tossed back against it and his knees bent, chilling like he was supposed to be here. The reason for the chill that had run down my spine: Jahad.

I swallowed and again ran my hand down my neck. Since I hadn't seen or heard from him in a little over a month, seeing him now was intense. That pull was strong. He felt it, too, because he lifted his head from the door and looked right at me. He pushed himself off the floor, stood, and advanced toward me while I stood in the middle of the hallway, stuck. His walk was different. He didn't have that stride of a god. His shoulders weren't squared off. And his chin wasn't cocked back a little. He walked with the pace of a man who was defeated. I felt it. I noticed it. I wondered if anyone else would have seen what I did. A warrior without his armor. A soldier wounded.

When he made it to me, he didn't greet me with a hello. He immediately wrapped his arms around me. I didn't protest. I wrapped my arms around his neck and hugged him back, willingly melting into his touch. I let him hold me because I felt how much he needed it. We stood in the middle of the quiet hallway like that for a while. For how long, I didn't know. Time didn't move the same with him. It didn't exist. We just . . . *were*. Him and me. No time. No problems. No wife. No wounds. No trauma. No loss babies. Just . . . us. Everything faded. I missed this so much. More than anything. This feeling was addictive. Nothing in the world felt better than this. When we connected, body to body, *soul to soul*, it was beautiful. It was fucking euphoric.

Next thing I knew, I was off my feet. Literally. I wasn't floating. None of that supernatural, high shit. He'd literally picked me up, and what did I do?

Wrap my damn legs around his waist and let him. He carried me down the hall to my apartment. I didn't have to put the code in. I kept my arms wrapped around his neck and my head rested on his shoulder. He put it in, and I didn't even have to tell him the code. Nosy bastard had to peek over my shoulder at it that night he brought me home from Vault.

When we got inside, he didn't put me down. He didn't come out of his shoes. I didn't come out of mine, or my coat, or hang my purse. He carried me straight to the bedroom, in the dark. The only light illuminating the apartment was the one I kept on in the guest bathroom. He sat on the bed, with me still wrapped around his waist. All of this was done in complete silence. The only noise between us was the loud smell of tequila literally oozing from him. He was drunk. He didn't just smell strong to me because I was sober. He literally smelled like a gallon of tequila. How was he able to stand, carry me, and without a stagger? Better yet, how did he even make it over here as drunk as he smelled?

"You're drunk," I said, finally breaking the silence.

"I miss you."

I sighed and rested my head on his chest, listening to the racing of his heart. He needed to leave. I should have told him to leave the minute I saw him at my door. Diamond would be so disappointed in me. Shit, I was disappointed in me. But this man, he was my fucking kryptonite. And he was in pain. What was I supposed to do? Neglect him? Even if I was that evil, I wouldn't do that because I couldn't. Literally, it would be physically impossible to.

"Do you miss me?" he asked as he began to caress my back.

"Does it matter?"

He pulled me away from his chest and cupped my face. With raised brows and his bottom lip pinched between his teeth, he nodded. His eyes . . . oh God, his eyes. They were bloodshot red and so got damn sad. I cupped his face and ran my hand over his beard.

"Jahad, are you okay?"

He gave me a lazy smile and nodded. "I wasn't. I'm good now, tho'."

I understood.

He delicately caressed my cheek. "Tell me you miss me too," he begged.

I ran my fingers through his scruffy, thick beard and cocked my head to the side. "I miss you too."

He gripped my chin and pulled me closer to his face. I didn't resist. Should have. But couldn't. He owned me, remember? I was healing. I wasn't healed. I still had a lot of fucking work to do.

When his lips touched mine, I wrapped my arms around his neck and deepened the kiss. I was back to jumping off that cliff. And man, it felt good.

For a second. I didn't let myself hit the bottom. Before I did, I saw her. Not Leighton. Leia. And then . . . I saw Leighton.

I pulled away, swallowed, and put my hand against his chest, pushing him away. "Jahad."

"That's new," he stated.

"What's new?"

"Resistance. You hate me too?"

I drew back with pinched brows. "What? Hate you, *too*? What are you talking about? How could I hate you?"

He didn't respond. He fell back on the bed and placed his hands on the sides of his head. He was so got damn drunk. I'd never seen him like this before. But then again, I hadn't seen many sides of Jahad. I didn't know much about this man but I'd fallen, anyway. Wasn't that crazy? I couldn't understand it, either. Mahogany's voice whispered in my mind. That part about us being predestined. I shook that thought away and crawled from his lap. I laid next to him, and propped my head up on my fist, digging my elbow into the mattress.

"Jahad."

"She told me she hated me," he suddenly said. "Said it was my fault Leia died." He turned to face me, bit down on his bottom lip, then asked, "Can you believe that shit?"

I couldn't. I *really* couldn't believe that. Leighton . . . really? I couldn't imagine her saying anything like that. Really? I was speechless. Literally loss for words. I didn't say anything for a while.

"You know that's not true, right?" I finally asked after studying him for a couple of minutes, because it seemed he really believed her. Like he'd let the ugly shit Leighton had likely said out of pain and anger get to him. "You should take what she says right now with a grain of salt. Right now, she's . . . she's not herself. Neither are you. You both went through something really traumatic. That makes people say ugly things. She didn't mean it. Leighton was high risk. Very high risk. She had multiple miscarriages. Multiple D&Cs so her cervix is damaged. The chances of her carrying to term, even with bed rest, were very low, Jahad. You know all of this, though. She does, too, so I don't have to expl—"

"Nah." He cut me off with a pause. He then turned away again and those red, sad eyes of his were on the ceiling. "She's right. Her reason for me being the reason might be wrong, but . . . she's right. It's my fault. It's my fault ours didn't make it, either." He turned to face me. With drowsy eyes, he slowly blinked with his mouth slightly turned down. "Don't even fix them pretty-ass lips to lie to me and tell me it wasn't mine. It *was* mine. If it wasn't, you would still have it."

I didn't know what the hell was going on.

He caressed my cheek before his arm lazily dropped back down onto the mattress. "I'm sorry, love."

He sighed and turned away again, closing his eyes. He slowly licked his lips and rested his hands on his chest. I grabbed them and interlocked my fingers with his. Electricity. Always electricity. The good kind. Not the kind that made you want to pull away.

"Is that the only reason you think the baby was yours?" I asked him with tears in my eyes.

He shook his head. "I just knew. I know shit. When it comes to you. I. Just. Know." He ran his fingers over the palm of my hand. "I wish it wasn't, though. You don't deserve what happened. You don't deserve this curse."

I blinked tears away and put my own sad eyes on the ceiling. "I was cursed before I met you. What happened wasn't your fault. Not to me. Not to Leighton."

"Yes, it was." He paused. *"Sa ou fè se li ou wè,"* he drunkenly mumbled.

"Hm?"

We turned to face each other at the same time. "You reap what you sow," he whispered as he brushed a tear from my cheek. "Karma. No one escapes karma. Not me. Especially not me."

This was . . . it was too much. I didn't like it. I didn't like the weight of our conversation. I would rather straddle him. Would rather have a mouth full of dick. Would rather swallow his nut than lie beside him, pouring our guts out like this. I wondered if when the sun rose he would regret this conversation. Jahad was a closed-off man. It took him a minute to even tell me why he was at Pandora's. Now he was in my bed, telling me his wife told him she hated him and blamed him for the miscarriage. He was too open. Most likely because he was drunk. I didn't like it. I liked him better closed-off because Jahad, with his wounds on full display, cut me wide fucking open. Not because I had wounds of my own. His pain was mine, too. I felt it. His on top of my own was just too much. I had to look away. "Stop talking like that."

"Stop crying," he told me as he brushed away another tear.

"Stop talking like that," I repeated.

"Stop talking like what? Stop telling my truth?"

"That's not your truth."

"How do you know? You don't know me. You don't know what I've done."

"You've done nothing to cost you the life of your child," I told him as I grabbed his hand to stop him from wiping another tear. I kissed his fingertips. I didn't know why. I wasn't the fingertip-kissing type of bitch. But I did it. Felt compelled to. "Children are innocent."

"I wish that was true, beautiful," he said, pulling his hand from mine to wrap it around my neck. "I've done a lot of shit. A lot of fucked-up shit that's cost me the lives of a lot of my children. *Ours* included. Nothing's excluded from karma."

He pulled me closer. We were nose to nose. So close. But I wanted to be closer. I wanted to crawl inside of his fucking skin but I needed to take him home. He was drunk. I was in love. We were in love . . . maybe? I didn't know. It was something. We couldn't keep our hands off each other. He couldn't stay away from me, and I couldn't resist him. It was . . . maybe it was a soul tie. Maybe we were predestined.

"Jahad, you're drunk and you're talking crazy. I need to take you home."

His face softened and he brushed his slender nose against mine. "I *am* at home."

"I know. Me too," I said with my eyes closed, enjoying the feel of him.

He was home for me too. Our eyes met and they said what our mouths couldn't. We might've felt at home, but we weren't really home. Home for him was that big-ass house in the suburbs with his wife. The one he needed to go home to.

I was backtracking, and it was easy. Very easy because Jahad felt so good. But the shit that was wrong for you always did, didn't it? How easy it was for me to give in to temptation didn't make me hate myself. It didn't make me want to crawl inside of a dark hole and stay there forever. It made me want to do better. I was aware of where I was going wrong, and I wouldn't have been if I had gotten drunk at the bar earlier.

Jahad was married. He was drunk. He'd just loss his child. He was in pain. Leighton was in pain. I was in pain. This was *still* a mess. A mess I didn't need to be a part of. Regardless of how fucking good it felt. Regardless of how in love I was. Regardless of how much I loved the way electricity transferred between us. And how much I floated with him. And how at home he felt. It was a big fucking mess I did not need. I already had a mountain of glitter-covered shit to clean up.

I opened my eyes and backed away. "Come on. Let's go. You need to go home to your wife."

I didn't know what I would say to Leighton, but I had a thirty-minute ride to figure something out. Shit, he was drunk as hell and smelled like a barrel of the finest tequila. Telling her I saw him at the bar would work perfectly fine.

He turned over on his back and put his hands back on the sides of his head. "*My wife* ain't there. She left."

I looked over my shoulder at him and felt so sorry for him. I almost let him stay. *Almost*. But I couldn't. Whatever they were going through, *they* were going through. I had put myself in the middle of it enough already. I was taking Jahad home.

It took a while, but eventually, I got Jahad inside of my car. He must have drunk most of the tequila when he made it to my apartment because getting him downstairs was nearly impossible. He was a staggering, Haitian-speaking mess. I could barely get him to the car, he was so heavy. I was tempted to say fuck it and let him stay, but letting him stay would lead to me fucking him and that would be no good for me. So, I used every bit of strength I had to keep him steady. Once I got him in the car, I rummaged around in his pockets for the keys to his car and found them so I could get the garage opener to the house. I figured, since he was drunk, using the key to the garage would be easier than asking him for the code to the front door.

The ride to his house was quiet. He was snoring ten minutes into it. My thoughts were all over the place. On Leighton mostly. I'd noticed the mean streak in her but I didn't know she was like that. Maybe she wasn't. She had just loss her baby. She was under a lot of pressure. But damn! To downright tell your husband you hated him and to blame him for the death of a baby you both loss was a bit much. Evil, honestly. Every now and then, I'd glance over at Jahad and the deep creases between his bushy eyebrows would make my heart ache. He was in so much pain. I couldn't imagine how that must've felt. I wondered how long he'd been at home alone, suffering through the loss of Leia by himself, with those feelings on his heart.

I opened the garage, pulled in, and shook him awake. It took another five minutes to wake him. Once he was up, he was a little disoriented.

"Can you walk?" I asked him.

He dragged his hands down his face. "Fuck."

"Jahad—"

"Yeah, I'm good. I'm smooth."

He wasn't smooth. He tried to get out of the car without taking off the seatbelt I had to put on for him. I reached over, unbuckled it for him, then he finally got out. I shook my head and quickly got out to rush over to his side to make sure he wouldn't fall.

He laughed. "Man, I'm good, shorty."

"No, you're not," I said as I tossed his arm over my shoulder and hooked my arm around his waist.

He really wasn't. Jahad was, just like before, a staggering fucking mess. I couldn't believe the day I was having. I had to be at work in the morning at eight and it was almost two in the morning. A couple of hours of sleep before work when I was nineteen, twenty was easy! A bitch was turning twenty-seven in a few weeks. That was pushing thirty—I needed my rest! I hadn't gone a night without rest all month. All it took was for this man, this beautiful disaster, to show up to throw things off. He was no good for me. So good for me, but no good at all. What sense did *that* make?

We made it into the house and through the kitchen without a problem. It wasn't until we got into the hallway near the elevator that we had an issue. He knocked over one of the floor vases, getting glass everywhere.

"Fuck it. Hated that shit, anyway," he slurred before reaching over to push the up button on the elevator. He leaned against it and eyed me up and down. "You staying with me?"

I shook my head. "No. I'm not staying with you, Jahad."

"Why not? You can sleep in the guest room, love," he said with a smile and a wink.

I turned my face up at him and crossed my arms over my chest. He was the playful type of drunk at this point. His emotions were tucked, and I was happy. I preferred this version of him over the other. This one kept a bandage over both of our wounds.

At the sound of the elevator coming, he pushed off the wall and was back by my side with his arm draped over my shoulder. I snaked my arm around his waist again. Wasn't sure if I really needed to or not, just did it because it felt good. We stepped onto the elevator and stayed that way. I even laid my head on his side and he dropped a kiss on top of it. We felt real. Like this was my house and we'd come home after a night out and my husband had too much to drink. Fantasy felt good as hell.

After stepping off the elevator onto the second floor, we headed down the long hallway with him lightly staggering. He sighed every now and then, drifting back and forth between goofy drunk and emotional drunk. He kept lowering his head, and then he would put it back up again. Even with that stagger, I could tell he was defeated and broken.

When we walked into the dark bedroom, he immediately stripped down to his boxer briefs. It took everything in me to keep my eyes on his.

"Can you at least tuck a nigga in?" he slurred before getting into the bed.

I shook my head and walked over to the bed to "tuck him in." I knew exactly what he was doing, and since I wasn't quite ready to leave him just yet, I played along with his little game. I stood at the bed, pulled the cover over his body and leaned down to kiss him on the forehead, but before my lips could touch it, his lips met mine.

I pulled back and cocked my head to the side. "Jah—"

He grabbed my arms, pulled me into the bed with him, and immediately wrapped his arms around me. "Stay."

"I can't stay," I protested. "I have to work in the morning, Jahad, and I can't . . . I can't stay with you. I don't feel right being here with you."

He didn't say anything. His hold on me grew tighter and he cuddled up closer to me. We were spooning. His dick was pressed against me. It wasn't hard but it didn't have to be for me to feel it. He was very well endowed. I needed to leave. I had to leave. I had no business in this woman's bed.

"Jahad." I nudged him in the stomach.

Nothing.

"I need to leave—"

"*Tanpri, renmen* (Please, love)," he grumbled before snoring filled my left ear.

I couldn't move. I was trapped. *Not really.* I mean, I could've moved. Especially when his snoring grew louder, and his grip loosened a bit. But I didn't. I fell asleep in his arms because . . . the fantasy . . . it felt so got damn good.

CHAPTER 33

Jahad

"The fuck—"

Whap!

Another blow to the jaw. I *wasn't* tripping. The first time I was hit, I thought I was dreaming. This time, I was wide awake and literally saw Leighton hit me in my shit. When I jumped up to grab her, she ran over to the other side of the bed where Sienna was sleeping. I grabbed her by the waist as soon as she jumped on the bed.

"Get off me! I knew it! I fucking knew it!" she screamed, kicking and crying, trying to get out of my hold. "But I didn't think you were that much of a bitch-made-ass nigga! And I didn't think I had a shady-ass, trifling, dirty bitch working for me! I come here to fix things and this is what I find!"

"Chill!" I yelled with my arms wrapped around her body and my face pressed against the side of hers.

Leighton was tweaking, and for what? This was a side of Leighton I hadn't seen in years. She had a mean streak and liked to run her mouth, but this wild, fighting shit? She hadn't been on this type of time in ages. For a minute, I forgot this side of her existed, so I was caught off guard. Both by her actions and her even being here. Leighton hadn't been home in over a month. The last time I saw her was at Leia's funeral. We had a small service with just her immediate family, Farrah, and my immediate family. Leia was cremated after. Yesterday, we picked up her remains, and when we left the funeral home, I went home alone to an empty house. That fucked with me. Tore me up, honestly.

Not even then did Leighton address me. She took Leia's remains with her. She let me rub and kiss the urn but that was it. When it was time to go, she picked it up and walked out of the funeral home without even looking my way. She had her girl with her. Farrah. Bitch had been enjoying every bit of what we'd been going through. Every second Leighton and I spent at odds was another second she spent getting back closer to her.

Nothing about Leighton's actions over this past month said she wanted to work on anything with me, so what the fuck was she even talking about?

"Oh, shit!" Sienna yelled, climbing out of bed, finally waking up. She scrambled to her feet and staggered as she tried to slide into her heels.

"Yeah, oh shit! Rise and shine, ho! Let me go, Jah, you bitch-ass nigga!"

See how she talks to me? I could never speak to shorty like that. Even at my angriest, I kept shit respectful. Leighton was viewed as this good girl. The perfect wife. One with grace, poise, and class because she listened to soulful shit, wore her hair in locs, and had an eccentric vibe to her, but she was bat shit crazy and didn't know how to control her emotions to save her life. In this case, her marriage.

Sienna didn't say anything. She ignored Leighton and continued to struggle to put her shoes on. Once they were on, she grabbed her phone from the nightstand and her purse. She looked over her shoulder at us, started to say something, but shook her head and headed out of the bedroom instead.

"You fake-ass bitch! You can't even look me in the eye! After everything! I let you in! I shared my world with you! I shared my pregnancy with you and you . . . you wanted a piece of my husband, too? You greedy, worthless bitch, you!" Leighton yelled.

She was hurt. So hurt, her entire body quivered. I didn't need to see her face to know she was crying, too. I heard the pain in her voice. She really liked Sienna. I hated this for her. My intentions were never to hurt Leighton. Sienna's neither. Despite the way it looked, we cared and tried to protect her from this as much as we humanly could. It was beyond us.

Sienna stopped at the door. I watched as she dropped her head. "I met him before I knew he was your husband, Leighton. I wasn't greedy. I just didn't know. And after I knew, I . . ." She sighed and shook her head. "I never wanted to hurt you." She looked over her shoulder at Leighton and then at me with tears in her eyes. "I'm sorry."

She walked out of the bedroom and Leighton continued to cry, kick, and scream. She clawed at my arms, drawing blood, telling me she hated me, calling me bitches and hos. I let her. I took the pain. Eventually, she'd tire herself out. None of it was new to me. Leighton had done worse. The hitting, the scratching, the name calling—she did the same shit back in the day. I took it on the chin then because I wasn't her husband. We were young, toxic, and wild as hell. Telling me she hated me back then was justified because she had every reason in the world to.

Today, she only had one reason to hate me. One reason that really wasn't even my fucking fault. She couldn't hate me because it was "my fault" Leia didn't make it. She could only hate me because I fell for another woman. She caused that, though. Another woman was the furthest thing from my mind until she forced that pass on me. Leighton and our baby were the only things I gave a fuck about. However, it would be selfish to put all the blame on Leighton. I did make the conscious decision to take it. I hated myself for a long-ass time for taking it. But shit, *I took it.* And I was happy I had. If I hadn't, I wouldn't have met her. I wouldn't have experienced *that.* Us. That pull. That electricity. Freedom. I loved that shit. Didn't want to go back to living life without it.

"You done?" I asked against her ear after she stopped yelling.

She was out of breath. The hysterical crying had subsided, and she'd stopped digging her nails into my skin. Once she nodded, I lowered her to the floor, stepped back, and rested against the dresser.

"Really? You fucked another bitch in our bed?" she asked, staring up at me with fire behind her eyes.

"She was fully dressed," I mentioned.

She approached me. "But she was in our bed."

I pushed up off the dresser and walked off to pick my joggers up off the floor. "Because I showed up at her house, drunk as fuck. She brought me home."

"That doesn't explain why she was in my fucking bed, Jahad!" she yelled, following me.

I leaned down and picked my pants up. With a deep breath, I slid them on and stuffed my hands into my pockets. Staring down at her, I asked, "You want to have a conversation or yell and have a conversation with yourself?"

I didn't argue. I didn't do the yelling back and forth and theatrical shit. Never had. Never would. Leighton knew how I was when it came to communication. If she wanted to talk, we would have to do it without screaming and disrespect. Otherwise, she wouldn't get shit up out of me.

"Go ahead," she said, gesturing at me. She put her hands behind her back and rocked back and forth. She was losing her mind. Shit was crazy. Sad, too, to be honest. I didn't want to bring the worst out of my wife. I'd tried not to. Had done everything in my power not to.

"She was in our bed because I asked her to stay," I honestly told her. Honesty was the only thing I had for Leighton. I had zero interest in sparing her feelings. We were past that now. I had no obligation to protect her heart because she hadn't given a single fuck about mine. "Like she said, we met before she knew I was your husband. I used the hall pass on her. Two weeks later, she walked into our bedroom as the new doula."

"And you let her work here."

"I asked her to quit. She wouldn't. Firing her wasn't an option," I said as I brushed a hand over the back of my neck.

"Why wasn't it? Because you wanted to keep fucking her? Because you—"

"Because I wasn't going to stop her bag because we had a one-night stand. That's why. What we did didn't have shit to do with her job performance. You wanted a Black doula, you got one. You liked her ass too. Loved her. Couldn't stop talking about her."

"You let me," she whispered with tight lips. "You let me like her and—" She paused and tossed her head back. "Oh my God. How fucking humiliating! You paraded this bitch in my face and you were fucking—" She looked at me with a squint. "Did you fuck her in my house, Jahad?"

I ran my tongue over my bottom lip and watched as she paced. She was spiraling. Her fists were balled, and she was crying again. Her locs had fallen from the bun she had them in, so they were tossed all over her head. Her hazel eyes were bulging, and her lips were tight. Leighton wanted to fight. I wanted her to leave. This shit was exhausting.

"I didn't parade her around you. You think I wanted her here? You think I enjoyed that shit? I didn't. That shit wasn't fun for me, Leigh."

"There you go again." She chuckled. "Ignoring my question. Just like you did at the gender reveal when I asked you if you were staring at her. It all makes sense now. The perfume I smelled on you. The same scent I smelled on her. The way you were looking at her. You . . . You fucked her in my house, didn't you?"

I stared at her for a minute, not intimidatingly. Literally just stared at her, searching for the person she used to be. Not the woman before we loss Leia. Nah, Leighton was gone long before that. I might've been gone off my ass last night but I heard everything Sienna said. I was lucid. I knew what I said, too, and had no regrets about it. She said Leighton had suffered a traumatic loss so she wasn't herself. Leighton hadn't been herself for years. And yeah, the miscarriages might've played a part—I was sure they had—but at what point does that stop being an excuse for being a fucked-up-ass person toward your husband, the muthafucka you're supposed to fight those types of battles *with*. Yeah, we rocked through problems together but that was all me. I was the one who kept us together. I'd held on by my muthafuckin' self in a loveless-ass marriage with a selfish woman who didn't appreciate any of it.

I snorted and dragged my top teeth over my bottom lip. "Yeah, I fucked her in the crib," I nonchalantly told her with a shrug. "In the kitchen you love so much. I would've fucked her in the bed you barely gave me pussy in, but I was too drunk to stay up."

I didn't give a fuck anymore. Stopped giving a fuck when she blamed me. I never knew what a broken heart felt like until she told me she hated me and blamed me for the loss of our child. Nothing I've ever done could ever compare to that shit. The love I had for Leighton was gone. She'd hurt me unimaginably. I could never forgive her for that. I had no obligation to spare her feelings anymore. She pushed me to a point of no return.

What Ms. Evaline say? I held on for as long as I could. Held on until my fucking hands bled. Until my skin was ripped to the fucking white meat. I was done. I couldn't hold on anymore. At some point, I had to do what was best for me. Holding on had a nigga suffering. The choice wasn't easy to make. Letting go, it was hard as hell for me to do that. To her, it might've looked easy. To her, it might've looked like I was choosing Sienna over her. But I wasn't. I was choosing myself.

Her jaw dropped and she stood up, then charged at me with wild fists. This time, I caught them and held her against my chest.

"You blamed me!" I yelled in her face with bulging eyes, so loud, my entire body shook.

I didn't yell. This wasn't me.

But she *had* to feel me.

I needed her to understand what that felt like. I needed her to understand why she needed to stop trying to fight me. She really had no reason to. She couldn't hurt me. Her small-ass fists didn't do damage, anyway. Still, she could grab the Drac' out the closet, squeeze off on me, and that still wouldn't hurt nearly as bad as her blaming me for Leia's death had.

I swallowed a knot in my throat, fighting back emotions. "You blamed me," I whispered, and pointed to my chest. "Told me you hated me. Blamed me. Left me. In this house . . . this big-ass house I didn't even fuckin' want . . . to suffer another loss by. My. Self."

"You . . . you fucked her—"

"Fuck her!" I yelled again, causing her to flinch. "This is about us!"

She didn't get it. I felt like . . . I mean, she had to get it. She couldn't be that fuckin' stupid. Leighton went to college. Had a nice-ass education. Me?

I had shit. I didn't get good schooling until I touched the States, and even my comprehension was better than hers. How could she not see what the fuck I was getting at? The root of our problems began long before I even knew Sienna existed. The fuck was she even talking about?

"I wouldn't have had to fuck her if you gave a fuck about me, dumbass," I snapped.

I was reverting. Untucking the young, wild, mannish, ignorant hood nigga I worked so hard to keep tucked. Just like I brought out the worst in Leighton, she'd brought out the worst in me.

"Dumbass? I—"

"Yeah, *dumbass*," I interrupted, steady staring into her eyes. "That's the only shit you care about. Me fucking another bitch. I fucked her. In your kitchen, on the island. And I'm gon' fuck her again. The same way I used to fuck you, but better because she give a nigga something you can't. Don't cry now, Leigh. This what you want to talk about, right? You don't want to talk about the way you hurt me. You don't want to talk about the way you treated me like a sperm bank for the past couple years. Me fuckin' Sienna is way more important than any of that shit, right?"

She pushed away from me and began to pace back and forth, wiping tears from her face.

Did I go too far? Fuck it. It was too late. I didn't give a fuck, anyway. Why should I? My feelings never meant shit to her. The past month had shown me that clear as day. She had a one-track mind. All she cared about was what I'd done, but not about what she'd done to make me do it. Shit was crazy. The lack of accountability.

"I can't believe you're talking to me like this," she cried.

My phone rang and I fished around my pocket to answer it. It was my pops. I stared at the screen and let it ring until it went to voicemail. He'd called me five times since yesterday. I didn't have shit to say to him. Nothing nice, at least. I was at my wits' end with him too. Samuel had been missing through this entire process. The loss of my child. I hadn't heard a single condolence from him. The crazy part about it was, I hadn't expected anything from him. That was how Samuel operated. He didn't show an ounce of weakness. That was why I was the way I was. Closed off. I kept the way I felt bottled up because he taught me to. Showing any sign of discomfort was seen as weak. Baptiste men were to hold their heads high and take losses on the chin. The only emotion we were actually allowed to freely express was anger. That was why Blaise was the way he was. Angry and unhinged all the time. Saint was different. He was the happy one. Lively and outgoing. And me . . . I was quiet. Rarely ever showed any type of emotion at all. That made me the worst because I had a lot of pent-up aggression. Toward my wife especially.

"You done?" I asked. "Because if all you want to talk about is what I did with my dick, then this conversation is over."

She looked over her shoulder at me. "I'm sorry, Jahad. Okay? I'm sorry!"

I nodded. "'Preciate that."

She drew back. "'Preciate that? Is that all you have to say?"

"Is that all *you* have to say?"

She walked over and sat on the bed. Wrapping her arms around her body, she shook her head. "I-I have a lot to say. A lot . . . A lot to apologize about."

I crossed my arms over my chest and hit the silence switch on the side of my phone when it began to ring again. Then I waited. Waited for Leighton to say something of significance. Waited for her to give me a thoughtful apology. Something worth listening to. Something from the heart. And ultimately, she gave it to me. When I knew she was ready to talk like married, civilized adults, I pushed away from the dresser and sat beside her. I owed her that much. A respectable conversation, face to face, without tension, frowns, and bad energy. And as she cried, I wiped her face clean of tears. Rubbed her back and held her when the heaviest shit came up. Despite the way I felt about Leighton, I'd always respect her. At one point in time, she meant the world to me. She was the light of my life. My world. My forever. The respect would always be there. Love, too.

After about an hour of talking, she took a deep breath and reached for my hands.

"Jah," she said. "Listen, I . . ." She lowered her head and shook it. "I didn't mean what I said. About Leia. I didn't mean it." She looked back up at me and she was crying again. "I don't hate you. I love you. And I hope you can one day forgive me. I—"

"I need you to look at me when you say that," I interrupted.

"What?"

"I need you to look me in the eye when you say you didn't mean it, Leighton," I reiterated.

Her grip on my hands tightened and her eyebrows rose a bit. That was enough for me. I didn't need her to look me in the eye and say anything. I pulled my hands out of hers and stood up.

"Wha-what's wrong? Jahad—"

"You meant what you said. Stand on that shit, Leighton. And I will never forgive you for that. Asking me to is wild. *Especially* since you meant it. That's the problem. The biggest problem."

She pulled her lips into her mouth and shook her head. "So . . . what are you saying?"

"I'm saying . . . this is the end for us, love."

She looked up at me and kicked her legs from underneath her bottom to stand. "Because of her? It's because of her, isn't it?"

I laughed and shook my head. "After everything we just talked about, you're *still* looking outside of us." I walked off and headed to the bathroom. "It's about *us*. Just us, Leigh."

I slapped hands with Blaise. *"Sak pase, fré."*

"N'ap boule." He pulled from his blunt before putting it out on the brick column and eyed me up and down with a squint. "This a friendly meeting?"

I smirked and pulled the glass door to my parents' house open and said nothing. After my shower, I walked out of the bathroom to an empty bedroom. Leighton was gone, as were a few more of her things. Good. She sent me a text a minute ago. She apologized again and told me she would give me an easy, painless divorce. I didn't have the emotional capacity to text her back.

"This nigga," Blaise grumbled as we walked into the house.

As usual, the smell of food greeted me at the door. Any time Momma got whiff of us coming through, she hit the kitchen. I appreciated the hell out of that but the furthest thing from my mind was food. Which was crazy since I hadn't eaten since yesterday afternoon.

As soon as Bebe saw us walk into the living room, she dropped her dolls and ran over to her father. He scooped her up and showered her with kisses. Bebe was the only person on earth Blaise had a heart with. Not even Moms got that type of love from him.

"Hi, Uncle Jah!" she bashfully said, as Blaise tickled her.

I kissed her on top of her messy, curly hair and pinched her chubby cheek. "*Bonswa*, Bebe." With a cocked brow, I waited for her response.

"Uhhh . . ." She looked around and twirled her hair around her finger. *"Bonj—"*

"It's not morning time anymore, is it, princess?" Blaise asked before she could finish.

With a big smile and raised brows, she said, *"Bonswa!"*

I put my hand up and she slapped it, giving me a high five. Bebe was four. Blaise didn't start teaching her our language until a couple of months ago. There was nothing wrong with that. At least she was learning it.

The minute I walked into the kitchen, my mother greeted me with a hug and two kisses on both cheeks. She asked me how I was doing and didn't mention Leighton at all. The shit Leighton and I were going through was no secret. It was for the first couple of weeks, but after the service, I couldn't hide it anymore. Since we didn't sit together and didn't speak, it was clear something was wrong. So, I said fuck it and told them. After the service, we came here and had a light meeting. I told them things weren't looking good and I didn't want to be asked about her again. They hadn't and I appreciated them for it. My mother the most. She might've loved Leighton, but she didn't tolerate anybody mistreating her children.

"I made your favorite," she said with a smile before hustling back over to the big pot on the stove. "*Joumou* (Squash soup)."

"Mesi," I said, with my hand over my chest. "Put it in a to-go container for me, little lady."

Both she and my father looked at me, both with concern for very distinct reasons. If I'd turned down my mother's cooking, then whatever I wanted to speak to him about was grave. My mother thought I was sick because that was the only reason I wouldn't eat as soon as I stepped foot in her house. When she approached, she untied her apron, took it off, and laid it on the island. "Are you ok—"

"I'm fine, *Manman*," I assured her, cupping her face with my eyes on hers. "I just have a busy day ahead of me."

That was only partially true. I did have a busy day, but I had time to eat. Just not now. The only reason I was here was for business. Nothing more, nothing less. I didn't want food. I wanted to have the conversation with my father I should have had with him years ago.

About ten minutes later, Saint arrived. Thank God. The ten minutes we waited for him in Samuel's office was intense. We sat in silence, with him staring at me, and me staring right back at him. Blaise paced back and forth behind us, oblivious to the tension between us because he was busy on the phone, smiling, talking shit to another bitch he was adding to his roster of cult members.

"Damn, what did I walk into?" Saint asked as we slapped hands.

"Sak pase," I greeted him, ignoring the grin he wore.

His eyebrows furrowed as he looked back and forth between Samuel and me. *"Sak pase . . ."* He let go of my hand and shook hands with Samuel before greeting Blaise the same way once he came out of the connected bathroom.

"Somebody want to fill me in on what's going on?" Saint asked, adjusting his jeans as he sat down.

Me in the middle.

Blaise on the right.

Saint on the left.

After today, that would change.

Blaise, leaning over to the side, stroking his short beard, said, "Yeah, bro. Fill us in."

I didn't have anything to say to them directly, but they needed to be here because the decision I had made affected them.

"Pops," I said with a squint. "When was my daughter born?"

He leaned forward in his chair and rested his elbows on the desk. After interlocking his fingers, he rested his hands there, too. "What?"

"My daughter. *Pitit fi ou* (Your granddaughter). Leia."

He lifted one of his hands from the desk and began to stroke his salt-and-pepper-colored beard with a grimace. "Last month."

"February seventeenth," Saint answered.

"I appreciate that, baby bro, but I wasn't talkin' to you," I said. Pointing at Samuel, I continued, "I was talkin' to him."

The room was quiet for a good five minutes before Samuel cleared his throat and offered up a poor excuse. With a light chuckle, he said, "You know me, I'm no good with birthdays. I don't even know your birthday. Or his. Or his. Or Natasha's. Not even your mother's."

"And you're proud of that?" I asked, with raised brows. I sat back against the chair and stuffed my hands into the pockets of my Amiri varsity jacket. "When I was a boy, I looked up to you. I wanted to be just like you. When you left and told me I was the man of the house, I became you. I put in work. I hustled. Made sure everybody ate. Made sure niggas knew that me being a li'l nigga didn't mean shit because . . ." I laughed. "I had big sticks on me. Big, big sticks and I knew how to use 'em, too. Thanks to you. You put me in the field young. Shit, it's sad that I'm really just realizing it, but even back then, you were grooming me." I cocked my head back with a frown. "Huh . . . I thought that shit didn't start until we came here—"

He stood up and slammed his fist down on the desk. *"Kiyès—"*

"Aye, let me talk," I interrupted with my eyes coldly shifted up at him. "That's the least you can do for me. You couldn't even tell me my dead daughter's birthday. Respect me enough to let me fuckin' talk."

From the corner of my eye, I noticed both Blaise and Saint run a hand over their heads.

Samuel slowly ran his tongue over his bottom lip and sat down with a menacing scowl on his face.

Nodding, I continued. "Like I was saying, I gave you everything. Every part of my life has been devoted to doing what you wanted me to do. You left,

I was in charge. You came back and got us . . . You played me, groomed me into this." I motioned at myself. "Made me believe we were bonding, but what you were really doing was grooming me again. I'm thirty, going on thirty-one and you've been the master puppeteer in my story all of my life. This life, this drug shit. Late-night calls, inconsiderate muthafuckas blowing my line down when I'm dealing with the loss of my fuckin' baby. This ain't for me, yo. I never wanted this shit. This . . . this was your dream, not mine. I've been miserable in this shit for years. *Years*, Pops. But I took it on the chin 'cause that's what I was taught to do. But the way you handled me this past month, the way you ignored what happened, what I been through . . . ignored my daughter, ignored my pain . . . Nah, I can't rock with it." I pinched the bridge of my nose and adjusted my posture. "Anyway, long story short, I'm done. I'm finished. Saint is better suited for the position. Blaise . . . nah, this isn't for him."

"Nigga, what?" Saint asked with a confused look on his face. "You didn't want to discuss that with me first?"

I didn't need to. Saint was ready. He may've been young, but he was mature and knew how to handle himself in a room full of people who didn't look like him. I didn't just pull the decision out of my ass because Blaise had refused. Nah, not at all. I could have mentioned Emu. But I didn't. I thought long and carefully about this conversation. I didn't just reach the decision to have it today. Any time my father called to talk about anything other than Leia, the decision to leave became clearer. I'd wanted out for a long time. The way he treated me when I needed him the most just made leaving easier. The timing was perfect. Not just for me but for them too. The love I had for my brothers would never allow me to walk away from the business if we were still dealing with the fallout behind that shit with Walker. Business was as flawless as business was before Walker's investigation. The trucks were moving, deliveries were on time, everything was copacetic.

"You want to quit because I didn't baby you? Because I didn't hug and kiss you and tell you it will be okay? You want a hug, Jahad? You want me to tuck you in at night too?" he chastised me. "*Fè yon moun* (Be a man)!"

I stood up from my chair and leaned over the desk. "Be a better father, nigga."

When he jumped up and raised his fist at me, I didn't move a muscle. Samuel didn't intimidate me anymore. He stopped intimidating me when he made me his equal. I respected my father, but I didn't fear him. Not like I did when I was a child. I was a grown-ass man who was fed up with being taken advantage of. I gave my father my whole life. Every bit of it. I didn't have a true identity of my own because, in a sense, he built me. Who I was, outside of the dope game, was overshadowed because I gave so much of myself to it. I wanted to pour more of myself into real estate. I wanted to go back home for a little while. Grab some land out there. Do something other than the illegal shit we did whenever we'd go back. I was tired of being Samuel's puppet. I was tired of demons I acquired fucking with him, riding on my back.

"I made you who you are because you are a warrior! Always have been! You were built for this!" he yelled, as I walked out of the office.

Warrior. That was what he'd always called me. I was prematurely born at three pounds and had a lot of complications during my mother's pregnancy. I wasn't supposed to make it, so because I survived, he thought that meant make me work harder? Treat me like I could handle anything without breaking? Like the weight of the world on my shoulders would be light because I had survived so much? What sense did that make?

"'Preciate it, sis," I said to Natasha as I climbed out of her car.

She smiled. "You know I got you," she said with a pause. "Hey, you sure you okay?"

I nodded and placed my hand over my heart. "I'm good."

"Well, what is your car doing—"

"Thanks again, sis. Hit me if you need anything," I interrupted before I closed the car door and walked away.

Her ass stayed in my business. If it wasn't for the way I ended shit back at my parents' house, I would have had Saint bring me. But I left right after I said what I had to say. With my bowl of *joumou,* of course.

I stood around the parking lot and scanning it, debating my next move. I flicked my wrist to check the time on my watch. It was after seven. She was home. Sienna, of course. Peeped her car when Natasha pulled into the parking lot. Instead of asking her to pull up at the entrance, I had her pull around to my car. Then I thought it would be best for me to hop in my whip and leave. I doubted if she wanted to see me. Shit didn't end well with us. My wife tried to fight her, and last night, I showed up at her spot, drunk as hell after not speaking to her for over a month.

I popped up on her because I had to. I could've called like a normal person, but a phone conversation wouldn't have sufficed. I had to *feel* her, too. I went a full thirty-seven days without seeing her. Without touching her. Without feeling her. Without hearing her. I couldn't go another one. It was torture and I'd had enough torture in my life. I needed *it.* The *thing* that only she could give me. So, I dropped by. I shouldn't have done that. I realized I shouldn't have done it the minute she rejected me. She was different. Something about her.

It was in her essence. For a second, I thought maybe she was in a relationship, but then I realized what it was. She was working on herself. Her apartment was decorated; she had new furniture. She had a different light to her. She was brighter. The brightest I'd ever seen her. Her aura, I mean. She wasn't that woman who cried when she thought no one was watching anymore. At least that was what she felt like.

Just as I was about to say fuck it and get in my car to pull off, I felt it. That pull.

It was light. So light that a nigga really could've imagined it. So, I ignored it and opened the car door. I got inside, set the bowl down, and pushed the start button. Before I shifted the car into reverse, I felt it again. This one was different. More aggressive than before. I tossed my head back against the headrest, shifted the car into park, cut the engine, and got out.

A couple of minutes later, I was in the building. Walked in behind someone else. She needed to move. It was way too easy to get in this bitch. The pull grew more aggressive the higher the elevator climbed. I rested my back against the wall and watched the fluorescent lights as the elevator climbed to the tenth floor.

Ding.

I stepped off and continued down the hall. The smell of fried chicken made my stomach growl. I ran my hand down over my waves as I made it closer to her door. I was nervous. Why was I nervous? Probably because I'd given her every reason to slam the door in my face when she saw me at it. Because since she'd met me, all it had been was bullshit.

I stood at the door, knocked, and waited. I thought about tapping in the code I wasn't supposed to have, but breaking in would've only made things worse. I leaned against the back wall with my hands in my pockets, heart racing, waiting. *For rejection.* I knew it was coming. I felt it. I couldn't leave, though. Something inside of me told me that regardless of the resistance she put up last night, she still couldn't *really* resist me. Was it arrogance? Probably.

I knew she was trying to do better. I knew I would potentially poison her life with the bullshit I had attached to me. But for a split second, I didn't give a fuck because what I wanted was more important. I wanted to be selfish. I wanted to use the power I had over her against her. I knew she was powerless against me. I knew regardless of how much she'd try to resist that pull between us, she really couldn't. I couldn't do that, though. Plotting to use what neither of us could control made me a bitch-ass nigga.

I shook my head and pushed up off the wall to leave. Just as I walked off, she opened the door.

She stepped out into the hallway and wrapped her arms around her body. Looking up at me, she said, "Hey. Came to get your car?"

Yeah, and to tell you just how painful those thirty-seven days were without you.

"Yeah," I said, with my eyes locked on hers. "I appreciate you makin' sure I got to the crib last night."

She smiled. "Of course. You did the same thing for me, didn't you?"

I nodded and bit down over my bottom lip. Time did that thing. *We* did our thing. Stood there, staring into each other's eyes until she took a deep breath and looked over her shoulder at the closed door.

"My best friend is here. She's waiting for me."

"My bad about this morning—"

"No need to mention it." She interrupted me as she ran her hands over her skin. I wondered if she'd gotten a chill too. "Shit happens. It happened."

"Right," I said, steady struggling to find my fucking words. What the fuck was wrong with me?

She pursed her lips together and nodded. "Yep. Goodbye—"

"We don't say goodbye," I interrupted her with furrowed brows.

We didn't. We never had. In the short time knowing Sienna, we'd never said goodbye. *Good night, see you tomorrow*, shit like that, yeah. Never *goodbye*. Goodbyes didn't apply to us. It never would. If life didn't purposely put us together, that pull would. It was fate. She was my destiny. For a while, I struggled with this. With trying to figure out what the fuck *this* was. I struggled with understanding why I didn't feel *this* with Leighton, someone I saw as my forever. And I had my answer. Because Leighton wasn't my destiny. She wasn't my forever. She wasn't for me.

Sienna was. Leighton was a pathway.

I was sure of it. Confidence came easily when it concerned Sienna.

She was for me, and I was for her. That was it.

"Today we do," she whispered, slowly lowering her gaze to the floor.

I gripped her dainty chin and lifted her head so her eyes could meet mine. "You want me to believe that, you gon' have to look me in the eye when you say it, love."

I waited. With a racing heart, I waited for her to reject me. Waited for her to resist me. Arrogance told me she wouldn't. The look of finality in her eyes told me she would. A look of finality that shook me to my core like nothing in the world ever had. I couldn't go back to a life without this. Every day of my life would be spent searching for something I knew I'd never find. And every day, I would live in agony without it. Without her.

But then I remembered, *this* . . . it wasn't up to *us*.

"Today we do," she said, this time with confidence. Head held high, shoulders pushed back, and gorgeous brown eyes on mine.

I nodded, closed the space in between us, gripped her face, and kissed her on the forehead. "Okay, my love."

I wanted to do more.

Wanted to kiss her on the lips.

Wanted to hold her in my arms and never let her go.

But I didn't do any of that. Instead, I walked away. I trusted that life would do its thing and bring her back to me. This time, I was going to leave it up to that. The universe. God. Whatever. Whoever. When thirty-seven days doubled, tripled, quadrupled and shit got too heavy, I would let it, with the confidence of knowing I would see her again.

This wasn't goodbye.

This was *see you later*.

CHAPTER 34

Leighton

Knock. Knock. Knock.

"Can I come in?" Farrah asked from the bedroom door.

I pulled the comforter over my shoulder and shrugged. "I don't care."

The bedroom door creaked open, and before she could, I told her not to turn the light on. I wanted to lie in the dark like I had since I'd made it back hours ago. I thought my days of lying in bed all day were over. Damn near every day since I loss Leia had been spent in bed. How ironic was that? I wanted to be out of bed so badly when I was pregnant. I couldn't wait to walk around and explore. But I hadn't done much of anything. The past month had been literal hell.

The first two weeks were spent crying all day, every day. I didn't miss a day. I didn't miss a minute. Every single moment of my life was spent crying. And when I ran out of tears, I still cried. Running out of tears, I didn't think that was possible, but when you cry as much as I cried without eating, sleeping, and barely drinking, it was. So, I cried tearless tears, cursing Jahad. Cursing God, asking Him why. I was depressed. I wanted to die. Wanted to be with my babies. All four of them. I hated my life. I didn't want to live anymore. I was ready to clock out. I had the pills and I had *several* unfinished beverages to wash them down with.

I got as far as removing the cap from the medicine bottle before my phone rang. There was nothing new about that. It always rang, but because the call came when it did, I wanted to see who it was. So, I reached over and checked. It was Rome. The first thing he said when I answered it was *"Create." Then "That's what we creatives do. When the world around us is at its ugliest, we create the beauty we want to see."* I didn't know what it was about what he said but it resonated with me in an unimaginable way. I told him I didn't have any supplies with me and he told me I did. He had some shipped to Farrah's house and they had just arrived.

That day, I found purpose. I finished a meal, drank two water bottles, got out of bed, and painted. Painted until the sun set and rose again. And it felt good. I created two beautiful pieces and called him right after. I wasn't happy but I felt alive. I felt like I could keep going. Hope? Didn't have any of that, but I had purpose. At that time, purpose was the only thing I needed to keep going. Hope would be pushing it. Hope would come eventually, I *hoped.* I thought finally going home to talk to my husband would bring me closer to it.

But nope.

Going home pushed me further away from it. Going home pushed me right back into the bed. I hated this damn bed and I hated being at this fucking house. I was miserable.

Miserable would be an understatement, honestly.

What's worse than being miserable? Whatever it was, I was that.

"I got Julio!" Farrah said with a smile as she climbed into bed with me. "Your favorite."

I could drink. Thank God, I could drink. I'd done a lot of that lately. It didn't do anything but make me emotional, but I slept good. I didn't have any nightmares. That was a plus.

She poured me a glass and I slid from up under the covers to lean against the headboard.

She handed me the glass. "What do you want to get for dinner? I was thinking pizza. You need to eat."

"Yeah, I guess that's cool."

I didn't want to eat, I wanted to go back home. To Jahad. My husband . . . who wouldn't be my husband soon. My heart broke every time I thought about it. Every time I thought about them. Him and . . . fuck. Sienna. Pained me to even think of them.

Sienna and Jahad. They were a thing. Well, not really. He used the pass on her. What were the odds? It was unbelievable. The story he told me about meeting her at the club and then how she just showed up as my doula was very unbelievable, and if the story would have come from someone other than Jahad, I wouldn't have believed it. But he had no reason to lie to me. Why would he protect my feelings when I hadn't cared about his? Jahad hated me. He didn't care about me. I realized that the minute he told me he fucked her in our kitchen. That tore me up. But again, I deserved it. I deserved every mean thing he said to me. Because I had been so mean and nasty toward him, and for so long, this situation I was in? I put myself in it. I couldn't do anything but lie in the bed I made.

I tossed my head back against the tufted headboard and softly knocked against it a couple of times. What was this? Why was this life? This felt like punishment. This whole thing. My entire fucking life. I had sisters who didn't give a fuck about me. Parents who kept making excuses for them, so I didn't want to speak to them. And a best friend who enjoyed my pain. She didn't think I noticed, but I saw it. She loved it.

When I told her I was going home to talk to Jahad, she was pissed. She barely said anything to me when I left the next morning, but when I came back with a face full of tears, she greeted me with fake-ass sympathy and open arms. I ended up telling her what I walked into. I told her everything. About the hall pass, too. And what did she do? Blame him. Blamed him for everything. Of course she did. I wouldn't have expected anything less from Farrah.

She slid underneath the comforter with me. "Did you do it yet?"

"Did I do what, Farrah?"

She pulled her phone from the pocket of her shorts. "Take the posts down and leave the reviews under the ad?" she asked. "It's been damn near a week. You should have done it by now."

"I told you I wasn't doing that," I said before taking a hefty sip of my drink.

She sucked her teeth. "I'll leave the reviews, then. The fuck? That ghetto-ass company. You need to warn people. She's a shady-ass bitch. Trifling-ass ho."

I cut my eyes at her and snatched her phone from her hands. "No, you're not, Farrah. Damn." With tears in my eyes, I took another sip of my drink. A big one. A heftier one than the last. I kept drinking. Drank until the glass was fucking empty.

She wanted me to delete the posts about Serene Mommy Doula Services from my page. She wanted me to leave nasty reviews about Sienna and the company on their page and under the sponsored ad they had running, but I couldn't do that. For a while, I wanted to. Initially, I wanted to rip the bitch's head off. I wanted to kill her. I wanted to kill them both. She and Jahad. I hated them. So much. But then, I didn't. I just hated myself for letting this happen. I opened the door for her to walk into my life long before she actually did. Long before I met her. I opened that door the minute I offered Jahad that pass. Before he accepted it.

"Did she not fuck him in your house, tho'? In your fuckin' kitchen? On your island? Bitch—"

"I've done things on that island, too," I reminded her. "*We've* done things on that island."

She looked over at me, pulled her lips into her mouth, and then took a sip of her drink. "That was years ago."

"It still happened," I pointed out.

She squinted at me. "He cheated on you. With your doula."

"I cheated on him. With my best friend."

"That's different! I knew you first. You were mine first."

"I was *never* yours, Farrah," I said with a stiffened laugh, snatching the bottle from between her legs.

Farrah rolled her eyes at me, took a deep breath, and sipped from her cup. "Whatever, Leigh. You know what I mean."

That was Farrah's issue. She always thought I was *hers*. We *really* did grow up close and people *really* did think it was weird. Because it was. We weren't the typical best friends. Initially, we were. At fifteen, things changed. We started to mess around. Our bodies changed, the world around us changed, and we got curious. Exploring sexual curiosity with each other made the most sense, so that was what we did. We went from kissing to touching, and then to humping. And then at seventeen, we were practically full-blown bisexual. Still virgins, but going down on each other on the regular. We were having fun, that was it. We weren't *together*. I wasn't hers and she for damn sure wasn't mine. We had boyfriends but we messed around too. It was our thing. Boyfriends didn't stop a thing. Not until I got with that fucking Jahad Baptiste.

Farrah hated him. Hated him for stopping something that had gone on for years. We didn't talk about it, though. It just stopped. She would say she didn't like him because "he changed me" and because "he had taken her spot." Shit like that. We both knew exactly what it was. "Jahad was never in the plan" because stopping was never in the plan. Years passed before we had sex again. Sometimes, I'd think back on it, feel like she planned it.

When the house was built, and Jahad was away on business, Farrah and I celebrated. We celebrated a little too hard and got a little too drunk. We got so drunk, we forgot we weren't teenagers anymore. Forgot we were grown-ass married women with whole lives and commitments. Grown-ass women who hadn't "played" in years. Well, I didn't forget. She did.

We were in the kitchen. I was sitting on the island, and somehow, she ended up standing between my legs. Before I knew it, her lips were on mine, and then they weren't. They were between my legs and under my dress, and I let them stay there until they were coated in my cream. Technically, *I* didn't do anything. Farrah did and I let her. Still, there was no excuse for my actions. I cheated and felt shame about it right after. However, she didn't. She didn't think anything was wrong with it. She wanted to "go back to how things used to be." I thought she was insane. But later, I learned that the only reason she didn't have an issue with it was because Mike was having an affair. I was happy in my marriage, though. The happiest I'd *ever* been in my marriage and didn't want to do anything to jeopardize it. After that, things got weird, and after her divorce, things got weirder. She got clingier, and getting her to keep her hands and mouth off me was harder.

I poured myself another drink and took a sip from it. "Like I said, I'm not doing it. I'm not going to bash that bitch or the company on social media. I blew my own life up. Everything I'm going through, it's all on me."

Leia too. Sitting alone, in silence, facing my bullshit head on made me face the facts. I had been so busy blaming Jahad for every wrong thing in my life, I hadn't stopped to look in the mirror once. I was the reason. Me. I should've stopped trying. I should've listened to my husband. He didn't want to try for another baby. I did. He brought up the option to adopt. I was stubborn. I didn't want a child if it didn't come directly from me. He mentioned a surrogate. I didn't want to do that. And when I saw that the best OB-GYN in the country wasn't taking on new patients, that should have been a sign for me to wait until he was. But I opted to go for anybody other than the one I had before. Because I was impatient. Because I felt like my biological clock was ticking and I wanted a baby. More than anything. But, after all of that, I ended up without one and without a husband too. Without a family.

I looked over at Farrah. *Like her.*

She shrugged and finished her glass off before setting it on the nightstand. "Fuck it, then. And it's not all on you. It's on them, too. But that's neither here nor there. We don't have to keep talking about that shit. It's not even important. What's important is getting through it, and the good part about that is"—she paused and winked—"you don't have to do it alone. I'll always be here."

Oh, I knew that. I was reminded of it every single day. I appreciated her. Loved her with my entire heart. But I couldn't just have her for the rest of my life. I wanted more. I wanted my husband. I wanted my family. The only reason Jahad didn't have to drag me out of our house kicking and screaming was because I'd done enough already. So, I let him go. I was peaceful because Jahad deserved that much.

She finished her drink, set it on the nightstand next to her, and reached under the cover to wrap her arm around my waist. "Mike left. Jahad left. But we never left each other."

The closer she got to me, the more I felt myself slipping. Us slipping. To a place of no return. To a place she was trying to take me. A place I didn't want to go. A place we wouldn't be able to come back from if she tried to take me there. Farrah was playing on my fragility. She wanted me weak. She loved that "I needed her." She wanted me right here, in this big-ass house, with her, forever. She wanted me all to herself because she thought I was hers. She wasn't a best friend supporting her best friend who'd loss her child and her husband in the same month. She was easing up on me, getting closer and closer to me, so she could get closer to what was between my legs. So things could go back to the way they used to be.

I wasn't a teenager anymore. I wasn't confused. I didn't need to explore. I was confident in who I was and what I wanted and I wasn't too drunk to see what was going on like I was that night in the kitchen. These days, I needed a lot more than two cups of tequila to inebriate me. She didn't realize that because I used to be a lightweight. I had never in my life felt the immense amount of pain I felt now. Back then, the liquor had nothing to drown. There weren't any miscarriages. No failed marriage. No stillbirth. Nothing. Now, the liquor had plenty to drown, so it took more.

"Farrah," I whispered, as a tear crept down my cheek.

I didn't want to believe that my best friend would prey on my pain. I really, really didn't.

"Hmm?" she mumbled, cuddling closer to me.

She wrapped her arm around my waist and cuddled into my side.

"I think I'm going to go ahead and grab a room."

She looked up at me. "A room? For what? Don't be silly. It's more than enough room for you—"

"Yeah, a room," I interrupted, tossing her arm from around my waist. I kicked my legs to the side of the bed and wiped tears from my face.

I was trying to save us from going to that place, that place we wouldn't be able to come back from. The end of our friendship. Because if I stayed here, I was sure Farrah would end up with her lips on me in some way. Either she would try to make a move on me, or I would end up with her face between my legs, and both scenarios would end with me beating the fuck out of her. And I didn't want to do that. So, I needed to leave. To save our friendship, I couldn't spend another day in this house with her.

Why did I even want to *save* this friendship? There was nothing about this friendship that was worth saving. The only thing that kept me in this friendship so long was fear. My fear of being alone. I was alone, anyway. I'd already lost everything. I didn't have my husband. I didn't have my baby. They were worth being afraid of losing. Not her. The only thing that kept her in this friendship was misery and control. She wasn't a friend. She wanted me at the bottom with her. Miserable just so she could have me all to herself. So, really, she didn't just want me miserable; she'd been preying on me too.

"Stop being silly," Farrah said from the bed, as I shuffled across the room to turn the light on. "You've been drinking and it's getting late. You are not about to leave and get a room when I have all of this space here."

"I'm not driving," I sternly said as I snatched a pair of pants up off the floor. "I'm getting an Uber. I don't want to stay here. I've stayed here long enough. I'm tired of feeling sorry for myself."

I grabbed my phone from the nightstand and clicked over to my Uber app. My heart raced against my chest as I felt her eyes on me. I wanted to end things as peacefully as possible. I did not want to leave on bad terms. Farrah was a lot, but I didn't want to fight her. She was complicated and a fucked-up person but she hadn't done enough for me to want to get into a fight with her. I was exhausted, physically, mentally, and emotionally. And honestly, my feelings were hurt. To me, this felt like a betrayal. I couldn't believe my best friend would try something like this while I was grieving the loss of my child. Not only that, but the man I loved wanted a divorce. Like, what about my life said I wanted to have sex with her? She needed to see a doctor, honestly. If anything, I felt sorry for her.

"Are you serious right now?" she asked, after the app sounded, letting me know they'd found me a driver.

I looked over at her and nodded. "Yeah, I think it's best . . ."

We made eye contact and, in that moment, I could tell she knew why I'd really decided to leave. She looked away and picked her glass up from the nightstand. She scratched the back of her head, took a deep breath, and cleared her throat. I grabbed the duffle bag I'd brought over my first night here and filled it as much as I could.

"Do you, um . . ." She got out of bed and looked out of the window.

She was crying.

It was awkward.

I didn't give a fuck.

She should be crying.

"Do you need any help?"

"Nope. I don't. I got it."

I slid my feet into my Crocs and hiked my bag over my left shoulder. "He's five minutes away. I'll get the rest of my things soon. I'll let you know." I wasn't coming back for any of it. I had everything I really cared about. My paintings were tucked underneath my armpit and Leia, she was safely tucked in the duffle. "I'm going to go out on the porch and wait for him. I need some air, anyway."

Farrah turned and faced me. With her lips pulled into her mouth, she nodded. "Okay, Leigh. I love you, okay? Call me if you need anything! Text me when you make it, best!"

I nodded with a forced smile. "Love you too."

When I walked out of the bedroom, I realized that was probably the last time I'd ever tell Farrah I loved her, and that made my chest hurt and tears fill my eyes.

CHAPTER 35

Sienna

ONE YEAR LATER

"Niggas ain't shit," Mahogany said.

"They really ain't. The ones that be doing the most cryin' and beggin' *definitely* ain't shit," Hazel chimed in.

I laughed and glanced at the family portrait on my Instagram feed. A little over a year ago, that picture would have had me crying, reaching for a bottle. Today, I felt nothing. It was all over my timeline, and I hadn't been bothered at all. I didn't want to log out for the day. I hadn't turned my comments off. I didn't block the people who tagged me, even though the people in the picture had absolutely nothing to do with me. None of that. Seeing pictures of Amiri with the woman he cheated on me with and the child he swore up and down wasn't his didn't bother me at all.

After exiting the Instagram app, I said, "I just pulled up. I'll call when I'm finished."

"Okay, sis. I hope this is the one," Hazel said, with her fingers crossed.

"It is!" Mahogany said, wearing a huge grin.

We said *I love you* and hung up.

Taking a deep breath, I flipped my sun visor down to check my makeup. I hoped Mahogany was right. This would be the seventh property I viewed this month. I was sick and *tied*. I needed a building for Utopia Wellness Center, my company. A shared office space wouldn't work because Utopia was more than just a doula company that housed doulas and sent them out to families. I needed something with space, and lots of it. I needed something big, with two or three floors and an open floor plan. Something I could add multiple rooms and a huge restroom to. It had to have space for a spa for facials, waxes, and massages too. Oh! And it had to have room on the main floor for Lamaze class. Lamaze on the main floor was *very* important.

My vision didn't just start and end with doulaship anymore. Nope. It had grown right along with me. Utopia was going to be bigger than anything I could have ever dreamed of a year ago. The plans I had for it were huge. Utopia was going to be a piece of paradise for mothers. Mothers like me, who weren't *quite* mothers, but were, in a unique kind of way. Mothers who needed grief counseling for babies they never got to hold and for the ones they did. And if the fathers wanted support, they could get it because their feelings mattered too. Pregnant mothers, mothers who needed a doula, mothers who didn't, overworked mothers who needed a break, mothers who weren't but took one anyway, pregnant mothers looking for a midwife, mothers who weren't. The point was made. Utopia was for mothers, *period.* So, a shared office space just wouldn't cut it.

I flipped the sun visor back up and squinted at the property with another deep breath. I really needed this one to be the one. Everything about it was perfect. The pictures, the description, the square footage, and, most importantly, the location. It was in downtown Detroit, on Woodward Avenue, not too far from Campus Martius Park. It literally checked off every little box on my must-have list, but none of it would mean anything if I couldn't compete with the highest offer.

That was another problem I had been having. I wasn't rich. Shit, a bitch was still very much struggling. The only reason I could afford to buy a property at all was because I moved out of that luxury apartment into a smaller, one-bedroom, one-bathroom in Midtown. I put a portion of the money I saved by downsizing into my savings, so in a sense, it was still like spending eighteen hundred in rent. But it was still less than twenty-five hundred, so I was fine with that. My savings, combined with the hefty business loan I secured, helped substantially.

I shifted my eyes to the rearview mirror when I noticed my Realtor pull up behind me. "Here we go," I mumbled before getting out.

The heels on my pink thong sandals tapped against the concrete as I treaded toward his truck with my pink Chanel bag draped over my shoulder. It was a beautiful seventy-eight-degree day. The sun was shining, and the sky was clear. Spring was in full effect, so I didn't need to wear a jacket over the white knotted tank I wore paired with stonewashed mom jeans.

"SiSi! Good morning, baby girl!" Keith, my Realtor, said, as he climbed out of his Durango. He was always full of energy. I couldn't recall a time when he wasn't.

"Good morning, Keith," I said with a smile, placing a piece of my hair behind my ear. I was rocking a blunt-cut bob. It looked good on me. So good, I hadn't worn anything longer than twelve inches in months.

He closed the door and hit the alarm. "You ready? Today is the day!"

He said that every time we toured a property. Keith had been my Realtor since I started searching, and sometimes I thought about finding a new one because I hadn't been able to get the job done with him. But because he was Black, I said fuck it and stuck with him because we didn't get a lot of opportunities and people usually gave up on us. I wasn't in a rush, anyway. The building that was for me would be for me, and I hoped and prayed like hell this one, this gorgeous, brick building with high windows and massive double doors, was mine.

"Mm-hmm," I said playfully as we headed up to the building. "You say that every time."

"Nah," he said with a smile. "Real shit. I feel it. This the one."

I laughed. "*Annnnd* you say that every time too. Just like that too." I made a face. "Which is pretty fuckin' weird."

He unlocked the door to the building and held it open for me. "Have some faith in me, woman."

We walked inside and immediately fell in love. The big double doors led into a vestibule that led to another set of oscillating doors I planned to keep *if* this building ended up being mine. I wanted it. I knew I wanted it, and I hadn't seen anything but the damn entrance. I felt like I didn't *need* to see anything else to make that decision. But we toured it, of course. It was beautiful. Open floor plan, white and gray faux marbled floors, high ceilings, lots of windows that created natural lighting that I knew would be absolutely gorgeous in the summer, and a kitchen! It had a fucking kitchen! Plus, room for so much more. And I needed the *more* because this mind of mine just kept formulating ideas.

Not getting this property would hurt, no lie. I'd lost many bidding wars, but this one? This one would hurt different. But something in my spirit told me this was the one. Something said, this one was mine. When I told Keith I wanted to put an offer in, I didn't get anxiety about the chances of me losing it to anyone else like I had in the past. I knew the chances were very likely, but something told me not to worry. I could literally see *Utopia* written in big, contemporary-style letters on the building with *Wellness Center* underneath it.

Yep, it was mine.

"Mm-hmm, yeah. It's nice, too, Dad. It's big and modern. It even has a kitchen."

Keith had put the offer in a couple of minutes ago, and now we had to play the waiting game. I hated the waiting game. We had a couple of other showings lined up, but the next one wasn't for another hour and a half, so we stopped at one of my favorite brunch spots, The Hudson Café, since they miraculously had a table open. I really didn't want to go to the other viewings, but I had to keep my options open just in case.

As soon as we got in the restaurant, I went straight to the restroom and called my daddy to tell him how the viewing had gone. He had been extremely supportive during this entire process and had even offered to give me money to help with the down payment. But I told him I was okay because I wanted to do this by myself. If it wasn't money from my savings or the loan, I didn't want it. This was going to be my first "big girl" purchase and I wanted to do it without his help. It might seem crazy to purchase a commercial property before a home, but I wasn't in a rush to buy a house. I was content with my little one-bedroom apartment. The house would come, eventually.

"A kitchen? What you gon' do now? Serve breakfast, brunch, lunch, *and* dinner?" He laughed, taking a jab at how I kept coming up with new ideas every other day.

I laughed. "No." Scrunching my face up, I said, "But a monthly or biweekly brunch did cross my mind."

"You might as well scratch monthly off. It's gon' be biweekly."

We laughed because it was funny and because it was true. I was like that. Walking around that gorgeous building gave me so much inspiration.

While we were laughing, I heard my momma walk into the room.

"Who is that? SiSi?" she asked.

I sighed and leaned against the wall.

Our relationship was still a little rocky. It took me months to speak to her again. If it weren't for therapy, I would have never spoken to her again. But I was on this whole healing, self-growth journey and establishing healthy relationships and boundaries was an important part of that. So, I called my mother and invited her to lunch one day. We talked for hours. I told her my love life and uterus were none of her concern. I asked her to respect my privacy and things of that nature and she apologized. She shed a few tears, said she just wanted the best for me and shit but understood and would mind her business going forward. But at the end of it, I felt like I hadn't gotten through to her at all. A few weeks later, she showed me I hadn't.

Eve didn't know what boundaries were and wouldn't stop asking me when I was going to start dating again. She masked meddling with playful jokes. Any time she'd invite me over for dinner, she'd ask something along the lines of "the new boo you're bringing . . . he doesn't have any food allergies, does he?" Shit like that. I didn't think it was funny. I always ignored it, but she was really treading on thin ice with me. I didn't play when it came to boundaries, especially when it came to the touchy subject of my love life.

I didn't have one.

Didn't want one.

Hadn't thought about one.

Because I couldn't stop thinking about him.

The him who didn't need to be named.

"All right, Dad, I'm about to go back—"

"Yeah, this her. You want to speak to her?" he said to my mother, ignoring me.

He heard me. I was sure of it. Big Reggie was sixty-six, but he could hear very fucking well.

A couple of seconds later, she was on the phone.

"Hey, SiSi!" she excitedly said.

I forced a smile and moved out of someone's way. "Hey, Ma."

"So, how was the viewing? Did you like it? What did . . ." She paused, and I could hear the bullshit coming. "*Keith* think?"

The way she said his name made me want to throw the hell up. She didn't know shit about the man. Didn't know how he looked or anything, but teased at us dating every chance she got. Eve didn't care who he was, or how I got him. If he had a dick with two working balls, she wanted me with him. The shit was pathetic and the exact reason I didn't want to talk to her. She was too grown to be so childish.

"It was good. I liked it a lot. I put an offer in. We're just waiting to see if it's good enough. Keith thinks we've got a really good chance. It just went on the market yesterday so we're confident."

I handled her with poise now. Straight-up ignored her ass, like I didn't hear the sauce she threw on his name, trying to imply that we should be romantically involved. That would never happen. Not in a million years. Keith wasn't ugly. He was very attractive. Tall, dark, waves, deep dimples. He was successful, charming, intelligent, had a nice car and a promising career. He was great, just not for me. He didn't have that *thing*. When our hands touched, there was nothing. When he touched the small of my back to escort me into a room, I felt nothing. There was no pull. Time existed in every room we stood in together. It didn't stay still. I didn't feel him before I saw him. I didn't float with him. I wasn't limitless. I wasn't free.

He was regular.

I couldn't do regular. Not after what I'd experienced with him. I wanted to float. I wanted to be free. So, nah, Keith would never work for me. Ever. Never. Not if he was the last man on earth. I'd die without ever sucking and riding another dick again if he was what I was left with. Yeah, it was that serious for me. Sad? That was what everyone said. That was one part of this healing thing I hadn't been able to conquer just yet. I didn't think I ever would, to be honest. Because I didn't think it was a part of me that needed to be healed. There was nothing wrong with *us*. Not together. Individually, yes. The situations around us, absolutely. But together? Together, we were fucking magic. And I missed that. I missed him. There was nothing sad about that. There was nothing sad about wanting that or nothing at all.

"That's good, honey! Maybe he'll take you out to dinner after to—"

"Do you want a relationship with me at all, or would you rather *never* hear from me again?" I interrupted, rubbing my forehead. "Because you're doing it. You're on a slippery slope of never, ever, ever hearing from me again, Ma."

She sighed and I heard my daddy in the background ask her what was wrong. She couldn't help herself. What the fuck was wrong with her? How was it this hard for her to mind her own fucking business? I didn't get it. I mean, I really couldn't understand it. My life was my life. That was it. The shit was annoying. She made me feel like I was doing something wrong. Like something was wrong with me because I was turning twenty-eight and single.

There was *nothing* wrong with me. It was very hard for me to accept that I would probably never get married. It was even harder for me to accept that I would probably never have children. I was okay with that now. Completely. Fully. I didn't just say it because it sounded good. I didn't say it one minute and then cry about it behind a closed door the next. I wasn't jealous of anybody with the life I wanted. I wasn't the "why not me" woman anymore. I was completely satisfied with the life I had. And before I allowed my mother to poison me with negativity that could potentially unravel me, I would cut her ass off and not lose a wink of sleep about it.

"I'm sorry, Si. I just want you to be happy. I—"

"I'm not happy because I'm not romantically involved with anybody?" I interrupted with a laugh. "You equate happiness with being in a relationship? Ma, that's really sad. Tell Dad I love him. Bye."

I hung up and stuffed my phone into my purse. I didn't have anything else to say to her. I didn't know if I was done talking to her, but for now, I needed a minute. She wanted me to be happy. I was happy! I was good. Was there something missing from my life? Of course! But I was happy. I didn't need affirmations. I didn't need a luxury apartment. I didn't need anything to validate that happiness, and I for damn sure didn't need a man to make me happy. The hell was wrong with her? My mother, man. She was . . . a lot.

Before leaving the restroom, I washed and dried my hands. I thought about calling Naoki back, but I'd already spent enough time in the restroom. I didn't want to be ruder than I'd already been.

"Damn, I thought I was going to have to send somebody in there looking for yo' ass," Keith joked when I sat down.

I laughed and picked my menu up. "Shut up. Did you order yet?"

"Nah." He shook his head. "I was waiting on you. You good?"

I frowned a little and looked up from my menu at him. "Yeah, why you ask that?"

He turned his mouth down and shrugged. "Before you left, you were smiling. Now you seem sad about somethin'. Nigga piss you off? You need me to spin?"

Keith wasn't the typical Realtor, if there was a such thing as a "typical" Realtor. He wasn't white collar. He was unapologetically a reformed hood nigga. He told me all about his past. He used to be heavy in the streets, in and out of prison, and shit like that. He wasn't stupid, though, and managed to go to school enough to get his diploma. This was his first year as a Realtor and he was still trying to get his first sale. That was another reason I didn't want to turn my back on him.

I sucked my teeth. "No, fool. My momma just . . ." I shook my head and looked down at my menu. With a sigh, I stroked the back of my neck, following a chill that ran down my spine. "She just don't know how to mind her business."

"Oh, you got one of them, huh?" he asked, with a smirk, biting on the tip of his straw. "What she on?"

I looked up from my menu and lightly huffed. "Yeah. She—"

My eyes catching *his* cut me off midsentence.

The reason for the chill that ran down my spine, and soon after flooded my body.

He was here, staring right at me, and I couldn't move. Time . . . it did that thing. He did what he always did to me. What only he could.

The *he* who didn't *need* to be named.

Keith waved his hand in my face and blocked my view.

"Sienna."

I wrapped my arms around my body and swallowed, coming back down to earth. "What?"

"You good?"

No, I wasn't good. I needed to catch him before he left. Before he walked out of my life for a second time, and for good this time, because he probably thought Keith was more than just my damn Realtor.

I grabbed my purse from the table and threw the strap over my shoulder. "I'll be right back."

"Girl, where you going now?"

"Order me a strawberry mimosa and the chicken and waffle. I'll be right back!" I yelled as I did a little walk-run.

Because the restaurant was pretty crowded, it was hard to get to the door without having to maneuver through people first. I had to bump into at least five people, a server carrying a tray of food included. Luckily, he had good balance and didn't drop anything.

When I made it outside, I looked around for his car, but shit, what was he even driving these days? I doubted if he was still driving the G-Wagon. Men were like that. I was still pushing my Range and had no plans of switching up anytime soon. I looked up and down Woodward Avenue, wondering which way he could have gone. Something in my gut told me to head toward Grand River, so I did. I was happy I listened to my gut because, as soon as I got to the corner, he turned it.

I looked up at him and wanted to jump *inside* of him. That was how much I missed him. I never wanted to be away from him again. Jumping inside of him, that would be a bit extreme, huh? A hug would suffice. A kiss. A subtle touch on my cheek would be good enough. Something. But I couldn't touch him. I had to respect the fact that I didn't know what the hell Jahad had going on. He could still be married. And if he wasn't, he could've been in a relationship. I didn't know, so I did the respectable thing and calmed my ass down.

"Hi," I spoke.

"Bonjou," said the little girl he was with. She was the cutest.

I looked down at her with a smile. "Bon . . . ju."

"*Bonjou* means hi, but only in the morning. In the afternoon, you have to say *Bonswa*. Ain't that funny?" she continued, with her head cocked to the side, twirling her braid.

I giggled. "Yeah, it is pretty funny."

I looked away from her and put my eyes back on Jahad.

"Introduce yourself, Bebe," he instructed, ogling me. His eyes were all over me. Every inch of me, like he was trying to make sure everything was just as he left it. As always, he made me unsure of myself. Like damn, did I look okay?

She looked up at him, moved closer to his side, then looked back over at me. "*Mwen rele* Bebe."

"Moy really Sienna." I struggled before biting my bottom lip.

He lightly laughed and said, "We'll work on that." He then paused, took a couple of steps forward, and closed the space between us. The scent of his cologne immediately filled my nostrils the same way I wanted him to fill *me*. "Hi."

"Hi, Jahad," I whispered with my eyes on his lips, wanting to put mine there. My mouth salivated. I wanted to kiss him so fucking bad. "Um, I was just . . . I was having brunch with my *Realtor*. We're in between showings, so we grabbed something to eat."

I was antsy. Why did I feel the need to give this man an explanation? I hadn't seen him in over a year. Did I really have to explain anything to him? Yes, I did. I really fucking did. I refused not to. I didn't want him to think Keith and I were anything other than what we were.

He lifted his hand and caressed my cheek. Electricity. Instant fucking electricity.

I closed my eyes and exhaled.

Finally. Oh my fucking . . . God. *Finally.*

This was why I couldn't and would *never* do regular. I was addicted to this. The feel of Jahad Baptiste. For a while, I thought maybe I could get this feeling from someone else. I was sure he couldn't be the only man with it. But after a few encounters, I realized he had to be. There was no way in hell someone else could have it. I had absolutely no desire to go out looking for it in someone else anyway because, realistically, the only man I wanted was him. I only wanted time to stop with him. I only wanted to float and to soar and to be limitless with him.

"You don't have to explain, love. I was coming inside to get you, no matter who he was."

"I like that one," Hazel said, nodding toward the black faux leather mini dress I had laid out on the bed. "That one screams *I didn't wear panties so bend me over the hood of the car and fuck me in the parking lot. I don't give a fuck who's watching.*"

"Okay, sis! Period!" Naoki agreed with a laugh, reaching over to slap hands with Haz.

"Both of you bitches lack class," Mahogany stated with her nose turned up, wineglass in hand just inches away from her scrunched-up lips.

Naoki and I shared a knowing look in the mirror, but said nothing. Mahogany's ass had some nerve.

"The long one with the high split. At least that one whispers . . ." She paused and whispered, "Ho." We cracked up laughing and she continued with a shrug. "*Classy* ho. The kind of ho that likes to be finger fucked underneath the dinner table in a restaurant full of people." She winked.

Okay, okay, that was a smooth recovery. I liked that. For a second, I thought Mahogany forgot I knew who the hell she was. I cackled, tilted my head to the side and picked the 'classy ho' dress up. Because I mean, I was a classy ho.

We were at my apartment, trying to find something to wear for my date with Jahad. Yes, date. Our first date. He asked me out before we sadly had to part ways. I hated to, but he had to take his niece back to his brother's house and I had business to handle. I was looking forward to later, though, that was for sure. I couldn't wait. A bitch felt eighteen again, sitting with her girls, gushing over a boy, trying to find something to wear. How childish. But that was how Jahad made me feel. Giddy.

"What you know about being a classy ho, Nene?" Naoki challenged before taking a sip of her drink. "Yo' ass been married for *fifty-'leven* years."

"So? What does that mean? I can't be a classy, married ho? How do you think I've *stayed* married for *fifty-'leven* years? The hell?" Mahogany shot back.

I cut my eyes at Naoki and took the other three dresses back into the closet, shaking my head. Naoki was still trying to get into Pandora's. She needed to give up. I wasn't asking Mahogany to get her inside and Mahogany would never tell her she was a member. She was trying to pull it up out of her, but Mahogany's been keeping that secret for a very long time; there was nothing Naoki could do or say to get it up out of her. Naoki would have to physically torture Mahogany to get her to tell her she was a member of an exclusive sex club.

Every time we got together, Naoki made some kind of attempt at pulling it out of Mahogany. It was getting old. Not only was it getting old, but I also didn't want Mahogany to pick up on it and realize I'd told Naoki about it. Like I said, she didn't tell me to keep it between us, but . . . yeah, maybe I should have. Our relationship was great. Like, I talked to her every single day now. I was open with her and not only because I had a secret to hold over her head, but I also just felt closer to her since we talked that day. I didn't want anything to come between that.

Naoki needed to leave it alone, anyway. She was in a relationship, trying to weasel her way into a sex club. Was I judging? No. I couldn't. I just wanted her to let it go. Isaac, the guy she was seeing, was decent. She didn't have any complaints about him. She said the sex was good, he was a surgeon, and he took very good care of her, and they had only been together for six months. I didn't understand the purpose. Naoki and relationships had never mixed well. She still bounced on Denim's dick every chance she got. More now than ever since she didn't travel anymore. She had been working at Beaumont Hospital as an ICU nurse for the last eight months, making more money than she had when she was traveling. So, we saw more of each other, and she had been seeing more of him. So much of Denim that sometimes, I forgot she was even in a relationship. I was honestly surprised when she told me Isaac asked her to be his girlfriend and she said yeah. I thought my friend had bumped her head and forgot she couldn't commit to save her life. But then she told me she said yeah because she didn't have anything else to do, and I realized she hadn't bumped her head at all. She was just crazy as fuck.

"Sis ain't got four kids for nothing," Hazel said with a laugh, as she climbed out of my bed. She stood behind me, sitting at my vanity, and touched my hair. "You gon' leave it straight? Or curl it?"

I ran my fingers through it. "What you think? Should I curl it?"

"Leave it straight. Blunt cut gives sexy," Naoki pointed out. "That's the look she's going for, right, Nene?"

Mahogany stood up from the chaise and joined me and Hazel over by the vanity. "Yes, ma'am!"

Naoki jumped up from the bed and dramatically snapped her fingers. "Ohhh, bitch!" She laughed. "Do you still have your mask? Wear it!"

How Jahad and I met wasn't a secret anymore. It couldn't be. Not after Vault. Hazel asked me how I knew her boss's brother and I told her. However, how I got the invite was still a "mystery." She was sure Jahad got his from Saint because she *heard* he was a freak. I felt like they messed around before, but she said they hadn't. Still, I had my suspicions. Naoki, too, which was the *only* reason she hadn't tried to sink her claws into him. Hazel was like that. As fluid as she was, she was private with her shit. She didn't bring people around. I'd never been introduced to anybody Hazel was dating. She mentioned a boo here and there but that was about it. I didn't think Hazel would ever bring anyone around. With a mother like ours, I wouldn't either. I loved that about Hazel. She didn't give a single fuck about what Eve thought about the way she lived her life. She was unapologetically free.

I looked at Naoki like she had lost her mind. "Bitch, if you don't get the fuck . . ."

Mahogany and Hazel laughed. "What is wrong with her?"

Naoki shrugged. "I thought it would be cute. Like, remember me?"

I laughed and pulled the drawer to my vanity open. "I don't have it, anyway. He broke the strap."

"Okaaaay! Freaky!" Naoki shrieked.

My phone rang and Naoki picked it up off my nightstand for me. "It's Keith!"

I jumped up from my chair and grabbed it from her. They stood around me, eager like little kids waiting for their turn at the ice cream truck. I loved how excited they were about this for me.

I took a deep breath and answered the FaceTime. "Hey, Keith."

With scrunched-up lips, he stared into the camera. "Aye, SiSi . . . what I tell you earlier?"

"What?"

He put his hand to his ear and put the camera up to it. "Tell me what I said earlier, my baby."

With wide eyes, I excitedly yelled, "Keith, stop playin' with me!"

He pulled the phone away from his ear and mean mugged at the camera. "I said today was the muthafuckin' day!" He paused and beat against his chest. "Today is the muthafuckin' day! Nah, baby girl, stop playin' with *me*!"

CHAPTER 36

Jahad

"So, what now? You about to ask her to marry you?" Saint asked with that dumbass smirk on his face.

I shook my head. "Not yet. I don't need to rush it. Eventually."

He turned his mouth down in shock. "Damn, I expected you to tell me to get my best man speech ready, how you been on shorty."

"I was on her ass because our future was uncertain," I admitted. "Shit's solidified now. I don't have anything to worry about. We smooth."

Three hundred and seventy-three days.

That was how long it took for the universe to put us back together, like I knew it would. When I felt her on my way out of The Hudson Café, I wanted to run back, grab her, and ask her what took her so fucking long, but I realized it wasn't up to her. That had always been a constant reminder when it came to us. It took three hundred and seventy-three days because it took that long for us to be ready.

When I saw her sitting, looking good as fuck, smiling and shit with another nigga, I thought the universe was trying to play a cruel joke on me. For a minute, I thought it was testing me. Either I was being tested or I had to witness her with another man because I was being told to let go. That was what I took from it and it pissed me off. *Almost* sent me into a blind rage. I waited three hundred and seventy-three days for *nothing*? Just for her to end up with another muthafucka? Nah.

The past three hundred and seventy-three days without her had been agonizing in the subtlest of ways possible. If it wasn't for burying myself in charity work, investing, and traveling back and forth between Haiti and Michigan, I would have folded a long time ago. I would have popped up on her three hundred and seventy-two days ago but I put my trust in the universe and chilled. Put my trust in the universe just for it to bring us back together with her in a relationship? Nah, I couldn't take it on the chin.

The only reason I didn't walk right up to the table was because I had to go back to the truck for Bebe's backpack in case the nigga Sienna was with tried me and I ended up catching a body.

On the way to the truck, I called Blaise and told him he needed to be en route and prepared too. When it came to shorty, I was taking the risk. I wasn't leaving the restaurant without her. That was nonnegotiable. Luckily, it didn't come to that because she met me at the corner. It was for sure divine intervention. A nigga was on a straight path. My hands were clean, but for her, I was ready to dirty them up again. What kind of logic was that? Logic didn't really apply to us, though, did it?

"Why you always expect me to be the best man, bitch?" Blaise said, and adjusted his shorts before sitting.

We were at Blaise's house in the living room, kicking it. When I brought Bebe back, I stayed, and Saint pulled up about thirty minutes later. It was just the four of us. His clan of cult hos weren't around. Blaise had made a few changes, changes I was proud of. On the days he had Bebe, they weren't in the house. The nigga had finally decided to grow up. It took him long enough, but late was better than never.

Saint cocked his head to the side with a squint. "Wasn't I the best man in the last one?"

"That one didn't count," Blaise dismissed with a wave of his hand.

I laughed and frowned at him. "This nigga. Fuck you mean, it didn't count? It counted, *idyot* (idiot)."

Things between Leighton and me might've ended badly, but I would never disregard what we shared. Ever. She was an essential piece to the puzzle of my life. How could she not be? She carried four of my children. I got it out of the mud with her. She was my *wife*, someone I loved enough to share my last name with. I would have laid down and died for that woman, but before I did that, I would have fought hard for it not to come to that, just to spare her the agony of losing me because she had lost enough already. That was how much I cared about her. I didn't hate her. Could never hate her. We just didn't work. She just wasn't for me. Our story ended. There was no bad blood between Leighton and me. I wished her well and prayed she was as happy as she deserved to be. It seemed she was.

Leighton was in New York. She moved out there shortly after our divorce was finalized nine months ago. We didn't talk much but the last time we did was on her birthday a few months back. She was excited about the possibility of having one of her pieces showcased in New York's most prominent art district. I was proud of her.

Blaise held his arms up. "No disrespect, but you know what I meant, bro."

He turned to Saint and scrunched his face up. "Like I said, bitch, you not the designated best man, ho nigga."

"Fuck out of here, *tét zozo*. Tell this nigga, Jah," Saint argued after sucking his teeth. "Bro already know what it is."

"You nigga's tweakin'," I said with a laugh, shaking my head.

"Nah, this nigga tweakin'," Blaise stressed. "You might as well tell 'em now, bro."

Saint laughed. "You didn't even know shorty existed until a couple hours ago. How you gon' be the best man at a wedding and you don't even know sis?"

I cut in. "How you niggas competing to be the best man at a wedding that's not even happening yet? Relax."

Before Blaise could say anything slick, Bebe ran into the living room and jumped into his lap. "You had fun with Uncle Jah today, Bebe?" he asked.

She nodded and the beads in her hair danced around her little head. Spending time with my niece gave me solace I hadn't realized it could before. Bebe brought joy into my life. She truly did. She was a hidden gem that had been in plain sight this entire time. Everything I wanted to experience with my child, I had been experiencing with her, with Blaise's blessing, of course. He shared his daughter with me because I didn't have my own. It was an unwritten agreement we had between each other. I would appreciate him for his generosity for the rest of my life.

After the meeting with Samuel, Blaise and Saint showed up for me in major ways. They didn't ask me if I wanted a hug. They didn't tell me they loved me or baby me. They didn't ask me if I needed to be tucked in at night. They were present. That was all I needed. The only thing I needed. Samuel was too much of a horrible fucking person to accept that. Instead, he chose to take a jab at my manhood when he knew I was more of a man than he could ever be. I didn't fuck with him. At all. That was shocking, coming from me. I was all about family. Would go to the end of the earth to protect them. But for Samuel? For Samuel, I would do nothing. He was dead to me.

"What did y'all do?" Blaise asked Bebe.

"We, ummmm . . ." She looked up at the ceiling. "We went to brunnnnch. And then . . . we saw the pretty lady. I taught her how to say *Bonjou*. She said *Bonswa* was silly, too, Daddy." She giggled. "And then . . ." She looked over at me, snickered, and cuddled underneath Blaise's armpit. "Uncle Jah kissed her!"

The minute my plane landed in Michigan this morning, I got on the phone with him to make sure he had her ready for me. Any time I came home, I had something planned. Some type of activity paired with lunch or dinner. Today, we chose brunch. In the past year, we'd never done brunch. How crazy was it that on the day we choose to, I see her?

It wasn't coincidental. Those didn't exist. Not between us, it didn't, at least.

"You some kind of spy, Bebe? Why you tellin' that man all my business?" I joked with a cocked brow. "Aw, naw. I gotta watch out for you!"

She laughed. "No! I'm not a spy, Uncle Jah!"

"You report to him after all of our little playdates, don't you?"

She drew back and frantically shook her head and those beads went wild again. "Nuh-uh! Nooo!"

"Yes, you do," Blaise said with a cocked brow. "You told me about the mall, too. About the lady at the register."

I dramatically dropped my jaw. "Aw, nah. See, it's over. You're a spy. No more playdates for you."

She poked her bottom lip out and crossed her arms over her chest. "I'm not a spy, Uncle Jah! Please! I'm sorry! Stop laughin', Daddy! It's not funny!"

I pushed up from the couch and grabbed her from Blaise's arms. "I'm playin', I'm playin'. There will be more playdates." I looked at her from the corner of my eye. "If you can count to five . . ."

"One, two—"

"Bebe," Saint interrupted.

She giggled. *"Youn, de, twa, tat, senk!"*

I gave her a high five. "All right, as long as you keep that up, the playdates will never end."

"You promise?"

I placed my hand on my chest, over my heart. "I promise."

She threw her arms in the air and yelled, "Yay!"

I kissed her on the top of the head and put her down. "I'm proud of you, Bebe."

I was. I really was. Sometimes I sat back, looked at my niece, and wished I would have had the opportunity to do all the things I'd done with her with Leia. I wanted to watch her grow up. I wanted to give her random tests and teach her how to speak our language. I wanted to chase her around the park, pull chairs out, and open doors for her. I wanted us to build an unbreakable bond.

Sometimes I wondered how it was possible to miss someone I never *really* got to experience, and I realize it wasn't the experiences I missed, it was the experiences I missed out on and the small things I did get to experience I missed. Like laying my head on Leighton's stomach to have one-sided conversations and the feeling of a foot or something jabbing against my face when I had those one-sided conversations. It was walking up the stairs, hearing her heart beating over the Bluetooth speaker when headphones weren't enough for Leigh. Shit like that. I miss that.

I stretched and ran my hand down the back of my head. It was cool, though. I was good. I coped well. I wasn't hitting the bottle heavy. None of that shit. I had never been a heavy drinker, and hadn't allowed stress, divorce, or child loss to turn me into one.

Saint's phone rang and he groaned. *"Kaka!"*

Bebe laughed. "Ohhh! Uncle Saint said a bad word!"

"Yeah, don't be like him, Bebe. The nigga's an animal," Blaise scolded as he ushered Bebe out of the room. "Let's get you something to eat."

Saint tossed his head back against the couch and glared over at me. "Why you do this to me, bro?"

"Why I do what?" I asked, feigning ignorance.

The day I walked out of Samuel's office was truly the day I walked out of the dope game for good. I gave Saint guidance every now and then, but that was about it. I didn't fuck with it. Shelby wasn't happy to hear about my decision to leave. Think I gave a fuck about what that nigga thought? Hell naw. I truly did not give a fuck about what anybody thought about any of it. He claimed doing business with anybody other than me made him nervous. He didn't know them like he knew me. Thing was, Shelby didn't know me. He knew a made-up version of me. A version of myself I created to make him comfortable. I didn't give a fuck about him and would have easily put a bullet in his head and attended his funeral service if I had to. He thought I was the easiest one in the family to deal with. I wasn't. I was the one who would get rid of you the minute you became a problem for us. Saint was his best bet. Saint would reason with him. I wouldn't have.

I was happy I wasn't that person anymore. A person wearing masks. I didn't have to do any underhanded shit to protect my family. I didn't have to get any blood on my hands. I didn't have to worry about karma—no new karma, at least. I was cool. The work I'd been doing back home was all legit. I had several communities in development. Schools, hospitals, and camps that offered dental and healthcare services too. There was a lot of work that needed to be done out there. I couldn't do it all, but I had a lot in motion, and I was happy to be moving bricks I could be proud of.

"Leave me," he complained with his face in his hands.

"Stand up," I ordered.

He pulled his hands from his face and stood up.

"I didn't leave you. I'm right here, Saint. If you ever feel like that shit is tearing you down, walk away." I locked eyes with him. "You hear me? I left it to you because it was better suited in your hands. You heard Blaise that night. He didn't want it. I wouldn't have mentioned you if I didn't think you could handle it. But if you can't, leave."

He held his head up high and nodded. "I can handle it."

Saint *could* handle it.

He was still fresh in his new position. Adjusting was taking a little time. He didn't want out. If I thought for one second it wasn't for him, I would have pulled him out of it with me. Him and Blaise, they liked it. Could possibly love it, even.

After the meeting, we talked and neither of them could understand why I would walk away from a million-dollar empire. They were young and didn't understand. Just as well as they couldn't understand how I could devote myself to just one woman. The drug game, it didn't excite me. It never really did. I was in it for the same reasons as them. Money. Power. Freedom. But what I really needed was peace, happiness, and sanity, and the drug business had never given me any of that.

The three hundred and seventy-three days we spent apart were worth it.

Three hundred and seventy-three days ago, I would have wanted her yesterday.

But we weren't ready. Today, we were.

Sitting across from her, watching her talk with light in her eyes and alfredo sauce on her chin, I knew she was ready. And I knew I was *ready*. When I thought to use power at the restaurant earlier, the universe stepped in and showed me I didn't need to do that. This time, it was different. If it wasn't, we wouldn't be here *together*.

Earlier, Saint asked me if I was about to ask her to marry me. I wasn't. Not yet. I didn't want to rush. I wanted to savor every single moment I had with her.

We were on our first date. I hadn't gone on a first date in years. This one was monumental. I didn't want to share the restaurant with anyone else, so I booked every table at Andiamo. I wanted to do shit like this. First dates, first vacations . . . I didn't want to jump straight into a proposal. We'd done enough *jumping*. We jumped in, headfirst. Love came fast. Life came fast. But now it was time to slow down and I wasn't afraid to. Before, I was. I was afraid of being without her because our future was uncertain.

I trusted that the universe had brought us together, yeah, but I didn't know for what exactly. I was confident then because I had to be. I was afraid of being anything but it. Afraid of having even a speckle of doubt because I needed this. I needed her. I needed us to be real. And as I sat across from her, watching her talk with a smile on her face and love in her eyes, I realized I had been rushing, worrying, and afraid for nothing at all. We were real. Always had been. I just needed to chill and trust the fucking process. Three hundred and seventy-three days waiting was a long fucking time but I was glad we waited.

"What? Why are you looking at me like that? I have something on my face, don't I?" She pouted and reached for a napkin, but I stopped her.

I leaned over the table and kissed the alfredo sauce from her chin.

She giggled and placed a piece of hair behind her ear.

"You've been doing that a lot," I mentioned with a smirk, as I rested against the back of my chair.

She looked over at me and sipped on her drink. "Doing what?"

"Giggling. Don't tell me you've gotten shy on me, love."

She drew back and made a face, waving me off. "Please! Me? Shy of you? Never!"

I laughed and pushed back away from the table. She looked at me as I rounded the table to sit beside her. She had gotten a little shy. I got it, though. I was a little nervous too. We were starting over. It was new. This was new. We weren't the same people. We weren't two masked people, mindlessly roaming around a sex club we had no business in. We weren't two broken people trying to put ourselves together by searching for a meaningless one-night stand. We didn't find that, did we, though? We found each other. We were broken souls who found each other when we needed each other the most.

I sat next to her, grabbed her hand, and interlocked my fingers with hers. Time did its thing. The thing it did when I didn't know her. The thing it did when I walked into that room when I didn't know her name. When I didn't know what she looked like under her gold mask. When she was just a fantasy. When she was just supposed to be a one-night stand. Someone I was using a hall pass I really didn't want on. Time stood still . . . the world and the noise in it vanished. Back then, I didn't know what the fuck it was. Didn't know what it meant. But now . . . now I knew what it was.

It was destiny. We were meant to be. That was the simplest way to describe what we were to one another. However, we felt like much, much more. When I was with her, I felt like there were no limits. Time honestly didn't exist. Nothing existed. But us. Just the moment. That would always remind me. There was no need for nerves.

"You feel that."

She locked her tear-filled eyes with mine and nodded. "Yes."

"You felt it then. In that room with that mask on."

She blinked. "I did."

Neither of those statements were questions. I didn't need validation. When it came to Sienna, remember . . . I knew shit.

I inched in closer to her and whispered, "Tell me what it feels like."

Tears trickled down her cheeks as she blinked. "Floating. It feels like . . . I feel . . . I feel free."

I grabbed the back of her neck and pulled her in for a kiss that made me float too. Three hundred and seventy-three days were worth it because nothing in the world compared to this. Floating with the freedom of knowing I could float without worry. I didn't have to worry about Leighton. I didn't have to worry about karma. I didn't have to worry about tainting Sienna's life. I didn't have to worry about shit but the moment. The moment in which only we existed and nothing else did.

EPILOGUE

Leighton

THREE YEARS LATER

I stood at my painting, ogling it as if I wasn't the one who'd painted it. It was just so . . . beautiful. It was my favorite because it was created during the ugliest time in my life. I saw its beauty back then, but I didn't really appreciate it. Not until now. Not until I was at a place in my life where I could. A place in my life where I was my happiest. The painting meant the absolute most to me. Sometimes, I'd stare at it and cry. Today, I kept my tears at bay. I couldn't stand in an art gallery full of folks, crying at a painting—my painting—like a crazy person. They would be tears of joy, though. When I painted that picture, I didn't think I'd ever feel joy again. But I felt it. I felt an immense amount of joy. Not sometimes—I felt joy every single day.

It took a while for me to get to that point. It actually took a little over a year. The past four years for me had been a roller coaster ride full of twists, turns, ups, and downs. It had been a hell of a ride, for sure. But lately, I'd been coasting. The ride hadn't been *nearly* as tumultuous as it was before this beautiful painting was created. Four years ago, I would have never thought I would be living in New York, standing in an art gallery, ogling a painting created by me. This painting wasn't the only one I had showcased here, either. I had several. I really couldn't believe it. Every time I woke up, I was happier with my decision to move to New York.

I didn't have *anything* in Michigan. Nothing but heartache and misery. My parents couldn't understand why I would leave. They couldn't wrap their minds around why I would move thousands of miles away from family. Family? What family? Sisters who never called or visited me? A best friend who really didn't give a damn about me? I didn't have a husband, and sadly, my parents were in their late seventies and had lived their lives already. They couldn't understand that Michigan had absolutely drained me of *everything*. I didn't need them to understand, though. I wanted to start over, and I did just that.

"Guess what?" Rome whispered, sneaking up behind me.

I flinched, nearly spilling white wine on my olive blazer. "What? You scared the hell out of me."

"You sold your first market-priced piece," he said against the back of my neck before kissing me there.

I turned around on my nude, four-inch Louboutin heels and wrapped my arms around his neck. "I did?"

"You did," he told me with a smile before kissing me on the lips.

Rome and I were a thing. I guess you could say we were *more* than a thing. We were married and had been for the past two years. Rome was on the roller coaster with me. When the ride was its scariest, at the top, right before the drop. When there was a dark tunnel to go into, one that seemed never-ending, like I would never come out of it, he was there. To hold my hand and to tell me everything would be okay. Rome never left my side.

That day he called and told me to create, there was a shift in our friendship. A pivotal shift. Especially when I left Farrah's house, feeling like I had no one, and he called me. It was like he showed up when I needed him most. He showed up for me as a friend. There weren't any conditions attached to his love. He was a true friend, someone I felt safe with. A friendship I valued. One worth holding on to, unlike the one I shared with Farrah.

I hadn't spoken to her since I left her house that night. Walking away from our friendship was one of the hardest things I ever had to do. We were friends for most of my life, since the first grade. I cried many nights, missing her. She was more than just my best friend; Farrah was my sister. But she was a poison. My life was already dark enough; I didn't need any more negativity in it and that was what she was. Just . . . negativity. A couple of years ago, I thought about calling to check up on her, but after a mutual friend told me she had been badmouthing me to people in our circle, calling me shady for getting engaged to Rome, I decided not to. Farrah hadn't changed at all. How in the hell was I shady? Because she had a crush on him and I ended up with him? She and Rome had never been together on any level. It was sad. After all of these years, she still had issues. I wished her well, though. As much as I missed her, I was happy I had ended our friendship. I couldn't imagine having that type of poison around me at this stage of my life.

People could think what they wanted about Rome and me. We knew what it was between us. We didn't come together based on anything but love. His love was real and raw. When I told him what happened between Jahad and me, he didn't judge me. He didn't blame me and he didn't blame Jahad. He didn't give a negative response. The only response he gave me was love and compassion. He told me there would be brighter days. He told me that, eventually, everything would make sense. At first, I didn't believe him. When the world around me was still just as ugly as it was when I created this beautiful painting, I didn't believe him. I didn't have a reason to believe him.

But years later, when the darkness around me faded and the sun began to shine again, and hope didn't seem so far out of reach, I understood. I saw it. And I began to see him and what he was to me. Love. In its purest form. Not because he loved me. Not because I cared for him. But because he helped me love me. He helped bring light into my life.

"Congratulations, baby," he said before kissing me again.

"Thank—oww!" I shrieked. "Rue!"

I looked down at the beautiful, busy two-year-old clinging onto my leg. I handed my wineglass to Rome to pick her up. "What did I tell you about running around here? Hmm?" I nuzzled my face into her chubby little neck, gave her wild kisses and tickled her ribs. "Hm? What'd I tell you?"

Rome truly did bring light into my life.

Not only did he love me at my worst, but he gave me a precious little blessing by the name of Rue Rose. She was two. And she was ours. I had her. She came from me. From us. And I didn't have to obsess over ovulation, or make sure we had sex in certain positions to get her. She was made out of love. Pure, unfiltered love. When I found out I was pregnant, I was petrified. I didn't want to be pregnant. I was mortified, honestly. But Rome did what Rome always did; he calmed me down and told me we would figure things out together. And that was what we did.

The doctor I couldn't wait for with Jahad was available. He was accepting new patients and I got in. I was put on bed rest again, but this time, I had a cervical cerclage put in. My pregnancy was completely stress-free. And yes, I had a doula. She wasn't Ms. Sienna Mills, but she was good enough.

I thought of Sienna. Often, honestly. Wondered where she was in life. Wondered if she'd ever gotten her rainbow baby. Wondered if she ended up with Jahad. Wondered if they'd gotten that rainbow baby together. Wherever they were, whatever they were doing, I hoped they were well. I wished them well. I had absolutely no hate in my heart for either of them.

Sienna

I picked my buzzing phone up from the patio table and checked my notifications. With a smile, I scanned over the email.

"You got it?" Jahad asked me from behind.

I looked over my shoulder at him. "Yep. It should be delivered within two weeks."

He ran his hand over my stomach with a nod and I set my phone back on the table. I bought a painting. A beautiful painting from a talented artist. I wasn't big on art like that, but I could appreciate a good piece. And that one? Baby, that one was fire. It was her first sale. I wished I could call and congratulate her. But . . . we were past that. Our friendship, or whatever it was, ended the day she found me in bed with her husband.

Mm-hmm.

I bought a painting from Leighton. I didn't know it was hers when I saw it initially. I was scrolling my Instagram feed, like I always do, when it came up on my feed. It was random. I didn't follow art galleries, but I had liked a few posts from underground artists, so I guess the algorithm was *algorithming.* Anyway, it caught my eye. I clicked on it and wasted no time clicking over to the website. I didn't see her name until I added it to my cart.

Life was funny, man.

"You really don't think it was a coincidence?" I asked, as I stared off into the distance, watching our family act a fool in our pool.

He kissed me on the side of my neck. "What I tell you about coincidences, gorgeous?"

"They don't exist."

"They do not exist."

I leaned into his touch and took a deep breath. "How do you think she's doing?"

"She's painting. She's happy."

I didn't say anything. Because . . . he was right.

We were happy too. I couldn't imagine being anything but it with Jahad. Three years flew by, but that was what happened when you were happy and having fun. I wanted time to slow down, though. I really, really did. I wasn't ready to grow old. I wasn't because I wasn't ready for this to end. I didn't want to live without him.

These days, I don't sit on Diamond's couch because I need her to heal me. I sat on her couch because I had been obsessing about the future. A future where he wouldn't be in it. I was worried about growing old and dying. How stupid was that? We were in our thirties. We weren't old, but I just didn't want this to end. I never wanted to stop floating. I never wanted to look up and the electricity was gone. I didn't want to look up and time existed, and I noticed everything around me. I didn't want to have a regular life.

I wanted to go first.

I told him that.

We talked about that.

Well, I talked about it.

He didn't like to, so we rarely ever did. Since we didn't talk about it, I thought about it and then he'd bring it up because he'd know it was on my mind, and then we'd talk about me not thinking about it. It was ridiculous.

Lately, I lived in the moment, though. When we were together, I basked in it. I overdosed on it. Him. The feeling. We were always like this. Skin to skin. Unless we couldn't be. Unless we were called to do something else, which we usually always were. We were busy.

Utopia was bigger. How crazy was that? The plans I had for it three years ago were already pretty big. But it had only gotten bigger. I expanded. There were several Utopia centers in Michigan, a few in Florida, two in California, and the grand opening for the Texas location was happening next month.

"He's moving," I whispered.

Jahad lifted me from his chest, and we switched positions. He laid between my legs and ran his hand over my stomach before placing soft, delicate kisses there.

"Bonjou, pitit gason . . ."

Business wasn't the only thing expanding. Our family had too. In more ways than either of us ever saw possible. I was seven months pregnant. I didn't need bed rest. I wasn't as high risk as Leighton because the miscarriages I had didn't always need a D&C, so my cervix was fine.

Everything happened when it was supposed to. I met Jahad when I was supposed to. We parted ways and came back together when we were supposed to. And when it was time to have children, and to be a wife, it happened when it was supposed to. You couldn't put a clock on shit like that. No one should.

I ended up speaking to my mother again after she pissed me off when she assumed I wasn't happy because I didn't have a man. I took a page out of Hazel's book and didn't immediately introduce her to Jahad. Purposely. I introduced him to everybody but her. I waited five months before I brought him around. The shit drove her crazy. I didn't even tell her I was in a relationship, and I told my daddy not to tell her. I wanted Eve out of my business. When she found out I had kept it from her, she was a little upset, but the lesson was learned, honey. I hadn't heard her say anything sideways to Hazel since. But then again, she really didn't have to.

Hazel was in a relationship. A full-blown relationship. With a woman. And she was open as hell about it. We could tell Momma was uncomfortable with it, but she hadn't said anything, and she hadn't been disrespectful about it either. Seeing Momma fight to keep her mouth shut over dinner every other Sunday had been fun as hell to watch, baby.

"Do not play with me! I swear to God if you throw me in that—Ahhh!" Naoki screamed as Saint wrapped his arms around her waist and jumped into the water with her, anyway.

I cackled. That was what her ass got. Who comes to a pool party and doesn't get wet? Her bourgeois ass. They were messing around. Heavy. I didn't know what was to come out of their situation, but my girl was happy. That little situation with Isaac didn't last long at all. At Jahad's birthday party three years ago, Hazel gave Naoki the green light. She told her she really didn't sleep with Saint and that she could have fucked him a long time ago. She had no reason to lie. That was all Naoki needed to hear. She still hadn't stepped foot inside of Pandora's and never would. When she asked Saint about it, he shut that shit down with the quickness and had her put on a banned list to prevent her from ever stepping foot inside of that freaky-ass place. She was pissed, but not nearly as mad as I expected her to be. That was because Naoki didn't need Pandora's anymore. Saint fulfilled every little kink she had. They were a mess together, but . . . the beautiful kind. They were having fun. Naoki was happy, so I was happy.

"Mwen renmen ou . . ."

Once Jahad finished talking to our son, he lifted and kissed me on the lips.

"They're about to be arguing all day," I said with a sigh.

"Not all day."

I nodded. "*All day.* She just got her hair done."

"He'll buy her ass another wig."

"That's not the point," I said with a laugh. "Men are—"

"Uncle Jah!" Bebe yelled, marching up from behind with a frown on her face. "Dream broke my phone!"

I placed my hand on my forehead and sighed. "Oh God. Another one?"

"Yes!"

Jahad stood up and looked up ahead. I watched with a smirk, wondering how he'd handle our three-year-old daughter breaking the third phone she'd broken within the past two months. Yes. Three phones in two months. She was bad. Bad as hell!

When I said our family had expanded in more ways than we saw possible, yeah. I got pregnant fast. I got pregnant after our first date and I wanted to wear the classy ho dress. For what? What's classy about getting pregnant on the first date? No, but seriously, I did. At first, I was afraid I was going to lose her. We both were. But then I had a dream I didn't and I wasn't afraid anymore. I had a vivid dream I gave birth to a beautiful little girl with big, brown eyes, beautiful brown skin, and a head full of unruly curls. I dreamed of her. Literally. When Dream was born, she was a spitting image of the child I dreamed of. So I named her Dream.

"She was supposed to be with her Auntie Mahogany," I stated, shaking my head once Jahad picked her up and babied her just like I knew he would. "What did she do this time, Bebe?"

He was soft as satin with his daughter. She had him wrapped around every one of his fingers.

"Mahogany? Oh, she was in the bathroom. I think I heard her crying," Bebe said with a frown, grimacing down at her broken screen. "She threw it against the wall because I asked for it back!"

Mahogany's life was . . . it was a mess. She and Duke were still married but she ended up seeing someone she met at the club, outside of it. Broke one of her rules and now she had found herself in a toxic situation. I felt sorry for her. I mean, I really did. But Mahogany really did have no business at that club. She should have stopped going a long time ago. I understood her reason for going but, after a while, she just should have stopped. Especially after she and Duke went to marriage counseling to work on their marriage for all the wrong he'd done. Mahogany hadn't told him anything. I didn't think she ever would. Honestly, pretty soon, she wouldn't have to. The skeletons were going to fall out of her closet on their own if she didn't stop before they did.

Jahad

I slapped hands with Blaise, and he pulled me into his chest. "Aight, I love you, bro."

I locked eyes with him and said, "Love you, too, fool. Be good. Don't act up in front of my niece."

He scrunched his face up and shook his head. "I'm good."

Bebe wasn't a baby anymore. She was eight and impressionable as hell. Blaise and Ari were, as always, at odds. Now more than before, since she was trying to move out of state with Bebe, and Blaise was against it. I wanted my brother to keep a cool head for the sake of always keeping one in front of his daughter. It was important that she always saw her father respect her mother. Blaise knew that, but when he was on one, he often lost sight of what was important.

"Good. Stay that way, bro," I said before pulling away from the embrace.

Blaise was Blaise. The growing he did three years ago was all the growing I think he was going to do. He might've been a wild-ass nigga but wasn't nearly as rebellious as he was five years ago. He listened more. Not as much as he should, but a little more was more than not at all. He finally started a business that wasn't attached to Samuel. Oddly, his decision to do so created bad blood between the two of them. Samuel accused Blaise of following me. As if that wasn't what he'd asked both of my brothers to do all of their lives. Now it was a problem because I no longer wanted to follow him.

I still hadn't spoken a word to him. My mother didn't like it. Especially since Samuel had been diagnosed with lung cancer six months ago. I'd made peace with the possibility of losing him years ago. I refused to speak to him now, just because he was sick. If I wasn't speaking to you when you were in good health, I wouldn't speak to you when you weren't. Him being my father didn't change that. Why should it? Samuel didn't give a fuck about me. He would've treated me the same way. My mother had to make peace with me making peace with it. She hadn't. So, our relationship was a bit rocky because of it. I loved my mother with everything in me and would until the day I left this earth. I called and visited her as much as she would allow, which hadn't been often. She stopped by a lot, though. Mostly to see Sienna and Dream. Our conversations were brief. It broke my heart, honestly, but I had to learn to live with that too.

Bebe ran up from the back of the house and wrapped her arms around me. "*Bòn nui* (Good night), Uncle Jah. Love you!"

"Good night, Bebe. Love you too. I'll bring your new phone over tomorrow, aight?"

"Okay."

I dropped a kiss on top of her head, and she ran off to get into the truck.

She was getting big and it scared me. The more she grew, the less time she wanted to spend with me. Our playdates weren't playdates anymore. We went to the mall more than anything. Sometimes I could sneak a movie in there, but Bebe didn't care for playing at the park anymore. She had even started to lose interest in the indoor amusement parks. Pretty soon, she wasn't going to want to do any of those things with me. Watching her grow was bittersweet, for sure. It wasn't too bad, though, because I had my own children to create memories with.

Sometimes I still couldn't believe it. Me? A father? I never saw it in the cards for me. I accepted it and everything. That was one thing that was hard for me to take on the chin. But I did and it was all for nothing. I used to think I didn't have children back then because I was cursed and because it was karma. Shit, sometimes I still think that. But I get to looking at my life and I realize the time just wasn't right. Shit lined up so perfectly for me it seems unreal. It didn't just take three hundred and seventy-three days for us to come together again. It took three hundred and seventy-three days for us to create our first child together, too.

Blaise saluted me and they pulled out of the driveway.

We had a little get-together. Nothing crazy. It was the first hot day of the summer, so we figured it was the perfect opportunity to use our new pool. I didn't have the big-ass house with the guesthouse anymore. I didn't need it. I wouldn't have kept it if I did. I sold it. I wanted to start brand new. I would never have started a life with Sienna in a home I shared with Leighton.

The past three years had been fruitful in multiple ways. Business paid for the house I had built on ten acres. This one and the second one in Haiti. A lot of times, when people hear Haiti, they automatically think of poverty, but there was more to Haiti than just poverty. Haiti was beautiful. Like everywhere in the world, it had poverty-stricken places. Poverty-stricken places I had been working toward rebuilding for the past four years. There was still a lot to be done. The nonprofit organization I started, Rebuilding Hope in Haiti, was working diligently every day to make changes.

"You look better without that long-ass wig, anyway. Stop trippin'," Saint fussed at Naoki as they headed toward his Bentley GT.

"I don't care. I still want a new one," she argued.

"The hell you need a new one for? Can't she just glue that one back on your head?"

"Yep! But I want a new one!"

I shook my head. Bro had his hands full with her for sure. Naoki was cool, though. Definitely a better best friend to deal with than Farrah was. We got along very well. She wasn't clingy. She didn't overstep boundaries. She didn't park in my spot. Shorty was cool with me.

"Bye, brother!" she yelled before climbing into the passenger side of the car.

"Good night, Naoki," I said with a head nod.

Saint walked over with his hand to his head. "Bro . . ."

"Why'd you throw her into the water if she told you not to?" I asked. "If a woman tells you not to do something—"

"I'm going to do that shit anyway," he interrupted.

"And that's why you gon' keep having issues, dumbass."

He looked over at me with a mischievous grin. "I like having issues. She run her mouth on purpose just so I can punish—"

"Chill," I cut him off.

He laughed. "Aight, aight."

Just like Blaise was Blaise . . . Saint was Saint. My brothers weren't changing anytime soon and that was okay. The only reason I matured so quickly was because I didn't have a choice. I was forced to grow up. They didn't have to. They were allowed to be children. Saint was all right, though. He was having fun.

The drug business had been very good to him. So good to him, he hadn't called me for guidance or with a complaint in months. The first couple of weeks, I felt slighted, to be honest. I looked forward to giving him advice about shit. But when he stopped calling, I realized he stopped calling because I'd done all I needed to do. My brothers didn't need me to take care of them anymore. They had it. It was a weird feeling, not having to take care of them anymore. I had my own family to worry about now.

"Should I get my best man speech ready?" I asked with a grin.

He looked over at me with a frown. "Fuck no. After the way you played me last time, fuuuuck no. Gave it to Blaise and you knew that was my spot. Fake-ass nigga." He laughed. "I'm calling Emu."

"You call Emu to be your best man, you won't make it to see your wedding day, bitch nigga." We shared a laugh and I seriously asked, "So, you'd marry her?"

He looked at me and shook his head. "Nah. I'm not thinking about getting married, bro. We chillin'."

Always chillin'.

"How long you plan on chillin'?"

He shrugged. "I don't know."

"Eventually, Saint, you gotta figure something out. You can't chill for the rest of your life."

He extended his arm, and we slapped hands. "I hear you, big bro. I hear you. I'll figure something out. Right now, I'ma chill and let you do the family thing."

It was my favorite time of day. My busy little princess was fast asleep. So, we could just be. Sienna and I. Because we were so busy these days, moments like this didn't come often.

We were lying in bed, in the dark. I was on my back, and Sienna was on my chest. My eyes were on the ceiling and hers were closed. I didn't have to see her face to know it. Her eyes were always closed when we were like this. Pretty soon, she'd be crying. Crying over something neither of us could control. The future. She worried about it. Life without *it*. This. These moments of floating. Electricity. Timeless moments where only we existed. I didn't like it when she worried.

"Si," I called out, cutting through the silence.

"Hm?"

"Wherever we go after this, we'll find each other," I told her, dropping a kiss on the top of her head.

"How do you know?"

"Because we always find each other, love. Don't we?"

"Yes, but it won't be like this," she whispered.

"How do you know? What if this is what it's like . . . *forever*?"

Tears wet my chest and I sucked in air.

"Sienna, please." I hated it when she cried. When she cried, I felt her pain immensely. We were connected like that. Always had been. Always would be. That was not why I hated it when she cried, though. I hated when she cried because the feelings I felt when she did, I didn't want her to feel them.

She kissed my arm. "I'm sorry."

I took a deep breath and decided to shift gears.

"How did they meet?"

Her eyes were open now.

Didn't need to see her because now, she was excited. Now, the wheels in her mind were turning because this part of our night was always exciting. I caressed her arm and waited for her to come up with a story.

"At the courthouse."

I frowned. "At a courthouse? Where you headed with this, *cheri*?"

She turned over on her side and looked up at me. "She's a lawyer and he's a criminal."

I made a face at her. "Why buddy gotta be a criminal?"

She smirked with a squint. "Why you think?"

I laughed. "Straight up? Keep going."

"He's a criminal and she's not a lawyer . . . she's a prosecutor! As soon as she walks into the courtroom and sees him, they feel it. That . . . pull. Time does its thing and the people around them vanish. The judge, she's banging on her gavel, but shit, Sienna and Jahad can't hear that shit. They're floating."

This was our thing. After making love, she'd get emotional and get caught up in the future. I'd let her feel what she needed to feel, even though I hated when she felt it, then we'd shift gears and talk about the possibility of us existing inside of some kind of parallel universe. It was something that came up after we watched one of those wild-ass Marvel movies. Might've been *Doctor Strange*. Anyway, we did it. We enjoyed it. It made her forget. I rarely ever did . . . about the future. I never forgot. I just didn't speak about it.

I worried about what life would be like without her all the time.

It wouldn't be torture in the subtlest of ways. It would be torture, just torture. I didn't like to think about it, so we did this. It made her happy, so it gave me comfort.

"You wild, shorty."

She laughed and looked up at me with a fading smile. "Do you really think Jahad and Sienna would love each other in every universe?"

I looked her in the eyes and kissed her on the lips. "Yes."

"You say it with so much confidence," she joked before kissing me again.

I could say it with confidence because I couldn't imagine there being *anywhere* in this *entire* universe where different versions of us existed, and I didn't love her in it.

Infinite
SOUL TIES
ILLUSIONAL LOVE

"I could say it with confidence because I couldn't imagine there being anywhere in this entire universe where different versions of us existed, and I didn't love her in it."

—Jahad Baptiste

. . . and he was right

GLOSSARY

Siren—Alarm Clock
Digibox—Laptop
Digipad—iPad/Tablet
Lushbumps—Goosebumps
Opicet/Opi—Percocet
Frost—Winter
Cluster—Condo
Dooh—Hood
Noaches—Roaches

Jahad

EARTH 333

I loved her.

That's what it was. That's what it had always been.

When she looked up at me, with sweat on her furrowed brows, and a lazy smile spread across her beautiful face, I loved her more. She laid back down and started to trace the drawings on my skin. Every time she laid there, her fingers glided over the same ones. The portrait of her, and then, she'd move over to the portraits of our children.

I closed my eyes and waited for her lips to touch my skin. When she placed a kiss on the portrait of our daughter, I exhaled and ran my fingers down the length of her spine. She was naked. Beautiful skin, dampened with sweat, sticking to me in a way that I always wanted her stuck to me. Flesh to flesh like this . . . shit was surreal. Every moment spent with her was surreal. Moments in time that I clung on to because the moments I spent with her . . . they were beautiful. Not nearly as ugly as the moments without her were.

Again, she lifted her head, her dainty chin digging into my chest. I opened my eyes, swallowed, and waited.

"I love you," she softly said before leaning her head on my chin.

I leaned down and kissed her on top of her head. The warmth of her skin against my lips felt better every time.

"I love you too, cheri," I told her before wrapping my arms tighter around her.

Her heart beat against my chest and I closed my eyes to bask in it. Only because I knew it wouldn't be long before the feeling came to a halt. It always did.

Beep! Beep! Beep!

The buzzing of my siren pulled me out of my sleep. I clenched down on my teeth before reaching over onto the bedside table to silence it. With the swipe of my thumb against the touchscreen, the beeping stopped, and I laid back down. I clasped my hands and locked them behind my head. With my eyes on the ceiling, I thought of her. Her smell. Her smile. The way she felt against me. The sound of her voice. The taste of her pussy.

Everything about the woman I'd dreamed of since I was a boy was real. But she wasn't. Not in my reality she wasn't. When I was younger, she was younger. She grew with me. As I got older, she got older and the more I dreamed of her, the realer she felt. Our life. It felt real as hell. I experienced everything. The tattoo. The feel of my daughter enveloped in my arms, and any time I would hold my son too. The pregnancies. The deliveries. The first *I love yous*. The kiddish arguments. The breakups. Every fucking thing. The life I lived in my dreams was sometimes more real than the life I lived outside of them. These days, I hated to wake up. I wanted to stay there, with her, forever. Whoever she was. I didn't know her name. Never had. But I loved her.

That's where I was at with it.

In love with an illusion. In love with a figment of my imagination.

The love I had for her made life difficult. I spent every waking moment looking for her. Not literally. I looked for bits and pieces of her in every woman I've been with. The feeling. The smell. The love. The magnetism. I was inching in on thirty and hadn't found her. Shit was lonely, to be honest. Because I couldn't find that, I was unattached. Emotionally, at least.

I looked down at the mess of golden curls resting on my bare chest and wished they belonged to her. The woman from my dreams. She was the reason I was so emotionally unattached. I had no desire for monogamy. For what? If she wasn't her, I couldn't imagine spending the rest of my life with her. The golden curls resting on my chest belonged to a beautiful woman. Leighton. I wasn't monogamous, but she was my favorite. I called her the most. She felt good. Smelled good. And shit, she tasted good too. She was beautiful, with eyes the color of toasted almonds, and full lips that were their sexiest when they were wrapped around my dick.

But . . . *she wasn't her*.

I was tripping. I was fully aware of that. But I wanted what I wanted. Chasing an illusion, someone who likely didn't even fucking exist was borderline insanity. But something in my spirit told me she was out there. And I wasn't going to settle until I found her.

As if Leighton could hear my thoughts, she groaned and tilted her head back to look up at me. She gave me a sleepy smile, with low eyes, the high from last night still lingering in her orbs.

"What time is it?" Leighton asked before pinching her bottom lip between her top teeth.

I smirked. "After nine."

"Oh shit!" She jumped up, her wild bush of curls hitting me in the face. "Why didn't you wake me? Shit! Shit! Shit!" she yelled, as she frantically shuffled across the white marble floors of my bedroom, holding the red silk sheet from the bed around her body. She was looking for clothes that weren't here. They were in the living room, and in the foyer, and on the front lawn, and in the hallway too. "Where are my—"

"Around. Not in here," I interrupted, as I sat on the side of the bed.

I reached over, grabbed my phone, and ran my free hand over my bald head.

"Fuck!" she yelled, as she retraced her steps, out of the bedroom.

With a smirk, I watched her freckled ass cheeks bounce out of the room after she dropped the sheet in a frenzy. Shaking my head, I put my attention back on my phone. It was after nine and I had somewhere to be. There was nothing new about that, though. I always had someplace to be. This morning, I had to meet with my family, and later in the evening, we had an impromptu meeting to attend. An impromptu meeting I had been looking forward to all month.

"Jahad!" Leighton called out; her soft, shaky voice carried through the massive home, up the stairs, down the hallway, and through the small crack she left in the bedroom door.

She was worried.

Soon, she'd be spiraling, and I didn't have time to deal with spiraling. So, I groaned and pushed up from the bed. Running my hand down the back of my head, I snatched my robe from the ottoman and headed out of the room. She was standing at the bottom of the staircase with tears sitting at the rim of her eyes, with the clothes she did find clenched against her butterscotched body.

"I can't—"

"I know," I interrupted, as I trekked by her, through the house until I made it to the front door. She couldn't go outside ass naked, so she needed me to help her find the rest of her clothes. Walking out, the bright *orange* sun greeted me before a soft breeze did. I looked down at the cobblestone porch, sighed, and picked her shoes up. I followed the trail, picking up her bra, and then her shirt before heading back inside. She was standing by the door, waiting for me.

"Why didn't you wake me, Jahad?" she asked, as I handed her her clothes.

"I was supposed to? You wake yourself, Leighton," I flatly told her, unmoved by the guilt she met me with after sucking my dick and drenching it in pussy juice all night.

Leighton was married.

She wasn't when I met her. When I met her she was single. The wedding . . . that happened once she realized I didn't want to be married. When she realized that the only way we could ever connect was pelvic to pelvic. Any other way was off the table. She was cool with it. Didn't give me a hard time. Kept fucking with me because I made her feel in ways no one else could. She'd married Rome for stability. Not because she loved him. Her love? Her love belonged to me. For a while, I hated that I couldn't reciprocate it. Felt like shorty deserved more from me. But I didn't force her into this situation. I didn't make her come to me. Leighton called me just as much as I called her.

She had a whole family at home but couldn't stop coming here.

That was her problem. Not mine.

If she was someone else, she wouldn't have had to worry about me waking her. If she was someone else, she would have been home before midnight. But . . . we had history, and she was my favorite. History was what made me delicate with her. I might've been delicate, but I didn't have to remind her of her obligations. Obligations she made on her own.

"He's going to leave me," she mumbled, as she dressed, following me out of the foyer toward the kitchen. "I don't even want to check my phone."

I didn't say anything. I didn't have anything to say.

"I was supposed to take the girls to school this morning. I—"

"You should head home then, love," I interrupted.

I didn't want to listen to her problems. I didn't care about them. My mornings were spent thinking in silence. Especially after dreaming of her, which was often. I liked to make coffee, sit, and think . . . about her. About the dream. And after thinking, I'd sit at the island, pull my phone out, and do what I did whenever time permitted. Looked for her. I was obsessed. I could admit it. I didn't have a name. Just a description. Her face was etched in my mind. Cemented there. Every morning, I searched the directory for her. I put in every intricate detail but always came up short. That didn't stop me from looking, though. It was insanity on my part. I knew I could very well be looking for someone that didn't exist, but that didn't stop me from looking. Because to me . . . she existed. Felt too real not to exist.

Leighton brushed a hand over her freckled cheek and sighed before walking over to me, standing at the cabinets. She wrapped her arms around me and laid her head on my back before kissing me there. The life she had with him, she wanted with me. She never said it, but she didn't have to. I understood her. And because she understood me, she knew that that was a life she would never get from me. Still, she came around anyway. We were in each other's lives for two completely different reasons. As complicated as it sounded, it worked. We didn't have any issues. We didn't argue and fight. We coasted through the mess because that's what we'd been doing for ten years.

I grabbed her wrist and brought her in front of me. I kissed her on the forehead and gave her what she needed. "He's not going to leave you. You're perfect. Go home and be perfect."

She looked up at me with eyes clouded with tears and nodded.

After Leighton left, I made my coffee, sat in silence, sipped, and browsed the directory for an illusion . . . with hope. After about forty minutes, I put my digibox away and retreated to my bedroom to bathe. As I stood under the water, I thought of her. Thought of the moments we shared bathing together. Thought of the time I spent with my mouth on her and inside of her. Devouring her. Tasting her. The taste . . . it was potent. Sweet. Creamy. She was so real. But . . . so unreal. It fucked with me. Fucked with me so much that as much as I enjoyed dreaming about her, some nights I loathed it. Some nights, I didn't want to sleep because I dreaded what awaited me after I'd awaken.

Loneliness.

A world without her in it.

Sure, I had Leighton, and a plethora of other beautiful women I could call to sleep with, but with them beside me, I'd be lonely still. They weren't her. As a man that didn't scare easily, I was terrified of dying without experiencing her outside of my dreams. I had to accept that the possibility was very likely. Many times, I thought about saying fuck it, and hanging that fantasy up. But I couldn't. My dreams wouldn't let me. It was like . . . *something* wouldn't allow me to. My mind . . . my soul . . . it wouldn't let me let go. As beautiful as it sounded, it wasn't beautiful at all. It was torture.

Three hours later, both the woman from my dreams and Leighton were off my mind. I was like that. I compartmentalized. Had to. The business I was in required me to. At home shit stayed at home. I was driving, on my way to my father's office for our weekly meeting. We had a variety of businesses. Legal and illegal. The illegal businesses required an immense amount of my attention. Mainly because I was second in command. My father was first, with my siblings falling in behind me. We were a family business. The business belonged to us; Samuel Baptiste and the descendants of him. But if you had

Baptiste blood coursing through your veins, you were a part of the corporation in some sort of way. Samuel made sacrifices and built the business on his back. When I was a boy, he left us in Gaiti to build a better life for us in the United Fates. While he was away, I was put in charge. I was given the responsibility to take care of my mother and my siblings. It took him three years to collect us. It wasn't easy. In fact, it was hard as hell for a seven-year-old boy, but learning independence and responsibility that young made a man out of me early. If it wasn't for those sacrifices, I wouldn't be half the man I am today.

After parking, I walked through the revolving doors into Baptiste Inc.

"Good morning, JB," greeted the receptionist, Monica, with a grin.

She stood from her chair and handed me a cup of coffee that I declined. "Good morning, Mo. No thank you, love. I had my caffeine for the day."

She dramatically stuck her bottom lip out. "Really? This is our thing."

I grinned and winked as I walked off toward Samuel's office. "Next week."

"Promise?"

With my hand on my chest, I turned and walked backward. "Promise."

A couple of minutes later, I was walking through the towering glass doors to Samuel's massive office. The sound of soft laughter as I walked down the long hallway told me my baby sister, Natasha, had beat me here. She handled things on the numbers end. She ran her own accounting firm but worked with us directly for obvious reasons.

"*Gro fré* (Big brother)!" she shrieked, climbing down from Samuel's desk once I walked through another set of glass doors.

She greeted me with open arms. I embraced her and kissed her on the cheek. "*Bonjou, ti sè* (Good morning, little sister)." I looked toward my father and greeted him as well. He stood up, walked from behind his desk, and met me with an open palm. We shook hands and embraced just moments before Blaise and Saint, my brothers, joined us and greeted us all the same.

After pleasantries, we got right down to business. Numbers.

While we sat at the conference table, Natasha walked around the room, digipad in hand, discussing revenue and the things we needed to change to make things better. The highlight of the meeting was our issue. Alex. The impromptu meeting we had to attend later was with him, a club owner we not only supplied with weapons, but protection, too. Protection came with a price, and he was late on payment. Since I was a child, I've despised problems. I didn't think anybody liked problems, but me, I absolutely detested them and made it a priority to get rid of them before they got out of hand. Alex should have been handled last month but because Saint was cool with him, he wanted to give him a chance. I didn't give those.

"His time is up," I said with my eyes on Saint, as I stroked my beard. "We've tried things your way. Your way didn't work. It's time we did things my way."

It wasn't often that we inserted ourselves in dirty work but on rare occasions we had to, as a reminder. Saint might've been cool with Alex but that didn't mean he wouldn't break a few bones and/or kill him if necessary.

Saint brushed his hand over his waves and sucked in air with a shrug. *"Konprann."*

Blaise looked up from his phone and said, "What time do we meet at Pandora's? Bebe has dance recital at five."

"We will meet later. Around eleven," I told him. "Send me the address."

I kneeled at eye level with Alex and swiped the towel I'd just cleaned my hands with across his bloodied forehead. "Tomorrow, when Emu arrives for payment, you'll have it. Right?"

Alex nodded, lazily looking up at me with terror in his eyes.

I grinned and stood up. "Good."

I stepped over him, snatched my white buttoned-up shirt and tie off the chair, and then walked over to the mirror hanging on the wall across from where he laid, heavily panting. I looked over at his men, standing off in the corner, and nodded at them. They frantically ran over to Alex's aid. Men that let me beat him near the brink of death because he only had them because of me. Because of us. The Baptiste Family. We ran the state of Richigan.

"We done for the night? The wife has been calling me nonstop since I left the damn house," Blaise complained, standing beside me, adjusting his tie.

I nodded with a light grin. "Yeah . . . we're done."

Blaise had a family. Saint was unattached because he had an aggressive appetite for whores. The whores that worked out of Pandora's, to be precise. I wanted a family but because I was obsessed with an illusion, I probably never would have one.

After finishing up, we left Alex's office and headed out. Saint was in his natural habitat, so he scurried off, on the hunt for pussy, while Blaise and I proceeded toward the exit. As tempting as Pandora's was, I had no desire to stay. I'd only come for business—not leisure. I could've slid off into a VIP room for a dance or gotten a private suite for pussy, but I wasn't interested. Tonight, I wasn't in the mood for unattached, random pussy. I wanted something real. I wanted her. That illusion. Tonight, if I couldn't have her, I didn't want anything at all. I got like that sometimes.

Up ahead, just about ten feet away, was the exit, and to the left was the stage. And for some reason, my eyes were drawn there. Pulled away from the exit and stuck there. Oddly, because my interest wasn't on any of these women. I was obsessed with an illusion, remember? But my eyes went straight to the stage. And when I took in the woman on it, I realized why.

There she was.

The woman from my dreams.

She wasn't an illusion.

Not at all. She was here. In the flesh. Beautifully, sultrily, twirling around a pole on the dimly illuminated stage with big, black angel wings attached to her back and a matching halo atop her head. And nothing else. Nothing but black pasties covering her nipples. But beautiful still. Just as magnetic as she'd been in my dreams.

As men stood at the stage, yelling and throwing money, mentally she seemed to be somewhere else as she sexily twirled around the pole with her eyes closed. When I was just about five feet away from the stage, she opened her eyes, and they met mine. She stopped twirling. Stood frozen, with her hand wrapped around the pole, staring directly at me.

And then time stood still.

Sienna

I pushed the door to the dressing room open and swiped tears from my eyes with the backs of my hands. My platform heels click-clacked against the tiled floors as I paced back and forth, out of breath, trying to control the racing of my heart. The fluorescent lights hanging over my head flickered and suddenly, the air in the dressing room turned cold and thick. Wrapping my arms around my body, I stopped pacing and just stood there. It was quiet. Too quiet. There wasn't a girl in sight. Everyone was out on the floor. It was Friday night and Big Hutch, the club manager, had cleared the dressing room out an hour ago, threatening to fire whoever didn't have their asses on the floor within the next ten minutes. He liked to run around here like he owned the place, but he didn't own shit. Alex, his brother did. But since he was the manager, he had the power to hire and fire so, the girls scattered like noaches.

I took my time. I waited for the crowd to clear. I refused to be knocked around by a bunch of bitches in fear of losing their jobs. Because well . . . I could do that. I had the luxury of sitting on my ass. I was Hutch's favorite. I was *everyone's* favorite. The men at least. The women hated me. All but one. But that was by default. She was my best friend and had been since first-level school.

Usually, when Hutch made his threats, I'd stay put for at least another fifteen, thirty minutes. But not tonight. Tonight, I only waited about ten minutes before I got up and went out on the floor. I wasn't sure if that was a good or a bad thing. If I would've taken longer, what happened five minutes ago wouldn't have happened. I would have missed him. He was on his way out of the building when I felt him. When our eyes locked. When he made me freeze. When his eyes on mine made time stand still and the music I'd been dancing to fade.

Whoever he was.

The door to the dressing room opened and I flinched. I sucked in air and slowly closed my eyes at the sight of my best friend, Naoki.

"What happened out there?" she asked, after closing and locking the door behind her.

Good thinking.

I should have locked it.

She meant well . . . but I just . . . I didn't want to talk about what happened because not even I knew what had happened.

"I don't know," I said, my voice uncomfortably, unexplainably shaking.

I walked off and leaned over against the vanity with my head down. My heart . . . it was still racing. Fuck. What the hell was that?

"Was it the pill?" Naoki whispered, leaning up against the vanity, next to me.

I looked over at her and shook my head. "It wasn't the pill."

"Are you sure? If Denim did something to that batch, I swear to God I'll—"

"It *wasn't* the pill, Ki," I interrupted, before putting my eyes on the backs of my eyeliner-stained hands.

I've always taken Opis before my sets. They relax me. Calm me down. Keep me out of my head. They made it easier for me to do the things I had to do on and off the stage. But they didn't make things move in slow motion. They didn't make music fade away. They didn't make my heart race—not anymore. How would that help me at all? If Opicets made me feel like that, I wouldn't take them every night.

"What the hell was it, then?" she mumbled.

I looked over at her again and dropped more eyeliner-tainted tears on my hands. I watched as they puddled atop the vanity and closed my eyes . . . remembering. I didn't know what it was. But I knew what it felt like. I knew what *he* felt like.

I stood up and crossed my arms over my chest, running my hands over my lushbumps-covered flesh.

"I don't know. But . . . whatever it was . . ." I paused and sucked in air. "My God, it felt good."

Naoki drew back with a frown. "Okay, bitch. You high. Yeah, let me call this muthafucka and curse him out because—"

I started to pace again. "No. Honestly, Kiki, it wasn't the pill. Nothing in the world has ever made me feel that free in my fucking life." I locked eyes with her, and a tear rolled down my cheek. I pinched my lipstick-stained bottom lip between my teeth and shook my head. "*Nothing*, Ki."

Free is a feeling that could never be associated with me. Nothing about my life had been easy. Absolutely nothing. But as I stood on that stage, frozen, staring into dark eyes that belonged to a man I did not know, I felt so . . . free. Boundless. And like nothing mattered. The problems, the sadness, the dark cloud that seemed to always hover over my head, and everything else wrong in my life . . . none of it existed. Nothing mattered. For a few seconds that felt like minutes, that really, *weirdly*, felt like hours, I was free. I was limitless. I wasn't Sienna. I was no one. I just . . . was. *We* just were. And it felt fucking amazing.

I wanted to feel it again.

I needed to feel it again.

I wanted to be addicted to that. Not the drugs and very subtly fruity alcoholic concoctions I had to drink every night to strip away both clothes and inhibitions.

Him.

That feeling.

I wanted to overconsume. He felt safe to overindulge on. Unlike the drugs. Unlike the liquor. Plus, he felt better than both, and he hadn't even touched me. What kind of shit was that?

Naoki looked at me like I was crazy, and I couldn't blame her because if things were reversed, I would look at her the same way. I sounded crazy. I could imagine just how crazy I looked up there. I was in the middle of my set. Dancing to my favorite Winter Walker song, "Girls Need Love Too," when I felt it. It was subtle at first. Almost as subtle as the juice I had in my gin a couple hours ago. But then . . . it was strong. Stronger than the shot of tequila I took before I hit the stage. A sensation. That was the easiest way to describe it. It ran through my entire body. Energy. It brought me to life. Made me open my eyes. Ignited the nerves in my body. Made my heart race and the finest hairs on my skin stand. I immediately stopped dancing. And I stood there, just . . . staring at him. We stood there, staring at each other. He felt it. What I felt. Otherwise, why was he standing there? I wasn't dancing. I was . . . frozen. And he was too. Not in a way that said he was trying to figure out why the dancer wasn't dancing. He was frozen in time, just like me. Probably full of my energy, just as I was full of his. I—

Boom! Boom! Boom!

"Unlock this damn door!"

I flinched and rolled my eyes at the sound of Hutch banging on the locked door. I walked away, in the opposite direction, toward my locker. Tonight, I was sure I was being talked about for reasons other than the way I could seduce a room with just eye contact alone. And Hutch was pissed about it. I wondered how many of my customers I would lose because of this.

"Here his ass go," Naoki mumbled before pushing up off the vanity to open the door for Hutch.

I unlocked my locker and immediately began to rummage through my purse for a pill. I needed something. I already knew what type of bullshit Hutch was going to be on. And I did not have the mental capacity to deal with his shit. Especially not after what I'd experienced. After experiencing that, knowing I'd probably never experience it again? It was heartbreaking. Nearly as heartbreaking as my ex-boyfriend sleeping with my little sister. Yeah, that happened. But as I stared into the eyes of the man that made problems disappear, the shit didn't even matter.

The pill was a sad replacement, but it would have to suffice because it was the only escape from reality I had. I stared at the small white pellet, rolled my eyes, tossed it to the back of my throat, and swallowed it dry. What a waste. The high I would get from it couldn't compare to the high I got from him. I wanted that. So bad.

Hutch barged in and I heard all three hundred and fifty pounds he carried stomping toward me. People didn't call him Big Hutch for nothing. He was a big man. Not just fat, but tall too. So he was solid. Solid and scary looking but he was just as pussy as all the pussy running around here. He was big for no reason. The only people he scared were people that didn't know his ass. Speaking down on women made him feel like a big man, though. We were the only people in this place that he berated.

"Sin!" He barked, calling me by the name I went by here.

Sin was the perfect name for me. If it wasn't dark and demented, I would have called myself Luci, short for Lucifer. Why? Because that's what I felt like on most days. I felt cursed. Isn't that what Lucifer was? Cursed? Happiness didn't reside here. I wore black angel wings and dark black makeup because *I* was darkness. I was empty. I didn't have a soul. Lucifer didn't neither, did he? I hadn't always felt this empty, though. Life . . . it gave me bits and pieces of happiness. Teased me with it, just to snatch it right away. Honestly, the dark cloud found me the minute I came out of my mother's pussy.

She hated me.

Hated me because my father loved me.

And because he loved me, whoever brought all of us here took him away from me.

I guess I could say God, since I spoke of Lucifer, huh? Well, yeah . . . God took him from me because he loved me. Everything I loved, God took, or made sure didn't love me back. My big sister . . . I loved her too. And what He do? Take her from me the same day He took my daddy. My little sister . . .

she was all I had left. And what she do? Hurt me. I let her move in with me and she broke me in a way I thought she never would. Fucked my ex, who I happened to love.

So yeah . . . darkness . . . it suited me well.

That was why I needed to feel him again.

I needed to feel that freedom. The feeling of nothing, but . . . everything. If that made any sense. Everything good, at least. Everything beautiful. I didn't feel that often. I wanted to feel it . . . again. Wanted to drown in that feeling.

"What?" I gloomily answered, as I pulled the halo headband off my head.

"What the fuck was that? Do you know how much money you left up there? What I tell you about gettin' too high?" He rambled off questions that I wished would fade away.

But they wouldn't because he wasn't here.

The man that made noise fade away.

How did he do that?

I shrugged and continued to disrobe, sliding out of the angel wings. I folded them and stuffed them into the back of the locker, before grabbing my shirt. I left my black pasties in place, and slid my T-shirt on, over my head, and ignored the pensive death stare Hutch gave me.

"Hutch, please—"

"Get back on the floor, Passion!" Hutch yelled, cutting Naoki off, pointing his chubby finger toward the door.

Grabbing my panties, I slid those on, and then shimmied my black tights on. Naoki's eyes met mine as she reluctantly walked out of the dressing room. If it wasn't for her obligations, she would have cursed Hutch out. But like most of the women working here, myself included, she needed the money. And unlike me, Naoki was pretty disposable. Not that she wasn't good at what she did. She just wasn't the sultry new girl. I was.

I was six months in and Hutch's prized possession. Most of the men only came to Pandora's to see me. After what had happened, you could say his anger was warranted. I just didn't give too much of a damn about it. The only thing I cared about was embarrassing myself. Pretty soon, I wouldn't care about that neither. Once the Opi kicked in, I'd be numb.

"Look at you," Hutch said, eyeing me with disdain, as I smoothed my hair over. "High."

I giggled and shook my head. Looking up at him, I said, "I wasn't high. Not off drugs. I was . . . I don't know what I was. But what I do know is that . . ." I paused and shrugged. "It happened, Hutch. Are you going to fire me? Should I see if Reese is hiring?"

Hutch looked down at me with a scowl. "All right now."

I scrunched my face up and grabbed the rest of my things out of my locker. I was leaving. I couldn't spend another minute here. I should've, considering I hadn't made nearly as much money as I needed to make. But after what happened . . . I just . . . I wasn't feeling it. I wanted to go home. Home to a spot that didn't remind me of them. Hazel, my little sister, and Amiri, my ex. I moved. Moved out and left the old place to them. They still stayed there. Ain't that some shit? What kind of sister . . . ? I just . . . I couldn't understand it. I was cursed. God hated me. I knew for certain now. After experiencing that . . . whatever that was with that man, I knew He did. Because what was that? How was something that beautiful possible? Why did He dangle it in my face like that?

I was so sure I'd never see that man again because I'd never seen him before. Men like him . . . they didn't come to places like Pandora's. Pandora's was for lowlifes and wannabes. He was the real deal. He walked with the air of a man who owned everything. The world. The universe. Like he was God Himself. He was a king. Kings . . . they didn't come here. I'd met Amiri here. That there was a testament to exactly what kind of place Pandora's was.

"Where do you think you're going?" Hutch asked, as I zipped my coat after sliding my feet into a pair of fluffy boots.

"I'm going home, Hutch," I told him with a sigh. "I did enough tonight, won't you agree?"

He looked down at me and his face softened a little. "You don't need to be drivin' like that."

"Like what?" I asked, feigning ignorance. "I drive like this all the time, Big Hutch."

I hiked my purse over my shoulder, closed my locker, and turned to walk away. Thank God he didn't try to grill me about what happened. I wouldn't have cared, but still. Who wants to listen to bickering? Not me.

"Sienna—"

I looked over my shoulder. "Sorry about tonight. Something just . . ." I paused and ran my hand through the long orange, brown, and golden tones of long extensions. "Something beautiful happened and . . . I . . . I don't know, Hutch. Something happened. That's all I can say. It won't happen again. I can promise you that. Tomorrow night will be a better night."

For dancing. Not for me, per se.

After talking to Naoki for about five minutes, I was out of the door. She made me promise to call her when I made it home, and I would. She was worried about me leaving so late, alone, off an Opi, but I assured her that I'd be okay. I didn't have a long ride home, so I was sure I'd be fine. Six months ago, I stayed thirty minutes away, in a lavish two-story cluster, with marble countertops, and wardrobes the size of the bedroom in the new place. I wouldn't say where I lived now was the dooh. However, it wasn't too far from it. Literally just about ten minutes away from it. My life changed in a blink of an eye.

On my way out, Moe, one of the security guards, lifted his arm for me to hook mine with his. I smiled at the gesture and gave him my arm. As soon as we stepped outside, the blistering cold hit me in the face. It was frost. Frost this season had been horrible. When we made it to my Geep Terokee, Moe helped me inside and told me to drive safe before he headed back inside.

I started the engine and immediately turned the heat on full blast, cursing once the cold air shot out of the vents. However, I didn't turn it off. I closed my eyes and rested against the headrest, waiting for the car to heat up.

And then I thought of him.

The guy . . . that didn't have a name but really didn't need a name anyway. He was a feeling. For me, he'd always be a feeling. A feeling I'd be searching for . . . longing for . . . for the rest of my life. I wrapped my arms around my body and went back there. To that moment on the stage, where time stood still and the melodic sound of Winter Walker's voice was fading. I went back to that moment on the stage where even the stage began to fade. A moment where just he and I existed. Where seconds felt like minutes and minutes oddly felt like hours. Time . . . time wasn't time. And then suddenly when Kev the DJ yelled my name, snatching me out of my trance . . . everything came back and I . . . I was me again. A silly girl, standing on a stage, frozen, with tears running down her face, with insecurities and want on full display. I wasn't Sin. I wasn't Sienna. I was no one. But then . . . I was someone. Sienna. The girl who never got what she wanted.

Now all I had were memories.

And God, the memories were good.

So good that I felt it again.

The floating. That pull.

The humming of the cold air that should've been heat coming from the vents faded and a chill ran down my spine.

Knock. Knock. Knock.

Soft knocks on my window pulled me out of my fantasy. Moe. He wanted me to pull off. I wasn't ready. I kept my eyes closed . . . tried to go back there. Tried to enjoy the feeling. But the knocking . . . it continued.

I sucked my teeth and opened my eyes, prepared to curse Moe out, but it wasn't Moe. It was him. The man with the dark eyes. The man with no name . . . the man who didn't need a name because he was a feeling.

Jahad

She was real.

I thought I was imagining things.

I thought my obsession with the illusion had made the line between reality and fantasy blur. But I was wrong.

As I stared at her through the thick glass of the passenger-side window to her truck, my heart raced. She was fucking real. I'd spent years searching the directory to find her, and tonight I find her in a place I never thought to look. What kind of shit . . .

She rolled the window down and gave me a light smile.

"Hi."

I chucked my chin back with a nod. *"Bonswa, cheri."*

With dipped brows and her head slightly cocked to the side, she gazed up at me with a puzzled expression. I was dazed. Had to be. Otherwise, I would have spoken to her in English. I wasn't myself. I was smitten. Caught off guard by the beauty just inches away from me . . . sitting outside of my dreams.

I cleared my throat and ran my hand down the back of my neck. "My apologies. *Bonswa* is Creole for 'good evening.' *Cheri* means . . . 'love.' Good evening, love." I extended my hand. A quivering hand. A hand that never quivered but quivered for her because she was real. I'd dreamed of her for years. And she was real. I could touch her. Couldn't wait to touch her. For years I'd imagined what she'd really feel like. I longed for her. I craved her. My mouth salivated as I waited for her skin to touch mine.

When she placed her hand in mine there was instant electricity. Electricity I expected only because in my dreams there was always electricity. However, it surprised her. Made her pull her hand away. But I reached for her hand again, in an unrushed, delicate way. A way to let her know that it was okay. And she believed me. In her eyes I could see that she trusted me.

"I'm Jahad," I said once she placed her hand in mine. "Do you mind if I get inside?"

She lifted her tear-filled eyes from our hands and shook her head before hitting the unlock button with her free hand. It would only be for a second, but it pained me to let go of her hand to get inside. I was afraid that the minute I let go of her, she would vanish. She'd go poof, into thin air, and my siren would sound. As real as she felt now was just as real as she felt in my dreams.

As I sat in the parking lot waiting for her to come outside, I pinched myself countless times. I thought I was dreaming the minute I spotted her on that stage. Especially since Blaise kept walking and said he hadn't noticed her when I asked him about her outside of the club. I thought I hadn't awakened at all this morning. I couldn't have. I thought, maybe I had slipped into one of those dreams where you'd awake, inside of a dream. I wasn't sure.

But I let go of her hand and she didn't disappear, and my siren didn't sound.

I took a deep breath and climbed into the truck. After closing and locking the door, I tossed my head back against the headrest and turned to face her. Her eyes were cemented on mine. I felt free. Free enough to be honest with her, so I did that. Didn't give a fuck about how soft or weak my words might make me seem, neither. Besides, this shit could very well be a dream anyway.

"Are you real?" I asked.

She frowned again. The same puzzled look from before. "Hm?"

"Are you real? You didn't give me your name."

She didn't. That spoke volumes to me. We didn't exchange names in my dreams. Never had. We had a whole life together but didn't share names. Not even our children had names. Just faces and feelings.

She giggled. "My name is Sienna, Jahad. Nice to meet you. I'm real. Very, very real."

I took another deep breath and closed my eyes. My heart raced and I mumbled. "Sienna."

She grabbed my hand and there it was again. Electricity. This time, she didn't pull away from it. She gripped my hand tighter and interlocked her fingers with mine.

"You feel . . . amazing," she whispered. "So . . . free. Better than . . . anything."

I opened my eyes and they met hers. We sat there, face to face, eyes locked, in a loud silence, connected with our fingers interlocked. The longer we sat in silence, staring, the more I felt. Just . . . felt. *Everything.* Pain, sorrow, happiness, love, heartbreak, desire . . . I felt everything. And I wondered if she felt it too. I wondered if in the midst of feeling free, she felt it too. What I felt . . . the everything. She had to. Because the feelings I felt, they weren't mine. Not mine alone, at least. I hadn't experienced heartbreak. Hadn't allowed anyone close enough to my heart to break it. She owned it. My heart. The woman from my dreams. The woman who had, up until tonight, been an illusion. A figment of my imagination, who wasn't an imagination at all. She was real. How was that possible? How could I have dreamed of an actual breathing woman I'd never met before? We had a life. A real life. We were in love. I loved her. Loved her so fuckin' much that I was prepared to die without having ever experienced love in the waking world, because experiencing mediocrity with a woman who wasn't her wouldn't suffice.

I sucked in air and shook my head. What the fuck? Last night I dreamed of her. Last night she looked up at me and told me she loved me and then . . . my siren sounded, and I woke up to Leighton. How was she all of a sudden here? All of a sudden . . . real? Despite having her name and feeling everything, I wasn't convinced. I . . . this just . . . it was too much to be real.

"Are you real?"

"Why do you keep asking me that?"

I closed my eyes and sucked in air. "I . . . this isn't real."

She pulled her hand away from mine and ran it along my cheek, brushing it against my beard. "I'm real. This is real. I'm real. What's . . . Are you okay? You crazy or something?"

I laughed and turned away, with the back of my head against the headrest. "I might be, *cheri.*" I ran my hand over the top of my head and took a deep breath. "I've . . . I've dreamed of you. Nearly every night since I was a boy. Since I was a boy I've loved you. Since I was a boy, I've looked for you. Longed for you. In my dreams, we grew together. We have children. We have a life. You sleep on my chest. You lay there and you . . . you trace portraits of you and our children etched on my skin until you fall asleep. And you smell. You smell amazing. Like vanilla. Like now."

I shook my head and ran my hands down my jeans. I was bugging. I was losing it. My mind . . . my grip with reality. This . . . it couldn't be real. I needed to see a doctor. I needed to be checked into a mental facility. This obsession with her . . . it had boiled over. It had tumbled over into reality, and I'd lost my grip. A man in my position . . . I couldn't lose my grip. My mind had to stay sharp, but this fixation with an illusion had made me psychotic.

"Jahad, look at me," Sienna sternly said before gripping my chin.

I turned to face her, and she gave me a light smile. Her eyes were lower than before. Glossed over with a tint of red I hadn't noticed until lights from headlights passing by flashed through them. She was high. That was new. Everything about this was new. This version of her. This version of us. This . . . dream. It couldn't be a dream. Because the dreams . . . they were different. We were different. Her hair was different. She didn't work at Pandora's. She wasn't a dancer. I wasn't in the same business. She was the woman from my dreams, but at the same time she wasn't. The woman from my dreams, she was perfect. Flawless. A bright light. Happy. Free.

Sienna? She was the opposite.

"I'm real," she said with a sad smile and a nod. "You have no idea how bad I wish I wasn't." Laughter . . . Not the type of laughter that came from humor. The kind that came from sadness. "I wish I was just . . . a dream. I'm not, though. I'm very real. But you know what? Being real. Right now . . . tonight . . . it doesn't feel so bad. Not like it did yesterday. Not like it did a few weeks ago. Being real tonight . . . it feels amazing." She paused again and whispered. "*You* feel amazing. That's why I let you in. Because I don't feel amazing . . . *ever*."

For the first time since laying eyes on her, I finally believed that she was real. Actually real. There wasn't a doubt in my mind about it. I wasn't dreaming. Sienna was real. This wasn't an illusion. I didn't believe just because we weren't who we were in those dreams. I believed because I felt it. Her. She felt real. Very real. Her feelings. Her pain. How much she needed to feel me. How much I needed to feel her. How much we needed to feel each other. Maybe I hadn't been able to find her in the directory all of those years for a reason. Maybe I was supposed to find her tonight. Because tonight . . . she *needed* to feel amazing.

"I won't feel like this for too long. The way you feel . . . it'll be taken away from me. You weren't supposed to come back. I wasn't supposed to feel this again. This . . . you . . . were supposed to be a tease. Just . . . a tease. But you know what? This is probably just another sick part of His game. He's dangling you in my face for a little bit longer. Eventually, He's going to take you away from me. Because good things don't happen to me." She got out of her seat and crawled into my lap. Hooking her arms around my neck, she laid on my chest. "So . . . please . . . stop asking if I'm real. And . . . let me feel. Let me . . . let me float. Let me be free . . . before he takes you away from me."

I wrapped my arms around her and let her float. I let her be free. I let *us* be free. I didn't ask if she was real. Because I no longer had to. In fact, I didn't say anything else. I had much to say, but I didn't. Instead, I planned to show her. I wasn't leaving her. How could I? Why would I? Because she wasn't perfect? Because she wasn't actually the woman from my dreams? I hadn't been searching for perfection. I had been searching for her. I had been longing for a feeling. *She* was that feeling. I didn't need perfection. I just needed her.

Now that I had her I was *never letting go.*

Infinite SOUL TIES
NEVER LET GO

"Why couldn't I have met him first? Before her? Before Amiri?"

—Sienna

GLOSSARY

Bloomday—Birthday
Seeyers—Glasses
Falsies—Contacts
Tunebox—Radio
Zone—Neighborhood
Towerbed—Bunk bed
Gruds—Drugs
Kodva—Vodka
Nissan Optima—Kia Optima
Grand Chevelle—Chevrolet Chevelle
Bop Music—Rap
Digidate—Calendar

Sienna

EARTH 111

There was this boy.

He wasn't a typical boy. The first time I saw him, I *knew* he was different. Very different. I was eight, and me and my family had just come home from The Big Store when we noticed him and his family moving in. The minute we turned the corner into our zone, my eyes found him. It was more like our eyes found each other's because when I looked at him, he looked at me. And then . . . that's when I knew *something* was different about him. Then, I didn't know anything about him, except for the way he *felt*.

How he *made* me *feel*.

He pulled me. Honestly. Except, he didn't touch me. I was . . . *we* . . . my family and I . . . we were still in the car. But . . . when my eyes met his, I felt a tug. The longer I stared at him, the harder he pulled. The harder he pulled, the quieter the car got. I'd never forget it. The music . . . it faded. The sound of Momma's laughter and Daddy's flirtatious jokes faded too. My sisters arguing over who would get their hair braided by Auntie Char first . . . yeah, you guessed it. Faded right along with everything else. That, coupled with the way he felt, scared me. So much that I cried. I didn't boo-hoo. I wasn't hysterical. I didn't know there were tears until my sister Hazel touched my face and asked me what was wrong.

That went on for years. The pulling. The emotions. Sound and the people around us just . . . drifting away . . . it went on for years. Every day since the first time. I *tried* to stay away from him because of it. But staying away from him proved to be impossible. If he wasn't in a room I was in when I entered it, shortly after, he'd walk right in. Goosebumps and the racing of my heart welcomed him any time he showed up. It was like . . . a hello. That hello we'd never spoken to one another. I didn't know him, but I *knew* him. Not in the way that everyone else in the neighborhood knew him. Not because he was treacherous and sold gruds. I knew him because since I first laid eyes on him, I felt him. When I slept. When I was thousands of miles away from home. I felt him. Not all of the time. But . . . mostly. When he was hurt. When he was in danger. When he was sad. Just . . . the bad stuff. Those were the nights that scared me most. Some nights, I'd awake in a cold sweat. Some nights, I'd awake, gasping for air, frantic, with tears pouring from my eyes. Some nights I'd jump out of bed and dress, in a frenzy, to head out of the door to go to him. My dad . . . he called them night terrors. But I knew what it was. It was him. By daylight, people would be talking about something happening with the Baptiste Brothers the night before. That's who he was. A Baptiste. Jahad Baptiste. He was more than just Jahad Baptiste to me, though. He was a feeling. He was a tug. He was a lot of things. An enigma, really. And now, at thirty-one, he was more than just a feeling for me. He was my husband, too.

I closed my eyes as I rested my head on his chest, listening to the subtle pitter-patter of his heart. A heart that used to race whenever we were close. I missed that. Listening to his heart race. These days . . . his heart . . . it didn't beat *nearly* as fast as it used to. In fact, for three hundred and seventy-two days, his heart rate had done nothing but decline. At one point, our hearts would beat in sync . . . these days, not so much. Not at all, really. However, I clung on to the hope that one day they would again. I liked to believe that the racing of my own heart kept his beating. As long as I stayed on him . . . connected like we've always connected . . . his would keep going. But my God . . . I was afraid. Afraid of moving. Afraid of looking at the heart monitor. Afraid that this little connection of ours was just a figment of my imagination, birthed by hope. Hope for more time when I knew that time was something we didn't have.

The door creaked open and ripped me out of my thoughts, forcing me to open my eyes. Tears I kept concealed behind my closed lids immediately soiled the thin white hospital gown he wore.

"Hey, Si," greeted my sister, Hazel.

I sucked in air and looked over at her, walking into the room wearing a familiar, desolate smile filled with both pity and sorrow. My eyes stayed on her for a moment. Long enough to notice the sympathy. Long enough to have seen enough. Every time someone walked into the room, they greeted me the same way. With sorrow. For me . . . and for him too.

People said Jahad had been holding on for me. The doctors . . . they called this a miracle. How? How was this a miracle when every day that passed, he slipped further away from me? They saw it. But me? I felt it. To me, that was worse than seeing numbers on some monitor decline. To literally *feel* the light being sucked out of him . . . that . . . it hurt. Because that light . . . it was being sucked out of me too. The pull? That touchless tug he'd given me since I was eight? It was fading. I couldn't feel him. Not like I did before. Not like I always had. I laid on his chest, connected to him, searching for it. Wanting to feel more of him. The thing that used to scare me? God, I wanted it so bad now.

"Did you eat breakfast?" Haz asked, as she walked over to the windows to draw the shades.

I didn't say anything. I closed my eyes and grabbed his lifeless hand. Gripped it. Waited for what would never come. Electricity. All I needed was a spark. A little one. Anything. Something. But . . . I got nothing.

Through trembling lips that were in dire need of water, I whispered a soft *"Please"* that only I could hear. I didn't know who I was pleading to, exactly . . . but . . . something. Him? Whoever . . . whatever put him in my life. Whatever created us. Whoever made him for me . . . us for each other. I just . . . I needed something. A little bit of anything. A sign that this wasn't the end of us. It couldn't be.

"You should eat."

There were a lot of things I should've done. Eating was on the top of that list, and drinking, bathing, and working were right underneath. However, I rarely ever left his side. I mean, unless it was absolutely necessary. To use the restroom, reposition him, or clean him. Because I was a physician myself, I took care of him. He didn't have an aide. I was that. When his family visited, I gave them privacy. Allowed them time to spend with him, but it was never too long—their choice of course—and I was never too far; just right outside of the door. I never left the hospital. I wasn't practicing at the moment. Refused to care for anyone that wasn't Jahad Baptiste. If he was lucid . . . if he was here . . . he would fuss at me about it but at the same time, he'd understand because if the roles were reversed, he would be the same way. We were like that about one another. Serious. Connected. One. Not just by last name. Not just by marriage. Our souls . . . they were tied. Interlinked.

That's what we came to realize. After years of trying to figure out what "it" was . . . that electricity. That pull . . . that . . . magic. We figured it out. We couldn't part ways. We had to come together. The running I used to do—it didn't matter. I could have run as far as humanly possible, we would have come together still because we were meant to be.

We were destined.

"You know what tomorrow is?" Hazel asked, cutting into that rambling that constantly went on in my mind.

"Three hundred and seventy-three," I mumbled, as a tear trickled down my cheek.

She was behind me. I could feel her eyes on me. Sad-ass eyes . . . pitiful eyes.

"No, the *day*, SiSi."

I didn't know what tomorrow was.

I just knew what number it would be.

Three hundred and seventy-three.

Day three hundred and seventy-three.

Tomorrow would make it three hundred and seventy-three days since I last heard his deep, baritone, drenched-in-Caribbean drawl. It had been three hundred and seventy-three days since I'd gazed into deep, dark brown eyes that could hold me captive for days if I let 'em. Three hundred and—

"Tomorrow is your bloomday . . . Cosmo Day," Hazel said with a smile in her voice, snapping me back into reality. Again. *Good.* I could get lost in numbers for hours.

I softly peeled my lids open and shifted my clouded eyes up at him. I didn't care too much about my bloomday. But Cosmo Day? *Wow.* A soft smile crept upon my face, and I wondered, could he come to me then? Cosmo Day was . . . magic. It was beautiful. Thirteen years ago, on Cosmo Day, I stopped running. Thirteen years ago, I couldn't run away from him if I wanted to. The pull . . . my God. The pull on Cosmo Day was . . . always too much to ignore. The electricity. The magnetism . . . it was . . . at its highest. Always at its highest on Cosmo Day. Electricity was what got us here. He and I. Electricity is what told me to stop running. Running didn't cross my mind, though. Not then. I didn't want to run because thirteen years ago, on Cosmo Day, the boy I was afraid of . . . I fell in love with him.

THIRTEEN YEARS AGO

"Come on, SiSi!" begged my sister Mahogany. "When's the last time you watched The Cosmo Show from someplace other than the window?"

I lifted my eyes from the romance novel I had my face in and pushed my seeyers up the bridge of my nose. "I can't remember."

"Exactly," she said before snatching my book from me and tucking it into her armpit. "And that's ridiculous." Pausing, she shook her head. "Actually . . . when you think about it, it's pretty sad, considering it is your bloomday, too."

I sat up and crossed my legs with a sigh. It was sad. Very sad.

"You're turning eighteen," Mahogany continued, steady trying to get me out of the house. "It's time to loosen up, Si. It's a beautiful day, too. You cannot and *will not* stay cooped up in this bedroom all day!"

Rolling my eyes, I swiped the floral drape hanging over the window to look outside. There were crowds of people, heading in the same direction. The entire zone was trekking toward the hill, where the best seats for The Cosmo Show were. They carried portable lounge chairs, tuneboxes, mini coolers, and big, fluffy throw covers draped over their shoulders or around their necks too.

Shifting my attention away from the crowd, I put it on the little blue house across the street. Instantly, my eyes found *his*. A cool breeze ran up the nape of my neck, making the thin hairs there stand. I swallowed and quickly swiped the drape back into position. Pulling my legs from underneath my bottom, I bent them and wrapped my arms around them.

Mahogany popped her lips and swiped at the curtain to look out of the window. "Worried about the crowd?"

Worried about him.

There was this boy. Well . . . ten years ago, when he moved into the zone, he was a boy. Today, he was a man. And he was . . . He was a lot of things but most of all, he was intimidating. I didn't like him. Really couldn't say I didn't like him. What I didn't like about him was the way he made me feel. He pulled me. He . . . made me feel things without any physical contact. Insane, right? Exactly. It didn't make any sense. So, I kept it to myself. Had been since the day he and his family moved in. I'd rather people assume I was just . . . shy. I would rather deal with that than deal with people calling me weird.

Instead of telling her the truth, I sighed and rested my head on my knees. "Yep."

She took a deep breath and stood at the towerbed I shared with her and my little sister Hazel, in front of me. Grabbing my arms, she pried them away from my legs and gripped my chin to turn my head in her direction.

"I know how to fix that," she told me.

I snickered. "Yeah, okay. How do you think you're going to do that?"

With a smile, she bit her bottom lip and glanced over at the closed bedroom door. "Liquor," she whispered.

"That's your plan?" I asked with my brow lifted.

She smiled and nodded. "Yeah, and a damn good one too." Pausing, she reached for my hand, pulling me up on my feet to drag me over to the closet. "So, come on. Let's get ready. Today is going to be a great day. We're celebrating your eighteenth bloomday at The Cosmo Show. You only turn eighteen once! It's the first day of the rest of your life!" she exaggerated.

Mahogany let my hand go and fingered through the unflattering clothes on my side of the closet, with her bottom lip pinched between her teeth, while I just stared at her. She had this hopeful, excited gaze in her eyes that made me pity her. There was no *fixing* my problem. Liquor would have worked if I was actually shy. I wasn't shy. I was actually pretty outgoing. Before he moved into town, I was a bright-eyed, bubbly little girl. But . . . then they moved into the zone, and I changed because . . . the air around me and everything in it changed.

Liquor couldn't fix that. I would be okay until he showed up. And he would show up because he always showed up. Everywhere I went, he would end up there. And that was where the true problem lay. I couldn't relax because there was the anticipation. I didn't look out of the window earlier because I was curious about the weather, or because I wanted to see who was heading up to the hill. I looked out because he was out there. Only looked over, because his eyes were on me. His eyes were always on me. Didn't do any of those things because I wanted to. Did it because he . . . *pulled me.* Had been for a while. Sometimes, I ignored it. Could only ignore it if something else had my attention. Today, my novel, *Tokyo and Haram: Solace*, kept me distracted for a good thirty minutes before Mahogany snatched it from me.

"Your bloomday outfit, SiSi," Mahogany pressed.

"I didn't get anything. Mom bought me a new dress for Saturday service. Maybe that'll—"

"Sienna Mills, you are *not* wearing a church dress for your eighteenth bloomday," Mahogany interrupted with a pinched-brow frown before taking a deep breath and turning to sift through more suitable clothes. Clothes that showed more skin. Hers. "Today, you're a woman. You're going to dress like the beautiful goddess you are." She paused, looked over at me, and smiled before shrieking with excitement. "Tonight is going to be amazing!"

"If you say so," I grumbled, fiddling around with my braid.

On cue, her eyes went straight to it. "And we're changing that hair too. Call for the girls! It's makeover time!"

I sighed and prepared for what I knew was about to be a draining day.

Hours later, I was dressed in an uncomfortable pair of light denim shorts, a sleeveless light pink shirt with a dainty white rose in the top left corner that showed too much cleavage for my taste, and strappy sandals with a low, chunky heel that showed off my freshly painted pink toes. None of the clothes belonged to me. The sandals neither. The only thing I had on that belonged to me were the clothes underneath.

Mahogany stripped me of my seeyers and made me swipe them out for the falsies I hated. She said the seeyers hid my natural beauty. I did look better without them, but I was a girl who was all about comfort. I hated the falsies. It always felt like I had something in my eye, because, well . . . I did! Anyway, Mo took the two braids out of my hair and straightened it.

I looked like a completely different person. So much like a different person that when our parents saw me as we were leaving, their jaws dropped. My father was concerned about my comfort, and my mother complained that I was dressed too provocatively. Mahogany was dressed in a skirt shorter than the shorts I wore, but that wasn't addressed. I got it. I was the quiet, quirky, reserved daughter. Well . . . that's who I was supposed to be. Who I've always been. However, I was more than that. The only reason I was seen as quiet and reserved was because I lived in my mind. I was constantly thinking. And . . . *feeling.*

We made it to Crescent Hill about forty minutes ago. The minute me, Mo, her boyfriend Duke, Hazel, and my best friend Naoki showed up, heads turned and this time, eyes landed on me. For the same reason my family's jaws dropped when they saw me. I looked different. In a head-turning, jaw-dropping way. Although I wasn't shy, all of the attention made me nervous. I didn't like it.

"Hell yeah!" Duke excitedly exclaimed. "I've been waiting for them fools to pull up all day."

Mahogany sighed. "Please don't lose all of your money to those Baptiste brothers today, Duke."

Duke grinned. "I won't."

He was here. Made it about five minutes ago. I knew he was here before any of them noticed. I felt how close he was before I heard the rumble of the engines of their 1970 Grand Chevelles.

"Mm-hmm." She rolled her eyes and turned her attention to me. Eyeing me up and down with concern, she passed my cup back. "Here, try it now," she said, after adding more juice to the cup of kodva she made me the minute we settled in.

Naoki climbed down from the hood of her Nissan Optima. "Are you going to go up the hill with me to watch them play later?" she asked.

I shrugged and ran my hand over the back of my neck. "I don't know, Nay. Maybe, I need to think about it," I said with an uneasy giggle. Giggling . . . I did that when I was nervous. When he was close, I was always nervous.

She sucked her teeth. "Why not, Si? Please. I don't want to look stupid just standing there with all of them."

I leaned my head over to the side. "Now you know you're too pretty to *ever* look stupid," I boasted, to stroke her ego, so she'd leave me the hell alone.

"Si." She pouted and placed her hands on her slim hips. "Come on, sis."

"Don't press her," Mahogany butted in. She briefly locked eyes with me before she went back to fixing herself a drink. "Sienna don't want to go, she don't have to go. Boys are easy for you, ain't they?"

Naoki was the only friend I had. To call her a friend would be an understatement, honestly. She was more like a sister. We grew up in the same zone and went to all of the same schools. We'd been inseparable since birth, first grade.

Naoki narrowed her eyes at Mahogany. "I was not trying to *force* her to do anything, Mo. What the hell do you mean, boys are easy for me? What are you trying to say, Mahogany?"

Mahogany sighed and turned her cup up to her lips. "Naoki, I'm not *trying* to say anything. I just think you should take it easy . . ."

I tuned their bickering out and looked over my shoulder into the crowd. The crowd he stood in. The crowd he *stood out* in, rather. God, he looked good. My eyes immediately caught his, as if they were *trained* to find him. And not because he was breathtakingly handsome. Not because he had dark skin that seemed to glisten like diamonds whenever sunlight hit him. Not because he had long eyelashes and hooded dark brown, almost black, dreamy eyes, and full lips. Jahad was very, very attractive but I wasn't attracted to him because he was handsome. I was attracted to him because I was *attracted* to him. Magnetically. Energetically. I couldn't help it.

Crescent Hill was packed with people, but we paid them no mind. He stood at the very top of the hill, looking down at me. And I stared right back up at him. That didn't happen often. I usually looked away. I was always the one who ran in the opposite direction whenever he would gain on me. It happened often. More than often, actually. Every time we were around each other. For a while, I wondered if he felt what I felt, but after a couple of years of this, I stopped wondering because I knew he felt it. Otherwise, what would explain *this*?

He held me captive. My eyes stayed trapped, stuck in his mysterious, tantalizing, dark browns. Time . . . sound . . . and *life* . . . it did that thing. That thing it's always done whenever my eyes got trapped swimming inside of his for too long. Things slowed down and the people around us? Everyone waiting for stars to shoot across the red, blue, and greens that covered our sky every day? They did what they always did when our eyes met.

They faded away.

The sound of my heart beating was loud in my ears. I could hear every breath I took. It was so loud. The only thing I could hear. Today . . . I was stuck longer than I'd ever been. I didn't know how long we stood there, connected like that, with the wind blowing in my hair, and the sun against his dark glistening skin, inviting me. Pulling me.

"Sienna!" I flinched at the sound of my name being called.

Turning around, I met the smiling face of the girl from the eatery I stopped at after school whenever I had the money.

"I can't believe you're here!" she exclaimed before throwing her arms around me.

"Hey, Leighton," I said, brushing her wild, golden hair out of my face.

Leighton was cool. I could call her a friend, I guess. So, in a sense, I didn't just have Naoki. I had Leighton too. She started working at the eatery a couple of years ago. When she started, I immediately took a liking to her. And she took a liking to me too. Sometimes, if it wasn't too crowded, I'd sit on the stools, study, eat, and talk with her. She'd help me with my homework, tell me stories about university and art. I'd listen, with bright eyes, in sheer admiration. To me,

Leighton was amazing. Amazing with a big heart, and a smile that could light up a whole room. She was too big for the eatery. Too big for this place. Sometimes, I felt like she knew it too. I caught her gaze drifting off a few times, while she talked about art and school like here was the last place she wanted to be.

She pulled away and looked at me. "You look so pretty. Where are your seeyers? You decided to use the falsies? You're wearing those shorts, girl!"

I bashfully smiled and looked away, my eyes briefly finding his. As always. This time, however, I didn't get stuck. I quickly looked back to Leighton with a sigh and placed a piece of hair behind my ear.

Leighton looked over in his direction. "Here we go," she sang.

"What?" I asked.

"You two," she said with a light smile. "I wonder if anyone else notices it," she whispered, with her head slightly cocked to the side, looking up with mystery. She took a deep breath and looked back at me. "Whenever he would come into the eatery, you'd leave. Like . . . every single time. At first, I didn't notice it. Thought nothing of it, actually. You've always been quirky and quiet, so I figured you were shy." She giggled and gave me a little grin. "But then"—she wiggled her eyebrows at me—"I stopped paying attention to *you*, and I started to pay attention to *him*. He never took his eyes off you. Ever. His attention was always on you. So much that, if there was a time that he'd come in, and you were heading out, I'd stand back and just . . . watch. Lean back against the coolers and just watch him watch you until he couldn't watch you anymore. Literally. Until you'd turn the corner onto Gilbert Court. I didn't watch just for the sake of watching. I watched because that was all I could do. Taking his order? Yeah, right. I tried that once. The first day you ran off I stood at the register, asking if I could help him. Attempting to get his attention, but . . ." She shrugged and looked over at him. "It was like he couldn't hear me. Like . . . watching you took away his senses . . . well . . . all but one. Sight." She looked at me. "Is it like that for you too?"

Watching me took away his senses. All but one.

Sight. What a perfect way to put it.

I bashfully shook my head and looked down. "I don't know what you're—"

"Leigh-Leigh!"

I looked up from the grass up at Leighton, who'd rolled her eyes to the back of her head. She turned around and forced a smile. "Yeah, Farrah?"

"I've been looking all over for you," said who I presumed was her friend, Farr. She eyed me up and down and stood beside Leighton. "Who's this?"

Leighton looked over at me and smiled. An actual one. With teeth and a sparkle behind her hazels. "Sienna. The girl I told you about."

"Oh . . . the *little high school* girl?" Farrah asked, steady ogling me.

Farrah. I'd heard about her too. *A lot* about her.

"Little high school girl?" Leighton repeated with a frown. "I never called her that, Farr. She's just two years behind us. But . . . yeah. She's not in high school anymore, though. Sienna graduated early."

"Oh. How adorable," Farrah mocked with a smile before taking a deep breath and turning away, disregarding me as if I was nothing.

I snorted but said nothing. I did that a lot. Kept quiet when people tried to make me feel small. Especially when I was in the presence of bitches like Farr. Mean girls.

I stayed to myself and didn't socialize because he was in *every* circle, and, well . . . you know how that goes. I wasn't a nerd, though. Just someone who shrunk herself because she didn't want to be seen. Seen in the way that Leighton had seen me. Open. Feeling. Fading. When he was near, at least. And he was always near. There was never a time that he wasn't, really. We had to be in the same spaces. We grew up in the same zone. Although we weren't the same age, me and his brother were, so we went to school together and he was there. All of the time. I couldn't escape him. Not ever. Not while I slept. Not while I was awake. If he wasn't around, I felt him. It was like . . . I was a prisoner, and he was my captor. And because I didn't like to be seen doing . . . that. Being pulled. Being controlled. Doing whatever it was that *we* did to each other. I shrunk. I hid. It was embarrassing. *She* wondered if anyone else noticed. I wondered too. All of the time. Wondering kept me in the house most of the time. Wondering made me avoid people because avoiding people kept me from showing them what *she* saw.

"Adorable?" Leighton mocked with a light huff before turning to me with a smile. "*Admirable.* She's like a little genius."

Farrah hooked her arm around Leighton's neck, pulling her into an embrace that she clearly didn't want to be in. She was nothing like Leighton described. The love she said they shared. How special Farrah was to her. I couldn't see it.

My eyebrows slightly rose when Farrah kissed Leighton on the forehead.

Oh. *Shit.* They weren't just friends. They were more than that. For some odd reason, it was clear that Farrah wanted me to know that. The public display of affection. The way she hooked her arm around Leighton's neck. Just . . . it was a bit much for a simple conversation. Made me wonder if Farrah was intimidated by my "adorable" ass.

Hmph.

"I guess," Farrah dismissed with a sigh. "I need a drink. Let's."

Leighton rolled her eyes and gave me a sympathetic smile. "See you later, SiSi. Hey . . . Don't leave tonight without letting a bit of magic happen, okay? It's Cosmo Day, after all." She winked and right after, Farrah dragged her away.

"Bitch, I didn't know you were cool with the bougie ho from the eatery." Naoki approached and spoke with a frown, eyeing Leighton up and down as they walked off.

I giggled and playfully bumped into her. "I thought you would be happy to know I had a friend other than you."

Naoki looked over at me with a fiery squint. "She's your friend?"

I laughed. "Oh God!"

We shared a laugh, and I took a sip of my drink. "She's nice."

"You didn't answer the question."

"I think she's a lesbian," I joked, steady evading the question, just to annoy her.

"Sienna!"

"Yes?"

"Yes what? She's your friend or . . . ?"

I giggled and shook my head before leaning over and draping my free arm over Naoki's shoulder. "Yes, but you're my best, best, best friend!"

She playfully pouted. "In the whole wide world?"

Laughing, I leaned my head against hers. "In the entire galaxy, you big baby."

"Whew!" She exaggerated before we shared a laugh. "I thought I was going to have to beat both of y'all up. Now why do you think she's a lesbian?"

On the short distance back over to where everyone else was, I told her about Farrah and the kiss. We were leaning up against Naoki's car when Mahogany walked over.

"You good, SiSi?" Mahogany asked with furrowed brows, concerned about me.

I nodded with a faint smile. "Yes, Mo, I'm good."

Her eyebrows dipped a little. Nodding toward the cup, she said, "Have another sip."

I looked down into the pink drink and put the cup back to my lips. Seconds later, Duke wrapped his arms around her waist and picked her up off her feet, pulling her away and sending her into a fit of giggles.

Naoki took the cup from my hand and took a hefty drink from it. "Can you believe she said that to me? *I'm* good with boys. Why would she say that to me?"

She handed me the cup back and I took another drink. From the corner of my eye, I noticed her watching Mahogany, with a frown and tears in her eyes. If Mahogany knew, she wouldn't have said that. She didn't know, just like Naoki didn't know why I didn't want to go up that hill with her. We all had something we kept from each other.

"She don't know, Nay," I whispered. "If she knew—"

"I know," she whispered back.

Naoki had friends. A lot of them. She was the social butterfly. Very likeable, loud, and funny. But she *wasn't* good with boys. Boys tried to get with her. All of the time. There were rumors spread about her, and because she was popular and constantly seen at all of the parties, people thought they were true.

At first, Naoki would defend herself and got into a lot of fights about it. But after a while, she stopped. She just let people think what they wanted to think. Naoki had been considered the boy-crazy girl since we were thirteen, but what people didn't know was that Naoki was very afraid of men. Her Uncle Anton was to thank for that . . . But . . . we didn't talk about Uncle Ant. *Ever.* But then there was this boy she started to like and well . . . she figured she'd take a chance on him.

I tossed my head back with a sigh, closed my eyes, and pushed up off the car.

Facing her, I smiled. "Come on. Let's go up that hill!"

Her eyes widened. "What?"

"What?" I mocked. "You heard me. Don't tell me you're scared. I thought I was the scary one. Today *we* bloom. Together."

She shook her head. "Yeah, I know, but you really don't want to. We do not have to—"

"You better come on before I change my mind, girl," I warned.

"Okay, okay," she rushed to say, with a big bright smile, the tears in her eyes long gone. She grabbed my free hand and pulled me away from the car.

My heart raced as we headed in a direction I was already being pulled in. I shifted my brown eyes to the green, prickly grass to avoid eyes that I knew were on me. The closer we got to the crowd, the harder it was for me to avoid. As soon as I lifted my eyes, they met his.

He was coolly leaned up against his car, cup in hand, surrounded by people who engaged with him while he silently engaged with me. *While we silently engaged with each other.* In the weirdest of ways. Ways I was sure neither of us could quite understand. Seconds ago, Naoki's voice was loud in my ear but the closer we got, the higher we trekked up that steep hill, the quieter her voice became. This time, I didn't get stuck. Wasn't allowed to. Someone stepped in front of him. Blocked my view and I was thankful for it.

I swallowed and put that cup to my lips again. This time, taking a heftier gulp than before. Swallowed it down completely. I needed it. Because we'd made it up the hill. We were so close. I'd never been so close to him before. It was so much. Almost too much. How close we were almost sent me crashing against his chest. I would have if it wasn't for her . . . She was in the way. But then she wasn't. And to stop myself, I latched onto Naoki. Grabbed her arm with so much force that she was startled. Looked down at me with furrowed brows and concern etched on her beautiful face.

"It's okay," Naoki reassured me with a whisper. "You look good. It's your bloomday. Tonight is going to be a great night. I'm so proud of you, sis. You should be proud of yourself too."

Should I be? Did I have anything to be proud of? Maybe. I had conquered a fear. Jahad was about three feet away from me. But I wanted to be closer. I wanted to touch him. I wanted to feel him. I wanted to be inside of him. How? Why? I didn't know. The closer I got, the closer I wanted to be. I didn't want to run. He didn't feel as scary. He felt good.

"Thank you," I said with a light smile. "You should be proud too."

"What do I say?" she whispered.

"I don't know, Nay," I whispered back, as we slowed our stride. "Just tell him you weren't feeling good when he asked you out the other day."

She really wasn't good with boys.

Mahogany didn't know how wrong she was about Naoki.

One of the boys from our zone had the biggest crush on Naoki. Naoki had a crush on him too but because guys made her nervous, when he approached her a couple of weeks ago, she was rude. She'd regretted it since it happened. And since today was a special day, she decided that today she would apologize to him and see if he was still interested. However, there was one big flaw in her entire plan—she wasn't good with boys. Despite what it might've looked like . . . she just wasn't.

"The truth? How do I tell him the truth? Just—what? Come out and say it or—"

"Yes, the truth. You'll be fine. Just . . . be your natural self. Be comfortable. Like you always are. And when the time is right . . . just . . ." I shrugged. "Tell him."

Naoki lightly smiled and nodded. "Okay. I—"

"Damn, Nay. Them shorts look good as hell on you, baby."

She looked at me with wide eyes before finally looking over her shoulder. Lucky her. She wouldn't have to approach him after all. He was a couple of feet behind us. Naoki was like that: magnetic. It wasn't just her looks that drew people in; she had an infectious, bubbly personality.

"I don't know why you're looking surprised," I whispered with a giggle.

She bashfully grinned just as he walked up beside her. Before she could say anything, he had his arm draped over her shoulder. I noticed her tense up a bit and gave her a reassuring smile.

"Hey, Denim," she spoke. "Thank you. You all on my hair, though, nigga. Dang!"

There she was. The Naoki everyone knew and loved.

He laughed. "My bad, baby. Come over here and blow on these dice so I can win and buy you some more."

"Don't forget you said that when you win neither," she flirted back, with a grin. Looking over at me, she quietly asked if I was cool.

I nodded. "Yeah, girl. I'm good. I'm about to kick it right here, though."

The dice game was too *in the mix*. Well . . . too close to *him*. I just . . . I needed a minute. It wasn't just about him. It was about being seen . . . the way Leighton had seen me. The way she seen *us*. I didn't want people to notice. I didn't know what that would look like to them. She said it was beautiful, I could only imagine it looking weird.

She moved Denim's arm from around her shoulder. "Hold on," she told him before turning to me, "I'm not leaving you—"

"You're *not* leaving me," I interrupted with wide eyes, giving her a look. "I'm right here and you . . ." I nodded toward in Denim's direction, where *he* was. "You're going to be right there."

Naoki glanced over her shoulder. "Can you believe he—"

"Duh!" I giggled. "Of course I can believe it. I told you, you're that girl!"

She rubbed her lips together, biting back her smile. "You sure you're going to be okay?"

I nodded, lying. I was a nervous wreck, but I couldn't let her know that. The liquor served a purpose after all. I had a little more courage. "Yes, I'm going to be fine."

"Are you going to come over?"

"As soon as I give myself the pep talk I don't need from you!" I lied with a light laugh. "Go blow on those dice, girl."

We shared a laugh. After about a minute, Naoki finally walked off and I turned around to gaze up at the mystical hues in the sky. The sun was setting. Pretty soon, at nightfall, The Cosmo Show would begin. People all over got together on the same day to watch the sky. Today the sky was more than its usual blue, green, and red at nighttime. Every year, today, the sky . . . it did something. Something magnificent. It lit up with shooting stars, from various directions. Today was the most magnificent day in the whole wide world.

Cosmo Day was all about intention setting. People got married on Cosmo Day, meditated . . . just about everything. Women prepared the most for Cosmo Day. Some even tried to make sure they had babies on the day . . . as if they could control that. To be born on Cosmo Day meant you were special. A miracle. Cosmo Day babies were deemed the "chosen ones." I wondered if that's what it was. Wondered if it was true. I wondered if I was magic. Wondered if I had superpowers. Maybe it wasn't him at all. Was it me? Did I—

"Happy bloomday."

The hairs on the nape of my neck stood and I tightened my grip on the cup, crushing it. He was right behind me. Wishing *me* a happy bloomday. Those two words were the best gift I'd received all day.

Hell, in all of my eighteen years of life.

A happy bloomday from Jahad Baptiste.

Simple. But not simple at all.

Turn around, Sienna.

I needed to. Wanted to.

He urged me to.

The racing of my heavy beating heart kept my eyes forward, with fear. But that pull . . . it grew. Quadrupled. Intensified. And before I knew it, I was twirling on the balls of my feet, being pulled by a force I was sure neither of us understood.

Finally.

For the first time since laying eyes on him, we were face to face. And everything around me slowed . . . yes, like before but absolutely nothing like before. I found myself trapped. My God, was it enthralling. At this distance, it was as if I was staring into a dark ocean with *me* at the center of it. He was quiet. Stuck, as usual. I wondered if it was for him, as it was for me. Wondered if staring into my browns was like staring into a vast ocean with him in the center of it, too. Wondered if time slowed. If his breathing slowed. And if his heart had gone from racing to . . . steady in a matter of seconds . . . like mine.

His scent was invigorating. He was all I could smell. Gone was the intoxicating aroma of barbecue, chicken, ribs, and hot dogs. He consumed my senses. I couldn't put a finger on the notes. I could describe it as refreshing. New. But familiar too. I wanted to be closer. I wanted to lay my head on his chest and bask in the scent of him. I wanted to ball his white shirt up in my hands and bring it up to my nose. I wanted to bury my face into the crook of his neck and just . . . inhale. I wanted to consume him.

After what felt like minutes but couldn't be more than a couple of seconds, he grabbed me, pulling me into his chest. Right after, a football went zipping behind me, missing my head by just an inch.

"Ay, watch where the fuck you throwing that ball, nigga!" Jahad barked at one of the guys I graduated high school with.

Amiri threw his hands up. "My bad man, my bad! I didn't see her!"

"Impossible," Jahad mumbled, with his eyes back on mine.

I was in his arms.

He . . .

My God.

He felt so got damn good.

I—

I couldn't put it into words. He . . . I . . . I had never felt anything like him before. I didn't want to leave. In that moment, I didn't care about anything I cared about before. Honestly. I was free. Completely. Nerves? Gone. Awkwardness? What they thought about us? Looking weird? None of it existed. Not even them.

"Hap—"

"Thank you," I interrupted before he could wish me happy bloomday for a second time.

"You're welcome," he lowly replied, those brown eyes steady, staring deep into mine. Penetrating me as if he could see through to the depths of me. Soul deep, even. And with my browns, I stared through him the same. Searching for answers. Sifted through the mystery that was him. The boy that made me feel funny. The boy that pulled me without ever laying a finger on me.

Until today.

He didn't just lay a finger on me . . . he laid ten. A hand. And I wanted him to. I wanted him to touch me . . . everywhere. I wanted to feel more of him. Before I knew it . . . before I could control it, I was melting into his arms. I didn't know what it was, or how to explain it, but I was immediately drawn closer to him.

I laid my head on his chest. And when I did, I exhaled.

He exhaled too, and tenderly enveloped me in his strong arms. He held me, gently, but with this . . . force. As if he didn't want to let me go. I let him. I let him hold me. Because . . . shit, it felt right. It felt like I belonged there. It didn't feel like we were meeting for the first time. It didn't feel like I'd been running away from him. It felt like I knew him. It felt like we were in love. I was stuck. We were stuck. Like two magnets almost. Hard to pull apart. Like . . . when that positive finally connects with that negative. The force of it.

It was funny, right? How not even an hour ago, I was terrified of him. Talked about running away every time I saw him. Couldn't bring myself to turn when I felt him behind me. But now . . . I didn't want to pull myself away from him. It was the connection. It felt . . . amazing. It was bliss. It was . . . freedom. Like soaring in the sky. Weightless. Soaring, with the birds. One with nature. *Free.*

"You good?" he asked, his deep baritone voice vibrating against my chest, sending a warm sensation down my spine.

"Hm?" I flinched and pulled away. "Ye-yeah. Sorry. Th-thanks again."

Wished I could stay like that forever. You know . . . stuck? Like magnets. With the beat of his heart against my body. His minty breath filling the air around me. Succumbing to that pull. But I couldn't.

Reluctantly, I struggled to walk away but before I could, he grabbed my hand, stopping me.

"Nah. I'm not letting you run away from me today."

Hours later, I was *still* with him, right beside him, sitting on the grass, a few minutes away from the start of The Cosmo Show. I couldn't run away from him if I tried. Not that I would have anyway. I wanted to stay. After that first touch, I couldn't imagine running away . . . ever again. That revelation . . . admitting that to myself . . . it made me a little nervous.

There was so much going on around us, but we were in our own little bubble, rarely interacting with anybody except each other. My sisters and Kiki checked on me a couple of times. Mahogany was worried, Hazel was confused, and Naoki was a combination of them both. However, she was proud.

Hell, I'd done more than interact. I was in the middle of it all. With him. Today, I didn't shy away from it. Didn't use the excuse of "too much going on." I just . . . existed, in the mix. And while, before, there was anxiety—*all because of him*—tonight there was peace—*all because of him.* How crazy was that? The flip side of things? I stopped avoiding . . . stopped running . . . and there was peace. And to think . . . all I had to do was stop resisting.

"I don't know why you fucking with this broke nigga, Nay-Nay," Saint, the youngest Baptiste brother, boasted. I looked over my shoulder at them. He blew on a pair of dice and tossed them atop his candy apple red Grand Chevelle. "You need to stop playin' with me."

In the middle of peace, there was a bit of that chaos I didn't too much care for. Just a few feet behind us, the dice game was going between the other two Baptiste brothers—Saint and Blaise—Denim, Duke, and a couple of other guys from the zone.

Denim huffed. "Nigga, you wouldn't know what to do with this. How old you is? Sixteen? Fuck out of here."

Saint smirked but said nothing before picking the dice up and tossing them out again. He shifted his eyes over at Naoki and said, "Give me a couple years. That's all I need, ain't it, Nay? Couple years. I'll show you exactly how to take care of her."

With a light giggle, I looked over at Naoki. Our eyes briefly locked, and she playfully rolled her eyes. Saint was cute. Since he was about three years younger, she didn't take him seriously. However, I could see how much she appreciated the coy banter. I could see him really swooning her. Out of all of the other boys in the zone, he was the only one who actually seemed to care about something other than what she had between her legs.

"Ay, *cheri*," Jahad whispered, swooning me with the simplest of Haitian Creole, lightly tapping my arm.

Looking away from Naoki, I turned my attention to him with a bashful smile. "Hm?"

He nodded toward the sky. "There is something I would like to share with you." He paused. "Do you mind?"

I shook my head. "Of course not."

Jahad was nothing like I expected him to be. He had a bad reputation. All of the Baptiste brothers did. But Jah was notoriously known for malice. Women said he was cold. Claimed he didn't know what chivalry was and only cared about one thing. However, tonight, he'd been nothing but gentle.

With a nod, he gestured for me to come closer. When I scooted over he lightly smirked, shook his head a bit, and pushed up from the ground. Before positioning himself behind me, he asked if it was okay to sit behind me.

I nodded. He tilted his head forward a bit and I took that as a cue for me to use my words.

"Yes, Jahad, it's fine. You can sit behind me," I said with a light giggle.

"Just making sure you're comfortable. You did run from me for ten years, *amou*," he joked before finally positioning himself behind me.

I giggled. "Has it been that long?"

"Ten years, two weeks, five days—"

I looked over my shoulder at him, taken aback. "*Really?* That's pretty precise."

His stoic expression softened to a smile. "I'm good with numbers." He paused and winked. "Plus, that is how long we've been in town."

I nodded with my mouth turned down, impressed. "Hmph. Impressive."

His eyes softened and I followed them, as they slowly traveled every inch of my face. "Impressive indeed."

Did I mention how intimidating he was? Yes? I'm sure I did. Did I mention how much more intimidating he was to experience up close? Like this? Face to face, eye to eye . . . Oh. I'm sure I did that too. To experience it was next level. Jahad honestly took my breath away.

"You wanted to—"

"I wanted to show you something . . . right," he interrupted, finishing my sentence. He cleared his throat and flicked his wrist to check his watch. Delicately, he gripped my jaw and turned my head. "Look up for me. It's beginning—"

"It's not. We have about five more minutes. When the north star gets its brightest and—"

"Nah," he interrupted with a light chuckle. "It starts before that. It starts with the moon. Look up, gorgeous."

With lightly dipped brows, I put my attention on the moon.

Jahad leaned in closer to my ear. "Five seconds," he mumbled.

His minty breath against the side of my face gave me goosebumps, sending yet another warm sensation down my spine. Against my back, I could feel it as the beat of his heart began to pick up. In turn, mine did too. I kept my eyes on the moon, marveling over how big and blue it was tonight. It was always its bluest on Cosmo Day. However, as Jahad began to count down, I noticed something more. It glimmered, as if it was a star, brighter than all of the stars around it. It wasn't *just* blue. There was depth. There was variety. It was marbled in hues of the brightest shades of blue I had ever seen.

"Two . . ." He paused, and my eyes widened. "One."

Lightly, I gasped. A subtle, soft white ring glowed around it. It didn't last long, at all. The glow. It was quick. But I saw it and it was magnificent. If you took your eyes off the sky for just a second, you'd miss it. But that second, for me, felt like minutes. The Cosmo Show had been a part of astronomical history for ages and not once had I heard of such magic. How could I have missed this?

"To me, it's the best part," he whispered into my ear. His hands slowly gliding across my skin.

"You don't like The Cosmo Show? The stars?" I asked, my breath accelerating every time his hand glided across my goosebump-covered skin.

His hands traveled down my arms until they met the palms of my hands, where he softly gripped. I lightly gasped as a subtle surge of electricity tingled through my fingertips and traveled through the rest of my body.

"The Cosmo Show is straight," he flatly replied, with little to no emotion.

That was new. The Cosmo Show was big around here. When I said everyone around the world participated in Cosmo Day, I meant it. We made a big deal about it. It was a national holiday. A day of rejoicing. Celebration. A day not to be taken lightly. Magical in every sense of the world.

"Oh, Big Bad Jah . . . too cool to care about The Cosmo Show, hm?" I joked, leaning my head back against his chest.

He lightly laughed. "Nah, it has nothing to do with being too cool, *amou.*"

Sucking my teeth, I laughed with him. "Okay? What is it, then?"

He was quiet for a bit. Too long of a bit. So long, I had to turn around to look at him. When I did, our eyes met. And I was lost there for a second. His expression softened and he stared into my eyes deep.

Ocean deep.

Jahad had this thing about him. A telling way of looking at me. I could always feel his eyes on me. If I was in a room with him, I always felt his eyes on me. When we were in our zone, in our circle, in a section filled with people, I felt his eyes on me. When I thought I was blending in . . . when I purposely shrank myself. When I tried to hide myself behind hooded jackets, sunblockers, or just . . . doing anything, anywhere. I felt his eyes on me. Before, it was scary. To be the focal point. To always be watched by him. But today, on Cosmo Day . . . on my bloomday, face to face, eye to eye, like this . . . close enough to touch noses . . . close enough to touch lips . . . it wasn't scary at all.

It was exhilarating.

No.

It was *levitating.*

The feeling.

Of his eyes locked on mine. To be the center of his attention . . . it took me off my feet. We were sitting on the hill, but we began to ascend. Slowly. Felt like we could touch the sky. If we stayed long enough. If we moved closer. If we met in the middle. If he dared to inch in closer. If I dared to let him . . . and his lips met mine . . . we would.

At least that's what it would feel like.

We'd be seated, still.

Held bound by gravity. But . . . like this . . . body to body, eye to eye . . . I—*we*—felt boundless.

"Privilege," he responded.

I drew back a little, confused. "Privilege? What makes that a privilege?"

He looked away from me. Just for a second, to gesture around us. "Look around."

I looked away from him to take in everyone else. Nothing had changed. People were partying. Dancing. Smoking. Drinking. Playing games. Amiri and his friends were on the other side of the hill throwing their football around. Mahogany and Duke were dancing. Hazel and her friends were standing at a grill Ms. Debra fired up, having hot dogs. The dice game was steady going, except this time, it was Denim and Blaise in a heated exchange. Saint stood beside Naoki with his arms crossed, probably flirting, while she playfully rolled her eyes and hid her blushing. There was life going on around us. Just . . . life. Good times.

Which only left me more confused than before.

"Okay?" I said with a laugh and furrowed brows. "What?"

"They didn't see it," he replied with a smirk. "While they stand, waiting for the stars, *we* got to see the moon." With that he winked.

I raised my brows. *"Hmph,"* I grunted. "Well . . . when you put it like that . . . it *is* a privilege. And you got to experience that every year."

He ran his tongue over his bottom lip and shook his head. "Nah. I get to experience *that* every day."

I laughed. "The Cosmo Show only happens once a . . ."

I stopped laughing, once I realized he wasn't talking about The Cosmo Show.

He didn't say anything . . . just continued to stare into me with those piercing brown eyes. I didn't know what was happening. Didn't know why it was happening. Didn't know what we were experiencing. But what I did know was that I didn't want it to end. Jahad had gone from the scary boy that "pulled me" to the man I never wanted to part ways with. He felt so good. *That* scared me . . . not him. How much I enjoyed this. How good he felt. How exhilarating. The rush.

"What is this?" I whispered.

"I don't know," he replied before brushing my chin with the pad of his thumb, leaving tingles with every stroke. "I like it, though. You like it too."

"So much it's scary."

"You have nothing to be afraid of," he reassured me.

"Okay," I responded with a bashful smile, believing him before he finally closed that very small gap between us.

Fireworks erupted inside of me. I had never been kissed before. I was eighteen and the first pair of lips to touch mine were his. How insane was that? Around us, the world carried on. The Cosmo Show started, but for us, it had started already. We were okay with missing out on the stars shooting across the sky. We'd seen enough of that. We had our own Cosmo Show going on between us.

PRESENT

"Good morning, Sienna."

I was jolted awake by the sound of my name being called.

Lifting my head from Jahad's chest, I peeled my eyes open and looked over at the doctor, standing at the foot of his bed in her *black* coat.

"Have you thought about our talk?"

Slowly, I looked away from her and laid back down.

No, I hadn't given what we discussed any thought. I hadn't been able to think about anything but him and not in the way they wanted me to think about him. I just wanted my husband to come back to me. I was a logical woman. Had attended university. Had my degree in medicine, just as she did. I was smart. I knew Jahad was slipping away from me. I knew the likelihood of a reversal was very slim. He'd been on life support for—I shifted my eyes over at the digidate on the wall—three hundred and seventy-three days. However, statistics didn't worry me. The seven bullets he took didn't worry me neither. I . . . *I couldn't feel him.*

Today . . . on my bloomday . . . I could feel him less than I could feel him just hours prior. He was slipping. Faster today than ever before. I knew I needed to prepare. I knew I needed to let go. But, I really, truly, did not want to. I wasn't ready. Couldn't imagine ever being ready.

"Si—"

"Please, Nay," I interrupted. "*Please.* I just . . . I just need a little time."

Naoki sighed, hung her head, and looked over her shoulder at the closed door. My best friend was Jahad's doctor. It was a bit unethical, but I wouldn't have had it any other way. Naoki was one of the best trauma surgeons in the country. For the most part, she tried to remain professional, but caring for him—for *us*—it was hard.

The talk we had the other day was about preparation for after. After for me was discharging my husband and preparing a homecare plan. Because she saw things I didn't, after for her was moving me in with her and her husband, his brother, Saint.

"Si, time is something . . . we don't have much time left," she struggled to say with a sigh as she approached the bed. "Tonight might . . . His heart is—"

"I know," I interrupted with a painful groan. "I can *feel* him leaving me, Nay-Nay," I whimpered, with my head pressed against his chest as tears poured from my eyes.

His heart didn't beat the same. I listened enough to notice subtle changes. Didn't have to count the beats to notice when something was off. Just . . . knew the way it sounded. Memorized the tempo, like my favorite tune. For fifteen years, I listened to it. Every night. Of course I knew what it sounded like. Of course I could tell when something was wrong.

I grew attached to him. We grew attached to each other. Painfully attached. Unhealthily attached. So . . . when this happened . . . when he was hurt . . . it shook me. It ripped me to shreds. Crippled me. I—I couldn't go on. I didn't leave this bed for days before I was convinced to shower and eat. I didn't want to let him go. I couldn't. I didn't know what to do without him. This was different from going to school. This was different from going to work. This was different from business trips and girl trips. This . . . this was very, very different. This was final.

He said he would *always* be a call away. He always had been. And when calls and videos weren't enough, and the pull urged us to meet in the middle, we did. Where was the pull now? Hm? Where was he now? I couldn't . . . I couldn't feel him. He—this wasn't supposed to happen. Not yet. Not like this. We were supposed to have children. We were supposed to grow old together.

He was supposed to leave the business to Blaise. But because he was devoted to her . . . loyal to her . . . his mother, when she begged him to wait another year, he listened. And because I understood his reason, I said okay. I said okay even though I didn't want to. I shouldn't have. I . . . had I said something. Had I spoken up, he would be okay. But he knew how I felt about it. He had to know. Jahad . . . he always knew. He just . . . he always had to take care of the family. But what about me? What about us? We were supposed to live happily ever after . . . together. The story was supposed to end with us.

"Do you want me to—"

"I just want us to be left alone. No visitors. No bloomday wishes. *Nothing*," I interrupted . . . again.

I was a nice person. A sweetheart, really. But now, my heart was broken. I didn't have an inkling of sweetness left inside of me. I was . . . empty. I didn't know what would become of me. I didn't know who I was without that . . . spark. Without that . . . pull. I couldn't remember life without it. I was eight when I first felt it. Can you remember what your life was like before age eight? I didn't have a personality then. I was just a kid. I didn't know . . . who would I be? How would I be? How would it be to never feel him again?

A second later, I felt Naoki's warm lips touch my cheek. "Okay, Si. I love you."

"Love you too," I mumbled, gripping his hospital gown.

Once she walked out of the room, I let out a gut-wrenching cry.

"Why didn't you take me with you? You said you would never leave me."

I was losing my mind. Losing him was breaking me in inexplicable ways. We were supposed to go together. Somehow, some way, that was supposed to happen for us. As unrealistic as it might sound, it didn't seem impossible for me.

I was born on Cosmo Day. I was magic. I was special. Wasn't I?

I didn't feel that way.

This didn't feel like magic.

This felt like a curse.

To experience that, with him, and then to lose it? I thought I was special.

I thought what we had was special. I thought it was because I was born on Cosmo Day. I really did think I was magic. After I embraced him. After I accepted what was. That we were for one another. That with him, time stood still. And that he could make me levitate. And that with him, I felt electricity. Because of the cosmos. Because they were perfectly aligned and shot across the sky when I was born. Because I was magic. Now what? What was I now? Who would I be? What would I be . . . without him?

"Attention family, friends, and patients . . ." announced the young woman over the hospital intercom. *"The Cosmo Show is starting in about fifteen minutes. We've been lucky enough to be stationed with one of the best views in all of Dream City. Today is a day of magic; let magic reign on Arcadia General."*

Magic probably would reign on Arcadia General, but it wouldn't reign on him. It wouldn't reign on us. I believed in magic . . . We were magic. But that had nothing to do with *this*. My ego . . . this big ol' ego I had from being a Cosmo Baby . . . it told me I could do anything. I thought I could bring him back. Thought we were magic enough to pull it off. But my ego lied. I couldn't fix this. *I* couldn't bring him back. Jahad was ready to go.

"You're strong," I whispered, as I brushed the pad of my thumb over his dry lips. "So got damn strong." I gasped and swallowed the lump in my throat.

This was bigger than just me. Hell, it was bigger than us. He fought for as long as he could. And so did I. I—I had to let him go. I had to give him permission. I had to tell him he could go. He wouldn't let go unless I told him he could. He was like that. Selfless. And I was the same with him.

I took in a deep breath and stared at him. I caressed the top of his head, running my fingers through his unruly, thick coily mane. He hadn't had a cut in over a year. Jahad stayed with a fresh cut—never missed his weekly appointments. The hair looked good on him, though. I smiled through my tears, as I brushed my thumbs over both his thick eyebrows, admiring them as well. I'd miss them. They complimented him very well. They were their thickest, untamed as usual. Slowly, I traveled over his eyes. Didn't stay there long. It was hard to admire them closed. I loved his eyes the most. I closed my eyes and remembered lying beside him, like this . . . staring into his mesmerizing browns, lost . . . soaring in the beautiful, mystifying hues that painted our nighttime sky, boundless, outside of time, free . . . without gravity.

I gripped his hand and felt a twitch in his.

I didn't let that excite me. Would have if I didn't have a degree in medicine. It was the myoclonus. The timing sure was impeccable. Because I was in love . . . and because I was a hopeless romantic, I wanted to believe that today played a role in the timing. I chose to believe he heard me. I sighed and my lids failed me as the tears I cried poured from behind them. I didn't bother to open my eyes again. Decided I'd rather remember him this way. In a memory instead. He was beautiful this way. We were beautiful this way. Nothing could touch us here. Nothing could take this away from me.

I inhaled.

Brought his flaccid hand up to my lips and kissed his knuckles.

I didn't know what I would do without him.

Literally hadn't a single clue.

Didn't know who I was without him. Didn't know who I would become. But what I did know was that I didn't like who I had become in holding on to him. I didn't want to hold on to him anymore. He was struggling here. Fighting because of me. Fighting because I wasn't ready. I needed to free him, despite how much freeing him would hurt me.

"You can let go, my love," I whispered, my lips brushing against his earlobe as I caressed his thick, scruffy beard.

The minute I said it, fear rushed through my entire being and I pressed my body against his. Had to because tomorrow, I wouldn't be able to. Lightly, I held his face and kissed his cheek because when tomorrow came, there would be no cheek for me to kiss. Then I kissed his lips, his forehead, his nose, and then his lips again. I let them linger there a while.

I was petrified. Had never been so afraid of anything in my life. But it was okay. I would be okay. Eventually. What other choice did I have?

Finally, I opened my eyes, exhaled, and just . . . laid there. With my body completely against his, I stared at the side of his face, wishing there was nothing in between us. I needed to *feel* him. Not just that pull—I knew that was over. I needed to feel the warmth of his skin. His arms wrapped around me. His lips on my forehead. I needed . . . *more* . . . More of everything. But what I had was what I had, so I had no other choice but to be okay with that. Acceptance . . . it wasn't easy.

Instead of complaining . . . instead of begging, and wishing, and hoping for a miracle that would never come, I waited. Waited for *him* to let go. Waited for that fading energy to dissipate. Waited for him to pull . . . *away*. He did, but it wasn't instantaneous. It was gradual. He was resisting, not because he didn't want to let go, but because he was worried about me. I knew because I knew him.

"It's okay," I told him, as I caressed his face. "I'll—I'll be okay, my love."

Would I be? Not today. Eventually I would be. I had to be. Couldn't imagine feeling *this* for the rest of my life. Tomorrow, there would be tears. Buckets of them. The day after that, the day after, and probably for three hundred and seventy-three days in a row, too. Enough to fill an ocean. But eventually . . . I would be okay.

"I love you, Jahad," I cried, as I felt what was left of him finally fade away.

It didn't take long for the nothingness to greet me. There was very little left in him, before. Almost a second after I told him I loved him, he was gone. His heart kept beating, but what was left of Jahad? The soul of him? What made him, him? Was *completely* gone. Felt like when he left, he took a big chunk of me with him. I wasn't surprised. That was the only thing about "after" that I was sure about.

I felt hollow.

Like something was missing.

Because something was missing.

There was a place inside of my heart where he belonged. What would I do with it? What would fill it now?

I turned over on my side and slowly swung my legs over to stand. I was numb. Felt like my head was in the clouds. But not in the way that it used to feel when I was "there" with him. With him . . . it was magical. This . . . it felt . . . scary. Like a disconnection. Like I was someone else. Like I was experiencing someone else's life. Because huh? This couldn't be my life, right? I . . .

I looked over my shoulder with pinched brows, head cocked to the side, in disbelief. He left? He was . . . gone? Wow. I couldn't feel that pu—where was it? I always felt a pull. Jahad . . . pulled me.

It's funny. There was this boy that pulled me when I was eight. I was in the backseat of the car. Me and my family had just left The Big Store and . . .

He always pulled me. I shuddered, looked away from him, wrapped my arms around my body, and rocked back and forth.

"It's okay. It's okay," I mumbled as tears poured from my eyes. "I'm going to be okay."

Would I be? I was so fucking sad. So got damn lost. So fucking empty. What in the . . . What would I do without him? I—I needed him. Didn't he know that? I—

"Attention, family and friends! We're at the five-minute mark!" announced the young lady over the intercom again. *"Get in position! If you're on the west wing, you're in for a real treat!"*

I couldn't move.

I stopped rocking. Just . . . sat there, staring off into the darkness with my head over to the side, listening as the alert on Jahad's monitor began to sound. His heart rate was declining.

The real show starts now.

With dipped brows, I looked over my shoulder at him and averted my eyes over at the monitor. Fifty beats per minute. Quickly, I looked away and got a glimpse of the moon. Yesterday, Hazel drew the shades. Left them open so I had the perfect view of it. And God, was it beautiful. Jahad's room was on the west wing, and the moon was positioned right outside of his window. It was so big . . . so bright. Mystical.

The real star of the show. I felt compelled to stand. Slowly, I walked over to the window. With my arms wrapped around my body, I stared out at it. Today was supposed to be magic. Something special was supposed to happen. Jahad was supposed to come back to me. It was Cosmo Day. Beautiful things happened on Cosmo Day, right? Why did he leave me then? Hm?

Tears streamed down the sides of my face as I watched the moon turn its bluest. And when it glowed for that second that felt like minutes, I felt *him.* Electricity and that pull at once. The tips of my fingers on my right hand tingled before my hand was filled with them.

I gasped, placed my left hand on my heart, and closed my eyes.

Privilege.

Was I hallucinating? Absolutely not.

I experienced true, unwavering, divine love, in its purest form with a man created by God, for me. We defied gravity. We stood outside of time. We were magnetic. Our love was destined. Boundless, even. Not even death could separate us. Our souls were interlinked, eternally tied. And if a person had yet to experience that, they would call it hallucination, but because I could feel, I knew it was him. I heard him . . . clear as day. But it wasn't about what I heard. Because I could hear him coding and the hospital staff rushing in to save him behind me, too. It was about what I felt. And my God, I could feel him. I could feel Jahad as if he was standing right beside me. And while it might've been a little different, I could feel him as if he hadn't left me at all . . . Immensely. Soul deep.

I wanted him to come back to me. Begged him to. He did.

Wanted to feel him again. I could.

Searched for that pull. Felt lost without it. Thought that after today I'd never feel him again. But I was wrong. I could feel him everywhere. All over. In my heart the most.

Today didn't go the way I wanted it to. It went the way it had to.

And it was magic still.

I'll never let go.

"Me neither," I whispered.

ABOUT THE AUTHOR

Miss Candice is a bestselling and award-winning author from the east side of Detroit, Michigan. Her debut novel, *If Not for Love,* was published in 2014, and she has written more than fifty books in the years since. She has a palpable passion for her craft and is a vibrant force in the world of Black romance literature.

Podium

FOR A GOOD TIME

follow us on our socials

podiumentertainment.com

@podiumentertainment

/podiumentertainment

@podium_ent

@podiumentertainment